Lovely Assistant

VID/VED!
THE "FUN
NAME" CLUB
HAS TWO
MEMBERS
NOW!

A NOVEL BY
GEOPH ESSEX

Copyright © 2012 by Geoph Essex
Art and Design © 2012 by Geoph Essex

Fifth Published Edition, May 2014
ISBN-13: 978-1468151374
ISBN-10: 1468151371

ГУЛЕ

ACKNOWLEDGMENTS

After starting a thousand projects and finally getting the chance to see one through, I think I owe a serious debt of gratitude to anyone and everyone who stuck by me while I worked out just what it is I wanted to do. So thanks, first and foremost, to every grade school teacher who helpfully pointed out, amidst the flawless academic assessments, that I was "not living up to potential." One who requires special mention is Dr. Gloria Sanok, a woman who probably understood what a bunch of weird kids were capable of far better than we ever did.

Another teacher who can take some credit (or blame) for my endeavors is Jim Nicholson, who managed to smuggle me through his playwrighting course and some pretty dark times no matter what trials and tribulations he was dealing with in his own life.

Thanks, too, to my family, who read and enjoyed this book no matter how far outside of their usual genres it may be. Special thanks to my parents for some alert and efficient typo patrol.

Also on typo patrol was my better-than-biological Big Brother, Tom, who has always been one of my coolest fans. Which is only fair, since I'm one of his.

As with any writer, there are people in my past and present who provided inspiration for specific characters, events, or even lines of dialogue in this story. To all of them: if you see yourself in here, it's because I found you that fascinating, and had to write about it.

Finally, absolute and unequivocal thanks to my freaking phenomenal wife, Gulya, who was in the frustrating position of reading this thing page by page, chapter by chapter, as I developed the story itself. She not only caught typos, but confusions and inconsistencies that are tricky to track from inside the creative process of one's own head, and all while she was working on her own creative endeavors. She also bought me a cupcake when I finished. Which was really all I wanted in the first place.

CHAPTER ONE

A pale horse clopped across the damp sand on Brighton Beach. The horse wasn't really white; in fact, it more closely matched the thready, ghostly yellow-white of the early morning sunlight coming in past the Rockaways and over the water. The horse, a very large and muscular stallion, wore a plain leather saddle and girth, and his reins swung loosely from a brown leather hackamore, leaving a delicate line of gibberish trailing through gaping circular footprints on the sand. Strapped to the saddle with a simple but solid series of leather ties was a sword. There's something to be said about the sword, but we'll get to that.

The horse's footprints, and the scrawl spidering down the center, overlapped smaller, bipedal footprints. Ahead of the horse, wandering eastward, was a man in a black robe like a monk's frock, a sweeping thing with a baggy hood and a cord cinched around his waist. The man was as pale as the horse, but with a blue tinge to his skin instead of the horse's blurry yellow, like the two of them had escaped from a pack of Sweet Tarts. The man's face was thin and tight, practically skeletal, and his black hair was cut so short and flat it looked painted on his round skull.

Every few feet, something would catch his eye: a seashell, or a stone, or a gum wrapper half-buried in the sand, or a tiny crab scuttling along the edge of the water, or a seagull shouting out to his mates, or a gang of gulls tearing into an early morning breakfast of tiny crabs that should have thought twice before their early morning scuttle. The man would stop short, stare intently at each object or event with his head tilted, and a curious smile would play on his lips. Then he'd slip back into gear and take a few more steps before another trivially interesting thing nabbed his attention.

The horse, for those adept enough at reading the body language of horses, was getting pretty fed up with this.

Officer Lewis and Officer Kopek didn't grok the body language of horses, but they knew there shouldn't have been a horse on Brighton Beach. The race track was torn down almost a century ago.

"What do you think, Al?" asked Officer Lewis.

Kopek didn't flinch. "It's a horse."

"Yeah," said Lewis. "On the beach."

"I noticed, Danny," said Kopek, still not moving. He stood with his hands on his hips. The belly his wife had given him through the gift of thirty years of phenomenal home-cooked meals hung contentedly over his belt.

Lewis, one of those ridiculously good-looking black men who go into public service because they're just that much nicer than everybody else and don't need to trade on their looks, stood a foot taller than his partner. He leaned like a swashbuckler and tapped on his belt buckle. "What's he doing?"

"The horse?" asked Al Kopek.

"No, the guy," said Danny Lewis.

"Walking." Officer Kopek never used even two words when one would do. When he could communicate entire complex sentiments in single syllables, he felt more comfortable. He and his wife Gracie had developed a shorthand over their three-decade marriage that required very little verbiage on Al's part.

Danny Lewis stared at the man in the black robe. "Yeah, but why's he stopping and looking at everything?"

"Outside of New York," Kopek said, "people take an interest in the world around them."

"He on drugs?"

"Probably."

"Approach?" asked Officer Lewis.

Kopek nodded. They slogged their way through shifting sand, caked from the morning humidity. The horse's ears twitched as the policemen approached, and he raised his head to look their way. His eyes locked on them. His posture clearly said: *Is there a problem, officers?*

"Morning!" Officer Lewis called out.

2

The man turned and smiled at them. "Yes, it is," he said.

The same smile on anybody else might have been a little less freaky, but this guy looked like a grinning skull. His accent was foreign, but not hard to understand. Kopek and Lewis exchanged a look; they didn't have a shorthand from thirty years of marriage, but four years as partners helped. Danny Lewis lowered a hand just behind his holster, while Al Kopek kept his arms studiously neutral and unthreatening.

"Just taking a walk, sir?" Lewis asked, raising his voice over the breeze coming in off the water.

The man nodded, then bent down so suddenly Danny Lewis nearly pulled his pistol and plugged him right then. The man straightened up and toyed with the shiny object in his hand. "Wow," he said.

Kopek and Lewis didn't even need to exchange a look. Kopek cleared his throat and said, "You live around here, sir?"

The man pulled his attention from the bauble in his hand and looked at the cops, his mouth open as if to speak, but his eyes pondering furiously. He snapped his mouth shut. Then he shrugged. "I don't know."

"Sir, have you had anything to drink?" asked Officer Lewis. "Or anything else today? Out partying last night?"

The man twirled the shiny thing in both hands—it was a piece of broken blue glass, worn smooth by sand and tides. "I don't think so," he said. By his tone, he genuinely didn't know. Lewis and Kopek decided, simultaneously and independently, that this sucker was high as the Chrysler Building.

"Maybe you should come with us, sir," said Officer Kopek.

The horse chuffed a bit, a low, growly sound from his muzzle. He stomped anxiously on the sand. The man smiled at the horse.

"This your horse, sir?" Kopek asked.

The man looked at Kopek, back at the horse, back at Kopek, and shrugged. "He's nice, isn't he?"

"Yours?" Kopek asked again.

The man shrugged. "He looks familiar. I'm not sure." He walked to the horse—Kopek and Lewis took a step back defensively, and the horse curved itself around the black-robed man protectively. The man fingered the leather straps holding the sword to the saddle.

"Sir!" shouted Kopek.

"Sir," Lewis called out, "do *not* remove that weapon." His hand was on his pistol; Kopek's was on his own.

The man in the black robe looked at the sword inquisitively, as if he hadn't even thought about taking it out before Lewis suggested it. "Huh," he said. With unexpected speed, his bony fingers danced across the straps and the sword was out. He held it in two hands, looking at it with wonder rather than brandishing it to attack.

Kopek and Lewis were trained police officers, and were taking no chances. Both had their pistols out in a flash, aimed low, not yet pointed at the man in the black robe. "Sir!" barked Officer Lewis. "Drop the weapon on the sand and step back!"

The man gave them an amiable look of confusion. He lifted the sword, the blade glinting in the pale yellow sunrise. The horse tossed his head and did the low, growly chuff thing again; Kopek could swear he saw actual steam puff out of the beast's nostrils.

The sword was odd and old. The hilt was almost precisely the same length as the blade, ending halfway up the length of the entire sword—the sword was almost five feet long if it was an inch—and was wrapped in black leather strips. A couple of lengths of leather hung down from a dense knot at the bottom; the top of the hilt had no guard or crossbar, just the blade slashing forward and curving nastily to the left like a waxing crescent moon. There was no engraving on the blade, no interesting lines or grooves—just a few discolored spots that could have been some kind of pattern, or could have just been as meaningless and arbitrary as an image of the Virgin Mary on a blueberry pancake.

"Sir!" Lewis shouted again.

"Put the sword down, sir!" Kopek demanded. "We don't want to hurt you. Let's all just calm down, and you put that sword down, okay?"

The man in the black robe furrowed his brow and focused on the sword, like he was trying to remember the Pythagorean Theorem but couldn't recall which letter represented the hypotenuse. "Huh," he said. "No, I think this is mine." He didn't say it as a refusal; more a reasonable justification for holding it.

"Sir, put the sword *down*," said Officer Kopek.

"Put it down, sir!" echoed Officer Lewis.

The man shook his head. "I don't think I am supposed to do that."

"You sure as hell *are* supposed to do that!" Lewis replied. "Sir, if you don't put down the sword, we'll have to open fire."

The man cocked his head. "I don't think fire can be opened."

"We *will* shoot you, sir!" Lewis insisted. Kopek tightened his grip on his pistol.

"I think," said the man. "I think...I am supposed to be somewhere. I think I have an appointment." He turned abruptly and walked calmly away along the water's edge, the strange old sword swinging in one hand.

"Freeze!" said Kopek.

"Sir, don't take another step!" Lewis ordered.

Without breaking stride, the man in the black robe glanced back and said, "But that won't get me anywhere." He kept going.

"Al...?"

Kopek sucked in a breath, his gun trained on the sand just below the man's black boots. "He goes somewhere with that sword, somebody gets hurt."

"Yeah, I know," said Danny Lewis.

"Yeah, rush him."

Kopek didn't need to say it twice. He thumped toward the man in the black robe, but Danny Lewis covered the distance in a second, leaping forward and grabbing the man by the shoulders, tumbling to the ground with him. The man let out a strange little squeak and his robe splayed out across the sand, making it hard to spot where his limbs were. Lewis wrestled with him as Kopek heaved across the beach and dove on the pile of flying sand and writhing limbs.

An unearthly shriek tore through the air. The pale horse came into the fray, clopping down on the sand with humongous albino hooves. The scene was a mess of thick black robe, flying pale limbs, cop uniforms, sand and horse sweat. Officer Lewis brought his gun to bear and fired upward—the horse let out a diabolical whinny and kicked out, grazing Lewis's forehead and leaving a bruise and a narrow gash. Kopek had the pale man in an arm lock, and held him tight on the uncomfortably wet sand. The horse looked at Kopek and the man in the black robe, then at Danny Lewis, slightly dazed and stumbling on dark streaks of dug-up sand, and charged in full steam to *yank* the sword from the man's hand with powerful horsey jaws. The pale horse gave the man a look—somewhere between disappointment and reluctance—then charged away through the surf, heading east toward the residential blocks of Manhattan Beach, its nimble mouth still clutching the weird sword.

"What the *hell?*" shouted Officer Kopek.

Officer Lewis held one hand to his forehead and stood on his knees, staring after the horse as it galloped over a rise and out of sight. "What just happened, Al?"

"I don't know!" said Kopek.

"Me neither," said the man in the black robe, still locked in Officer Kopek's grip.

Officer Lewis grabbed his radio from his belt. "Al, I don't even know how to *report* this."

Kopek kept a firm hold on the man in the black robe, who wasn't making any effort to struggle. The older cop raised an eyebrow and shrugged. "Suspect apprehended," he said. "Horse at large—armed and dangerous."

CHAPTER TWO

Life and death were mounting a sneak attack on Jenny Ng, but the best laid plans of mice, men, and abstract philosophical concepts often go awry. So when she stepped off the curb at Prospect Avenue, and a bicycle bell chimed angrily at her, and she dodged out of the way of a delivery guy, then tripped over the wheel of a stroller, staggered four steps while throwing "Sorry, sorry, excuse me!" at the bewildered Haitian nanny and her curly blonde charge, and wobbled, off-balance, into the middle of the intersection, the car that hit her was more the culmination of a pretty rocky week than the termination of a pretty rocky life.

Car horns blared and a collective gasp went up, and Jenny was surrounded by half the population of Brooklyn.

"Wow!"

"You okay?"

"You see that?"

"What happened?"

"Chick got creamed!"

"Is she breathing?"

"Is she bleeding?"

"Can you talk?"

"Can you walk?"

"Can you hear me?"

"Yes!" Jenny coughed, "I'm fine, I can hear you, I'm fine." She looked around wildly, trying to get a grip on what was happening. "What...?"

"You got hit by a car," a short Mexican man said flatly. His bored, matter-of-fact bedside manner was the next best thing to morphine.

"Don't move her!" commanded a middle-aged white lady with garish red hair.

"She's moving herself," replied the Mexican man.

"No, don't get up..." said a couple of girls who had cell phones out, either dialing *911* or texting their friends about the coolest thing they'd ever seen.

"I'm *fine!*" Jenny insisted, rolling over and picking herself up. She looked for her bag, then saw it half spilled at the feet of three burly guys in matching work uniforms ("Min's Moving Men," read the block letters on their chests). The biggest looked down and realized what Jenny was scoping out, and all three instantly crouched to help her collect her crap and stuff it back into her bag. "Thanks," she said, "thanks, guys."

"Ambulance on the way," said one cell phone girl while the other snapped a shot of Jenny with her phone.

"The ambulance is on its way!" declared the red-haired lady, taking charge of the situation by repeating any information relevant to it.

"Anybody a doctor?" someone in the crowd asked.

"Let me through, let me through," said someone else. "I'm a doctor! Let me through." The crowd parted, and a tanned Adonis stepped into the center where Jenny was kneeling and checking the strap on her bag. Jenny looked up and gulped.

The new guy was straight out of a movie: golden tan, hair like dark chocolate, eyes of crystal blue beneath manscaped eyebrows flanking a gracefully arched nose pointing down to fantastic lips parting to reveal even, straight, perfectly white teeth. It was a parade of perfect features, and it didn't end there: sharp cleft chin, corded neck muscles, broad shoulders, sculpted chest...there was more eye candy here than in the Macy's parade. He wore a powder blue golf shirt and khaki pants. His shoes were expensive and leather.

"Are you all right?" he asked Jenny, intense baritone music filling her ears.

Instead of blurting how much she loved him or embarrassingly admitting that she hadn't had sex with something that didn't require electricity in almost a year (Keith Heckler didn't count, and probably required electricity anyway), she nodded mutely.

"I'm Doctor Raymond," he said, with a reassuring smile of perfect white teeth. "You can call me Vincent. What's your name?"

"I'm," said Jenny. "Um," said Jenny. She knew her own name, damn it. There it was: "I'm Jenny."

"Jenny, you're going to be just fine," said Doctor Raymond. He took her arm and placed a firm, manly thumb where the ball of her hand met her narrow wrist. "Your pulse is racing a bit, but that's to be expected," he chuckled. His laugh was like warm honey dripping all over her body in some marble-decked palace of silk curtains and pillows, where she and Vincent would while away the hours talking about intimacy and commitment and half-Chinese, half-Perfect-Man-God children—

"I'm fine, really," said Jenny. "I don't need a doctor. I don't even feel hurt. Honestly!"

"Well, you should get yourself checked out," said Doctor Raymond.

Jenny avoided the easy punchline. "No really, I..." She smiled apologetically and lowered her voice. "I don't have insurance. I'm fine, I just—I don't want to bother dealing with, you know...."

Vincent Raymond nodded sagely like a Greek hero planning an assault on Troy. He pulled a slim leather wallet from his pocket, then plucked out a card. He placed the card gently in Jenny's palm and lingered, pressing the card on her skin. Even his fingers were tanned and muscular. "This is my card—my practice is in the city. Please, come by in the next few days," he said, "and let's just make sure nothing's falling off on you!"

Jenny laughed. "Sure, I'll be there," she said. "I mean, if anything feels off. Or falls off," she added with another laugh. She rose, and he went with her, guiding her to the top. He was over six feet tall, towering over Jenny. (She was barely over five—what her mother always called "a correct height for a Chinese girl!") She felt like a toothpick standing in front of a lion. Self-consciously brushing her fingers through her short, spiky hair, she smiled up at Doctor Raymond. "Thanks, Doctor—Doctor Raymond—"

"Vincent," he reminded her.

"Vincent," she agreed. "Thanks. I, uh, I really need to go."

The red-haired lady shook her head. "You can't leave, dear," she said with an air of self-proclaimed authority. "The ambulance is on its way."

"Crap," said Jenny. "Can we call them back, cancel it, I mean...I'm fine...."

"I'll take care of it," said Vincent. "Just a quick call and let them know it's all cleared up, false alarm."

Jenny flashed a grin his way. "Thanks," she said. "Vincent." She knew it wasn't necessary to address him by name—everybody, including Vincent Raymond, knew who she was talking to—but it felt good to hear his name coming out of her mouth again.

Apparently, she wasn't the only one. "Vincent!" a melodious voice called pleasantly. The crowd opened up again to allow a tall, leggy blonde through. She was wearing a summery dress and glittery pumps, and was the Aphrodite to Vincent's Eros. Not a mark, not a scar, not a flaw, not a blemish. What the girls back at Renova High would call "a bitch." The accusation of bitch, in Jenny's experience, had very little to do with a woman's personality or behavior, and a lot more to do with how much more easily she could turn men's heads than the accuser.

"No problems, Carrie," said Vincent. Tall blonde perfect Carrie moved gracefully to Vincent's side and smiled prettily at Jenny. "A minor accident, but she's just fine."

"That's good news," said Carrie the Friendly Bitch.

"This is my wife, Carrie," Vincent said, an arm around the blonde's creamy tan shoulders. "Carrie, this is Jenny."

"Hello, Jenny," Carrie Raymond sang cheerfully to the tune of I'm Tall And Blonde And Gorgeous And There's Zero Chance Any Of Your Fantasies About My Husband Will Come True. "You must be pretty tough, huh?"

"Uh," said Jenny. She shrugged. "Guess so, yeah."

"Oh, she's *fantastic*," sang Carrie in a chorus of You're Just A Little Chinese Girl With No Real Breasts To Speak Of, And I'm The Buxom Feminine Ideal Of Modern Western Civilization.

Jenny cleared her throat and shifted her feet. "Um, yeah, so—thanks for the help, and Doctor Raymond—"

"Vincent," said Vincent and Carrie Raymond on cue.

"Vincent," Jenny said quickly, "I'll, I mean, I may take you up on," she waved a hand at the antecedent.

"Oh, please, yes," said Carrie. "Vincent's wonderful—the best in Manhattan. Make sure you come in, he'll make sure you're doing all right."

A couple of teenage boys in baggy jeans, freshmen or sophomores in college, pushed through the crowd. "Hey!" one said. "Crap," the other said.

Vincent and Carrie eyed the boys appraisingly. Jenny squinted at them. "Yeah?" she said.

"Uh," said the shorter, rounder one. His taller, gangly friend hit him on the arm. They wore dark T-shirts with pop culture images on them: the short one had *The Crow*, the other had *Iron Man*. Iron Man Kid poked Crow Boy, who spoke up. "I'm sorry about the accident."

"Yeah, well," Jenny shrugged. "Not your fault. Thanks for stopping by."

"No, it *was* his fault," said the Iron Man Kid. "He was driving."

Jenny took a moment, then nodded curtly. "Whatever. It happens. You guys okay?"

Carrie Raymond smiled. "She's so generous!" Vincent Raymond nodded proudly.

"Oh, shit," Crow Boy said, relief pouring faster than sweat and sebaceous oils. "Cool. I thought you were going to sue us or something."

"*Us?*" Iron Man Kid pointed out.

"Shut up, Lloyd," said Crow Boy. He turned to Jenny. "Hey, could I, like, give you a lift or something? Or give you some money? Or, uh, get you dinner or something?"

Lloyd the Iron Man Kid was clearly impressed by his buddy's balls, and checked Jenny's face for a reaction. She kept her composure, and gave Crow Boy a tight-lipped smile. "No, *really*, don't worry about it."

The guy wiped his nose on his arm. "Cool," he said. "I'm Lyle." He waited expectantly.

Jenny nodded slowly. "Great," she said. "Doctor Raymond—I mean, Vincent...Carrie, nice to meet you. Lloyd, Lyle...nice, uh, being run over by you." Lloyd smacked Lyle on the shoulder again. Lyle hit him back. "I really have to go—thanks, everybody," she said to the crowd in general, hoping it would be a signal to disperse and let her get out and on with her life. "I've got to get into the..."

The crowd's murmur increased, but didn't drown out the approaching sirens. Vincent Raymond smiled at Jenny. "I should have called quicker," he said. "New York Methodist is only a dozen blocks away."

"Crap," said Jenny. "Are they going to make me go to the hospital? I *really* can't afford to—"

"I could help out," said Lyle, his hormones visibly aching. Lloyd nodded eagerly, staring at Jenny and scratching at chin fuzz that probably took six years to cultivate.

Great, she thought, *comic book geeks with an Asian fetish. That's new.*

"Don't worry, Jenny," said Vincent—Jenny winced as her name was devoured by Lyle's and Lloyd's mental processors for storage—"I'll let them know you're all checked out. Just let me do the talking."

"Yeah, but I have to go," said Jenny, "really. I'm on my way to a job interview. I *can't* be late." She frowned. "Again."

Vincent shook his head. "Now, you can't just leave."

"No, definitely not," said Carrie Raymond, glistening some beauty at Jenny.

"But once we get this cleared up, Carrie and I will get you where you need to go." Vincent delivered another sparkling smile. Jenny practically heard a bell ring as a glint spiraled off a perfect incisor.

"We could drive her," said Lyle.

"Yeah, we're going—uh," said Lloyd, "where you're...going."

Carrie Raymond gave the boys a regal smile. "I think Jenny would be much more comfortable with us, you know?" she said. "It's a girl thing." She winked at Jenny.

Jenny smiled back. Maybe the Amazing Amazon wasn't so bad after all.

The crowd opened wide. (The red-haired lady said "Move aside, move aside!" to people who had already got out of the way.) Two EMT guys moved in and scoped out the situation. The older one, short and muscular with a thick mustache, took a look at Jenny, Lyle, Lloyd, and the Raymonds. He looked at the Mexican guy, who shrugged dispassionately and walked away through the crowd. "Hey, people," said the EMT, "what's up?"

The other EMT, a lean guy with shaggy blond hair and a five o'clock shadow, lugged an equipment bag. "We got a call on a car accident...?"

"Hi, guys," said Vincent. "I'm Doctor Raymond, I was on the scene. This is Jenny," he put an arm around her shoulder, and Jenny melted a little. "The boys there gave her a little tap, and she got shook up a little, but no damage."

Mutters in the crowd multiplied. Lyle and Lloyd looked sheepishly at each other's sneakers.

The mustached EMT said, "Yeah, okay, let us just take a look...." The shaggy one put his bag down and started poking and prodding at Jenny, asking questions softly and so quickly she had no time to answer any of them.

She opened her mouth to speak, but Vincent Raymond cut in. "Listen, guys—Jenny's running a bit late for a job interview, and she wasn't planning on a trip to the emergency room today. If we could just bypass protocol, I'll take the heat if it comes up." Vincent offered the EMT guys another glamorous smile and handed the mustached one a business card.

The EMT guy read the business card and his face sagged; he looked like he'd found scraped-up sidewalk gum in his after-work beer. He rolled his eyes and handed the card to his partner, who developed a similar expression. The mustached guy nodded nonchalantly. "Yeah, whatever. We just need to get some information, have you sign off on this." The shaggy EMT pulled a case out of his bag and opened it to reveal more paperwork than Jenny would have to fill out at her job interview.

With the ambulance parked at the corner and Jenny and Lyle filling out paperwork (while she underwent a cursory physical at the hands of the shaggy EMT), the show died down and the crowd shuffled away bit by bit, like the audience at intermission when a mildly amusing *entr'acte* comedian competes with the lure of the bar in the lobby. The Raymonds chatted with the mustached EMT guy, and the shaggy EMT finished giving Jenny a once-over, then put his bag away and sat in the ambulance talking on the radio. Lloyd hovered nearby sneaking furtive glances at Jenny's butt, which was slightly exposed above the top of her pants as she sat on the curb filling out paperwork. When the crowd had nearly disappeared, the red-haired lady announced to nobody in particular, "Yes, move along, it's all over," and straightened her tastefully anal compulsive outfit. She gave Jenny a sickly attempt at a warm smile, threw a look at Carrie Raymond, and followed the crowd into the off-screen part of Jenny's life, presumably never to make a cameo again. She passed by a couple of cops, who'd finally arrived on the scene. "Hey, what's the story?" said the little Italian cop.

The Raymonds and the mustached EMT guy filled the cops in. The big Irish one looked down at Jenny: "So you don't want to do anything about this guy?" He nudged Lyle with his toe.

"No, really," said Jenny. "It's okay, nobody got hurt. I don't want him to get in trouble." She fervently avoided Lyle's puppy dog stare. The last thing she needed was a chubby, geeky fanboy who expected her to dress

13

up like Sailor Moon or something. The cops shrugged and started asking the EMT guy questions; he glanced at his partner in the ambulance, and confirmed that Jenny didn't appear to have any injuries.

With all the *T*s crossed (there wasn't a single *I* to dot, by chance), Jenny held her papers up to the EMT guy, who took them and helped her up. Lyle was still scribbling away, his tongue sticking out in concentration and his wallet unfolded on his lap, a New York driver's license sticking out of one fold. The two cops stood on either side of him like egregiously mismatched bookends at a flea market. Vincent and Carrie Raymond smiled at Jenny, and Carrie said, "All right, Jenny, let's get you to that interview."

The EMT guy said, "Okay, Miz Ng, remember, you start feeling anything weird, any pain, any soreness, if anything shows up, bruises or anything—just head over to the emergency room. Here's my card. You tell them they can call my dispatch if they need any details."

"Thanks," said Jenny, holding his card and Doctor Raymond's like a pair of aces.

"Mister Raymond," the EMT guy nodded goodbye.

"*Doctor* Raymond," Vincent chided him goodnaturedly.

"Yeah," the guy said curtly. "Missuz Raymond."

"Thanks so much!" Carrie chirped harmoniously.

"Uh huh." He wandered behind Lyle to wait for his paperwork. "Let's hurry it up, kid. The cops'll want to have a word with you." The cops grunted and nodded.

"Shit," muttered Lyle. Lloyd valiantly stifled his laughter and smiled goofily at Jenny.

"Our car isn't far, Jenny," said Carrie Raymond. "Walk this way!" She linked arms with Jenny, guiding her along Prospect Park West toward the circle. Jenny mused silently that she'd be able to "walk this way" a lot better if she had a few extra inches in her legs, an actual ass, and heels to match Carrie's, but the Blonde Bombshell didn't seem to care. Vincent Raymond walked along on Jenny's other side, and the Beautiful People kept up pleasant conversation, asking and answering, learning about Jenny and giving her little bits and pieces of their way too perfect life. They were interested but not too invasive; interesting but not too intimate. It was the kind of conversation Jenny would watch in cocktail scenes in movies. She felt nervous not knowing her lines, but the Raymonds fit every awkward utterance of hers into their seamless script.

They turned at the circle, walked half a block on Prospect Park Southwest, and Vincent pulled a keyring from his pocket and pressed a button. A sleek black BMW by the curb *bleet-booped* and flashed its lights, and Vincent Raymond opened doors for the ladies. Carrie Raymond helped Jenny into the back seat and shut the door, then got herself in the front while Vincent strolled around to the driver's seat.

The car started with barely a growl, the engine purring loud as a cat in the vacuum of outer space. Vincent buckled his seatbelt and asked, "Where are we headed, Jenny?"

Jenny shuffled through her bag and came out with a blue Post-it. "It's on Madison, near Fortieth," she said. "I just need to get to the corner, it's right there."

Vincent got them on the Brooklyn-Queens, headed for the bridge. He was a safe and polite driver: not driving granny-slow, but no reckless daredevil, considerately letting other motorists change lanes ahead of him or make their turns as needed. Jenny hadn't been in a car since the last time she visited her mother. As a gritty transplanted New Yorker, there was something decadent about the experience, but she liked it.

"So what's this job you're going to get, Jenny?" Carrie Raymond asked.

"Well, I don't have it *yet*—"

Carrie clucked her tongue. "Now, I asked what job it is you're *going* to get, Jenny," she said. "You'll get it—after a day like this, you deserve it!"

Jenny smiled dubiously. "Well, yeah, okay," she said. "It's just a receptionist job. At a law firm." She played it down to keep her expectations low. "It's no big thing. Just a job."

"Is that what you do?" Carrie asked earnestly. "You work as a receptionist?"

"No," Jenny said, a little too quickly. If Carrie noticed, she politely kept quiet. Jenny said, "No, I mean, I just do whatever—you know, just to pay the rent."

Vincent Raymond shook his head. "But that's not what you should do with your life," he said.

"No, no," agreed Carrie Raymond.

"You should be doing something you love!" said Vincent. "The more you love it, the harder you'll work, and the rent will seem to pay itself."

Jenny shrugged. "Sure, I guess," she said. "I mean, you're a doctor, you don't have to worry about that stuff."

"I went through the same hard times we all do, Jenny," said Vincent.

Carrie laughed like a flute section playing a song about daffodils. "And *I* took care of *him*, then," she said. "I worked as a receptionist, too. And a secretary. I worked at a library, and an antiques store. I even worked in a butcher shop!"

"Exactly," said Vincent. "We all put in our time, we all pay our dues. We all have our hopes and dreams, and in the best of all possible worlds, we aim for them, and we do whatever's necessary to achieve them. Even if it means toiling in the dirt for a while," he laughed, and his wife joined in.

Jenny smiled. "Yeah," she said. "I mean, I guess I always figure, people like you—"

"Like us?" Carrie asked.

"Well," Jenny backpedaled, "you know...rich. Or, you know, just doing fine. You guys don't have to worry about the rent every month, or count your change to pay for lunch for the week, and I guess it's hard to keep in mind that you guys were there once, too. Here, I mean." She spread her hands. "Where I am."

Vincent and Carrie shared a moment. "Yes," said Vincent. "We're all people, and people are people. All these little differences, they don't matter so much on a...cosmic scale."

"It would be nice," Carrie Raymond added, "if all the differences could just be stripped away. We could all be together, just one perfect unity, in peace and happiness. All in one."

"Consumed by love," said Vincent.

"Consumed by love," murmured Carrie.

Jenny paused. It was kind of a nice thought on the one hand; on the other, it was just a little bit *Rosemary's Baby* the way they said that. "Uh," she said. "Yeah, exactly. I guess."

A cab driver on the FDR cut them off and flipped off Vincent with some angry unintelligible words. Vincent Raymond waved pleasantly back. "So," he said with a friendly glance in the rearview, "what is it you *really* do?"

Jenny sighed and looked out the window. "I don't know," she said. "There's stuff I want to do, but it doesn't seem like...."

"Yes?" Carrie prompted her.

"I like photography," said Jenny. "I'm into it, I mean. And I do it, I mean. I mean—yes, I'm a photographer," she finally said. "It's just hard to break in there, in the arts. Everything's so subjective, you just have to hope that the right person sees the right photo in the right place at the right time, and likes it, and then maybe you start getting some exposure."

Vincent and Carrie laughed, catching Jenny off guard. They saw her expression and stopped laughing. "Sorry," said Carrie Raymond, "we thought you were making a joke."

"Oh," said Jenny. "Right, no, sorry," she smiled, but it lasted as long as a cloud's dim shadow through the living room windows on a lazy Springtime Sunday afternoon. "It's just that—I spent so much time in school, learning all this stuff, art history, and photography, and lighting, and color, and composition, and *fashion*, for Christ's sake...and I'm out here in the real world, and none of it *means* anything. Because what I didn't learn was how to get a job."

"But you have!" said Vincent Raymond. "Haven't you? You've had jobs since college, right?"

"A few," Jenny admitted.

"A few jobs in a couple of years is a pretty good average," said Carrie Raymond.

"A couple...?" Jenny laughed sharply. "I'm twenty-eight."

"Oh!" said Carrie. "You look so young, I'm sorry!"

"Yeah," Jenny groused. "I know."

Vincent angled the BMW off the FDR and took the ramp to Forty-Second Street. "It's not a bad thing, Jenny," he said. "Our society is obsessed with youth."

"And how," Carrie Raymond said emphatically and adorably.

"You have something many people want."

Jenny scoffed. "Yeah, ask them how much they want it when half the bartenders in Manhattan won't believe their totally real license isn't fake." She smiled ruefully. "I get carded at *weddings*. They don't even ask the flower girls or the little boys in tuxes for ID there, but me...?"

They headed down Second Avenue, and Vincent took a right on Thirty-Ninth. "Almost there," he said. He glanced at the digital clock lodged between a GPS readout, satellite radio, and a dozen other luxury features Jenny couldn't have identified. "What time's your interview?"

"One o'clock," said Jenny. She looked at the dashboard, too. "Oh, cool. I'm on time!"

"See? We told you there was no reason to worry," said Carrie Raymond. "You're going to get this job, Jenny, I can *feel* it."

"Carrie has a great sense of the future," said Vincent. "It's like she's psychic! She always knows."

Jenny had to smile. "Yeah, hope so," she said. "Listen, thanks, you guys, *so* much. This is just—really, just thanks. It's been a bad week. You guys are life savers."

"No, certainly not," said Vincent.

"Certainly not!" repeated Carrie.

"We just like to help, however we can."

"Exactly," said Carrie. "You were in a tough spot, and just needed a hand. We're glad to help." With a sparkle in her eye, she added, "Better than twenty minutes in a car with Lyle and Lloyd."

Jenny laughed. "Better than *one* minute in a car with Lyle and Lloyd," she said.

"Madison Avenue," Vincent announced. "Which side of the street?"

"Oh—uh, right side, near corner," said Jenny. "Wow. Thanks, Vincent. Carrie—thank you both so much!"

"Don't worry about it," said Vincent. "Life has a way of turning round and round."

"Sometime, someday," Carrie said, "*you* might be the one helping *us* out."

"Everything is circular," said Vincent.

"Ends are just new beginnings," said Carrie.

"And new beginnings are only possible when the old has ended."

They nodded and smiled at each other and at Jenny.

Jenny smiled politely. "Sure, yeah," she said, hoping they weren't about to sell her AmWay or *Dianetics*. She slung her bag over her shoulder and checked her Post-it. "So, hey, I'll totally get over to your office later this week. Like I should take you to dinner or something," she said, "both of you."

"Well, you can go to dinner *with* us," said Vincent, "but you don't get to pay unless your rent is already covered."

"That's the rules," beamed Carrie.

"Okay, okay," Jenny surrendered. Vincent pulled over, and she put a hand on the door handle. "You guys drive safe, and thanks again, thanks *so* much, for the ride, for everything."

"You just go get that job, Jenny!" Carrie said.

"And come by my office any time," Vincent said, "we'll make sure Lyle didn't do any permanent damage."

"Thanks!" said Jenny, opening the door. "I gotta go—I'll be there. See you guys!"

"So long!"

"Go get 'em!" Carrie Raymond called after her.

Jenny raced into the building, bag over one shoulder, Post-it and two business cards in one hand, the other ruffling through her hair in an effort to make herself at least somewhat presentable. She felt a moment of envy toward Carrie Raymond, who probably got out of bed looking like a movie producer's wet dream, but shook it off as she stepped into the elevator. Jenny looked at the mirrored back wall and took some time to fix her hair and makeup, adjust her blouse and pants. She checked the suite number on the Post-it and shoved it in her bag. She looked at the two business cards. One was for the EMT guy, Thomas F. Hillman. The other was for Vincent Raymond, Doctor of Chiropractic, Licensed Physical Therapist.

A chiropractor? Vincent wasn't even a real doctor! With her Chinese heritage and her no-nonsense mother, Jenny was wary of the bullshit that was passed off as "alternative" medicine. Her mother had pounded into her that traditional practices like acupuncture might have some effect, but the explanations were just metaphors. Americans, her mother complained, thought the metaphor had to be taken literally. They had little grasp of the art of Chinese science *or* poetry.

Jenny shook her head, put the business cards in her bag, and took a deep breath. The elevator door opened, and she gracefully swept out to *get* that job.

CHAPTER THREE

Or not. A half hour later, she stood at the corner, regretting nearly every word she'd said to the man with horn-rimmed glasses who'd interviewed her. Rationally, she knew she didn't say anything wrong. He just had another candidate in mind. A tall, buxom, blonde candidate. A carbon copy of Carrie Raymond who knew how the phone system worked and how to bat her eyes at bitter old men going through divorces or real estate deals or mergers and acquisitions or whatever it was that bitter old men went to law firms for.

"Crap." Jenny leaned back against the wall of the office building. It was only Wednesday, and she'd had four rejections this week, not counting when she got fired from Spank's on Sunday. She hated waitressing anyway, and she wasn't about to apologize to the fat couple who had not only complained about everything on the table, but spit when they were talking, swore at her repeatedly, and actually threw a fork at her. Mister Cullie was not an understanding manager. His motto, in a nutshell, was "The customer is always deserving of a nice big puckery kiss on their ass." Employees ranked lower on his sympathy scale than the cockroaches he chased out of the kitchen every night.

Still, that left Jenny with a quarter of this month's week-late rent in her bank account, a few hundred dollars of credit card debt, a few *thousand* dollars of student loan debt, and a couple dozen articles of clothing in the fancy closet that, according to the real estate people, was her studio apartment in Brooklyn. She hadn't admitted to Vincent and Carrie Raymond that she sold her Nikon a year ago to pay for a few months of non-essentials like rent, utilities, food and toothpaste. Jenny Ng, aspiring photographer, hadn't snapped a shot since. Her cheap cell phone didn't have a camera.

She pulled out that cheap cell phone and stared at it; she knew anything in the bank would be going toward this, the only bill she made sure to pay on time, every time. Credit card and student loan debts, she could live with. No apartment, she could crash at Heckler's place until he made her feel bad enough to have sex with him. (Which, she admitted, she probably would out of guilt.) But without her phone, she was done— finished, game over. There was no way she could even *look* for a job if employers had no way to contact her. She was reluctant to provide her address, since she ended up skipping out on leases so often. She usually jotted down her mother's address back in Philadelphia, but a couple numbers off, so Hua Yao Ng wouldn't receive mail intended for her daughter and open it out of motherly concern, better known as "a federal offense." Some random person on Spring Street was probably getting fed up with receiving collections notices and credit card offers addressed to Jenny Ng.

Jenny ran through her contact list and landed on Keith Heckler's entry. She set her jaw, but she wasn't going to call now anyway—her free minutes didn't start until seven. Maybe in the next five hours, she'd find a way to avoid calling him. She wandered through the rest of the short list of names and numbers. Dana had moved back to Seattle to take care of her grandmother; Charlie and Angie were married and gave up on the whole Take New York By Storm idea, moving down south somewhere. Tammy was still living with that jackass, Rick; Lisa was still living with that jackass, Matt (and sleeping with Rick on the side); Abby had gone back to school to get a law degree; nobody had even *heard* from Ramona since a few weeks after she moved to the city to Take New York By Storm with them (Jenny mostly kept her entry out of nostalgia).

In only six years, her friends had melted away into a city of nine million strangers.

Jenny sniffed and refused to let herself cry; her eyes stung from tears itching to break free. Nothing was working out the way it was supposed to. In college, everything seemed ready and waiting. Life was theirs for the taking. Instead, life took her, chewed her up, and spit her out.

She wiped her eyes with the back of her hand, took a deep breath, and straightened up. A remarkable number of cats was lined up along the sidewalk, staring at her. Overhead, across the street, a row of at least a hundred pigeons lined a cornice on the building opposite. Jenny froze, looking at pigeons and cats. She laughed at herself; there was no way they were all staring at her. She adjusted her shoulder bag and shuffled a couple of steps to the left.

A hundred beaks shifted in unison; a couple dozen shining cat eyes followed her.

Jenny froze again. She shuffled right. The cats kept their eyes on her; the hundred beaks shifted back like Rockettes phoning it in.

"Stop that," she said, softly but sharply. The afternoon bustle of the city whirled around her, cars and people and vendors and exhaust and a pretty decent early Summer breeze. The cats didn't move, and the pigeons didn't move, and Jenny did her best not to move. A handful of pigeons flapped into view and took their places on the cornice with the rest. Another cat trotted up and sat next to the line of cats. A delivery truck pulled up, but did not stare at her.

Jenny centimetered, then inched her way around the cats, watching twenty-six eyes and over a hundred beaks follow her. She stepped off the curb just as the rear door of the truck swung up and a couple of crates, having shifted in transit as the door warned might be a possibility, tumbled out right on top of her.

"Ow!" she cried.

The crates were a lot bigger than Jenny, and weighed a lot more than thirteen cats and a hundred and sixteen pigeons. The edges were bolted with strips of metal with jagged bits where the die cut hadn't run as smoothly as it could. They smashed down on her leg and the street, and the sharp edge of the first, teamed up with the weight of the second, sliced right through her thigh.

Jenny gasped. She was accompanied by the flapping of two hundred and thirty-two wings as every pigeon across the street took flight simultaneously. Most of the cats scattered; a few lingered, watching the proceedings intently.

Propped on one elbow on the curb, she looked down at her own severed leg, sticking out from under a crate like the Wicked Witch's striped socks and ruby slippers. She wiggled the stump of thigh still attached to her hip and gibbered.

She wondered why it didn't hurt that much.

Shock, she figured.

But it was still odd. Her thigh tingled, and the ghostly sensations of her severed leg felt astonishingly real. She reflexively "flexed" her "foot"—and watched the foot on her severed leg extend and wiggle inside her boot.

"What the...?" The bustle of New York City continued around her—in the span of seconds, nobody had even noticed her predicament, but she heard footsteps coming around the truck. Instinctively, with no real clue what she was doing, Jenny braced herself on the curb and kicked out with her remaining leg. There wasn't really much blood to speak of, an unusual lack what with the severed limb and all. With a couple of swift kicks, she shoved the crate over—proud that she thought to wear her Doc Martens today—and her soggy, squished leg *squelched* out from under it, landing right next to her.

It was her leg, all right. Cut right off. Still sheathed in the leg of her nice gray pants, the cloth frayed where the sharp edge of the crate had bitten through. Jenny marveled that she wasn't more panicked than she felt. One of the cats looked at her inquisitively: *What's your next move, Little One-Legged Chinese Lady?*

She put a hand on her disembodied leg and pulled it closer, shifting on her butt to examine it—but as soon as her stump moved within a few inches of its severed associate, she felt a sensation like yarn being pulled through all the major cavities of her body, tugging and tickling in places where she couldn't scratch the ticklish itch. She coughed as if an actual spool of yarn was dragging through her throat, tickling the insides, and watched as spurs of bone and veins and muscles and tendons reached out and entwined in unbloodied knots, her severed leg and stump pulling at each other. The force of the twisting bits of innards dragged the leg the few remaining inches where it butted up against the stump, and Jenny saw the skin on her leg melt and mold and reform into her own perfectly smooth leg. She was whole. The only sign of the incident was the ragged rip in her pants around the entire circumference of her thigh.

"Hey," said a voice. Most of the remaining cats scattered. Jenny looked up. The delivery guy winced when he saw the two crates on the street. "Shit, did that damn thing open again?"

Jenny nodded, still a little stunned.

"Sorry about that, lady," the delivery guy said, swatting a crate. "Thought they fixed that permanent-like, this time." He grinned apologetically. "It's been giving me trouble for months."

Jenny gave him a stiff mannequin smile.

"You okay?"

Jenny looked at her leg and nodded, slowly at first, then with more speed and enthusiasm; maybe too much. "Yeah!" she squeaked. She took a breath and cleared her throat. "Yeah, I'm fine."

"Aw, shit," said the delivery guy, "you tore your pants."

"No!" Jenny said quickly. "I mean, uh, that was already like that. It's a new thing. Fashion. Thing. New one."

The guy shrugged and checked his crates. "If you say so." He muttered about kids today, with their loud music and weird clothes. He was probably about thirty.

Jenny stood and gingerly tested her reattached leg. The last lingering cat looked at her with distaste: *What are you, new?* It turned its nose up and pranced away. Jenny defiantly pushed down on her leg, felt no twinge of pain, nothing broken, nothing sprained. Her leg was whole and healthy and functional. It was like nothing had happened.

Except she knew it had. And her pants leg, riding down to a toroid heap around her ankle, was evidence of that. She bent over and yanked her pants leg back up, straightening it out as best she could to cover her thigh. It wouldn't stay, of course; in one fist, she held a frayed handful to her thigh, keeping her pants mostly together. She thought she might have some safety pins in her bag, but she didn't want to check here and now. Avoiding the delivery guy's eyes, she crossed the street and walked into an easy, well-lit diner. The girl behind the counter got her a small table in the corner, where she ordered a coffee as a lease on the table.

It only took about ten seconds to decide that this was the most unusual thing that had ever happened to her. It took another five to wonder if it was going to keep the record. Her leg had reattached itself— *Okay*, she figured, *I can deal with that*. But was that the extent of what was happening? What was up with the pigeons and cats?

Focus, she told herself. One thing at a time. The leg thing. Her leg had been chopped off, and she put it back on. Was that a one-time thing? A Get Out of Jail Free card she was given as an exclusive, limited time offer? Or was it going to last?

Would it work a second time?

Hacking off her leg in the middle of a diner might raise some eyebrows. She decided to start small, and see what the limits of this strange new phenomenon might be. She caught the waitress with a wave and a half-smile.

"Coffee'll be right out," the waitress said.

"Right, thanks," said Jenny. "I just need a steak knife."

The waitress paused. "A steak knife?" Jenny's table was empty, and she'd only ordered coffee. Both women knew this, because the waitress's question mark told that story in full, with embellishment, in epic form.

"Yeah, a...yeah," said Jenny. "A steak knife. Please."

The girl chewed her gum thoughtfully, then shrugged. "'Kay," she said. She got a steak knife from a shelf and dropped it off on Jenny's table the next time she walked by.

Jenny smiled gratefully at her, then picked up the knife. She was right-handed, so she figured she'd try this out on her left—she'd have better control of the knife, and if it didn't work out, her dominant hand would be unscathed. She looked around the room furtively, then unfolded her paper napkin on the table and tucked her hands underneath it with the knife.

She decided her pinky was the least important finger. She pressed the edge of the knife on top of her finger and steeled her nerves. She pressed down. Then she pressed down harder. She really pushed it in.

Nothing happened.

"Oh, god." She cringed. She uncovered her finger and saw only a deep gray mark from the pressure of the knife. Her skin wasn't even broken. The steak knife wasn't really that sharp—if this was going to work, she was going to have to *saw*.

"Eww," said Jenny.

She reminded herself that she *really did* lose her leg and reattach it. That it barely hurt at all, and then only right when the metal-edged crate sliced through it. Compared to a whole leg, a finger was nothing. Less than nothing. Over in an instant. Could put it right back on. Wouldn't feel a thing.

Jenny didn't believe herself for a second.

She thought about sneaking into the kitchen to grab a sharp cleaver, but that was doubtful. If she was caught, she couldn't very well explain *why* she was borrowing the cleaver. There wasn't any alternative explanation she could give. Hell, chopping off her finger as an experiment in exploratory existentialism was hardly a convincing explanation, even if it was quite nearly true.

She braced herself and snuck her hands under the napkin again. The waitress brought her coffee, a collection of sweeteners, and some creamers.

Jenny thanked her, fishing her hands out but leaving the knife hidden under the napkin. She poured a few pink packets in her coffee, emptied out one little plastic cup of Half-n-Half, stirred her coffee, and took a sip. It was hot, but not scalding. Jenny thought for a moment, then put her hands back under the napkin with the steak knife.

She put on her game face and picked up the knife, resting the blade on her little finger. She pressed down and pulled the blade along the width of her finger...and lost her nerve. She withdrew her hands and took another sip of coffee. An idea hit her. She stuck her pinky in her coffee and let it simmer for a moment; the heat became uncomfortable, even a little painful. With her other hand, she grabbed a second napkin from across the table, wadded it up, and shoved it in her mouth. She yanked her hand out of the coffee, slipped both hands back under the napkin, and picked up the steak knife. Holding the knife ready, she winced, closed her eyes and dragged the blade forcefully across her finger. The napkin in her mouth muffled a tiny squeal as the blade broke skin.

Jenny'd gone too far to turn back now. She pushed the blade forward, sawed backward, forward, back, tearing through flesh and muscle and bone, feeling a little damp seep of blood pour from her sliced finger. She cut through it faster and faster, and realized she wasn't silently screaming through the napkin in her mouth anymore, more focused on getting through her finger with this damn, dull steak knife. It was hanging on by a flap of skin now; now by a thread, like a loose tooth just *begging* to fall out. And, like that, with a click of stainless steel knife on formica table, she was through.

She gasped, then almost choked on the napkin in her mouth. She pulled out her uninjured hand and yanked out the napkin, leaving behind damp bits of paper that she spent the next minute spitting out or swallowing. Jenny's left hand was partly uncovered—she took a panicked look around the room and hid it beneath the unfolded napkin.

Sitting out in the open on the table, though, was her chopped off pinky.

Jenny shoved it under the napkin just as the waitress passed by—the girl slowed and looked at Jenny. "How is every—how's the coffee?" she asked.

"Fine, thanks," Jenny said, smiling too broadly. A little strand of shredded paper napkin dangled from one tooth.

"Great," said the waitress as she floated off to her other tables.

Jenny took a peek under the napkin. There were tiny spots of blood, and one jagged line of red on the table where she'd sawed through her finger. But neither the ragged stub nor the severed finger was bleeding. She wiggled her absent finger through the "ghost pains," and the pinky under the napkin twitched.

Psyching herself up, she picked up the finger beneath the napkin. Without fanfare or hesitation, she jammed it right into her hand, where it belonged. She waited a moment.

She waited another moment.

"Shit," she whispered ferociously. "No, no, no, *shit!*"

And then the weird feeling came through her again, pulling her insides out to tangle with her severed finger, a tickle that begged to be scratched and never could be, as her finger wove a network of bone and veins and sinew and flesh while tiny slithery crackling noises provided a soundtrack, her skin filling in the gaps before her eyes until her finger was reattached, functional, and completely unmarked.

She smiled a giddy little smile and let the napkin fall away, lifting her hand and flexing her fingers. She rubbed her reattached finger, and it felt fine. She looked down at the steak knife and the tiny red spots—she swept the blood away with the napkin, and it was like the whole thing had never happened. Her finger, her leg—nothing could hurt her. Not permanently, at least. She'd be just fine. Jenny Ng was indestructible. She smiled at her finger. "Kick *ass*," she said, and she took another sip of coffee.

CHAPTER FOUR

She left the knife and the slightly bloodied napkin on the table with her empty cup and a dollar tip, safety-pinned her pants leg to the frayed edge at the top of her reattached thigh (she used only three of the seven safety pins wandering free-range in her shoulder bag), and paid for the ninety-seven-cent coffee. A slightly more than one hundred percent tip would seem excessive if she thought about it mathematically; but even in her impoverished circumstances, Jenny wouldn't leave less than a dollar. For one thing, that was just tacky. For another, she'd been on the receiving end of crap tips.

She headed west with no particular destination, a spring in her regenerated step, an intoxicating buzz in her head. The sky was a cheerful shade of blue; the smell of street hot dogs boiling in car exhaust was mouth-watering; the nattering of tourists and business drones on cell phones was almost bearable. She'd miraculously got a new lease on life, and despite her leaseless situation in Brooklyn (Doc Kolachek kindly let her go month to month with no deposit and nothing to sign), she was feeling good. It wasn't every day you discovered you were indestructible— in fact, by definition, and barring even more peculiar scenarios, you could only discover something like that once—and Jenny felt this was the beginning of something. Anything, really. What could go wrong?

Then again, nothing was guaranteed to go right. It just didn't feel like a Wrong kind of day anymore. That thought itself, that gut feeling, kept Jenny's feet moving toward a distinct but unknown destination.

Blocks passed in grays and blacks and the gleam of windows, and she arbitrarily swung right at a corner. She watched traffic speed by and playfully skipped across the avenue, weaving between wildly swerving cars with blaring horns. She guiltily glanced around—it probably wouldn't be a *great* idea to draw too much attention. Cops might have some questions; or they might just want to slap some cuffs on the crazy jaywalker.

Jenny controlled herself, despite the giddy Monarch butterflies performing abridged Cirque du Soleil routines in her stomach. She waited at the crosswalk and walked casually and cautiously with the rest of the crowd. Then she resolved to go back to Spank's and demand that Mister Cullie give her back her job.

She hurried down the subway stairs and grabbed a C train downtown, practicing a powerful and moving monologue the whole way, vehement *F*s and *S*s in her revolutionary speech slashing viciously at her fellow passengers without warning as she subvocalized the most inspiring call to battle since William Wallace. Some kinder faces looked ready to offer spare change to the muttering Chinese girl if she only asked.

With each stop, though, her resolve dipped a bit, like riding a burlap sack down successive plastic drops on an amusement park slide. By Twenty-Third Street, her monologue had dwindled down to vague and insubstantial muttering liberally sprinkled with some choice profanity gleaned from years of listening to her mother's *mah jongg* games. Any Cantonese speakers who'd overheard her would have been shocked; any Mandarin speakers would have looked around for a bowl made of cheese and filled with tiny hammers; any linguists who spoke both dialects would have enjoyed a brief chuckle.

She slunk off the train, defeated before the battle had even begun, and sulked up to the street. It wasn't yet four o'clock, but a slight overcast darkened the day and matched her mood. Mister Cullie wouldn't be impressed by a show of spine anyway; Mister Cullie was genuinely offended by employees with spines. Affirmative action was perhaps all that prevented him from exclusively hiring invertebrates. Storming Spank's with an impassioned challenge to his hiring and firing practices would get her nothing but some loud invective and a quick trip to the exit. At best, she might steal some silverware and cocktail napkins.

She wandered aimlessly down Eighth Avenue, past posters which, regardless of the subject they advertised, almost invariably depicted very sexy and scantily clad men with no interest in her gender. A silken-skinned shaven-headed black guy implored her to change her cell phone service; two twinks with frosted tips suggested she join their gym; a muscleman wearing only a bow-tie and an outdated mullet (the poster cut off at his waist) asked her to fight toxic waste. Chelsea advertisers played to their demographic, if nothing else.

One poster tugged her eye simply because it was absent any half-naked men. A lonely globe of the Earth sat in a wastebasket, presumably expanding on the Chippendale guy's environmental message, but it was the graffiti that caught her eye: a hastily Sharpied comic strip word balloon had the globe declaring: "I hate (most) humans—die already." She couldn't help but think that the poster likely conveyed the planet's actual opinion of her species.

Distracted by the poster, she didn't see the guy until he'd grabbed her arm. "Miss!"

She whirled and smacked him with her bag.

"Ow!" he said. "Wait, sorry, wait!" He held up his hands in submission. His submissive hands hovered three feet over her head, which wasn't ideal as a sign of submission, but he tried to hunch his lanky six-and-a-half-foot frame to better make his point. "I'm sorry, wait!"

Jenny glared at him, bag held ready for another counterattack.

"Please, I need your help," the guy said. Bright green eyes peered from a spectacularly freckled face—with a touch of orange in his bright red hair, he was bucking for Irish mascot status and had just overtaken a drunk, potato-starved leprechaun cop who owned a bar. He was dressed almost formally, like he'd been wearing a tuxedo but took off his jacket to reveal he'd been cheating with a short-sleeved shirt. Little sparkles on his bow-tie and vest glinted in the neon light overhead, but his black pants were clearly a cheap substitute that didn't come with the rest.

"What the hell?" said Jenny, defensive anger firing up her expression.

"My assistant didn't show," said the guy. His eyes were panicked and sincere. "I'll pay you!" He dug deep in his pockets but came up empty, spreading his hands. Jenny noticed that his fingers were just this side of grotesquely long and thin. "My wallet's inside," he admitted with a weak grin.

Jenny didn't follow. "Your *what?*"

"Listen, if you have, like, ten minutes, and you can just stand there and hand things to me, I'd be really, really," he took a deep breath, "really really really really really grateful. *Really,*" he finished emphatically.

Jenny blinked. "Your *what?*"

"I'll pay you twenty bucks."

"I'm in," said Jenny.

"Great," the tall guy said. He yanked open the nearest door and ushered her in. Jenny still didn't quite get it, but twenty bucks was twenty bucks, and twenty bucks was a few meals or a third of her phone bill, and if it just involved ten minutes of standing next to this tall skinny guy in the crappy tux, she wasn't going to argue.

She followed in his wake across a red-carpeted lobby with old-style doors, the paneling inlaid with *bas relief* sculptures of *bas relief*. He held open another door, and Jenny slipped through into darkness.

It took a moment for her eyes to adjust to the stark contrast in the room—a midnight dark audience of red cloth seats facing a bright yellowly lit stage. Two dimly lit figures, one stout and one slight, sat in the middle of the audience; a half dozen others slouched about in the front row, off to one side. On stage, in front of old-school red curtains, a drag queen with an overly punctual five o'clock shadow and a giant orange-winged parrot on his wrist snidely reported: "And I told him—darling, that's not my baseball bat!" A tinny imitation of a rimshot rattled out of the parrot's throat as it shifted on its hairy, bejeweled perch.

The stout man in the audience nodded and whispered something to the other. The other said, "Thanks very much!"

"You're beautiful, sister, don't ever change," the drag queen said in a sequined baritone, and he minced behind the curtains to the sound of applause coming from the parrot.

The thinner man in the audience consulted a clipboard. "Calvin Quirk?" he called toward the closed curtains.

"Here!" replied Jenny's companion. "Back here," he said, scrambling down the aisle, "sorry, just warming up with my assistant." He paused at the foot of the stage and looked back—Jenny still stood at the back of the small theatre. "My *assistant*," repeated Calvin Quirk with a meaningful look at her. She looked around, and Calvin made a wild and unsubtle gesture for her to follow him to the stage. "My *lovely assistant*," he said, gritting his teeth.

Jenny sighed: *Why not?* She jogged down the aisle after Calvin, who stepped easily up onto the three-foot-high stage and held out a hand. She put a little effort into her jump, and his helping hand sent her soaring over the lip of the stage to land gracefully at his side.

They looked at each other and shared a smile at their unplanned but effective opening choreography. They turned, and Jenny was blinded by the footlights. The audience beyond them was lost in total blackness.

"Hello! Good evening!" said Calvin, stretching upward to his full height. "*I*...am Calvin Quirk. Magician extraordinaire!" His overly long fingers flicked a flourish of epic proportions, and his tie and vest scintillated in the bright lights. Spinning like an ungainly quadriplegic spider with four good limbs remaining, he presented Jenny. "This is my lovely assistant...uh..."

He gave her a wide-eyed look. She produced a tight-lipped smile. "Jenny," she said quietly.

"*Jade!*" Calvin said, his booming introduction covering hers.

"...Jade," Jenny corrected herself, slightly louder. Calvin froze in a dramatic pose, and the pitch dark audience was silent. With nothing to go on, Jenny curtseyed. Calvin cleared his throat, and she followed his desperate eyes to her bag, still in a death grip in front of her. She caught herself and chucked the bag to one side, then—catching the spirit—mirrored his pose as best she could.

"Yes, thank you, Jade!" Calvin said unnaturally loudly. His tone of voice suggested he was talking to her; his volume and stance indicated otherwise. Jenny had flashbacks to the two shows she'd done in college, where the most highly regarded bad actors favored projection and facing the audience over character development and portraying emotions. Perhaps for this kind of performance, projection and facing the audience *were* the primary concerns. She made a mental note.

Calvin whirled with more wild, spirally motions, looking like a cuttlefish with a muscular disorder, and swept half the red curtain aside. He missed the actual break in the curtain, though, and instead swept one half of the curtain into the other half, creating a crimson velvet mess as he poked repeatedly into the folds, hunting for the opening.

Jenny held her pose, facing the audience. If she knew her lines, she would surely have projected them.

"Uh," said Calvin. "Uh, Jade..."

Without turning, Jenny shuffled backward and threw a hand back, quickly finding the separation and pulling her half aside. She held her tight smile, though it looked more like the rictus of death than the dazzling beam of a showgirl.

Calvin leaned through the opening and pulled a rolling table downstage. It was covered on three sides by posterboard ruthlessly molested with glitter glue, and large fancy *Q*s were crudely cut out of tin foil and pasted on each board. As it rolled past, Jenny saw that the back was open—the table was just a dolly with three shelves. An assortment of items filled the middle and lower shelves; the top shelf served as the top of the table, and was artfully covered with white paper towels. Jenny briefly thought about the napkin beneath which she'd chopped off her own finger. Her finger twitched; she tried to play it off as a melodramatic flourish to match Calvin's, and danced forward with big, swishing steps, presenting the magician and his table.

Calvin's smile turned sickly and he glanced at Jenny; she was overdoing it. She tried to think back to magician's assistants she'd seen on TV, and assumed a neutral pose with her feet perpendicular and her hands on one hip. As he spun about the table, Calvin Quirk shot her an appreciative smile.

"Now, ladies and..." He paused. "Now, gentlemen, I will endeavor to amaze you with the tricks of my trade. But my tricks, and my trade...are *magic!*" He punctuated this with a clap and a sudden flash of smoke and flame that exploded between his hands. Jenny squeaked and lost her pose, but quickly regained her composure and watched Calvin out of the corner of her eye. It was a simple trick, but it was a nice one; she belatedly decided that Calvin really was a stage magician, and this wasn't just some ploy to get her to go out with him or accompany him to an unmarked, windowless van. She wondered when he'd palmed whatever made the tiny explosion.

Sidelong, Calvin mumbled: "Rings." Jenny pivoted smartly and pranced behind the table, face forward and smile fixed. She bent down, her smile plummeting from her face as she furiously scanned the two lower shelves, then grabbed the shiny metal rings and resumed her pose and expression. She straightarmed the rings into Calvin's side—he winced, but worked it into a dramatic, wide-legged extension and grabbed the rings, presenting them upward as if he intended to throw them into a fiery volcano and restore peace to a kingdom of hairy-footed fairy folk.

"These rings are an ancient Chi—" he coughed and caught himself, not daring to look over at Jenny. "Child's toy," he amended, clearly improvising, "but that child was a high prince of a kingdom so secret, that...that you will not find mention of it in your history books. None dare speak its name," said Calvin, his grin and tone dialing for ominous, but mistaking a couple of digits and connecting to ambiguous and slightly goofy. "But I have visited with scholars and wizards who have preserved the secrets of this kingdom through generations. And now I bring those secrets here before you, to give you but a *glimpse* of the mysterious world beyond the veil of your natural human senses."

There were ten rings, each larger than the one before it, ranging in size from little girl's bracelet to soup bowl rim. Calvin Quirk's flexible fingers interlocked and disconnected the rings quickly and easily, seemingly passing them through one another with no regard for the fact that solid matter doesn't do that sort of thing. Even Jenny, a few feet away, was unable to see the seams. The rings flashed and clicked as Calvin worked, connecting them in a linked chain from smallest to largest, which he held up for the audience to admire.

"Now, that," Calvin Quirk said, "you may have seen before. But I guarantee you that you've never seen *this*...."

He let the largest ring go, and the chain dangled from the smallest still gripped in his thumb and forefinger, gently swinging back and forth. Then he tapped across the smallest ring in a rapid and intricate pattern...and let go. The entire chain hung unsupported in mid-air, the smallest ring caught in the invisible vise grip of nothing at all.

A collective gasp erupted from the audience, and was echoed by Jenny, who couldn't help but gape at the levitating chain of rings. Once again, just six feet stage left of the action, she had a particularly impressive view.

Calvin took two steps back. He stuck one arm through the largest ring, swaying at the bottom of the links. He tapped carefully on the edge of that ring, and it began to shrink, tightening slowly but steadily around his arm. As it dwindled nearly to the width of his wrist, Calvin yanked his arm back out, escaping the snare. There was a click and a funny little pop, and the bottom ring suddenly reversed, dilating back out to its original size—at the same time, the unseen grip on the top ring was released, and the links instantly collapsed and fell. Calvin Quirk's other hand swept forward with stupendous agility to snatch the rings just as they dropped.

Several voices murmured low in the audience; somebody laughed nervously. Jenny swished her arms in a half-stupefied denouement. There was no applause, but she heard the two guys in the middle of the theatre whispering hard.

Calvin Quirk basked in the non-existent adulation. "Thank you!" He bowed. "Thank you very much!" He turned toward Jenny and tossed her the rings, then winced as she completely missed the catch and they clattered on the floorboards. She knelt and scrambled to pick them up, looking up at Calvin apologetically. He gave her a little shrug and mouthed: "Cards." Jenny nodded and moved behind the table.

"For my next trick..."

Calvin was good with card tricks. The deck Jenny found on the middle shelf, swapping it for the rings, was a normal, everyday deck of cards—she couldn't spot any suspicious gimmicks, though she certainly wouldn't claim expertise. Calvin coaxed one of the men in the first row up on stage—these were apparently other hopeful acts waiting to audition, and this man wore a leopard-pattern unitard and fuzzy cat ears—and the magician did a few quick *Is This Your Card* tricks, including a bit where the seven of clubs (not, as it turned out, the Cat Guy's card) rose out of the deck of its own volition, bent over itself, and pushed the four of spades (confirmed as the Cat Guy's card) out of the bottom of the deck, where Calvin caught it in mid-flutter on its way to the floor. His long, lithe fingers made the required sleight of hand look easy. The Cat Guy was completely in the dark about each trick, though he pretended he'd totally figured it out in a jaded New York art scene kind of way. Jenny was similarly clueless, but forgot that she was part of the act, and failed to pretend she'd totally figured it out in a jaded New York art scene kind of way. She stared in amazement, her arms still limply held in her glamorous showgirl pose.

The card tricks concluded, the Cat Guy lumbered back into the audience with none of the grace of a cat, nodding with a sage little smirk like he'd taught Calvin all these tricks personally. Calvin caught Jenny's eye and mimed putting on a hat as he kept up the showman patter. "Thank you very much, sir! And thank *you*, ladies and gentlemen!" He'd given in to the fact that his audience was gender-lopsided, and decided to ignore it. It was a burlesque in Chelsea; at least half the guys there probably preferred the feminine address anyway.

Jenny strutted to Calvin, starting to feel her character, and handed over the traditional black top hat she'd found in the table. Calvin graciously took it—hiding his mouth behind the hat, he quietly said: "Bag." Jenny winked at him, smiled at the audience, and headed back upstage.

"For my final trick this evening, ladies and gentlemen," Calvin announced proudly, "I will turn to one of the better known practices of magic. All magicians, from all cultures, share a love of making things disappear..."

He held the top hat to one side and riffled the entire deck of cards across a foot of empty space with impeccable aim, the cards springing from his hand and sputtering through the air with the sound of unpopular center-fielders in bicycle spokes as they tumbled into the hat. Fifty-two cards in less than five seconds.

Calvin upended the hat, and not a single card spilled out. He beamed at the audience. "And just as much, we magicians share a talent for making the disappeared...appear again." He placed the hat atop his goofy shock of red hair and reached out as Jenny returned with the crushed velvet bag she'd retrieved from the table.

The bag wasn't large, but was bulky and wrinkled and luxuriously velveteen. The lights played over dark swirling patterns that danced across the velvet when Calvin took it. "A lot of magicians," Calvin declared, "work with rabbits." He dug one hand into the velvet bag as he spoke. "Me? I like to get down to the more basic elements of magic."

He pulled out a hand and held it up for the audience to see the three small white mice on his palm. One mouse shivered by his thumb; the other two trepidatiously explored the farther reaches of his fingers, definitive evidence that these were real live rodents. The magician smiled at his audience. "It doesn't get much more basic than this," he said, moving behind the glittery table. He plopped the mice unceremoniously back into the bag and put it on the table. Then he swept off his top hat, holding it carefully and blatantly away from the table. "But as all good magicians know," he continued, "when you take the most basic elements—" he fished in the bag and pulled out a couple of mice "—and add them together...."

He tossed two mice in a highly visible arc—the little white furballs dropped right into the black top hat. He fished back in the bag and grabbed another handful of white mice, showing the wriggling things to the audience before chucking them into the hat. "And you mix in a little bit of arcane knowledge...and magic..." He kept withdrawing mice from the bag and tossing them into his hat, one after another—he must have tossed at least a dozen mice in. "You can really work some wonders!"

He turned the hat over, the open end facing the floor—as with the cards, not a single mouse came tumbling back out. Calvin turned to Jenny with a projected smile. "Jade, let's make sure we got all of them," he said.

He stepped away to let Jenny pose behind the table—she picked up the bag and turned it upside-down, dramatically bobbing it up and down to shake out any lingering white mice. Calvin winced, but kept his smile and very slightly shook his head *No* at her, mouthing: *Inside-out.* Jenny stopped shaking the bag and rolled down the lip, turning it completely inside-out to prove its emptiness. It was still heavy and warm in her hands.

"And when you're working with the most basic elements of magic," said Calvin Quirk, "it's just like working with the basic elements of any craft. A house is made of bricks and mortar. A shirt is made of cloth and thread. And *my* rabbits..."

Calvin tilted his head at Jenny, then dramatically waved a hand over the hat and flung a gesture at the bag. Jenny nervously took the cue and reached into the inside-out bag—and felt something warm and soft, not at all velvet. She pulled out an adorable snow white rabbit and let out a tiny *squee*, cradling the bunny in her arms. The animal's nose twitched incessantly, its whiskers tickling her wrist.

"...are made from a simple formula," Calvin went on, "of thirteen mice...and a dash of magic."

He bowed to an unexpected but welcome smattering of applause from the front row. Jenny curtseyed daintily, clutching the little white rabbit with childlike glee.

"Thank you!" said Calvin.

"The Amazing Quirk!" Jenny declared loudly, presenting him with a sweep of the velvet bag.

Calvin faltered for a split second, but recovered nicely and returned the flourish. "And the mysterious Jade, Jewel of the East!" he announced.

They smiled at each other, feeling a little awkward in the less than thunderous applause of five pairs of hands, and Calvin nodded toward the wings. Jenny one-armed the rabbit and the velvet bag, grabbed her own bag off the stage, and scrambled off. Calvin followed her, putting the hat down on the table, which he rolled ahead of him.

Jenny dropped her bag and threw a hand up in the air—Calvin high-fived her and they both laughed. "That was awesome!" said Jenny. "You're really good!"

"You did great," said Calvin. "Thanks—thanks a lot! You were way better than Monica, and you never even had a rehearsal."

"How the hell did you do that ring thing?" Jenny asked. "And the cards—and the *mice!*" She held up the rabbit and stared at it in wonder. "Where the hell did they *go?*"

Jenny held the rabbit gently by the scruff of the neck, lowering the animal into the black top hat on the rolling table.

"*No!*" shouted Calvin in horror. He smacked the hat with a sweep of his arm, sending it tumbling across the floor as the rabbit landed harmlessly on the white paper towels.

Jenny jerked her hand back and froze. "Sorry!" she said automatically. "I'm sorry. Wait—what? I'm sorry!"

Calvin took a deep breath and raised his hands. "It's all right, it's okay," he said. "I'm sorry. It's okay. Just—don't put anything in the hat." He let out a sigh of relief. "It, uh, doesn't work that way."

"Sorry," Jenny repeated. "But..."

"Mister Quirk?" a nasal voice pierced the air from the audience.

Jenny and Calvin exchanged an excited look. He turned and peeked around the proscenium. "Yes?"

"Don't go anywhere," said the smaller guy in the audience. "If you could hang out in the lobby for a minute...?"

"Sure!" said Calvin. "Sure thing." He turned back to Jenny with wide eyes. "I've never gotten a callback before." He grinned. "I'm doubling your twenty bucks!"

Jenny smiled back. "They said wait in the lobby...."

Calvin nodded and turned the table so they could reach the shelves. Jenny put the velvet bag on one shelf and Calvin grabbed his top hat and put it on another one. The rabbit burbled impassively on the top, its nose and whiskers twitching. The skinny magician pushed the table through a thick door, nudging it over the doorstep. Jenny grabbed her bag and followed him.

The lobby was back down a short hall, and Jenny waited with Calvin, who paced back and forth with about a hundred amps of nervous energy. She'd agreed to help for the money, but the excitement was infectious, and now she was hooked—she wanted to see how this turned out. She idly ran her fingers through the bunny's soft fur while they waited. Calvin produced a large silver coin and absently flipped it from finger to finger as he paced.

"What's the bunny's name?" Jenny asked.

Calvin waved off his distraction. "Uh, oh...Colby."

"He's cute."

"She," Calvin said. "Yeah. Short for Colby Cheese. She likes it." His real life voice was very different from his on-stage persona; less sure, much softer and higher.

Jenny rubbed Colby between the ears. The bunny's eyes drifted shut. "Did you name all the mice?"

A dark shadow crossed Calvin's expression, and the coin teetered before resuming its oscillating path along the magician's knuckles. "No," he said.

"Where'd they *go*, anyway?" Jenny asked.

The click of the theatre door cut short Calvin's tight-lipped silence. The guy with the clipboard came out, and the light of the lobby revealed him to be a bony guy with a crewcut and bad skin. The clipboard was revealed to be a clipboard. The larger guy followed; he had a deep tan, a hairy chest, and a silk Hawaiian shirt. Two gold chains snaked through the jungle poking out of his collar, and his fingers did slow-motion weight-training with the heavy bling they bore.

"You're *very* talented, Mister Quirk," the big guy purred, drinking Calvin in from behind half-tinted glasses.

"Thank you," said Calvin. Jenny smiled pleasantly.

"The girl needs some work," the guy said, "though I adore the *faux* punk K-mart look." Three pairs of eyes followed his to the safety pins on Jenny's pants and bare skin through the tear. "But we like what you do. It's just the direction we're looking for—classic burlesque always includes a good magician."

"That's—that's great!" Calvin said. "I've got all sorts of ideas worked up, a lot of traditional—"

"Right, sure," the guy said, oozing the lascivious grease that keeps show business lubricated. "We'll need to make some stylistic changes, but I think you could work out *fabulously.*" He nodded to the other guy, then made a little bow to Jenny and winked at Calvin. "Lovely of you to stop by."

He moseyed back into the theatre, and the guy with the clipboard made a few pen marks on a printed grid. "Can you come in on Friday for a run-through?" The boss was all royalty and molasses; the assistant was bureaucrat and acid.

"Uh," said Calvin. He looked at Jenny—she shrugged a very genuine shrug. "Sure?" he replied. "I mean, what time?"

"Plan on being here at three. We'll go over everything then, and the run-through will start around nine. Bring all the tricks you're sure about. We'll help you decide which to do. Number?"

"Um," said Calvin. "Maybe twelve or fifteen...? I'm working on a few more."

"*Phone* number," the assistant said testily.

"Oh, right, okay!"

Calvin gave the guy his phone number. A few mildly unpleasant pleasantries were exchanged, and the assistant retreated into the theatre. Calvin looked at Jenny with one-hundred-point bold-faced Times New Roman amazement printed out in his freckles.

"Congratulations!" said Jenny.

"Thanks," said Calvin, still dazed. "Wow. You were great! I don't know what to say."

"You could say 'forty bucks,'" Jenny suggested. She smiled to make sure he didn't take the joke as mercenary as it sounded.

"Oh! Yeah," Calvin said, folding nearly double to bring his frame low enough to search through the lower shelf of his table. He pulled out a wrinkled green jacket and grabbed a wallet from an inside pocket. The Vel-Cro flap opened with a *vvratch!* and he thumbed through some bills. "Yeah, I got it, here it is."

"Cool," said Jenny.

"Listen, though," Calvin handed her forty dollars, mostly in fives and singles, "what are you doing this weekend?"

Jenny took the money without hesitation. "Uh," she said. "I'm looking for a job."

"You've got one!" Calvin smiled the smile of a million children presenting their non-smoking parents with distorted ashtrays sculpted through sheer determination and fired by bored art teachers.

Jenny's smile was more the mom putting unidentifiable crayon artwork on the refrigerator out of parental loyalty variety. "No, I mean a *real* job. I got fired Sunday. Been trying to find something since." She stuck his money in her bag and waved a hand semi-apologetically. "Gotta pay the rent."

"I could *totally* make this a real job," said Calvin. "I'll pay you. I mean, I don't have much, but we can split what we make fifty-fifty. And until we make something, I'll pay you forty bucks every time we do a show." He shrugged. "You're a natural, Jenny."

"Well..." Jenny scratched her chin.

"Colby already likes you," the magician said. Colby the rabbit sniffed nonchalantly and took a step across the table. A tiny brown pellet sat on the paper towel where she'd been lounging.

Jenny surrendered a small laugh. "You really are good, Amazing Quirk."

"It's McGuirk," he said. "Calvin McGuirk. Quirk's just my stage name."

"It works," said Jenny. "I'm Jenny Ng," she stuck out a hand. "My stage name's Jade, the Jewel of the East."

He caught the implication and devoured her tiny hand in both of his giant ones, pumping it up and down gratefully. "That's great! That's great! This is going to be, uh..."

"Great," Jenny smiled and nodded. "Okay, Calvin, so we're in business."

"I promise you won't regret this," said Calvin McGuirk, throwing his jacket over one shoulder and wheeling his table toward the exit. He kept one hand on Colby to make sure she didn't fall off. "I've got a few tricks up my sleeve. I mean, not like the joke, I mean..."

"Yeah, I get it," said Jenny. "One thing, though—seriously, where did the mice go?"

Calvin slowed and tensed, his head wobbling back and forth between an honest answer and a careful dodge. Finally, he pushed the door with one long leg and backed the table onto the sidewalk. He gazed levelly through the doorway. "Let's go grab a bite and I'll tell you."

"Dinner *and* a show?" Jenny raised an eyebrow. "I'm in."

CHAPTER FIVE

In a small Irish pub nearby, they stowed Colby the rabbit inside the sparkly table to avoid a health code violation, or at least to avoid getting in trouble for it. Calvin bundled his absurdly long limbs onto one side of their booth, one leg stretched out by his rolling table, and Jenny slid in across from him, her tiny figure nearly lost on the giant wooden bench. They ordered fried mushrooms and Buffalo wings, beer for Calvin, and water for Jenny. The cute waitress smiled warmly at both of them through thick glasses. She knew a first date when she saw one. Even if she was utterly wrong.

Calvin started them off on the casual Get To Know You path, working through hometowns (Jenny was from Philly, Calvin was from just outside of Baltimore), college (hers in the midwest, his up in Vermont), and general timelines. She was surprised that he was four years her junior; he was surprised that she was any older than twenty-one. The fried mushrooms moved in during discussion of college majors (Jenny was a Fine Arts major in photography, Calvin had a Bachelor's in history), and made their exit once they knew which borough each was currently calling home (Brooklyn for Jenny, Queens for Calvin). The wings lingered through an exchange of political views (both unsurprisingly and unapologetically liberal), sibling counts (Jenny had one little brother, Calvin came from a good Irish Catholic family of seven kids—he was fifth), parental rosters (Jenny's dad died when she was eight, Calvin's parents were still kicking down in Maryland), and chocolate preferences (Jenny liked dark, Calvin was partial to milk). Calvin nursed his beer the whole time. Jenny had at least a dozen refills on her water, and didn't take one bathroom break. Calvin snuck a few pieces of celery off the plate of wings and into the magic table for Colby to munch, sipping his beer nonchalantly to cover up feeding the illicit varmint.

"So," said Jenny, "how does a history major end up being a struggling stage magician?"

Calvin laughed. "The better question is: how does a magician end up majoring in history?" He took another small sip—Jenny recognized him as a fellow Every Penny Counts Club member. "I went to college 'cause—well, 'cause everybody goes to college," he said. "And I needed a major, but I'm no good at math or science or business or law...." He threw his hands up in a resigned shrug. "It was either something 'smart' like history, or the same English or psychology degree everybody graduates with and never does anything with."

At least half of Jenny's friends had English degrees—half of the other half had psychology degrees. She was familiar with the phenomenon. If college actually dictated career paths, the world would be mainly populated by angsty novelists and the therapists who helped them through their writer's blocks. For better or worse, most of them instead ended up behind a desk or in front of a blackboard—or both.

"But magic," Calvin said, leaning back. "I don't remember not being into magic. First time I ever saw a magician, I must've been, like, three or four or something. I remember the guy had this crazy Evil Spock beard and a big black cape, and he could pull *anything* out of his cape. But, well...." Calvin smiled and shrugged. "He actually wasn't that good. I mean, everybody else was impressed, but I was so into the tricks that I was, like, staring. The whole time. And I realized—I'm this little kid, and I realized—whenever he was making stuff disappear or appear, he was distracting the audience so they wouldn't notice the trick. Like he made a big wave to this blonde lady he had with him, and she pulled a curtain or something, but meanwhile he was switching hands or hiding something in his cape, and everybody was looking at her the whole time."

"Except you," said Jenny.

"Yeah," said Calvin. He sat forward, one hand on the table. "I mean, I was three, I didn't care about the hot girl in the sexy costume, and I didn't care about the sexy costume on the hot girl. Didn't care about the curtain. Any of it." He sipped his beer. "What *I* thought was cool was that everybody fell for it. 'Cause he controlled where they were looking. The best magicians don't need to have the best hands or the best tricks," he explained, "they're just really, really good at making you look the other way."

Without warning, he flipped his palm off the table and a bouquet of daisies sprang up.

"Ha!" exclaimed Jenny. She stared at the flowers in amazement.

Calvin grinned. "See? Everybody else is distracted by me drinking my beer," he said, "and you were distracted by having to pretend not to notice me feeding Colby. Nobody's looking when I drop the celery for Colby and take the flowers out of the table. Sure, the rest takes practice—and good hands help—but making sure nobody's looking at the right place at the right time is really how any magic works."

"What about all the hocus-pocus?" Jenny asked. "The abracadabra? I mean, the stuff that isn't just a surprise, but really looks like it's 'real' magic?"

Calvin laughed and handed her the flowers. "It's the same thing! The trick is you're *always* looking in the wrong place. And the best magicians are just messing with your expectations—you could totally explain how the trick was done, but you're *expecting* that, so you're looking for *that* trick...and you miss the one the magician's really doing."

"Well, yeah," said Jenny. "There's no *real* magic."

Calvin McGuirk pursed his lips. "Hm," he said. "Well, I guess. Depends on what you mean by 'real.' My best friend as a kid was obsessed with the 'real' thing, like sorcerers and wizards and all that. We played a lot of *Dungeons and Dragons*," he said with a guilty smile. "Griffin was convinced magic was real, and we just had to figure out how to do it."

"Ha," said Jenny, smelling the daisies. They were real, if a little wrinkled, and smelled fresh. "What, did he go crazy, blow himself up?"

"Maybe," said Calvin. "Probably. I dunno. We lost touch when we went to college. But the thing is, that was *his* distraction—he was looking so hard for the 'wizard-y' type of magic that it was easy to do something simple and mundane right in front of his eyes...and he'd miss it."

"Okay," Jenny arched her brows. "So where was I looking...and where did the mice go?"

Calvin chugged half his remaining beer and swallowed hard. He avoided her eyes, idly playing with a chicken bone stripped of its meat. "Right," he said. "Where did the mice go...."

"You said you'd tell me," Jenny feigned offense.

"I know," said Calvin. "I know. It'll just take some explaining, I mean. It's...tricky."

"No pun intended?"

He grinned. "Right." He set himself, finished his beer, then set himself again, and shuddered. "Okay." Calvin stared hard at Jenny, lassoing her eyes through sheer force of will. "What I'm going to tell you can't leave this table. Or, I mean, well, it's just between us. Hell," he said, "I can't believe I'm telling you this."

"Calvin, I'm broke and unemployed, and you're currently my only shot at a steady paycheck," said Jenny. "I'm not going to screw you over. I promise."

Calvin nodded. "Okay," he repeated. "So, see...um. Okay," he said again. Jenny hoped he'd get past the false starts and just *talk* already. Mercifully, he continued: "So there isn't any real magic. Not the wizard-y stuff, anyway. But like anybody smart could tell you, if you just don't get something, it'll *look* like magic."

"Any sufficiently advanced technology is indistinguishable from magic," Jenny said automatically.

"Hey, yeah!" Calvin looked surprised. "Right!"

"That's Arthur Clarke," she said.

"I know," said Calvin, smiling at the shared connection. "That's a good one. And it's right. So, basically, the same thing's true in magic. Like, stage-magic magic. If you don't get how a trick is done, it looks like magic. But that doesn't mean it is. It just means you don't know how it's done. But," he patted his chest, "the same thing is true about magicians, too. If we don't get a trick—even though we *know* it's a trick—it looks like magic to us. Real magic."

"Wizard-y magic," Jenny adopted his terminology.

"Right, yeah! Wizard-y magic. So the thing with the mice is...um."

"Yeah?"

"It's, well," Calvin waved a hand ambiguously. "I don't know how it's done. So...it's magic."

Jenny stared blankly.

He clarified, "It's a trick I don't understand."

"But it's *your trick!*"

"Right," said Calvin. He hunched his shoulders sheepishly. "It's a found trick. I mean, something somebody else did, and I just figured out what to do with it."

"So where did the mice *go?*" Jenny insisted. "Fuck, Calvin...!"

"Okay, okay, I'll tell you," said Calvin. "It was a few months ago. I've been in the city for a while, looking for some kind of gimmick that'll work for me, something that'll give me something to stand out. Auditions suck. I hate 'em." He smiled self-deprecatingly. "You never really know what they want, or what they don't want, and they could say 'no' if they just don't like your nose."

"The mice," Jenny prodded.

"*So,*" Calvin continued, "I go to pawn shops and antique stores and novelty places a lot. Sometimes people sell stuff they don't realize is actually a pretty good magic trick. The best magicians are also really good amateur engineers, or they work with one. All those boxes and locks and everything, every device and machine you see on the stage, somebody had to build it. Somebody had to think of it, and put it together. And sometimes, they get sold, and sold again, and collectors trade 'em around, and then they end up with somebody who doesn't know the first thing about magic, and nobody knows what they do. I met a guy who bought a cabinet that turned out to be a famous trick from the Twenties..."

"And you bought the mice, or the thing you disappeared them with, or—"

"Okay," Calvin surrendered. He gave Jenny a very serious look. Then he reached into the magic table and snagged the top hat, putting it on the booth table, open end up.

Jenny wrinkled her nose. "You're kidding," she said.

Calvin picked up a fork and dropped it into the hat. There was no clatter; no sound at all, in fact. He picked up the hat, turned it over, and— no surprise—nothing came out.

Jenny knew enough to know that doing a trick like that so close-up was pretty impressive. And she still couldn't see how it worked. "So where's the fork?"

Calvin put the hat down. "That's the point," he said. "I don't know."

Jenny stared into the depths of the hat—it was *awfully* dark at the bottom. Or the top. Whichever. A deep blackness, poking her with the loudest silence she'd ever smelled, peered back up at her. The profound sense of synaesthesia was dizzying. She looked away and blinked off the vertigo. "Can you make it come back?" she asked.

Calvin McGuirk shook his head. "I could fake it," he said. He held up one arm, palm facing away from her, then twisted his wrist and produced a fork from nowhere. "But I just palmed this one while you were staring at the hat. It's yours. Mine's gone."

Jenny glared at the hat as if it had tried to patronizingly psychoanalyze her in a coffee shop in Williamsburg. "What do you mean, gone?" she demanded. "What the hell, Calvin? Where did Colby come from?"

"The pet store," he quipped. He apologetically warded off Jenny's irritated look. "She was in the bag the whole time. That was the easy part— it's a reversible bag. That's why I needed you to turn it inside out. You turn it inside out, it looks like you're being thorough, getting all the mice out, and that unfolds the part that Colby's tucked into, so now it's a right-side-in bag with her inside it. Everybody's more interested in where the mice went, so nobody stops to think that you never reversed it back the other way."

"*I'm* more interested in where the mice went!"

"They went in the hole!" he blurted. He looked around defensively, suddenly aware of the rest of the pub, but everyone was too focused on one of three different televisions to care about the stretched out leprechaun hollering in the corner booth. "It's a hole. It's what I found—*one* of the things I found, I mean, at a shop a few months ago."

"A hole?"

"I'm not sure how else to say it," he admitted lamely. "You saw it. It's a hole. Just a hole. I'll show you later—I can't take it out here, I don't want anybody else to see it."

"A hole," Jenny repeated, more thoughtfully.

"Like, just some kind of tear in space and time or something," Calvin explained helpfully. "It's got some kind of weird edge on it, feels like rubber or plastic. On one side, it's a sheet of that stuff, that plastic. Floppy, like a tortilla. The other side's just—a hole." He made an *O* with one thumb and forefinger. "Stuff goes in," he pushed a finger through the *O*, then flapped his hands away, "and just goes away."

"To where?" Jenny asked quietly. A day or two earlier, she might've laughed in Calvin's face, walked out, and stiffed him with the bill. After reattaching two severed body parts in one afternoon, though, she was inclined to be a bit more charitable toward his personal brand of crazy.

"I can't see through, or it's too dark in there," said Calvin, "but wherever it is, it's really, really cold." He saw her inquisitive eyes and made an unhappy expression, like a rough kid's deep regret for flooding an ant hill with the garden hose. "I tried some experiments. Stuck some stuff through on a string, and pulled it back out—it was frozen solid."

Jenny nodded slowly. "Wow." She stared at the black top hat.

"It was a little too perfect," said Calvin. "I fitted the hole into the hat, and *presto*—magic bottomless hat."

"So...the mice?" Jenny frowned.

"Yeah," Calvin frowned back. "I checked—they come back frozen solid, too. And their eyes—"

"*Don't* need to know," Jenny said firmly. "So your trick is just that you're...you're throwing the mice away, and then you take Colby out of the bag?"

"Basically," said Calvin. "And the rings...."

Jenny looked up. "Yeah?"

"Found them with the hole. They were in this weird wooden box at the shop. Some other stuff in there too. The guy couldn't open it—I could. He didn't think it opened at all, and I didn't tell him, so he sold it to me really cheap."

"What do the rings do?" asked Jenny.

"Just like you saw," said Calvin. "Figured it out accidentally, then practiced until I figured out how to do it right every time. You just have to tap these little symbols on the edges in the right order. The little one 'anchors' itself, and the big one shrinks down if you put something through it."

"How far down?"

"Tight," Calvin grimaced. "Glad I didn't experiment with my arm *first*." He smiled ruefully.

"Weird." Jenny thought a moment. "And the cards?"

"That's just me," Calvin shrugged. "I *am* a magician, I mean."

"You're really good," Jenny said sincerely.

"Thanks."

"I think I should show you something."

"What?" asked Calvin.

"Do you have a really, really sharp knife?" Jenny asked.

Calvin cocked an eyebrow. "Plenty of 'em, back at my place," he said.

Jenny nodded and raised a hand over the back of the booth. "Check, please!"

CHAPTER SIX

The third time Jenny Ng was dismembered—only the second time she did it herself—was alarmingly easy. Calvin McGuirk's big flashy knife, part cleaver, part ninja sword, was just the ticket. After warning him not to interfere, Jenny slammed the knife down, chopping off three fingers and the very tip of the pinky that had already been through this ordeal once before. Jenny flinched, but only barely; she wondered what it said about her that she'd already got used to dismembering herself, quickly and casually.

Despite the warning, Calvin couldn't stifle his most unmanly scream. He instinctively moved to help, but she waved him away with the knife, which was as much an unintended threat as a wave, coming as it did from a woman who'd just nonchalantly chopped off her own fingers. Calvin backed off obediently. Jenny gathered up her fingers (the pinky tip had skittered off the table, but she found it on the dirty rug beneath) and arranged them next to her hand. It only took a four-count or so before that now-familiar scratchy yarn feeling pulled through her body and her fingers knitted themselves back onto her hand, melting into shape until there was no trace of the injury.

Calvin stared at her the way she'd stared at the conjured daisies. "How...?"

"Got me," said Jenny. She wiggled her fingers at him. "I don't even have a 'went to the store' story to tell. It just happened."

"So the truck—your leg—that was the first time?"

"Uh huh," she nodded. "I did my finger at the diner to see if it worked."

"That's incredible!" said Calvin. He laughed and spun away, doing a strange and silly kind of dance that looked all the more strange and silly featuring his goofy elastic body.

Jenny smiled pleasantly, humoring him. She'd already been through the giddy realization of her indestructibility. She was more interested in what she might be able to do with it...now that she'd met the Amazing Quirk.

"We could really do this, couldn't we?" Calvin said. He gibbered and paced back and forth in a sort of half-hop, half-skip, half-jump. "With my stuff and your...your...your *you!* We could put together the most incredible magic act the world's ever seen!"

"Well, yeah," Jenny said. "You know what's weird, is I think I might be able to control my parts when they're cut off. That would be useful, too, right?"

"Definitely," said Calvin. "Definitely! Oh, man, this is incredible."

"Okay, okay," said Jenny. "Calm down. We need to work this stuff out."

Calvin visibly got a grip and stopped short in the middle of his apartment. The place was a mess except for a giant bookcase against one wall, and the cleared space before it. The bookcase held boxes and gadgets and strange bundles and thick books on every shelf. One clear plastic case had hundreds of identical decks of cards inside, stacked neatly in columns, each deck turned ninety degrees from the one below it.

"Hey, yeah," said Calvin. He reached up to the highest shelf. "Let me show you the rest of the box stuff."

He retrieved a small wooden box and joined Jenny at the coffee table. Colby sat imperturbably on the floor, gurbling a bit and twitching her nose. She hopped lazily toward her small cushioned bed in the corner and plopped herself down, apparently happy to be home. The magician folded his legs uncomfortably to sit across from Jenny, and placed the box on the table.

"See, this was the first part I had to figure out," Calvin said. The box was dark brown with swirling woodgrain, fixed with small brass ornaments along each side. It had a roughly square footprint, only half as high as it was wide. Calvin pointed at the brass fixtures. "The guy didn't want to risk damaging the box—thought he wouldn't be able to sell it—so when he couldn't figure it out, he just left it closed. He probably never studied stage magic...." Calvin swept his fingers over the fixtures, and started pivoting them in a very deliberate sequence, like he was solving a Rubik's Cube. "Like a lot of cool magician's tricks, it's just math. You can't turn this one here until you turn this one to there, but you can't turn this one to there until you turn that one here...they're all interdependent, so you have to do at least three of them together right away, before you start the rest of the pattern. And the pattern is mathematical." He grinned as he moved the fixtures in a very practiced script. "Magicians do tend to have long fingers. I guess some people wouldn't even be able to do this. At least, not alone."

Jenny nodded and watched Calvin's fingers fly. "I thought you said you were bad at math," she said.

"Well," Calvin shrugged, "the math you have to do in school, yeah. But a lot of simple card tricks are about math. Those were the first ones I learned. And some of the cooler stuff is math too. Ever see that David Copperfield one where he tells the home viewing audience what their...oh." There was an audible *clack*. He smiled across the table at Jenny. "And there we go," he said, lifting the top off the wooden box with a dramatic flourish. Two of the brass attachments went with the lid—the other two were attached to the box itself.

There were just three items in the box; the hole was still inside the top hat (Jenny did her Show-and-Tell right when they got to his apartment), and the rings were still in the magic table. A long, shiny black stick—looking unequivocally like a traditional magician's wand—bisected the box from one corner to the other. In one triangular half was a thick pair of spectacles with antique metal frames. In the other half was a dusty square of glass.

Jenny reached forward, then paused, looking at Calvin. He nodded, and she pulled out the wand. "What does it do?"

"Not a clue," said Calvin. "The hole was obvious—at least, the obvious part, and I figured out some details—and I got lucky with the rings. I've tried messing around with these, but they don't do a whole lot. Well," he amended, "the glasses do *something*. With the little window thing. But nothing that helps."

Jenny waved the wand, watching yellow lamp light play up and down its length like one of those pens where the lady gradually gets more and more naked when you turn it upside down. She pulled her attention away and looked at the two remaining items. "What's 'something'?" she asked. "What do they do?"

"Here," Calvin snatched the spectacles and handed them over, then picked up the tiny window pane. Jenny made as if to put the spectacles on, again checking with Calvin. He nodded. "Yeah," he said, holding up the glass in front of her. "Then look at this through them."

Jenny slid the spectacles on; the stems hugged her ears uncomfortably, and the thick lenses were surprisingly heavy, weighing down the wire over the bridge of her nose. They weren't prescription, and they weren't X-ray—they were just a bit warped and dusty, and made the room in front of her look a bit warped and dusty. No real change.

Until she looked at the small square of glass in Calvin's hand.

"*Diu!*" she swore.

Floating just behind the small window, glowing symbols filled the air. Calvin grinned—obviously, he'd already seen this phenomenon. He took her hand (staring curiously at her reconnected fingers for a moment) and pressed the glass square into her grip. "Look around," he told her. "Look through the glass around the room."

Jenny pushed the spectacles down her nose an inch and peered through the tiny window pane: nothing unusual. She pushed the specs back in place, and the glowing symbols snapped into view behind the little window. She turned back and forth, holding the glass square in front of her—wherever she looked, glowing symbols shimmered in front of the scene, as if they were just behind the glass. It was like they were written everywhere, all around her, but were only visible through this small square window...and only while she wore the spectacles.

"I know," Calvin said. "I don't know what they mean, either. I mean, I see some repeats, so it's gotta be *some* language, but I don't think it's—"

"Mmu, kamark damidel mooz gursh slafneets," Jenny said, or words to that effect.

Calvin looked at her askance. "Huh?"

Jenny's eyes went wide. "I can read them," she said. "I know what they say!"

"No way!" said Calvin. "Are they...uh, Chinese or something?"

"No." Jenny shook her head. "They're not any language I know, but...somehow, I can read them. Some of them, anyway."

"That doesn't make any sense."

"Tell me about it," said Jenny. She passed the window in front of Calvin's face and peered at him through the spectacles. "It gets weirder," she said. "I can read them—*and* I know what they mean."

"You know what 'moo camel damn gross slave knees' means?" Calvin's jaw dropped.

Jenny gave him a look.

"That's what it *sounded* like," Calvin said defensively.

"Okay, wait," said Jenny. "Your birthday wouldn't happen to be..." She looked up into that middle distance just above the head where people check for data like phone numbers and calendar dates. "March Eleventh?"

The magician jumped, but his long legs got tangled up under the coffee table and tripped him up. "Holy shit!" he said from a semi-prone position. "You got that from those little glowing letters?"

Jenny nodded. "There's more than that," she said. "You want to..." She suddenly trailed off. She pulled off the spectacles and rubbed her eyes.

"Want to what?" asked Calvin, extricating himself from his own knees.

"Forget it." She shook her head. "Just forget it."

"Uh uh," Calvin insisted. "I've been trying to figure that stuff out for months! If you've got a handle on it, I wanna know! What is it?"

"Calvin, this is all really crazy," Jenny said. "The hole, the rings, this stuff. I'd be careful with that wand, if I were you."

"No you wouldn't," Calvin said. "You're indestructible."

"This is serious!" Jenny snapped. She closed her eyes and sighed some tension out, but she was bailing the Atlantic Ocean with a soup ladle. "I'm sorry," she said, opening her eyes. Calvin stared at her cautiously, not daring to do or say the wrong thing. She looked at the window in one hand, the specs in the other. "Calvin...the letters..."

"Yeah?"

"Everything's got letters," she said. "When you move the window around, you're seeing letters telling you *about* what's behind them. I can't read all of them—it's like they're in more than one language—but I get some of them. Like they're in 'my' language. Your apartment was built in nineteen-eighty-two."

"Nah, it's older than *that*—"

"The *building* was built in nineteen-forty-six," Jenny continued, eyeing him earnestly. "Yeah. And...this building is going to be gone—torn down—in a little over thirty years."

"Wait," Calvin knocked concepts out of the air around him like Kong swatting biplanes, hoping that one would land in an accessible spot. "You're saying that those letters are telling you the *future?*"

"Not all of it," she said. "Just certain moments. Like beginnings." She looked glum. "And endings."

"So you know when the building's going to 'end,' and when...oh." A biplane finally hit his forebrain. He smiled a gentle, mysterious smile. "You know when *I'm* going to end. When I'm going to die."

She nodded and gulped an unchewable lump of empathy.

"Do I want to know?" Calvin asked.

"I don't know," Jenny shrugged. "Why would you want to know that?"

"I guess if it's soon," said Calvin, "I'd want to get as much in before I went as I could. And if it's gonna be a while, I guess that'd be a pretty nice thing to know. I mean, we all die eventually, right?"

"Right," said Jenny. But she wasn't so sure.

"I mean, yeah," Calvin said. He set himself and nodded firmly. "Go ahead and tell me. If it's soon, at least we'll be able to see if it's right, right?"

Jenny Ng looked long and hard at the magician. She smiled a little. "You're an interesting guy, Calvin," she began.

"Thanks."

"And you're going to be around for a pretty long time."

Calvin nodded his head, not with gravitas, but more like Alex Trebek had just explained the correct Final Jeopardy response, and the clue given thirty seconds earlier suddenly made sense. "Cool," he said. A thought spread across his freckled face. "What about you?" he asked.

Jenny smiled wider, then shrugged. She put the spectacles on, bent over, and peered through the window at her own body.

"Well?" Calvin said.

Jenny shook the window out like she was forcing a Polaroid to develop. She peered through it again. "Maybe it doesn't work on the person who's reading it," she said. "I don't have any letters at all."

"No, that's weird." Calvin reached across the table. "Here, let me try." Jenny handed over the specs and the window; Calvin stared through them at his own body. "I've got letters," he said. "The same ones I always see on me." He pointed to a sheet of college-ruled paper taped to the wall.

Jenny looked up and saw that he'd drawn the same symbols the window revealed on his own body, though they *were* upside down. "So you see the ones on you?" Jenny asked. He nodded. She boldly set her jaw: "Okay, then—look at me."

"Right," said Calvin. He held the window up and peered at Jenny, squinting hard behind the spectacles as if extra effort might pierce through the mystical effect and write some letters on her. He stared for a full ten seconds. Then he lowered the window and looked darkly off to one side.

"No letters, huh?" asked Jenny.

Calvin shook his head.

"It's okay," Jenny said. "Maybe it doesn't work on Chinese people."

"How does that make any sense?"

Jenny smiled. "We don't need it. We've got fortune cookies."

"If you tell me my lucky numbers, I'm calling you a cab home," Calvin groused playfully.

"I won't," said Jenny. "But you *can* learn to speak Chinese." She stood up and smiled. "*Maan on!*"

"What?" Calvin scrambled to his feet—he had a longer route to take than she did—and stared down at her, dumbfounded.

"It's 'good night,' duh," Jenny teased him.

"Oh!" said Calvin. "Right, wow—it's after eight?" He put the spectacles and window back in the box, then stretched impressively, crackling like a cereal that stays crunchy in milk. "So what's the plan?"

"I can try to be back here by noon, and we can figure out what to do for the act." Jenny grabbed her bag from the beat-up old couch.

"You could crash here," Calvin offered brightly.

Jenny rolled her eyes. "Calvin. We're going into business together. My spending the night is *not* a good way to start things off."

"Nothing would—okay, right," he cut himself off at her exasperated sigh. "But it wouldn't," he insisted.

"Good to know," said Jenny. She tapped her chin thoughtfully. "You know, I thought you were gay at first."

"What?" He tried balancing his acceptance of homosexuality with his shock at the affront to his own heterosexuality, and succeeded about as well as any liberal straight guy ever does.

55

"You were auditioning at a burlesque theatre in Chelsea," she reminded him. "And wearing a bow-tie."

He laughed. "Yeah, well," he spread his hands, "it's a living."

"Let's hope so," said Jenny, grabbing one of his hands and shaking it. "Okay, Amazing Quirk, let's do this!"

"Tomorrow, noon," he confirmed. "I'll try to clean up the place."

"Don't try too hard," Jenny said. They smiled and exchanged quick *Good Nights* at the door, and she slipped out into the hall as he locked up. Calvin's apartment was a third-floor walk-up—she'd carried Colby the bunny while Calvin had carefully navigated the two flights up with the magic table. As the *clonk* of Calvin's bolt echoed behind her, she made her way back to the stairs, then headed down and outside.

It was a short walk to the Astoria Boulevard subway stop. Jenny debated whether to save money taking the roundabout way through Manhattan, or time by getting off at Queensboro Plaza and hopping a G train back to Brooklyn. The giddy rush of the evening's discoveries, bolstered by the unplanned forty dollars in her bag, pushed her to get home quicker—the G train wouldn't eat much of the cash Calvin gave her, and it was less than ten short blocks from Queensboro Plaza.

The city raced by as her mind raced with ideas for the magic act. Calvin could do card tricks and conjuring, and they could work out something with the rings—perhaps even cutting off Jenny's hand to get it out of the tightened bottom ring. Maybe they could rig a way to get stuff back out of the hole, like a safety net stuck through and fastened to the hat; nothing living, of course, since it would be dead when they pulled it back out. Jenny—or rather, Jade, the Jewel of the East—could use the Magic Spectacles and look through the Window to Your Soul to mystically divine audience members' birthdays. She toyed with mystically divining their death days, too, but decided that would be both too morbid and less impressive by way of being not so easily proven.

If they could figure out what the wand did, they could add some more stuff to the act.

Jenny never thought of herself as a performer. She didn't get stage fright; she just wasn't attracted by the lure of applause, and she felt awkward pretending to be something she wasn't. Photography was her art, and she had no illusions about her skills on a stage. Still, if they could make some money, she and Calvin could both pursue whatever true ambitions they had in mind. She promised herself that, once her rent and daily living were under control, the first few hundred she saved would go toward a new camera. Not top of the line, at that price, but she might get a good deal on a used one. She thought idly that Vincent and Carrie Raymond would be proud of her for making that promise.

The train slowed down for her stop. Jenny picked up her bag and twirled around a center pole, light on her feet and mildly disturbing a skinny white guy, a black couple with three young kids, and two Mexican guys who were just trying to get from their first jobs to their second jobs. Smiling prettily at all of them, she let her momentum around the pole launch her through the opening doors and tripped lightly up the platform to the exit.

Traffic was heavy this close to the bridge, but Jenny didn't pay much attention to it. Blocks flew by as she kept thinking about the act and the possibility of actually being able to afford three meals a day. The Court Square stop loomed in front of her before she knew it. Her mood was only slightly dampened by the twenty minute wait for the G train. When it came, the announcer's muffled *wamp-wamp-wa-wa-wamp* speech was as intelligible as an integral calculus lesson in Charlie Brown's classroom, and Jenny didn't catch a word of it. *Whatever*, she thought. *Just a couple dozen stops 'til I'm home.* She tucked herself into a backward-facing seat near the rear of the last car and watched the station disappear down a long, dark stretch of subway tunnel, her imagination wandering through the hole in Calvin McGuirk's hat to explore the mysterious world on the other side.

Her reverie was broken just nine stops later by another *wampa-wamp* dissertation that sounded a little more urgent and declarative. The handful of other people on her car all gathered their things and started exiting to the platform. Jenny was confused—they'd only reached Classon Avenue. An MTA worker, a big black woman with smooth skin and a bumper crop of dreadlocks, stuck her head in. "All out! No passengers, no passengers!"

"What?" Jenny asked, eyes flashing minor panic.

"Last stop," said the MTA lady. "No passengers!"

"I'm going to Prospect Park..." Jenny tried.

"Construction on the G," the MTA lady said, as if Jenny should have been fluent in *wampa-wamp* and already known. "Last stop, no passengers."

Jenny tested fate and humor. "No passengers?" she asked, with mock astonishment.

The MTA lady did a slow burn and crossed her arms. "*No passengers.*"

"Oh!" said Jenny. "Right, so, no passengers." Jenny hopped the gap to the platform. Two of her safety pins tore through, leaving her pants leg just barely hanging on and a lot of leg showing. The MTA lady shook her head with the disdainful "Nn, nn, nn" that big black ladies on commercials throw at cheerfully ignorant white folks who are using the wrong household cleaning supplies.

"*Puk gai!*" Jenny said into empty air, just loud enough for the MTA lady to hear. If they could speak their *wampa-wamp* at her, she could throw some Cantonese back at them. She headed for the turnstiles, looking for a subway map along the way so she could figure her route home.

The map turned out to be past the turnstiles, but it didn't matter anyway; there weren't any transfers at Classon. There was a C train a couple blocks away, but she didn't want to waste *another* fare after the first two just to avoid the walk. "Damn it," she whispered, wishing she'd taken the long way through Manhattan. She strapped her bag securely across her body and resigned herself to walking clear across the park to get home.

It wasn't even ten o'clock yet, so Brooklyn wasn't exactly dead. Still, Jenny was iffy on which neighborhoods were okay for a five-foot-tall skinny chick to roam without fear, and which were likely to be teeming with dangerous people with dangerous thoughts. Her indestructibility wasn't totally comforting; there were worse things than being cut or hit or shot, especially when indestructibility didn't come with any magical black belt in karate. She kept her eyes open and walked as tall as she could. A little late, she also did her best to cover the tear in her pants with her bag.

The park was a pretty straight shot from the subway. It was a bright night; the moon was near full, and the usual glowing signs of delicatessens and banks lit the street up like harsh fluorescent day. She did the Stop-and-Go Jaywalk across Eastern Parkway and followed it past the museum—easier to head right into the park than to go around the Botanic Garden. She cut over just before Grand Army Plaza and sank into the clean, cool green of Prospect Park.

She wasn't alone in the park, but everyone else seemed to stick to the paths; she walked boldly down the middle of Long Meadow, which was unnaturally empty. The stark moonlight cast a silver sheen on the lawn, marked only by her own crisply outlined shadow. The grass beneath her Doc Martens crushed satisfyingly with each step, like a smooth jazz snare drum keeping time for an imminent bass solo. The snare was accompanied by deep, double-time, reverb-laden bongos.

She pulled up short. Bongos?

Jenny kept walking, but looked over her shoulder, trying to be casual. There was nobody there. The *clip clop* of the bongos echoed out of the near distance. Jenny slowed down. The bongos slowed down. Jenny sped up. The bongos sped up. Jenny broke into a nervous jog. The bongos broke into a syncopated tango.

She nearly fell over the guy before she saw him. "Fuck!" he snarled. He was tall and lean and had dark tattoos on his pale shaven head. His two friends were fun-house mirror copies of him, one skinnier, one chunkier, all with the same tattooed skulls and sleeveless black T-shirts.

"Sorry," Jenny said, trying to avoid the issue and all three guys.

"Where you running?"

Jenny set her jaw. She didn't need this tonight. Or, she admitted to herself, any night. She realized that whatever night something like this happens, that's exactly the night you really don't need it. Whether it was the lingering euphoria of the magic act audition and the time spent with Calvin, or just some serious balls from knowing that she was indestructible, she kept a cool head and stared the first guy right in the eyes. "Just going home, man," she said. "G'night."

"Night's young," the guy said. His buddies laughed like cartoon characters. "We got beer."

"Congratulations. Have a good time," said Jenny, edging over to walk around them. She was acutely aware that they'd formed a loose triangle around her.

"Wanna beer?" It wasn't the most offer-y sounding offer she'd heard.

The other two giggled like idiots. "Wanna beer," one of them repeated like he'd just learned a new swear word.

Jenny taught him another one. "*Diu lei*," she said. "Let me—"

"We got plenty," the guy held up a hand. One of the others tossed a bottle into it. He yanked on a chain that was leashed to his belt, and pulled a big multi-tool army knife deal out of his pocket; a flick of his thumb unfolded a bottle opener. He popped the top and took a swig. "And you owe me one," he added, pointing to an open bottle lying at his feet, slowly pouring itself out in the grass.

"Open a tab," Jenny snapped.

"Uh uh, *chink*." The guy loomed forward, army knife in one hand, bottle in the other. Chunky and Skinny moved to flank her.

Jenny snorted. "What the hell, guys? What *year* is this?" The two flunkies seemed to seriously work out the answer to her rhetorical question, so she saved them the trouble. "It's not the middle ages, for fuck's sake! What are you...skinheads? Didn't you guys go out in the Nineties? Gimme a break!"

The other two goons faltered, but the Head Goon seethed.

"I scream once, and people come running," said Jenny, glaring back at him.

"What people?" the Head Goon smirked.

Jenny quickly checked left and right. The guy had a point. It was suddenly very quiet and empty in the park. Jenny wasn't sure her voice would carry much farther than the trees, and she was even less confident that the average New Yorker would consider one scream to be far enough out of the ordinary to venture into the park and investigate. She instantly regretted her bravado. Being able to reattach her limbs would only remain useful provided she could locate them.

"Listen," she backpedaled, "I'll give you ten bucks. For the beer." She made no move to open her bag.

"Nah," said the Head Goon. "You can pay the old fashioned way, chinky bitch."

"Chinky bitch," giggled the Assistant Goons, like a Greek chorus with one too many traumatic head injuries.

"Guys," she was struggling to avoid falling back on pleading. She silently cursed sexual dimorphism. The goons moved in; light gleamed on the army tool and flashed in their dull eyes. She couldn't catch her breath to scream. She had no hope that the cavalry was on its way.

With a piercing cry and a pounding rhythm, the cavalry—or rather a tiny percentage of the cavalry—flashed across the meadow in a pale silver fog. The goons backed away from her; Chunky Goon fell on his ass with a piggish grunt.

Protectively circling Jenny Ng with high, clipped, deliberate steps, a humongous horse eyed the three goons angrily. The presence of the giant white stallion alone would have been more than enough to strike fear into the hearts of cowardly and superstitious criminals. The fact that the beast clutched a wicked, curving sword in his mouth was just a bonus.

Of course, Jenny wasn't any more prepared than the skinheads for the arrival of her equestrian savior. She froze in the muddy circle carved out by his sharp, forceful stride. Each time the horse's tail flicked by, Jenny saw the Head Goon staring daggers at her, his jaw working soundlessly, before the horse's muzzle blocked her view again in his relentless looping path.

The horse came to a decisive stop at Jenny's side, stomping the ground to make his point. The Assistant Goons flinched. The Head Goon steamed, his fingers working over the bottle and the multi-tool.

The horse waved his head. The long hilt of the strange sword poked out in front of Jenny. She was still frozen. The horse chuffed and poked the sword hilt at her again. She looked at him out of the corner of her eye.

He rolled his eyes. It was a strikingly blatant *What—do I have to spell it out for you? I don't have thumbs. You do.*

Jenny reached out and took the sword; the leather-wrapped hilt felt warm in her hands. The horse let go, and Jenny raised the sword in front of her.

"Shit, Barry!" said Skinny Goon, and he bolted. Chunky Goon stuttered a bit and struggled to get on his feet.

"Barry?" Jenny echoed in disbelief. "Your fucking name is fucking *Barry?*" She laughed and waved the sword, feeling its comforting weight on her thin wrists.

Barry the Head Goon snapped his mouth shut and ground his teeth in impotent rage.

"Let me show you something, *Barry*," said Jenny. She smiled obnoxiously and held out one hand, swiping the sword downward to chop right through her own wrist.

The horse whinnied and butt-checked her shoulder, throwing off her aim—she nicked the back of her hand with the very sharp sword, and it hurt. A *lot.* Jenny shouted a sharp "Ouch!"

"Chinky bitch's crazy!" yelped Chunky Goon, scrambling on the wet grass and dashing for the trees without a thought for Barry.

Jenny glared at the horse, who gazed back with a laconic air.

"I'll fucking *kill* you, bitch," said Barry.

Jenny and the horse looked back at him. His resolve wavered in their collective withering gaze. "You know what, Barry?" said Jenny. She tried to think of some badass movie action hero line, but nothing came to mind. "Good night. It's over. *Go home*," she ordered.

He itched with trampled machismo, and it was clearly written in his snarling face. He dropped his gaze, turned—then whipped around and hurled the beer bottle at her, a perfect arc of glittering glass and swirling beer that would end right at her forehead.

Except it never got there. The horse let out a growly chuff and wrapped around in front of her; the bottle shattered on his head. Jenny only saw the horse in profile, beer spilling down from the other side with little shards of glass. Past the horse's head, she saw Barry, his eyes wide and staring at the horse. Without a word, he took three shaky steps back, then turned and ran.

Jenny and the horse stood alone in the moonlight, the beer fizzing in the grass at their feet.

She moved around the horse; he obligingly turned his head to let her see the other side. A couple of tiny crumbs of glass were stuck to his pale yellowed muzzle, and rivulets of beer ran down in veiny trails to drip off the bottom of his chin. In between the trails of beer she saw smudges. She smeared one with her thumb and rubbed the tacky fluid between her fingers. The moonlit color made it tough to tell, but it hit her as she stared at the fluid on her fingers...and then the still bleeding cut on the back of her hand. The smudges were blood—the horse's blood.

"Shit," she said in a genuinely concerned tone. She swept away slivers of glass and rubbed moon-grayed blood smears from the horse's head, looking for the wounds they'd oozed from. As she wiped away the last of the smudges, though, she realized there weren't any wounds—or, more likely, they'd disappeared before Barry's eyes, stitching themselves up with a ripple of flowing flesh that Jenny would have found very familiar. She smiled and leaned in close to the horse, smelling the ripe, leathery citrus scent of his sweat. "You're just like me," she murmured.

The horse chuffed and swung his head down to look her in the eye. *Duh.*

Jenny rolled her shoulders, pushing out the tension that had built up in the goon encounter, and looked at the sword. She was no connoisseur, but it wasn't like any sword she'd ever seen, in person or in pictures. The hilt was too long, and the blade curved off just inches past where there should have been a crossbar. The black cords wrapped around the lengthy hilt made a comfortable grip, stiffened by what must have been many years of sweaty palms. Jenny had just contributed some sweat herself.

The horse was wearing a simple saddle, and a casual leather harness on his snout—none of those tight rings and straps she saw in the movies, just some loose loops and long reins. This horse wasn't just some random horsey hero wandering through the park. He belonged to somebody.

"Well," said Jenny. "Um." She patted his cheek; it was rock hard muscle and bone. "Thanks."

The horse chuffed.

"I have to go," said Jenny.

The horse stomped the grass.

"It's been a long day," said Jenny.

The horse tossed his head. His reins slapped gently against his neck and shoulders.

"Here," said Jenny, holding out the sword. "Um, thanks, you take it back."

The horse pulled his mouth away from the sword, refusing her offer.

"No, really!" Jenny insisted. She felt ridiculous arguing with a horse in the middle of Prospect Park. Even one that had just saved her life. "Take it back. Whoever owns you owns it, right?"

The horse snorted. He stomped again.

"Take it," said Jenny. She tried to jam the hilt in his mouth.

He wriggled his lips away.

"Take it!" Jenny said.

But he refused.

"Fine," Jenny said sternly. She turned the sword upside down and jammed the blade into the ground. Because of the peculiar curve of the blade, the hilt leaned at an odd angle. "Well," she said, "thanks again. Take the sword and go home."

She turned away and started walking across Long Meadow.

The bongo beat struck up again.

Jenny stopped and turned on the horse. He'd plucked the sword from the ground and followed close behind her. "No!" she scolded. "Bad horse! Stay!"

She turned and walked away. The horse followed.

"Stop! Stay! Bad horse!" Jenny put on her best angry face.

The horse didn't care. He stared impassively at her.

"Damn it!"

The half-silent argument between horse and girl devolved into a bizarre sport of zigzagging across the grass, whirling, reprimanding, dodging, weaving, scolding, running, galloping, rebuking—the score was hard to follow, and the rules weren't totally clear, but Jenny felt she was losing the match. She lost ground, too, quickly finding herself evading the horse on the east side of Prospect Park, the side opposite from her apartment. In the excitement, her last safety pin gave up, and her pants leg collapsed to her ankle, tripping her. "Gahh!" she exclaimed. She yanked the heap of cloth off, over her shoe, and stuffed it in her bag. She made growling and yelling noises at the horse, but he was unfazed. He followed her out onto Ocean Avenue. The few passersby who even took notice just shook their heads or laughed. Most studiously ignored the crazy girl yelling at the huge white stallion.

Jenny realized she was making a scene; worse, she realized they might get in *real* trouble for the sword, if a cop came along. She snatched the sword out of the horse's mouth and held it tightly to her side, willing it to camouflage itself against her body. The blade felt cold against her bare leg. She switched sides; it still felt a bit cold through the cloth covering her other leg.

"Stop it," she hissed at the horse through clenched teeth. "*Go away!*" The horse trotted along behind her, taking in the sights of Brooklyn.

Jenny looked around; she was only a short walk from Heckler's place on Lenox Road. At this point, she just wanted to get out of the street and away from the horse. The choice between a couple of miles around the park to her place or a few blocks away to Keith Heckler's apartment was a no-brainer. She weaved through a couple of turns to Lenox. The horse kept pace easily, hooves smacking the pavement behind her as they went.

She plodded up the steps to Heckler's building and jabbed at his buzzer. The horse waited patiently.

"Jenning!" Heckler's voice called down from his second-storey window. Keith Heckler liked to think he was really clever, contracting *Jen Ng* to a proper gerund. He nearly always called her that. Outside of a bedroom.

She didn't look up. "Can I come up?" she shouted, trying to be loud enough for him to hear, and soft enough to not draw attention from the neighborhood.

Heckler had no such concerns. "Sure!" he yelled down cheerfully. "Nice horse! Yours?"

"Heckler, shut up and let me in!"

He pulled back inside. After a moment, the door buzzed, and Jenny pushed it open. She turned sharply—the horse was caught mid-step, and sheepishly lowered his hoof to the concrete with a gentle click. "Go home!" Jenny told him, and she slammed the door.

She wearily tackled the stairs up to Heckler's apartment. The sheer volume of weirdness in one long day made even Keith Heckler's smarmy grin a welcome change, at least because it was something normal, something she was used to. Heckler's teeth were brilliant white, a high contrast to the deep brown of his skin. He kept his tight kinky hair shaved almost bald, and he usually greeted her wearing some form of clothing, but tonight was apparently special.

"*Lan yeung*," Jenny said.

"There's at least two feet between my dick and my face," said Heckler. "And you've been all up and down that path."

"Damn it, Heckler, not now!" She pushed him aside, making sure to avoid touching any prominent bits, and threw the sword and her bag by the couch, which she collapsed on.

He shut the door and walked very much in front of her face on his way to the refrigerator. "Drink?" he suggested.

"Anything," Jenny said. She closed her eyes and rubbed her temples furiously. When she opened her eyes, Heckler was standing in front of her, wearing gym shorts. He held a shotglass like a peace offering. "Fuck it," she said, surprising both of them, and she took the shot and slammed it back. Her expression skipped. "Uh, that..."

"Was water," said Heckler. He grinned. "In my only clean glasses." He did a shot of water himself, then refilled from a plastic bottle he'd put on the floor in front of the couch. Heckler had no coffee table. His studio apartment was populated by the couch—which folded out to a bed—a few folding chairs, a kitchenette, and a few foldable cardboard dresser drawers. Clothing and magazines were scattered about like an L.L. Bean warehouse had exploded in the center of the room. In one corner was an electric guitar and a small amp; across from the couch was a TV supported by a milk crate. A few posters were taped roughshod to the walls; many of them were scribbled on with bright neon-colored marker.

The total eclipse of the television passed, and Heckler sat down next to Jenny on the couch. "So you're really up for something stronger?" he asked her. He waggled his eyebrows suggestively.

"Fucker," she replied. She leaned against his shoulder, not out of any real affection, but out of a basic human need to let loose.

"The horse brought 'er, but I'll be happy to," Heckler grinned, putting an arm around her, farther than actually required.

She slapped his hand off her breast and sat up. "The horse! *God!*" She buried her face in her hands.

"Yeah, I was gonna ask," said Heckler.

She looked at him, deadpan. "Yes?"

"What's with the horse?"

She let out a giant sigh that turned into a spectacular *plubba-lubba-lubba* of the lips that would do the horse proud. "This has been a really, really weird day, Heckler. The horse isn't even the weirdest part." That realization doubled its efforts and smacked her right between the eyes. "*Diu!* A goddamn *horse* that saved me from skinheads and brought me a...a magic sword, and followed me home—"

"You're moving in?"

"—*isn't* the weirdest part of my day," Jenny finished, completely ignoring Keith Heckler.

"So what *was* the weirdest part?" he asked, refilling her glass.

"Toss up," she said, and did another shot of water. She wiped her mouth with the back of her hand and noticed the dried blood and jagged cut still there near her wrist. "Between joining a magic act and being dismembered."

"Whoa," Heckler whistled, "dismembered?"

"Only three times," Jenny explained. "And two of those I did myself."

"What are you smoking, and where can I get some?"

"Forget it," said Jenny. "Listen, can I just crash here tonight? I don't want to walk all the way back home."

"Sure, Jenning." He stretched and hopped off the couch. "I'll open the bed."

"Can I grab your College shirt?" She got off the couch and out of his way, dragging her bag and the sword to one side.

"Back of the bathroom door," said Heckler.

Jenny went into the bathroom and shut the door, double-checking to make sure it was locked. Her friendship with Heckler baffled her as much as it had always baffled the rest of their friends. She didn't love him; she barely liked him; she wasn't that attracted to him, though he was cute enough, and definitely in shape—he occasionally worked as a fitness trainer in the East Village.

The thing about Keith Heckler was that, while any other guy was secretly an asshole behind every charming smile, every kind word, every clever joke, and every generous gift, Heckler was totally up front about it. No secret: he was a straight-up asshole. It was refreshingly honest.

She squeezed some toothpaste onto her finger and brushed her teeth as best she could. She stripped down to her panties and slipped into the gray T-shirt she found hanging from a hook on the door—a shirt that just said *COLLEGE* on it in classic frat letters. It fit Heckler's broad chest snugly; it was Jenny's preferred nightwear when she crashed here, because it hung nearly down to her knees, like a dress.

She washed her face and ran wet fingers through her hair, hoping that Heckler would just let her sleep in peace tonight. It wasn't unheard of. She *had* spent nights here without any sex involved. That was part of the refreshingly honest asshole phenomenon—unlike most guys, if Heckler wanted sex, he just said it up front. There weren't any hidden catches. She dried off on a Mets towel and opened the door.

"Wanna fuck?" asked Heckler.

"No," Jenny answered. "I just want to sleep, okay? No tricks, no bullshit. It's been a rough day." She looked at him, painfully exhausted. "Please, Heckler?"

"Sure, Jenning," he smiled. "I'll keep my shorts on."

"Thanks," said Jenny. She flopped down on the fold-out—the springs shook beneath her.

"Is that really a magic sword?" Heckler asked her in his inimitably careless style. It was leaning against the wall. He nudged it with his toe and it toppled onto her bag.

"Good night, Heckler."

"Night, Jenning," he said. He turned off the light, slipped under the sheets with her and put an almost entirely not completely innocent hand on her thigh.

"No," Jenny reminded him.

"No problem," said Heckler.

Two minutes later, Jenny declared, "No."

"Right," said Heckler.

Six minutes later, Jenny mumbled, "No."

"Okay," said Heckler.

Twelve minutes later, Jenny whispered: "Where...?"

The condoms were under the couch.

CHAPTER SEVEN

Heckler had never sprung for window shades or air conditioning—he claimed that black people didn't need cooling or shade—so Jenny wasn't sure which thing woke her up with a start: the blinding sunlight, the dull roar of chattering voices outside the window, or Keith Heckler's morning wood pressing into the back of her thigh. It was a six of one, half a dozen of the other, quarter of two dozen of the *other* sort of situation. Her urgent need to pee added up to another square root of three dozen.

Jenny rubbed the groggy crust from her eyes and blinked, adjusting to the light. She gently extracted herself from beneath Heckler's arm and slid off the bed. The College shirt was dangling inside-out from one of the tuning pegs on the electric guitar in the corner. She was relieved she couldn't remember exactly how that happened. Picking her way through magazines that stuck to her feet if she stepped down too hard, she plucked the shirt off the guitar and went into the bathroom.

She slipped into the T-shirt while she sat on the toilet, getting rid of all the water she'd drunk with Calvin McGuirk at the pub and the shots of water she'd shared with Heckler. She briefly entertained the suspicion that Heckler had spiked the shots, but she knew the answer was much simpler than that: she was worn down, desperate for something mundane, and wanted a little human contact. Heckler's advances were Ghengis Khan and the Mongolian Hordes laying siege to a Smurf village hung over from a wild night of smoking Smurfberry leaves. It was a lopsided battle; the end was never really in doubt.

Jenny pouted. She'd put up a good fight, at least.

For twenty minutes.

Ngong gau.

She finished up, swished some toothpaste in her mouth for a minute before gargling and spitting, and splashed her face and hair with cold water. Her hair was a mess, but that was why she kept it short and spiky— it was hard to tell what was intentional and what was a bad hair day. She exchanged looks with her mirror image and hoped she was faring slightly better than Mirror Jenny. They stuck out their tongues at each other. Jenny reached over and flicked the light switch.

Movement caught her eye before the bathroom went pitch dark. Jenny immediately flicked the light back on and looked around. Nothing there. She checked the mirror. Mirror Jenny nodded at her. That was a little disconcerting; Jenny hadn't nodded.

Jenny tightened her lips and made an executive decision to ignore this particular incident until further notice. She vehemently looked anywhere else, shut the light off again, and huffed back out of the bathroom.

Heckler was leaning on the window sill, still naked. "Hey, Jenning," he said without looking at her, "your horse has fans."

"Shit," she muttered. She shoved Heckler over with her hip and looked down from the window. On the walk below, the horse stoically and patiently stared up at her. On the sidewalks on both sides of the street, and on the front steps of buildings a fair distance up and down the block, people had gathered in knots and groups, gesturing at the horse, chatting, shaking their heads. At least forty locals, waking up for a morning coffee, a jog, or just to head off to work or school, had abandoned their daily plans to stand around and gawk at the large, pale horse. "Why's he still *here?*" Jenny whined.

"Dude's hung," said Heckler.

"You're just jealous," Jenny replied, hurrying from the window. She picked up her torn pants and frowned. "Could I borrow some shorts or something?"

A couple of minutes later, Jenny yanked open the front door of the building, wearing Heckler's College shirt and kitty-print boxers that were in danger of slipping right down her slim hips. "Yah!" she yelled at the horse. "Go! Go away! *Puk gai!* Go away!"

The horse stared impassively back. He leaned down and took an experimental nibble out of the front yard.

"Run!" shouted Jenny. "Home! Giddyup! Vamoose! Bad horse! *Waai! Jau boy!*" She was hotly aware of the onlookers chuckling and pointing, talking to each other in low voices punctuated by loud laughter.

He watched Jenny with an aloof sparkle in his eyes, chewing thoughtfully on the inferior grass in his mouth.

Wheeeeet! Whoot-woo, the cop car bleated as it pulled up alongside the curb. Some rubberneckers dispersed; the interest of the rest was only compounded by the arrival of the police. The cops took their time opening doors, creaking out of the car, straightening up and putting on hats. Jenny wondered if they were giving her time to jump on the horse and escape so they could avoid the paperwork. Unhurried, they strolled up the walk. Both were big guys; the black one was beefier, the white one a bit leaner. They wore nearly identical mustaches.

"Morning," the black cop said.

Jenny played it straight, like this was the most normal thing in the world. She moved around the horse toward the cops. "Hi. Sir."

"This your horse, ma'am?"

The white cop said nothing, but sidestepped around the horse on the opposite side from Jenny.

"No, sir," said Jenny.

The horse chuffed anxiously as the white cop got too close, and clopped over toward Jenny, where he platonically nuzzled her shoulder.

"Seems to know you," said the white cop.

"Nope," said Jenny. "Never seen him before." The horse started nibbling at her hair, gently tickling. "Never seen him before last night," Jenny added quickly, watching her fibs dissolve in the horse's sticky saliva.

"Where'd you see him?" said the white cop. The horse kept a wary eye on him, and the sentiment seemed mutual.

"In the park," said Jenny. She tried unsuccessfully to tilt her head out of reach. The horse leaned further and whiffled wet bursts of horsey breath down the back of her neck.

"Sure he's not yours?" said the black cop.

"I swear," said Jenny.

"Sure," said the black cop.

"Would you mind coming with us?" said the white cop. Behind them, a much larger vehicle pulled up next to the police car: a big white truck with a silver trailer attached. Two guys in gray uniforms got out.

"Um," said Jenny. "Where?"

"Just back to the precinct," said the black cop. "Hey, Mike," he called to one of the gray uniforms.

"Jim," the guy greeted him. He had slicked back black hair and an earring in one ear. "Nice horse."

"Big fucker," said the other. His hair was also slicked back and black. No earring, though.

"Fits the description," said the white cop.

Jim the black cop nodded. "Yeah, take him in, guys."

"What are you going to do with him?" Jenny blurted before she could convincingly exhibit some sensible detachment.

The white cop waved her off. "Don't worry, they're just from Animal Control, ma'am. So would you mind coming down to the station with us, answering a couple of questions?"

"Um."

The Animal Control guys approached the horse wielding long poles tipped with flexible loops. The horse chuffed and grumbled, not at all happy with this new development. "Easy, boy," said Mike. "Rico, round the other side."

Rico moved swiftly to flank the horse. The horse wasn't interested. He bolted and vaulted right over the two cops, landing on the sidewalk. Then he paused and waited by the big truck.

The crowd was vocal; some broke out in applause. Mike and Rico swore; the cops stopped ducking and turned to look at the horse, hands at their holsters, though they didn't draw their guns.

"Extend it!" Mike told Rico. "Take the back end!"

"Wait, wait!" said Jenny. "Hold on!" She felt responsible for the horse. He *had* saved her life. "Listen, I'll get him in. In the trailer, right?"

The Animal Control guys nodded sullenly. The cops eased back, but kept their hands by their holsters. Jenny approached the horse and looked him in the eye. "It's okay," she said. "It's okay. *Syu wun.* It's okay."

The horse didn't seem particularly worried. It dawned on Jenny that it would actually be much worse if the cops shot the horse—not because he'd get hurt, which he wouldn't, but because the fact that he instantly healed from the gunshot wound would raise questions substantially more interesting than what he was doing here in the first place. She resolved to get him in the trailer as quickly as possible.

"Okay, horse," Jenny began. She felt awkward speaking so intimately to the animal without something to call him. "Okay, uh, Rex," she picked a name at random. "Listen. You and I both know the *last* thing we need is any complications. We'll figure this all out later. But for now, let's just get in the trailer and avoid any...um. Complications." She was fairly certain that professional horse whisperers made better and less repetitive speeches to their subjects.

The horse shook out his mane and whinnied at her. The cops twitched reflexively. The Animal Control guys held very, very still.

"So, uh," Jenny continued. "Let's go." She waved the horse toward the back of the trailer. He didn't move. She took a couple of steps. He moved to follow her. "Right," she smiled weakly. She walked around to the rear of the trailer, and Mike and Rico opened up the back for her. After a few awkward seconds of trying to get the horse to march up the ramp himself, Jenny gave in and ascended, moving all the way into the trailer. "Come on, Rex!" she called, patting her thigh, assuming she looked ridiculous treating him like a dog. The horse agreed. He rolled his eyes, but followed her in. It was dark inside, but the shade didn't cool things off—the metal walls captured the heat and made the air stuffy and stifling. Jenny patted the horse's nose and looked him in the eye. "Just hold on," she said. "We'll work it out. Don't make any trouble." She was almost positive the horse nodded. She squeezed her way past him and out to the street.

The onlookers applauded again, impressed by her talent in whispering at horses, or at least softly conversing with this one. Mike and Rico closed up the trailer. Inside, Rex—as Jenny had started thinking of him—snorted and stomped a bit, but remained calm.

"Nice," said Jim the cop.

"You *sure* that's not your horse, kid?" the white cop asked her.

Rico from Animal Control concurred. "You talk like he's yours," he said. "And he listens like he's yours."

"I swear," said Jenny, a sinking feeling in her stomach.

"Well, we'd just like you to come down and answer a few questions," said the white cop.

"Can I grab my stuff?"

"Sure," said Officer Jim. "We'll wait. Take a couple minutes. Officer Bergen will help you."

Jenny knew that Officer Bergen would be there to make sure she didn't run away, not to carry her luggage, but she nodded her thanks and headed back to the door, conscious and self-conscious that all eyes were on her as the white cop followed. She grabbed the doorknob and pushed—the damn thing was locked. She glared sharply up at Heckler, who was leaning out the window and grinning at her. His expression tripped and skipped, and he smiled apologetically, then pulled back into the apartment. A moment later, the door buzzed, and Jenny and Officer Bergen went inside.

"Which one's yours?" he asked gruffly.

"Oh! No," said Jenny, "I don't live here. I was just...visiting a...." She tried to think of the right word for Heckler, but settled on: "Friend. Second floor," she added.

Jenny knocked on Heckler's door, and he opened it for them—she was relieved to see he'd put on some pants and an undershirt. "Morning, officer!" Heckler greeted cheerfully. "Nice thing with the horse," he told Jenny.

"Shut up, Heckler," she grouched.

Officer Bergen watched carefully as she picked up her blouse and panties from the floor. Her eyes searched frantically, but she tried to keep her panic from showing on her face.

"Man, Jenning," Keith Heckler called cheerfully from the kitchenette. "My shoulder was all *sored* up from all the *thrashing*," he sliced through the air with a stiff chopping motion. "I iced it down. With ice. Ice from the *refrigerator*."

She looked at him. He winked. She shook her head at his imbecilic code talk, but at least he'd been thinking ahead. "Right," she said. "Sorry about your shoulder. *Keep it on ice*," she said, hoping all of the less than subtle emphasis passing back and forth wasn't picked up by the cop.

Officer Bergen wasn't an idiot. He did, however, fortunately and completely misinterpret their attempt at secrecy. "'Shoulder,' huh?" he smirked. "Try a warm bath, pal—cold's not good for *that* sort of thing."

Jenny's torn pants only reinforced the police officer's misunderstanding, though to be fair, he was correct in his presumption of the previous night's dalliance, as much as Jenny may have wished otherwise. She borrowed a fancy dress shirt from Heckler and used a black leather belt of his to make an impromptu dress of it. Complemented by her Doc Martens, the outfit looked well within the ordinary for New York—it wouldn't warrant a second glance. It wouldn't warrant a *first* glance in some parts of the city, even assuming it wasn't a parade day. Coming out of the bathroom after changing, she stuffed her blouse and torn pants in her bag and nodded at the officer.

"All right, then," he said, opening the door for her.

"I'll be back later," she told Keith Heckler, leaning in for a hug and a kiss on the cheek. Nothing in their mutual history indicated that Heckler should expect that at all, but he was happy enough to reciprocate. Locked in his arms, Jenny leaned close and whispered: "Don't play with it. Seriously."

She pulled back and looked at him meaningfully. He nodded solemnly. She turned and walked past Officer Bergen into the hall.

The cop looked at Heckler. "Huh. She's right, pal," he said. "Playing with it'll just make it worse. Give it a rest for a day or two."

"Sure thing, officer," Heckler smiled politely. "Thanks for the advice!" It was the same smile that frequently prompted mothers to ask about "that nice Heckler boy" when their daughters knew better.

Officer Bergen followed Jenny out to where his partner was waiting. Mike and Rico had already driven off in the big truck, taking Rex away with them. "Is he okay?" Jenny asked.

"Don't worry," said Jim the cop. "The horse'll be fine. Bill?"

"All clear," said Officer Bergen. "Miss, just follow Officer Tell into the car, and we'll be on our way."

Jenny allowed Jim Tell to help her into the back seat. There was a solid wire mesh between her and the front seat. Tell and Bergen got in the front and pulled away from the curb. The last of the horse show crowd drifted away. It wasn't even seven o'clock; the air was still glazed with that bright white that tends to burn off before noon. Officer Tell drove fast, but didn't bother putting the lights and siren on; Officer Bergen was on the radio, saying, "Dispatch, six-seven-Adam-ten. The boys on West Eighth still want our witness? Over."

The radio crackled, and a woman's voice pushed the static aside: "Adam-ten, dispatch. Yeah, six-zero's waiting for her. Will let them know you're on your way. Over."

"Dispatch, thanks—we're *en route*. Adam-ten out." He put the radio back and turned halfway round to look at Jenny. "What's your name, miss?"

"Jenny Ng," she told him.

"Miss, uh...Jenny," said Officer Bergen, "we're going to bring you down to Coney Island. Don't worry, that's just where they're asking us to take you. You may be a key witness in a case they're working down there."

"A case in Coney Island?" Jenny wrinkled her nose. "I don't get it."

"It's about the horse," Bergen explained.

Shit, Jenny thought.

"Don't worry," his friendly smile came out a bit off-balance from under his spectacularly porn-ish mustache. "I don't think you're in any trouble. They just want some things cleared up. They'll get you back up here when you're through."

Jenny nodded anxiously and stared out the window. She suddenly felt highly claustrophobic in the back of the police car.

It wasn't a long drive down McDonald toward the beach. Within sight of the Cyclone and the aquarium, the car made a quick U-turn and pulled into a lot overflowing with black-and-whites. Officer Tell maneuvered into a spot near an imposing building. The cops helped her out of the car and led her through the main doors to a large reception desk.

Officer Tell smiled at the woman behind the desk, who could easily have been his mother. "Hey, we're from the Sixty-Seventh, bringing in a witness for Monaghan."

"Mm hmm," said the lady. She wore a smart blue suit, but it wasn't a uniform. "I'll get him for you, sweetheart."

"Thanks," said Tell. He nodded at Bergen, who brought Jenny over to an uncomfortable bench and stood next to her while she sat.

Some hustle, some bustle, and a lot of people went this way and that through the lobby. Jenny held her bag tighter. She noticed the back of her hand again—the cut she'd made with the sword, when Rex had knocked into her, was still there. Now *that* was confusing—shouldn't it have healed? Or did she need to chop it off completely in order to do her Indestructible Chick Trick?

Or did it have more to do with the sword?

Jenny decided that seemed most likely. She'd have to ask Calvin to help her test her theory later.

"Miss, ah, Nig?"

A man in a light gray suit walked over from the desk, where the lady waved him in Jenny's general direction.

"Jenny Ng," said Jenny, pronouncing it correctly for him. "Yes?"

Officer Tell trailed after the man in the gray suit. "My partner," said Tell, "Bill Bergen."

Gray Suit shook Bergen's hand. "Thanks, ah, Bill, I can take it from here."

"Detective," Officer Bergen said, brusquely professional. He looked at Jenny. "You'll be fine, kid. Just tell 'em whatever they ask."

Jenny gulped and nodded. Officer Tell smiled and tipped his hat, and the two cops walked out the door.

"Miss Ng," said the Gray Suit, hitting the pronunciation a bit closer to the target, "I'm, ah, Detective Monaghan." He was an older man—probably in his sixties—and almost skeletally thin, with a worn face and bony cheeks. His thinning hair was grayer than his suit, and his watery blue eyes squinted through reading glasses at the file folder he held in his hand. He hunched his shoulders a bit, and had a weak old grandpa kind of voice. Jenny instantly felt pity for him, though she couldn't say why. "It, ah, looks like you may be able to help us out, ah, a bit. Ah...if you wouldn't mind? Just follow me, we'll, you know, find a room to talk." He pulled compulsively at his necktie, not really loosening it so much as stretching it.

It turned out not to be the interrogation room that Jenny expected it would be—the one with the giant mirror on one wall behind which the chief and a couple of district attorneys were obviously hiding, listening in on the interrogation while a soft-spoken but cunning psychologist who worked for the police calmly suggested to them that the suspect might be broken by mentioning his mother, or a cigar, or his mother smoking a cigar, or anything else that might have got Freud all hot and bothered. On the contrary, there were no mirrors; just a giant window to the hallway, and if any of the people who passed by were chiefs, district attorneys, or sagacious psychologists, they made no attempt to spy on her conversation with Detective Monaghan. He even left the door open, and the blinds were raised on the exterior windows, letting in plenty of slowly warming morning light. It occurred to Jenny that he was doing everything he could to not stick her in a scary room and rough her up out of view of any witnesses. That reminded her that the cops kept referring to her as a *witness*, not a suspect. Some of her nervous energy eased a bit, and she sat down calmly to answer Monaghan's questions.

The first four answers were: "Sure," "Okay," "I guess," and "Water's fine." This further alleviated any lingering impression that she was going to be tied to a chair and tortured for information while a bright light shone in her face. Detective Monaghan was like an old-timey grandfather in a movie where kids come of age against a backdrop of beautiful summer days and weeping willows swaying in uncannily revelatory breezes. He was a little scattered, a little out of it, and had a terrible time collecting his thoughts for each question. If it was a clever ploy to put her at ease, it was working like gangbusters. If not, then Monaghan was perhaps a few years overdue for retirement.

He returned with her water and she sipped it as he ruffled through folders on the table. "So, ah, Miss Ng," he said in a voice like a startled vuvuzela. He had the old-fashioned accent of cops and street vendors in Fifties movies. "The, ah, horse...?"

Jenny swallowed another sip of water and shrugged. "I was walking home through the park last night, and—"

"Which park?" Monaghan asked, taking notes.

"Prospect Park," she said. "There were a couple of guys in the park who, um...." She made an ambiguous gesture with her head. "You know."

"Ah, gang members?"

"Maybe, I don't know," said Jenny. "I mean, they were harassing me. Nothing serious," she added quickly when Monaghan looked up with sharp, grandfatherly concern. "Just being jerks. And then the horse just came out of nowhere, and scared them away." She was editing her story on the fly, not sure how much to reveal. One thing she *knew* she didn't want to mention was the sword—she needed to keep that under wraps for now.

"Did the, ah, animal have a, ah, sword with it?" asked Detective Monaghan.

Jenny winced, and tried to cover it with a small coughing fit. She took another sip of water, collected herself, and put her best light and breezy face on. "Uh, no," she said brightly. "A sword? I didn't see one. How does a horse carry a sword, anyway? In his mouth?" That might be pushing it, but she was trying to walk a fine line between not knowing anything about the sword and not being a complete idiot.

"I, ah, guess so, heh," Monaghan gave her a little smile. "Miss Ng, do you recognize, ah," he paused to sift through his files, and slide a photograph across the table, "this man?"

The photo was a classic mug shot, a man holding a plaque with a name and serial number on it, standing in front of a wall of lines marking off his height. According to the marks, he was over six feet tall. According to the plaque, his name was John Doe. He was remarkably thin, even more skeletal than Detective Monaghan, with a tightly drawn face and a sharp nose. His jet black hair was cut close to the smooth round top of his head. His dark eyes were round and friendly, if a bit dim, but his skin looked like it had been sculpted from Play-Doh—not quite real, as if Monaghan had handed her a picture of a bust in a museum.

"No, I've never seen him before," Jenny answered honestly. She kept staring down at the photo. The pale man wore a distant smile. There was something about him—not something familiar, Jenny didn't think, but something she felt she should recognize, if only she could pinpoint what it was. "Who is he?"

"We're not sure," said Detective Monaghan. "He, ah, claims not to know, himself." At Jenny's dubious look, Monaghan shrugged and took a deep breath. "It's possible he's got amnesia, or, ah, just a mental disability," he explained. "But he may be the horse's owner. Or, ah, he may have stolen the horse from its actual, ah, owner. You're sure you've never seen him before?"

"Definitely," said Jenny.

"Would you mind if I brought you to, ah, see him?" Monaghan asked tentatively. "To see if maybe *he* recognizes *you?*"

Jenny protested, "But I've never met him..."

"There are, ah, any number of reasons why one person might recognize another," said Monaghan in a gentle tone, "even if they, ah, haven't previously met. It could really, ah, help us out—at least give us a clue, or eliminate, you know, an avenue of investigation. Would you mind?"

"No, sure," said Jenny. "Yeah, I'll see him."

"All right, ah, thanks," said Monaghan. "Just a couple more questions, Miss Ng, and we'll go, ah, down to holding."

Jenny took another sip to cover her nervous reaction at having to answer more questions. Her mind raced to make sure her story was hanging together so far. It wasn't that she was lying so much as omitting. Well, except for the sword. She'd outright lied about that.

"So after the, ah, gang members left," Monaghan continued, "what happened?"

"I tried to just go home, but the horse kept following me," said Jenny. She didn't think that would get Rex into any trouble. Stalking didn't seem like a crime horses could be convicted of. "I, um, got a little sidetracked, 'cause I kept trying to run away from him. I think he was just playing," she defended, careful about how she painted Rex's personality. "But I ended up on the wrong side of the park. And it was a long day, so I went to my friend Heck—uh, my friend Keith's apartment so I could get some sleep."

"What's Keith's name?"

"Keith." She flinched at her obviously dimwitted answer.

"His, ah, full name?" Monaghan asked patiently.

"Keith Heckler," said Jenny.

"And he lives on, ah, Lenox, where the horse was, ah, taken into custody?"

"Yes," said Jenny. At the detective's prompting, she gave him Heckler's street number and apartment.

"Thank you," Monaghan marked that down in his notes. "And you spent the night there, ah, at your friend's apartment?"

"Uh huh," Jenny said. "We woke up because everybody was outside, talking about the horse."

"Which was, ah, standing at your doorstep," Monaghan said.

"Heckler's—Keith's doorstep, yeah," Jenny corrected him.

"And you live at...?"

She gave him her address on Seventeenth Street.

"Ah," said Monaghan, adding to his notes. "The, ah, officers said you showed a, ah, affinity for the horse. That it listens to you."

"I just didn't want anyone to get hurt," Jenny said. "Or him. I guess he likes me."

"Ah," Monaghan nodded. "So you helped calm him and get him into the Animal Control vehicle."

"Yes."

"And, ah, then...?"

"Then the cops—the, uh, policemen asked me to come here, so I got dressed and came." Jenny spread her hands as a conclusion to her story. *That's all, folks.* She hoped.

"All right," said Monaghan, scribbling some more notes. "All right." He stopped writing, clicked his pen and dropped it in his shirt pocket, and retrieved the photo. Straightening his files, he stood and smiled at her. "So, if you'll, ah, just come on down to holding with me, we'll take a look and see if Mister, ah, Doe gets any, you know, spark of recognition."

"Okay," said Jenny.

He waited a moment while she gulped down the last of her water, then escorted her through a series of hallways and down a flight of stairs. He stopped to check in with a cop behind a small counter; they exchanged a couple of casual jokes, the kind that people who work together and have never had a single drink together exchange, and the cop buzzed them through a barred door. Monaghan led Jenny a short way past two small holding cells, and stopped at the third. "Ah, Mister, ah, Doe?"

The man from the photograph was lying peaceably on a cot, staring up at a half-window near the ceiling. He had a beatific smile that was rarely seen outside of saints and ten-year-old cancer patients, and he didn't appear to have heard Monaghan at all.

"Ah, *sir?*" Monaghan said.

The thin man craned his neck to look at them. "That is right," he said in a vaguely unplaceable accent straight out of an independent film about life and love behind the Iron Curtain. "I forgot that I am Mister Doe," he grinned. He pivoted and planted his feet on the floor, then took a few steps to greet them at the bars. He wore a flowing black robe with a hood. Jenny flashed on the discussion of "wizard-y" magicians she'd had with Calvin McGuirk. This guy looked like he'd done a few alchemy experiments in his day. He looked just about lucid enough to have transformed gold into lead, though the reverse was probably well beyond his skill set.

"Mister Doe," said Monaghan, "this, ah, is Jenny. She came to say hello."

The guy stared at Jenny expectantly.

There was a very long, very awkward pause. Jenny cleared her throat and said, "Hello."

"Thank you," said John Doe, quite sincerely, and he turned back toward his cot.

"Ah, no, ah," Monaghan verbally scrambled, "Mister Doe..."

"Yes?" the guy turned back to them.

"I'd like you to, ah, take a look at Jenny," Monaghan explained. "Do you think you may, ah, have seen her before?"

John Doe looked at Jenny openly but emptily. Jenny looked back. There *was* something about the guy, not something she knew...but something she knew *about*...if she could just put her finger on it. He gazed at her thoughtfully, his eyes glazing over with the effort of pushing through the foggy walls of lost memory. Then his eyes snapped wide, and he smiled broadly.

"Mister Doe?" Monaghan prompted him.

"No," said John Doe.

"Ah...?"

"I have not seen her before," said John Doe.

"Oh," said Monaghan, disappointed.

John Doe sniffed, and said: "But I think that I was supposed to."

Monaghan and Jenny exchanged confused looks. "What do you, ah, mean by that, Mister Doe?" asked the detective.

The man behind the bars looked down at Jenny curiously and said: "*Ngaan lai lai gam mong sat ngo soeng dim?*"

Jenny's jaw dropped. Aside from profanity, her Cantonese had always been very limited—to her mother's eternal dismay—but she understood precisely what John Doe had just said. Half of her shock was from his proficiency in speaking it, and the other half was from her ability to understand it.

"Ah, what?" asked Monaghan, out of the loop.

Jenny clapped her mouth shut and shook her head. "I don't know," she lied. "I don't speak Cantonese—mostly just some swear words I used to hear my mom use." Until this very moment, that would have been the truth. It was going to be hard to keep track of her lies if the truth kept transforming like that.

"Ah," said Monaghan. "Well, then." He asked John Doe, "What do you mean you were 'supposed' to, ah, see her, Mister Doe?"

"I do not know," said John Doe.

"Right, ah, okay." Monaghan patted Jenny on her shoulder. "Thank you, Miss Ng. We'll, ah, head back out now. Mister Doe, thanks for trying."

"You are welcome for trying," said John Doe. To Jenny, he smiled and said, "*Hou hou hoi sam sik zi dou dou nei.*"

Jenny laughed nervously and looked at Detective Monaghan with an exaggerated wide-eyed shrug, as if the man in black was spouting crazy gibberish. She waved at John Doe, and he waved back, as she and the detective headed back upstairs.

At the front desk, Monaghan had her fill out some paperwork and confirm the notes he'd scribble out. She provided her cell phone number. Monaghan put his reading glasses back on and squinted down at her information. "Do you have a, ah, work number, Miss Ng?"

"I'm looking for a new job," Jenny said. "I was, um, 'downsized' this week." Euphemism felt better than pessimism.

"Oh, ah, sorry," said Detective Monaghan. "Well, good luck finding a new, ah, job." He shook her hand and waved toward the door. "We've got a cab waiting outside to take you home—NYPD's treat."

"Thanks, Detective," Jenny said. She headed for the exit.

"And you should probably get that, ah, sword wound looked at, heh," Monaghan called after her with a light laugh.

She froze and turned. "Um," she said. She held up her hand. "This? Ha," she forced a smile, "sword wound, right. Just cut myself."

"With what?" asked Monaghan. "Looks, ah, pretty bad."

"Caught it in the fold-out couch," was the first thing Jenny thought to say.

"Ooh," Monaghan winced sympathetically. "Those things are, ah, dangerous, yeah. Make sure you get a, you know, a bandage on that. Don't let it get, ah, infected." Jenny started to wonder if maybe Monaghan was a *lot* farther from retirement than he seemed to let on.

"Right," said Jenny. "Thanks!" She turned and walked out as quickly as she could, trying not to make it look like she was walking out as quickly as she could. She felt Monaghan's weepy blue grandpa eyes on her back until the heavy door closed behind her.

CHAPTER EIGHT

"Watch this," Jenny said, turning on the clock radio next to the futon that served as Calvin McGuirk's bed.

Calvin stood by the open door that she'd just pushed through like some swirling desert wind he used to know the name of. "Uh, *ni hao* to you too," he said carefully.

"Not bad, but that's Mandarin," said Jenny, sharp and fast. "It's not the same. Nice Googling, though. Now shut up for a second and watch." She turned on the radio and started dialing through stations.

"You mean listen?" Calvin asked. She looked up but kept turning the dial. "'Cause it's a radio," he explained lamely. "Not a TV."

"Shh," Jenny said, and she found a station that would do. "Listen."

A deep man's voice on the radio clearly said: "...*tenista americano* Tommy Norquist *ganó su juego—y la adoración de los espectadores—a los cuartos de final del torneo de* Wimbledon *tras superar cómodamente al suizo* Jonas Eicher, *que no tuvo ninguna opción ante el cincos veces ganador...*"

"American tennis player Tommy Norquist," Jenny interrupted, "won the game, and the love of the fans, on the court for the final match at Wimbledon, after comfortably beating Swiss player Jonas Eicher, who had no chance against the five-time champion." She smacked the radio in triumph, shutting off the rapid-fire Spanish sports coverage, then crossed her arms and looked at Calvin expectantly.

"Um," said Calvin. "Bravo for Norquist?"

"I understood every word of it!" said Jenny. "I've been watching *Telemundo* all morning at the Mexican place near my apartment. I had a conversation with the waitress. She didn't know I could speak Spanish."

"I didn't know you can speak Spanish," Calvin said.

"I *can't* speak Spanish!" Jenny hollered. "I mean, I couldn't," she waffled. "I've never spoken Spanish in my life. I mean, *amigo* or *gracias* and stuff like that. But I never took Spanish. *Ahora, hablo español como un natural.*"

"So you speak Spanish now?" asked Calvin.

"I speak *everything!*" Jenny declared dramatically. She threw her hands up and collapsed on Calvin's couch. She closed her eyes tight to block out the world.

Calvin straightened the clock radio and squatted in front of his raving magician's assistant. Colby the rabbit crept out from under the couch to hang about his feet. "Jenny, what're you talking about?"

Her eyes snapped open and drilled through his. "Do you speak any other languages?"

"I know a little Gaelic," he admitted with a shrug. "Uh, *cad is ainm duit? An bhfuil tu damhsa liom?*"

"You already know my name," Jenny said in a bored, tedious tone, "and no, I don't feel like dancing."

"Wow," said Calvin, impressed. "You speak Gaelic?"

Her withering stare drove home the new point that Calvin was missing the original point.

"Right," he corrected hastily. "Everything. Every language." He stood up. "Really?"

"If you have any books in other languages, I can show you," said Jenny. "But whatever. Yes. Every language. I never really learned Cantonese—my mom was always pissed about that—but now I speak it fluently. And this guy today...fuck." Jenny collapsed deeper into the couch, totally drained.

Calvin sat next to her, his hands on his knees, which jutted comically upward. He took a deep breath, then said: "Okay, Jenny. What?"

The whole story poured out. She'd already told him about her miraculous powers of regeneration, and he'd trusted her with knowledge of the magic hole, the rings, and all that, so there wasn't much to hide with Calvin. In less than twenty-four hours, they'd each become the only person who knew the other's most incredible secrets. Jenny had always thought it silly how quickly the action hero and the distressed damsel fell in love in real time over the course of a two-hour adventure movie, but she had to admit: intense incidents inspired instant intimacy. Not that she was planning on getting actually *intimate* with Calvin; it was just that their relationship had clearly progressed from a twenty-dollar offer on a sidewalk to an actual bond in a short amount of time.

She finished up with the story of her subway ride over, during which she read the newspaper over a Chinese man's shoulder until he commented softly on her poor upbringing, and she snapped back in perfect Mandarin a remark comparing his manners to those of a maggot that aspired to be a louse. "*Mandarin!*" she emphasized. "I barely know Cantonese, and my family's from Hong Kong—my mom never spoke any Mandarin around me. Ever. In my *life*. Gah!" she concluded, leaning on Calvin's long arm and actually feeling somewhat tension free for the first time in five years.

Calvin, on the other hand, was a little tight, his shoulder tensed like a coiled, pent-up, perhaps sexually deprived spring beneath her head; he cleared his throat. "Yeah," he said, "I get it. Wait!" He stood up abruptly, leaving Jenny to sprawl on the couch. Colby bolted across the room to avoid Calvin's huge feet. "If you can speak any language, and *read* any language...." He walked to his bookcase and retrieved the special wooden box from the top shelf.

Dawn slowly broke on Jenny's face. "The letters!" she realized. "That's why I can read what it says through the window!"

"Yeah!" said Calvin McGuirk, his face similarly aglow with discovery.

"But," Jenny wondered aloud, "how come I can only read *some* of them?"

Calvin shrugged. "Maybe they're not languages?" he suggested. "The ones you can't read, I mean."

"Hmm," said Jenny. "Maybe. I don't think so, though. They definitely look like letters. I mean, as much as the other ones do. Sometimes they even look like the *same* letters, but I just can't understand what they say." She stood on her knees on the couch, facing the wall. "Look at this," she said, pointing to the paper that Calvin had taped up—the one where he'd copied down the letters that appeared on himself through the window. Jenny pointed at one series of characters: "That's your birthday, right there," she said.

"It actually *says* March Eleventh?" Calvin asked dubiously.

"No," Jenny explained. "It's more like a...well, a description of the world the day you were born. I just kind of 'translated' it from that to March Eleventh."

"Weird."

"Hold on," Jenny shifted and pointed to another set of characters. Two of them were identical to two of the characters in the part that described his birthday, though they weren't in any discernibly equivalent order. "See these?" Jenny pointed to the two repeated symbols. "They're just like those..."

"Yeah," said Calvin, scratching his chin.

"But I don't know what any of this part means," said Jenny. "I don't even know if those symbols have the same meaning here that they do in the part I understand. It's like everything can only be read all together, or it can't be read. Like, if the letter *B* had no sound outside of a word—and had a different sound in each word you put it in. And you had to learn what sound it made in each word."

"*Really* weird," Calvin elaborated his earlier assessment. "Well, wait, though—so what does, like, *that* one mean?" He pointed to one of the two repeats they were looking at in the bit that referred to his birthday.

Jenny grimaced and sucked in on the air as if the curious tilt of her head ran on pneumatics. "It's weird to explain," she said reluctantly. "You know, like some languages have words that other languages don't have a direct translation for? So you have to say a whole definition just to translate it...I don't think you'd fully understand."

"Okay," said Calvin, disappointed.

Jenny realized that the magician felt cheated, not being able to understand the symbols he'd discovered before she ever came along. She gave it a try: "Okay, that symbol," she placed her palm on the wall and traced the contours of the character with her finger. "It kind of refers to the way that the spinning of a certain star in a really far away galaxy is changing direction in a pattern that matches the motion of something that's kind of like water on a planet that's in a totally different galaxy in another part of the universe."

"You're right," Calvin said, wide-eyed. "I don't understand."

"Well, it's just that, in my head," Jenny continued, "that 'literal' meaning of all the letters put together kind of gets jumbled up into more like...well, like a figure of speech, and that figure of speech kind of pinpoints the location of a bunch of stars in the sky, and just knowing where they are...I suddenly end up thinking of your birthday. The month, the day, even the year." She pushed away from the wall and inched up a bit, studying the other characters. Distracted, she added, "I'm not totally sure how I even know that, though. It's kind of just the way you know that, in English, the letters *T, H, R, E, E* mean that you have one thing, and another thing, and another thing."

"Still weird," Calvin said. "But I think I know what you mean there."

"Uh huh," said Jenny. She stabbed at a few of the letters on Calvin's paper. "Damn it!"

Calvin stepped back, startled. "What, what?"

"It's like I can *almost* figure out what some of these other ones mean," said Jenny, her frustration bordering on anger. "Like when you see Spanish words like *invitación* or *televisión* and you know they've *got* to be 'invitation' and 'television' because they're so close...." She pounded the wall with her fist, startling Calvin again. Whispering, she repeated: "So close." She hung her head and sagged on the couch a little.

Calvin McGuirk stood behind her for a long, silent moment, clutching the wooden box. His fingers rapped a nervous, idle rhythm on its edge. Finally, he cleared his throat. "Uh...hey, we should put a Band-Aid on that."

Jenny turned and looked up at him without a clue.

"Your hand," Calvin pointed. "From the sword."

Jenny nodded with a tiny, grateful smile. She sat back down on the couch as Calvin went into the bathroom—he came back with a box of Band-Aids and a tube of ointment. He squeezed out some ointment on the back of her outstretched hand—it smelled like plastic oatmeal cookies—and started smoothing it out along the short but jagged cut she'd given herself with the sword. With the non-stop excitement of arcane linguistics dying down, Colby the bunny wandered over to sniff at Jenny's feet. "So yeah," Calvin segued, "why *didn't* this thing just heal right up?"

"I don't know," said Jenny thoughtfully. "I was going to ask you if I could borrow your knife—maybe if it's just a cut, my...thing...doesn't work."

"Or..."

Jenny nodded. "Yeah, or maybe it's the sword." She scowled. "Which means that my thing..."

"You can go ahead and call it your 'power,'" said Calvin. He grinned at her annoyed expression. "That's what it *is*," he insisted.

"Then my *power...*" she said hotly.

"Yeah!"

"...has something to do with the sword," Jenny finished. "And the sword...and the horse...probably *both* belong to the guy the cops have. Or they have *something* to do with him."

"And he's got the same language thing you do," Calvin said, smoothing a Band-Aid over her cut, "so *that* power's connected to all this too."

"What?"

He finished sticking the Band-Aid firmly to her hand. "Well, come on, Jenny," he said like he was explaining that water is wet and dirt is dirty. "You said the guy looks like Count Dracula. What are the odds that he *just so happens* to speak Chi—uh, Cantonese?"

"Oh," said Jenny. The light snapped on in her head. "Yeah—good point."

"So maybe he does the healing thing, too," said Calvin. "And if the horse and the sword are his, then maybe that's why the sword can cut you. And," he suddenly realized, "why the horse likes you! You're just like the Count!"

"Damn it," said Jenny. "Give me a knife."

"I just finished patching you up!" Calvin pretended to complain, but he went to the bookcase and brought back the same knife she'd used to chop off her fingers. He held it out to her, handle first.

Jenny took the knife and sighed. "Okay, let's just see...." She drew the tip of the blade across one fingertip. "Ouch!" she said reflexively.

But it didn't really hurt much. After a couple of heartbeats, the perfectly smooth, curved incision began to weave itself together and disappear, until all that was left was a bright red line of blood. Jenny wiped it off with her thumb, leaving not a trace of the wound.

"I think that answers that," said Calvin. "It's the sword."

"It's the sword," Jenny agreed. Though she tried not to show it, she was royally relieved. She'd been a little worried that perhaps she'd "used up" her new power, and that was why the sword was able to cut her. Finding out that she was still indestructible, and just had to be careful of one particular magical sword, was a load off her mind.

"So, hey, we can still do all the cool stuff in the act," said Calvin. Obviously, he'd thought of the same possibility.

Jenny smiled, then stood up and tried to artfully twirl the knife in her fingers; she failed spectacularly, and the knife slipped and plunged to the floor, stabbing into the rug and whanging back and forth as they both twitched their toes out of the way automatically. "Eep," said Jenny. Colby the bunny hopped over to sniff at the knife curiously. It wagged back at her.

"Um," said Calvin pointedly. "But how 'bout you leave the sleight of hand to me?"

CHAPTER NINE

Saturday night was opening night, and Jenny felt about as ready to roll as a chained-up bicycle with both wheels stolen. Calvin took five minutes out of every hour to reassure her that the act was solid, her costume looked great, their rapport was sparkling, and her performance was, at the very least, passable.

They'd spent Thursday evening working out the act, proposing and discarding ideas with the rapid-fire pace of late-term lame duck senators just trying to look busy. They experimented with Jenny's powers (as she reluctantly agreed to call them), and came up with some new tricks involving Calvin's magic hole. Jenny tried seeing if she could make the magic wand do anything. The long, thin stick was a little flexible—Jenny sensed she might break it if she bent it too far—but didn't do anything obvious. She suggested using it as a prop, like a traditional stage magician, but Calvin pointed out that suddenly discovering what the wand did in the middle of a show might be a bit dicey, especially if it turned out to shoot deadly laser beams or magically erase noses off of audience members' faces. They agreed the wand was off-limits until they knew what it did; but the hole, the rings, the specs and window, and Jenny herself were all fair game.

By the time they'd ordered some cheap Chinese take-out, they had a general structure worked out. They juggled the order of the tricks over chicken lo mein. They ran over their staging—and Calvin's lines, which were Jenny's cues—while munching greasy egg rolls. They put together shopping lists for costumes and additional props as they drank won ton soup. (They'd saved it for last to let it cool—New York was hellishly hot this late in June.) They really felt like they'd accomplished something by the time they cracked open their fortune cookies. Jenny confirmed for Calvin that *xué xiào* on the back of his fortune did, in fact, mean "school." She even managed to teach him to pronounce the Mandarin tones correctly.

As comfortable as she was with him at this point, she still opted to head back to her place around eleven. Jenny still firmly agreed with herself that starting any romantic or even merely physical relationship with Calvin would do nothing but ruin their chances with the magic act. Calvin still only half-heartedly agreed with Jenny and Jenny's self, but wasn't about to push it since he was conceptually outvoted. The issue was left unspoken but not unthought, like a long trail of snot dripping down your companion's face on a first date.

Jenny had crept into her apartment without alerting the Ecuadorian family who lived below her, who not very secretly reported on her comings and goings to Doc Kolachek. If everything with Calvin and the act went well, and she found a second job at a restaurant or an office, she should be able to catch up on rent in a month or two, and pay on time and in full from there on out. Calvin had offered to put in a good word for her at the office where he wageslaved, but she declined.

Her free minutes had started well before she got back to her place, so she called Heckler and asked him to keep the sword in his fridge until she came by to pick it up. She wanted to retrieve it as soon as possible and show it to Calvin; between the two of them, they might start piecing together the puzzle of the sword, Jenny's new powers, Rex the wonder horse, and Count Dracula down in his Coney Island jail cell. Plus, the idea of leaving anything of hers—or something she was holding onto for the horse—at Heckler's didn't sit well with Jenny.

Friday morning was a whirlwind of thrift shopping as she put her costume together in time to meet Calvin at the *Beau Regardez*, the theatre where they'd auditioned on Eighth Avenue and would be playing Saturday night. They knocked the socks off the producer, David Dennis—the round, purring gay man with the open shirt and chest hair from Wednesday's audition—and his prissy assistant Kevin. Both begged to be let in on the tricks; Calvin and Jenny politely refused. "You know how it is with magicians," Calvin had said pointedly. David, his eyes running up and down the lanky magician like he was mentally licking him, agreed not to pry. Kevin eyed Calvin and his assistant suspiciously, but stuck to his boss's decision. "You're the closing act tomorrow night," he told them as they packed up. "Be on time to watch the acts before you. You can head backstage to get ready two acts before yours—that's Roberta and Verbena."

Roberta and Verbena turned out to be two very large women—Jenny was fairly certain of their gender, at least—who read poetry out loud and welcomed audience participation: every time the audience caught certain patterns or rhymes in their poems, Roberta or Verbena had to strip off an article of clothing, like a drinking game where readers take a shot for every time Robert Frost mentions a road. Jenny and Calvin snuck out the back of the theatre when Verbena, or possibly Roberta—Jenny couldn't figure out which was which, and they hadn't said—decadently stripped off a fluffy pink boa. Whether the audience member who had caught her alliterative metaphor involving cats was genuinely interested in seeing the obese lady's naked splendor, or merely in inflicting the view on everybody else, was up for grabs. Campy trumpet music leaked out through the theatre door as Calvin held it open and followed Jenny through.

Backstage, Jenny felt a nervous buzz and a dizzying excitement at the same time. The world's first successful example of cold fusion twirled in her stomach. She took off her coat to reveal the sexy black bustier beneath, and pulled her jeans off of sheer black leggings; she wriggled into the stiff red tutu she'd bought on Saint Mark's Place and wrapped a velvet choker around her neck. Standing in front of a mirror teasing her hair into the most glamorous wavy spikes she could manage, she looked over Mirror Jenny's shoulder at Calvin's reflection. She coldly ignored the fact that Mirror Jenny took a quick glance back over her own shoulder to see what Jenny was looking at.

Calvin was in his magician's outfit again, though Jenny had found him slightly nicer black pants. He grinned at her through the reflection. "Sounds like the, um, poets are done," he said, as applause wafted through the proscenium arch. "You ready?"

"As I'll ever be," Jenny smiled tightly. She wondered if it was unusual that an audience of several dozen people made her more nervous than the idea of Calvin chopping her hand off. She decided it very likely was. At least, for people who weren't her. Or Rex. Or, probably, the Coney Island Count. The slowly growing list of people (or animals) who likely shared her powers was making it increasingly urgent to investigate just what was going on. The sword—retrieved from Keith Heckler's place the night before—was currently wrapped up in three big green garbage bags and stacked with the rest of their stuff backstage.

She checked her slutty stage makeup, and put some foundation and rouge on Calvin despite his protests. Jenny knew plenty about lighting and faces, and she knew his fair complexion and red hair would look almost completely washed out in the bright stage lights. He'd be a blank white blob with freckles. Holding his chin tight as he squirmed, she applied some dark eyeliner to compensate for his nearly invisible eyelashes. She used the same pencil to darken his eyebrows.

"You're gonna make me look like Mister Spock," Calvin complained.

"Better than Richie Cunningham," she replied, finishing up. "You look great."

They heard laughter and catcalls from the audience, though they weren't sure what the two rotund poets had just done or said. One of the ladies called out in a cigarette-scratched voice, and the audience broke into applause. David Dennis rolled his pudgy figure on stage from the opposite wing as Roberta and Verbena shuffled off toward Jenny and Calvin—both ladies were down to mercifully opaque negligees and thigh-highs.

"Adorable," Verbena, or Roberta, commented on Jenny's outfit.

"Thanks," said Jenny.

"Break a leg," said Roberta, or Verbena.

"You too," Calvin said, before realizing his timing. "Um, I mean, great job."

The big women smiled burlesquely at him through heavy makeup and long fake lashes—Jenny reassessed her perception of their gender—and left to circle around to the back of the theatre and watch the show. On stage, David Dennis introduced the next act, and the audience applauded as somebody began singing in Italian from the back of the theatre. The *basso profundo* voice moved closer, and a wiry little guy tumbled onto the stage, his shape completely at odds with his deep and powerful voice. As he sang, the audience started chuckling, then laughing broadly—Jenny listened closer: the Italian was fake, and the lyrics were actually satirical political commentary meant to sound like traditional Italian opera. She and Calvin were on next, though, so she was a little too distracted to work out the narrative.

Calvin started patting himself down, making sure everything he might need was stowed away wherever it might be needed. They both went through the magic table, checking and re-checking the props. Colby Cheese the bunny was tucked away in the secret compartment of the velvet bag; a number of white mice Calvin had picked up at the pet store were crawling about in the more mundane part of the bag. The "feeder mice," as the pet store clerk called them, would have been purchased by snake owners as pet food anyway, but this didn't make either Calvin or Jenny feel better;

they avoided the little red mouse eyes the way you avoid an ex you may have inadvertently infected with herpes. The less emotional connection they felt to the doomed rodents, the better.

It wasn't long before the operatic satirist rolled through an impressive rhyming list of nearly every right wing conservative in Congress, using clever wordplay to match them to the precise vices each politician vociferously decried in public (and therefore most likely engaged in). With one giant high *A* held for twenty seconds, the guy sealed the deal, and the audience applauded enthusiastically.

The bottom dropped out of Jenny's stomach as the opera man skipped past them. Calvin gave her a comforting smile and rolled the magic table to the edge of the curtain as David Dennis ambled into the spotlight.

"Thank you, ladies and lovelies," he purred to the crowd as if the applause for every act was aimed at him. "And now, for the final act of the evening, you've got an incredibly rare treat—the kind of act that's supposed to be in Vegas. Lucky for us, I know they've never been there. Because what happens there, stays there." Weak laughter acknowledged the outdated joke. "Please welcome to the *Beau Regardez*, for his world premiere, the Amazing Quirk, and his lovely assistant!"

The applause exploded again, and Jenny felt for just an instant like she'd forgotten the entire act. The moment passed, though, and she sashayed on stage with a twirl, her scarlet tutu bouncing as she presented Calvin Quirk. Calvin boldly shoved the magic table out to center stage, where Jenny caught it and spun it into place as Calvin marched into the light and smiled warmly at his audience.

"Ladies and gentlemen!" Calvin boomed in his Powerful Magician Voice. "And visitors from other realms," he added with a sly smile. "I am the Amazing Quirk!"

His hands came together in a clap and an explosion of multi-colored flame and smoke. Light applause rippled through the theatre, more from the audience getting into the spirit of the show than because they were at all impressed.

"This," Calvin swept his hands toward Jenny, "Is my lovely assistant: Jade, the Jewel of the East!"

Jenny beamed at them with her best showgirl expression. She got a bit more applause, probably out of admiration for her outfit.

"I made the acquaintance of this mysterious lady on my recent journey to the Orient," Calvin said, spinning the tale they'd worked up. "Where I furthered my studies in the ancient and arcane arts of magic and mysticism." A mock *oooh!* swept across the audience—this was the kind of crowd that appreciated melodrama. "Jade was living in the tallest tower of a secret stone castle where only the wisest and most powerful of mystics are allowed to enter. There they study mystical artifacts and divine the mysteries of how they work. But Jade was no mystic, there to study the artifacts." The Amazing Quirk moved to stand behind her and took her wrists, spreading her arms outward on display. "You see—Jade herself *is* one of the artifacts."

Jenny lowered her arms and slyly glanced at the audience. She couldn't actually see anything beyond the dim first rows, but the effect was what mattered. Some catcalls and whistles hit the stage—the story was going over well.

"A thousand years ago," said Calvin, walking back to the magic table, "there was a young prince who was obsessed with capturing the beauty in everything he saw." Calvin reached into the table and pulled out a long, thin knife and an apple. "The prince was a talented sculptor," the magician continued, "and he would spend hours, days, even *months* cutting away at wood or stone—" he started peeling the shiny red skin off the apple with his sharp knife "—to create exquisite duplicates of the best examples of beauty he could find in nature. He would sculpt birds with outstretched wings, willows with drooping branches swaying in the breeze, a tumbling waterfall spilling over a cliff on the rocks below...."

As he spoke, Calvin quickly but carefully whittled away at the apple, cutting bits and pieces away in a marvelous demonstration of manual dexterity. "He would create sculptures that captured everything he saw, like the lovely ladies who welcomed visitors to the royal court, and waited on his royal father hand and foot. One lady, in particular, caught his eye, for her eyes sparkled like the jade dragon the prince had sculpted as a birthday present for the king. Her name...was Jade."

They'd quibbled over that part; Jenny's eyes weren't green. Calvin figured nobody in the audience would notice, and he convinced Jenny that dramatic license was pretty forgiving.

"The prince made many, many sculptures of the beautiful Jade, out of wood, or stone, or clay...or anything he happened to have lying around," Calvin said. "Like an apple from his father's royal orchards!"

Calvin made one last slice and held the apple up sharply. He had cut the core into a rough, misshapen but recognizably humanoid figure.

He grinned weakly. "Okay, yeah, so his probably looked a lot less like Yoda than mine does," he admitted in a voice more like his real one. The crowd laughed appreciatively, and even clapped a bit. "But," the Amazing Quirk returned to his dramatic performance tone, "the prince's brothers challenged him. 'You may be able to capture beauty,' they told him, 'but you can never keep it. Beauty always fades.' The prince was frustrated—what good was capturing all this beauty if it would always fade?"

Jenny caught her cue—she moved swiftly back toward the magic table as Calvin took center stage, still holding the knife and apple.

"He studied and studied, learning more about art, and the materials that he used," said Calvin, still displaying the mediocre apple statue and sharp knife. "But that wasn't enough. He talked with the wise men and wizards of the kingdom, and even consulted with the demons who lived in the deepest, darkest caves where you can actually smell the Gates of Hell. But wood weathers, and stone crumbles, and apples..."

He tossed the apple figure into the air, then jabbed upwards with the knife and caught the core on the tip, where it stuck. "They rot away."

Behind Calvin, Jenny hoisted herself up on the magic table. It rolled a little, but she wiggled her hips and swiveled it back into position, trying not to distract the audience from Calvin's story.

"The prince traveled far and wide, looking for the answers he needed," Calvin walked a slow but definite arc, heading up to where Jenny sat on the magic table. "And he realized that there was no material that would last forever. The laws of the universe wouldn't allow it. Everything, or anything, that he made his sculptures out of would eventually break down, and that beauty would be lost. But," Calvin paused dramatically as he approached Jenny, facing the audience the whole time, holding up the knife with the apple core stuck on its sharp point. "Maybe that was only because the beauty itself—the beauty that he captured—wasn't in the sculpture at all. It was always in the original."

Calvin ran a finger from Jenny's wrist down to her waist, barely touching her. The audience sighed some more melodramatic *oohs* and *aahs*. "If the prince could preserve the beauty of the original," said the Amazing Quirk, "then what would it matter if the sculpture turned to dust? In fact, if the original lasted through the ages, eternally beautiful...why even make a sculpture at all?"

Jenny propped her hands behind her on the edge of the magic table and artfully arched her back. She felt like she was in a yoga class, holding this position until Calvin's story ended.

"The prince changed his questions," said Calvin, "and looked for new answers. Preserving his sculptures no longer mattered. If he could preserve the original beauty that he saw, he would never make another sculpture again. He studied darker arts, scarier arts. And when he was sure he had it, he came to the most beautiful girl in his father's court—Jade."

Carefully keeping her balance, Jenny turned her head to gaze at the audience mysteriously.

"He gave her his potion, and cast his spell on her, and made sure that her beauty could never fade," Calvin said, his voice getting lower and quieter and more urgent. The audience hung on every word. "She would never grow old; she would never know disease. And no sword or spear could ever..."

He looked at his assistant, then back at the audience. "*Ever*," he emphasized, "mar her beauty."

With a giant upswing, the knife glittered in the stage lights before Calvin thrust it downward, dead center in Jenny's bare belly, between the bustier and the tutu.

Gasps erupted; even a few screams pierced the darkness. Jenny closed her eyes and doubled over dramatically as Calvin backed away, his hands up and commanding silence.

Jenny knew to count to three, like Calvin had instructed, but it felt like forever before she finally uncurled and arched her back again. The audience had a clear profile view of the long knife—it was driven through the apple core and into her stomach, pinning the fruit to her skin. She pivoted on her hips to face downstage. She opened her eyes and offered a mystical little smile.

"Ladies and gentlemen," Calvin boomed, "Jade—the Jewel of the East!"

Wild applause thundered through the theatre. The crowd of struggling artists and Chelsea debutantes realized they were getting a *lot* more than expected at this evening's performance.

Calvin took Jenny's hand and helped her off the table, where she gracefully curtseyed, the knife still driven into her belly. The magician kissed her hand politely, and spun her away across the stage where she struck a pose, the knife sticking out.

"I'd like a volunteer from the audience," announced the Amazing Quirk. "Jade, if you could?"

Jenny nodded—with an exciting thrill running through her, she yanked the knife out, holding the apple with her other hand to ease it off the blade.

"If the apple's in your hands, you're my volunteer," Calvin told the audience. Jenny tossed the apple into the darkness, and happy shouts rang out until one voice claimed victory. "Come right up," said Calvin. "Just hop up on stage." He leaned down to offer a hand over the edge.

A young woman with a bulky sweatshirt, curly hair, and stylish glasses took his hand and clambered onto the stage. She dropped the apple as she got to her feet, to the amusement of the crowd. Calvin played the role of power and waited patiently as the girl sheepishly retrieved the apple. Jenny gave her a little wink—the girl looked about Calvin's age, with the façade of confidence that was a girl's only means of survival in the New York art crowd. She exuded a cultivated air of self-deprecation which was a familiar counterattack against deprecation from others, like a Kamikaze blowing himself up to demonstrate his piloting skills. Jenny felt a connection, or at least some common ground.

She danced back to the magic table as Calvin started right in—this next spiel had to move quickly before the blood on Jenny's belly dried up.

"What's your name, young lady?" Calvin asked the girl who was probably at least his age.

"Sarah," she declared proudly; despite her attempt at projection, her voice sounded tiny in the wake of Calvin's booming magician character.

"Thanks for coming up, Sarah," Calvin said. "You're welcome to eat the apple, if you like." Sarah's pretend revulsion and plenty of audience chuckles kept the patter going; the crowd was into him now. Calvin and Jenny had won them with the first trick.

Calvin made small talk as Jenny pulled a deck of slightly oversized cards from the table. She handed them to the magician as he said, "Sarah, do you want to see the most personalized card trick you've ever seen?"

She nodded. "Sure," she said cheerfully, putting on a show for the audience.

"We have lots of ways to identify ourselves," Calvin began, spinning another yarn for the crowd. "Almost everyone here has a driver's license, or some other way to get past the bouncers here in Chelsea." He graciously paused for the whoops and hollers, which came as expected. "We have the names our parents gave us, or the names we choose for ourselves. We can sign our signatures, whether they have any resemblance to our names or not!" Some more laughs. "But there's one form of identification that stays with us from the day we're born, to the day we die." He stuck up one long thumb. "Our fingerprints!"

Ambiguous sounds of appreciation and inquiry washed over the stage as Calvin reeled them in. Jenny started walking off into the wings.

"I'd like you to take this deck of cards, Sarah," Calvin said, handing it over. "Shuffle through them, cut the deck, do whatever you like to mix them up. Then I'd like you to pick one card—any card—out of the deck." Calvin abandoned the girl and headed to the magic table. "Show it to the audience—don't let me see it!" he told her, rummaging inside the table. "But when you've picked that card...hmm...wait a second..."

Jenny had almost walked off stage.

"Jade!" Calvin called. "There's no ink!" He turned to the audience. "We can't get Sarah's fingerprints without ink, right?"

The audience cheered in agreement as Jenny turned back inquisitively, feigning ignorance.

"We need ink, Jade," said Calvin. He froze, musing. "Did we forget the ink?"

Jenny approached Sarah and struck a pose—her belly, bare between her black bustier and red tutu, was smeared with blood.

The audience went nuts—they loved the idea. "Perfect," said the Amazing Quirk. "Sarah, once you've picked your card, just press your thumb on Jade's stomach—get it nice and red—and press your singular, unmistakable, uncopyable thumbprint right on the card you chose."

Calvin walked downstage and kept up some patter while Sarah ruffled through the deck, shuffling inexpertly. She picked her card; Jenny smiled and presented her belly. The girl faltered, but like anyone in the audience, she assumed the blood was fake anyway—the complete disappearance of the knife wound confirmed her incorrect suspicions. The audience egged her on with cheers and hoots. Sarah gamely pressed her thumb against Jenny's skin, swirled it around in the blood, and pressed her thumbprint firmly on the Six of Diamonds.

"Shake it," Jenny told her, demonstrating as if shaking out an old Polaroid to develop the photo quicker. The girl did, and then returned her card to the deck.

"Go ahead and shuffle, cut—mix it up," Calvin called from across the stage.

Once the deck was thoroughly mixed, Calvin returned and Jenny walked quietly off stage. This part of the show was all his. After some clever bits of trickery and misdirection, he was going to pull the Six of Diamonds from the deck...with no thumbprint on it. Then he would reveal a card—not at all the Six of Diamonds—with Sarah's bloody thumbprint on it, and on cue, the crowd would go crazy.

While the card trick continued, however, Jenny had work to do. She rushed to her bag and pulled out the specs and the magic window, along with sheets of paper and a Sharpie marker. She sat down just off stage— Sarah was facing the other way, toward Calvin—and put on the spectacles.

One by one, Jenny went through the second row of audience members, peering through the magic window and writing down their birthdays, which she read in the glowing letters hovering around them. A slight twinge hit her when she glanced at a pretty, slightly overweight blonde girl, but she kept going. She finished marking dates in large block letters and arranged the sheets in the order that the individuals were sitting in the second row. She clipped the sheets to a clipboard and put enough blank sheets in front of them that the Sharpie didn't show through, then folded the corner of the second page just slightly. By this time, the audience was happily applauding Calvin's card trick and Sarah was returning to her seat with a souvenir: the Jack of Spades with her own bloody thumbprint on it.

Jenny sauntered back on stage with the clipboard and the Sharpie as Calvin started the next bit.

"Now, Sarah's had her thumbprint since the day she was born," he mused, "just like any of you. Anything that's been with you since birth is something you outright own—we can't take that away from you, right?" He smiled. "But maybe...just maybe...I can get those birthdays themselves!" He twirled another flourish and called: "Jade!"

Jenny handed over the clipboard and Sharpie and struck a pose.

Calvin barely glanced at the folded corner of the second page before showing the clipboard's blank white pages to the audience. "The clipboard?" He shrugged. "It's just a clipboard. There's no magic there. But the trick you're about to see...that's magic!" With his other hand, he swept through the air and conjured a deck of cards. The audience applauded. "Can I have another volunteer?" he asked. "Anyone will do, just come right up."

A handful of folks perked up, but one reached the stage first, a skinny hawk-nosed guy who had played a few songs on a ukulele earlier in the show.

"You're Igor, right?" Calvin said, remembering the guy's name. He got a warm smile in return. "Igor, if you'd be so kind to help us out—pick a card, any card!"

The audience giggled at the cliché, and Igor the ukulele player obediently yanked a card from the deck.

"What card is it?" Calvin asked loudly.

Igor displayed the card and announced, "Two of hearts!"

"Igor picked it—would the *second* row, center section, please come on up?" The magician flashed a smile at Igor. "Thanks for helping us out!" He gestured, and Igor hopped off the stage as the second row of the audience shuffled up. Some of the overeager and more agile ones jumped up out of order, but Calvin had a contingency plan. "Everybody on stage, please," he requested, "face your own seat!" This would put them in reverse order, but he could accommodate that.

Calvin again displayed the blank paper on the clipboard, then paraded in front of the people lined up on stage, handing a sheet of paper to each of them. Trailing behind him, Jenny handed each of the fifteen audience members a colored marker.

"I'm sure you all know your birthdays," Calvin quipped. "If you could, please go ahead and write them down—month, day, and year—on the pieces of paper you've been given." Calvin distinctly and blatantly strode downstage, looking away from the participants as they scribbled their birthdays down. "No use lying about the year," he admonished them over his shoulder. "At least *one* of us is going to get it right anyway!"

The audience laughed as the participants finished writing.

"Now go ahead and crumple up those pieces of paper," said Calvin. "That's right, crumple them up—uh, no!" In a flash, he caught in mid-air a crumpled ball of paper that one guy had chucked. "Don't *throw* them, just crumple them up," he clarified, tossing the paper back to its owner. The guy grinned as the audience jeered him. "And hold onto them," Calvin said, shooting a pretend-angry look at the guy who'd thrown his. "That way, we've got proof." He winked at the audience.

Keeping up the jokes and dramatic tension, Calvin walked behind the participants, from one to the next. Behind each, he'd make a few quips, pretend to "psychically" concentrate on the back of the audience member's head—he stood at least five inches taller than any of them—and scribble across the paper on his clipboard. Then he'd yank a sheet off the clipboard, fold it over and hand it to the participant in front of him. Standing off to the side, even though she knew how the trick was done, Jenny was amazed that she couldn't see Calvin's clever hands pulling sheets of paper out from under the sheet he was scribbling on. It looked like he was always taking the top one—the one he was writing on—even though she knew better.

When he was done, he pulled off one more sheet—the *actual* top sheet, which was covered with his random scribblings—and crumpled it up, improvising: "See, if you do this," he chucked the ball of paper off stage and gave the wiseguy a reproachful look, "we'd never be able to match them up. These papers," he displayed the empty now-top sheet of the clipboard for everybody, "are going to match the ones you've got. That's the whole trick!"

The audience liked him; they expected the trick to work, but were still looking forward to seeing it. One by one, each participant unfolded the paper Calvin had given them, uncrumpled their own ball of paper, and showed them to the audience. The dates matched all fifteen times. More applause rang out as the participants left the stage to return to their seats.

Her gaze lingering on the round blonde girl, Jenny almost missed her cue. A verbal nudge from Calvin got her back on track, and they started in on the hat trick.

It was old hat for Jenny, regardless of the pun. They'd worked on it during rehearsal, and it went off even better than it had during the audition, since Jenny knew her role this time around. By the time Calvin's recipe of "eleven mice and a dash of magic" (they had less mice with them this time) had produced wriggling, sniffling Colby the rabbit, the audience was thoroughly convinced that Calvin was a hell of a magician.

That left one last trick, and Jenny cleared away the hat, bag, and bunny as Calvin set the scene for his audience. At this point, they were lapping up every overdramatic flourish and silly-sounding phrase Calvin Quirk could throw at them.

"You've all met Jade," said the magician, "and you know about her mysterious and ancient history. But things weren't always so easy for her. Remember that, while Jade's beauty lasts forever," he shrugged wistfully, "the rest of us are still mortal. Like her prince was."

Jenny took the rings from the table and marched forward with a very serious expression on her face.

"Her prince died not long after he cast the spell that made her beauty eternal," Calvin went on. "It was a dark and dangerous time, back then, especially for a woman—even one as unusual as Jade. The prince's brothers fought over her, and eventually, one of them won. He was an evil prince, though." Calvin walked behind Jenny and placed a comforting hand on her shoulder. "Not at all like his brother. The evil prince didn't care about capturing beauty...he just wanted to own beautiful things. Beautiful things...like Jade."

Jenny gazed downward and extended a hand, releasing all the rings except for the small one. The chain of rings jingled and swung ominously in front of her.

"These rings," said Calvin in a low, secret voice, "were created by the evil prince's blacksmiths. Magical rings, created by magical blacksmiths, for a very special purpose."

Calvin plucked the small ring from Jenny's fingers. He began connecting and disconnecting the rings in a fast and intricate pattern as he spoke. "For while Jenny's beauty—" He faltered, two rings catching for longer than he intended. "While Jade's beauty never fades," he quickly corrected, "Jade herself can slip right through your fingers if you're not careful. Like that evil prince, I know that Jade isn't mine to own. But unlike that evil prince," he reconnected the full chain of rings in order, and held the small one high over his head, "I know that any *attempt* to own her is doomed to fail."

With a quick series of taps, Calvin let go, leaving the rings suspended in mid-air, swaying. The audience clapped prematurely, but Jenny couldn't blame them.

Calvin focused on the audience as he went back to get the table and rolled it forward beneath the rings. "The evil prince tried to imprison Jade in his castle, high above the castle walls. As a trophy," he suggested darkly, "or a prize." He extended a hand to Jenny and steadied the table as she climbed to stand on it. "He thought that keeping her there would be a sign to everyone: I've got the most beautiful thing in the world, and it will never escape. And when Jade's arm was shackled..."

Jenny stuck her arm through the largest ring, trying her best not to wince in anticipation.

"...it truly seemed like she never would," Calvin finished. He tapped the bottom ring before pulling away quickly.

The ring began to contract and Jenny couldn't help but grimace. They'd rehearsed this one five times in Calvin's apartment, and done it for David Dennis at the callback, but even though she knew it didn't hurt much, and she'd be fine when it was over, that didn't make it any less scary.

Fortunately, the audience's attention was on her arm, not her face. The ring tightened around her wrist and squeezed with an audible *crunch*. The audience was stunned; heavy breathing and squeaks of amazement were all that reached the stage.

"The chains were magically locked high above the evil prince's castle," Calvin declared, reaching down for the magic table. "And there she hung for years...or centuries!" He yanked the table out from under his assistant, and she dropped a short way before jerking to a halt with an ugly *crack*, suspended by the chain of rings clamped tight to her wrist. Jenny let out a strangled yelp. Her feet dangled several feet above the stage.

The audience roared in an outrageous combination of amazement and sympathy for the girl in the story, the girl dangling by an obviously broken wrist right before their eyes.

Calvin was visibly upset. The trick had been his idea, but he wanted to call it off after they'd rehearsed it the first time. Jenny insisted that it wasn't going to be a problem—she insisted they keep the trick the way it was. She repeatedly claimed she was starting to not even *feel* pain anymore, let alone be permanently damaged by it. Even so, Calvin rushed through the rest of his lines to get to the climax.

"What the evil prince didn't know," he said, "was that the mystics, the very same mystics who taught the good prince how to cast his spell, had their own reasons for teaching the prince their magic. And that they wanted this eternal beauty for a very important reason." He glanced at Jenny and decided to cut several lines on the spot. "A reason that remains a mystery to this day!" he proclaimed. "And they sent the youngest and most talented of the mystics to go and rescue Jade, and bring her back to their castle, where she would be safe." He pulled a huge knife from the table and took only a moment to let the light glint off it dramatically. "The youngest mystic knew what to do—Jade's beauty is eternal, after all," Calvin shook himself and put some speed on, "and-any-damage-is-only-temporary-so-he-did-what-he-had-to-do-and-with-one-swing-of-his-sword-he-*released* the girl!"

As he spoke, he slashed downward with the knife, slicing right through Jenny's wrist. Her hand fell to the floor; her arm slid out of the ring and Jenny dropped mere inches before Calvin was under her, catching her gently.

The audience shrieked, cheered, clapped, even cried out. Calvin was breathing heavily, looking down at the girl in his arms.

Jenny looked weakly up at Calvin...and winked. His relief was palpable—she was putting on an act. He almost laughed, but caught himself and continued.

"Here, Jade," he lowered her to her feet, "let me give you a hand."

The audience loved it. Calvin reached down and picked up Jenny's hand, still freaked out every time he picked up her disembodied parts, and returned it to her. She turned upstage and held her severed hand to her wrist as the audience kept cheering and applauding. Calvin smiled broadly, glancing back to check on her progress. When her hand had nearly stitched itself up completely, he pulled away, shouting over the noise in the theatre: "Ladies and gentlemen—Jade, the Jewel of the East!"

Jenny whirled around to show off her reattached hand and beam at the audience. "And the Amazing Quirk!" she shouted, presenting the magician. She wiggled her reclaimed fingers and winked at the crowd. The volume in the room increased. David Dennis had a giant grin on his round, tanned face as he stood in the thunderous throng and clapped with the rest. He nodded proudly at the magician and his lovely assistant. No doubt about it: they were a hit.

CHAPTER TEN

The Popular and Incredibly Witty Host of A Very Well-Liked Late Night Television Talk Show tapped his pencil on his desk as the band played him in and the audience cheered. He caught sight of himself on the monitors as the camera crane flew overhead and honed in on his face, and he playfully tossed his hair back as if he cared about appearances. Of course, he *did* care, but he had to keep up the pretense that he didn't, so that the pretense that he did would seem like actual pretense, rather than narcissism. The television comedy world is a sticky tightrope to walk.

"We're back!" he exclaimed to a studio audience of many and a home viewing audience of millions. The millions wouldn't see any of this for another seven hours, which technically meant this entire message—forty-four minutes of glib repartee, obsequious affirmations of his celebrity guests, and humorous commentary on current events—was his legacy to the future. Not the far-flung future of jetpacks and robot maids, but at the very least, the future of tonight's midnight snacks, college stoners, and couples having sex with the TV on. He often mused that it was better than not leaving a legacy at all, like the "brooding" member of any given boy band.

"Hey, Sycophantic Sidekick," said the Incredibly Witty Host to his Sycophantic Sidekick, "do you like magic?"

"I'm a *huge* fan of magic," said the Sycophantic Sidekick.

"That's great, because there's—"

"Love it," said the Sidekick, who kept up his end of the conversation whether people were paying attention or not. He had only one real responsibility on the show—to agree with, repeat, or confirm everything the Host said—and he damned well did it at every opportunity, on the off chance that some Hollywood producer looking for a pudgy forty-three-year-old comedian was going to be having a midnight snack or sex with his wife in seven hours.

"That's great," said the Host, "yeah." He mugged at the camera, emphasizing his Sidekick's oblivious interruption, because he knew he was being considered to host the Big Entertainment Awards Ceremony later this year, and the Big Entertainment Awards people were big on midnight snacks and sex with the TV on. He suspected most of them were stoners, too, but he was careful not to push that, since even late night television has prim and proper sponsors and the FCC breathing down its neck.

"Who *doesn't* like magic?" the Host continued.

"Not me," said the Sidekick. "Love it!"

"Right, I've heard," said the Host. He glanced at the audience: "It's like having him on instant replay any time I want."

Laughter. Light applause.

"Oddly Quiet Bandleader, *you* like magic?" the Incredibly Witty Host asked his Oddly Quiet Bandleader.

The Oddly Quiet Bandleader nodded.

"Enthusiastically, I see," concluded the Host.

The band's drummer hit a rimshot for him. Laughter. The Oddly Quiet Bandleader was lightly stoned and focusing more on his upcoming tour schedule with a Major Rock Star friend than the ongoing antics of the Late Night Television Talk Show.

"So, yeah," said the Host, "I don't know about you guys, but I *love* magic."

"Me too," burbled the Sidekick.

"...And I think you're all going to *love* my next guests, one of the most talented magic acts to come along since...uh..."

"The Three Stooges," the Sidekick supplied.

The Host did another take. "*Not* a magic act," he pointed out to effusive laughter, "but sure. Sure! Please, everybody, put your hands together for the most talented magic act since the Three Stooges...the Amazing Quirk, and his lovely assistant!"

Applause signs went wild, and the crowd clapped obediently, hooting and hollering in support of whoever was getting the endorsement of a Late Night Television Talk Show.

Glittery blue curtains parted, and Calvin Quirk strode across the shiny stage floor, followed by a lovely but very bewildered assistant. "Um," said Jenny Ng, looking around at the lights, the crowd, the band, the distracted smiles of the Host and his Sidekick. "Are we...?"

"Ladies and gentlemen!" Calvin proclaimed. "I am the Amazing Quirk, and this is my lovely assistant—Jenny!"

Jenny looked at him sharply. "Jade," she quietly corrected.

He didn't seem to hear her. "Are you ready for some magic?" he shouted to the crowd. They answered with a resounding cheer.

"Calvin!" Jenny hissed quietly.

He turned to her with a plastic smile and a very large sword. It was, in fact, the sword that Rex had brought to her, the strange magical sword that could hurt her. "As you'll see," Calvin joked to the audience, "my assistant comes with some assembly required."

Laughter. Mild applause.

"Calvin!" Jenny's eyes went wide. Alarm bells were ringing in her brain.

With a swipe of the sword, the Amazing Quirk decapitated his lovely assistant. Jenny's head went tumbling across the studio, rolling to a stop at the feet of the Sycophantic Sidekick. He picked it up and placed it on the Host's desk.

"So, I hear you can read the future," said the Incredibly Witty Host. "Can you tell us the Nielsen ratings for tonight's episode?"

Wild laughter. One lady laughed so hard she pounded the seat in front of her. The man sitting there disintegrated into a pile of grayish dust.

"I don't...wait," said Jenny. Nothing seemed right. The audience members all looked blurry.

"She needs her glasses," said the Amazing Quirk. He wrapped the stems around her ears and the world snapped into focus. "Just look through the window, Jenny!"

The Sidekick rolled a framed giant-sized version of the magic window across the floor, placing it between Jenny and the audience. Through the window, glowing letters floated this way and that across people, chairs, and walls, like a PowerPoint presentation by Cheech and Chong. Jenny's eyes swam.

Laughter.

The people in the audience were animated corpses in varying states of decomposition. Each had a stamp across the forehead, like an expiration date on a milk carton, but glowing and implicitly more sinister. One corpse was a cute but pudgy blonde girl in her early twenties. She shook her wristwatch and listened to it, as if trying to get it started again. "I think I have an appointment," she said. Jenny could hear her clearly through the raucous laughing and cheering.

"If you're not using your body anymore..." said Lyle, the kid who'd run her over with his car.

"...can we have it?" finished his skinny friend, Lloyd.

"You see, Jenny?" said Vincent Raymond, sitting beside the Sycophantic Sidekick.

"They're all the same!" said Carrie Raymond, sitting on the Host's lap. She smiled a Stepford smile so contagious it spread to the entire audience.

"Calvin!" cried Jenny.

As the members of the audience smiled, the smiles turned fake and plastic like Calvin Quirk's, then spread to the rest of their faces. Their bodies hardened and began to melt like Barbie dolls in an E-Z Bake Oven.

"Stop!" yelled Jenny.

Laughter and cheering. The audience continued to melt. A horse whinnied somewhere.

The Coney Island Count Dracula burst through the door at the back of the audience and raced down to the stage. Calvin handed him the sword. The Count offered a sheepish look to the cameras. "I'm sorry," he said in his unplaceable accent. "Am I late?"

Laughter. The Count's faced melted and flowed and turned into a skull grinning from the monitors.

Jenny Ng screamed.

She woke up on her futon, tangled in sheets and sweat. "*Diu*," she said softly. She'd had weirder dreams, but not many. And, if she were honest, most of the weirder ones she'd had were in the last couple of months.

The sword glistened in the corner of the room, hit by moonlight through the window as if the Gods of Dramatic Lighting had taken a special interest in it. In the two months since she'd got the sword and the powers she suspected were inextricably linked to it, Jenny had caught up on the rent and bought a used futon mattress (off a friend of Keith Heckler's, so she suspected Heckler had a history with the futon itself). The magic act was going well; David Dennis knew the goods when he saw it, and he paid Calvin and Jenny a fairly decent sum to keep performing at the *Beau Regardez* every Wednesday and Saturday. Even David's uptight assistant Kevin seemed to grudgingly respect them, and reserved a private room for them to prepare in before each show. Jenny also got a part-time job translating legal papers into various languages, trading her new power for a decent paycheck. Between magic show money and hourly wages from her translating job, she felt like she was almost back on her feet again—not too comfortable, and certainly not living in the lap of luxury, but actually not *struggling* for the first time in years.

Her social life picked up again too, to an extent. She and Calvin saw each other every show night—they also got together at least twice a week to work on the act, and ended up having dinner more days than not. It was still strictly professional—or at least strictly platonic—but they'd grown very close over the stifling New York summer. They also went to a few after show parties, socializing with the freaks and queers and artistic nutjobs who frequented the *Beau Regardez* both on and off stage. They had a small fan following in the underground theatre community, and David Dennis even had posters printed to advertise the magical duo and their headline show at the *Beau.*

The mysteries of June had morphed into the nagging concerns of August. Jenny still didn't understand how or why she got her powers, where the sword came from, or how Rex or the Count tied into all of this. Still, life had become a routine of chopping off body parts, reattaching them, smiling prettily, prancing across the stage, translating legal documents, and reading people's birthdays.

It was unavoidable that she also saw their death days.

Jenny got up and went to the mini-fridge she'd found in the street. Heckler had graciously carried it home for her (and graciously accepted a blunt refusal when he asked her to sleep with him in return), and Calvin— his magical hands just as good with machines as they were with cards and coins—took an afternoon to fix it up enough that it kept things colder than lukewarm. It hummed a bit louder than she might like, but she could live with that; a cold Diet Coke in the middle of the night was a luxury she hadn't been able to afford in a long time.

She sat back against the wall, took a long pull on the soda, and stared thoughtfully at the sword. She flashed back to the blonde girl in her dream; the girl from the audience at their first magic show. The girl who was probably dead already, if the date Jenny had seen through the window during the show was correct. She had no reason to assume it wasn't.

Plenty of audience members since then had imminent death dates; the sight of one scrawled across a smiling face in glowing letters never failed to tug at Jenny's heart, giving her a little *ping* in her stomach as she thought of them—happy people out for two hours of entertainment on a beautiful summer night—dying just weeks or months later. Some were old, some were young. She wasn't sure what they were going to die of—the letters never said (at least, the ones she could read). All she knew was that they would be dead and, curiously, the exact location where they would draw their last breath, think their last thought, and pump their last two ventricles' worth of blood.

Jenny tried to be philosophical about it. Everybody dies; she knew that. Still, most people got through life without thinking about it—or *by* not thinking about it. With no end to her own indestructible life in view, but a clear view of everyone else's end, death was preying on Jenny's mind night and day. It had become a sort of hobby of hers, the way some people are drawn to stamp collecting or Civil War reenactment. With no Internet access, and little time to get to the library, she didn't have much of an outlet for her new interest, no opportunity to read up on causes of death or near-death experiences or actuarial tables; but she thought about the subject constantly.

Despite visions of the Grim Reaper dancing in her head nightly—like sugar plums but decidedly more grisly—Jenny kept a generally positive outlook. She had reliable income, a close friend, and a modicum of local fame, along with some secret superpowers that actually found practical use in her daily life. She and Calvin tweaked the magic act as they went; each week they tried new tricks, got rid of old ones, or changed things around to see how they would work. The one thing they hadn't tried yet—though they'd toyed with the idea enough to make David Dennis salivate at the potential box office numbers—was actually sawing Jenny in half. Lopping off a limb was one thing; Jenny still felt like Jenny, just with a limb over *there* instead of over *here*. The idea of getting chopped in half or—more nightmarishly—having her head separated from her body made Jenny break out in a cold sweat. They were relatively sure the classic magician's trick would work with her power, but if not, the consequences would be pretty disastrous—especially if, despite being halved, Jenny continued to live. Or whatever it was did now; living usually included the inevitability of dying on its long-term To Do list.

No mysteries had been solved, and none had gone away. Life just chugged onward, as was its tendency, with no regard for aspiring Nancy Drews who needed their clues tied up neatly in a penultimate chapter preceding a touching scene of paternal appreciation. Jenny stood and picked up the sword, sipping Diet Coke as she leaned on her window sill and let the moonlight play off the curved blade. Stars filled the clear sky like a connect-the-dots puzzle with no specified order.

She sighed. It would be nice if she could connect a few dots here or there. She fleetingly wondered whatever became of the Count or Rex. The spooky guy was probably in an institution somewhere. The spooky horse was probably shipped off to a farm, she thought, just like all the dogs of all the kids who ever cried themselves to sleep years later when they saw through their parents' little white lies.

She shook herself from idle thoughts and placed the half-empty soda can on the window sill, wishing she saw it as half-full. Dropping the sword in the corner with a heavy *klunk* that was sure to bug the Ecuadorians downstairs, she flopped down on her futon to drift off into more strange dreams of unintelligible symbolism and ambiguous portent.

CHAPTER ELEVEN

Jenny skipped lightly upstairs from the Eighth Avenue station and hit the early evening sunlight with a smile and a sigh. Days like this almost made her forget the craziness—her powers and Calvin's mysterious magic props, puzzles still left unsolved, everything just faded away in the warm pink glow of a summer sunset. She felt almost normal again.

Normality was knocked off its pedestal as she glanced at the large window of the bank by the subway entrance, where Mirror Jenny gawked at the tall buildings of Manhattan like a tourist on a double-decker bus. Mirror Jenny caught Jenny looking, and quickly shifted her pose to match Jenny's. An apologetic smile and shrug ruined the effect.

Jenny scowled at her mirror image in the glass. Mirror Jenny's frequently unsynchronized behavior had become just another fact of life since the start of the summer, but it was never a welcome one, since it pulled Jenny out of the ordinary and threw the inexplicability of her bizarre circumstances in her face. To exacerbate matters, the strange effect couldn't even be put to good use in the magic act—Mirror Jenny just did whatever Mirror Jenny felt like, so there was no guarantee she would coordinate with Calvin and Jenny to participate in the act. The effect was therefore not only as disconcerting as a three-legged cat, it was definitely more useless.

She'd talked to Calvin about Mirror Jenny, though he'd never caught her moving independently of Jenny—which made Jenny wonder if the effect was visible to anyone besides her. Calvin didn't doubt her claim for a second, though, and had suggested trying to start up a conversation, but all of Jenny's attempts had been fruitless. Either Mirror Jenny would frustratingly mimic Jenny's every move, pretending to be nothing more than a run-of-the-mill, ordinary mirror image, or she looked bored and casually glanced around the room to avoid Jenny's eyes or, in fact, any discussion whatsoever. Jenny was experiencing, first hand, what it must have been like for her mother when Jenny decided to give her a week or two of the Silent Treatment. Her mother had it easier—teenaged Jenny always broke down within thirty-six hours, while there was no end in sight when it came to Mirror Jenny's wordless obstinance.

Jenny rolled her eyes at her mirror image. Mirror Jenny rolled her eyes, too—but a moment later, and the wrong way. Jenny shook her head and walked away, turning up Eighth at the corner.

She was a little early for the show, but she felt like getting away from her apartment. If Calvin showed up early, too—he usually did—they could work on some tricks before the show. Calvin had been teaching her sleight of hand, with the eventual goal of being able to add her talents to his in the act. Jenny wasn't a natural like he was, but she was catching on to the easier stuff, and Calvin was optimistic.

She slowed as she approached the *Beau Regardez*. In the midst of pedestrians strolling up or down the avenue, a short man with a round belly and a large bald spot was standing right in front of the big poster of the Amazing Quirk and his lovely assistant, Jade.

It gave Jenny a giddy thrill when people she didn't know looked at the poster. She still wasn't interested in a long term career in show business, but she had to admit that her big fish in a small pond celebrity was kind of exciting.

She stopped in front of the poster to look. The photo was liberally Photoshopped—Jenny knew her skin didn't look that good in real life, no way, no how—but it looked like a spectacular show. Calvin, the Amazing Quirk, stood dynamically in the center, displaying his hat to the camera; the blackness of outer space oozed like cold fog from the dark depths inside it. Jade, the Jewel of the East, hung overhead, her wrist suspended by the chain of rings, a very *Charlie's Angels* pout on her seductive face. In the foreground was an extreme closeup of the magic window, which had become an actual feature of the act—the mystical Jade even wore the spectacles, which Calvin and Jenny had added as a permanent accoutrement. They wanted to avoid revealing the connection between the specs and the window, so that no curious fans got it into their heads to try them out. The window by itself seemed like an ordinary square of thick glass; if Jade only wore the specs when she peered through the window, it would be a strong clue to the link between the props. The chance of someone else seeing the glowing letters was a risk they didn't want to take, so Jenny wore the specs whenever she played Jade, with or without the magic window, to hide the connection.

The whole poster was splattered with graphic explosions and mystical smoke, and a bold logo streaked across the top, *The Amazing QUIRK*—below that, in *faux* Oriental type, was the more demure and mysterious *...and his Lovely Assistant...JADE the JEWEL of the EAST.* Attention-grabbing captions called out *The Chains of PERIL!*, *The BOTTOMLESS Hat!* and *The Window to Your SOUL!* with appropriately gaudy graphics and fonts.

Jenny grinned as the man took a step closer and reached toward the poster, one finger tracing down the paper from the top, coming to rest on the magic window, tapping an idle rhythm. "It's a good show," she told him.

The man was slightly startled. He looked at Jenny, looked back at the poster, did a subtle double-take, and stared at Jenny again.

"Starts tonight at eight," said Jenny.

The guy was probably about fifty; his hair was mostly mouse gray. He wore a lemon yellow short-sleeved Oxford and business casual brown pants—his scuffed and worn Converse sneakers didn't quite match. Neither did his mute and honestly pretty creepy expression.

"So, um," said Jenny. The man's lack of response was unnerving.

"Eight o'clock?" the man asked. His voice was hoarse and he had a thick Brooklyn accent.

"Yeah," Jenny nodded. "Admission's twenty bucks. I think there's an Internet discount, if you go to—"

"We'll be back," said the round little man. He turned and walked away up Eighth Avenue, disappearing into the early evening crowd.

Jenny was a seasoned New Yorker, but that guy was definitely a few ice cream cones short of a truck that was really a front for a serial killing pedophile. She made a face and took one last look at the poster before heading inside.

Calvin was there, of course—if they didn't rehearse at his place and have dinner three or four nights a week, she might almost believe he *slept* here at the theatre. He gave her a big hug as she walked into their dressing room. "Agents!" he shouted.

"What?" Jenny asked. "Let me put my stuff down."

"Agents!" Calvin repeated, as Jenny put down her bag and the long instrument case she carried her sword in. The case was ostensibly for some sort of long woodwind or something—she was a little fuzzy on the terminology the second-hand store guy was using—but the sword fit into it quite nicely, allowing her to carry it around with her. She didn't anticipate any confrontations with dragons or other mystical beasts, but she'd decided that, just in case someone broke into her apartment, she would keep the sword with her instead of in the closet. Potential burglars were welcome to her clothes and makeup and even the mini-fridge full of Diet Cokes; the sword was distinctly irreplaceable, and she would probably have trouble finding an insurance company that would cover it, no questions asked.

Calvin went on. "Tonight! Here! The show!"

"Agents?" asked Jenny.

"Kevin told me." Calvin tried to settle down, but his energy was up, and his long loose limbs were all over the place. "Two different agents! They heard about the show, about us, I mean, and they called to ask if there's an industry discount!"

"Is there?"

Calvin shrugged. "I dunno," he said. "Who cares? They want to see us!"

"Wow," said Jenny. She collapsed in a chair. "Cool."

"Uh," said Calvin. He stopped fidgeting and looked at her. "It doesn't *sound* cool. You okay?"

Jenny smiled. "It *is* cool, Calvin," she assured him. "I mean, yeah— agents? I'm just a little out of it. And...you know..."

"Still not really into the show business thing. Right," said Calvin glumly.

"Hey, it's not you!" Jenny said. "You know I love doing the show with you. And it's a great way to pay the bills. It's just not really my thing. We both know I won't do it forever. But whatever, right? You can always find another assistant..."

"Jenny, the show *is* you!" Calvin insisted.

"Come on—"

"Without you, I'm just a good closeup magician," he said. He pulled a coin out of the air. "Coins, cards, little tricks."

"Magic hats that lead to nowhere, chains that float in the air!" Jenny looked at him pointedly.

"Sure, there's those," said Calvin. "But the show isn't *about* those anymore."

"Calvin, you got the callback without using *any* of my—powers," Jenny said. She still tripped over the word *powers* a little every time the subject came up. "You're also an incredible showman. You *made* the show. I'm just a prop."

Calvin flinched, a twinge of guilt on his face.

"Which is *fine*," she said gently. "This was never my dream, Calvin. I like being your lovely assistant—I don't need to be the star. But I also don't want to do it forever."

"I know," Calvin said. He frowned, but he clearly understood. "Well, yeah, that's something else."

"What?"

"I was going to save this for after the show," he said, taking two easy steps across the entire room and rummaging through his backpack, "but now that you bring it up...I know the act isn't your dream, Jenny. And I totally want you to be able to do what *you* want to do. Here."

He held out a package wrapped in Christmas-themed wrapping paper, snowflakes and reindeer and bright green pine trees. Jenny took it and raised her eyebrows with a big, inquisitive smile.

"It was the only wrapping paper I had around," he admitted with a schoolboy grin.

Jenny ripped through the paper to reveal a shiny cardboard box; the pictures and words on the outside of the box made it pretty clear what was inside. "Holy shit!" she said. "Twelve megapixels...SLR..."

"It's not top of the line, and it's used, but I got a good deal on it," said Calvin. "I got you a spare memory card for it, too."

"Calvin!" Jenny squealed gleefully. She leaped up and wrapped her arms around his neck, her legs swinging well above the floor. He hugged her back. "It's only the *best* camera I've *ever* owned in my *life!*"

He pulled his head back to make eye contact. "Well, then," he said, "I'm glad you like it."

Jenny *squee*'d soundlessly, pumping her legs around in excitement until Calvin let her drop to the floor. She picked up the box to read the camera specifications.

"So, I mean," Calvin puttered a bit, "you've got a camera, and you can get back to taking pictures. Do *your* thing, I mean."

Jenny smiled up at him. "I'm not leaving the act, Calvin," she said. "Maybe I *don't* want to be in show business—but *you* do, and if I can help you make it big, I'm not going anywhere."

"You're staying?"

"How many guys do you think I'll meet who won't mind chopping off my hands and feet twice a week?" she said, throwing mock desperation at him. "If I don't get my daily dismembering, I get cranky—you know that."

"Cool!" Calvin jumped in the air to celebrate. "Agents!" he exclaimed.

"Agents!" Jenny cheered.

"Man, we get an agent, we can start booking some really cool stuff," said Calvin, resuming his energetic pacing. "Maybe play some bigger theatres, get a whole show of just us! Oh, man, we could do the late night talk shows!"

A cloud passed over Jenny's face.

"Or not," Calvin quickly added.

Jenny shook it off. "Just a bad dream last night. Don't worry about it. Hey—agents!"

"Agents!" Calvin beamed.

"Let's put the order together for tonight," said Jenny. "Something that'll really impress them."

Calvin nodded, and they started discussing tricks and stories. They had a collection of standard tales that introduced certain tricks, and a number of segues to slide seamlessly from one trick to the next. Calvin was good at going with the flow when he had to tie one trick's story into the next—he successfully relied on a vaguely recalled encyclopedic knowledge of fantasy and fairy tales derived from a youth of watching anime, playing *Dungeons & Dragons* and reading sword-and-sorcery novels with his friend Griffin. Amazingly, with the exception of some early concepts they'd thrown into the first few shows, the invented mythology of the Amazing Quirk and Jade hung together very well, even cobbled together as it was from the tales and ad libs Calvin presented in each very different show. Calvin was casually careful about avoiding contradictions in his stage patter, and Jenny rarely spoke on stage. There were even some die-hard fans who could recite stories of the Quirk and the Jewel of the East from memory, like geeks spouting their favorite *Monty Python* lines.

By curtain time, they hammered out a strong show that included a new trick Calvin had worked out with the bottomless hole. The *Beau Regardez* line-up still wasn't exclusively about them, though they were consistently presented as the final act. Plenty of fringe performers were clamoring to get into the show at the *Beau*, because Calvin and Jenny drew a real crowd, and the chance to be seen was a siren song to struggling artists. Occasionally, another magician even showed up in one of the earlier acts; but none could hold a candle to the Amazing Quirk.

The preceding acts went by with the usual rowdiness and fun. The large stripping poets, Roberta and Verbena, were there, along with a number of faces that came and went at the *Beau*. At least a few of them were blatantly aware that agents were present tonight, and the performances—or at least, the energy behind them—were knocked up a notch or two more than usual. David Dennis was in rare form, delivering introductions and jokes that seemed like he put some thought into them for once (rumor had it that his anal retentive assistant Kevin had written the jokes this time around), and he got a good response from the packed audience. When the performers two acts before theirs started up—a trio of young ladies who juggled everything from balls and bowling pins to cell phones and pineapples—Calvin and Jenny snuck out the back and went backstage to get ready.

After the jugglers was a rock string quartet called Sex and Violins, three guys and a girl that Jenny and Calvin knew from the *Beau's* after parties. They riled up the crowd with classic punk on classical instruments—Ellie, the girl on the stand-up bass, also added effective percussion by liberally beating the crap out of her bass. As they finished off a Sex Pistols homage, with Mark the violist shrieking obscenities past the bridge of his viola, the crowd started going crazy.

David Dennis didn't bother getting up, and Jenny quickly realized why: pre-recorded music started playing, the opening to Mussorgsky's *Night on Bald Mountain*, and David's recorded voice spoke in slimy, slithering, sinister tones: "Ladies and gentlemen! Prepare yourselves for dark mysteries, for miraculous feats, for mystical visions the likes of which you have never seen, and will never see again! The weak of stomach are excused. The weak of heart are advised to excuse themselves. The weak of mind have no excuse."

Titters of laughter and murmurs of anticipation infiltrated the space between the aggressive notes of Mussorgsky's first big crescendo.

"What you are about to see," continued David Dennis's voice, while the actual man smirked in the front row, all too pleased with himself, "is nothing short of *amazing*. But it's no freak occurrence. No fluke. Consider it a...perk of our spiritual universe. A *quirk* of nature."

The crowd started cheering.

"Prepare yourselves!" the recorded voice of David Dennis demanded in a dizzying frenzy. *"For the Amazing Quirk, and his lovely assistant!"*

Lights flashed and whirled and spiraled, *Bald Mountain* hit the second crescendo, and thunder sound effects filled the theatre. Jenny and Calvin looked at each other, dumbfounded—David hadn't mentioned any of this was going to happen. With the audience screaming for them, though, they didn't have time to ask questions. Jenny donned her spectacles and dashed out to center stage, and Calvin shoved the magic table across the floor toward her as he bounded into view himself.

The audience response bowled them over, and it was all Calvin could do to shout loudly enough to be heard. "Ladies and gentlemen!" he hollered. "I am the Amazing Quirk!"

Jenny set the table on its mark.

"And this is my *amazingly* lovely assistant, Jade—the Jewel of the East!"

The cheering subsided after a minute or so, and they went into the act. The tricks were flawless, and Calvin was really on his game with the storytelling. They opened with their William Tell bit, which concluded with an arrow shooting right through Jade's belly—after a moment for the audience to cringe, the bespectacled Jewel of the East straightened up and pushed the arrow all the way through and out her back, where it clattered to the floor. Jenny hadn't really stopped to draw any conclusions, but she *had* noticed that the slight pain of her temporary injuries was becoming less of a bother to her. She wasn't sure if it was a physical phenomenon, or if she was just becoming cynical. She refused to entertain the term "jaded."

A neat trick with the hat followed, that actually relied on Calvin's phenomenal fingers rather than the hole inside the hat: participants signed their own ten dollar bills, which the magician threw into the hat one by one, never to be seen again. A quick upending and thumping of the hat confirmed the disappearance. Then the Amazing Quirk demanded that Jade return the money; with a slim silver knife, she cut a hole in the palm of her hand and, one at a time, the Amazing Quirk pulled bills from her palm and returned then to the participants in a random order. Each was amazed to unfold the same bill they had supplied, with the same serial number and their own signature still written across Alexander Hamilton's face.

Jenny didn't think she was actually becoming a masochist, but she had to admit that a bit of "Jade chopping" always got the audience going. With a New York art crowd full of hardcore body piercing enthusiasts, fake nihilists and wannabe punk anarchists, it was hardly surprising. Play to the audience, she and Calvin had decided weeks ago, and it seemed to be an effective strategy.

A series of cards tricks was followed by the mystical Jewel of the East peering through the Window to Your Soul and divining the birthdays of audience volunteers, along with the places where they were born (another factoid she could glean from the glowing letters). It was Calvin who had wanted to expand Jade's part in the show, giving her a more active role than just Human Pincushion. She had become a sort of mythological figure, a mystical oracle, and they quickly dropped the pretense that it was the Amazing Quirk who divined volunteers' birthdays—Jade read them herself, passing in front of the volunteers one by one, peering at them through the Window. One of the volunteers tonight was a college kid wearing a funky necktie and a high-tech digital watch on a wide leather strap. Jenny's throat caught as she read his birthday, because she also saw his death date: tomorrow night, in the Hudson River. As the volunteers returned to their seats, she looked long and hard after that one boy, wondering furiously why she was given this arcane knowledge of the future if there wasn't anything she could do about it.

Then again...maybe there *was* something she could do about it. Jenny smiled to herself; then she heard Calvin shouting out her next cue, and put her focus back on the show.

She and Calvin affectionately referred to the next trick as the Popsicle Trick. A volunteer from the audience held the magician's hat upside-down on top of her head, the opening oriented upward. The Amazing Quirk poured perfectly normal orange juice—both he and the girl from the audience took sips as proof—into a clear plastic bag, and stuck a wooden chopstick into the bag. He closed the bag, securing the opening around the chopstick with a few coils of duct tape, and shook the orange juice around to demonstrate its liquid properties inside the makeshift balloon. Then he carefully lowered the bag deep into the hat, holding on to the end of the chopstick; on cue, the audience counted to three, the Amazing Quirk shouted some magic words, and he pulled a giant, misshapen orange popsicle from the hat! It looked like a frozen orange asteroid, with puckers and craters marking half the surface. Jade peeled off the plastic with a knife, and the audience volunteer received the popsicle as a souvenir to snack on for the rest of the show.

They'd been worried, when Calvin first proposed the trick, that whatever was going on at the other end of the hole to freeze everything that went through might also make the frozen orange juice inedible, or even poisonous. Making sure the seal on the bag was airtight, though, Calvin was confident enough to try it himself the first time—and it was delicious. Further experimentation had also taught him to make sure the bag was less than half full, or it would sometimes burst during those brief seconds inside the hole, and the frozen block would come back with a nasty blue tint.

The Rabbit Recipe trick was next; it always elicited a strong reaction—partly for the nostalgia, partly for the skill with which the trick appeared to be performed. If the audience knew that the mice never came back, they might shudder as much as Jenny did inside each time Calvin threw one into the hat. Snuggling Colby when the bunny emerged was a consolation Jenny counted on to get past the guilt she felt over several handfuls of dead mice.

Calvin had convinced Jenny to be brave, and the penultimate trick involved appearing and disappearing coins, with Jenny using her newly trained skills in sleight of hand to assist the Amazing Quirk as he magically made coins appear or disappear in the strangest places. She only made one mistake, which Calvin expertly covered with a bit of misdirection and a well-timed joke.

For the finale, of course, the Amazing Quirk told the audience the tale of the evil prince, and reproduced Jade's captivity by suspending her from the ring of chains. When the magician freed her with a devastating slash through her wrist, the audience broke into wild chanting and cheers, and music erupted from the sound system again. "Ladies and gentlemen!" boomed David Dennis from the speakers. "The Amazing Quirk, and Jade—the Jewel of the East!"

Jenny barely had a moment to reattach her hand. Lights swirled around them and the exciting, uplifting end of Stravinsky's *Firebird* played them off as the audience roared and whooped and whistled. Calvin and Jenny were buzzed. Blood pounded in their ears, and the pure energy was enough to keep them coming back for one more hit. They bounded back onstage for a few more enthusiastic bows before rushing off and dragging their stuff back to the dressing room. Through the walls, the music was still riding high and they could hear the crowd chattering loudly in the wake of the spectacular event.

"Holy shit!" Jenny exclaimed, throwing a shirt on over her bustier and pulling her tutu off.

"Brilliant!" said Calvin. "You nailed the coins!"

"I fucked up the—"

"*Nailed* it," he insisted. "That was incredible! Where did David get all those lights? And the music! And the...the...wow!"

"Wow!" Jenny agreed. "Come on, I want to get out there. You can meet the agents!"

"Yeah!" Calvin was grinning like an idiot. "Agents!"

Jenny smiled and pulled her jeans up over her leggings. She was so distracted she didn't even take off the velvet choker, though she remembered to return the spectacles to the box with the magic window. She slung her bag over one shoulder, the case with the sword over the other, and swung the door open, pausing to make sure Calvin was following her. The magician tucked Colby Cheese into a fluffy towel on the makeup table and hurried out after Jenny.

A wild cheer filled the lobby as the two of them came sauntering down the hall. Congratulations and claps and whistles flew around them, everyone getting in on the excitement. Like most performers, the usuals at the *Beau Regardez* were excited to be part of such an incredible show, even if they weren't the part that made it incredible, if only because they could bask in some second-hand adulation. Those from the audience— many of whom were also performers, and had also played at the *Beau*— were just as stoked, and the air was crackling with jokes and compliments and the witty social tactics known in Show Biz as "networking."

David Dennis was front and center, moving through the crowd with an air of royalty while anyone with hopes for a spot in the *Beau Regardez* line-up parted to make way. Kevin trailed behind him; Jenny was positive this was the first time she'd ever seen the producer's assistant with a smile on his face.

"Amazing as ever!" David oozed professionally. "You live up to your name, darling!"

Calvin smiled, barely able to hear in the noisy crowd. "Thanks, Da— thank you!" he interrupted himself to respond to some vociferous fans. "Thanks, David! Thank you *so* much!"

"You may have heard—"

Jenny cut in, forceful but friendly: "Just point him to the agents already, David!" She smiled prettily, and David Dennis gave her a smooth little smile and nod back.

As David led them through the crowd, Jenny scanned faces, looking for one in particular. Toward the vending machines, she saw him: a goofy-looking bow-legged college kid with a funky necktie and an overlarge wristwatch weighing down one arm. He was smiling and enthusiastically gesticulating to some friends, reliving some of the high points of the show—he looked like a nice kid. A messy shock of black hair hung in his eyes and over a very big nose.

Jenny slipped quietly off the trail blazed by David Dennis, smiling graciously at faces in the crowd who offered cheers or congratulations; she shook hands, offered a few quiet *Thank yous*. She apologized twice for accidentally knocking a shoulder or an elbow with the long case slung over her back, but otherwise met no obstacles as she forged through the crowd to reach the vending machines. The tremendous noise continued unabated, but it was happy noise, the kind that can give you a hangover headache after the fact, but feels too good to hurt when you're in the middle of it.

"Oh my god!" said the college kid. He was barely inches taller than she was, and almost as skinny.

Jenny smiled. "Hi," she said, trying to make herself heard over the din without screaming. "March Eighth, right?"

"Yeah!" the kid said enthusiastically. He was just the kind of adorable energy-filled nerd that kept the money circulating and the slushees flowing at Comic-Con. He probably knew an awful lot about computers and *Star Trek*.

"I'm Jenny—you know, 'Jade,'" said Jenny.

"Yeah, yeah! I'm John!" he said. "This is Meg and Callie and Ryan and..." He went around an irregular polygon of seven friends, and Jenny didn't want to be impolite.

"Cool," she sent smiles all around. "Nice to meet you."

"You were awesome!" said one of the girls. She had thick glasses—Jenny suspected that Jade was a big hit with the Geek Chic set ever since the lovely assistant started wearing her spectacles.

"Thanks!" she said sincerely. "So, you guys go to school?"

John nodded his funny little muppet head wildly, as if the nod would be better heard over the noise if he exaggerated it. "Yeah, we're at Empire Tech!"

"Cool."

"I mean, I am, and Ryan and Callie, but Meg and Mike go to—"

"Wait, yeah," said Jenny, trying not to be rude. "You guys going to the after party?"

"Wow!" said one of John's friends. "Really?"

"It's open to everybody," Jenny said. She looked at John. "You coming?"

"Sure!" John said, his eyes wide and an orgasmic smile plastered on his face. She might as well have just asked him if he wanted to make out right then and there.

"Cool," said Jenny. "Just ask around, somebody will know where it is—"

"Jenny!"

Jenny whirled at the unexpected voice—it hit her ears like a chocolate sundae on a perfect date. In the crowd, easily gliding through chattering, celebrating art types, Vincent Raymond approached like Hercules parting the Red Sea, if Moses had been out sick that day.

"Oh my god!" said Jenny. "Doctor Raymond—Vincent!"

"Vincent!" he reminded her as she corrected herself. He smiled warmly, his porcelain-white teeth gleaming in the lobby lights. "She's over here, honey!" he called.

Carrie Raymond blew breezily through the crowd, no one daring to stand in the way of such glamour as she lithely followed her husband to Jenny's side.

"Carrie!" Jenny greeted cheerfully. She looked down. "Oh my god! You're—"

"Six months," Carrie said proudly, patting her belly. She barely raised her voice, but it was crystal clear through the chatter, as if the cacophonous noise itself knew not to get in the way of a goddess. "I just started to show around the Fourth of July." The Astonishing Amazon's skin glowed doubly bright—impending motherhood had endowed her with some kind of divine halo.

"Wow, congratulations!" said Jenny.

"To you too!" said Carrie Raymond. "I hear you've had some wonderful publicity from all this."

"A dear friend of ours told us about the show, and we knew we had to come," said Vincent Raymond. "You were outstanding!"

"Simply wonderful!" echoed his wife. "You looked so beautiful up there! And some of those tricks..." She pretended to shudder. "I don't know, they looked awfully *real*."

Jenny laughed it off. "Just smoke and mirrors," she said.

"How in the *world* do those chains work?" Carrie Raymond asked.

"And that hat of his is very clever," added Vincent Raymond.

"Wait," said Carrie, "what happened to your glasses, Jenny?"

"Oh!" Jenny laughed. "They're just, you know, for the character. I don't wear glasses, really."

"Of course," Carrie said, laughing lightly. Her beautiful gray dress flowed gracefully around her smooth round belly. "They just looked so charming on you! I loved seeing you in them."

"I'll, uh, wear them at the after party," said Jenny. "You guys are invited! You can come, right?"

Vincent smiled avuncularly and put an arm around his wife, who shook her head. "No, sorry, Jenny," said Carrie. "No late nights for me right now! I've got to keep my strength up for the big event." She rubbed her pregnant belly. Vincent put his hand over his wife's.

"Aww," Jenny needled them. "You guys are still young."

"No," Vincent said apologetically, "I'm afraid the party's over, Jenny."

Carrie beamed at her. "But we'll see you again, real soon—we'd love to take you out to dinner and celebrate your new career! And we'd love to meet your magician friend—"

"Career? Uh..."

"Jenny!" It was Calvin, launching across the lobby, his hand reaching her arm miles before the rest of him in an inverted demonstration of Lorentz-Fitzgerald contraction.

"Calvin! This is Doc—uh, Vincent and Carrie, they're friends of mine..."

Calvin flashed them a grin. "Nice to meet you."

"And this is John and..." Jenny looked around—adorably nerdy John and his friends had melted away into the crowd. "Oh..."

"Jenny," Calvin said urgently, "they want us to come in."

"Agents?" she said.

"Agents!" he crowed. "They're almost fighting over us! They want to see us Friday, one in the morning, and one in the afternoon."

"Wow." Jenny turned back to the Raymonds, but they had drifted off through the crowd as well, bronzed Vincent and his glowing golden wife drawing eyes as they made their way to the exit. Jenny felt a little lost, but focused on Calvin. "That's awesome! Calvin, this is great!"

"Nothing's definite or anything, and I don't even know really what they can do, but it's *something*," he said. His face swarmed with forty racing emotions, excitement in the lead.

"Wow!" said Jenny.

"You're free on Friday?" Calvin asked.

"Of course!"

"Cool—oh! Hold on, there they are," Calvin jumped straight up and waved, as if he needed any extra height above the crowd to be seen. With his bright red hair soaring over every head in the room, he could have done stunt double work as the Olympic torch. "Hey! Mister, um, Carson, uh, Car—uh—hey!"

The agents strolled through the crowd like they owned the place, and David Dennis strolled through the place like he owned the crowd. Introductions ping-ponged around, and Jenny met tall bald Barry Carter and short squat Abe Roman. Carter was all business and acted like he had at least five far more scintillating conversations he could be attending if he could only break way from this one; Roman was much older, white-haired, a bit scatterbrained, and seemed to have enough trouble following the conversation he was in, preferring instead to compare Calvin and Jenny and Barry Carter (whom he kept mistaking as another performer he was scouting) to old time movie stars who featured heavily in his non-stop allegedly first-hand stories of scandalous behavior. David Dennis smiled regally, content in his firm belief that everything and everyone here owed its very existence to him, the Big Gay God of New York Fringe Theatre.

After some verbal rustling back and forth, Carter consulted his smart phone and Roman's pretty young assistant took over his end of the conversation for scheduling purposes; Calvin and Jenny were slotted in for an appointment with Abe Roman at eleven on Friday morning, and an appointment with Barry Carter three hours later. Roman wandered off to corner some other aspiring performer with tales of escorting Miss America 1956 to Liz Taylor's birthday party. Carter excused himself and vacated the premises the way a homeowner does before a bug bomb is deployed.

David Dennis meandered into the crowd to lustfully accept congratulations on the amazing job he did sitting in the audience while various talented young people displayed their talent on a stage he controlled access to.

"Party?" said Calvin, grinning from cartoonishly large ear to cartoonishly large ear. He looked like the giddy love child of Howdy Doody and a Manhattan skyscraper.

"Party," Jenny said, grinning back.

"Yes!" Calvin shouted, and he threw his hands into the air in an explosion of flashing *pops* and confetti. The crowd in the lobby cheered him like the rock star he was.

CHAPTER TWELVE

David Dennis lived on West Twentieth in a high rise crowned with a huge rooftop garden of patios and trees that even included a sauna. His boyfriend Paul was, to the surprise of those who'd seen David eye every young male performer like Wile E. Coyote scoping out an aviary, at least fifteen years David's senior. He was the inevitable result of stuffing Nordic genes in business suits and high-risk venture capitalism for forty years—tall, blond, in perfect health, and obscenely wealthy. David's ability to while away his time dabbling in the theatre world with no discernible source of income suddenly snapped into sharp relief.

Paul was also exceedingly sincere, impeccably polite, and the first person anyone present had seen David Dennis defer to on anything. He was a quiet but firm leash on David's more outrageous and narcissistic behaviors, which kept the *Beau Regardez* boss in check and gave others their chance to take a turn in the social limelight.

Jenny hung back from the limelight, less for lack of interest—which was genuine—than to keep tabs on her target: John, the dorky college kid who'd shown up with half his friends in tow. He was an animated guy whose smile had set up permanent residence on his face for the night; he kept doing full three-sixties as he mingled, soaking up the brave new world around him. Paul and David's apartment was huge—three storeys with direct access to a private section of the rooftop garden—and tastefully decorated in Austere Manhattan Gay Couture. Framed black-and-white photos flooded the eyes with bleak and beautiful landscapes; abstract marble sculptures gave the distinct feeling that they depicted something erotic, though viewers couldn't quite tell what, which itself reaffirmed the likely randy nature of the oblong curves and jutting angles.

John and his friends looked as out of place in this private museum as Jenny felt, but the driving techno music and incessant buzz of three dozen overlapping conversations kept the energy flowing as freely as the booze. Jenny flitted from one knot of conversation to the next, warmly accepting accolades and contributing just a few words, which suited everyone just fine—they were there to be seen and heard, not to see and hear, and the verbal sparring featured thrusts, parries and fancy footwork that would shame an Olympic fencer into hanging up his foil and taking up needlepoint. She stayed within three conversational archipelagos of her nerdy quarry for most of the night, without getting too clingy. The last thing she needed was for John to think her interest in him was romantic.

The few times she found herself in the same eddy of social current as John, she managed to make some small talk, fishing a little more information out of him each time. He lived in the East Village. He was a computer science student at Empire Tech. He was an avid amateur juggler (he'd come to the *Beau* because he was friends with the three juggling girls who had performed before Jenny and Calvin). He was originally from Illinois. He had a dentist appointment on Friday.

Sifting through the biographical detritus like a bearded Forty-Niner panning for gold, Jenny tried to see if anything she came up with added up to John being dead in the Hudson River in less than twenty-four hours. If she could discover something—an undiagnosed ache or pain, a romantic rejection, a predilection for illegal drugs, anything that might suggest a cause of death—then maybe she could figure out a way to warn the kid or keep him out of harm's way. But John didn't drink or smoke, he seemed too socially awkward to make any advance that could be rejected, and the dentist appointment was just a routine cleaning. Jenny was racing a painfully slow but final clock, and she was running out of clever segues to ask John about his schedule for the rest of the week without sounding suspicious.

Calvin frequently touched base with Jenny as he made his own rounds through the party. The gangling magician beamed, humbly accepting compliments and trading jokes, winning friends and influencing people. He occasionally pulled off some outstanding prestidigitation, conjuring a filled wine glass from thin air or suddenly presenting a girl with a necklace that was, the last time she checked, still around her own neck. The success of the Amazing Quirk had given mild-mannered Calvin McGuirk a boost of confidence, and he played the room like a fledgling hawk doing loop-de-loops on its first day out of the nest. Every loop around the room, though, he made sure to give Jenny a big hug and a high five, and the two made waves through the party like the latest tabloid couple giving the paparazzi a free lane for the money shot.

By one in the morning, the half-life of the party proved to be approximately three hours, and the life of the party proved to be the guy who had sung political opera on the Amazing Quirk's first night at the *Beau*. A ring of women hung on his every word and witty turn of phrase, though he seemed more intent on catching Jenny's attention whenever the opportunity presented itself. Jenny was more than happy to let the other girls take him, and returned only a distracted smile as she glanced away across the room. John was heading out the front door with two of his friends.

"So in case of emergency, *I* break *wind*," said the opera guy, pushing his posterior into firing position. Jenny was sure the comment must have been remarkably quick and clever in context, judging by the cackling and giggling ladies all around. She laughed perfunctorily, throwing her head back and following it in a quick twist to the next crowd over.

"Calvin," she whispered in the magician's ear.

He smiled at her. "Agents!" he said.

"Right, agents," she replied. "Listen, I've got to head out—could you bring the you-know-what home with you?"

Calvin looked at her with a puzzled expression.

"It's in David's bedroom, with the magic table and Colby," she told him, raising her eyebrows as if to psychically batter him with the reminder: *The sword, the sword, the sword....*

He got it. "Right," he said. "Sure thing! But where are you...?"

"I'll see you tomorrow," she said quickly. She smiled to soften her abrupt farewell. "Just something I have to take care of."

Calvin hugged her. "Your camera's in the table," he reminded her. "Don't worry, I'll grab it."

It was only natural to gave him a quick kiss on the cheek, but she paused after doing it. Calvin's smile was still frozen on his face as she slipped through the dwindling crowd and out the front door.

The elevator answered her summons with all the speed of a mildly palsied tortoise filling out paperwork at the Department of Motor Vehicles, and Jenny worried that John would be out of sight by the time she reached the street. A couple of other *Beau* folks came out of David Dennis's apartment right when the elevator *dinged* and opened up; she anxiously but politely made small talk on the way down. She said good night when the elevator reached the lobby, and she dashed outside to look both ways.

John was gone. Elevator luck had screwed her.

The other two elevator passengers walked awkwardly past her and into the night as Jenny dawdled, making up her mind. Her bag was slung over her shoulder; Calvin would take care of the sword and her new camera. There was no reason to head back up to the party, but she wasn't sure which way John had gone. She shrugged the tension out of her shoulders, tightened the bag's strap around her, and picked a direction.

Jenny found herself drawn west, toward the Hudson River. She reached the West Side Highway and aimlessly headed south. She pretended that she was drawn by the glow of the fantastically warped IAC Building, but she knew her destination was much farther south, a bit farther west, and substantially wetter. Without meaning to, she was heading toward the future final resting place of John, the lovable geek.

Twenty minutes down the road, she crossed to the river side of the street to avoid passing right by a strip club, one of the few vibrant signs of life this far down West Street after one in the morning on a week night. Two beefy guys were enjoying a smoke with a bleached blonde in a giant coat, bare legs, and six-inch heels. Jenny didn't feel like taking a moment to even give them the simple eye flick and nod that acknowledges a member of your own species. As the driving beat of *chunka chunka* music bounced off her bones, she crossed over to the big Pier 40 building and kept heading south.

A couple of people were leaning against the railing halfway along the pier to the Holland Tunnel Exhaust Tower. Probably kids sharing some pot, or crackheads sharing a needle, or just some adventurous couple sharing a moment, even though the pier was closed to the public this late at night. Jenny passed Canal Street. Across the highway, she saw someone waving in her direction—but it turned out to be Mirror Jenny reflected in big gas station windows, gleaming in the white lights by the pumps. The mirror image was waving her hands around wildly. Jenny set her face and looked straight ahead, ignoring her reflection.

Past a few silvery park benches, farther down along the bike paths, Jenny veered off toward a construction site right on the water—maybe a new pier, or some development that would cater to the upper class desire to live within view of the Statue of Liberty, a message to all the huddled masses and wretched refuse that they, too, can achieve success, greatness and wealth if the successful, great, and wealthy feel like giving them a shot. She couldn't get past the fencing to the construction, but she leaned against the adjacent rail and stared out at the water, right where she knew John the geek would take his last breath tomorrow night. New Jersey blinked back at her sympathetically; Jersey City had seen more than its fair share of tragedies staring across this river. Her circle of yellow light faded to sickly green and eventually a dim gray before giving up against the onslaught of a dark summer night. The lights of Jersey City tried their best to meet it halfway, but the deep center of the Hudson was swathed in dark waves on their inevitable journey to swim under the Verrazano Bridge and out to the ocean.

Jenny watched the rippling surface of the river as it smacked into the foundation below her. She followed the waves in and looked straight down at the surface of the water, which was orange and purple in the harsh yellow light overhead. The wavelets interlocked and intercepted each other like someone trying unsuccessfully to put together a complicated shopping mall stereogram on the fly. Extra, incongruous movement within the dark swatches and shining spidery wavetops caught her eye, but it was just Mirror Jenny bothering her with another mute, mischievous round of Charades. The reflection was so broken up by ripples and swirls that Jenny couldn't work out any second syllable of a third word of a movie title anyway, so she shook her head and stuck her tongue out at her reflection.

Her tongue still out, she lifted her head and saw dark forms on the water. For a moment, she thought they were boats—garbage barges or late night ferries—near Jersey City, but as her eyes adjusted, she realized they were much closer than that, and much smaller. The shadows bobbed up and down, but not like water; more like hard work, a steady and inexorable pace marching atop the river. The rhythm was familiar; she'd seen it on film hundreds of times before. In fact, she'd seen it very recently, in person—it was the gait of a horse plodding forward across rough terrain.

The shadows came closer, and there was no mistaking them—horses, pushing hard across the water, stomping on its surface like it was soft clay or craggy rock and not something they should easily fall through with a splash and a justifiably irate whinny. Enough light reached them that she could see they were very pale, like Rex, and Jenny had to admit that the yellowish tint of their hides probably wasn't a trick of the construction lights. They had the same blurry tinge as Rex, and they were extremely large, just like he was. They could have been his twins. Or his fellow quadruplets—there were three of them, each remarkably similar to her equine hero.

The most striking difference was that these horses had riders.

Jenny bit her tongue, and reflexively jerked it back into her mouth. No mistake, no trick of the light, no illusion of splashing waves—shadowy cloth flapped sharply in the strong wind strafing the Hudson, and dark figures swayed slowly on horseback, heads knocking up and down in rhythm with the hooves thrusting down onto a surface they had no business standing on.

The horses, heedless of the defined properties of solids and liquids, marched closer. The riders were almost completely concealed in billowy black folds, save for very pale white hands held in front of them like talons, loosely clutching their leather reins.

Jenny jerked back from the railing. She wasn't sure if the riders had seen her, but she suddenly felt very paranoid about the possibility. Saying there was something ominous about three dark riders on pale horses walking across water on a windswept night was like saying there was something sticky about peanut butter. It was better left unsaid, and smarter to simply make tracks. She turned and ran across the street.

Ahead of her, Mirror Jenny jumped up and down in the glass doors of a towering co-op. Jenny glared at her—Mirror Jenny gestured and pantomimed, but the meaning was unintelligible. Jenny rounded the corner and dashed along North Moore, away from the river and the sinister figures riding horses on top of it.

She heard footsteps behind her. She froze—footsteps? The riders were on horseback, and probably weren't wearing sneakers, judging by their Nouveau Dark Sorceror style. The telltale *squeak* of sneakers on the polished marble steps of the co-op spun her around, wondering who was there, hoping it was someone who might keep the dark riders at a comfortable distance.

At the corner was a short man in a blue windbreaker. A lemon yellow shirt collar flopped out of the top of the windbreaker and shifted in the wind. His bald spot glinted in the nearest streetlight; he was unmistakably the creepy guy who fondled her poster in front of the *Beau Regardez*.

Jenny's eyes widened as she recognized him and gasped. The little man's eyes narrowed. He took a step, and she bolted.

The streets were heart-stoppingly empty, the kind of empty streets that are made to order for nightmares starring crazed chainsaw-wielding lunatics in hot and impressively relentless pursuit. Her pursuer didn't have a chainsaw, that she knew of, but she wasn't waiting around to find out what made him confident enough to come after her without one. Like the night in Prospect Park—when Rex had saved her from the skinheads—Jenny didn't think indestructibility would get her out of whatever psychotic plans this guy had in mind for her in his proverbial ice cream truck. If anything, an instantly regenerating victim might give him an all new menu of depraved acts to work with. Running was her best option.

Every passing window or shiny metal surface danced with Mirror Jenny's urgent contortions as she tried fruitlessly to catch Jenny's attention. Jenny didn't care—now wasn't the time to play around with her unusually autonomous reflection. She zigged south on Greenwich, then zagged across and raced down Franklin.

Franklin Street was an odd little throwback in the midst of Tribeca's urban progress. It had fewer streetlights, making it dark and claustrophobic between tall warehouses and unlit buildings. Cars and trucks lining the curbs threw sharp shadows across the street in a silent game of rock-paper-scissors-lizard-Spock, and whatever other symbolic shapes they could muster. The uneven cobblestones, splattered with asphalt where the stonework had given in to the passage of decades, would have been quaint on any other night. Running for her life, Jenny found them less quaint and more a pain each time she stumbled over a loose brick or jagged edge and silently swore. She absurdly wished she had her sword with her; not that she was Bruce Lee or even just Errol Flynn with the thing, but the sight of an angry Chinese girl with an exceedingly sharp and wicked sword might at least make the Ice Cream Psycho think twice, if not convince him to back off entirely and look for some unarmed kids who might be coaxed into his van with the promise of Neapolitan ice cream and flat wooden spoons.

Unarmed and not interested in ice cream of any flavor, Jenny scrambled down Franklin Street, angrily glaring at Mirror Jenny in every storefront. Her reflection's behavior was getting wilder, more forceful, and more insistent. One store—filled with statuettes, wicker furniture, and works of art that were charmingly but unconvincingly pretending to be authentically Native American—had a giant gilt-edged mirror displayed prominently in its main window. It was the double reflection that caught her eye—faint Mirror Jenny in the window backed by vivid Mirror Jenny in the mirror, each of them moving entirely independently of the other and jumping up and down like a little girl trying to persuade her mother to watch her next spectacularly failed dive in the public swimming pool.

"What?!" Jenny hissed vehemently, demanding at least a little respect as she slowed to look at the next reflection down the line. Looking back from a tall windowed door, the reflection very clear thanks to the pitch darkness in the store behind it, Mirror Jenny curled her fists in frustration. She pointed straight down in front of her in a devastatingly communicative *Come here.*

Jenny looked back up the street—she had perhaps seconds before the Ice Cream Psycho hit the corner; she could hear squeaky footsteps pounding down Greenwich. She let out a sound between a growl and a groan, and jumped up the steps to the door.

"What do you want?" she whispered.

Mirror Jenny gestured toward herself: *Come on.* The reflection didn't bother speaking; she never did. Perhaps sound couldn't break the reflective barrier between worlds, or maybe the reflection had no voice of her own.

"Inside?"

Mirror Jenny gave her an ambivalent wobble of the head and a shrug—the kind of expression and posture that said: *Close, but not really.*

Jenny tried the door. Locked, of course.

The reflection threw up her arms in exasperation. She shook her head, and made a more forceful, more deliberate *Come here* gesture with both hands.

Jenny looked back toward Greenwich Street—a pot-bellied silhouette had just swung around the corner. He peered down the dimly lit street and put on some steam, running her way with surprising speed on short chunky legs.

She turned to her reflection. Mirror Jenny mirrored her pose, but tilted her head forward, her eyes earnest and pleading. *Trust me*, her expression said. Jenny took a deep breath and put her palms flat on the surface of the glass; Mirror Jenny matched her, palms pushing out to meet Jenny's.

A swirl of light and wind and dust distracted her from the feeling of pulling her own arms inside out and gagging on her lungs. The world squeezed itself into her visual cortex and exploded again in substantially duller contrast—the cobblestones, buildings, even the streetlights looked like relics from a nineteenth century Daguerrotype. The air roared, like when your ears are *just* about to pop as your plane reaches altitude but they never do. Jenny staggered back from the door and tripped down the steps, catching herself on the cobblestones—her footsteps echoed hollowly, as if her feet were a great distance away and behind studio-grade professional soundproofing.

Jenny steadied herself and looked around in a panic, sure she would see the Ice Cream Psycho bearing down on her, his stubby fingers reaching out to grab her shoulders...

...but she was looking the wrong way. She was looking at Hudson Street instead of back where she'd come from. It made no sense—staring at Mirror Jenny, Greenwich Street and her pudgy pursuer had been to her right; now Greenwich was to her left, and the little man was nowhere in sight.

Neither was Mirror Jenny. The glass on the door was sleek shiny black, reflecting everything across the sepia-toned street, but not Jenny herself. She tentatively waved a hand, and knew what it felt like to be a vampire in a campy Eighties movie—no reflection peered back at her, let alone glanced past her or gesticulated independently.

The roar of pressure in her ears was constant and disorienting. Blurry cars were there and not there at the same time, like the creator of this dull dun-colored world had drawn the outlines but hastily and half-heartedly filled them in. They were mere suggestions of vehicles rather than the real deal. Looking directly at one made it almost disappear while all the others snapped into focus; but shifting her gaze to one that was in focus reversed the effect, so that she could never get a clear look at any one car or truck.

Except in the glass. In the reflections she could still see the cars, solid and clear and distinctly defined. In fact, every reflective surface she could spot—windows, metal bars, the gilt-edged mirror in the store window back up (or down?) Franklin Street—gave her a clear view of everything on the block. The reflections were more *real* than the world around her.

So was the Ice Cream Psycho, running through the reflections on the windows and slowing to a stop right in the frame of the door Jenny had just touched. He stood there in the glass reflection, in the middle of the street, breathing heavily and scratching his bald spot. He looked up and down the street. He looked through the glass, straight at her.

Jenny tensed and froze.

The man narrowed his eyes and frowned.

Jenny's panic caught in her throat.

The man tilted his head, smoothed out his fringe of mousy gray hair, and straightened his disheveled windbreaker. He rubbed at his jaw with one hand, and looked away.

He hadn't seen her. He'd looked straight at her, through the glass, and it was like she wasn't even there.

And then it hit her: she *wasn't* there. Not where the man was, anyway. She was literally Through the Looking Glass, in a Wonderland that existed on the other side of the mirror. She *was* Mirror Jenny—and Jenny was just gone. The man had run to where he'd seen her, but she'd disappeared. All he'd seen in the glass was his own reflection, which was probably much better behaved than hers.

Jenny hesitantly took a few steps up to the door, watching the Ice Cream Psycho through the glass. He pulled out a cell phone and made a call; she couldn't hear him, even if she didn't have the alien whirlwind in her ears, and she wasn't banking on a talent for reading lips. Whoever he was calling remained a mystery, but the call itself suggested one thing: this guy wasn't working alone, and this was more than just a random stalking. Perhaps he was just calling his doting mother to let her know he'd be home to clean up his basement bachelor pad in an hour; but judging by his stance and the cold expression he wore as he spoke calmly into the phone, there was something much more disquieting going on.

His conversation wrapped up, and the man put his cell phone away. He did one full, slow turn in place, looking around, and ended facing the glass again. He scratched his chin thoughtfully, as if trying to puzzle out Jenny's disappearance, and then pivoted and walked back the way he'd come.

In Wonderland, Jenny kept pace alongside him, watching him walk in the clear reflections on each window surface. The cobblestones on her side of the mirror seemed slick with fresh rain; she absently wondered if it had just rained in this version of the world, or if it only experienced precipitation when the real world did. She was playing by all new rules now, and didn't have a copy of the rulebook.

The man turned north at Greenwich Street, and Jenny felt entirely turned around when she turned left to go "north" in the Looking Glass world. She did her best to follow him, despite an unnerving sense of universal misalignment. The signs for the deli across Greenwich—in fact, the street signs themselves—were all written backwards, in mirror image letters. That, at least, made sense in context.

The man turned on North Moore, heading back to where he'd first started chasing Jenny. Jenny counterintuitively turned right to return to the Hudson River—

—and found herself face to muzzle with a snuffling, steaming horse snout.

The giant horse clopped one huge hoof down on the street and chuffed at her. On its back, one of the black-cloaked riders leaned forward, any distinguishing facial features lost in the deep folds of a dark hood. A gravelly voice emerged from the hood: "*Gong dung waa?* Or would ya prefer English?"

Jenny was speechless.

"*Deutsch? Español? Fdtt-tt-dtt-tttt-ft! Chto bi ti vibrala?*"

"Uh," said Jenny. "English is fine. I mean, yeah, English." Her voice echoed and twisted strangely in the rustling wind-tunnel atmosphere, just like his did.

"Well," the man said, leaning back in the saddle and turning his horse sideways. He didn't use the word *well* the way Jenny had ever heard anyone use it before. It wasn't a verbal pause, and it wasn't an implied question, or an invitation to speak. It was simply an acknowledgement. It set her on edge.

She had no real response.

The man in black seemed to sense this, and one pale hand reached up to pull down his hood, revealing a craggy, square face with an untrimmed, unkempt red beard. His hair was long and as red as his beard; his eyes were dark and burning. "Ya got an appointment about the island this night?" he asked her.

"With you?" asked Jenny.

He stared hard at her. "Are you escortin' someone?" One hand fell to his hip. Jenny saw the long sword secured to the horse's saddle with an intricate series of leather ties and knots. It was just like her own sword—the one Rex had brought her.

Jenny raised both hands as a show of cooperation. "I'm just lost," she said quickly. "I had a little trouble—this guy back there...." She rewrote her map in her head. "Over there, I mean. He was chasing me."

The burly man with the red beard chewed his mustache with a clear *Does Not Compute* show of consternation. "He weren't yer charge?" Put an eyepatch on this guy and he could be an extra in the latest blockbuster pirate movie. Of course, he'd need a change of wardrobe first. Right now, he was dressed like—

"The Count!" Jenny said.

Now it was Redbeard's turn to remain silent. He stared at her blithely.

"Uh," said Jenny. "Listen, yeah—I *do* have an appointment. There's somebody who's going to die tomorrow night, right over there." She aimed to point at the river, and got it right on the second try.

"Well," said Redbeard.

"I have to save him," Jenny said urgently.

"For why?" asked Redbeard.

That wasn't the question she'd expected. "Because, uh," she tried to come up with an answer that would make a dent in someone for whom the obvious answer didn't suffice. "He's a friend of mine."

"Which now?"

"He's too young to die," Jenny tried.

"How's that?"

Jenny worked her jaw soundlessly. The conversation was slinking toward a corner to crouch down and hold its head in its lap. She was sure she'd chosen English from Redbeard's original options, but now it seemed like they were speaking totally foreign languages to each other. "Um," said Jenny. "Who are you?"

Redbeard turned his head and glared at her hard from one eye, like a vicious bird about to get down and dirty. "What're ya talkin' at?" he demanded. "What's yer means here?"

"Shit," Jenny muttered. "I—fuck, could you just tell me where 'here' *is?*"

The big man's face softened from diamond hard to quartz. "Yer an accident, then," he said. It was consistently hard to tell his questions from his statements. "Yer just happenstance."

"Guess so," Jenny said quietly, barely hearing herself over the howling in her ears.

"Well," said Redbeard. "Ya need t' orient. This ain't the place to talk on this. I ain't the one to speak at." He raised one meaty hand and pointed. "Take yerself to the lake. Past sunrise and sunset. Stand yerself atop the wall. Walk the smooth road."

"The lake?" she asked. Then she started puzzling together Redbeard's strange way of speaking. She deadpanned. "The reservoir—the reservoir in Central Park. Tomorrow night."

"Well," Redbeard said. "I ain't got a tongue for makin' grace, and no mind for lessons. Bring yer sword an' steed. Caravel shall set ya right."

"Caravel?" asked Jenny.

"She talks it plain," he said simply. He raised his hood, hiding his boxy face and red beard in shadows once more, and pulled his reins.

"Wait!" Jenny called. "Steed? I don't have a horse." She considered that for a moment. "Well, I mean, I guess I do, but I don't know where he is."

Redbeard's giant stallion sauntered down the street. Over his shoulder, he shouted back to her: "Regain him! He's in bad means on the rough road."

"Shit," said Jenny. "Wait! How do I get him back!" But Redbeard had already galloped out of sight around the corner. Jenny was alone in the windy Wonderland on the other side of the mirror. She ground her teeth nervously. "How do *I* get back?" she wondered.

She supposed it could be as simple getting back to the real world as it was getting into this one. She approached the floor-to-ceiling windows fronting the lobby of Wonderland's counterpart to the co-op on West and North Moore. She could clearly see the Hudson River flowing in the reflection, with the lights of Jersey City beyond it. Behind her, the mirror image of Jersey City blinked dully in brown and beige light against craggy black terrain.

Jenny moved close to the windows and tried to think of what muscle to flex or what direction to travel in. She had no ruby slippers, and wasn't sure what magic words would trigger them if she did. Ignoring common sense, which was growing more irrelevant to her experiences by the minute, she placed her palms on the window and pushed. It felt solid and unyielding. She pushed harder, not just with her hands, but with her eyes, with her *soul...*

She felt herself twisting inside-out, spilling through dust and wind and a howling flash as the world snapped into focus and full color. She was back. The rushing pressure in her ears ceased, replaced by a gentle breeze and the distant sound of car horns. A truck downshifted and zoomed by, a welcome blast of the mundane after her foray into another world.

Everything was in the right direction again, and staring back at her from the reflection in the glass, Mirror Jenny gave her a friendly little smile. "Thanks," Jenny whispered. Without losing the smile, her mirror image sighed and shrugged, as if to say: *Well, if you'd been paying attention....*

Jenny turned and took in the cool summer wind coming off the river. If she could meet with this Caravel person tomorrow night, maybe she could learn how to save John. Maybe Caravel would even help her.

According to Redbeard, though, she needed to have both her sword and her horse to join the super-secret club of horse-riding, sword-swinging, mirror-traveling weirdos. The sword wasn't a problem; but Rex was still a guest of the New York Police Department, or whatever outfit they passed horse crimes off to. Jenny Ng made another in a series of decisions that would have had her mother shouting and smashing dishes in the sink. She took out her cell phone, scrolled through her contacts, and rang through.

"Hello...?" Calvin's voice was wrapped in a gummy cocoon of sleep. Jenny pulled the phone away from her cheek and checked the time—she hadn't realized it was already nearing three o'clock.

"Calvin, it's me," she said. "Sorry it's so late."

"No, 'sokay," he slurred. She could hear him trying to wake himself up. "Wha's goin' on?"

"It's been a long night," said Jenny. "I'll tell you all about it. But I need your help."

"For what?"

"I need to get Rex."

There was a pause. "The horse?" asked Calvin.

"Yeah," said Jenny. She thought about how best to phrase her next question. "So, uh—how hard do you think it is to break a horse out of jail?"

CHAPTER THIRTEEN

They didn't have much time to practice. Despite the urgency, Jenny knew she should at least get a few hours of sleep before they started plotting Rex's jailbreak. Despite the necessity of sleep, she could barely shut her eyes while the anticipation of the next day poked at her like a chubby kid on a bus hoping for a bite of your doughnut. A mere few hours flew by during an uneasy cease-fire between excitement and exhaustion, and by eight o'clock the next morning, she was at Calvin's apartment with a fancy retail coffee for herself and a chocolate milkshake for him. (He didn't drink coffee.)

She filled him in on Wonderland, Redbeard, John the doomed college kid, and the Ice Cream Psycho. Calvin absorbed another tale of Jenny's crazy adventures with wide eyes and an open mind. "You really think we could save him?" he asked Jenny. He vaguely remembered John from the party.

"I think it's worth a shot," Jenny said. "I mean, in all the movies and TV shows and everything, whenever somebody gets powers like this, they sort of have to go—"

"Yeah!" Calvin interrupted happily. "With great power comes great responsibility, right?"

"Or at least a major guilt trip," Jenny admitted. "If you *can* do something, and you *don't*...well...."

"Right," said Calvin. "So you need to get Rex back, and bring the sword."

"And meet Caravel—whoever she is—in Central Park. On the wall that goes across the reservoir."

"Tonight, after dark?"

Jenny shrugged. "That Redbeard Guy was hard to understand, but I can't think of what else 'after sunrise and sunset' might mean."

"Right." Calvin nodded slowly, jumpstarting his morning-groggy thoughts. "So where's Rex? And how do we get him out?"

Jenny stretched out on his couch, her toe nudging Colby Cheese, who nibbled on her sock. "Listen, the cops have to have *some* kind of procedure for this kind of thing," she mused. "They don't know who owns him, and they probably want to find out. They can't just boil him for glue if somebody might come looking for him."

"Well, they kill dogs and cats, right?" said Calvin, petting Colby's pristine white back to reassure her that she wouldn't cruise Euthanasia Road any time soon. "I mean, they put them to sleep. You know, if nobody comes to get them. I don't know how long they wait, though."

"Wouldn't they have to wait longer for a horse?" Jenny asked. "He's a lot more expensive, at least."

"Maybe."

"Okay, so we've got to find out where he is."

"But then we've got to get him *out*," Calvin reminded her.

Jenny sat up and ran her fingers through Colby's fur, momentarily bumping up against Calvin's fingers and leaving her hand there for a moment.

She stood up quickly and ran her fingers through her hair. "At this point, I think we can start trusting that I can do some pretty weird stuff," she said with a grin. "I can sneak in most places if I go Through the Looking Glass, and it won't matter if they shoot me *or* the horse as long as we can get away. I just need to make sure they can't see my face or anything. If anybody can pick me out of a line-up later, I'm screwed."

" *We're* screwed," Calvin loyally corrected her. "So, uh." He looked like a kid begging to unwrap Christmas gifts the night before. "Could I see you do it? The mirror thing, I mean?"

"I should practice it anyway," Jenny agreed.

She showed off her latest power by heading through the mirror in Calvin's bathroom, emerging moments later from the reflection in his oven window. Calvin was floored. "It's like you just *poof* right out of the room!" he exclaimed. "Do it again!"

They experimented—Calvin, as always, thought of interesting ways to test and stretch her powers, coming up with ideas and urging Jenny to see how far she could go. As a magician, he was already hooked by the prospect of anybody appearing and disappearing, especially without the aid of a hat (or a mysteriously serendipitous hole). Maybe there was a perfectly reasonable explanation, but from his perspective, this was *magic* magic—"wizard-y" magic—and Calvin couldn't wipe the goofy grin off his face after watching Jenny literally disappear into thin air and reappear out of the thin air of an entirely different room.

"Wait," said Calvin after Jenny made a few forays through Wonderland. "You can bring stuff with you—I mean, your clothes and everything go with you—so what if you brought something there and *left* it there?"

Jenny responded with a curious look. "Good point," she said. She wondered why someone like Calvin hadn't gotten her powers. Someone who would think of clever ways to use them; someone whose idealism and optimism would drive them to use their powers to help others. That would make more sense, from a cosmic perspective, or at least a narrative one. Instead, they'd landed on her, after a lifetime of broken plans that had left her twice as cynical at half the age of the average cynical New Yorker.

Then it hit her: she *was* trying to use her powers for others. She was trying to save John the juggler from a fate not worse than but exactly equal to death. Maybe Jenny Ng could be the good person she wanted to be after all. The kind of good person Calvin McGuirk was. The thought made her feel lighter, practically floating, and she continued practicing with a renewed sense of purpose.

They started with a spoon. Calvin always happily accepted utensils at restaurants and from delivery guys, even when he didn't need them, and he had a stupendous pile of plastic forks, knives and spoons in one drawer. Jenny went through the bathroom mirror and placed one of his spoons on the floor of the living room in Wonderland. When she pushed her way back out to the real world, the spoon wasn't there—presumably still waiting on the other side of the mirror. They double-checked: there was nothing on the floor next to Calvin's couch, even though she'd put the plastic spoon right next to the couch's mirrored twin.

"Wait right here," said Jenny. She went back to the bathroom, slipped Through the Looking Glass, and skipped back to the mirror-image living room. The pink plastic spoon—the only bit of pure color in the place other than Jenny herself—was still lying on the floor. She snatched it up and dove through the glass reflection on the front of Calvin's giant case of playing cards. "Got it!" She waggled the spoon at Calvin like a first prize trophy from a yogurt eating contest.

"Awesome!" Calvin clapped. "Okay, now...what about bringing somebody else with you?" He spread his long arms and smiled hopefully.

"What?" Jenny's high spirits deflated. "Well, wait. I mean, what if it does something weird to you?"

"Start with one of the mice," Calvin suggested.

A cage of doomed mice—their execution date set for Saturday's show at the *Beau Regardez*—was on a shelf with an assortment of other magic props. Each squirmy little white furball was either dozing or happily gnawing away at the stale popcorn, sunflower seeds, and giant hunks of carved watermelon that Calvin and Jenny had supplied them with: one last fantastic meal for the condemned. After the first few performances in July, this had become routine—they still felt bad about the mice, but they'd accepted that at least the little creatures were receiving a last week of luxury and a shining moment in the spotlight instead of a one-way trip down the intestinal tract of a pampered reptile.

Jenny screwed up her face and her courage, lifted the lid on the cage, and plucked one of the bigger mice from the bedding of tissue and wood chips. "Sorry, Mickey," she said. They never actually named any mice—ever—but she felt the need to call him *something* to apologize for using him as a guinea pig.

"I bet he'll be fine," said Calvin. "*You* go to the other side with no problem, right?"

"I'm also indestructible," Jenny reminded him. She shrugged and rubbed the mouse between the ears. "But let's see what happens."

She was most comfortable entering through the bathroom mirror, where the image was crystal clear regardless of the lights and angles; reflections on glass in a dim daylit room were faint and harder to make out, and they made her feel like she was leaping blind. Jenny held the mouse close to her chest and leaned forward to place her other palm on Mirror Jenny's. Her reflection winked at Jenny—the mouse's reflection wriggled pitiably.

She slipped through into Wonderland, the now familiar rush of air in her ears tuning itself to her ragged breathing. She immediately looked down to see a perfectly whole and healthy mouse crawling up her shirt, sniffling whiskers tapping along as he went. Jenny let out a burst of relieved laughter that echoed strangely off the tintype walls of the Wonderland bathroom.

Calvin was standing near the bathroom door, not sure which direction she might come from, when Jenny came right back through the bathroom mirror. "Mighty Mouse lives!" she cheered, holding the mouse over her head. Calvin almost accidentally high-fived the hand with the mouse in it, but stopped himself awkwardly and smacked the wall instead.

"Yes!" said the gangly magician. "Now do me!"

Jenny took a deep breath. "Okay, we'll do it," she said. "I mean, you should be fine, right?"

Calvin nodded his head up and down so quickly his face was a blur wrapped in a pointy chin and a tangle of red hair. "Come on," he said. "There's no reason why it would hurt me."

"There's no *reason*," Jenny said pointedly, "that I should be able to walk through a mirror at all." She put the mouse back in the cage with his fellow Death Row inmates, and turned back to Calvin. "But yeah—let's do it." She smiled nervously at her partner in horse crime.

They went back to the bathroom, and Jenny took hold of Calvin's hand, their fingers interlocking. Calvin squeezed her hand and grinned at her in the mirror. Mirror Jenny was exasperatingly compliant with Jenny's every move, as usual, preventing even Calvin from seeing her abnormal behavior.

"Ready?" Jenny said.

"Let's go," Calvin said.

She pushed forward physically and mentally, and shifted through the explosion of red sound and loud dust to the pounding pressure of Wonderland. The grip on her hand didn't go away, and she realized she'd reflexively shut her eyes tight. Opening them up, she glanced tentatively up and saw Calvin standing beside her in full Technicolor glory, a stark contrast to the dull sepia of Wonderland.

"Yeah!" she shouted, her voice ringing dimly through the incessant roar of the mirror world.

"Jenny?" cried Calvin. He looked around wildly. "Jenny?"

His voice sounded panicked. "What's wrong?" Jenny asked him, grabbing his other hand and holding tight, reassuring him with her presence.

"I can't see," he said, his voice high and tight. "What's happening?"

"Shit," Jenny said. "Okay, wait. You can hear me?"

"Jenny?" he said. "I can't see!"

"Or hear," Jenny realized. She squeezed his hands tight, squeezing and unsqueezing to get his attention. Calvin squeezed back; he could feel her hands, and respond. "Okay," she said, even though she knew he couldn't hear her, "let's go back, come on!" She wrapped an arm around the magician's skinny waist.

Calvin put his hand on her shoulder and held tight. "I feel okay," he said in an oddly-pitched voice. "I just can't see anything. And there's this weird noise...."

Jenny patted his hand, hugged his waist, and pushed through the mirror. A snap, crackle and pop later, the lights flared white and the real bathroom locked in. Calvin staggered next to her. "Whoa!" he huffed, grabbing the counter for balance.

"You're okay," said Jenny, leaning in and rubbing his arms soothingly. "You're okay! Are you okay?"

"I think so." He focused on her face and grinned. "You keep telling me I am."

Jenny smacked his shoulder playfully. "Dummy," she teased. She looked over his shoulder at the mirror; Mirror Jenny looked over Mirror Calvin's shoulder at the real Calvin, shaking her head and letting out a voiceless sigh of relief. Jenny pulled back and looked him up and down. "You can see me?" she asked. Her concern was tangible.

Calvin felt it, and held her hand comfortingly. "I can see you," he said. "I can hear, too." He glanced over his shoulder at the mirror, where Mirror Jenny had carefully matched Jenny once again. "That was *weird*."

"I don't get it," said Jenny. "You couldn't see or hear anything? What did you see? I mean," she shrugged off her own stupid question, "what was it like—for you?"

"Not sure." He bit his lip thoughtfully and raised his eyebrows. His face was even paler than usual behind the army of strategically deployed freckles. "It was like everything just went blank. You know, like when you close your eyes and all you see are those specks and weird dots and stuff? And I couldn't hear anything—I mean, it was like...I don't know," he searched for a description, then perked up as he hit it. "Like when you play an old cassette tape that nobody recorded anything on."

"That kind of hissing, empty silence noise?" Jenny asked.

149

"Yeah." Calvin eased himself off the counter and held the back of his head like he'd just whanged it on the top of a doorframe, which wasn't a terribly unusual occurrence for him.

"Well, that answers that," Jenny said glumly, taking his arm and leading him back to the living room. Calvin sat down on the couch, still a little psychologically disheveled, and Colby the bunny hopped curiously over to check on him. He affectionately tickled her between the ears as she plopped her chin on his thigh.

The magician gazed up at the ceiling, calculating his abstract magician's voodoo in his head. "Well, it kind of does," he said slowly, "but there's one good thing there."

"What?"

"I'm alive." He smiled at her and gave a little shrug.

"Yeah," said Jenny, sitting crosslegged on the floor in front of him.

"No," said Calvin, leaning forward carefully to avoid jostling Colby. "I mean, I can survive in there. Yeah, I can't see or hear, I can't get around...but I *can* go in and come back. The mouse probably had the same problem I did, right?"

"Makes sense," Jenny agreed.

"So you can *bring* other people in there," Calvin continued, "but they can't really do anything without you."

Jenny picked at her sock aimlessly. "Yeah. So I guess we could use it in an emergency."

"What happens if you leave me there?" Calvin asked suddenly. "Like the spoon!"

"No," Jenny shook her head and emphatically crossed her wrists in a universal *No Entry* gesture. "No way. I'm *not* leaving you in there."

"But—"

"We can try it some other time," said Jenny. "But let's be done for now. Let's figure out how we're going to find Rex and break him out."

Calvin seemed about to push it, but surrendered when he saw how worried Jenny was. "Okay," he said. "But you know—it'd be really cool if you could make me disappear in the act!"

Jenny rolled her eyes at his giant grin. "At least you're staying focused, huh?" But she smiled back.

They discussed how to track Rex down, and the best course of action once they found him. A lot of their strategy depended on where the horse actually was. The cops had taken him into custody at Heckler's, so the nearest precinct should have some information on the horse. Jenny hated to admit it, but a plan had started to formulate in her mind—and it involved getting Keith Heckler to help out.

CHAPTER FOURTEEN

Calvin McGuirk pulled at a necktie that was too short for his towering frame and leaned over. "I hope this works," he muttered.

"Just keep them distracted, Mister Misdirection," Jenny Ng whispered back, pulling her borrowed baseball cap over her eyes and snapping a few more pictures with her awesome new camera. She'd grabbed it before they left his apartment.

"So is this, like, a regular thing with you guys?" asked Keith Heckler.

Calvin's eyes slowly smoldered at Heckler. He was aware of Jenny's tangled history with the slacker playboy—even if he didn't know all the details—and he didn't approve. It just wasn't his place to say so.

"I mean, I'm all for Stickin' It to the Man," Heckler continued, "but carjacking a horse?"

"How is it 'carjacking' if it's a horse?" Jenny said glibly.

Heckler grinned. "My people were in carjacking way before there were cars, Jenning."

"I hope this works," Calvin muttered again.

"I still don't know what 'this' is," said Heckler.

"Would both of you shut up?" said Jenny.

"Quiet back there, please!" called the tour guide.

The small group of tourists glanced back at Jenny and her friends with the stern reproach that the American white middle class reserves especially for irritatingly law-abiding riff raff. The riff raff smiled and lowered their heads contritely.

The tour guide continued his prepared speech, guiding them through the exhibits in the old administration building at Floyd Bennett Field. This was not where Jenny had expected to end up by lunch time, but Rex's twisty trail had led them here.

Heckler had been unfortunately instrumental to the plan, not just because he had a car, but also because he had access to student ID cards. More accurately, he had access to co-eds, who had student ID cards, but the result was the same. Calvin and Jenny had worked up their nerve and marched into the police station around the corner from Heckler's apartment, where she'd slapped down an NYU student card identifying her as Elizabeth Park. She was reasonably sure that the desk sergeant wouldn't be able to tell the difference between a Korean girl with long black hair and a Chinese girl with a baseball cap on, and that particular gamble paid off. He listened to their story with a big, patronizing smile on his pleasantly round face.

"You know, that horse who was picked up a couple months ago?" Jenny had prompted.

Yes, he remembered the incident.

"We're doing an article on weird police cases," Jenny had lied, holding up her camera. Calvin backed her up—he was the Woodward to her Bernstein, looking quite uncomfortable in a necktie that barely extended below his chest. "And how you guys handle them," Jenny added. Her sweet smile indicated that she thought the cops handled their weird cases quite well, even heroically. The desk sergeant was won over more with flattery than with subterfuge.

As it turned out, Rex had been transported to a horseback riding place down by Jamaica Bay, which promised to babysit him (in exchange for a decent sum of taxpayer money) while the police worked out his status. Unfortunately, the giant stallion proved to be a little too much for old farmhands, college interns, and teenaged volunteers with braces, pastel-colored shirts, and an overabundance of equestrian daydreams. After less than a day (and three escape attempts), the police took matters into their own hands. They shipped the horse right down the Shore Parkway to Floyd Bennett, home to the NYPD's own fleet of helicopters, where special arrangements were made to keep him in an abandoned hangar large enough to afford him some exercise and strong enough to keep him locked in. He'd been there ever since; he was slated to be destroyed by the end of September unless someone could legitimately claim him.

"That would suck," Calvin had lamented on their way out of the precinct.

"Yeah, because they wouldn't be *able* to destroy him," Jenny had pointed out. "They'd learn a lot more about him when they tried. So we've got to get him out of there."

Calvin understood Jenny's emotional connection to the captive horse, and the importance that the horse played in the plan to save the juggling college kid later that night. That understanding held a jumpy Mexican Stand-Off with the creeping realization that he was about to steal something from the NYPD. Diving head first into another dimension where he couldn't see or hear didn't seem to give him pause, but committing a crime raised the hairs on the back of his neck. He was running on adrenalin and stark fear, trying to keep his mind off what he was doing.

Heckler didn't seem too bothered, though it seemed likely that Heckler had hunted down and killed his conscience in some tribal rite of passage when he'd smoked his first cigarette at thirteen. If any moral core remained, it was huddled in a dark corner of the attic in his mind, running a near-toothless comb through tangled thinning hair, rocking back and forth and mumbling eerie sing-song lyrics to forgotten nursery rhymes. That thought alone made Heckler's perpetually cheerful grin seem downright petrifying.

They hadn't given him all the details, but they did tell him about the horse. He was already familiar with that part of the story, and filling him in on that end seemed like the right thing to do, in case they needed his help handling Rex once they got him out of here. Jenny had never shared with Heckler most of the strange happenings of the past couple of months. He only knew some weird shit was going down; he'd seen Rex and the sword, of course, and he'd come to watch the magic act at the end of July, after which he'd smiled at Jenny with a funny expression, like he was trying to peer into her brain and figure out how the tricks worked and where she'd learned them. "Hey, are there any other parts you can chop off?" he'd asked her. "'Cause there are a couple I'd wanna borrow, if you're not using them right now."

Calvin, overhearing Heckler's joke, got off on entirely the wrong foot with him.

Trailing along behind the bulk of the tour group, Jenny looked around, making a mental note of every reflective surface she could see. Mirror Jenny checked in occasionally, a quirky smile on her face as if she was waiting to see how this turned out. Jenny wondered if there were tricks and tips that people like Redbeard—and, presumably, the Coney Island Count—used to manage these things a bit more efficiently. Maybe Caravel, whoever she was, would give her a few pointers tonight, if Jenny reached Central Park with Rex and the sword.

Calvin and Heckler covered for her, acting interested and asking questions to keep the tour guide happy. Calvin wasn't a big fan of Heckler's, but he knew they needed his help, or at least they needed his car to get here and back in a reasonable timeframe. He feigned a cordiality and comradeship that, simply by virtue of his general gregariousness, became more genuine as they went. Heckler was, if not a friend, at least on the same team—the Free Rex team—and Calvin had trouble being overtly mean to anybody in the long term.

There were plenty of holes in the plan—Jenny carefully avoided counting them—but she was relying on her powers, Calvin's talent, and Heckler's patented Balls of Steel to leap those chasms when they came to them. If she wanted to meet Caravel and join the "club" in time to save John, then this was by necessity a rush job. In the movies, smooth-talking pretty boys pulled clever heists like this in less than two hours. All Jenny lacked was liberal editing and an off-screen mastermind to keep the authorities from getting wise.

She figured she was screwed. But at this point, it was an all or nothing deal.

Finally, Jenny saw her opening: the group was following the tour guide around a large display case with model planes almost large enough for a human pilot, and at the tail end of the group, Jenny would be out of the backwards-walking guide's sight for at least a moment. She grabbed Calvin's hand and squeezed. "Okay, I'm going," she whispered. "Keep your phone on vibrate." To Heckler, she said: "Be good." He winked and turned to follow the tour group.

Jenny pulled her hand from Calvin's and sprinted four steps to the shiny window of a small office adjoining the larger hall. The room behind it was dark enough that she could see Mirror Jenny overdramatically scrambling to meet her there. They placed their palms against each other's at the surface of the window, and Jenny focused, still not sure what conscious effort was required to get her to Wonderland, but confident after so much practice that it would just *happen*.

A whirlwind of brown dust and blobs of light later, the familiar roar pounded in her ears, and the hall was replaced by its dull sepia Looking Glass copy. Mirror Jenny had disappeared from the reflection in the window, though she saw Calvin and Heckler rounding the corner of the display case. In Wonderland, the model plane counterparts behaved just like the cars and trucks on Franklin Street—not quite all there, but somehow still present.

Remembering her confusion the night before, Jenny paused to reorient herself to the mirrored compass of Wonderland. Doing it over and over in Calvin's apartment had been easy; it was simply a matter of memorizing two "different" apartment layouts. In this unfamiliar setting, it took her a moment longer, but she got her bearings. She aimed for an emergency exit which she figured should open up to the parking lot sprawled beside the airfield. The *EXIT* sign was written backwards and lit with a dim tan glow. Jenny pushed through the indefinite scenery like a mime walking in the wind, only with less pathos, and looked at the door.

She suddenly realized she wasn't sure if she could open it. She hadn't tried that at Calvin's apartment.

If Wonderland was merely a reflection of the real world, then how could she open a door here that was shut on the other side? Would it stay shut, emulating its real world double? Would the door in the real world mysteriously swing open when she pushed through this one? Worse— would the emergency alarm sound off, if it did?

Her practice traveling through Wonderland didn't offer any answers, but she had to risk it. She winced and tentatively pushed the bar on the door.

Like the vaguely filled-in cars and trucks and planes, the door became strangely unfocused, there-and-not-there. Her eyes gave her entirely conflicting information: a stilted, half-filled-in image of the door still closed, and a near-identical image of the door wide open. It was like looking at the world through Schrödinger-colored glasses, seeing all possibilities at once, a cat simultaneously dead and alive.

Jenny didn't stop to write a dissertation; she took advantage of the phenomenon and slipped outside, heading for the mirror image of the parking lot.

The sky above her was like a photo negative, black clouds on a brilliant clay-colored expanse; the clouds suffered from even worse There-And-Not-There syndrome than the emergency door or even the vehicles she'd seen. Haphazard, unfocused shading and sketchy outlines scattered from horizon to horizon, making it completely uncertain where any clouds actually were, or where there was genuinely clear sky. The dizzying effect gave her upside-down vertigo just looking at it, so Jenny kept her eyes on the ground ahead of her.

She hurried by the parking lot, moving with the worrisome easiness one feels in a dream—the slightest intention sent her hurtling forward in a blur, or maybe it sent the world hurtling backward in an amateur illustration of relativity. Either way, Jenny soon found herself stepping lightly on blurry burnt-umber grass beneath her feet. The grass crunched with the same distant echo her footsteps had produced the night before, the same hollow reverb her voice threw in the Looking Glass version of Calvin's bathroom. The intangible wind pushed hard on her eardrums.

They had scoped out the place when they'd arrived, and Calvin and Jenny had done some research on his laptop computer earlier, taking advantage of the WiFi that came free with their purchase of one coffee, a fruit smoothie, and a couple of sticky square cakes at a megacorporate coffee franchise. South of the administration building stood the majority of the original Floyd Bennett hangars, the ones that hadn't been turned into tourist traps or sports venues. The airport was once pushed as the primary travel hub for the five boroughs, but LaGuardia soon beat it for convenience, and Floyd Bennett Field served various other purposes—including military—before being handed over to the National Parks Service. While campgrounds had been set up in the woods at the corners of the airfield, and a crew of die-hard aviation buffs had taken over the big hangar across the field for the restoration of historic aircraft, these smaller hangars had been left for dead, and quickly accomplished that mission. Overgrown with weeds and cracked pavement, the structures sagged with age and missing windows, like a broken old man with a depressingly toothless smile on the front porch of an Appalachian shack. One of these disused buildings had to be the hangar that the desk sergeant referred to—the one that housed Rex.

Off to the east—disconcertingly to the right as she made her way south through the mirror world of Wonderland—lay row upon row of partitioned lots, the community garden tended by locals with green thumbs, green intentions, or Greenpeace aspirations. Distorted crops of various simultaneous sizes shifted jerkily in the dreamlike wind like a time lapse nature documentary edited all out of order.

The first hangar building looked pretty bad; Jenny walked past it, and the second one looked even worse. She went back around the first; on the broad walls above the hangar doors, she made out faint writing, which was even harder to read in mirror image. Squinting, she worked out that the one on the left was Hangar Four, and the one on the right, closer to the runways, was Hangar Three. The two were connected by a central structure of brick—a normal-sized door led inside. Jenny pushed the door into a weird ambiguous state between open and closed and walked inside.

She wasn't sure what the real world hangar looked like yet, but the mirror world version was a shock of disjointed shapes and lines, blurred vegetation overgrowing the sensible boundaries between man and nature, and sections of roof smeared out of existence to expose failing support beams like broken ribs. She walked through a crumbled section of wall and knelt down beside a cracked pane of glass leaning against a pile of debris.

A very large horse stared back at her through the reflection.

"Rex!" Jenny shouted, though she barely heard herself under the thumping rush of Wonderland's weird air pressure.

The stallion definitely saw her in the glass—he stared straight at her. He tossed his head and sniffed inaudibly, a subtle but firm: *It's about time.*

Jenny reached out to press her palms to the glass, but paused. She moved left and right, up and down, aiming for different angles to look around the horse in the real world and see if he was alone. During practice, Calvin had pointed out that she should take advantage of looking back into the real world through the mirrors in Wonderland. Seeing nobody in the hangar with Rex, she went for it—she pushed through the glass and whatever dimension it was that she used to switch worlds, felt her heart in her mouth and her kidneys in her toes for a brief squirming moment, and found herself back in the real world with an inaudible but shockingly visible *pop*. The real hangar didn't look much better than the Wonderland version; it was a bit less jittery, but still covered with trash and fallen roofing and plants that had settled in more firmly than an unemployed roommate on your couch.

She rushed to the horse and put her arms around his neck. "I'm sorry," she said softly. "I should've...you know."

He nibbled on her hair and nuzzled her shoulder. His big black eyes placidly suggested: *Whatever. Are we going now?*

Jenny put a hand on his nose and a finger to her lips. "Let me check outside," she told him. She crept to the door and peeked through a broken slat. Sitting on a folding lawn chair just outside of the hangar was a uniformed cop. He had a magazine and a soda, and he yawned as he thumbed through an article on the latest advancements in golf shoe technology.

"*Diu*," Jenny swore. She looked back at Rex.

He scraped the garbage at his feet with one hoof like Clever Hans counting apples. Jenny followed his gaze down to the tilted pane of glass. She furrowed her brow and asked him out loud, but quietly: "I can get you in there with me, right? I mean, you're not too big or something?"

The horse gave her an old familiar look: *Duh*. It was comforting that some things hadn't changed. Of course she could bring the horse with her, Jenny realized—Redbeard was riding his own horse through Wonderland last night. It was obvious in hindsight.

Apparently, nobody had been brave enough to remove Rex's saddle, and the simple leather reins were still secured to the giant horse's snout. Jenny had ridden on horseback only twice in her life. Despite Philadelphia's honored place in the history of the American Revolution, Midnight Rides were a thing of the distant past and whimsical poetry, no matter how many lights were burning in a church almost three hundred miles away from the City of Brotherly Love. Jenny hadn't had a lot of opportunities for random equestrian excursions, and was never really interested anyway. The first time she'd been on a horse was at her friend Melanie's tenth birthday party—Melanie had filled the role in Jenny's fourth grade class of the quiet girl who did her homework reliably enough that she could spend most of her time daydreaming in the back row and drawing horses. All of the kids had been forced to wear ugly black helmets, and Jenny found it hard to feel the Thrill of Adventure with a chinstrap on. In college, she went with a group of friends to a ranch not far from school, where they were very slowly led on a circuitous trail through some wooded hills. The horses, as bored with the walking tour as their passengers, wearily trudged the path, each following the one before it without giving a damn about the scenery or the gaping monkeys jabbering on their backs.

Jenny knew she wasn't exactly the Lone Ranger. She wasn't even Eddie Arcaro. She didn't know the first thing about real horseback riding. She fingered Rex's reins tentatively.

The horse leaned down to meet her eye to eye. *Trust me*, he was clearly saying.

Jenny gritted her teeth and reached up around his neck.

Rex jerked his head up so suddenly that she had no choice but to hang on—she swung up and over, clinging to the stallion for dear life, both legs unfortunately on the same side of the horse. Rex waited a moment as she threw one leg over the saddle, situating herself slightly more comfortably on his back. She had seen enough popular movies to remember the stirrups, and quickly jammed her toes through as Rex sidestepped across the hangar to stand in front of the pane of glass. Jenny's knuckles were pale white, gripping the reins and the front of the saddle like she was hanging off the edge of a tall building.

She looked nervously down at the reflective glass. Her own terrified face stared back at her. Then Mirror Jenny stuck her tongue out and crossed her eyes. "Wait," she said softly, "I'm not sure how I...I mean, if I can't touch the glass...I can't reach it...how do I...?"

Rex turned his head just enough to glance back at her with one eye. If he'd been human, he would have flashed her the rakish smile of a scoundrel with a heart of gold. He winked, or maybe blinked—she couldn't see his other eye, so she wasn't sure—and then bucked forward with a triumphant whinny, galloping straight through the pane of glass.

The pane of glass shattered, and Rex skidded to a stop through weeds and trash.

"Quiet down in there!" came the cop's voice from outside. "Stupid horse," he nattered on to himself, magazine pages flipping audibly. "Stupid captain. Stupid...huh. With a lob wedge? No way! Never would've thought..."

Shards and slivers of broken glass tinkled to their final resting places. There were tiny cuts on Jenny's shins and the horse's legs and neck, but they instantly healed up and faded away. Rex looked sharply back at her and growled an indignant *chuff.* Jenny gibbered apologetically. "I don't know!" she protested, keeping her voice to a whisper. "How does it work? Do I do it, or do you do something, or what? Do we do it together?"

The horse looked skyward. Apparently, no matter what your species, the deities who helped you cope with stupidity lived above the clouds.

"I'm new at this, okay?" said Jenny.

He puffed a little sigh and turned around, scanning the room. At the far end was a torn sheet of metal with one twisted corner, leaning against the wall. It was reflective, to a point, but the brushed metal surface distorted and blurred the reflection.

"Uh," said Jenny uncertainly.

Rex gestured with his nose. In the streaked reflection on the metal, a striated Mirror Jenny on a big blurry horse gave her a jaunty little salute to reassure her.

"If you say so," said Jenny. "But I still don't know what I'm supposed to do."

Outside, the *skutch* of the lawn chair on concrete sounded off. The cop called out: "Hey!"

Jenny froze, and Rex cocked one brow.

"Afternoon, officer," said another deep voice outside.

"That the horse feed?" asked the cop.

"Yeah, just gotta get it inside."

"Okay," the cop said. "You been here before? You know the drill?"

"Uh huh," said the other guy.

The cop's footsteps approached the central door between the two adjoining hangars. "Okay, let me get him closed off so you can get in there," he said.

Rex looked back at Jenny. Jenny echoed the horse's assessment: "Shit." She took a deep breath. "Okay," she told him. "I guess it's now or never." She focused all of her energy on the sheet metal across the room. A grayed-out, distorted Mirror Jenny applauded silently and pumped her fist in encouragement.

Rex huffed and growled, lowering his head and pawing the ground with one enormous hoof. With a powerful kick, he launched himself forward and raced for the surface of the sheet metal as the outside door rattled.

A tremendous *clang!* rang out in the hangar as Rex bore straight through the sheet metal and rebounded off the wall, knocking himself for a loop. His legs buckled and wobbled, but he stayed upright, if just barely. Jenny was flung forward and to the side, finding herself dangling from Rex's neck with one foot propped on his shoulder and the other tangled in a stirrup. Her baseball cap fell to the floor next to the crunched sheet of metal.

"The *hell*—" said the cop outside the door. "Chill out, you stupid horse! Wait, I've gotta pull the door, one sec..."

Jenny twisted around to look past Rex's throat at a huge sliding door along the wall adjoining the center room of the building. It was huge, made of oak, and much newer than the rest of the hangar. A cable was hooked to the top of the door, stretching across the wide doorway through a series of metal rings fastened to the framework, snaking a trail toward the front of the hangar where it exited the building through a hole in the wall. On the floor just through the doorway was a wide trough of water and the remnants of a pile of hay.

Jenny saw the slack on the cable tightening up—the cop was using the cable to pull the door shut, so the horse guy could enter to refill the trough without having to worry about Rex. The cable pulled taut and the door began sliding across the archway. "Oh, no," she whispered. "Go!"

Rex shook himself lucid and gave her an unmistakable look: *Hang on.* Jenny hugged herself tight to his neck and jammed her foot more deeply into the tangled stirrup. With barely a pause to make sure she was set, Rex leapt through the rapidly closing doorway like Indiana Jones, knocking into the trough and sending it hurtling end over end. Jenny's bones rattled, but Rex didn't slow down—he skidded down the short hall and threw his shoulder into the front door at full gallop.

The door burst apart, flying from its hinges as the cop and a tall guy in overalls dropped to the blacktop and covered their heads. Jenny hung tight to Rex's side as bits of shattered wood rained down on her, pelting her head and shoulder. She shrugged them off—if severed limbs couldn't take her down, she wasn't going to fret over mere bruises or conscussions.

Rex burned the horsey equivalent of rubber and zoomed past the administration building in seconds, headed for the airfield criss-crossed with defunct runways. Jenny felt like she was on a terribly unsafe rollercoaster, the thrilling rush of speed combining with the stark terror of knowing she wasn't at all strapped in. She turned her head and found herself looking down at grass skimming dizzyingly by beneath her; the speed was overwhelming, and she quickly turned away to look up at the sky, which proved difficult through eyes shut tight with abject fear.

In less time than it would've taken to pee her pants—a thought that crossed her mind more than once—shadows flitted across her face, and she opened her eyes. Rex slowed down, picking his way through trees in a fairly dense wooded area. As he hopped and jumped over roots and shrubs, Jenny was jerked this way and that, dangling from his side.

"Okay!" she said. "That's cool! We escaped!" The horse swung around another stand of trees. "Hold up!" Jenny insisted. "*Whoa!*"

Rex stopped short, leaving Jenny swaying slightly on the tangled stirrup. He curled around to look directly at her.

"Yeah," she said. "I don't know how to ride a horse, okay? Gimme a second," she grumbled, extracting herself from the muddled twist of the stirrup. She tried to keep her arms on the horse's neck, but as her foot came free she collapsed to the ground, banging her hip on a distended tree root. "Ow," she said, but without much passion for it—exclamations of pain from an indestructible girl seemed petty.

Her cell phone buzzed in her shoulder bag.

She was relieved she'd zipped it up so nothing had fallen out during the bumpy ride across the airfield. She pulled her bag around to the front, unzipped it and fished inside for her phone, which was now playing a chirpy little tune some Swiss sound engineer thought was groovy enough to inflict on the world. Jenny flipped it open. "Hey," she said.

"Holy cow!" Calvin exclaimed in an excited whisper. "What was *that?*"

Jenny rubbed her hip; it already wasn't sore, but the habit felt natural as she stretched her legs. "What? What are you talking about?"

She heard Heckler's voice in the background, but couldn't make out what he said. "I don't know, hold on," Calvin said away from the phone. "Jenny! The whole place is going crazy. People saw you running away, everybody was taking pictures through the window, it's a big thing!"

"Crap," said Jenny, panicking. "They got pictures?"

"I don't think anybody really saw you," said Calvin. "Just the horse. It looked like you were hanging onto his side, away from the building." Heckler chimed in, and Calvin shushed him away. "Heckler says 'Nice riding.'"

"Yeah, thanks," said Jenny. "Where the hell am I?"

"What do you see?"

"Trees."

"You're probably in the woods at the north end of the airport," said Calvin. "You know, up near the bridge back to the horse place." They'd scoped the map out online.

"Right," said Jenny. "Okay, listen—can you guys get out of there? I mean, without anybody checking you out?"

"I think so, yeah. The tour's kinda broken up, everybody's doing their own thing. I don't know where the guide went."

"Okay," Jenny traced a trail in her mind. "Get back to the car and start driving back up Flatbush. I can meet you guys in the woods, right after...well, right *before* the Toys R Us."

"Woods before the toy store, check," Calvin said.

"Call me when you get there," said Jenny, "we'll find each other."

"Got it." She could practically hear his grin through the phone. "Good luck!"

"Hope so, bye." Jenny flipped the phone shut and shoved it in her bag. Recalling the rough ride so far, she zipped up the bag again, too. She hoped her phone and her new camera would play nicely, and not end up smashing each other to bits.

Rex waited for her attention. She looked up and shook her head guiltily. "Sorry," she said. "I just didn't know how to get through. Usually I touch the mirror or whatever." This was true, although "usually" amounted to the dozen times she'd tried it so far, including her first foray into Wonderland. If there was some way to go Through the Looking Glass without touching it, Jenny hadn't yet figured it out.

The horse's aloof posture softened, and he *whuffed* quietly, stepping toward her and nuzzling her hair.

"Thanks," said Jenny. She rubbed his muzzle warmly. "Come on, let's get going. Gimme a hand—well, some help, would you?"

Like a circus show horse, Rex knelt down on his front legs, his rump sticking up in back. Jenny still needed to jump to get a leg over the huge horse's back, but she settled into the saddle and got her feet in the stirrups as he straightened up. She grabbed hold of the reins and patted his side lightly; realizing he probably couldn't sense that at all through the thick cords of muscle beneath his sweat-slicked skin, she slapped down harder, giving him enough rough affection that he might actually feel it. He tossed his head and peered back at her with a friendly look. "Okay," she told him. "Let's go—but take it easy!"

His hindquarters twitched, and he bopped off through the woods, weaving through the trees and jumping bushes and roots. Jenny's butt bumped up and down on the saddle; she instantly flashed on a firm though medically inaccurate understanding of the phrase "saddle sore." The woods ended at a wide runway stretching from Flatbush Avenue toward Jamaica Bay. Sirens sounded in the distance to her left, and Jenny felt nervous about crossing right out in the open; still, if they were going to meet Calvin and Heckler, they had to keep going. Rex's hooves *clopped* solidly on the tarmac, Jenny cringing at every thunderously loud step. There were several cars parked by a small clearing before the woods on the opposite side of the runway. She didn't see any people, but hunched her shoulders instinctively anyway, as if that would somehow disguise the fact that she was riding a giant, pale yellow horse across a runway in south Brooklyn. "Uh," she said, trying to be more equestrian about this, but worried that yanking the reins on an intelligent horse might be condescending. She pulled just slightly, and Rex obediently headed for the clearing, trotting between a red Honda and a gray mini-van. Jenny started to feel more comfortable giving him direction, and sat a bit straighter in the saddle.

They tripped lightly off the runway, and the muted sound of Rex's hooves on the grass and dirt relieved Jenny's paranoia. Several paths led from the clearing into the woods; unpaved but smooth, they bore the tell-tale signs of bike treads. Jenny knew she eventually wanted to head west, so she picked the left-most path and aimed Rex that way. Self-doubt made her falter for a moment, but she realized she was just reorienting herself back from Wonderland to the real world. Maybe Rex was used to that in his riders; he ignored her minor twitch on the reins and loped up the path without hesitation.

The stallion picked up speed, and they cantered through what could have been a lovely summer day in the woods if it weren't for the grand theft horse charges looming on the horizon. Jenny knew she couldn't really hear sirens anymore, but they still bellowed in her head, overpowering the light and breezy chittering of birds and bugs and scurrying woodland creatures. They reached a fork in the winding trail, and another, and turned left both times. Jenny heard traffic noises nearby. The trees were less dense here, no longer crowding around the path like so many deciduous bullies on the first day of school sniffing out the shrubs who will readily hand over their milk sap money, but more distant gangs of aspen and birch blocked any view of roads. The ground looked soft and spongy, even wet in some spots.

"I think we're looking straight at Flatbush," she told Rex, as if the street name would mean anything to him. "But we shouldn't be too far from the parkway." She pulled the reins to the right. Rex left the comfort of the smooth bike trail and struck out across muddy grass and rocks. His hooves *squelched* unhappily with every step; he had to work a little harder, but he kept up a decent pace.

Jenny felt something on her thigh and jumped. Rex halted and looked back at her: *Do you mind?* She gave him a weak apologetic smile and fished in her bag for her vibrating phone. She flipped it open and read a text message from Calvin: "Where?"

She tapped in a response: "Not sure yet. 1 min."

The sound of cars was louder now. Through the trees ahead, Jenny could see flashes of motion and a bright strip of highway. Across the Shore Parkway were trees, marshland and eventually the giant toy store right next to the marina. Jenny only remembered this from the map and the drive down—she couldn't see it through the thick leaves and branches. What she *could* see, as they drew closer, was the highway...with cars zooming by in both directions.

"Shit," she muttered, pulling gently on the reins. Rex slowed down and stopped on a dry patch of grass. He nipped at the blades like he was just stopping for a quick bite anyway.

Past the trees were a paved bike path, an entry ramp, three lines of highway in each direction and an exit ramp before the dark safety of the woods on the other side. There was no way they could get cross without being seen, if they could get across at all. Jenny worried less about reaching the other side in one piece than about damaging cars as they went—Rex was indestructible and likely outweighed some of the smaller cars on the road. The chance of causing a major pile-up was lurking in Jenny's mind like a smirking serial killer on a foggy Victorian street corner. Forget being seen; they'd be lucky if they didn't end up on the six o'clock news.

To the left, through more woods, was Flatbush Avenue: most likely the direct route the cops were swarming down to the scene of the horsenapping, but also the only place she could meet the car without crossing any roads. She grabbed her phone and speed-dialed Calvin.

"Hi!" said Calvin. His phone voice was buffeted by the wind of an open window.

"Change of plans," said Jenny.

"What?"

"Can you guys stop just *before* the highway? Find a spot where you can pull off onto the grass or something?"

"Uh," said Calvin. He muffled the phone; Jenny heard a muted conversation with Heckler. "Yeah, wait," he returned, "you mean coming from the airport?"

"Yeah."

"Hold on, yeah," Calvin said quickly, and he shared another exchange with Heckler. Heckler shouted something—Jenny couldn't tell if he was happy or angry—and Calvin came back to the phone. "We need to turn around. We'll be there in five minutes."

"Okay," said Jenny. "Hurry!" She tried to keep from sounding too anxious, but she was starting to realize that this hadn't been the smartest plan, even if anything had actually gone according to it. She'd been flying blind since she found Rex. Jenny put her phone back and zipped the bag up. "Come on, big guy," she said, patting the horse's flank hard enough for him to get something out of it. She turned him around, parallelling the highway ramp back toward Flatbush.

The boys made it in less than four minutes—Jenny hoped Heckler wasn't speeding, with all the cops heading down to the airport. She hadn't heard any more sirens, but she was sure she saw some black-and-whites cruise by while she and Rex hid in the trees near the bike path.

Heckler veered off Flatbush to the ramp for the parkway, then pulled off the ramp, crossed the grass, and parked on the bike path, completely illegally. Jenny trotted Rex to the edge of the woods, closer to the scrappy gold-colored Toyota. "Heckler!" she whispered harshly, feeling the need for stealth even though the passing cars couldn't possibly hear her. Her phone buzzed, and she answered it just as it started chirping.

"Hey—"

"I'm right behind you guys," Jenny interrupted. "Can Heckler back up to the trees?"

"One sec," said Calvin.

The doors opened on both sides of the car, and Calvin and Heckler raced over to the trees.

"Holy shit!" said Heckler.

"Wow!" Calvin agreed.

"I don't think this guy's gonna fit in the car, Jenning," Heckler said, his eyes popping at the size of the horse.

"Funny," said Jenny. "Listen, I just need you to back the car up to here. I don't want anybody to see...um...."

"Right," Calvin swept in with the assist. "Heckler, back her up."

Heckler's eyes ran down the horse to trashcan-lid-sized hooves, then back up. "He's bigger than I remember."

"You were one floor up last time," said Jenny. "Don't worry, I'm not going to hurt your car, I promise. Just back up to the woods. Calvin...."

Jenny reached out for Calvin's hand; he helped her jump off the horse as Heckler got back in the car and repositioned it across the bike path, the back toward the trees. He backed up until he'd completely blocked the paved path.

It only stood to reason that a cyclist came around the bend right then and there.

Heckler froze halfway out of the car; Calvin looked like he'd just been caught rummaging in his sister's underwear drawer.

Jenny gulped, then waved. "Hi," she said. "Sorry about the car—we're just doing a photo shoot." She showed off the camera suddenly in her other hand and snapped a picture of Calvin and the car convincingly. Rex retreated furtively into the woods, hidden in leaves and shadows.

The cyclist just shook his scruffy head; he took the long route around the front of the car and continued down the path.

"That was close," Calvin said. He smiled at Jenny. "Quick thinking!"

"Just make sure you get my good sides," said Heckler.

"Get back here and help us," Jenny said.

"Hey, you may've just pulled off a pretty cool horse heist," Heckler said, "but you're still not getting that thing in my car."

"She doesn't need to," Calvin grinned broadly. "You can do this, right?"

"I think so," said Jenny. She slapped her thigh like she was summoning a puppy, then felt stupid for treating the Wonder Horse like that. "Rex, come on."

The horse poked his way through the trees and looked at her skeptically.

"It'll work if we do it my way, okay?" Jenny said. She reached out a hand; Rex snorted, but moved closer so she could grab his reins and guide him to Heckler's sideview mirror.

"Wait, the horse can drive?" asked Heckler. He shrugged. "Huh. Shotgun!"

"Shh," said Calvin. "Jenny, go ahead. I'll fill him in on the way back."

"I've got to get to Central Park," said Jenny. "You guys meet me there. Like, around Belvedere Castle or something."

"I'll bring the elves, m'lady," said Heckler.

"Yeah, well," Jenny smiled slyly, wishing she could see his face in five seconds. "Hold the wizards. We don't need 'em."

One arm on the horse's neck, Jenny leaned in toward the Toyota's sideview mirror. She and Mirror Jenny nodded at each other, and she put her hand on the mirror, pushing through and yanking Rex with her into Wonderland. The burst of bloody light and deafening sound seemed heavier than before, as if Rex's extra weight made a bigger splash in the mirror. Jenny stumbled slightly on re-entry; Rex's tree-trunk legs stood solid and firm on the starkly orange grass. She could almost see a superior little smirk playing about his lips.

"Whatever," she scolded him gently. "I got us in, didn't I?"

Rex whiffled softly.

"Well, I'll learn how to do it your way later." She moved to his flank. "Let's just get to the park, okay?" The giant stallion knelt down again; she found it easier to climb up this time, though she wasn't sure if that was due to experience or the oddly buoyant sensation she felt when she jumped from the ground here in Wonderland.

She wasn't surprised to notice that Heckler's car had no counterpart here beside the Looking Glass version of Flatbush Avenue. There was the barest hint of some kind of sketchiness, like the cars on Franklin Street last night, or the airplane models back at the Floyd Bennett administration building; but it was only *just* there, out of the corner of her eye, and when she tried to look, there was nothing but the blurry wind of Wonderland and the smear of a million blades of grass that individually added up to nonexistent, but gave a good impression of grass when taken all together. Jenny still wasn't sure how the world behind the mirror worked, but she'd at least figured out that some things in the real world just didn't leave any kind of impression here.

Neither do people, she thought to herself. The only people she'd ever seen in Wonderland were the ones who'd come through from the real world—Redbeard, who'd come in just like she had, and Calvin, who she'd brought with her through his bathroom mirror. If Wonderland was populated at all, it wasn't by mirror images. Of course, that made her wonder where Mirror Jenny went when Jenny invaded her world, and that cascaded into a mind-screw of elephantine proportions, and she already had enough weighing on her mind, so she cut that train short, ignored the mirrored elephant in the room, and clicked her tongue softly at Rex. The noise echoed like dripping water in a slasher flick, but was drowned out by the crashing railroad sound of Rex's galloping hooves.

One advantage of the lack of cars and people in Wonderland was clear: no traffic. Rex shot up Mirror Flatbush like he was plummeting downward along the face of a cliff. The weird, shifting, hurtling vertigo Jenny had felt before was back in full force, as the scenery seemed to burst past her in fits and starts. In mere minutes, they'd covered half of Brooklyn, and Rex was bounding across the reflection of Long Meadow—where they'd first met—taking a shortcut to avoid the kinks in Flatbush Avenue. A minute later, they galloped across the Manhattan Bridge, which took only seconds to cross. The murky water below sparkled with dazzling flashes of reflected light, and she could see the heavy traffic on the Brooklyn Bridge to her right—not on the Wonderland version of the bridge, which was empty, but in the watery reflection below it, her window on the real world. Jenny smiled and hugged Rex's powerful shoulders; Wonderland Transit was evidently the fastest way to travel in New York City, like a subway that always ran express and never let other passengers on, and she had an unlimited Metro Card.

Rex barrelled off the bridge and careened through the archway at Canal Street. He veered left and flew through Chinatown and the Bowery without missing a beat; in moments, he was in and out of Union Square Park and racing up Broadway on a whirlwind tour of New York City's beige and eerily empty twin. The Mirror Empire State Building towered over the flashing scenery on her left, and seconds later, Rex made a slight left at Seventh Avenue to gallop straight up to the park. In no time at all they were enveloped in the crisp clay and maroon reflections of hazily illustrated leaves, a welcome change from the baffling salmon-colored sky slashed with pink and gray and black.

The horse stuck to the path at first, but there was no need—no Looking Glass Cops were likely to show up and raise a fuss if they cut across the grass. Solid trunks and sketchy leaves flashing past them, Jenny and Rex raced through the trees, sped over the big rocks and across the baseball fields, dashed through Sheep Meadow, and leapt back onto a path to cross the bridge over the Lake. After a quick jaunt through the Ramble and more trees that looked like Vincent Van Gogh had painted them on a less lucid day, the horse made a giant leap across the entire width of the Seventy-Ninth Street Transverse. He honed in on Turtle Pond, skidding to a fantastic mud-flinging, rock-hurling stop between the pond and Belvedere Castle.

Jenny noticed that the rocks and mud weren't entirely there as they flew through the air, giving more of a mere "vibe" of wild movement and chaos rather than a solid visual.

She looked up at Belvedere Castle, the mini-golf course of fortresses, which actually looked more ominous and authentic on this side of the mirror than it did in the real world. Jenny rubbed Rex's neck vigorously; it suddenly occurred to her that she'd barely directed him, and didn't know if he really understood enough English to register it when she'd mentioned their destination to Calvin and Heckler. Somehow the horse just knew her goal, and headed there as fast as he could. If they were both impervious to harm and able to travel through another dimension, she decided that horse telepathy or whatever wasn't that much of a stretch. She smiled and put her face in his shaggy blond mane. He pushed back affectionately.

"Okay," Jenny said, "let me try this without falling." She pulled her feet out of the stirrups, needing to use her hand to get the left one out, and swung herself sideways on the saddle. She slid off Rex's back and dropped lightly, feeling almost skillful. Then she lost her footing as she hit the ground, and fell over. "And another perfect dismount," she said ruefully, picking herself up.

Rex gave her a sympathetic look.

Jenny patted his side. "It's okay." She looked around. "I need to find a..."

Her eyes came to rest on the pond.

"Mirror," she finished. "Yeah." She walked lightly to the edge of the water. Close up, she saw how strangely smooth water was in Wonderland—with waves and ripples firmly in the There But Not There category, a clear and flat surface was perfectly visible beneath the haze of sketched lines. Through the reflection she saw clear blue skies, fluffy white clouds, and dazzling green leaves.

Rex crept up behind her and put his muzzle over her shoulder. Jenny absently reached a hand up to scratch his chin, then turned abruptly: "You should stay here."

He gave her a look.

"You can see, right?" she said. "Not like Calvin. So you'll be fine in here. Just for a little while." She took his face in her hands, like she was trying to convince a small child to hold out just another few weeks for the latest gaming console. "It'll be weird enough if people see *me* suddenly appear out of thin air. You'll be a lot harder to explain. Right?"

The horse couldn't argue with that logic, even if he could talk. His chin dropped and he looked away in an all too human expression of concession.

"Okay," said Jenny. "Not long, I promise. And I'll come back in with some lunch." She rubbed his nose and gave him a little kiss on the cheek.

Jenny turned back and knelt at the edge of the pond. She tried to see if anybody was hanging around nearby, in the real world, but it was hard to get a decent angle. "Well, here goes nothing," she said. She leaned over and placed her hands above the flat, colorful surface of the water. She took a deep breath and pushed.

GEOPH ESSEX

With a squirming of worlds through her eyeballs and the same old inside-out feeling, she found herself perched precariously on the edge of Turtle Pond in the real world, leaning out over the water, face to face with Mirror Jenny, who cringed and gasped without a sound right before Jenny toppled over and splashed spectacularly into the pond.

Surfacing and sputtering, Jenny let out a sharp string of Cantonese profanities as she scrambled back to the brush-lined shore.

Up a rocky slope next to the real Belvedere Castle, three college girls with beach towels, a tall skinny black guy, and a couple with four small children looked at her with big eyes. The littlest child laughed.

"Um," said Jenny, crawling back on land. "Heh. Oops?"

The mini-crowd seemed willing to accept that excuse, and went about their business. One of the girls seemed to briefly consider loaning Jenny her towel, but the others tugged at her arm and they kept walking along toward the Great Lawn to get some sunbathing in on their lunch break. The skinny guy called out and started toward the slope, but she waved him off: "I'm fine, thanks, sorry about that!" He shrugged his shoulders and walked off behind the castle.

Jenny sat by the pond and wrung herself out, shaking water out of her hair and checking her bag. While wet, it was in one piece and not soaked through—she sadly pulled out her camera and her phone, but was pleasantly surprised to find out they were both still functional. The camera turned on and the LCD screen lit up with no problem. She flipped open her phone—the screen was a little swimmy, but the digits were visible. She dialed Calvin.

"Hey!" he said, sounding only slightly wet.

"Hi!" she replied brightly. "I'm here."

"Where?"

"At the castle."

"No way!" the phone warbled in a damp imitation of Calvin's cheerful voice. "We just hit Bedford!"

"There's no traffic in Wonderland." Jenny smiled to herself. "Listen, can you guys pick some stuff up?"

"Sure," Calvin said. "Heckler wants to see if he can get his parking spot back. Then we'll grab the subway to the park."

"Cool." Jenny clambered up the rocks at the base of the castle and looked around for a park bench. "Could you guys pick up some lunch? And get some extra stuff for Rex. Like apples or something. Oh, and bring your laptop?"

"Can do," said Calvin. "Anything else?"

Jenny looked down at her soaking wet outfit. "Yeah, I could use a change of clothes," she said, stifling a self-deprecating laugh. "And a towel."

CHAPTER FIFTEEN

It was nearly three by the time Jenny Ng sat down on the grass across the pond from Belvedere Castle. In the rippling reflections by the opposite shore, she could see a pale figure waiting proudly but glumly, occasionally twitching his tail. There was no horse on the actual shore, of course; Rex was still waiting in Wonderland.

A nice girl at the Delacorte Theater box office let her use the bathroom, though it was hours before the doors would open for tonight's show, and Jenny was mostly dry and comfortable in one of Heckler's club night Oxfords and a pair of pants she'd been fortunate and unfortunate enough to leave at Heckler's sometime last month. Fortunate because they fit and were dry; unfortunate because of the uncomfortable glances she exchanged with Calvin when Heckler cheerfully handed them over. She wanted to protest that she'd just crashed there one night to get away from magic acts and mystic powers, but then, she also wanted to protest that she was six feet tall and a virtual twin of Carrie Raymond, which was quite nearly as true. Heckler, with his usual regard for etiquette in the face of solipsism, had winked and said: "Lucky you forgot these, huh?" Jenny had grimaced, snatched the dry clothes and towel, and zipped off to change.

By the time she got back, Calvin and Heckler had laid down a thin blanket and started a picnic. Sunbathers and other picnickers lounged on the grass around them, families relaxing, students reading, hard-working folks taking a well-deserved moment to soak up some sun. Jenny wondered briefly if any of them could possibly have stories as strange as hers. It was hard to imagine that they did, but Jenny supposed that none of the other people enjoying a sunny day in Central Park imagined that the Chinese girl lunching with a mismatched set of guys was regularly

174

dismembered and could travel through mirrors. If her life was that invisible to them, perhaps their lives were just as invisible—and just as unusual—to her.

But she still doubted that any of them had an ancient, mysterious, very sharp sword hidden in an instrument case next to their picnic lunches.

Calvin McGuirk had filled Heckler in on some of the details during the trip to meet Jenny. At this point, keeping Heckler in the dark was more likely to create problems than avoid them. Jenny felt blithely unconcerned, though. With Heckler's typical grasp on reality, it wasn't going to completely blow his mind, and with his typical interest in people more than four inches away from the center of his own brain, he wasn't likely to spill their secrets.

"At least now the sword makes sense," Heckler said through a mouthful of cheeseburger. "So you're like the *Highlander*, right? There can be only one?"

"Um, no," said Jenny. She nibbled at her chicken sandwich, too anxious to eat much. "I've already met another one. And we're *here* so I can meet another one tonight."

"Right." Heckler mashed half his cheeseburger into his mouth at once, and still managed to talk clearly. "This Carnival chick. Sounds sexy. Brazilian and shit."

"Caravel," Calvin corrected him. He was working on his ham sandwich more politely than Heckler, but more hungrily than Jenny.

"Hey, Jenning, if she's all Tarzan, Jane, loincloths and swords, get some photos! Huh," he paused thoughtfully. "Hey, does the camera work—over in the mirror place?"

Jenny was actually impressed. "Good question."

"Actually, yeah," agreed Calvin. "I mean, I'd bet it doesn't, because it's not you. You know, like me—the camera probably can't see anything."

"And takes a while to develop," grinned Heckler, scratching the stubble on his chin. Like a lot of fair-haired guys, Calvin's own facial hair wasn't very noticeable, what little there was of it.

The magician made a face at Heckler, but said to Jenny: "I think you should try. Tonight, when you go in, I mean. Taking a picture."

"Sure," Jenny spread her hands. "I'll meet Caravel and tell her: 'Say cheese!'" She mimed clicking a camera. "Sorry," she said quickly, cutting off any hurt feelings. "I'm sorry, Calvin, I'm just tense."

"Massages all around, then?" suggested Heckler.

The afternoon passed like a normal afternoon among three friends, rather than the precursor to a meeting with some mystical being from an alternate dimension. Jenny kept the peace between Heckler, who didn't care, and Calvin, who tried his best not to. They talked openly about the weird events of the summer, now that Heckler was in on it, and it was Heckler who pointed out that carrying mirrors around might make good sense for a superhero who could travel through them. The idea struck the magician and his lovely, superheroic assistant as a pretty sound one. While Heckler watched their stuff—not as closely as he watched a trio of nearby sunbathers, but with acceptable vigilance—Jenny and Calvin made a quick foray out of the park to a pharmacy to pick up some mirrors.

"I wonder if any of the others do this," Jenny said as they crossed Central Park West.

"Other whats do what?" asked Calvin.

"The other, um, people like me," she said lamely. "Redbeard and Caravel and the Count. Do you think they carry around mirrors with them, just in case?"

"In case there aren't any mirrors or windows or something around?" Calvin nodded. "Yeah, that makes sense. What happens if you're in a spot where you've got to get to Wonderland, but there aren't any mirrors? Or windows, or...or ponds?" He playfully ruffled her hair, which had long since dried.

"But they'd have to be, like, emergency only," Jenny thought out loud. "Like when that guy was chasing me. And I'd need a bunch of them. 'Cause they wouldn't be there on the other side, and I don't think I could bring them through with me. Could I?"

"I dunno."

"Wait, that's weird." She tapped her chin and pondered the middle distance where strategic thoughts frolic, waiting to be hunted down, caught, stuffed and mounted in chains of logic. "I mean, stuff I carry or 'pull' with me comes through. But I've never tried to bring the mirror or window or whatever through with me. If I did, what would happen?"

"Could you really rip my bathroom mirror off the wall?" Calvin asked incredulously. "Or out of the world, even?"

"Damn, I need to practice," Jenny muttered.

Calvin grinned. "Does that mean we can put new stuff into the act?"

They found a small but well-stocked pharmacy on Columbus, and browsed through shelves looking for something ideal. Calvin found a bin full of mirrored compacts for teenaged girls just learning about makeup—they were overbearingly pink and flowery on the outside, but each half opened up into a clear and reflective mirror. "Will these work?" he asked Jenny.

Jenny opened one and stared into the two small circular mirrors. A Mirror Jenny looked back from each—one winked and the other stuck her tongue out. Jenny couldn't help but smile as she snapped the compact shut. "Yeah, these'll work," she said.

They picked up five at a dollar each, realizing that a quick break of the plastic hinge would get Jenny two emergency escape routes for the price of one. The gray-haired lady at the counter smiled maternally at Jenny. "You'll only need one, dear," she said warmly. "Would you like me to show you how to use it?"

"Uh, no," said Jenny graciously. "I got it, thanks."

Calvin choked back his laughter, but not so successfully that Jenny didn't elbow him in the gut when they exited the store. All she did was trigger an explosion of Irish glee. "Come on, it was funny!" said the magician, catching his breath and wiping at tears.

"Yeah, try living with it for ten years," Jenny replied with only half-felt irritation. "Eh, whatever. I shouldn't complain. The Raymonds said it, I guess—a lot of people wish they looked young."

"The Raymonds?"

"Remember?" Jenny gestured to the past behind them. "They came to the show last night. You met them. The totally incredibly good-looking guy and his impossibly awesomely beautiful wife?"

"Uh, yeah...." Calvin scrunched his shoulders and expression, drawing a blank.

"Don't worry about it," said Jenny. "Remember I got hit by a car when all this started?" Jenny threw *this* around the world in general, but the antecedent was unambiguous. "He's the doctor...well, sort of, but whatever. They're the ones who helped me out."

"Oh."

"Nice couple. Kinda bland."

"Cool," said Calvin.

They walked past the Museum of Natural History. Through the trees, they could see the Rose Center, the giant white globe of the planetarium imprisoned in a colossal cube of crystal clear windows. Calvin smiled and swung his arms boyishly as he walked. "Ever go there?" he gestured with a nod.

"The planetarium? Yeah," said Jenny. "A couple times when I first moved to the city. I went once when I was a kid, too, when my mom and I came up from Philly to visit my cousins."

"In Chinatown?"

"Racist," Jenny teased. "But yeah, they were in Chinatown."

"I came when I was a kid, too, a few times." He didn't slow his pace, but craned his neck to track the planetarium as they passed. "And when I moved here, I tried to go to all the places I remembered from back then. You know how everybody always jokes about how tiny everything gets? You know, when you go back and see places you went when you were a kid?"

"Yeah," said Jenny. "I was going to visit my elementary school once." She smiled feebly and shrugged. "The playground was so weird—it was so *small* from what I remembered—I just got kinda creeped out about it and didn't even go inside to see if any of my teachers were still there." She pulled a deliberately farcical robot impression: "I Fear Change," she said in monotone.

"Right," Calvin chuckled. "Been there." He took another look over his shoulder at the planetarium. "Yeah, it was like that with all the stuff in the city, when I got here. I went to Central Park, and a couple of the bridges, and Yankee Stadium. Even that big blue whale in the museum. Everything seemed a lot smaller now than it did when I was a kid. Except the planetarium." The magician's gaze drifted far away, more through time than space. "I went in to see the show, and it was still just...*huge*. I still got that kind of...vertigo or something...you know, when you think about how big the whole universe really *is*."

Jenny nodded quietly, falling into an easy rhythm beside Calvin McGuirk. They might have been walking together like this for years.

"I guess I think about that stuff a lot," said Calvin. "Like, the stuff you can't really think about. What's out there. What's possible. All the big stuff that we'll probably just never know." He flashed a grin. "But then I found the box. And the glasses and the window, and the chains, and the hole. And then *you*." He put a hand on her shoulder. "It's kind of like somebody said: 'Sure, man, here's some of the big stuff. Take a look! Get used to it!' And you know what?" He took his hand away before it got too awkward. "Even though I got to look—even though I got *a* look—it *still* doesn't make it any smaller. All it did is make me see how much *bigger* everything is. You know?"

Jenny took his hand and held it as they walked. It was just—she was sure—two really good friends who had the right connection. "I know," she said. "I've been trying to fight it, I think. Maybe because it was all too big to fit." She spread a palm over her head. "In here, I mean. I tried to pretend all of this was just little bits. Being indestructible. Reading the letters through the window. Wonderland." She laughed. "You and all your stuff, the chains and magic hole and all. But if it's all happening, here and now...and the universe is just really that big...well, I guess it's all part of the same thing. Maybe we found each other for a reason."

"Maybe," Calvin said softly.

"All this stuff is just part of the big picture," Jenny continued without a pause. "On a cosmic scale, it's all one big thing, I guess. It's *got* to be connected, even if we can't see it. So maybe there's a reason, after all. Your stuff, and my powers, and us meeting. Maybe it'll all fall into place. Maybe it'll all make sense."

A long pause was filled only with passing traffic, drifts of other conversations, and a clean summer wind sweeping out from the park. As if it was just the cue they needed, their hands let go naturally, dropping to their sides, and they walked side by side without touching.

Finally, Calvin spoke. "Yeah. Um."

Jenny answered just as succinctly. "Uh, right." The light changed at Central Park West, and a glowing green man frozen in mid-step implied that they could walk forward, even if he never could. "Let's get back before Heckler eats all the chips," Jenny said.

Heckler hadn't eaten all of the chips. He was lying on the grass next to the three sunbathing girls, looking like he'd just missed the cut for the latest sexy firemen calendar, but only because he'd kicked the Dalmatian off the truck. He waved lazily at Jenny and Calvin as they walked across the lawn, a vague gesture that translated loosely as reassurance that their stuff was okay. Jenny winced at the thought that he'd left the case with the sword lying on their picnic blanket where anybody could've just come along and snatched it, but nothing was missing or disturbed.

Leaving Heckler to his nubile young string-bikini'd reindeer games, Calvin and Jenny settled down on the blanket and started breaking mirrored compacts in half, chucking each half in Jenny's shoulder bag like discarded oyster shells after the wriggling mollusks have already forged their way into the stomach to herald the arrival of more powerful aphrodisiacs.

"He's not a *total* jerk," said Calvin, crunching some chips and breaking the last compact in half. "Here's the last two."

"Thanks," Jenny said, holding her bag for Calvin to drop the mirrors into. She glanced over at Heckler; he was rubbing lotion on one of the girls. "No, he *is* a total jerk. But that's the thing—you can trust him. I know it's weird, but he's not hiding anything, and that's...I don't know. Comforting, I guess. 'Cause you know if he's letting all *that* hang out, there couldn't be anything worse."

"No, I get it," Calvin said. He tried to comfortably fit his long legs on the blanket as he sat back, but the odds were against him. "Really, he's okay. And I think he actually likes you. It's funny—he's the kind of guy I would trust with nuclear missile launch codes, but I wouldn't trust with my daughter."

"Or your mother," Jenny grinned.

"Right!"

Jenny stood and grabbed the bag of apples the boys had brought with them. "I need to feed Rex," she said. "I promised."

Calvin perked up. "You want to try one of the, um, Emergency Exits?"

"Maybe later—I'll just use the bathroom mirror at the theater." She affectionately scratched his head and smoothed out his wavy red hair, then jogged toward the Delacorte. The box office girl wasn't there, but the door was unlocked, and Jenny knew where the bathroom was. She snuck in quietly, not sure if sneaking was necessary. The bag of apples rustled gently, bumping her thigh with each step. Inside the bathroom, she looked in the mirror.

For a moment, she wondered if she could go Through the Looking Glass without touching it, as Rex seemed to suggest in the hangar. She figured it would probably be a pain for the other folks in the horse-riding, sword-swinging, mirror-traveling club to have to get off their horses all the time just to put their hands on a mirror—there must be *some* easier way they all used. She stared at Mirror Jenny, who looked back expectantly but unhelpfully. She tried focusing on the mirror, pushing with her brain, lasering the surface with her eyes. After thirty seconds, she realized she wasn't doing anything besides holding her breath and popping her ears, achieving only a headache and a purple face. Sighing, she put a hand on the mirror and ignored Mirror Jenny's sympathetic looks. A flash of blobs and a gooey drip of thunder later, she was in Wonderland, the crinkling plastic bag of apples making funny *swutch* sounds in the echoing wind.

Jenny reoriented herself—she had to admit it was getting a bit easier each time, though it took just as much effort to orient herself when she returned to the real world—and retraced her steps back to Belvedere Castle. She scrambled down the rocks as Rex impatiently stomped the ground and flared his nostrils.

"Sorry, boy," she said. If he could see in Wonderland, she was pretty sure he could hear, too. "It's hard to get away sometimes."

He accepted her apology mutely, and eyed the plastic bag.

"Yeah," said Jenny. "Lunch." She held the bag open by its handles, letting Rex stick his nose in to pluck out apples and crunch them in his devastatingly fierce jaws. His teeth were the size of school lunch milk cartons, and probably exceeded the Recommended Daily Allowance of calcium.

As Rex's munching sounded off in the strange pounding whoosh of Wonderland, Jenny's mind wandered. *Hard to get away....* A thought struck her, and she shifted the bag to one hand—annoying Rex, who was digging for another apple—and dug into her shoulder bag for one of the Emergency Exit mirrors. This was the first time she'd ever brought a real world mirror into Wonderland, and her mind raced with questions. Would it show a simple reflection of the real world, like the other reflective surfaces in Wonderland? Would it be a reflection of Wonderland? Would she see Mirror Jenny in it? Would it be just a normal, mundane mirror? Or would it be—

She fished out one of the mirrors and stared.

—something much, much weirder.

The surface itself seemed to ripple and warp, like silk being twisted and untwisted, tightening and flowing across a flat table. Beneath the surface, smoke and amorphous shapes roiled and coiled in a sinuous dance of eerie angles and diabolic parabolic curves. She flashed back to Wednesday's show, strains of *Night on Bald Mountain* playing dark and fiery chords in her head. This, she determined, was not at all normal behavior from a mirror. It wasn't even normal considering what she'd come to *accept* as normal, which was itself pretty far from normal. She would've given anything to see Mirror Jenny swish into view, tongue waggling, eyes rolling, fingers in her ears; but her feckless reflection was nowhere to be found in the smoky void through the little mirror.

A shimmer of sound cascaded through Wonderland like rainfall, and a horse growled and whinnied miles away. Her fingertips hovered just above the undulating surface of the mirror, pushing closer...

A fearsome shriek pierced the fog as a massive shoulder slammed into her hand, knocking the mirror to the ground. Jenny snapped out of her trance and looked up; Rex's eyes were wide and panicked, his breath coming in short snarls of steam from both nostrils. He flicked his eyes at the mirror lying face down on the ground, pink and shiny and innocent, gleaming dully in an unseen white light overhead.

Jenny shook herself and looked at the mirror, not far from the apples that had rolled across the blurry grass when she'd unconsciously dropped the plastic bag. "Right," she said to Rex. "Thanks." She rubbed his neck gratefully. "What *was* that? What *is* that?"

Rex might have had answers, but they required more detailed language than even his expressive eyes and body language could convey. He snorted quietly and lowered his head to nuzzle her hair.

She patted his nose but pulled away. A couple of steps over, she bent down to pick up the pink plastic shell. Jenny felt the urge to flip it over and stare at the mirror, and found herself shifting it in her fingers to turn it—she heard a growly *neigh* behind her and steeled herself against the draw of the dark and smoky place. Shoving the mirror in her shoulder bag, she gave Rex a tight-lipped smile. "I'm fine." His dark eyes doubted her. "I'm fine, I promise," Jenny said. She shuffled her way back to the horse, picking up apples as she went and rolling them toward the plastic bag. He got the nearest one and crushed it loudly at her between his giant yellowed teeth. "Yeah, I know," said Jenny. "Whatever it is, it's off limits."

She handed him an apple, and his extraordinarily adroit lips grabbed it and threw it behind his teeth to meet the same mashed up fate as its colleagues. Jenny hugged him and put her face against his leathery, sweaty hide. Rex curved his body around her and tickled the back of her neck with his fuzzy chin. Though Jenny had never had a thing for horses—she hadn't even gone through the unicorn phase half her friends had gone through—she understood the attraction, at least where Rex was concerned. He was a huge, utterly loyal masculine force that only wanted to protect her. Maybe all those girls who got into horses just had major daddy issues. Jenny wouldn't know; she never really had a daddy. Her father, Dewey—he'd accepted an Anglicized name more readily than her mom—was a hard-working guy, and she didn't see him much even before he died. She was pretty sure her brother Peter had no real memories of their dad at all. Jenny never saw it as a disadvantage, though. To her, a father was a strong, quiet presence that kept everything running smoothly, even in its absence. She'd never had to learn that even fathers have feet of clay and unfair high school dating policies.

Jenny cleared her throat and sniffed, pulling away and straightening herself out. "So," she said. "You'll be okay in here a little while longer? Sunset's not too long now."

Rex stoically accepted his lonely burden.

"Okay," said Jenny. "I'm sorry. We'll figure out something better for the long term." She had no idea where she was going to keep over a ton of horse flesh that needed to be fed and, put politely, "walked," but she didn't like the idea of leaving him in Wonderland all the time. Getting him in and out of her apartment would be a simple matter of going through her bathroom mirror, but keeping him there might be a bit too much to handle—for both of them.

We'll figure it out, she thought, and she gave him one last pat on the nose and slipped away. She picked her way back up the rocks, rounded the more sinister Wonderland version of the castle, and headed for the theater to go back through the bathroom mirror to the real world.

CHAPTER SIXTEEN

A creeping blue-green glow wasn't enough to illuminate the infinite depths of inky blackness, but dim light reflected waxily off a constellation of two hundred or so glistening frozen corpses. The human talent for finding patterns in completely arbitrary sequences would handily supply an appropriate name for the constellation—but there were no human eyes to witness it, and no human minds to come up with clever figures to trace over it. There was only inky blackness, frozen corpses, a few odds and ends floating in the void, and the sickly blue-green glow.

The blue-green glow moved.

It uncurled and uncoiled in several dozen directions at once, coherent and massive on a scale that would baffle human minds into forgetting the word for the power tool or exotic breed of parrot they were going to name the morbid constellation after. Aphasia would give way to incontinence, followed by emesis, hypoxia, syncope, cyanosis, ebullism, and finally expiration, in a parade of fancy terms that would get any medical student laid within four hours of dropping them at an undergrad kegger. Unfortunately for the medical student, no amount of clever wordplay would stave off the near absolute zero temperatures and lack of oxygen in the inky blackness, and the cold sheen of the constellation Keg Stand would be the last thing they saw before their puckered, blackened eyes withered in the most horrific gaze this side of a basilisk, unseeing and fixed perpetually on the mass of flesh, slime and radioactive ooze that swam through the bleak and thready solar winds of stars so far distant that the Inverse Square Law choked the life out of their brilliance, leaving nothing but a jet black ambience to illuminate the jetter and blacker inky blackness.

The blue-green glow created its own light. And moved. Swimming through quantum fluctuations, gliding on matter popping in and out of existence, huge swaths of wrinkled meat and shiny carapace scaled virtual matter, surfing wave functions that would have had old Hendrick Casimir slathering zinc oxide on his nose and hanging ten. Strange, unkind gases fumed from orifices better left undescribed.

A huge column of fleshy tendrils swiped through the grim constellation of crispy cadavers, sending little bodies twirling through the blackness. Noxious vapors carried the unmistakable odors of consternation and impatience. Approximately four hundred tiny, crunchy eyeballs and half as many gaping mouths were frozen in terrified shrieks, minuscule screams torn from miniature lungs before being horribly cut short.

The writhing lambada of trillion-mile-long curves and coils recognized the corpses for what they were; there was no mistaking the remains of organic beings, the smoky tang of carbon and effervescence of boiled nitrogen. The things were dead and done, animated only by the application of advanced physics equations to the blue-green glowing thing itself.

But—and this was the point—they were *there*. This was the impetus for the unholy brimstone signaling leviathan frustration.

The little corpses had been there for only an instant, the blink of a behemoth's eye. Nothing new had floated through this inky black neighborhood since at least a behemoth's yawn or two ago. Time was a bother; with no points of reference, no stars shifting in their seasons and no planets spinning on their axes, the passage of time was all internal, with events like this one chiming intermittent and unpredictable hours. A vague recollection (too vague to be called memory) persisted in the fabric of local space: non-visual images representing more momentous chimes in ages past, incidents that involved more than mere tiny corpses and frozen knick knacks. The images were largely inconsequential in the context of a synaptic network wider in diameter than the orbit of Venus, and would set fire to any brain smaller than the orbit of Mercury; the only minds capable of understanding them would have next to no interest in them.

Still, in those images were clues; and in those clues, answers; and in those answers, a way to restore perfect, undisturbed emptiness to the inky blackness. Glowing and oozing, the thing in the void scanned the farthest reaches of its domain, casting outward with an instinctual understanding of integral calculus to pinpoint the origin of the fuzzy corpses.

It was quite a distance, but it was there—a few degrees warmer than the surrounding space, something gave off a blurry luminance just four shades lighter than the black nothingness. It was infinitesimally small, relative to the senses reaching out to investigate it.

Like a brontosaurus lumbering across Pangaea in search of a single thumbtack, the glowing, slithering, burbling, steaming colossus set off in a surprisingly graceful breast stroke for one with no breast to speak of, riding the quantum waves in an undulating pachanga. The source of the withered little bodies demanded investigation. And, if necessary, retribution.

CHAPTER SEVENTEEN

Even with a young college student's life in the balance, even while anxiously anticipating meeting her very own otherworldly Obi-Wan Kenobi, Jenny had to admit it was a gorgeous sunset, and she'd be a fool not to appreciate the golden glow boiling away behind the Delacorte Theater. Feel-good funk played nearby: an electric guitar snapping chords like popcorn, a smooth bassline dripping gooey yellow butter substitute on top, and a skilled drummer shaking up a slushee in one of those sassy blue flavors that had less to do with whatever fruit they were named for and more to do with giving your tongue wet dreams involving scandalous and scantily clad sugar cane. Summer cicadas joined in the song like karaoke enthusiasts with a broken teleprompter stuck on one page of unintelligible but suggestive lyrics. Evening conversations buzzed, swirling in snatches and drifts over grass and between trees, as all-day frolickers and sunbathers worked out dinner plans, subway routes, the GPS directions to tonight's indie music scene, and the best tactics to wind up naked and out of breath with a fellow frolicker on sweat-soaked sheets in the perfect breeze of an undeniably phenomenal summer night.

Keith Heckler played his tactics like a Chess Grandmaster, heading off with Tara, Gina, and Alyssa for a club that was guaranteed to provide them with enough alcohol and temporary hearing loss to make fun and meaningless sex their only viable option. The three girls had come prepared—they wrapped skirts and loose tops over their bikinis and pulled high-heeled shoes from their enormous beach bag. Heckler introduced them to Jenny and Calvin and said goodbye in practically the same breath. As the girls swayed their hips down the path toward hedonism, Heckler gave Calvin a fist bump and hugged Jenny loosely and easily. "Hey," he said earnestly. "Tell me how it goes, Jenning."

His concern was touching. "Right," said Jenny. "Have a good time."

The well-tanned sirens called, and Heckler followed, pausing only to shout back: "If she's hot, I get photos!" He faded into dark trees and darkening dusk accompanied by a trinity of light feminine laughter.

It was nearly seven, and the sun was almost down. "Listen," Jenny began, "it's pointless bringing you with me. You won't be able to see or hear any of it anyway."

"Yeah," Calvin admitted.

"But you know what you could do for me?" The magician met her eyes hopefully. Jenny said: "You could go to John."

"John?" Calvin scrunched his face. "How'm I supposed to find him?"

"Well, we know where he's going to be around nine o'clock tonight," Jenny pointed out. "The Hudson River, just above Battery Park City. Calvin, really—it would make me feel a lot better knowing you're there, just in case. I mean, I don't know what's going to happen here, or how long it'll take, but if anything goes wrong...maybe you could...I don't know...."

"Okay," Calvin said. He grabbed her hands. "I don't know if there's anything I can do, but I'll be there." He grinned. "I'll have a front row seat when you ride to the rescue!"

"It might be a walking rescue," said Jenny. "I still suck at riding."

She hugged him tight, then pulled away and secured her shoulder bag across her body. She reached down for the instrument case that held her sword and slung it over her shoulder. She felt weirdly comfortable knowing she had it with her, even if she did look like an experimental jazz musician on her way to a gig.

"Wish me luck," she said, setting herself.

"Lots," said Calvin. "I'll grab the rest of this stuff. Go, uh, meet your destiny."

"Right."

Jenny headed back to the Delacorte entrance. Crowds had been gathering for the last few hours, waiting on line for free tickets to see Hollywood celebrities pretending to return to their roots by memorizing the lines to sixteenth century shows they pretended to revere. The exceptionally large paychecks they received as acknowledgement of their huge—and perhaps even deserved—box office draw were the only motivation they needed to pretend to dredge up the appropriate sense memory in passable iambic pentameter. Even if Jenny could find the helpful box office girl now, that particular font of generosity probably dried up in the body heat of a hundred entitled Shakespeare aficionados. Rather than coaxing her way past disgruntled New Yorkers grumblingly wondering what made *her* so special, Jenny decided this was the perfect opportunity to try out an Emergency Exit.

She wandered away from the theater toward the relative secrecy of the trees, dodging trunks and amorous couples who sought similar secrecy for different reasons. She found a shady spot and looked up through the trees at a sparkling array of stars. There was only the faintest hint of purple light from the west; the sun was well and truly set.

Jenny rummaged through her bag and pulled out an Emergency Exit, flipping it over in her hand tentatively. She was half afraid to see the smoky, swirling place again, but only Mirror Jenny looked back at her, miming a Trapped In A Box routine with the edges of the small round mirror. "Ha, ha," Jenny whispered facetiously. Mirror Jenny cut it out and put her game face on. "Okay—let's go." Jenny touched two fingers to the mirror, and her reflection followed suit. After the usual hurricane of squishy blobs and threnody of searing light, she found herself in the woods in Wonderland. As she'd predicted, the Emergency Exit was nowhere to be seen; it hadn't come through itself with her, and it left no counterpart in Wonderland. At least she was spared looking into the scary smoky place.

Half joking, Jenny gave a shot at the kind of ear-splitting whistle cowboys use to summon an obedient Appaloosa to the balcony of a brothel for the time-honored Old West tradition of blunt-force self-vasectomy. The whistle sounded strange, partly because of its spidery ricochets through the rushing noise of Wonderland, and partly because Jenny wasn't good at whistling. Perhaps with a magical mind-reading horse, it literally was the thought that counted—a moment later, thumping hoofbeats echoed, and Rex cut through gnarled trees and blurry leaves in a full-on gallop, skidding to a magnificent stop just in front of her, sending There But Not There rocks and sticks not quite flying through what wasn't, strictly speaking, the air.

"Good horse," Jenny said warmly.

Rex posed. *Of course I am*, his preening suggested. He knelt down to let Jenny clamber onto the saddle in less than circus-caliber style. She clucked her tongue and tapped Rex's sides with her heels, trying to feel a little more equestrian. That turned out to be a lot easier without a chinstrap.

Rex weaved a long and twisty trail through the trees, breaking into full speed as he soared across baseball fields that looked like old World Series photographs in the desaturated brown tones of Wonderland. For the first time, Jenny felt at ease on horseback; she had no illusions that she was a capable rider, but she had a feeling that as long as she wanted to stay in the saddle, Rex would find a way to keep her there. She relaxed her arms, loosened the reins and gave in to the thrill of the wind and the machine of powerful muscle and sweat beneath her. She stopped hunching over in terror at the thought of falling off. She straightened up and even leaned back a bit, opening her eyes and breathing in a moment of actual happiness.

Happiness turned to euphoria as she took in a view of the giant sky overhead.

Where the daytime sky of Wonderland was dominated by unnerving slashes of discolored clouds smearing and slicing the darkness beyond them, Wonderland at night lived up to its name. Fear and confusion had guided her actions the previous night, on her first trip to the mirror world; now relaxed for the first time in a long time, she saw the dazzling display of light and color above her, like a collaboration between Jackson Pollock, Thomas Young, and a Lite-Brite. Giant spots of brilliance replaced stars, generating wave after wave of rainbow-colored concentric circles from each that melted into the others in an interference pattern that lit up the sky. The effect faded toward the horizon, where blackness took over, but the sparkling patterns above looked like holes punched through the sky to a world of color and light beyond.

"Rex!" she shouted. "It's beautiful!"

The stallion leapt magnificently over an infield, nailing first base like he was spiting Mark Teixeira. Of course, in Wonderland, it felt more like third base, relative to home plate, so Mark might have let it go. There was no bag, anyway; just the shimmering suggestion of one.

A second later, they dashed madly through trees again. Rex vaulted a path, snaked through another short stretch of forest, and palpably downshifted as he reached the edge of the woods. As they slowed, Jenny saw a small structure ahead—the South Gate House of the reservoir. Rex crossed an overpass and came to a dead stop at the gate house. A large, simple clock was set into the stone atop the building, but instead of hands, it had a swirl of translucent motion in front of its face. There was no way to tell time by it, but Jenny knew it couldn't be much later than seven, or much earlier than seven-thirty.

"Well," she said. She frowned—she sounded like Redbeard. "Here we go, Rex." She patted his neck and scruffed his mane. "Um...where—?"

The horse jerked left around the gate house, rounding the corner and jumping lightly over a short fence onto the smooth surface of the reservoir itself. *Of course*, Jenny realized. She remembered the horses marching atop the Hudson River. It stood to reason that Rex could pull off the same stunt.

The There But Not There ripples above the surface licked intangibly at the horse's legs as he tramped steadily across the water. On the other side of the gate house, a long retaining wall—its top barely level with the surface of the water—stretched across the water to the far shore. Jenny remembered the wall; it had featured heavily in a photo project she'd worked on when she'd first moved to the city. That was why Redbeard's references to a "lake" and a "wall" clicked so quickly.

When she'd taken pictures of the reservoir, there hadn't been a huge pale horse and black-cloaked rider perched midway along the wall. That had changed.

Visible gusts of wind swept across the reservoir between Jenny and the other rider; the black robe fluttered and twitched, but the rider sat in the saddle with a stillness generally reserved for the dead. Rex trekked diagonally to the wall, his steps reverberating emptily in the wide open space. Jenny heard a distant snort, and saw steam rise from the other horse's nose. It didn't take long to close the distance. Rex knelt down for her, and Jenny slid off, sprawling on top of the wall. It was crisscrossed with hazy patterns of things that had washed up onto it and been removed, things that weren't all there but weren't all not.

Jenny cleared her throat, not sure where to start. "Um." She felt like a sixth grader at the threshold of the principal's office. She pushed a little more strength and confidence. "Caravel?"

"That's me," said the figure in black. Her voice was hoarse and sexy, with a hint of tough street accent beneath more cultivated tones, like a Spanish Harlem stripper putting her tips toward an Ivy League law degree. Caravel removed her hood, and Jenny was surprised that she *looked* like a Spanish Harlem stripper putting herself through law school. She looked a little older than Jenny; her skin was dark and flawless, her hair all rich brown and kinky curls. Her golden brown eyes scanned her surroundings with laser precision. She also had a French manicure and large hoop earrings. "You're the one Ketch sent?"

"Ketch...?"

"Big man, red beard—"

"Right," said Jenny. "Yes. I met him last night. Here in...uh." She realized that *Wonderland* was her nickname for this place, that she and Calvin had taken to using. If there was an official name, she didn't know it.

"No idea what's going on. Right?" Caravel asked her.

Jenny shook her head vigorously. "Not a clue," she said. "Red...uh, Ketch said you could help."

"Mm," Caravel said ambiguously. She swung one leg over her saddle and slid off; her horse leaned ever so slightly to assist her. She took three solemn steps to Jenny and held out her hand. "Caravel," she introduced herself.

"Jenny," said Jenny, taking Caravel's hand uncertainly.

Caravel shook hands normally, then pulled hers away. "So, Jenny," she said. "How long has it been?"

"How long? You mean since I've been indestructible?" Jenny asked, feeling snarky. "Since I found a magic sword and a giant horse...? Since my mirror image stopped mirror imaging me?"

"Do you want the quick, blunt answer?" asked Caravel. "Or do you want me to sugar coat it?"

Jenny clenched her teeth and tensed herself. "Quick and blunt's fine."

"You're dead," said Caravel. "You just don't know it yet."

Jenny paused. "Wait." She hugged herself, feeling her skin crawl. "What? Is this, like, the afterlife or something?"

"No," said Caravel. "This is the world, it's real, and you're here. Dead doesn't mean gone. In some cases, *menina*, it doesn't even mean 'dead.' At least," she tilted her head quirkily, "not the way *you* mean it."

"So, uh, *you're* dead too?"

"As dead as you are," said Caravel. "I got an offer that sounded good. Some of us get a choice, and some of us get picked. And some of us," she gave Jenny half a smile, "are just accidents."

"Gee, I wonder which one *I* am," Jenny said with the other half of the smile.

"Mm," said Caravel. "Here's the point, Jenny—you have a job to do. We all do, whether we're picked, or we choose, or we just fall into it. We're *anjos da morte*. Death's Little Helpers. We need to bring the living to their next stop along the way."

"So we're what?" Jenny cocked an eyebrow. "Like grim reapers?"

"It's not that grim," Caravel said lightly. She walked along the wall with an unspoken invitation. Jenny followed; Rex and the other horse walked softly behind them. The dark woman continued: "Think of us more like guides. Death is confusing—"

"No shit," Jenny said.

"—and people need help working out what comes next. There are rules, and you'll learn them, but our job is just to help people follow those rules and find out where they need to go next."

"Next," Jenny repeated.

"Well, it's not the *final* stop." Caravel sensed Jenny's meaning. "It's just the next one along the way. And each stop has plenty of roads leading forward, to different stops, for different reasons. We're not dead, and we're not 'Death,' because it's not really the end. If there *is* an end, it's a long, long way past us. We're just here to help them get past this one crossroad."

"So what's after this?" asked Jenny. "Where do the roads go?"

Caravel shrugged and smiled—her teeth were sharp and white. "*Não sei*," she said. "You think dying is the gateway to some deep cosmic knowledge about the universe?"

"Well, kinda, yeah," Jenny said. "Isn't that how it always is? Some guy dies and goes to heaven or something, and then All His Questions Are Answered?"

"Is that what you thought would happen?"

Jenny shook her head. "I didn't think anything," she said. "I was an atheist."

"So am I, now," said Caravel.

"How can you—"

"There are no gods that I've seen, Jenny," Caravel interrupted. "I was a good Catholic girl. God made sense, for a while. But the truth—the Truth with a capital *T*—is clearly a lot bigger than any gods that anybody has ever prayed to. Gods just aren't necessary, and I've never seen one. It's completely reasonable to be an atheist in an afterworld with no gods."

Jenny thought about that. "I guess." She waved a hand at Caravel's black robes. "But then why do you all look like the Grim Reaper, anyway?" She pointed at the horses. "'Death rides a pale horse,' right? And the swords? How come you guys—the *real* guys—look just like all the paintings and stories everybody always does?"

"Where do you think we got them from?"

Caravel walked on and left Jenny in pause mode on the wall. Rex caught up and tickled the back of her neck with his lips. The other horse walked right past her, following Caravel. Jenny shrugged Rex off, calling: "Wait." She jogged to catch up. "Wait!" Falling in beside Caravel, she asked: "So you guys look like this *because* it's what everybody thinks you should...?"

"The human species has always created its own gods," said Caravel. "It's one of our talents. I think the jump from 'animal' to 'person' might be all about creating some gods to explain away the world. Once you can do that, you've got a reason to wake up in the morning besides eating and *foda*. That's when things get interesting."

Jenny zoomed in on one phrase. "*Our* talents..." She looked at Caravel. "You're a person, too. A human, I mean."

"I am," Caravel said. "I was among the living, too. Not that long ago."

"You said you got an offer."

Caravel folded her arms inside her wide sleeves. "Where—and *when*—I was, there weren't a lot of opportunities for women. Not far away, women were doing okay, but those with my skin color were *macacos*."

"I thought you said it wasn't that long ago," said Jenny.

"It isn't," said Caravel. "Jenny, *menina*, when you're ten years old, a week takes forever. When you're sixty, *years* fly by in the blink of an eye. When you've got all of eternity, a century or two just doesn't add up to a lot."

"Eternity," Jenny repeated. She was tired of playing the supporting role in this Socratic dialogue. She pushed forward proactively. "You're immortal."

"You too," Caravel said. "This isn't the kind of job that can be done in one lifetime. So we get as many as we need."

"So you got an offer," Jenny pushed again.

Caravel sighed and dropped her arms, swinging them as she walked like a bored child trailing her mother in a department store. "It wasn't a hard decision to make," she said. "Take my daily beatings, squeeze out some *bebês*, grow old and die. Or live forever, never get hurt, see the world and help the people in it."

"That sounds a lot more romantic than it looks so far," Jenny said. "I mean, really, whatever you want to call it, aren't we basically killing people?"

Caravel stopped short and turned to Jenny. "Killing? No," she said quickly. "Whatever death is, it's not a person, Jenny. It's not *us*. It's just what *happens*. All we do is go where we're needed." She clasped her hands together. "We *catch* the ones who are dying, like a safety net, to make sure they land okay. If we weren't there...." Caravel's expression went dark. "Well, I'm not sure what would happen, but I don't think it's a good thing."

"So you don't know all the rules either?"

"Of course not, *menina*," Caravel laughed. "I just work here."

Jenny grabbed the strap of her sword case with both hands to keep from fidgeting. "But how did *you* learn about it? What you *do* know, I mean?"

"From Voitas," Caravel said. She sat on the edge of the wall, her legs kicking in the strange flat water, and gazed out across the Wonderland reservoir. Jenny sat down beside her as Caravel went on: "He was one of us, one of the *anjos da morte*. He offered me his sword and his horse. He told me how it all worked. I agreed."

"How does he do the, uh, job...all this stuff...if he gave you his horse? And his sword?"

"He doesn't." Caravel's horse stood calmly over her, and she reached up to tickle the stallion's chin. "He quit."

"How do you quit?"

"You stop doing it," said Caravel. "You move on. Somebody else takes on your sword—your role as a guide—and leads you to the crossroads *you* need to take."

Jenny swished her legs back and forth; she felt no resistance from the spectral water beneath the smooth surface. "So he's gone, and you took his place. But nobody offered *me* the job. Why am I...one of you?"

"Some of us are asked," Caravel explained again, "and some are picked. That happens when there's a need and it's...eh, it's just not filled. But sometimes," she said, eyeing Jenny, "things just go a certain way. Whatever decides these things...along comes you. And here you are." She pursed her lips—she was strikingly beautiful, though not in the modern sense, with a strong, narrow jaw and wide curves in all the right places. The flickering, fluttering ambience of Wonderland played across her face the same way it echoed her words. "Did anything happen, before you found your sword and horse?"

"Uh, *yeah*," Jenny said rudely. "I found out I'm indestructible."

Caravel blinked. "You discovered your Gifts *before* you found your Tools?"

The capitals were audible. Jenny felt like a farm boy in Fantasia about to learn the illustrious history of his Magic Plow. "Yeah," she said cautiously. "My gifts, and my tools. Right. Is...um, that's not how it works?"

"It shouldn't," said Caravel. "But accidents don't work the same way. When did you discover your Gifts? When did you find you were indestructible?"

"A couple months ago," said Jenny. "Same day I...oh. Oh!"

Caravel nodded. "What happened?"

"I got hit by a car," Jenny said. "Hard. And I got up and just walked away! I must have been indestructible then, too. I just didn't know it yet!"

"No, Jenny," said Caravel. "You weren't indestructible yet."

"Then how did I survive the accident?"

Caravel chuckled and patted Jenny's knee. "You didn't, *menina*."

"I...." Jenny finish the sentence.

"You died," said Caravel. "Or, you were supposed to. Something went wrong. Nobody was there to guide you, and you...guided yourself."

Jenny fixed her jaw firmly. She wasn't reeling from the revelation of her death, partly because she didn't *feel* very dead, and partly because her definitions of life and death had been irrevocably broken in the past few minutes. She wasn't even too upset about it. Instead, her mind turned and searched, putting puzzle pieces together. For the first time, some bits fit, new bits she hadn't known anything about, and the bigger picture was making sense. "The Count," she finally said. "I mean, of course he's one of you. But he was supposed to be there. Wasn't he?"

"The who?" asked Caravel.

Again, Jenny had to adjust to discussing these topics with somebody who actually knew the correct terminology instead of her own made-up vocabulary. "There's a guy in jail. He's weird, and he says he doesn't remember anything. But he's wearing a robe like yours. And I think R—my horse, I mean, and my sword, I think they were his. Tall skinny guy, short black hair. He—"

Jenny broke off as Caravel let out a sigh and smiled. She leaned back, palms flat on the top of the wall, and said one word: "Pauzok."

"What?"

"He disappeared. Not long ago." Caravel shook her head. "We can't be everywhere at once, and we aren't all-knowing or all-seeing. Once he was off the map, we had no way of knowing where he was. Some of us thought he'd offered his sword to someone new."

"Well, kind of," Jenny said. "I mean, I got it."

"Yes," said Caravel. "He's in jail?"

"Uh huh," Jenny confirmed.

"Not the biggest surprise, with Pauzok." Caravel laughed. "He's a funny one. And not all too smart. Nice man, though."

"That sounds like him," said Jenny.

"He doesn't remember anything?"

Jenny shook her head. "He speaks different languages—you know, like we do." She felt an odd but warm feeling referring to herself as part of the group. "But the cops said he doesn't know his name, and he doesn't remember anything about Rex or the sword."

"Rex?"

"Um." Jenny grinned sheepishly. "It's what I call my horse."

Caravel smiled back. "Meet Zé," she said, tickling her horse under the chin again. Zé *chuffed* at them. Rex stood opposite his colleague, looming protectively over Jenny's shoulder.

"Hi," Jenny said to Zé. A thought struck her. "Wait, but what was his name before? Rex, I mean. Didn't Pauzok give him a name? What if he's pissed at me that I'm calling him Rex this whole time?"

"Jenny, *relaxe*," Caravel laughed pleasantly. Her easy voice sounded like melted butterscotch in the electrified echoes of Wonderland. "He's called whatever you want to call him. He's a part of you. You might say he *is* you, or an 'extension' of you."

"I don't get it," said Jenny.

"You will," said Caravel. "In fact, we should get started. It won't take long to teach you the basics."

"Really? That's great!" Jenny scrambled to her knees and stood up. "I need your help—I need to figure out how to save somebody. He's going to die tonight, and I figured with my powers, maybe I could—"

197

"Save him from what?" Caravel asked. She stood up next to Jenny.

It was like dealing with Redbeard—or Ketch—all over again. These people had no sense of mortality. "He's going to die!" Jenny repeated.

"And?"

"Gah!" Jenny threw her hands up. "He's too young. He's—he's just a kid. I have to save him!"

"Jenny—Jenny!" Caravel took Jenny's arms and lowered them, trying to calm her down. "You have to understand. There's no such thing as too young. There's no such thing as too good, or too bad, or too young. There's no fair or unfair. Death just happens. If it's his turn, then it's his turn."

Jenny's mouth opened, her eyes crinkled in righteous indignance. "But—"

"No, it doesn't work that way," Caravel said firmly. "We don't get to pick and choose. It's not up to us. The rules are what they are, and when someone is appointed to move on, they're going to move on. It's our job to help them do that—not to stop it from happening."

"But I *have* to, he's—"

"Just another person, *menina*," said Caravel, not unkindly. "Another special person. He's smart or he's pretty or he's young or he's important. He's all those things, to all different people, just like everyone is to *somebody*. But he's just another person. We don't break the rules—*ever*. We don't take these decisions into our own hands. It's not our right, and it's not our responsibility."

Jenny was silent. Her eyes burned with tears she refused to let fall.

Caravel held her hands. "It's good that you care. You wouldn't be human if you didn't." She gave a slight but understanding shrug. "But if you've been given the appointment, you have to keep it. You can't break the rules."

One part stood out. "Appointment?" Jenny asked. "What do you mean?"

"Your horse is drawing you to him, *sim?* The boy who's going to die?"

"Uh," Jenny said brightly. She glanced at Rex. He gazed levelly back at her. "I don't get it," she said.

Now Caravel was confused. "How do you know he's going to die?" she asked. "You don't have an appointment?"

"I, um...no. I don't know what that means, Caravel," Jenny protested. "I was reading his letters. The glowing ones, through the window. They said he's going to die. Tonight, in the Hudson River."

"The glowing what?"

Jenny was at a loss. She and Caravel stared at each other for ten full seconds as more puzzle pieces fell into place, while some she'd thought fit perfectly popped back out from the strain. Jenny had been assuming for months that all of the strange and bizarre things she'd experienced were part and parcel of the same specific fantastic mess. "Wait," she said carefully, "wait. You don't read the letters to find out when people are going to die?"

"What letters, *menina?*"

"The glowing letters," said Jenny. She spoke as if she could pull answers out of Caravel if she just showed some patience and restraint, but she'd already realized this line of questioning was a dead end. "The ones you see if you put on the glasses and look through...crap." Her tears slipped by the border patrol, and Jenny was powerless to stop them streaming down her face. "Oh, crap! Oh no, no, no—oh crap!"

"Jenny," Caravel began.

"Fuck this!" said Jenny. She spun around as Rex knelt behind her, and she climbed up into the saddle.

"Jenny!" Caravel warned.

Jenny ignored her and spurred Rex on. He took off across the reservoir. Jenny was disoriented, meaning to head for the Hudson and not thinking she was, but Rex had it under control—despite the flipped compass of Wonderland, he aimed straight and true. Like an avenging angel, Rex burst out of the park, searing a trail along Eighty-Sixth Street and not even pausing as he bounded across Riverside Drive, the Greenway, and the West Side Highway before letting out a Wonderland-shattering scream and hurtling out over the mirrored Hudson River. His hooves slammed into the water and kept pumping as he raced across the smooth surface marred only by sketchy waves and currents. At this speed, it took some effort to swerve right, but in moments he was racing south down the middle of the river, flying across the water like Christ running to catch the ferry to Weehawken.

In minutes, they drew even with the construction site where Jenny had stopped the night before, where she'd looked out across the water and seen a trio of Death's Little Helpers riding their horses across the Hudson.

She'd felt drawn to the place then because she knew it was the future site of John the juggler's ultimate heartbeat. She felt pulled to it now because she wanted to stop that from happening.

Rex pulled up and sent sketches of not-all-there spray sluicing up from the flat Wonderland water. Jenny wondered if she could perform the messianic water-walking feat herself, but was too worried to chance it now. She turned Rex toward the shore and he shot up and over the fence to the sidewalk. If she'd stopped to think, she would have been impressed by his prodigious leap, and by her own faith in his ability to accomplish it. All she wanted now was to change the rules, stick it to whoever qualified as the man, or—barring any of that—scream and howl and beat Fate into submission.

Her eyes spun furiously as Rex turned quickly to let her take in everything around her. She needed a reflection to touch, so she could shift back to the real world, find Calvin, and the two of them could save John. Across the highway she saw the high-rise co-op—the same one where she'd slipped back out through the lobby windows after her meeting with Redbeard, the guy that Caravel called Ketch. Gratefully, Jenny urged Rex toward the windows and he leaned forward at the foot of the steps to let her tumble off his saddle. The instrument case bopped her sharply on the back of the head, but she ignored it and dashed for the glass.

Rex growled softly behind her. She caught herself, realizing she was acting like a madwoman, and held up a steady hand to reassure the horse. "I know," she said. "I have to. Wait here—I promise I'll be back." He didn't seem keen on the plan; he took a couple of steps forward, his hooves ringing out in the rushing, pounding white noise of Wonderland, but Jenny turned and pushed through the glass.

Inside-out, upside-down, she squiggled between dimensions and felt the warmth and light of the real Manhattan seep back into her eyes and ears. An older couple at the door of the lobby gasped and stared at the short Chinese girl who'd just appeared from nowhere. "Sorry," she apologized perfunctorily. Without another word, she raced across the road to the construction site, narrowly missing two cars, a sport utility vehicle, and a motorcycle that all swerved to avoid her one after another. Jenny paid them no attention. The yellow lights overhead hit her in the way that places do when they're only just familiar enough, but not frequently visited.

She stared hard at the water as a few last horn honks bleated irately from the highway. The river stretched away into rushing blackness broken only by white-capped eddies. Even if she knew what to do to save John, she realized the chances of even seeing him out there—in the exact spot in the Hudson River predicted by the glowing letters—were next to nothing. She grabbed the fence railing in an iron grip. Her eyes were feverishly hot, the tears on her face boiled away to smudges of damp salt. She stared.

"Hey," said a voice next to her. She had no idea how long she'd stared at the dark water, but Calvin's voice in her ear was just what she needed right at that moment. "I was calling you—" he began.

"Calvin!" Jenny threw her arms around him, her face buried in his shirt. He was startled for a moment, but recovered and wrapped his arms around her tightly, gently swaying and soothing her with an unsure hand on her back.

"It's okay," he whispered in the meaningless but comforting way that people use when it really is by no means okay. "It's okay."

Jenny sniffled and tried unsuccessfully to avoid getting snot all over the front of Calvin's shirt. "I'm sorry, I'm so sorry," she babbled.

"It's just a shirt," said Calvin.

"No, it's not," Jenny kept on, "it's not the shirt. I can't do it, Calvin. I can't save John!"

"What happened?"

Jenny shook her head and held on to Calvin as a lifeline. "It's against the rules or...or something. I don't know," she sobbed. "I don't get it. But Caravel said he's supposed to die. That it's just his turn, or his time, or...fuck!" She closed her eyes and put her face against his chest again.

"Well," Calvin said, trying not to jostle his lovely assistant. "Maybe Caravel's right."

From behind him came a rough, silky voice: "*Obrigada, menino.* Thanks for the vote of confidence."

Still holding each other, they turned to face Caravel. Her black robe flapped in the breeze from the river, her hood down. Her eyes looked like polished bronze in the harsh aspirin-colored light of the construction site.

"Jenny," she said. "I know it may be hard to accept. Especially when you didn't come into this the usual way. Please, *menina,* I'm not trying to make this hard on you. It's just how it is."

Jenny wiped her eyes and sniffed. "I'm sorry," she said. "I just...I'm sorry. I wanted so bad...."

Calvin watched Jenny trail off, and squeezed her tighter. He looked at Caravel. "There's nothing we can do?"

Caravel gave the magician a maternal smile that was older than any living parent could offer. Despite her young and beautiful features, the wisdom of the ages looked perfectly at home on her face. She shook her head.

"So John's going to die," said Calvin.

"Very soon," Caravel said quietly.

"Can we stay?"

Caravel nodded. "I'll stay with you."

Jenny looked at Caravel, then up at Calvin. Through the remains of her tears, she managed a painful but necessary smile. "Thank you," she whispered to Calvin. He smiled at her. Jenny turned back to Caravel. "Thank you," she said to the *anjo da morte*.

"I'm on your side, Jenny," said Caravel. "But we can't break the rules."

Jenny nodded, biting her lip to keep it from quivering. Clinging to Calvin's shirt, she turned to look out on the river. Caravel stood on her other side, not touching her, but warming her with tangible compassion.

Traffic passed, water rushed, and pedestrians wandered by without giving much thought to the trio looking out at the river, still as statues.

After a long, deep time, Caravel said: "He wasn't your appointment, Jenny."

Jenny looked at her blankly.

"Someone else will come soon," Caravel explained. "One of ours. To guide him. If this is where he dies, then this is where it will be."

Jenny looked back at the river. Calvin, understanding enough, kept holding her. His armpits had soaked through his shirt. He smelled like sweat and citrus and fresh bread; Jenny found the scent comforting.

A longer, deeper time passed.

Calvin's hand tensed on her shoulder, and Jenny knew the minutes were ticking down to John's proverbial deadline. A swatch of movement across the river caught Jenny's eye. She glanced at Caravel, who nodded and pointed. A giant pale horse marched across the Hudson River, but Jenny found it much less eerie this time around. The rider in black was hard to make out, but a pure white hand emerged from the folds of the black robe and removed the rider's hood. Reaching down to the water like he was plucking a flower, the rider pulled upward, extracting a skinny human form from the rushing river by one wrist. The rider sat his charge behind him on the saddle, and redirected his steed toward Manhattan where Jenny stood breathlessly with a wide-eyed magician and a sad-eyed Not-So-Grim Reaper.

"Hello, Caravel," the rider called as he neared land.

"Hello, Curach," said Caravel.

"I've heard o' she," the rider named Curach said, with a head nod toward Jenny. "The mishap Ketch mishappened upon, aye?" His voice was charmingly twisted in an ancient brogue. He had a giant mass of curly blond hair and eyes that twinkled in the darkness.

Caravel smiled. "This is Jenny." She looked past him, at his passenger. "How is your charge?"

Behind Curach, his bowlegged frame molded perfectly to the saddle, sat John the juggler. His face was pale, and his hair poked out in all sorts of odd directions. He wore a striped T-shirt and a bewildered expression. John's dark eyes searched the darkness and found Jenny—a spark of recognition flared, and he gave her the tiniest smile, more a suggestion of regret than happiness.

"This one made himself a choice t'night," said Curach. "The first o' many t' come." He looked over his shoulder at John. "Are y' ready, man?"

"Jade?" John called out. "Wow!"

Jenny choked back a sob. "John," she said. "Hi. Are you okay?" She mentally kicked herself—he wasn't okay, he was dead. "How do you feel?" she amended.

"Okay, I guess," said John. "I kinda wish I didn't do it, though."

"Do...?" She stopped herself. Calvin hugged her close.

"It's no' the end o' the journey, man," said Curach.

Caravel added, "Just the end of this part."

John considered that, and nodded decisively. "Okay," he said. "That's okay."

"It is," Curach said definitively. "Let's be off! Caravel," he tilted his head.

"Have a good ride, Curach," said Caravel.

Jenny reached out, without any hope of reaching the young man riding Curach's horse down on the river's surface. "Goodbye, John," she said.

"Good luck," Calvin offered.

"Thanks," John said brightly. "I think it's okay. I really think it's..."

His words faded in the wind as Curach's horse wheeled around and galloped across the river into the darkness.

Like clouds receding after a storm, the normal world crept back into focus, and the still and private scene they'd shared slipped away into the night to follow Curach and John the juggler into the next world. Jenny and Calvin still held each other. Caravel folded her arms into her sleeves.

Calvin broke the silence. "Wow."

"Yeah," Jenny quietly agreed.

"So, uh," Calvin looked at Caravel uncomfortably. "Now you're going to...you know, wipe my memory or something? So I can't look 'behind the curtain' anymore?"

Caravel laughed her deep crushed velvet laugh. "You watch too many movies, *menino parvo!* There's nothing wrong with knowing the truth. The truth," she turned her penetrating gaze on Jenny, "never really hurts. It may seem like it, at first. But that's before you get to know it." She smiled and winked at Jenny.

Jenny said nothing. She felt numb and a bit overwhelmed.

"Take her home," said Caravel. "Let her rest. Jenny—we'll meet again, in the same place, in three nights."

Calvin counted. "Uh...."

"Sunday," Caravel clarified with a smile. "I've got no appointments then."

Jenny ran her hands through her hair wearily. "Okay, yeah," she said. "I'll be there."

"Don't forget Rex," said Caravel.

"I won't," Jenny promised.

"I mean tonight," Caravel said, waving toward the lobby windows across the road. Jenny saw two horses standing side by side in the reflections: Rex and Zé.

"Right," said Jenny with a guilty start.

Caravel laughed warmly. She looked at Calvin: "You're a good one, I can tell. Don't let her work herself up. These things have a way of sorting themselves out."

Calvin nodded wordlessly.

Caravel danced across the road, missing cars by inches but never making them swerve, and took three quick leaps up the steps and through the glass. Jenny watched her fold up into herself, like an invisible curtain spreading out from the center and hiding her behind nothing, and realized that must be what Calvin saw when Jenny went Through the Looking Glass. What Calvin didn't see, though, was Caravel seamlessly appearing inside the reflection itself, effortlessly mounting Zé, and galloping out of view.

"Calvin?" Jenny said.

"Yeah?"

"I'm really tired."

"Okay."

He took the subway to her apartment in Brooklyn to tuck her in. Jenny rode Rex to get there, under the extraordinary art-filled night sky of Wonderland.

CHAPTER EIGHTEEN

Squiggles of dust danced through a beam of shockingly bright light that could have easily filled in for the Bat Signal on a sick day, if it took the time to get into makeup and wardrobe and learn its lines first. Rather than a mysterious oval emblazoned on the sky, though, it created a rhombus emblazoned on Jenny Ng's apartment floor. And rather than rendering an iconic bat symbol in the center, it didn't.

Jenny stretched and rolled over, blinking herself into focus. Her loose pajama bottoms and T-shirt sparked a dim memory of Calvin McGuirk adorably banishing himself to the stairwell outside until she'd sleepily changed her clothes. When she let him back in, he tucked her into bed as her consciousness packed up and left town for the night.

She sat up and yawned. Morning tapped its toes impatiently, but Jenny let it glower and check its watch as she slowly shifted off the futon. Her cell phone was charging on the window sill—Calvin must have plugged it in. She smiled and grabbed it, flipping it open to check the time: almost nine. She'd gotten yesterday off for the horsenapping by promising to show up to work for second shift today. That gave her enough time to meet both agents with Calvin before taking the subway back to Brooklyn; Miller & Barash, where Jenny translated legal documents, was just a hop, skip and a couple of subway stops away in Prospect Heights.

A big bag of raw vegetables sat on top of the mini-fridge with a slip of paper. Calvin's overdramatic signature—he actually dotted the *i* with a star, like a third grade girl or a Venice Beach debutante—swept the bottom half of the paper below his compact block letters:

> *Skip the first agent—I'll go—you need to
> sleep! Carter's business card on your
> bag—see you there at 2. Horse food on
> fridge.*

Jenny stood. Her joints made noises like plastic packaging bubbles accosted by obsessive compulsives. She glanced at the bag of vegetables and rounded the corner to the bathroom alcove.

Rex stared down at her passively. He puffed very wet vapor from his nostrils: *Morning.*

Jenny's face dropped into her hands. "I didn't," she said. She looked back up. "I did. I brought you inside."

Rex sniffed. *Evidently.*

Jenny sniffed, too—magical otherworldly horse or not, he digested food just like a real one. A small pile of crumbling manure steamed on the floor at his tail end, by the bathroom door. The smell was quickly signing a lease with an eye on permanent residence. Her apartment would never be the same. "I don't suppose you're toilet trained?" Jenny asked with little optimism. Rex tossed his head, and she gave in, scratching his muzzle and pressing her forehead to his nose. "We'll work it out. But I get first shower." She patted his neck and inched around him to the bathroom, gagging a little on the stench of manure.

Twenty minutes later, showered and refreshed and wondering why she even *got* tired if she was indestructible—shouldn't the two be related somehow?—she heard a knock on the door. Someone spoke on the other side: "Miss, ah, Ng?"

The voice was familiar. Jenny's mind raced. "One sec!" she shouted. She tore off the bath towel and tossed it over Rex's head; the disguise might fool a severely disabled kindergartener with both eyes taped shut, but probably wouldn't cut it in her current situation. "Go!" she whispered frantically, pushing on the horse's shoulders. He outweighed her by nearly two thousand pounds, and wasn't going to budge involuntarily. "Come on," she pleaded in a hissing whisper. "Just get in the bathroom. Please!" After all she'd been through, this may have been the most surreal moment yet: naked, dripping wet, and trying to push a humongous horse with a towel on his head into her bathroom.

Beneath the towel, Rex heaved a gigantic horsey sigh that rattled his lips, and tried turning around. His hooves clomped on the hardwood,

207

making Jenny wince anxiously with every step. The small alcove leading to the bathroom was tight, but he squeezed through and ducked under the top of the doorframe. There was no room to close the door, but unless someone went past the corner, he was out of sight. "One sec!" Jenny called again. "Be right there!" She reached into the bathroom and yanked the towel off Rex's head; he looked back, fully embarrassed. Jenny shrugged a weak apology and snapped the towel up, spreading it downward over the pile of manure. She wrestled with a pair of shorts and a clean T-shirt, scrambling to get dressed and straighten herself out. "Coming!" she announced. Finally, she opened the door part way.

On the landing outside her apartment, wearing a gray suit more colorful than his sallow face and thinning hair, was the old detective who'd questioned her at the Coney Island police station. He smiled weakly and gave a little wave; he carried a thick folder under one arm. "Miss Ng, ah, good morning," he said in the same old halting, grandfatherly manner. He squinted at the sharp contrast from the dark stairwell to Jenny's brightly sunlit apartment.

"Detective...!"

"Ah, Monaghan, Detective Monaghan, yes," he said.

"Right," said Jenny. "Detective Monaghan, hi." She blinked in what she hoped was the most surprised and innocent expression she might possibly own. Two dozen *Law & Order* episodes flashed quickly through her mind; none of them ended well for the perky young suspect being questioned in her apartment.

"Do you mind if I, you know, come in?" said Detective Monaghan.

"I was—actually, I was just on my way out!"

"Don't, ah, go out with a wet head, Miss Ng," the detective joked feebly, with a tiny laugh.

"Right," Jenny pulled at her wet, spiky hair. "Just got out of the shower. I'm in a hurry, 'cause I have a meeting. For work."

"You found a job!" Detective Monaghan beamed. "That's a, ah, very good step. What are you doing?"

"Oh, a bunch of things," Jenny shrugged modestly. "I'm working at an office, and doing a show, you know, whatever pays the bills."

"This shouldn't take too long," said the detective. "If you wouldn't, ah, mind?"

Jenny bit the bullet, hoping it wouldn't end up a literal one. "No, sure, I mean, yeah," said Jenny. She opened the door wider. "Come in."

Detective Monaghan shuffled inside and reeled, his face going sour. "That's quite a smell!" he exclaimed. "What is that, that's, ah, that stuff...you're making, ah, *kimchi*, yeah? That's what they call that?"

"Yes!" Jenny latched on to the alibi like a starving leech on a femoral artery. She tried to inconspicuously keep herself between Monaghan and the bathroom. "Yeah," she said more calmly. "Making kimchi. It gets pretty smelly, yeah!"

Monaghan chuckled pleasantly. "Yeah, I've, ah, smelled it before, I think," he said. A thought visibly crossed his face. "Funny, though—ah, isn't kimchi a, ah, you know, a *Korean* dish? From, ah, Korea, yeah?"

"Uh huh," Jenny smiled blankly.

"You're, ah, Chinese though, right?" he said, stirring the air like he was digging for memories in a bowl of porridge. "Cantonese, yeah? Not Korean?"

Jenny paused. "Well, yeah," she said. "But lots of people eat kimchi. My mom always used to make it."

"Ah," the detective nodded sagely. "This is her, ah, recipe?"

"Nope," Jenny shook her head and grinned, hoping an ear to ear row of teeth would sufficiently camouflage her nerves. "All mine."

Detective Monaghan gave the room a once over, not slowing down as his eyes swept past the bathroom alcove and the towel on the floor.

"Sorry, the place is a mess," Jenny laughed nervously.

"Right, you're on your way, you know, out, ah, to your job," said Monaghan. "Your meeting."

"Right."

"How long does the kimchi take?"

Jenny skipped a beat. "Huh?"

He smiled. "It's for lunch? Or can you, ah, leave it? You know, all day?"

"It's for the weekend," Jenny decided. "It takes a few days. You know, it has to...ferment." She was pretty sure about that. Her mom *had* made kimchi a few times, though more the way a Jewish mother might make spaghetti marinara than out of any personal cultural tradition.

"Ah, I got it," said Detective Monaghan.

Jenny wondered helplessly if he actually had.

"So—you're probably, ah, wondering why I'm here," Monaghan began.

"Yes?"

The detective looked at her expectantly. "You are?"

"Uh," Jenny lost the thread. "I'm what?"

"Wondering why I'm, you know, here?"

"Oh—yes!" Jenny exclaimed. "Yeah, what can I do for you?"

"It's the darnedest thing," Monaghan said, shuffling through his folder. "You remember, you know, that horse? The, ah, horse you helped us out with back in, ah, June?"

Jenny nodded slowly, building up speed to give the impression of a rapid approach toward an exceedingly distant memory. "The horse," she said. "Right, I remember. He was...big."

"He was big, ah, yeah," Monaghan agreed. "Fact is, we had to really work to find a, ah, place to keep him. Regular, you know, stables—he was a, ah, bit too much for them."

"I can imagine," Jenny poured on some sympathy for hardworking folks dealing with tremendous problems like gigantic horses and where to put them. The sympathy wasn't hard to muster.

"So we've been, ah, keeping him in one of our own places," Monaghan went on, "to, you know, see if his owner will, ah, show up. Maybe shed a little light on the situation."

Jenny once again found herself performing a careful balancing act between not seeming like she knew anything and not seeming like an idiot. She wondered if all of her conversations with the police were going to be like this. If so, simple seemed like the best solution: "Right."

"Vegetables?"

The non-sequitur jumped up and bit Jenny on the nose. She tried not to panic. "What?"

Monaghan looked down at the top of the mini-fridge. "That's a, ah, lot of vegetables there," he said.

Jenny stared at the raw vegetables overflowing the plastic bag. "Yeah." Her synapses played an impromptu round of word association to see if they could win a suitable excuse for the vegetables, or at least a lovely parting gift.

"For the, ah, you know...kimchi?" said Monaghan.

"Yes!" Jenny said thankfully. "Fresh vegetables are best."

"So it's a big, ah, party this weekend then," the detective suggested. "Lots of folks, ah, for kimchi."

Jenny's face was bright and empty. "Uh huh," she said. "Everybody likes kimchi." She cocked an eyebrow at her own absurd sales pitch, wondering just how much of an idiot she sounded like.

"I'm sure," Monaghan smiled. "It's a little much for me. Have to, you know, stay away from the spicy, ah, foods. Doctor's orders."

"Oh," said Jenny. "Sorry."

"So you'll never believe what happened yesterday," Monaghan forged on, "with, ah, the horse. Did you, ah, see the news last night?"

Jenny shook her head.

"Funny thing, ah, the horse," Monaghan began. He sniffed and played up an overpowering lightheadedness: "Hoo, boy! That kimchi, it's, ah, pretty powerful! What a smell!" He slammed back into first gear with just as little warning. "The, ah, horse, he was, you know...stolen. Yesterday afternoon."

"Oh!" Jenny wasn't sure what tone of voice would best reflect equal parts surprise, passing concern, and complete ignorance. She aimed for three parts light and one part bland, figuring no real opinion equated to no real risk.

"Somebody just rode away on him," said Monaghan.

"Wow," Jenny said. "I don't even know how to ride a horse." She felt that was pushing it, and added: "Like, who does, in the city, right?"

"I suppose, ah, it'd be a job requirement," said Monaghan, "for a, you know, horse thief."

Jenny tried her ponderous face. "Hm, good point." She nodded as an afterthought.

"So I'm just following up," the detective continued. "Ah, checking in with all the, you know, folks, the witnesses, we had the, ah, first time around. When we got the horse."

"Right," said Jenny. "Yeah, that's weird."

"Ah, what's weird, Miss Ng?"

Jenny fumbled a bit. "The...horse," she said shortly. "Somebody stealing him. Right?"

"Yeah, of course," Monaghan smiled. "So, if you could, ah, just let me know—where you might have, you know, been yesterday. Around...ah, noon?"

"What?"

"Just covering our bases, Miss Ng," he assured her. "It's, ah, standard procedure. Just need your whereabouts, you know, on record. As somebody who, ah, knew the horse. Or, you know, *about* the horse."

"I was with my partner," Jenny blurted.

Monaghan perched his half-glasses on his nose, plucked a pen from his jacket pocket and held up the folder. "Her name?"

"His," Jenny corrected. "My, um, *business* partner. I do a show with him."

"That's, ah, great," Monaghan smiled. "What was his, ah, name again?"

"Calvin. Calvin McGuirk."

"Can I get his, ah, you know, his number?"

"Sure, one sec." Jenny rushed to her futon and grabbed her cell phone. She scanned through her contact list and read off Calvin's number. "We were rehearsing yesterday," she explained.

"What sort of show?" Monaghan asked. "The, ah, show that you and Mister McGuirk do?"

"It's a magic act," Jenny said, faltering humbly. "Just something fun we do a couple nights a week."

Detective Monaghan beamed. "That's great!" he said. "I'm a, ah, big fan. Love magic shows."

"Sure, you should come see it," said Jenny. She smacked herself mentally. If Monaghan was already suspicious of her, having him at the *Beau* asking questions about her wasn't the best idea. "I could get you tickets," she offered. She smacked herself harder inside her own head.

"That'd be nice, ah, very nice, thank you." Monaghan poised his pen over the folder. "Where's the show?"

"At the *Beau Regardez* in Chelsea," said Jenny, kicking herself in disbelief. "On Eighth."

Monaghan scribbled on his folder and nodded, "Uh huh. Uh huh." He pushed his glasses down his nose and peered over them at Jenny. "So, ah, you and Mister McGuirk were, ah, rehearsing yesterday?"

"Yeah."

"And he'll confirm this, then, yeah?"

"Yeah," Jenny repeated. "Definitely."

"Then I've, ah, got all I need here, Miss Ng." Monaghan scribbled a little more and put his pen away. He took his glasses off and smiled like he was showing off new dentures. "Thanks so much. Sorry to, ah, be a bother."

"No, no bother," Jenny said, laying it on thick.

Monaghan put his glasses away and shoved the folder under his right arm; he stuck out his left hand. "Thanks again for your, ah, time, Miss Ng." Jenny awkwardly offered her left hand to match, and shook his. Detective Monaghan glanced down and turned the back of her hand upward. "Looks like that, ah, cut cleared up no problem."

Jenny tried not to flinch. "Cut?"

"From the fold-out couch," Monaghan said. "I was, ah, worried it might leave a pretty bad scar, but, you know, there's almost nothing, ah, left." He peered at her hand. "Just a mark. It, ah, healed up nicely."

"Right, yeah," Jenny said, pulling her hand back. "I'm a pretty fast healer."

"Good thing," said Monaghan. He looked over at her futon. "Got rid of the, ah, couch, huh?"

"It wasn't here," she said truthfully. "That was at a friend's place."

"Oh, of course," Monaghan shook his head at his forgetfulness. "At your, ah, friend's place. Mister Heckler's place."

"Yeah," said Jenny. "Right."

"My mistake, sorry," the detective said. "Thanks again." He headed for the door.

Jenny followed, and a thought hit her. "Detective?"

He paused and turned with a friendly smile. "Yes, Miss Ng?"

"That guy," she said. "The one you had me go see in the jail."

"In the, ah, holding cell," he said helpfully. "Our Mister Doe, yeah?"

"Yeah." Jenny tried to make it seem like a mere thought passing through with no plans to settle down. "What happened to him?"

Monaghan let out a wistful sigh. "He was transferred over to a, you know, medical facility. No change, but he seems, ah, happy enough. The doctors'll see what, ah, you know, what they can do for him."

"Oh," said Jenny. "Cool. I was just...I felt bad for him, I mean."

"Yeah," said Monaghan. He paused. "Yeah, it sounds like a, ah, tough spot. Not knowing, ah, who you are. You know."

"Um, yeah," Jenny said. "Thanks, though. For letting me know."

Monaghan smiled at her, his watery eyes reflecting the bright sunlight at the window. "Sure, of course. Thank *you*, Miss Ng. Have a, ah, nice day. Enjoy that kimchi," he added. "Me, I can't, ah, stomach the stuff." With a cheerful nod, he walked out and closed the door.

Jenny let out a giant breath that must have been all that was holding her up, because she immediately stumbled over and caught herself on the fridge. Last night had been rough enough, and the deceptively doddering detective's passive interrogation techniques put her on edge. She grabbed a soda from the mini-fridge, snapped the tab and took a long gulp. She planted the can on the floor and let out an impressive burp. Like a well-considered response, a soft, growly nicker echoed off the tile walls in the bathroom. "Coming!" said Jenny, rounding the corner to the alcove.

Rex stared back at her over his shoulder; his front legs were in the bathtub, while his rear legs stomped on the floor right by the door. She'd left his saddle on, partly because she wasn't sure how to take it off, but mostly because she'd completely crashed without giving anything much thought after Calvin tucked her into bed.

Calvin—he'd probably be getting a phone call from Detective Monaghan very soon. Monaghan would ask questions, and expect matching answers. While Calvin would surely say whatever he had to, to help cover Jenny, his fabricated alibi might not match hers, and Monaghan would be on top of that like David Dennis on an ambitious chorus boy.

Her phone was on the small shelf by the door. She grabbed it to speed dial Calvin, but suddenly slapped the phone shut. The same *Law & Order* episodes paraded through her head again; half of them prominently featured cops scanning phone records to track down all the calls their suspect made. A call to Calvin immediately after Monaghan left would be a big red flag on her phone records. She was trapped—either call Calvin and tip her hand, or don't call him and risk mismatched alibis.

"Crap," she said, scowling at the phone like it had presented her with Sophie's Choice. Jenny paced back to the bathroom and harrumphed at the giant horse's ass aimed squarely at her.

Rex *chuffed* a bit and gave her a laconic look. *You think you've got problems?*

"Okay, wait," Jenny put her thoughts into words to make them come clear. "How fast *can* you go?"

The horse's eyes narrowed with a mischievous gleam.

It took only a minute to shove a change of clothes in her bag, grab her sword case, and hug Rex tight as she pushed through the bathroom mirror to Wonderland. Mirror Jenny sported a supportive thumbs-up before the world turned inside-out and the color drained from the walls. Rex backed up uncomfortably through the alcove to the wider room of Mirror Jenny's studio apartment. She pulled the door into its ambiguous midway phase, simultaneously open and closed like a photographic double exposure, and rushed down the stairs, leading Rex by the reins just as she'd led him up the night before. Outside, with the dodging and darting air of the mirror world skittering by them, Rex knelt for a moment to let Jenny mount up, then looked back at her with a twinkle in his eye. The message was clear; Jenny grabbed on and held tight.

The dull colors of Wonderland flashed by like a kinetoscope run by an arthritic epileptic, shifting and halting and speeding in a blur of indiscernible shape and motion. Jenny had trouble tracing their path, but they spent a minute rushing up the East River beneath several bridges before making a sharp left and rocketing up into Queens. Jenny wasn't surprised to see they were on Calvin's street seconds later; when Rex skidded to a stop outside of the Wonderland version of Calvin's building, she was ready—the horse leaned forward and she slid off the saddle, trying valiantly to hit the ground running. She immediately stumbled and fell over on the sidewalk. Recovering, she scrambled to her feet, securing her bag and the sword case. "Be right back!" she called behind her, running up the steps to the front door.

She got the point of Wonderland doors by now; she pushed through it without hesitation and barely registered its wavering state. She took the stairs two or three at a time, racing up to Calvin's floor, and dashed through his glitchy open-and-closed door without pause. Once more in a familiar environment, she got her bearings quickly—Jenny ran to Calvin's bathroom and practically jumped through the mirror, the squirming explosion of red noise and screeching light catching her in mid-air as she tumbled through multiple dimensions to spill out on the bathroom floor.

"Calvin!" she breathlessly hollered out into the apartment.

"Ack!" Calvin shrieked in response.

He was in the shower, holding a bar of soap between his legs.

"Oh god, oh god," Jenny babbled. "I'm sorry! Sorry! I'll wait outside!"

"Um," Calvin said, water dripping down his long skinny frame. "Yeah." He calmed down a bit. "It's okay," he said nervously. "I'll be out in a second."

Jenny averted her eyes, which brought her face to face with the mirror, through which she was staring straight at Calvin anyway. She blushed and walked briskly out, ignoring Mirror Jenny, who waggled her eyebrows and leered at the magician in the shower.

In the living room, Jenny collapsed on the couch. She saw Calvin's cell phone lying on the cushion, and checked the screen: no missed calls. Monaghan hadn't called yet. Jenny looked at the time—she felt a giddy shiver of pride when she realized she'd gone from Park Slope to Astoria in under seven minutes. It was no mystery why Caravel and Ketch and the others traveled the Wonderland Express.

Thinking of the other Not-Grim Reapers, Jenny's mind wandered to the Count—Pauzok, she remembered—cooped up in a psych ward somewhere in the city. Immortal and indestructible, he could be there for the rest of eternity...until doctors started wondering why his records stretched back decades and he still didn't look a day over forty. The thought gave her chills. What would they think? What kind of experiments would they conduct to figure out his secret? Worse—what if they never even realized his remarkable longevity, and he ended up institutionalized for the rest of time...or longer? She struggled to come up with reasons why it just wasn't her problem, fighting with herself to keep out of it, to just stop getting so caught up in everybody else's problems. She hadn't helped John. He was dead, his body probably swept out to sea by now. She winced angrily, chastising herself for not thinking of calling the police last night; maybe she couldn't save John's life, but she could have at least reported his death. Maybe the authorities could have found his body, let his family have some closure...she resolved to do something about that. Today.

The Count—Pauzok—would have to wait. At least until tomorrow.

Calvin came out clad only in cargo shorts and scrubbing his hair dry with a dark blue towel adorned with yellow stars. "Hey, good morning!" he said cheerfully.

"Morning," said Jenny. She scrunched up her face. "Sorry about...."

"Yeah, whatever. The only problem with really pretty women looking at me naked," said Calvin, "is that it doesn't happen very often."

216

Jenny clamped down on her smile, pretending she didn't catch the compliment. "Liar," she teased. "What about that blonde girl at the party?"

"I guess my manly super-attractive Irish Sex Freckles didn't work on her," Calvin swept his hands melodramatically, showing off his pale, skinny chest.

"Total lesbian," Jenny declared.

"Nah, she left with that opera guy," Calvin admitted with a self-deprecating grin.

"That just confirms it." They laughed as the magician tossed the towel over a chair. "Listen, you might get a phone call today. I mean, probably will."

"From?"

"Remember I told you about the cop in Coney Island? The one who asked me about Rex, who—"

"The guy who showed you the Count, yeah," Calvin said. "What? Why's he...oh." He slapped his forehead and collapsed on the couch next to Jenny. "Oh, man."

"He just wanted to cover his bases, he said," Jenny assured Calvin. "I told him we were rehearsing yesterday. Nowhere near the airport." She threw a meaningful look.

"Right," Calvin said drearily. "Rehearsing yesterday, here, all afternoon. Got it." He sat back and spread his arms across the back of the couch. "I can't believe I'm lying to the cops."

Jenny patted his thigh. "You're already guilty of grand theft horse."

"*Accessory* to grand theft horse," Calvin corrected her. He smiled broadly. "You're the mastermind around here."

"The cop said we were on the news," said Jenny. "You see anything?"

"I got home pretty late," Calvin pointed out. "We can go to Starbucks and check online later. Maybe somebody put your escape on YouTube!"

"Ugh."

"Don't worry, I don't think anybody got a shot of you. Just Rex, and he's so fast he's probably just blurry." Calvin stood up and stretched. "You want to grab breakfast and go meet Abe Roman with me?"

Jenny shook her head. "You were okay going without me, right?"

"Yeah, well, Abe doesn't seem like the right guy anyway," Calvin said. "If you can only make it to one of them, I'd rather you come to Barry

Carter's. He looks more like a real agent. I just figured if you're awake already, and you're here, then maybe...?"

"I just needed to let you know about Detective Monaghan," said Jenny. "I didn't want to call, 'cause I thought the cops would trace the call and think it was funny that I called my alibi person right after telling the cops my alibi."

Calvin nodded, impressed. "Good thinking."

"So I rode over. Rex is waiting outside." She saw Calvin give a start, and quickly added: "In Wonderland. There's some stuff I need to do today, and I've got to go to work after we meet Barry Carter, so I don't have too much time."

"'Sokay." Calvin was entirely agreeable. "You have Carter's address, yeah?"

She'd actually forgotten the business card in her rush, but Calvin rewrote the address on a slip of notebook paper, which she folded up and put in her bag. He went into his bedroom to get dressed, and Jenny took the opportunity to change clothes in the bathroom, putting on a more presentable outfit with light pants and a nice summer blouse. She stuffed her shorts and T-shirt in her bag, and stuffed her socked feet into her Doc Martens.

Dressed and ready, Calvin tried to convince her to at least eat breakfast with him before riding off into the reflected sunset, but Jenny had a goal in mind, utterly unaccompanied by a plan, and she wanted to figure it out as soon as possible. She promised to meet him at Barry Carter's office. Calvin squeezed her tight, then pulled back and looked at her with a silly grin. "Agents!" he said.

Jenny smiled back mock condescendingly. "Agents," she echoed. "Go have breakfast. Make sure you get to Abe's on time."

"Yeah, *some* of us still have to use the subway," he groused playfully.

Jenny grinned. "I am *so* not apologizing for that," she said. She was pretty stoked that she had a new mode of travel, faster and more direct than anything public transportation could manage.

Calvin saw her to the bathroom mirror, where they said goodbye and she shoved through it, back into Wonderland. The matter-of-fact procedure was starting to feel quite normal.

She went downstairs and out the front door, not quite so rushed now. She knew where she wanted to go, and using the Wonderland Express, she wasn't worried about travel delays. Rex waited on the Wonderland sidewalk, flutters of sketchy, halting shadows tracing trails over his back as the bizarre clouds scraped across the sky. He knelt, and Jenny hefted herself up and into the saddle. With enough practice, she might even improve her riding skills.

Across the street, the real world gleamed in the broad window of a soup and salad place. Past cars and early morning pedestrians, Jenny saw Calvin McGuirk emerge from his building, patting himself and his backpack in a mental checklist to make sure he hadn't forgotten anything. Jenny smiled, a catch in her throat and a flush on her face. Calvin was a great guy; she'd gotten really lucky bumping into him. She wondered how the past couple of months would have gone without him, dealing with all of this strangeness on her own.

She waved to the magician, knowing he couldn't see her, and clicked her tongue, turning Rex around. The horse was off like a shot, Jenny clinging to the saddle so she wouldn't roll right off his back.

Jenny knew where Empire Tech was; she'd even considered enrolling a few years back, to pick up some skills more practical than photography and a degree that would pad her résumé better than a Bachelor of Fine Arts, which might give her a chance to make a decent living without being shackled to a cubicle somewhere. As trade schools went, it was fairly well-known and had a great reputation, a notch or two above the joints that took aim at the unemployed and unsatisfied on late night cable TV commercials. The tuition was as formidable as the institution, though, and Jenny had no easy way to gather the paperwork required to prove she qualified for financial aid, so it ended up being one more in a long line of scenic detours that circled right back around to a life of scraping to get by.

The main building of Empire Technical Institute was on the Lower East Side, a stone's throw away—for certain values of stone and throw—from the bulk of the properties owned by New York University. It was a subtle jab at Empire Tech students: you're not good enough to shine the shoes of *real* college students, but you're welcome to bask in the ambience of their fascinating conversations at local coffee houses. According to some Empire alumni Jenny knew, the students at Empire Tech had two terms for NYU students: the adequately clever "nyoobies," and the significantly more revealing "assholes."

Rex took a long, leisurely run through the mirror world, Jenny's wandering thoughts translating to a meandering trail down the East River. A leap from the water took them over the FDR, shooting straight down Avenue C. The horse knew just where to take her, and Jenny started to get an inkling of what Caravel had suggested the night before: he really was *part* of Jenny. That accounted for the apparent telepathy, the exultant feeling she experienced when he ran flat out, and how he always knew where to run without Jenny giving it much thought. He was practically another limb of her body, if perhaps one with a much more sarcastic personality than her usual arms and legs. The realization only further confused her, though—if Rex was originally Pauzok's horse, how could he so suddenly and easily be an extension of Jenny? It was a good question for Sunday night's lesson with Caravel.

The stallion made a sweeping arc at Tenth Street and sauntered another block to Tompkins Square. Jenny patted his shoulder, and he looked back at her. "You know I hate doing this," she told the horse. "But you're kind of a wanted, um, horse. It's not safe for you to be out there."

Rex shook his mane out vigorously. He would comply, but he didn't have to like it. Horses were meant to roam free across lush green grassy plains, and eat them; not stagnate in disjointed, sepia-toned worlds where the grass itself inconsistently existed. Still, Jenny made a good point. Until his status was clear, he would stay parked in Wonderland when they were out and about in the city.

He knelt down to let Jenny off; she managed a bit more grace this time, tripping twice but staying on her feet, and rubbed his nose as he rose. "Stay close," Jenny whispered; her voice stretched and wobbled in the slippery Wonderland wind.

She left the park and looked for helpful reflections—around the corner was a restaurant with broad French doors alongside an outdoor seating area; the full-color world went about business as usual on the other side of the mirror image. Jenny saw enough people walking the street that she decided not to chance a sudden reappearance. She passed the restaurant, a broad-windowed store front, and a mural featuring cartoonishly painted clocks, as if Salvador Dali did community service as part of a Clean and Sober program. Past the mural was another restaurant—the entrance was set back in a recess, slightly concealed, and Jenny figured it would do. Moving close to the reflecting glass in the front door, she focused, pushed, and slipped through...then moved straight forward away from the door in the real world, trying to act natural, like she'd just left the restaurant. She glanced over her shoulder; the restaurant was closed, locked, and dark. Nobody seemed to notice that she'd just walked out of a locked door; nobody even gave her a second glance. Mirror Jenny laughed silently in the reflection, and the world kept spinning.

Readjusting to the real world compass, Jenny saw she was a block down and a block over from the Leonard L. Breem Building, the squat square monster that took up half a block of Lower East Side real estate and housed the administration and most of the classrooms and workshops for Empire Tech. Dodging other pedestrians—the usual varied city folk on their many and varied Friday morning missions—Jenny still wasn't sure what her plan was, but the first few steps had developed in her mind.

She caught sight of Rex in the reflection off a van window. The horse was shadowing her in Wonderland, keeping pace easily as he trotted alongside Mirror Jenny. Her jaunty reflection waved to her and patted Rex's flank solidly. Jenny returned a tiny smile, but suddenly thought to wonder exactly what Mirror Jenny *was*—was she actually there, in Wonderland, with Rex, right now? Did Rex see her walking next to him? Did she really just touch him? Was she an actual person? And where did she go when Jenny went Through the Looking Glass? More items piled up on the list to present to Caravel on Sunday.

Jenny approached the glass double doors of the Breem Building and gave a subtle waist-high gesture to Rex and Mirror Jenny, signaling them to not distract her. Empire Tech students in assorted shapes, sizes and colors knocked this way and that like a junior high science fair simulation of air molecules. A cute guy with round Lennon glasses and a big Marx nose held the door for her; she smiled graciously and went through.

The atmosphere inside the Breem Building was very busy, full of rushing people, the stiff musty detergent smell of fresh textbooks, and funny echoes incompletely baffled by unusual architecture and metal panels. Jenny walked directly to the front desk, a dully gleaming brushed metal torus between two sets of stairs that each led upward and downward in square spirals. The lean guy behind the desk had bleached blond hair and an unattractive scar twisting his upper lip. His long, thin wrists swung back and forth quickly as he shuffled through papers, and he gave off a distinctly feminine air. Jenny was sure he was wearing eye makeup. "Can I help you?" he asked her, not even looking up. He clearly thought that knowing she was there without looking was a talent on par with fire eating or lion taming.

"Hi," Jenny said, ignoring the fact that the exchange of pleasantries was one-sided, and therefore not an exchange. "I'm looking for a guy."

"Get in line, honey," the kid behind the desk quipped.

Jenny put on the obligatory smile his cliché deserved. "Ha, right," she said. "No, I mean, there's a student here, who I need to get in touch with. Or, well—one of his friends."

The guy blew errant spikes of hair out of his eyes, annoyed. "Sorry, we can't give out student information—"

"No, I don't need—I mean, you could just give them my number, right?" Jenny tried to keep her tone sweet. "It's really important. I just need one of them to call me back."

"I can leave a tag in his digital inbox." The unsaid final *dub* was very nearly audible.

"Cool, yeah, thanks," said Jenny.

"Name?"

Jenny paused. She wanted some way for John's family or friends to get in touch with her, but a message left for him might never be seen. She didn't know his last name, anyway, and there were probably at least a hundred Johns at the school. She flashed back to the lobby of the *Beau* on Wednesday night and mentally crossed her fingers. "Uh...Callie?"

The receptionist's fingers paused over his keyboard. He waited, looking at Jenny expectantly. He cleared his throat. "*Last* name?" he finally said.

"Um." Jenny cringed. "Listen, can I be honest?"

"Only if you don't lie," the blond guy answered.

"I met a bunch of people at a party the other night," said Jenny, "and I think something...I'm worried something happened to one of them. I barely know them, but I just wanted to make sure he's all right." She pushed the sincerity with a wide-eyed expression. "Maybe there's just a few Callies? I could describe her—you know, like match her picture or something," Jenny suggested.

The guy sighed rudely. "Lamest...stalker line...ev-ar," he intoned.

"Please," Jenny said. "If I could just give you my number for her to call."

He smiled patronizingly at her, leaned his elbows on the desk, and propped his chin up on his fingers. "So," he smiled like a crocodile inviting a gazelle into the river for a quick swim, "describe her."

"She's uh," Jenny thought back. "She's a little taller than me, a little bigger. Short brown hair. Glasses."

"And that's Callie?" He didn't move from his smarmy pose.

"Um. Yeah."

He curtly returned to his paperwork. "You just described half the comp sci queens in the school. Nice try, though."

Jenny almost unleashed a barrage of swears in twenty languages, but she grappled her outrage with both hands and wrestled it into submission. If this slimy bastard only knew she could pull a very wicked sword out of the case on her back and slice him in two, he might be a little more polite. She was pretty sure, though, that "Don't slice people up just because they piss you off" was probably very near the top of Caravel's Guidelines for Grim Reaping Newbies.

Firmly ignored, Jenny turned away, at a loss for how to proceed. She'd faced death itself, even if she hadn't realized it at the time, and barely flinched; she'd learned to wield strange and superhuman powers, and even ride a horse, despite her shaky dismounts. The last thing she'd expected was to have her game plan stymied by a pissy bureaucrat. It was the kind of mundane obstacle she'd completely forgotten existed. Most of her other problems these days seemed easily solved by chopping off a limb, walking through a mirror, or speaking a foreign language. It was quite possible that her everyday problem-solving skills were suffering from severe atrophy.

Confidence bruised, she walked slowly out to the front doors. Before she pushed them open, she saw Mirror Jenny at the reflected desk, shaking her fist and mutely screaming at the bitchy receptionist's reflection. Jenny wished it were that easy.

Somebody rushed after her. "Hey!"

She jumped and turned to look.

A guy with sandy blond hair and an admirably failed attempt at a goatee opened the door, ushering her through and following behind as the door closed. "J.P.'s a dick," he said. "Fuck 'im. You're looking for Callie? Callie McDonough?"

"Uh, I'm not sure," said Jenny. "I don't know her last name."

"Short, brown hair, glasses," the guy said rapidly, "Just like you said." He had a breathless way of speaking, as if he'd actually forgotten the human lung's occasional need for a fresh batch of oxygen. "Wears jeans and sweatshirts. Going out with that Mike guy, hangs out with Ryan and John—"

"Yes!" Jenny cried. "That's her! You know her?" She jumped at the possible reprieve, and this guy's rapid-fire pace was infectious.

"Yeah, she's in my circuits workshop," he laughed. "Fuckin' J.P. She's not comp sci. She's an electrician."

"Can you give her my number?"

"Sure," the guy said. "If you do something for me."

Jenny returned his devious smile with a playfully suspicious gaze. "What?"

"Give me your number." His grin widened.

Jenny laughed. That was good enough, she decided. She rattled off her digits and made sure he had them right. He introduced himself as Rob. "Do you know where she is?" Jenny asked. "I mean, can you call her, or...?"

Rob shrugged. "I don't know her that well—but I've got circuits at ten. I can give her your number then."

"Oh, wow," Jenny shook his hand. "Thanks—thank you!"

"And who should I tell her she's calling?" Rob's eyebrows rose.

"Jenny," she said, but she thought twice. "Well—tell her it's Jade, from the magic show."

"All right, Magic Jade," said Rob. "She'll be out at twelve. I'll let her know it's important."

"Thanks, Rob," she shook his hand again.

"And I'll hang on to your number," he promised with a boyishly innocent expression. "In case you need *me* to call you really desperately some *other* morning."

Her confidence back in the saddle again, Jenny found a little bakery around the corner with sidewalk seating and excellent coffee. For the first time all week, she took a moment for herself, out in broad daylight, to simply sit and wait. For a dead girl, her life hurtled forward at a particularly lively pace. If she couldn't relax and be still every once in a while, she might run out of eternity.

Shortly before eleven, she texted Calvin: "Good luck with Abe!"

He texted back: "Agents!" Jenny couldn't help but laugh.

She sipped at her second cup of coffee and watched the cars pass by, people roaming the sidewalks for every important reason in the world. It was the first time all day she'd been out and *not* in Wonderland. Jenny decided she was getting a little too used to the eerie, stuttering world behind the mirrors; she resolved to spend more time in the real world, even if it meant she had to take public transportation. There was something so empty and static about Wonderland. It was a dead place, which made sense, but it wasn't grim or deathly—just dead; complacent and unchanging. The more she thought about it, the more she thought that the people around her, the cars zooming down the street, coffee being served and slurped down, traffic lights changing color, all of it changing and moving and populating the world before moving on to the next—*this* was what it meant to be alive. Impermanence. Uncertainty. A place where a door might be open or it might be closed, but not both at the same time.

It was only a few minutes after noon when her phone rang. She sighed with relief and answered. "Hello?"

"Hi—Jade?"

"Callie?"

"Yeah," said Callie, nervous laughter trailing her words. "Um, Rob gave me your number, said you needed me to call...?"

"Uh huh, yeah," Jenny said. "Do you have some time? I'm right nearby, at this bakery near your school. On Tenth?"

"Vinetti's?"

Jenny checked the painted window behind her. "Right!"

"Sure," Callie said. "I'll be there in a couple minutes."

Callie McDonough turned out to be just the Callie she was looking for. Jenny recognized her as she turned the corner, and waved to get her attention. Callie smiled back uncertainly and squeezed into the sidewalk café through a gap in the corner of the temporary railing. Her sweatshirt got caught on the corner, but she tugged it loose. "Jade! Hi!" she said.

"It's just Jenny," Jenny said politely. "Jade's the mysterious lady on stage. Jenny's just me."

Callie laughed lightly but genuinely and sat down. "So, um, what're you doing here?"

Jenny's face got serious. "Okay, this is weird," she said, "and I don't want you to get the wrong idea, but have you heard from John today?"

The girl nervously pushed her glasses up her nose and squinted her mouth to one side. "Oh. Were you there yesterday?"

"Yesterday?" Jenny was sure Callie couldn't be talking about last night.

"Those guys were pretty terrible to him," Callie said quietly. Her voice dropped an octave, shifting from carol to dirge.

"Wait—what?" Jenny was flying blind. "What happened?"

225

It didn't take long to get the whole story, or at least the parts that Callie knew. John Herron—that was his name—was already a misfit, a hyperkinetic ball of nervous energy with a string of geeky hobbies guaranteed to chum the alpha-male-infested waters of any social climate. Even at a school attended mostly by underachievers with an interest in technology and an encyclopedic knowledge of *Star Trek*, Monty Python, or both, John stood out as a geek. So he was already a magnet for teasing, bullying, and other social tortures.

The next to last thing he needed was for his father to be arrested, very publicly. The very last thing he needed was for the charges to be so serious.

It had filled the newspapers and swamped the major networks all day. While Jenny was stealing a horse and picnicking in Central Park, John's life was turning cartwheels so fast he was flung out of his comfort zone and into a grisly nightmare. The press gleefully reported, in that starving hyena way that saved them from slow news days, that John's father had been caught with a very young boy. Further investigation had uncovered photographs and videos proving it wasn't a one-time incident. Mister Herron had been hunting kids for at least half his life.

The shock of the revelation, coupled with the cruel suggestions some of his less evolved classmates had needled him with, had sent John running from the Breem Building yesterday with a stark, stunned look on his face. The last time Callie had seen him, he'd dropped one of his textbooks and just kept going. On one side, John was receiving the full heat and hatred of victims needing to lash out, people with no sense of the irony inherent in "sins of the father" painting John and his family as just another branch of the evil his father had perpetrated. On the other side, he was getting merciless teasing and unbearable insults from troglodytes who couldn't differentiate between Reality TV and reality *on* TV. The few folks in the middle could offer only empty, comforting words that produced more emptiness than comfort.

The regret on John's face last night—his pale, drawn expression as Curach's horse carried him into the darkness across the river—gelled in the wake of Callie's story. Jenny couldn't know the exact details, but the image of John choking back tears and hurling himself into the Hudson sprang into her mind, uninvited and unwelcome.

The possibility that there was more to the story than Callie knew—like personal memories John had of his father, buried deep, hidden away until the scab was torn off by the media storm—seared Jenny's heart like a branding iron. Maybe Caravel was right; maybe death wasn't wrong or right, fair or unfair. But Jenny hoped to never think it wasn't ugly.

Her phone vibrated. Jenny asked Callie to give her a moment and read the text from Calvin: "Abe = old + older. 1 hr of stories about famous dead people. Didn't even ask any questions."

She tried to laugh, but the story of John's life and death leeched away any amusement. She texted back "Sorry, be there at 2" and shut her phone.

"I feel terrible," Jenny told Callie. "I mean, I didn't really know him, but he seemed like a really good guy."

Callie smiled sadly. "He is," she said. "I don't know if...you know, maybe there was something there. About his dad and him." She shuddered.

Jenny put a sympathetic hand on Callie's arm. "I know." She wondered if she was doing the right thing...

...but with the sudden clarity of sunrise slicing through the dissipating morning clouds, it occurred to her that she wasn't. Closure might be a good thing, but learning about John's death—especially if it was suicide—wasn't going to close the book for John's family and friends. It would just open up a whole new chapter with too many questions and too much pain, which would never end because, no matter how much they knew, they could never know the answer to one simple question: Why?

All at once, Caravel's words washed over Jenny and filled her with profound understanding. They weren't saviors or heroes, these *anjos da morte*, Death's Little Helpers. They weren't demons or killers. They weren't meant to interfere with the living, or to keep them from dying, any more than they were meant to hasten their imminent ends. They weren't even there to bear witness, or to offer comfort—the living had each other to depend on, and all of the funerals and cemeteries and wakes and toasts and stages of grief were for *them*, the living, to work through the turmoil brought on by the departure of the dead. The dead, on the other hand, had nobody. Death was single and solitary, and Jenny understood for the first time the trite expression: we all die alone.

That was her job: to be there for the dead, not for the living. She couldn't offer the same overused meaningless phrases others might use to comfort the bereaved, because she knew better; she knew death intimately. What she could do, what only the Angels of Death on horseback could do, was be there for the dead, helping them make their decisions wisely, guiding them forward to wherever they were destined to go next.

Like it or not, Jenny had found her purpose. Comforting Callie or giving John's family closure wasn't it. She'd done her part last night, with Caravel and Curach. She'd seen John forward, to someplace else. He wasn't a part of this life anymore. And neither was Jenny.

She pulled her attention back to Callie. "Hey, um." She felt awkward, having called Callie so urgently, and now realizing she never should have. "That was work," she said lamely, gesturing to her phone and the recent text message. "I'm running a little late."

"Oh," Callie said, surprised. "Sorry. You have to go?"

"Yeah," Jenny said, shoving her phone in her bag and rising. "But Callie—thanks. I really had a good time at the party the other night, with you guys all there. I didn't know about...about John, and all that. I don't have a TV. And I was working...um, at home, all day yesterday."

"It's okay," said Callie. "Thanks for calling, though. I know John really likes you. I hope he'll be back at school soon. It's not his fault...all that stuff."

"He'll be fine," Jenny said. She knew she meant it. Just not in a way that was comfortable or comprehensible to the living.

"I'll let him know you came!" Callie said enthusiastically. "He totally thought you guys rocked at the show. We're totally going to come see you again!"

Jenny tried for a light, easy smile, but the one that came out was much older and heavier than a girl her age should be wearing. "Cool," she said. "Then I'll see you guys soon." She grabbed her bag and sword case, and slalomed through the outdoor tables. Callie called out behind her, and Jenny turned: "Yeah?"

"Wait," Callie said. "But then, why did you call? You didn't know about any of this?"

"Oh," Jenny said. She'd painted herself into a corner. "I, uh, saw a picture of him on TV this morning when I went to breakfast. I didn't know what they were talking about, but I was worried about him."

Callie considered that. "Oh." She shrugged. "Yeah, they've been running the story, like, every half hour. That and the horse thing."

"Uh, right," said Jenny. "Guess that's what I saw."

"I'll tell him 'hi' from you!" Callie promised. "When I see him."

"Cool," said Jenny. She waved and rushed down the street. She may not have done what she'd set out to, but she'd learned the valuable lesson that she shouldn't have tried to do it in the first place. As it turned out, an old dog—or even a dead one—*could* learn new tricks. Sunday night's lesson with Caravel couldn't come soon enough.

CHAPTER NINETEEN

Calvin nearly knocked over the magic table as he opened the dressing room door. He caught the table before it tipped over, but dropped his backpack, which crashed into the table anyway and sent two decks of cards shuffling across the floor of the *Beau*'s back hall. "Aw, *agents!*" Calvin swore.

"Agents" had become their neologistic curse word of choice, replacing most of the juicier profanities through sheer relevance. When they'd met outside Barry Carter's office ten minutes before their appointment, Jenny's quiet contemplative bemusement had fit Calvin's glum anxious disappointment like a warm, comfy sweater-vest on a starchy, pressed school uniform. Abe Roman, as Calvin's text implied, had spent over an hour spinning stories of bantering with Barbara Billingsley, dallying with Doris Day, rambling with Rosalind Russell, and sharing a birthday—as well as several outrageous parties—with Mary Pickford, all of whom were conveniently dead and unavailable to either confirm or deny Roman's tawdry tales. Among the few show business subjects that *hadn't* been discussed were the aspirations of the Amazing Quirk (and his lovely assistant), or any plan to make those hopes and dreams come true. If his celebrity claims held water, Abe Roman may—once upon a time—have been a well-connected figure in the entertainment industry; these days, with all his connections retired or deceased, he spent his days absently reminiscing with any desperate soul unlucky enough to walk into his office. His young assistant kept his schedule going, occasionally tried to find his clients work, and mostly tried to push her headshot photography services on said clients during their hasty retreat from Roman's deluge of name-dropping and Hollywood fantasies. Calvin suspected that many struggling performers probably gave in and threw their money at Roman's assistant hoping it would buy them a speedy escape from another dicey, dubious story about drinking with James Dean.

With all their eggs hastily and unexpectedly shoved into one basket, Calvin and Jenny had strapped on some bravado and marched proudly into Barry Carter's office hoping to turn their luck around. Their bravado sagging below their knees, they'd walked out less than thirty minutes later relatively certain that they would never hear from Barry Carter again. The tall, bald man only vaguely recalled who they were and what they did, and insisted that he only took on established acts or "triple threats," though he might "freelance" with them to see if they got any bites. Jenny had entertained tempting thoughts of punching him, kicking him, and slashing him with her sword to establish just how triply threatening she could be— not for herself, but more because of the crushed look on Calvin's face as he gamely tried to keep the conversation going. "Freelancing," according to the explanation they were given, meant that Carter might give them a call sometime if he found a good gig, but that he was under no obligation to even look for one.

Jenny sincerely wondered how anything ever got done in show business. Nepotism and sex seemed the two likeliest candidates.

Despite the setbacks, and their newly dour view of agents, they knew the show must go on; they spent Friday night commiserating, and showed up at the *Beau* on Saturday two hours ahead of curtain time to run through a few tricks on stage.

Kevin, David Dennis's prissy assistant, always made sure of their privacy when they needed to rehearse. Calvin insisted it was part of the Magician's Oath; of course, Calvin didn't associate with very many other magicians, wasn't aware of any oath, and had never sworn one. It was more a careful ruse designed to safeguard the secrets of Jenny's powers and Calvin's strange devices.

"Calvin," Jenny said as she collapsed on the big, beat-up orange easy chair in their dressing room. "I think we should probably talk."

Calvin rolled the magic table inside and shut the door. He offered a tiny, wistful smile. "I know," he said. "We're not going to do the act forever."

Jenny tucked her legs up under her and looked at Calvin affectionately. "Damn it, I hate always talking about this *right* before the show!" She sighed. "I really do like doing the show, Calvin."

"I know," the magician repeated glumly. He dropped down on a folding chair, his legs splayed out in two different directions.

"I do," she said earnestly. "It's not about the act, and it's not even about, you know, photography anymore."

"It's not me, it's you," Calvin grinned.

"Well, *yeah*," said Jenny. She shrugged plainly. "Calvin—I'm dead. Deceased. Not living. I'm...I'm...whatever I am now! And there's this whole other thing going on, a whole 'nother *world*, and it looks like I'm part of it. And I've got a job to do."

"But I don't get it," said Calvin. "What do all the other people do? The other...Deaths? Where do they go when they're not, you know, um...deathing?" He gestured feebly, at a loss. "Do they have apartments? Do they, uh, go to the movies? Do they get jobs, or have money, or buy stuff, or—hey, do they *eat?*"

"Whoa!" Jenny held up her hands. "I'm trying to work all this out, too! I mean, I still sleep and eat and all...but I don't know what would happen if I stopped. I haven't tried."

"Oog," Calvin said, squeezing his expression up. "Yeah, what if you *do* need to eat, and you try to go a week without it..."

"Well, I can't die," said Jenny. "Or, um, I can't die *again*. We know that, at least. So I don't really know what happens. That's why I'm going to go see Caravel tomorrow night. I need to ask about all this stuff. I need to find out what I'm supposed to do."

Calvin idly toed a rip in the carpet. "And then you'll...um," he hunted for the right words, "go do the death thing full time?"

"If I'm supposed to."

"But don't *you* get any choice in it?" Calvin protested. "I mean, you didn't go to a job fair and sign up for it or anything! You just kind of got forced into it."

Jenny nodded soberly. "Caravel said...some of us choose it, and some of us are chosen, and some of us...are just accidents. So if it's an accident— if *I'm* an accident, I mean—then I guess I *don't* get a choice. Like if you're in a plane crash or something, you don't get to choose that, right? Or if you're born with some kind of disease? Or just one arm? You accept it. You see what you can do with your life even if you *don't* get to choose which life it is."

"But you can do stuff about those!" said Calvin. "Okay, not the plane crash," he amended, then raced on, "but you can get a prosthetic arm, or treat a disease—"

"No cure for death," Jenny pointed out. She smiled gently at his attempt.

Calvin sat sullenly, long arm dangling below the chair, magician's fingers dancing idly. "So."

"So," Jenny agreed. She nudged his foot with hers and caught his eye. "Hey, I'll be your lovely assistant as long as I can."

"And when you find out the rules? And it turns out you're not allowed to do any, uh, freelance work—outside of Grim Reaping, I mean?"

"It's not that grim," Jenny borrowed Caravel's line.

"And then it turns out you have to sacrifice a tall, red-headed Irishman to complete your transformation?" Calvin gaped in mock horror.

Jenny grinned darkly. "We'll cross that bridge when we—"

A quick knock interrupted them; Kevin's muffled voice came through the door: "Ladies, you dressed?"

Calvin had gotten used to the *Beau Regardez* practice of referring to just about *any* performer as a lady. "We're dressed, Kevin!" he called.

"Damn," said Kevin, opening the door and leaning in. "Some fans in the lobby to see Jenny. Absolutely *delicious* guy and his supermodel baby factory?"

"Oh my god!" Jenny perked up. "Yeah, sure, let them in!" Calvin looked at her with a question mark. "It's the Raymonds," she explained, "remember? I told you about them—they came Wednesday night."

"They're hard to forget," Kevin meowed. He headed back down the hall.

"Right," Calvin remembered. "Cool—you've got fans!"

Moments later, a glowing blonde peeked in and a sparkling white smile illuminated the dressing room. "Here they are, Vincent!" she trilled prettily.

Vincent Raymond's chiseled features popped into view beside his wife's gloriously tanned face. "Jenny!" he said.

"Vincent! Carrie!" Jenny jumped up and skipped cheerfully over to the Golden God and Goddess. She hugged Vincent, trying to ignore the fact that he smelled like Christmas Eve and first-time sex combined, and pulled away to look at Carrie. "Wow!" she exclaimed, staring at the lovely round belly beneath Carrie's flowing floral-print dress.

"Just a few months now," said Carrie, "but it's already huggable!" She gave Jenny a big squeeze. Jenny felt the smooth, solid belly between them and marveled at the sensation.

"This is Calvin," Jenny said, pulling the beautiful people into the room. "You guys met really quickly the other night."

"The Amazing Quirk," Vincent said, his mellifluous voice washing over them as he stuck out a hand.

Calvin shook it. "Hi! Nice to meet you, sir."

"Just Vincent, Calvin," Vincent Raymond scolded him goodnaturedly. "And my wife, Carrie."

Carrie Raymond offered a hand simultaneously dainty and strong. "The Amazing Quirk," she fawned. "You were wonderful Wednesday night!"

"Thanks, ma'am." Calvin shook her hand—at her reproachful look, he corrected: "Um, Carrie. Thanks!" He nodded down at her belly: "And congratulations! When are you, uh, due?" Like most men, Calvin worked through this kind of script by rote; pregnancy wasn't really in his repertoire.

"November," Vincent answered, his arm wrapping around his wife's shoulders.

"But I think this one's in a hurry," Carrie beamed, patting her belly. "It won't wait that long!"

Jenny stood by the easy chair, gesturing for Carrie to take a seat. Long lithe legs swished gracefully, and the beautiful blonde sat lightly, crossing her legs in a ladylike fashion. Calvin pulled over a folding chair for Vincent as Jenny asked: "Do you know if it's a boy or a girl?"

"We've got a pretty good idea," said Vincent.

Carrie smiled up at her husband. "But we're keeping it a secret," she added.

"That's right," Vincent smiled back. "No fun spoiling the surprise."

"It would be like you telling everyone how you do your tricks!" Carrie suggested to Calvin.

The magician laughed. "Yeah, well, anybody could figure out my tricks," he said modestly. "You guys having a baby, that's a trick nobody could work out!"

A confused moment generated an awkward pause.

"Uh," Calvin said weakly, "except for...parents. Heh. Who have kids," he clarified.

The Raymonds laughed warmly. Jenny smiled cheerfully at Calvin.

"How *do* you do those tricks?" Vincent asked in amazement.

Carrie nodded and looked at Calvin McGuirk approvingly. "You really are amazing," she said sweetly. "Could you show us some tricks right now? You could warm up for the show!"

"Um, well," Calvin started.

"Oh, I'm sorry," Carrie said hastily. "How silly of me. All of your props are probably out on stage."

"No, no," said Calvin. "We keep all our stuff here."

"Don't want anybody poking around and finding out the secrets," Jenny pointed out.

Calvin patted the top of the magic table. "It's the Magician's Oath," he said dramatically. "I can't reveal my secrets or...uh..."

Jenny finished for him: "He gets sawed in half, and never gets put back together!"

Vincent and Carrie laughed pleasantly. "Oh," said Carrie suddenly, "are you going to do that kind of trick tonight? Sawing your lovely assistant in half?" She smiled suggestively.

Jenny raised her eyebrows and looked innocently upward. Calvin shrugged. "We've been thinking of working on it," he said. "Not tonight, no, but we might add it into the act later."

"My favorite trick was the rings," Vincent said. "They really just *hang* there—amazing!"

Carrie touched his hand excitedly. "Oh, yes! And Jenny does such a wonderful job with that 'window'—guessing all those birthdays!"

"Really," said Vincent. "Incredible, Jenny."

"Oh!" Carrie put a finger to her perfect pink lips. "Could you do that one? Could you tell us our birthdays, Jenny?"

Jenny made a show of resisting, but the Raymonds coaxed and cajoled, and even Calvin joined in. She couldn't say no forever. "All right!" she surrendered. "But I, uh, need to be in character first." She gave Calvin a look.

"Right," he said.

The magician pulled the spectacles and the Window to Your Soul from the magic table, and handed them over. Jenny dramatically leaned forward and put on the specs, straightening with a flare and flourish.

"Ladies and—well, lady and gentleman," said Calvin with a humble shrug, "the mysterious Jade!"

The Raymonds applauded, and Jenny presented the window in a melodramatic style that fit the brightly lit and badly carpeted dressing room as well as Armani on a squirrel. She raised it and peered through at the Raymonds. As always, the glowing characters exploded into view, spread across everything behind the small square of glass. Jenny focused on the ones she knew, the ones she could translate, as they danced on Carrie Raymond's face. She faltered for a moment, her jaw loose and her eyes frozen, but shook it off and played as if she were communing with her private spirit world. "Carrie, your birthday is...July Twenty-Sixth," she proclaimed.

"She's right!" Carrie's glee rang like a bell.

"Happy birthday," Calvin said. He hiked a thumb over his shoulder: "Belated, I mean."

"Thank you, Calvin," said Carrie graciously.

Jenny shushed them petulantly, grinned, and snapped back into character. "Vincent," she passed the window over his tall body as if reading lines from head to toe, though she'd already read his birthdate near his left shoulder. She gulped and blinked her eyes rapidly behind the magic spectacles, then said: "Your birthday is November Fifth."

Vincent grinned, his teeth far whiter than the fluorescent lights or dingy walls of the dressing room. "Phenomenal!" he said.

"Ooh," Carrie burbled, a thought bursting into her mind. "Can you do the baby? Can you tell us what date the baby will be born?"

Calvin looked inquisitively at Jenny, genuinely wondering.

"Um," said Jenny. "No, I can't—it doesn't really work that way."

Calvin and the Raymonds shared a collective disappointed *aww*.

"But Calvin and I have to get ready soon, anyway," said Jenny, removing the glasses and rubbing the bridge of her noise.

"We—" Calvin started it as a question, but saw Jenny's face switch gears: "—*do* have to get ready, yeah." He shrugged and smiled. "Getting close to show time!"

"Oh, that's a shame," said Vincent.

Carrie allowed her husband to help her up, and smiled at Jenny and Calvin. "It was lovely of you to see us, though," she said.

"Are you staying to see the show?" asked Jenny.

"Oh, no—sorry, Jenny," said Carrie. "We can't tonight."

"We have a previous engagement," said Vincent.

"But we'd love to take you out for dinner!"

"What are you doing next Friday?"

Jenny and Calvin agreed to meet the Raymonds for dinner the following Friday, exchanging cell phone numbers and targeting a vague midtown destination—Vincent assured them he'd find a nice restaurant that wasn't too stuffy or formal. After a flurry of goodbyes, some more *oohs* and *ahhs* over Carrie's belly, and promises to make sure next Friday's dinner happened, the Raymonds left and Calvin shut the door. He faced Jenny and raised an eyebrow. "What's up?" he said pointedly.

Jenny casually put the spectacles and window back in the magic table. "What?" she asked.

"Come on," said Calvin. "It's me. I know you well enough by now...."

Jenny looked down. "I didn't want to say anything," she said. "I mean, I don't know if the window would've worked on the baby or what, but...well."

Calvin nodded and touched her arm. "You saw their deathdays. Uh, deathdates. The days they're going to die."

Jenny looked up at Calvin sadly. "I don't think that baby's going to be born, Calvin," she said quietly. "Carrie and Vincent...they're both going to die before it's due."

"Oh, man," Calvin hugged Jenny comfortingly. "I'm sorry."

"It's probably a car accident or something," said Jenny. "They both had the same time, just a couple seconds away, on the same day. October Thirty-First."

"Ow," said Calvin. "Halloween? Man, that sucks. I mean," he added, "it sucks on *any* day. I just always liked Halloween."

"Yeah, me too," said Jenny.

"Dammit," Calvin whispered. He cleared his throat. "They seem pretty cool. That sucks. Hey," he asked abruptly, "are they famous or something?"

"Famous?" Jenny pulled back to look up at him. "I don't think so. Why?"

"Eh, nothing," said Calvin. "Just, she looked familiar."

Jenny rolled her eyes and grinned. "You met her on Wednesday. Remember? She's pretty hard to forget!"

"Well, yeah," Calvin said. "I know, right. I just had the weirdest feeling of *déjà vu*, seeing her."

"You were distracted by visions of agents at the time," Jenny reminded him.

"Agents?" Calvin said, pretending to dredge up the memory. Then he scowled and swore: "*Agents.*"

"Agenting mother agents," Jenny added for good measure. They smiled.

Show time crept up soon after. The *Beau* filled up quickly; a lot of favorites were performing tonight, including the Amazing Quirk and his lovely assistant, Jade. Calvin and Jenny got ready and went out to the audience to watch the earlier acts. There were musicians, singers, comedians—all sorts of variety acts, featuring plenty of regulars and a few new faces—but the majority of the crowd was there for the main attraction: the magic show. Jenny tapped Calvin's shoulder when their turn was two acts away; a couple of guys who made interactive art using audience participation were barking strange requests and one-liners at the highly responsive crowd. Calvin lingered to see how one of the sloppy paintings turned out—surprisingly well, as it happened—and followed Jenny out the back of the theatre to head around backstage.

They were waiting in the wings when the audience applauded the act just before theirs. It was the team of juggling girls that had performed Wednesday—John's friends. Jenny felt a tiny pang deep inside, like someone doing maintenance in her brain had dropped a wrench and it fell way, way down, all the way to the bottom of her stomach, clanging against railings and catwalks as it tumbled. By the time it hit bottom, though, she could barely hear the echoes clinking through the steel corridors of her internal edifice. The same way she felt less and less pain every time she was stabbed or cut or chopped, she felt numbed to the once overwhelming regret and desperation that had driven her to save John. Whether it was aftershocks from the moment of enlightenment at yesterday's meeting with Callie, or just the natural transition from the world of the living to the world of the dead, Jenny was gradually experiencing a kind of disconnect, pulling away from a world that couldn't much affect her either physically *or* emotionally. She wondered what would happen when the cord was completely cut—would she end up as out of touch with the living as red-bearded Ketch? Maybe he'd been at this a long, long time; maybe Caravel wasn't the veteran he was, and that was why she still had a tenuous connection to sympathy, compassion, and a basic understanding of how to communicate with others in plain English.

The jugglers finished on a high note, flashing swords dancing and spinning from one to the next. The audience was hyped up, and the cheering was in overdrive—a booming combination of applause for the juggling girls and the anticipation reserved for the act everyone knew was next. David Dennis rolled onto the stage; *Night on Bald Mountain* started playing softly in the house speakers, but the dramatic pre-recorded voiceover was apparently a one-time thing.

"You know them," David proclaimed regally, like he was offering Christians to lions, "you love them." A chorus of squeals and shrieks played out of the center of the theatre, and David smiled patronizingly. "Some of you more than others." Appreciative laughter washed in over the stage. "Ladies and lovelies, put your hands between your legs and just scream your love—the Amazing Quirk, and his lovely assistant!"

He'd obviously been carefully timing his delivery, and the first climax of *Bald Mountain* hit right then; Calvin slid dramatically onstage into lights that were bright and flashy, but not quite as showy as they were Wednesday. Jenny shoved the magic table across the floor and twirled on after him.

They had a good show—not the rock star extravaganza of the last one, but they did a great job with a solid set of tricks, and the audience was smitten. Jenny was excited when she absolutely nailed her end of the sleight of hand tricks. Being thrilled by such a tiny thing made her feel better; she wasn't completely cut off from human emotions yet, if she ever would be. She'd practiced palming and producing and flipping coins all day, relaxing in her apartment while Rex chewed contentedly on carrots and cabbage. They twice rode through Wonderland to some woods out on Long Island so that he could do his business. Jenny wondered if something so trivial was the best use of the Emergency Exits, which she used in order to get back into Wonderland from Long Island, but she decided that getting her horse out for some fresh air qualified as important.

The show flew by, and before she knew it, Jenny was peering through the Window to Your Soul at audience volunteers to divine their birthdays. Over the weeks since they'd started doing it, they'd had to institute limits on the number of volunteers per show. Many people who showed up at the *Beau* were the same old faces time after time, and announcing the birthdays of people she'd already done would quickly lose its appeal. Jade and the Amazing Quirk had to work harder and harder to pick through the audience and find new people who'd never come up for the Window trick before.

She went through the first two volunteers like calling out ticket numbers at a deli, quick and easy...but when she got to the third, she paused before declaring, "April Seventh!" The skinny Goth chick waved her hands over her head, extending her fingers in Devil Rock signs to celebrate another win for Jade. On the next volunteer, Jenny took an even longer pause. She swallowed hard and took a deep breath, then shouted: "December Fourteenth!"

It was another correct answer, of course, and the crowd loyally *ooh*ed and *ahh*ed and chanted Jade's name. Jenny took brief pauses before each of the last two volunteers, but accurately announced both birthdays and finished the trick. Stiffly, she returned the Window to the magic table.

If Calvin noticed anything, he kept it buttoned up; the Amazing Quirk was on his game tonight, and he kept the act moving right along. After a round of stupendous card tricks, they moved on to the Rabbit Recipe, and Calvin tossed white mice into the hat one by one, never pausing in his showtime patter. Jenny felt a little bad that she couldn't recognize which of the mice might be the one who had made a brief trip into Wonderland with her; like all the rest, he would be condemned to the frozen Hell inside the hole without any mouse monuments erected to honor his daring adventure. When it came time to reveal Colby Cheese, Jenny hugged her close and felt Colby's soft white fur on her cheek. One quick moment of Fuzz Therapy picked up her mood enough to finish the act.

As it often was, the final trick was the Tale of Jade, the story of ancient princes that ended with the magic rings suspending Jade three feet above the floor by one wrist until the Amazing Quirk slashed off her hand and freed her. The crowd went nuts, *Bald Mountain* boomed, and Jenny reattached her hand as she and Calvin took their bows. She noticed a group in the middle of the theatre jumping up and down, wearing matching T-shirts and holding up signs, but she couldn't make them out past the bright footlights. Calvin waved enthusiastically, leaping into the wings like a horribly miscast Peter Pan; Jenny turned briskly and rolled the magic table off without fanfare.

Calvin waited backstage. "What's the matter?" he said seriously. His face was soaked and lathered with concern.

Jenny shook her head. "Hold on," she said. "Let's get back to the room."

The post-show noise still pounding the walls, they hurried back to the dressing room. Jenny rolled the magic table over by the easy chair and stood still. Calvin shut the door and took a second as the sound of the crowd dropped to a more bearable muted hum. "Jenny...?"

She turned and stared at him. "October Thirty-First," she said.

"What?" Calvin squinted as if sharper focus would reveal Jenny's implication.

"Something's going on," said Jenny. "Something on October Thirty-First. This Halloween."

Calvin held out a hand. She took it and held tight. Her lips clamped together almost as tightly; the skin around her mouth faded to a bloodless white. "The Raymonds," Calvin said. "That's when they're...um. Right?"

Jenny nodded. "Not just them, though," she said. "I thought it was weird, for a second. Birthday number two—"

"The fat...um, big guy," Calvin observed politely.

"Yeah." Jenny's hadn't taken a step since entering the room. She held on to Calvin's hand like she was practicing for Vulcan Self Defense class. "I noticed it on him. His death date. October Thirty-First."

"Holy cow."

"It didn't hit me until the third one," Jenny said. She looked at Calvin solemnly.

"The Goth girl...? Wait—*her* date was the thirty-first, too?" Calvin's jaw dropped.

"And the girl after her," Jenny went on, "and the two guys at the end."

Calvin stared at her. "*All* of them?"

"I don't know about the first one," she admitted. "I wasn't paying attention. I noticed it on the fat guy, and thought it was weird, and then I saw it on the Goth girl, and the next one, and...." She shook her head and sank into the easy chair, still gripping Calvin's hand as she held her head with the other. "All of them, same date. Same time, even. Off by seconds, or maybe minutes here or there, but right about the same time."

"Holy shit," Calvin said, dispensing with his usual boyish avoidance of full-on profanity. "What could be...? I mean, what happens that so many people...?"

"I don't know." Jenny shook her head again, slowly. "But it's just—"

"Wait," Calvin said. "Can the dates change? I mean, are they always the same, or do they maybe change? Like in the movies, when people time travel, and then the things that were going to happen don't happen, because—"

"I don't know!" Jenny repeated. "Calvin, this is all just as new to me, right? You're the magic whiz—you figure out how all this stuff works. What can we do?"

"Check me," Calvin said immediately. Jenny opened her mouth, her eyes wide. The magician waved off any protests: "You remember my date, right? So...see if it's changed. And if it's...the thirty-first." Jenny bit her lip, but Calvin knelt down and looked her right in the eye. "Hey, if it *is* changed, then we know that maybe we can change it *back*. Yeah?"

She tried to smile, but just pulled away and went to the magic table. She grabbed the spectacles and the Window and put the specs on. "Okay," she said. "Let me look." She passed the Window over Calvin, who was still on one knee by the chair, and peered through. Her arm dropped to her side and she clenched her teeth, looking at Calvin blankly.

He tilted his head. "October Thirty-First?"

Jenny nodded and removed the spectacles.

"Okay," Calvin said slowly. "Okay!" He stood up and grinned at her. "Jenny, that's a good thing! That wasn't my date before, was it? My death date the last time you saw it? The first time, I mean?"

Jenny shook her head. "No...."

"So," he spread his arms in a six-foot *quod erat demonstrandum*, "that's great!"

"Great," Jenny said sarcastically, putting the props away. "You're going to die."

"*Or*," said Calvin, "we look at this more like a warning. A warning that only *you* can see. Something's going to happen on Halloween—something big—and it's supposed to kill a bunch of people. Right?"

"Yeah, but how come all these different people? You don't have anything in common," Jenny said, vigorously scrubbing her hair like she was trying to jumpstart her brain.

"Yeah, except we don't really *know* how many people are supposed to die," Calvin pointed out. "Maybe it's a lot more than just me, and the

Raymonds, and those people in the audience. Heck, maybe it's the whole city!"

"Or the whole world," Jenny mumbled.

Calvin shrugged. "There's that, sure," he said. "But if you *know* about it, maybe you can *do* something about it."

"Calvin, I couldn't even save *one* person from death," Jenny began heatedly. "It's—it's against the *rules* or something! How am I supposed to save *everybody*, if I'm not even supposed to save one guy?"

"Maybe it's different," Calvin tried. "I mean, if the dates change, then nothing *is* set in stone, right? I mean, Caravel's whole thing about when it's your time, it's your time...that goes out the window, if you can...um...reschedule your time anyway."

Jenny thought, then started slowly coming around. "Okay, yeah," she said. "And Caravel doesn't even know about the letters. The glasses and the Window," she replied to the magician's quizzical look. "Caravel doesn't know anything about them. Whatever they are, they don't have anything to do with the, uh, Reapers. I'm supposed to find out about people dying some other way. When I do the job, I mean—the Reaping or whatever. She didn't have a clue what I was talking about when I asked her about the letters!"

"Right, okay," Calvin kept the train going. "So as far as *Caravel* knows, there are these rules, and everybody dies right on time, as planned. But *you* can see that the dates change. So *you* know that maybe it *doesn't* work that way. Maybe some people die when they're not supposed to. And we *can* change it—you know, we can save them!"

"You," Jenny said softly.

"Huh?"

"Save *you*," she said. She smiled a sorrowful smile at him.

Calvin just shrugged uncomfortably. "Yeah, well, me too." He grinned back. "Jenny Ng," he said formally, "will you save my life? And, uh," he waggled a hand as if carelessly referring to an afterthought, "the whole rest of the world, too?"

Jenny tried not to laugh, but wasn't entirely successful. The gravity of the situation was losing ground to the absurdity. Stifling a giggle, she said: "I'll see what I can do."

"Thanks," said Calvin, and he walked over to hug her. Despite the light humor, the hug was wholly serious, and the two held each other for a long and quiet minute.

"Um," Jenny said eventually.

"Yeah, we should go do the crowd thing," said Calvin. They detangled themselves and started taking off bits of costume. "Do you feel like the party tonight?"

Jenny shook her head. "Not after all this," she said. "And I should get a decent night's sleep. Caravel tomorrow night," she reminded him.

"Okay, sure," said Calvin.

"Hey," Jenny said as she pulled her jeans on over her tights, "Could I take the glasses and Window with me tonight? I was thinking...maybe I should try looking around some more, see how many people have Halloween death dates. And I could show them to Caravel, too. See what she thinks."

"'Kay," said Calvin, "that sounds like a good idea, yeah."

Jenny finished dressing and Calvin handed her the Window to Your Soul and the magic specs; she wrapped them in a pair of socks and stuffed them in her bag. Slinging the sword case over her shoulder, she headed for the door. "Ready?"

"Sure," said Calvin.

She suddenly realized that all his replies were largely monosyllabic. "Calvin," she turned her full attention on him, "are you okay?"

Calvin gave her a pained little smile. "I'll be okay," he said. "You know, it's just..." He waved an arm at their conversation. "I mean, I just found out that probably everybody I know is going to die in a couple months. And, well, me too. So...I just...you know."

"Calvin." Jenny walked straight to him and took his hand, just as he'd taken hers. She looked up into his eyes, hard. "I promise you," she said clearly and simply, "I am *not* going to let it happen. Whatever it is, I'm going to stop it."

"What if you can't?" Calvin said.

It was the first time she'd ever seen him give in to pessimism. Jenny felt like she'd witnessed a child learning the terrible truth about Santa Claus the day after catching his parents stuffing cash under his pillow and absconding with his tooth. She opened her mouth to reply, then closed it, then opened it again. With a sustained shrug, she said: "If I can't save you from dying, then I'll make sure you head in the right direction after that."

Calvin hugged her. "You know," he said, "that actually feels better."

"Good," Jenny replied. "Let's get out there and meet your fans. Those girls in the T-shirts looked pretty cute...."

The girls in the T-shirts turned out to be part of a self-appointed fan club calling themselves the Charmed Quirks, with an overdone logo on their shirts bafflingly featuring the standard icon of electrons whizzing about the nucleus of an atom. A non-scientific mind would have pondered the connection; a scientific mind would have complained loudly about the inaccuracy. The gaggle of grinning girls—and three guys—didn't seem to care, and happily shook posterboards over their heads as Calvin and Jenny walked into the lobby. The posters bore messages like "Amazing Quirk You Made My Heart Disappear!" and "The Window To My Soul Is Unlocked (And My Parents Are Away For The Weekend)." The cheesiness of the whole affair was genuinely charming, and the magician and his lovely assistant drank in the cheers of the crowd, grinning as they read each poster.

After putting in enough of an appearance so as not to seem ungrateful, Jenny slipped through the crowd to nab Calvin, who was surrounded by a knot of Charmed Quirks. She pulled his shoulder to reach his ear. "I'm going to head home," she stage whispered over the noise of the packed lobby.

Calvin nodded. "Okay!" He hugged her, to the swooning delight of several Charmed Quirks and the seething jealousy of several others. "I'm gonna go to the party. Do you want me to come tomorrow night? I could wait in the park...?"

"No, don't worry about it," said Jenny. "I'll call you after."

"Okay," said the magician. "G'night, Jenny."

"'Night."

She escaped the *Beau Regardez* with only a few more polite words to adoring fans as she made her way out. The street was a breath of fresh, cool air after the stuffy theatre. She headed straight for the subway at Fourteenth. Despite the weekend schedule, she didn't wait long, and boarded an L train in minutes. She walked to an F train one stop later and sat back for the long ride to Park Slope.

The car was half full of New Yorkers: couples heading home from a romantic Saturday evening, musicians heading for Brooklyn venues, boisterous college kids and post-college kids pretending that how they felt after a half dozen shots and several beers confirmed their deep personal significance in a massive universe that couldn't care less. A homeless guy sprawled across four subway seats at one end, and a bouquet of stale urine and months or years without a shower set up an invisible force field that kept most of the other passengers crammed into the other half of the car.

Jenny sat down opposite the homeless guy. Her nose wrinkled and her eyes watered, but there was something very *vital* about the stench, and she was drawn to it like a vampire moth to a living flame. She stared at him thoughtfully, and without really thinking about it, she pulled the spectacles and the small square of glass from her bag. She wrapped the stems over her ears and looked at the smelly sleeping man through the Window. Sure enough: October Thirty-First. His death date—his deadline—was the same as Calvin's, and Vincent's and Carrie's, and the people on stage at the *Beau.*

She turned and let the Window to Your Soul play over the rest of the passengers, some sitting, some standing, some jumping with drunken excitement and overindulged hormones. One after another, they all revealed the same date: October Thirty-First, October Thirty-First, October Thirty-First...there were two exceptions. One was an older man sitting with his wife—his death date was in September, which probably just meant that he would die before the mysterious event on Halloween—and the other was one of the drunk guys, whose deadline was November First. That threw her for a moment, but his time was only hours after midnight on Halloween, and she started thinking that whatever the big event was, it wasn't going to kill everybody instantly. Maybe it was a nuclear bomb, and some people would survive the original explosion only to die out in the days and weeks that followed. She shuddered.

As they neared Prospect Park, one of the drunken party guys noticed Jenny staring at them through the tiny square of glass. "Hey!" he called. "Hey, you gonna take a—" he burped acid and grimaced, but didn't let that stop him "—a picture?" He grabbed another guy in an awkward headlock and smiled: "Cheese!"

"Dude!" the other guy protested, wrestling out of the headlock.

"She's takin' a picture," the first guy said.

"That's not even a camera, dude," the second guy eyed Jenny and the small pane of glass she held. The alcohol in his system made it hard to focus, and he stumbled a bit as the train started slowing down.

Jenny removed the specs and put them in her bag with the Window. "Sorry, just a thing," she said vaguely. A more thorough explanation—even, or especially, the true one—wouldn't matter to these guys.

"Hey, hey, hey," the first guy tried to get a full sentence out.

"Hay's for horses," said Jenny, "and I've got to get home and take mine for a walk." She was all too amused that her quip was entirely true.

Fortunately the guy was too drunk to read her barely constrained amusement. "You goin' home?" the guy said, disappointed. "You should come out with us. Come out with us!" he commanded rambunctiously.

Jenny looked at the state of the species she was going to save from extinction, personified by the loud, obnoxious, ignorant fool in front of her. With a strange detachment she hadn't even realized she felt, she decided that even a worthless life was worth more than no life at all. She looked at the guy with a friendly smile and a weary sigh. "Have a safe and happy Halloween," she said, and she slipped out as the doors opened.

Behind her, the guy turned to his friend. "Wha...? Halloween?" He scratched his head and peered through thick mental fog. "Dude, how long were we at that bar?"

The subway doors whisked shut, and the F train carried them off to their next drunken adventure.

CHAPTER TWENTY

Arguments over which day any given deity may have taken a breather after a week of creative entrepreneurialism may orbit close to the center of the most divisive issues to ever plague humankind and pad the salaries of theologians, but the fact remains that Sunday is a definitive day of rest for the city of New York as a whole, if not for individual New Yorkers themselves. By fiat or trend, businesses shorten their hours, subways trim their schedules, restaurants close earlier, and a colorless malaise envelopes the city, slowing things down and putting the City that Never Sleeps into the moral food coma that inevitably follows the gluttonous feast of Saturday's nightlife. The air itself seems paler, thinner—ponderous and meaningless at the same time, like a snail trying to decide what to wear to the office Christmas party before her husband finally makes his way from the bedroom to the bathroom sixteen hours later to remind her that she neither wears clothes nor works at an office, let alone celebrates the birth of a hairless hominid who lived in a desert two thousand years earlier. Those who do celebrate the birthday of a man who died seventy or more generations before their grandparents guilted their parents into dunking them underwater in his honor often spend half of this day trapped in a building with old men who feel that reciting stilted Olde English translations of ancient Latin texts in a paralyzingly dull monotone is the best way to celebrate the rapturous joy they feel just thinking about a dead Jew whose attempt to popularize the Golden Rule has since been used to justify everything from slavery to cures for baldness. Whether or not their attendance is meant to atone for snorting cocaine off a transgendered Vietnamese hooker's ass during Saturday's bacchanalia is a mystery best left to the theologians, who are never invited to those parties regardless of their padded salaries, leaving them with more time to unravel such mysteries and announce their conclusions in theses read only by other theologians and atheist bloggers looking for a laugh, a fight, or both.

Whatever activities the living choose to participate in—or not—on Sundays, the day itself feels like a tantalizing taste of what it is to be dead: no pressing concerns, no urgency, no destination, and no motivation to do much more than idly wonder about what Monday might bring. The slowly building hysteria and anticipation that kick in sometime between sunset and bedtime might give some good reason to believe that the dead are just as anxious at the prospect of living as the living are at the prospect of dying.

Jenny Ng was anxious about actually starting her life as a personification of death. After two months of puzzling and unexplained phenomena, the past week had been the first driving orchestra hits after a disjointed half hour of violins noodling and woodwinds tuning up in the pit. She woke up surprisingly refreshed, and decided to take advantage of her Angel of Death perks and take a day trip. She grabbed her sword case and shoulder bag, plus a sandwich, a couple of Diet Cokes, and a bag of apples and pears for Rex, and she mounted up. They rode through Wonderland all the way to Montauk and shot across the Atlantic Ocean to a tiny island just short of Martha's Vineyard. Rex really let loose, showing off power and speed Jenny had only suspected, and in barely two hours, they splashed through the reflection off a small lake on the largely undeveloped island.

They found an isolated spot on the south side, set off from the rest of the isolated spots with which the island was heavily unpopulated, and Jenny managed another less than graceful dismount, tumbling into the brush that fringed the shore of the island. It had rained overnight, and the sand was wet and dark, caking to her bare knees and Bermuda shorts. The ocean breeze was working out and gaining muscle rapidly, and smelled like it was perspiring salty sweat from the effort.

Jenny thought about taking off Rex's saddle—she was pretty sure that horses weren't supposed to wear their gear all the time, and it was probably both uncomfortable and painful in the long term. Of course, Rex was as indestructible as she was, and Jenny had no idea how to remove the saddle *or* put it back on again. She could ask Caravel about that later, but for now, she'd just leave it alone.

Rex didn't mind. He ate his fruit and felt his oats, prancing across the beach, stretching his legs and tossing his mane in the wicked wind whipping in off the ocean. While he had resigned himself to dwelling in Jenny's apartment, he relished his trips outside, and made the most of them. Jenny brought a book to read—a photography book she'd grabbed for a fair price at the Strand—and took some shots with her new camera, enjoying the challenge of relearning techniques she hadn't employed since she sold her old camera the previous year. She spent the day taking pictures, playing tag with the horse, lounging on the beach, and practicing her sleight of hand. After enjoying her sandwich, she ate an apple down to its narrow core and offered it to Rex, then deftly disappeared the fruit with a flick of her wrist. Rex gave her a hard, pithy stare until she sheepishly smiled and re-conjured the apple core for him. The horse was less interested in her show of dexterity than he was in the crunchy apple core, on which he quickly performed a cruder but more effective vanishing act himself.

Even the sun bummed lazily across the sky, though perhaps that was a reward earned when you had the day to yourself *and* named after you. As it wound down toward its own spectacular vanishing act, Jenny finally checked her phone and saw that it was getting close to five. She packed up and called out to Rex, who pounded up the shore from where he was teasing frothing breakers that hectically chased his hooves only to splash against them like liquid kamikazes. He knelt down, but Jenny put an arm over his neck and slipped through an Emergency Exit to Wonderland before clambering onto the saddle. With the rushing, thumping Looking Glass wind pounding in their ears and the scudding clouds above even sketchier than usual, they took off across the flat smooth surface of the mirrored Atlantic Ocean, headed back toward Manhattan.

Jenny had been true to her word since Friday, taking regular routes through the normal world when possible, so slashing through Wonderland on horseback was now a special treat she reserved for when she took Rex out for his walks. Making less use of the place restored some of the breathless adventure that tingled at the back of her neck when she went Through the Looking Glass; it was the difference between eating birthday cake for breakfast, lunch and dinner, seven days a week, and having it only ten times a year at an assortment of birthday parties. The rarity of the event added flavor to the otherwise dull and listless buttercream icing.

In barely a half hour, the flat splashing ocean whipped away to be replaced by the shores, then streets, then highways of mirror Long Island, entirely devoid of cars as usual. With no obstacles or traffic laws, Rex skipped barriers and cut through woods as he pleased, drawing a generally straight line west. Jenny didn't spend a lot of time on Long Island, so the reversal of north and south as she swept by towns and streets didn't disorient her; she had no frame of reference to confuse.

As they flew through Queens, Jenny noticed a peculiar sight: the strange, sketchy clouds were slowing down, almost screeching to a halt. For all she knew, they actually did make a sound, which she couldn't hear over the pounding in her ears that she'd become accustomed to after so many trips through Wonderland. Like a movie projector losing power, the clouds slowed and flickered and inched to an unnatural and unsettling stop. An explosion of light burst out of the horizon ahead of her, spilling through the sky and replacing the vague cloudy smears of Wonderland's day with the blazing pop art of Wonderland's night, like some god of fine arts dragging a brush across the sky after dipping it in swollen Van Gogh stars. Jenny witnessed sunset in Wonderland for the first time; as opposed to the slow and gradual shift from day to night in the real world, nighttime hit Wonderland with a speed and suddenness that was exhilarating. She hugged the galloping stallion tight and let a blissful smile stretch across her face.

Rex sliced across the East River minutes later, leaping over Roosevelt Island in practically a single bound, and then galloped along Seventy-Ninth to the park. They crossed the threshold and the horse wheeled left, swinging northward around the reflected version of the Metropolitan Museum of Art. They raced through the trees, covering the clearings between them in split seconds as Wonderland jittered by, and Jenny looked up to see the South Gate House rapidly approaching. Rex didn't even pause this time—he vaulted the fence, hit the reservoir running, and charged across the water. Out on the low wall, another horse and rider waited.

"Jenny!" Caravel called as Jenny and Rex drew near.

"Hi, Caravel," said Jenny. Rex slowed and clopped up onto the wall near Caravel's horse. Zé nattered a greeting, and Rex nickered in return. He knelt down, and Jenny tumbled down onto the oddly patterned top of the wall, spilling herself and her bag. "Gah," she yelped darkly. "I suck."

Caravel helped her gather her items and return them to the shoulder bag. "You may need to work on your dismount, *menina*," she said sweetly.

"I know, I know," said Jenny. She sighed and straightened. "I'm getting the hang of riding, at least. Or at least Rex is getting the hang of carrying me."

"Almost true," Caravel said, smiling enigmatically. "Remember, *nossos cavalos* are really just a part of us, Jenny. You need to learn how to guide him. How to use him like you use your arms and legs."

"I felt that," Jenny said excitedly. "The other day. I started feeling that—like he just does what I need him to do, and I don't even really need to think about it."

"*Muito bom*," said Caravel. "Now you just need to get used to cutting *him* off the way you can cut off an arm or a leg without worrying about it."

"Huh?"

"That's how you dismount." Caravel flashed a secretive grin.

Jenny screwed up her face. "Um, sure. I don't get it."

"You will." Caravel turned and walked north atop the wall. "Let's talk."

Jenny caught up and walked beside her black-cloaked mentor. Rex and Zé followed close behind. "I've got a lot of questions," she said. "I mean, lots of stuff I need to figure out, I guess, but some stuff you could probably help me with." She didn't want to seem overbearing or completely helpless.

"Let's begin with your Tools," Caravel said simply.

Caravel showed Jenny how to tie her sword neatly and easily to Rex's saddle, with the intricate knots and bonds arranged just so. Jenny allowed the *anjo da morte* to guide her through tying and untying the sword, and did it several times herself. While she wasn't as quick and fluid as Caravel, her sleight of hand practice with Calvin paid off—her fingers were more cooperative and coordinated than they'd ever been, and danced along the knots almost as fast as Caravel's.

The sword itself, she learned, was more than Jenny had realized. "*Sim*, it's a weapon," Caravel conceded as Jenny practiced binding and releasing it, "but it is much more than that. Look at the blade."

It occurred to Jenny that she'd never taken the sword out in Wonderland before. The realization that the silvery metal was reflective startled her, and she cringed to think she might see the spooky, smoky place in the surface of the blade—but the metal was bright and shining, displaying the real world reflection of the dull Wonderland around her, as clear and unmarked as a window. "It's a mirror!" she exclaimed. "But—it *stays* a mirror!"

"Yes, *menina*," said Caravel. "The sword is one way we *always* have to take passage from the rough road to the smooth road, and back again. It's a permanent portal from one to the other."

"Then what's that—um...that other place?" Jenny asked. "I brought some mirrors with me, here, to the...uh, smooth road. I looked through them here, and they weren't...well..."

"It's another place," Caravel said carefully. "Not one that you or I need to visit any time soon. It is, sometimes, a place we must guide others to. Once they've died."

"Is it...Hell, or something?"

Caravel shook her head. "It's a place to reconsider your choices," she said. "I can't say more than that."

"Because I'm new?"

"Because I don't know," Caravel shrugged. "Remember what I said: we only know what we need to know to do our jobs, *menina*. Anything beyond that isn't given to us."

"But then how do we know where to send people?" Jenny insisted. "Hell, how do we even know when we're supposed to go *get* people?"

"Your horse," said Caravel. She patted Zé's muzzle; he leaned over her shoulder. "They aren't merely limbs, Jenny. They are eyes and ears, too. They know when you have an appointment. They'll guide you there."

"How?"

"How do you move closer to the fire on a cold day?" Caravel laughed at Jenny's unimpressed expression. "No, really, *menina*. It's only that simple. Let him speak to you the same way your eyes and ears and skin do. Listen to the world he paints for you, just as you know which way the wind blows when it touches your hair."

Jenny cocked her head skeptically, then closed her eyes and tried to focus.

"You may not have an appointment yet," Caravel pointed out.

Jenny opened one eye. "Am I supposed to just *know?*"

"It will make sense the first time you feel it," said Caravel. "You probably won't get many appointments at first. Whoever or whatever is in charge, they go easy on you until you have a bit more experience. I only had nine appointments my entire first year."

"What do you do when you get an appointment?"

"You'll sense it when it's a few days away. It will come closer through time, and you'll go through space to meet it. The horse will know the way."

"And you just go there to meet them?"

"And guide them through, yes."

Jenny snorted. "How can I guide them when I have no idea what *I'm* doing?"

"You open up their paths," said Caravel. Before Jenny could retort, the dark woman untied her own sword from Zé's saddle and slashed it through the air in a looping pattern.

Nothing dramatic happened.

"Um," said Jenny. "Like I said, how—"

"By itself," Caravel stared Jenny in the eye, "the sword is only our Tool. Once we bring an appointment here to the smooth road, our sword is just as much theirs as it is ours. It will open new roads for them, leading to different choices and more roads. All we have to do is open those roads so that they can make their own choices."

Jenny furrowed her brow. "Well," she said, "okay, but how can I tell them which choice to make?"

"You don't," said Caravel. "You just look at the choices with them, *menina*, and let them decide which is best."

"I thought you said we help them," Jenny insisted. "That we *guide* them."

Caravel laughed again. "We do!" She rapidly tied her sword back on Zé's saddle. "We certainly do, Jenny. You'll truly see it when you do it. Just remember to *talk* to the person you escort here. Care about them—care about the job—and you'll see what it is we actually do."

She wasn't happy about the slippery answer, but Jenny let it go. Caravel either couldn't or wouldn't tell her more, but the woman did seem to have her best interest in mind. "Okay," she finally said. She decided to be more proactive. "Okay, I have a question. What's with my mirror image?"

"Your mirror image?" Caravel's pursed lips popped a question mark on the end.

"She's all—you know, she does all her own stuff, instead of being *me*." Jenny realized that in any other context, this sounded entirely psychotic. "Instead of being my reflection, I mean."

"Oh," Caravel said, the light dawning. "You haven't taken control of your reflection yet, *menina?*"

"What do you mean, 'take control' of her?"

"Your reflection is just another extension of you," Caravel explained, "like your horse, or your sword. You have just as much control over it as you do your own body."

"I don't have *any* control over her!" Jenny protested.

"You do," said Caravel pleasantly. "You just haven't used it. It—she—is yours to do with as you wish."

Jenny frowned. "Have you *met* her?"

"You'll get the hang of it," Caravel said.

"If you say so." Jenny went through the mental checklist she'd been building for the last few days. So far, Caravel's answers had been hit or miss on satisfaction, but she wanted to try getting everything down before springing the Big Question on her teacher: the issue of all of the imminent Halloween deaths. "Okay, so also—do I need to eat and sleep and...you know, stuff like that? I was wondering about that, and Calvin asked, too. I mean, if I'm indestructible and everything...?"

"Eat when you're hungry," said Caravel. "Sleep when you're tired. After some time, you'll feel hungry and tired less often. It's not that you *need* to, *menina*—it's that you'll want to. They're habits." She shrugged. "I still enjoy a drink every now and then. But as time goes on, you'll find less to connect you to that kind of thing. Less to connect you to *any* of the things of the living world."

"How long does that take?" Jenny was genuinely curious—her slow but steady disconnect from physical pain and social ties was noticeable, particularly every time she nonchalantly sliced or chopped herself up in the magic act.

"As long as a lifetime," Caravel mused. She spread her arms. "The world still has a claim on you, Jenny. Because there are those who still remember you. As they go, one by one, so will any need you have for the world of the living."

That hit harder than Jenny thought it would. For the first time, immortality sank in. It wasn't just a cool superpower that let her walk through anything unscathed. It was the guarantee of seeing everyone and everything she'd ever known or loved grow old, break down, die, and disappear in the dust of centuries. Calvin, her mom, her brother—all her college friends who'd scattered to the four winds. Even Keith Heckler. As she kept on, ageless, unending, they would meet their deaths and be swept into history, until no one—perhaps not even Jenny—remembered them.

She felt a hard and immediate despair. She suddenly missed her mother terribly. She hadn't talked to Hua Yao Ng in weeks. She hadn't talked to her brother Peter since before any of this stuff began; he was at school in California, living the life of a single guy several thousand miles away from his family. Phone calls weren't his priority, and Jenny wasn't as good as their mother at forcing the issue through guilt or frequent phone calls herself. She occasionally got e-mails from him, but with no computer, e-mail was a luxury she checked at an Internet café or on Calvin's laptop. Her mother called once a month whenever she hadn't heard from Jenny— who, like any grown-up American child, had better things to do than cater to a parent's need for periodic filial contact. Now, more than ever, she wanted to call her mother and cry, and remind her how much she loved her.

Caravel understood. "They won't suffer, Jenny," she said tenderly. "Any more than any of the living do when the dead have gone. You know," she added thoughtfully, "you have a sort of special luck, in a way. You have a chance to say goodbye." She smiled and put a hand on Jenny's arm. "Those of us who aren't accidents, we all 'die' before we move on to any of this. As far as they're concerned, *you're* still alive."

Jenny nodded wordlessly. She wiped at potential tears with the back of her hand, just to be safe.

"It might be a good idea," Caravel said, "to say goodbye to them. Let them know how you feel. You'll need to stop seeing them soon, anyway, before they notice you don't age like they do anymore."

"Right," Jenny whispered. She wondered what she could say that her mother's sharp ears and penetrating gaze wouldn't see through.

Caravel leaned in and scanned Jenny's face. "*Menina?*"

"I'm okay," said Jenny. She shook herself and took a deep breath. "I mean, I should have realized all...I should have known. So, yeah." She walked away and stared across the unmoving water. Abruptly, she cleared her face and turned back. "Caravel!"

"*Sim?*"

"I need to ask you something," said Jenny. She walked back to Rex; her shoulder bag and the instrument case hung on his saddle. "Remember I told you about the letters?"

"Letters?" Caravel said. "The ones you read the appointment in? That boy's appointment, from the other night?"

"Yeah," said Jenny. She fished out the magic spectacles and the Window to Your Soul and showed them to Caravel. "This is them," she explained. "My friend Calvin—the one you met—he found these...and a bunch of other stuff. I thought they had something to do with you guys. I mean, *us*," she corrected herself. "Because I could read the, you know, death dates on people. I figured that's what you guys did, but then you didn't know what I meant, and...well," she shrugged. "Do they look familiar? I mean, do you know anything about them?"

Caravel took the props gingerly and stared at them, turning them over in her hands. "No, *desculpe*," she said. "They mean nothing to me, *menina*."

"Here, put them on," Jenny gestured. Caravel put on the specs. "Now look through the Window at stuff," said Jenny.

Caravel looked through the Window at her. "Ah," she said, "what is it I should see here, Jenny?"

"What?" Jenny reached for the specs, and Caravel took them off— Jenny wrapped them onto her face and held Caravel's wrist, raising the Window between them and looking at the scenery around them. Through the Window, she saw no glowing letters—only the blurry shimmer of Wonderland and Caravel's bewildered face. "It doesn't work here," Jenny said. "The glasses and the Window...they don't work in Wonderland." She shook her head. "On the smooth road, I mean."

Caravel handed the Window back, and Jenny took off the spectacles. She looked down at the magical props in disbelief. "Okay," said Jenny, "but here's the thing. I mean, I know you told me there are these rules and everything."

Caravel gave her a look. "Rules?"

"Like we can't save them," said Jenny. "When somebody's going to die, we have to just let them die. But that's 'cause that's their, you know, appointment. It's their time."

"*Sim, menina.*"

"But what if it's *not* their time?" Jenny asked. "What if they were supposed to have a *different* time, but something happened? Something *changed* their time?"

"I don't understand," said Caravel.

"The letters," Jenny explained. "When I look through these at people—living people—in the regular world...on the rough road, I mean. I see these glowing letters, and they tell me about the person. I can't read all of them, the letters, but I can read their birthdays. And," she added importantly, "I can read the day—even the time—that they're going to die."

"This is how you knew about Curach's appointment with the boy," Caravel concluded.

Jenny nodded. "Yeah," she said. "And I see anybody's death dates. *Everybody's*. But the thing is," she paused and took a breath. She held up the specs and Window for emphasis. "I've been seeing a new death date. A new death date for *everybody*. The *same* death date."

"The same...?" Caravel eyed Jenny expectantly.

"Almost everybody I look at now dies on Halloween. This Halloween, this October Thirty-First. Even Calvin, and I already knew his death date *before*. Before—it was different! Before, he wasn't going to die for years and years. He was going to be an old man." Jenny gave Caravel an imploring look. "But it *changed*, Caravel! Now everybody's going to die on Halloween. Or...well, around then. So if their death dates *changed*, then how do you know if it was meant to be? What if their time," asked Jenny, "*isn't* their time?"

Caravel considered this, then shook her head, slowly at first. "*Menina*, it makes no sense," she said. "Why would their appointment change? How *could* it change?"

"Maybe we did something wrong. Maybe *I* did something wrong," Jenny said nervously. "I mean, I've been one of you all this time, and I didn't know it. Maybe I screwed something up, and now everybody's going to die when they're not supposed to."

"You can't blame yourself, Jenny."

Jenny laughed sharply and unhappily. "I can if it's my fault."

"There could be another reason," Caravel suggested.

"Well, fine," said Jenny. "But whatever it is...you said before, if it's their time, it's their time. And we can't do anything about that. That it's the rules. But, well...what if it *isn't* their time? Can we save them *then?*"

Caravel's arms dropped limply. She gazed into the dark Wonderland night. "I don't know, *menina*," the beautiful angel of death said softly. "This is uncharted territory. I have no idea what any of it means."

"You believe me?" Jenny asked hopefully. "I mean, you believe me about the letters?"

"I believe you," replied Caravel. "I just don't know what to do about it. Jenny, if they are meant to die, I'm not sure what we can do to change this."

"But it already changed!"

"But the people you wish to save—"

"*Everybody*," said Jenny.

"*Que?*"

"*Everybody*," Jenny repeated. "Everybody I've looked at. Nobody lives past whatever happens. Nobody, Caravel! Maybe it's everybody in New York...maybe it's the whole world!"

Caravel was silent.

"*That* can't be according to the 'plan,' can it? I mean, everybody can't all die together, right?"

"It seems wrong," Caravel admitted. "But we can't interfere. We aren't meant to."

"But we interfered already," said Jenny. "Or...or *I* did, maybe. Can't we just *fix* whatever I messed up, so everything can go back? You know, the way it was supposed to happen? Then, everybody's time *will* be their time. Right? I mean—"

"*Menina*," Caravel stopped her, putting a hand on each of her shoulders, holding her still. "I told you before. I *am* on your side—but we can't break the rules."

Jenny nodded solemnly. "Maybe you can't," she said. She shrugged Caravel's hands away. "But then I'll just have to do it on my own."

Caravel looked sad. She walked past Jenny to Zé—the big stallion leaned just a bit, and Caravel rolled right up into the saddle. "Jenny," she called. "I like you, *menina*. I won't stop you—I'm not sure if I could. But be careful."

"Of what?"

Caravel looked down at her. "Our rules never change," she said. "If the appointments have changed, then we're playing by someone *else's* rules now. We don't know whose—and we don't know why. It could be very dangerous, *sim?* Whoever can change the rules like that is someone powerful. Someone very dangerous." She leaned over and stared hard at

Jenny. "And someone who's even more powerful—more dangerous—than the *anjos da morte*...is someone I would not like to go up against."

Jenny gulped. "Right."

"If you need to talk, *menina*, just come here. If I am not here, leave a note—I will find it, and find you."

"Thank you, Caravel," said Jenny.

"*Boa sorte, menina*," said Caravel. She gave Jenny a friendly smile, and Zé took off into the shifting night.

Jenny stood with her horse in the mirror image of Central Park, feeling small, lost, and very, very alone.

CHAPTER TWENTY-ONE

Less than two months away, October Thirty-First was on Jenny's mind like a hungry wolf stalking a nervous rabbit. Every audience member at Wednesday night's show was marked by the looming deadline, written in glowing letters that burned metaphorical symbols into Jenny's brain—symbols which resolved themselves into a definite time and place: Halloween in New York City. At Calvin's urging, she'd also been looking around at buildings, streets, cars—all of the city scenery surrounding them. While some larger structures had appointments with destruction still farther into the future, the ominous date continually popped up on buildings, cars, trees, benches...all sorts of objects or edifices that might be simply incinerated in some sort of explosive cataclysm. Calvin McGuirk's money was still on nuclear bomb or asteroid collision, and he constantly combed newspapers and online articles in an effort to piece together patterns that might add up to a terrorist plot or government conspiracy. Jenny had her doubts that an unenthusiastic history major with a talent for prestidigitation and showmanship could spot the missing clue that every intelligence and security agent in the nation missed, but at least he was giving it a shot—she just watched calendar pages flip by and wondered if she'd be up to the challenge of stopping whatever it was that was going to destroy her world at the end of October. With September strolling into town, the pressure only increased.

She'd gone to Boston on Monday, riding through Wonderland in a blur, and looked through the magic spectacles and Window at people and places up there—something she and Calvin had discussed after her lesson with Caravel on Sunday night. Sure enough, nobody in Boston would live past November Second; most died on Halloween or in the dark hours after midnight on the First of November. Whatever the horror to come was, it was very likely huge—perhaps even a worldwide event.

Jenny had also called her mother before the trip to Boston, and again before Wednesday's show, diplomatically ignoring her mother's outstanding vocal performance as a woman in shock at getting two calls in the same week. She kept the conversation light, just skimming the surface with stories of her new job (she left out what she actually did there) and the magic act (she left out how the tricks worked). Jenny knew that Maternal Radar Sensitivity was cranked up to the maximum on the other end of the line, and that Hua Yao Ng was well aware that deep, important secrets swirled beneath the aimless and easy words, but her mother kept the dialogue sharp and clean—she made sure Jenny was eating enough and didn't need any cash, but didn't pry into any obscure corners of Jenny's life beyond asking a few pointed questions about Calvin. "Is he Chinese?"

"Yeah, Mom, Calvin *McGuirk*," Jenny had answered. "Totally Chinese. Grew up in Beijing. On a rice farm."

Her mother had muttered in Cantonese about ungrateful children; Jenny pretended not to understand. "Don't forget to call your brother. He's starting senior year this week." Jenny promised to call Peter. Her mother's expert guilt trips were deadly accurate even when tripping from the world of the living to the land of the dead.

On top of all that, on Tuesday afternoon Jenny had started to sense her first appointment. She now understood what Caravel had described: it was another sense, beyond sight or sound or anything she was used to, that registered something on the distant horizon of time and space. In a strange and unsettling way, she "saw" her appointment a few days away, on Friday evening. It was much less exact than reading glowing letters through a Window, the difference between taking a high-resolution digital photograph and doodling with crayons—the picture still meant the same thing, but one was easy to intellectualize, while the other was purely conceptual. The appointment crept closer, minute by minute, coming into range and focus like a distant traveler cresting a hill. An electric tingle shimmered down her spine whenever she was with Rex, as if proximity to the horse boosted her reception and sharpened the focus—he was the rabbit ears on the television of her Death Sense.

Sensing her first appointment with death was a rite of passage more unnerving but less messy than Jenny's first period. Calvin didn't appreciate the comparison, but chivalrously attempted to roll with it. She politely refrained from pointing out that she hadn't gotten her period since she'd died. Her cycle had always been a bit erratic anyway, but she *had* been slightly nervous for a week or two at the prospect of raising a tiny Keith Heckler—her meetings with Caravel had settled that question, though, when she discovered that she was, technically speaking, dead. Jenny was pretty sure the dead didn't get pregnant any more than they menstruated.

Meanwhile, a few pleasant phone calls had pinpointed their dinner reservation with the Raymonds at six o'clock Friday night, just hours before Jenny's appointment. The timing didn't thrill her, but there wasn't much she could do about it without putting the Raymonds off *again*—she rode Rex across Wonderland's glassy East River and left him waiting outside the mirror image of the restaurant where she and Calvin were meeting the Perfect Couple. She marveled at her new ability to use her shining sword to simply and easily switch from Wonderland to the real world and back again. The sword came right through with her, no hassles; in Wonderland—the Smooth Road, as the other Angels of Death called it—the blade was a bright, clear window to the real world, with no sign of Mirror Jenny. Jenny had brought her sword case along, too, and put the sword back in after emerging from the ladies' room mirror. She looked thoughtfully at Mirror Jenny, who looked thoughtfully back without actually reflecting her. Jenny headed out through the restaurant to the front door; if anyone noticed that a slim Chinese girl in a simple dark green dress had come out of a bathroom she had never gone into, they didn't say anything.

Calvin was waiting at the door—he'd taken the subway to meet her there. Jenny needed Rex ready and nearby to head to her appointment when they finished dinner with the Raymonds. Along with the sword case, she had a bulky backpack slung over her shoulder with a change of clothes, like an Upper West Side debutante ready to bolt from the restaurant to the gym to work off a hundred-dollar, six-ounce dinner.

The magician shared her Fish Out of Water take on the restaurant. "Fancy," he said. He tugged at his collar. "This is the second time I've worn a tie in two weeks. Ugh."

"You wear a tie at every show," Jenny teased him.

"That's a bow-tie." He made a face. "And a clip-on. It doesn't choke like this one."

Jenny rolled her eyes. "Here, let me," she said. She reached up to adjust his tie and collar, making him look slightly more comfortable and slightly less stylish. The Ward and June Cleaver moment hit both of them at about the same time, and they laughed nervously. Jenny patted down

Calvin's suit jacket and put her hands back on her backpack straps. "You look nice."

"You look really great," he replied. "I like your...." He searched for anything that wouldn't directly imply he was checking out her body in the form-fitting green dress. "Shoes," he picked, without looking at them.

"Thanks." She was wearing the plain black heels she used in the show. They didn't really match her dress, but Jenny's wardrobe wasn't big on options. She was forced to face the fact that her lifestyle wasn't very conducive to small talk, either; she and Calvin were so often discussing mammoth cosmic issues, and their friendship had gelled and hardened so quickly, that she suddenly felt very awkward trying to relate to him in a context that was almost but not exactly just about very similar to something that someone might call kind of a date.

They smiled at each other. They laughed again, simultaneously, softly. They smiled at their simultaneous laughter.

Dinner plans came to the rescue. "There you are!" Vincent Raymond's silky voice flowed through the glass doors as he held them for Carrie. The incredibly attractive pregnant woman entered like some noble animal crossing an African veldt, graceful as ever despite her big round belly, and reached out to hug Jenny enthusiastically. Jenny delivered what enthusiasm she could; the pressures on her mind, including the imminent deaths of Carrie and Vincent, sapped a bit of excitement from the moment like a tax collector swooping in on a triumphant gold miner.

"Your outfit is adorable!" Carrie beamed. "It really accentuates your figure."

Calvin cleared his throat and said, "Uh, thanks."

"Not yours, Calvin Quirk," Carrie shot another big smile his way. "But you look *very* handsome. I love your tie!"

"Calvin!" Vincent stuck out a hand, his perfect white teeth competing with his wife's for Shiniest Surface in the Room. Jenny was positive she could've used his smile to make a trip to Wonderland.

"Hello, sir," Calvin said, shaking hands.

"Just Vincent," the bronzed Apollo of chiropractors reminded him. Despite being a few inches shorter than Calvin, Vincent towered over him on charisma alone. He smiled at the hostess, checking in for their reservation. The perky blonde girl stared and smiled the kind of smile reserved for movie stars who have studiously avoided tabloid scandals.

"I'm so glad we could finally do this," said Carrie, grabbing a hand each from Jenny and Calvin. The Jungle Queen—even her dress, tight over the top and flowing gently over her belly, bore a spotted leopard pattern—emanated a warm invisible glow that was too enticing to resist; Jenny and Calvin smiled and relaxed. "Jenny, you never did come see Vincent after your accident."

"Oh!" Jenny paused, smiling blankly. "I, um—turns out I was okay. Nothing broken, nothing bruised."

"Just stuff falling off sometimes," said Calvin, absently.

Jenny whispered fiercely: "Calvin!"

He smiled fecklessly. "In the show, I mean. Chopping, um..." He made a chopping motion, cutting off the end of his sentence and Jenny's hypothetical limb.

Carrie nodded. "How's the show?" she asked with keen interest. "And didn't you meet with some agents last week? I remember you talking about them after the show...."

"Ladies? Calvin?" Vincent held out an arm for his wife, and led the group to follow the young pretty hostess to their table.

The restaurant was large and coolly lit in blues and whites; brushed chrome-colored surfaces filled the space with tables, chairs, a long bar down one end of the room, and a riserless staircase leading upward. The place took up two opulent floors in the corner of a building on Forty-Seventh, and the magician and his lovely assistant trailed after the two mortal avatars of erotic deities as the hostess brought all four of them up to the mezzanine, situating them in a comfortable booth set off from the other tables. The booth was all shiny table and posh leather. Jenny and Vincent scooted in from opposite sides; Calvin needed the leg room on one end, and Carrie needed a quick route to the bathroom on the other—just in case. Calvin kept Jenny's sword case and backpack right by his side, pinning the straps to the floor with one enormous Size Fourteen foot.

A perky black girl with very short hair—she could easily have been the perky blonde hostess with a deep tan and a haircut—pranced over to take their drink orders and recite a list of specials that were all encrusted or glazed or served on a bed of broccoli rabe. She interrupted her own recital several times with personal opinions on the various dishes, which ranged from "Yummy" to "One of my favorites!" Jenny smiled politely, Calvin nodded attentively, and the Raymonds kept up their usual sparkling banter with each other and the waitress.

By the time she returned to discreetly deposit their drinks on the table and slip away without interrupting, they were talking about last week's meetings with the agents.

"Well, that's just not very polite," Carrie Raymond decided. "If they're going to go through all the trouble of seeing your show, you'd think they might like to really work with you."

"Meh," said Calvin, trying to play it off. "I don't know if they actually work with magicians. I mean, I know there are agents who specialize in magicians and stuff, or, you know, 'acts' instead of actors. Maybe they just heard about the show and wanted to see what we could do."

Jenny snorted. "Whatever," she said darkly. "They just didn't really care. I mean, maybe Abe did, but he's just...*old*." The Raymonds laughed appreciatively. "Barry Carter didn't care at all. He's like those agents you see on TV—just keeps talking and talking, and none of it really means anything."

"Well," Vincent mused, "that's often just a kind of compensation for being uncertain. A lot of people cover up a really good, genuine person with a tough exterior—as a defense."

"A lot of people cover up a total jerk with an even bigger asshole—as a defense," Jenny pointed out bluntly. She stopped and smiled guiltily. "But I'm just saying that to cover up my good, genuine person."

The Raymonds and Calvin laughed big.

The waitress returned for their orders. Jenny opted for something encrusted and Vincent went for something napping on broccoli rabe. The menu was mostly seafood, but Carrie chose one of the few pasta dishes— wary of some of the more exotic fish dishes because of her pregnancy— and Calvin ordered chicken. The lanky magician wasn't keen on fish outside of the fried variety served with chips and a healthy dose of malt vinegar.

Over salad, the conversation drifted to the magic act itself. "You really are quite a talented magician," said Vincent.

"Well..." Calvin hedged modestly. "I've got some good tricks. And Jenny makes me look good."

Jenny blushed and bit her lip, hiding her flattered smile behind a sip of Diet Coke. Carrie Raymond was drinking spring water, and Vincent had water as well, showing solidarity with his expecting wife. Calvin had a beer—he was no alcoholic, but a strapping Irish lad who enjoyed his suds.

Jenny wanted to keep her head clear, though she wondered if she even could get drunk anymore. Did indestructibility apply to liquor, too?

"How did you make all those 'devices'?" Carrie asked brightly. She pursed her lips at a sudden thought. "Oh! Or did you buy them?" She was an amazing conversationalist—the full focus of her attention was right smack in the middle of Calvin's face.

"Yeah," Calvin admitted, shrugging and spearing some leaves of lettuce with his fork. "I'm okay at making stuff—"

"He's *really* good at it," Jenny interjected proudly.

"—but I got a lot of that stuff at a pawn shop," Calvin went on. "You can find all sorts of stuff at the pawn shops and antique stores in the city."

"Oh, hey," said Jenny. "Carrie, didn't you used to work at an antique store?"

Carrie gave her a tiny, conspiratorial smile. "Guilty as charged," she said.

"Oh," said Calvin. He scratched his chin thoughtfully. "Um...oh."

"Carrie's had a wide variety of careers," Vincent said, putting an arm around her.

She cooed back at him. "Well, not careers," she corrected. "Those were just jobs, really. *This* is my purpose in life," she cradled her round belly, which peeked over the edge of the table. "Bringing something new into the world!"

Vincent looked at his wife with adoration in his crystal blue eyes. "Out with the old, and in with the new," he said gushingly.

"Oh, Jenny!" Carrie suddenly switched topics. "How *did* that interview go? Did you get the job?"

"Job?"

Vincent nodded. "The day we met! You were going to a job interview."

"Oh, right!" It was only months ago, but the day of her accident—the day she died—seemed like ages ago. Maybe if she'd known how momentous it was at the time, it would have stuck in her head more clearly. "No, I didn't get that one. But I did get another one a little while ago."

"She's a translator!" Calvin said enthusiastically.

It was all Jenny could do not to kick him under the table, but she barely concealed her cringing expression. Calvin immediately realized something was wrong, though he couldn't put his finger on it—he left his smile on autopilot and glanced aside at Jenny.

"That's lovely!" said Carrie. "What other languages do you speak?"

"Um, just a couple," said Jenny. Outside of her job at Miller & Barash, she avoided any mention of her pan-lingual abilities. Trying to explain their source might tangle her up in explanations she wasn't ready to provide. She'd lied on her résumé to get the job, claiming a linguistics degree that was all too easy to demonstrate on the spot, thereby avoiding any challenges to its veracity.

"Vincent speaks fluent Japanese," Carrie proclaimed. "And some Spanish, too—right, dear?"

"*Sí, mia cara,*" Vincent purred as the sexiest Zorro ever. "But Carrie is the polyglot in the family," he added. "She even speaks Latin!"

Carrie laughed off the praise humbly. "Twelve years of Catholic school does that to a girl!" she said. Calvin laughed, and Jenny nodded a little less tightly, feeling her tension ease a bit—nobody cared about her linguistic abilities or where they'd come from. Carrie took a sip of her water and lightly asked: "So, Jenny, what do you speak?"

So much for not caring. "Like, Cantonese," Jenny said. "You know, from my mom. And some—" she thought of a language, any language, and Caravel's honey-glazed voice came to mind "—Portuguese."

"*Muito bom!*" Carrie exclaimed, clapping her hands. "*Português europeu ou português brasileiro?*"

Merda, thought Jenny. "Um," she said, "both." In for a penny, in for *uma libra*, she figured. "But I translate stuff all day," she explained. "It's nice to just hear everybody talking in plain English after work, you know?"

"Of course, dear," Carrie said sympathetically. "I used to feel the same way after sitting through a good old-fashioned traditional Latin Mass."

"Ugh," Calvin blurted out behind a forkful of lettuce. He caught himself. "I mean, you know, no offense...."

"Don't worry, Calvin," Carrie said with a breezy laugh. "Forcing schoolchildren to sit through Latin Mass is offensive enough!"

Another laugh made the trip around the table, carrying them through to their main course. As always, Vincent and Carrie Raymond kept the conversation going effortlessly, transforming the awkward and clumsy contributions of their less refined guests into the sparkling repartee of a prime time television drama brilliantly written by the latest Hollywood upstart with a sociopolitical axe to grind and ninety words per minute to grind it with.

Vincent somehow maintained his divine class and style even while shoveling floppy greens into his mouth with his seared mahi mahi. "So, Jenny," he said after politely swallowing, "have you caught the show business bug now? Or are you still going to pursue photography?"

Jenny wasn't surprised that he remembered; part of the Perfect Couple Package was a flawless memory for personal details and flattering conversational topics. "Oh, no, I'm not really into acting or anything," she said. Calvin said nothing, and Jenny added: "Calvin got me a new camera, though—it's the best camera I ever had!"

Calvin smiled gratefully. He understood where she was and where she was headed. Even if he wished it could be otherwise.

"That's great!" said Vincent. "We'd love to see some of your photographs. Do you have a portfolio?"

"Vincent could hang some of your work in his office," Carrie suggested. "If that's all right with you, of course!"

"I don't really have a lot of stuff right now," Jenny said. All her old stuff was either lost or stored at her mom's to make it easier for Jenny to move from apartment to apartment, and her new stuff involved a giant horse that nobody was supposed to know about and a deserted beach that she shouldn't have been able to visit. Not for the first time, she remembered that she *still* hadn't tried taking photos in Wonderland, and reminded herself to try it tonight. Of course, that wouldn't yield any more portfolio-ready material.

"Oh, that's too bad," said Carrie. "I'm sure your pictures would look lovely on his walls."

"I'll make do with yours, darling," Vincent said sweetly. To Jenny and Calvin, he explained: "Carrie paints beautiful pictures."

"Oh," Carrie dismissed the compliment with a casual wave.

"Cool," said Jenny. "What do you paint?"

"Just whatever I see," Carrie wrinkled her nose in an adorably modest expression that seemed out of place on the woman Nietzsche would have deemed an appropriate bride for his *Übermensch*. "I only paint when the mood strikes me. Once in a blue moon, really!"

Calvin smiled brightly. "Maybe you could paint a new poster for us?" he suggested. "Me and Jenny doing our magic stuff, I mean. For the show."

Carrie shook her head. "My paintings are more abstract," she said. "I don't really paint people. Just feelings—or concepts."

"Oh," said Calvin. "Well, that's cool."

"Yeah," said Jenny. "We should come to the office sometime and see them."

"Certainly!" said Vincent.

Carrie nodded. "It would be so nice to have you there. And to see what you think of my paintings!"

Jenny only picked at her encrusted whatever, as yummy as the waitress might think it was; she had little appetite, and wondered if this was just part of the natural process Caravel had explained: letting go, bit by bit, of the living world and its physical requirements for things like food and sleep. More likely, she was just nervous about her first appointment as an Angel of Death. She tapped Calvin and said quietly: "Could you grab my phone?" He took it out of her bag and handed it to her, and she checked the time—she had more than a half hour to go, but she wanted to get there early and prepare for whatever she needed to do.

"Do you have an appointment?" Carrie asked.

"What?" Jenny stared. "No. I mean, yeah. Um, it's a work thing."

Vincent arched an eyebrow. "This late?" he asked.

Calvin chimed in: "It's the time difference." Jenny looked at him, frozen for a moment, and he smiled. "Those lawyers in China are just getting up now."

"Yeah!" Jenny seized the story. "I was hoping I could stay for dessert, but I should probably go pretty soon."

"Oh, that's a shame," said Carrie, pouting playfully. "But we'll definitely get together again soon!"

"Right," Vincent agreed. "You two have to promise us! No sneaking off this time, Jenny." He smiled.

"I promise," Jenny nodded. "So, how much can we—"

"Uh uh!" Vincent shook his head.

"Certainly not," Carrie insisted. "We invited you out to dinner—it's our treat. In fact, we'll drive you to your office so you can get to work."

"Yes, of course," said Vincent.

"Um, no, that's okay," said Jenny. "It's not far. Um. They pay for the cab, anyway." In a way, her travel *was* covered by the job she had to do.

"Well," Vincent said, "Calvin, at least we can get you back home, if Jenny's running off to work."

Calvin nodded. "Sure—thanks!" The prospect of getting a ride home was one of the less grim things the magician had endured lately.

Jenny nudged Calvin, who stood up to let her out of the booth; Vincent slid out after her. Carrie kept her seat. "I'd get up," the gloriously glowing goddess said, "but it might take longer than you have." She grinned and patted her belly.

Jenny doubted that, but smiled. She leaned down to give Carrie a quick hug. "Thanks so much for taking us out," she said. "Thanks for dinner! And for, well, you know. Everything."

"Of course, Jenny!" Carrie pointed two mischievous fingers at Jenny and her magician companion. "I told you things were going to turn around for you."

"Everything runs in cycles," Vincent said. "It's important to take on the rough roads to reach the smooth sailing ahead."

Jenny paused. "Yeah," she said thoughtfully. She looked at Vincent, then Carrie, then back at Vincent. "It's, uh, nice when you can get onto a smoother road. Right?"

"It sure is," Vincent agreed easily.

Carrie nodded. "Everyone has to go through rough times to appreciate what they really need," she said philosophically. "Without trouble, there's no end to it."

"Without fire, there's no putting it out," Vincent added.

"Without destruction, there's no creation," said Carrie.

"It's all a great big circle, of endings and beginnings," said Vincent.

Carrie nodded. "Endings and beginnings," she echoed.

Jenny was getting that eerie AmWay feeling again; she looked up at the expression on Calvin's face. He looked as if the couple had just suggested a wife swapping session back at their place, and he was trying to figure out how to politely decline. "Um," he said.

"Yeah," said Jenny, trying to help. She had slightly more experience with the Raymonds' strange interludes than Calvin did. "Good point. Well, um, I've got to get going. Calvin, could you come down with me for a second? I just want to, um, freshen up, and you could hold my stuff outside the door."

Calvin jumped off his uncomfortable train of thought and nodded rapidly. "Yeah! Sure."

The magician leaned down to pick up Jenny's sword case at the same time Vincent did. After a moment of confusion and a polite tug-of-war, the case suddenly fell open and dangled from Calvin's hands—the sword clattered to the floor.

Jenny *eeped* and scrambled for the sword. Calvin knelt instantly and tried to help her slide it back into the case.

"Wow. That's a beautiful sword, Jenny!" said Vincent.

"Um, yeah," Jenny said, trying to close the case quickly. "It's—for work."

"Work?" asked Carrie. She leaned past the table to get a look.

"Yeah, it's...um...part of a legal case." Jenny knew it sounded lame, but she had no other story in mind. "They asked me to...polish it up."

"Get it polished," Calvin clarified helpfully. "There's a place around the corner that does stuff like that, and the bosses needed the sword cleaned up, so Jenny took it there for them. She has to get it back tonight for a...um..."

"Video conference!" Jenny finished victoriously. She gave Calvin a quick smile of gratitude. "Which I'm translating at," she explained to the Raymonds.

"It looks very old," Carrie observed.

"Yeah, it's, uh, some old Chinese sword. From China. Like, ancient China," Jenny tried to avoid digging her hole any deeper, but the edges kept crumbling in on top of her.

"Chinese?" Carrie said. Her eyes played over the blade as Jenny clamped the case shut and flipped the latches. "That's nice." She smiled at her husband prettily, batting her eyelids at him in a private Morse code.

Vincent smiled broadly. "We'll take care of the check," he said, "and meet you downstairs. Sorry about the sword, Jenny."

"No, it's okay," Jenny said, slinging her backpack over her shoulder and giving Vincent Raymond a hug. She got lost in the smell of orgasms and Girl Scout campfires, tried to shake off the disturbing place in her mind where those two things met, and pulled away. "Thanks again for dinner. We'll see you guys soon!" she promised.

Calvin smiled. "I'll wait for you guys downstairs," he told the Raymonds. He carried Jenny's sword case and followed her down to the ladies' room.

At the door, he touched her arm. "Jenny..."

"What?"

"I remember where I remember Carrie Raymond from."

Jenny squeezed her expression into confusion. "What do you mean?"

"I don't remember them coming to the show," said Calvin. "Not really. But I *have* seen her before."

"Where?"

"At the pawn shops."

Jenny raised an eyebrow. "Which pawn shop?"

"No, the pawn *shops*," he emphasized. "Lots of them. The shops and antique stores and all. I remember seeing her a bunch of times."

"Yeah, well," Jenny threw off, "she used to work at an antique store, right?"

"I guess," said Calvin. "But she was different there."

"What do you mean?"

"She wasn't as...nice," he said, with an expression inspired by very sour lemons. "She would get really bossy with the shop guys. Had a big argument with one of them."

"So?" Jenny's hand was on the bathroom door. "People have arguments, Calvin. And she's nice to us because we're out to dinner with them—you know, like friends. Everybody acts nice to their friends."

"I guess," Calvin said, dropping his arm. "Yeah, sorry. Okay, you go get changed—I'll wait out here."

Jenny turned to enter the bathroom, then stopped and looked back at Calvin. "Okay, you know what?" She put a hand on his chest and he looked down at her. "I'm not going to be stupid anymore. There's enough crazy shit going on in our lives that I should really stop ignoring something just because it's a 'coincidence.'"

Calvin looked at her inquisitively.

"Fuck, those two have had this weird Stepford vibe ever since I met them," she confessed, feeling a huge relief just letting the words out. "And whenever they start in on that whole Circle of Life thing, endings and beginnings...it feels like bugs crawling under my skin."

273

The magician nodded with exaggerated distaste. "Yeah, I know what you mean."

"Maybe they're just weird," said Jenny, "but it's pretty weird that you've seen her before at the antique shops and stuff. And it's pretty weird that they were there the day I...you know." She narrowed her eyes. "And it's pretty weird they came to the show at all, really."

"You told me they said a friend told them about it," Calvin pointed out.

Jenny eyed him levelly. "What friends do people like the Raymonds have in the Chelsea fringe theatre crowd?"

He gazed back just as seriously. "Well," he said carefully. "Us?"

"I—I don't want you going with them," Jenny told him.

"What?"

"I don't want you riding home with them," she repeated. "I just don't."

Calvin smiled and put his hand over hers on his chest. "I'll be okay," he said. "It's not like they're serial killers or something. Probably just Far Right Republicans. The worst thing they can do is evade more taxes than me."

"Well..."

"Jenny, don't worry," Calvin reassured her. "I'm just getting a ride home. It'd be rude if I didn't, now. You just get changed—you've got to make your appointment."

Jenny took a deep breath. "Okay," she said. She reached up on tiptoe and gave him a quick kiss on the cheek. "Wait out here." She dashed through the door.

In the ladies' room, she picked a stall and turned the lock, hanging her backpack on the hook inside the door. She wriggled out of her dress and nudged her shoes off, pulling another outfit out of the backpack: black jeans, a black tank top, a black hoodie, and her Doc Martens. She wasn't sure where the other Deaths got their fancy black robes, and decided to improvise for now, sticking as close to the company image as possible. Other Deaths probably didn't have cell phones in their pockets or digital cameras slung around their necks, but she wanted to bring the devices along—she needed her phone on her when she was done, and she wanted to finally experiment with taking pictures in Wonderland. She got dressed, tightened the laces on her boots and stuffed her high heels into her backpack with the dress, then straightened herself out and exited the stall. Looking in the mirror, she wasn't as satisfied as she thought she'd be—she looked more like a hard luck junkie in an award-winning European independent film than the Grim Reaper. Mirror Jenny looked down at her own arms and picked at the sleeves, looking back up at Jenny in disbelief. *Is this really all we've got?* her expression clearly asked.

"Best I could do on short notice," Jenny whispered back. Her reflection rolled her eyes and put her hood up. Jenny left hers down and headed out the door.

Calvin was outside, smiling. She traded him the backpack for the sword case. "Let me get it out, and you can bring the case with you," she said.

"No, wait," said Calvin. "Now they think you're going to work with it. You have to bring the case with you."

Jenny glowered. "Crap, you're right." She took her fingers away from the latch she'd opened partway. "I guess it'll be okay—it's not like I've got the right outfit, either."

"I think you look cool," Calvin said emphatically.

"Let's hope my appointment doesn't have any preconceptions about what I'm *supposed* to look like," said Jenny. "Okay—wish me luck."

"Luck," said Calvin. "Call me when you're done—let me know what happens."

"I will." Jenny pushed back into the bathroom, but looked back. "Be careful with those two."

Calvin laughed. "Jenny—"

"Just be careful," Jenny insisted.

He nodded solemnly. "I will. Go. Good luck."

Jenny ducked inside and psyched herself up. Mirror Jenny gave her a professional nod from beneath her hood, like a fellow gunslinger reassuring her: *I've got your back.* She unlatched the case and pulled out the sword, watching Mirror Jenny's sword glint dully behind the mirror. With a quick sweep, she held the blade before her eyes and placed her palm against it.

And Jenny Ng, Angel of Death, embarked down the Smooth Road to her first Appointment.

CHAPTER TWENTY-TWO

Rex knew where to go. It was like Caravel said—as easy as reaching for an alarm clock in the morning darkness, your arm unerringly guided by your ears no matter what spinning blackness cloaks your vision. Rex was her ears, honing in on the incessant buzz of the imminent appointment. He was also her arm, steadily and surely approaching her target. The thrill of the visceral, intimate connection with the horse galloping powerfully beneath her made Jenny's nerves sing.

He flew up Broadway, headed north. For an instant, Jenny caught sight of another horse, and another black-garbed rider, dashing away on a cross street. The rider was too far away to recognize if it was Caravel or Curach or Ketch—the only necromantic colleagues she'd met—but it seemed Jenny wasn't the only one with an appointment in the city tonight. It was spooky to think of other Angels of Death thundering solitarily through the rushing, swirling emptiness of Wonderland, all with their own appointments to meet.

Broadway slashed diagonally up Manhattan, then curved slightly left and straightened out, parallelling the other avenues on the West Side. Rex slowed, the *cloppity-clop* of his pounding gallop stepping down to the *clop-clop-clop* of a brisk canter, downshifting swiftly to the simple *clip-clop clip-clop* of a decisive trot. Beneath her hoodie, the digital camera kept time, awkwardly tapping the front of Jenny's waist. A tall building loomed over her. The windows had that dull brownish glare that most Wonderland windows had, somewhere between fully lit and pitch dark. The place looked like a cross between a hospital and a hotel. Bold letters on a dark awning made Jenny catch her breath as she flipped the text in her head to read it: the Madelyn Coleman Foundation Assisted Living and Care Center. It was housing for senior citizens; a place for people to spend the twilight years of their lives before night fell one last time.

She was dishearteningly certain that her appointment would be someone very old; a grandma or grandpa, with little life left to stave off the death she was here to witness. Jenny wasn't sure if this was a simple assignment to ease her into the job, or a devastatingly hard assignment to toughen her up for more difficult ones to come. It was like figuring square roots in math class—the result could be positive or negative, even if it was the same answer.

Rex didn't pause as they approached the front door; he ducked, and Jenny followed suit, leaning over his broad neck as they swept beneath the awning and through wide double-doors that fidgeted in the blurry state between open and closed. A long mirror behind the reception desk showed the mostly empty lobby in the real world: the back of the receptionist's head, an orderly unfolding a wheelchair, and a couple of wrinkled old folks in old-fashioned clothes shuffling spryly across the linoleum floor. Jenny thought about leaning over near the mirror, searching the receptionist's desk to see if she could match a name to the irresistible pull coming from a few floors up at the opposite end of the building, but even if she could spy the right page in the right register, she didn't know the room number. The pull was a simple direction, not a notion of factual information like numbers or names—she hadn't seen this death date through the Window. Rex nickered softly and turned for the stairwell. Jenny glanced over her shoulder at the elevator; if doors were constantly between two states in Wonderland, she wondered how elevators could possibly work. She agreed with the horse; the stairs were a more comfortable option.

At least, they were for her. Like most buildings in the city, these weren't built with large quadrupeds in mind; the architects hadn't foreseen any giant horses with a pressing need to visit one of the higher floors of a nursing home. Rex took each flight the same way—a few tentative steps to get started, then violent kicks upward to reach the next landing before the steep angle could send his heavy body sliding right back down. Jenny had no doubt he could make it, though it did look pretty frustrating. She rubbed and clapped his neck to encourage him. The horse doubled his efforts, making the fourth floor in very little time.

They emerged into a wide corridor that was nevertheless a bit claustrophobic for a two-thousand-pound stallion, or even a hundred-pound rider on top of one. The long fluorescent lights overhead didn't cast light so much as give off the color of light in the dim, sepia-toned hall. The inside of the building matched the outside—a hybrid of hospital and hotel. The wide corridor and the nurses station near the stairwell and elevator said hospital; the dingy *fleur-de-lis* patterned wallpaper and little wooden tables arranged periodically down the way said hotel. The emergency kits fastened to the walls outside every door smirkingly reiterated: hospital. The fake flowers on the tables and fancy mirrors hung on the walls petulantly insisted: hotel. The square tiles on the linoleum floor made a convincing final argument for hospital. Case closed.

Jenny held the reins loosely, knowing that Rex would follow the call of the appointment and not her unhorsemanlike pulls and tugs. He went past the nurses station and trotted down the corridor to the corner, turning to follow the structure of the halls around to a room on the opposite side of the building. Jenny flipped the mirrored number on the door in her mind: 315. The Madelyn Coleman Center numbered their floors the European way.

Rex knelt down. Jenny somberly swung one leg over—and promptly spilled off the horse, thumping the floor with a ghostly echo off the Wonderland air. She grumbled softly to herself and sighed; the horse gave her a sympathetic look. "Here," she said to him, "hold on to this." She balanced the empty sword case precariously on his saddle and wrapped the strap around the saddle horn tightly to hold it. Rex helpfully backed out of the way of the door; the case wobbled a little, but stayed in place.

The sword itself was tied in place on Rex's saddle—Jenny wanted to do this thing right. She wondered if she should bring the sword in with her, but decided that some old man or lady would be less scared by her appearance if she wasn't brandishing a weapon. She left the sword tied to the saddle, and pushed her way through the door to Room 315.

It was pretty much what she expected: as cozy as a small suite could be and still leave space for a crash cart or a gurney. There was a fancy set of shelves on one wall, but its contents were smeared into a sketch of hundreds of overlapping knick knacks, unidentifiable in their Wonderland forms. A similarly disconcerting bedspread lay on a wide bed in the center of an adjacent wall. A small writing desk was wedged beneath a tall window, and the area nearest the door was given over to a couple of comfortable looking chairs and a low circular table. Another door by the entrance led to a private bathroom, wide enough for a wheelchair and fitted with enough handicap-accessible bars and railings to hold a Special Olympics gymnastic event.

Jenny peered through a mirror on the wall over the sitting area; in the real world, an old woman sat heavily on the edge of the bed. She held something in her hands, and her shoulders hunched as her head slumped down to look at whatever it was she was holding.

Jenny reached for the mirror, but a chuffing growl made her stop. Rex stood in the doorway, staring at her, puffing air through his wide nostrils. *Not yet*, his expression told her.

Jenny let out a deep breath and nodded. It made sense—she wasn't here to visit the living, she was here to escort the dead. Until the old lady was dead, Jenny should leave her alone. If the dull buzz of her Death Alarm Clock was any indication, it wouldn't be much longer now anyway. The woman deserved her last few moments in peace.

Through the mirror, the old woman closed her hands on the object—Jenny still couldn't glimpse what it was—and reached toward the small bedside table. Her fingers never touched the drawer, though. With an eerily graceful slowness, she rolled back on the bed, slightly twisted, one arm still extended toward the bedside table and the other bent up across her belly. Her legs dangled uncomfortably off the bed, small feet hovering inches above the floor, slippers skewed slightly off her tensed toes. Her chest moved up and down, just barely, in quivering fits and starts.

Through the Looking Glass, Jenny bit her lip anxiously. Even if the affairs of the living were no longer her primary focus, she didn't like watching the old lady suffer. She reached for the mirror again, but a ruckus from the door made her falter. Rex whinnied and huffed, stomping one huge hoof on the floor with a whooshing Wonderland echo. The horse made his opinion on the matter utterly clear.

Jenny stared hard at him. "Is it a *rule?*" she asked pointedly. "One of the ones we don't break? Or just standard operating procedure?"

The horse stared back coolly.

"What are they gonna do?" Jenny snapped. "Fire me?" She placed her palm on the glass and pushed through, swirling along odd and unplaceable dimensions to the real world.

The old woman's twitching fist was hanging just off the bed, still in mid-reach for the bedside table. Her fingers struggled to close tight, but spasmed and flipped open like they'd all been instantly magnetized with the same polarity. A flash of shiny white fell from her hand, spinning down to the thin carpet below.

Jenny's small, slim-fingered hand caught it. She looked kindly down at the old woman. "It's okay," Jenny said. "I got it."

The woman stared from bulging, nervous eyes, glancing past her lower eyelids at the black-clad girl beside her bed. Jenny reached down and raised up the old woman's legs, guiding her into a more comfortable position lying on the bed. She took the woman's arm and folded it slowly over her nightgown, trying to get her into a more natural pose. The woman's cloudy, pale eyes stared back with wonder, curiosity, and a strange glint that Jenny couldn't interpret.

Jenny looked down at the object in her hands. It was the cap from a jar—silvery metal on the inside, painted white on top with red lettering: *Gelman's Sweet Gherkins* in cheerful block letters. Around the opposite arc, the cap claimed: *You're in a Pickle Now!* Scrawled across the middle in faded black, smeared but still legible, was a name and a series of characters: *Sam GR5 9033.*

Love at a pickle store. Jenny smiled. "He was your husband?" she asked quietly.

The old woman made a small sound in the back of her throat.

"Don't," said Jenny, "I'm sorry. I didn't mean to make you—don't talk. You can tell me all about it later. I'll wait here."

The woman's expression didn't change—Jenny realized she might be paralyzed from the heart attack or stroke or whatever it was that had taken her.

"I'm not going anywhere," Jenny reassured her. "I'm staying right here."

Eyes the color of rain stared back, unmoving. There was a calm and understanding light in them, pale sunbeams sneaking through the thunder-gray clouds, knowing that no storm can last forever and they'll be back to bake some rainbows in a bit. The light was dwindling, shrinking to a tiny gleaming pinprick like the last challenge of a boxy old television that's just been turned off, the bright star in the center of the screen promising the heroic return of the Lone Ranger, Howdy Doody, and Uncle Miltie. And just as easily, just as smoothly, that final light went out. There was no angelic chorus and no dramatic glowing form bursting free from the empty body. Just a very quiet moment. That moment was broken by the next.

"So that's it then?"

Jenny jumped and looked at the foot of the bed. The old woman stood there, looking down at her former body, her expression less that of the recently departed and more that of a discerning shopper assessing the quality of a used car. Her voice was stronger and deeper than Jenny would have thought from the old woman's thin frame and bony limbs.

"Um," Jenny answered expertly.

"That's all we get?" the old woman asked. "Seems anticlimactic to me."

Jenny gave her a half-hearted smile. "Yeah, I know. I didn't even *know* it when *I* died. Didn't even blip on my radar."

The old woman turned from her own peacefully resting corpse and examined Jenny. She pursed her lips. "Are you an angel?"

"No..." Jenny began.

"Didn't think so," said the old woman, nodding confidently. "So what's next?"

"What?"

"What do I do?" the woman asked. She wasn't abrupt or rude—just fast. If she still approached everything with a breakneck sense of urgency after her death, Jenny wondered how fast she must have lived. "Do we take a look at my whole life?" she went on. "What I did right, what I did wrong. Or do I have to go on trial? Defend my choices? I think I can do that. I don't regret a lot. Just George. And Harry, and the other George, and that one boy with the freckles."

"Um." Jenny wasn't sure how to get a hold of the situation.

"No, don't get the wrong idea," the woman said quickly. "I don't regret what I *did*, I regret what I *didn't* do. With *any* of them. George or George or Harry or that freckled boy. Or Matthew. Oh! And Leo...or Lenny? Or—what was his name?"

"Right, no, that's—"

"And I certainly don't regret what I *did* do with Sam. He was such a sweetheart. Oh! Do I get to see him again? Or any of them? Well, I don't suppose all of them have gone now. Some of them might still be kicking. The freckle-face boy was a whole lot younger than me. But don't judge me for that. Are you here to judge me?"

Jenny almost missed her opening. "No!" she said hastily. "No, I'm just here to help. To bring you to where you need to go next."

"Where's that?" the old woman asked.

"Uh," Jenny thought about how to answer that question. "We're going to find out together," she answered, hoping it sounded appropriately mysterious rather than totally uncertain.

"Oh, good then," replied the old woman. Her train of thought came to a sharp stop. "Are you sure you're not here to judge me?"

"I'm not here to judge you," Jenny confirmed.

"Then I wonder," the old woman dawdled for the first time, "do you know if Maggie's gone on yet? If I might see her again? I don't regret what I did with *her*, either." The woman gave Jenny a coy smile. "I know modern standards are a bit different, but it was still a pretty big whoop for me, you know. Back then, that sort of thing didn't go on." She tilted her head. "Well, I suppose it did. After all, I *know* it did. But nobody talked about it. Or threw parades."

"Right," Jenny tried to rein in the conversation. "It's okay. Sounds like you had a...good time. A good life," she corrected herself. "Now we just have to move forward. Well, *you* do, I mean. You've earned it. Sounds like."

"All right, then," said the old woman. She looked down at herself. "Well, I'll be!"

Jenny looked too—the woman wasn't wearing the same nightgown and slippers as her recently deceased body. She wore a very smart, very tightly cut skirt and jacket, an old style that Jenny recognized from any number of classic films where fast-talking career women proved they could get the job done as well as any man before proving that the producers still required them to end up married and lovingly doting on a man with a face like a leather couch before the closing credits.

"I was wearing this the day I met Sam!" the woman said cheerfully.

Jenny raised the jar cap. "Sam the pickle man?"

"No, he didn't work there," the old woman explained. She reached for the cap—Jenny tried to hand it over, but the woman's shimmering fingers slipped through it like it was air. "Oh!" She shrugged and moved closer to look down at the hastily inked number on the cap. "He just didn't have a piece of paper to write on," she explained. "I was buying groceries for Mother, and he wanted to give me his telephone number. Not everyone had telephones then. I thought he was showing off!"

"But he—"

"No, he was, as it happened," the old woman said. "It wasn't even his number. It was his neighbor's down the block. He pestered them for a week, waiting around and answering their calls whenever their phone rang. People started to think the Klineks had hired a secretary. It was scandalous!"

"But you—"

"Yes, I called." The woman's smile flashed like fluttering tinsel on a Christmas tree. "He still fooled me into thinking it was his phone. I didn't find out until I called a second time. Mister Klinek was *not* very polite about it. Elena—that was his wife, Elena—she thought it was charming, though. She told me the truth, and told me where Sam lived. I stormed over there like I was going to give him the business!"

"Business?"

The old woman laughed. "But I was all talk. I thought it was charming, too. He was so adorable, after all. How many other fat men can you name who are so full of bravado and yet still perfect gentlemen?"

"I—"

"Didn't think so." Another confident nod, like it was her trademark.

Jenny leaped in. "What's your name?" she asked, a bit too shortly.

The old woman blinked. "Oh! I'm Dolores. Dolores Meisel."

Jenny smiled tightly. "Dolores—I'm Jenny. I really want to hear all about this, but we need to go. I don't think they can bother you anymore...but if I'm still here when somebody walks in, I think that would be bad."

"Oh," said Dolores. "I'm sorry. Yes, let's go. Where are we going? Is there anything I need to do?"

"Just stick with me," said Jenny. She put an arm around Dolores's shoulder and guided her toward the mirror on the wall. Jenny's arm tingled where it lay across Dolores's back. The woman was just about Jenny's height, though not as thin—she had all the respectable curves of an old school Hollywood starlet, even if her face was a bit too plain for the flickers. In ghostly form, she hadn't regained a youthful face, but her body was strong and unbent, and she walked with a spring of tempered carbon steel in her step. She was a little translucent; the corner of the room peeked through her like nervous high school actors spying the audience through a scrim.

"Just hold on to my arm," Jenny told Dolores.

"Funny," said Dolores, wrapping her arm around Jenny's elbow, "how come I can touch you, but not the jar top?"

Jenny smiled. "I'm different." To prove it, she pushed the mirror and pulled Dolores through with her, spinning into Wonderland with a puff of bells and the ringing of dust.

283

Dolores gaped, then laughed. "Ha!" she exclaimed. "Didn't think so!"

"What?"

"I always figured everybody was wrong." Dolores gave her a big grin. "My family was Jewish. So was Sam's. And my best friend Arlene was a nice Methodist girl. Jo Ellen—she's the head nurse here—she's a Baptist. All of them so sure about what happens next—you know, *after*. I figure, any time somebody's *that* sure, they must be wrong."

"Guess so," said Jenny.

"So where do we go next?" Dolores asked.

Jenny pointed to the door. Rex stood proudly in the corridor, his expression unmistakable. His lips were tight and his eyes narrowed. He was miffed at Jenny for ignoring his recommendation, but he was trying to act professional in front of their appointment. If he were her husband instead of her horse, Jenny knew she'd be in for a hell of an argument on the drive home.

"Fantastic!" said Dolores. "You have a horse!"

"*We* have a horse," said Jenny—it felt like the right thing to say. "Climb on, and we'll get going." She toyed with putting her hood up for authenticity, but at this point, presenting Dolores with the whole Grim Reaper look wasn't going to matter. It would be hard to give her the right dark, mysterious, hooded mood when she'd already seen the skinny Chinese girl inside it.

Dolores followed Jenny out the door to stand beside Rex. Jenny absently handed her the jar cap so that she could mount up with both hands free, and Dolores took it without thinking. "Oh!" the ghost woman cried out. "I touched it!"

"Um, yeah," Jenny pretended it was all perfectly natural to her. "Bring it with you, if you like." Rex knelt down and Jenny climbed on, making sure the sword case was secure. She held out a hand.

Dolores hugged the shiny cap to her breast in one hand and took Jenny's hand with the other. She climbed on behind Jenny, side-saddle. Rex stood abruptly, but was careful not to throw Dolores off.

"It's been a very long time since I've ridden a horse," Dolores whispered.

"Don't worry," said Jenny. "He's really good at this. Hold on tight." She patted Rex's neck, happy to have him there, even if they were in a spat. He grumbled and tossed his mane; he was willing to let it go. He turned with a gentle jolt and took off, trotting back around to the stairwell. Down was much easier than up: Rex scrambled down each flight, not worrying much when he slipped and slid a little, always catching himself firmly at each landing. Dolores laughed as they jostled and bumped down each step. "He's just like a real horse!" she said.

"He *is* a real horse," said Jenny. "He's just a little extra."

"I'll say," Dolores replied, giving the giant stallion an appraising look.

They reached the lobby, and Rex bolted through the wavering double-doors; Dolores caught her breath sharply as they went through with no shattering of glass or splintering of metal. Outside, Rex burst into full speed, slicing down the sidewalk and racing to the corner before veering quickly eastward. The Looking Glass city thundered by them in a blur of buildings and twitching air. Dolores and Jenny both looked upward to the phenomenal night sky of Wonderland. "It's beautiful!" Dolores shouted. Actual joy lit up her face; Jenny wasn't sure if she'd ever seen actual joy before, on the face of any living person. Maybe all that joy was stored up for moments like this one, after the arduous task of living was done, and the rewards for all that hard work were earned.

The horse streaked into Central Park and curved just barely left, heading south and shooting out across the Lake. Dolores whooped and squealed as sketchy half-existent jets of water sluiced in their wake. Rex suddenly leapt and skidded to a stop at the opposite shore, vaguely illustrated water splashing all around them as the echoes of Wonderland wind died down to the usual dull roar.

Dolores's face glowed with delight. "We're here?"

Jenny tried to cover her own confusion. "Yeah," she said. "I'll help you—"

Dolores slid right off the saddle and landed solidly on the smeared stick figure grass on the shore.

"—down," Jenny finished. She scrunched up her face and prayed she wouldn't make a fool of herself on the dismount; Rex bent over and Jenny spilled out of the saddle, but she quickly grabbed the horse's neck and swung around to his other flank in a way that might almost seem natural, if not intentional. She landed lightly on the ground, tripping only barely and catching herself quickly. To keep up the pretense, she continued around the horse the long way, coming around behind his tail and smiling at Dolores.

The old woman stared up at the sky, idly flipping the jar cap in her hand.

"It *is* beautiful," Jenny said softly. "But it's not the end."

Dolores looked at her expectantly, a serene smile on her face.

"This is just a road," Jenny explained. She was making it up as she went, going off everything she'd learned from Caravel and little bits she'd overheard from Ketch and Curach, but she was surprised at how easy it was to just talk. "It's just one path along the way. And you've got a lot of paths left, Dolores. It's not the end."

The woman nodded. "Didn't think so." She smiled wider.

Jenny reached for the saddle, and her fingers danced over the ties to release her sword. The blade flashed as she raised it up, and she slashed through the air in an improvised figure eight.

Laughter echoed in the throbbing Wonderland atmosphere. It wasn't coming from Dolores or Jenny. There was a vague smell of grass and sweetness, and Jenny felt warm sunlight on her face.

"The beekeeper!" Dolores said, astonished.

Jenny paused. "Who?"

"I was only a little girl," said Dolores. "My class went on a trip to see a beekeeper. He taught us all about the bees, and honey, and how we could make them go to sleep with a little puff of smoke. It was my favorite day of school! I didn't have many—I quit school early to help Mother at home." She looked around, feeling the warmth of an easy Spring day on her skin, but not seeing much more than art-drenched sky and the dark surface of the Lake. "Is that what this is? Do I go back to where I was?"

"No." Jenny shook her head. "It's not that day. Wait." She wasn't sure how she knew any of this, but it was coming to her as needed. Maybe it was just a natural part of her role as an Angel of Death, like immortality, sensing her appointments, speaking languages, and traveling through mirrors. She sliced her sword through the air again, dancing a few steps away, and a splash of music filled the air, like big band music played through a tiny old radio. The smell of wine and floor wax filled their noses, and tiny lights flickered in their eyes, flashing for just a moment and disappearing into the darkness of the Smooth Road.

"The week before Sam left," Dolores said. She was smiling, but a tear trailed from the corner of one eye. "We went dancing."

Jenny smiled back, trying to put the arcane knowledge swimming in her head into concrete concepts and useful words. "It's not the day itself, Dolores," she said. "It's...think of it as a key. Or like a sign on a door. You've got a lot of doors in front of you, and you can choose which one you take. Each one will mean something different. But they'll only mean those things to *you*. You make the choice. Let the signs tell you how you feel about what's behind each door."

"I'm not sure I..." Dolores spread her hands helplessly.

"The paths you have to choose from," Jenny explained, "are things we can't understand. They're not like anything you've ever seen before, because they're an entirely different world, where...um...*seeing* isn't anything you've ever seen before. Everything you've experienced as a human being...it's only the way it works in *our* world."

She swung her sword through the air, skipping lightly along the shore of the Lake. She felt what Dolores felt: the soft thrashing and crunching and brushing of cut grass and fallen leaves, tingling in her nerves rather than actually touching her skin. She heard what Dolores heard: bounding footsteps and shouting. She smelled what Dolores smelled: the tiniest hint of warm breath carrying the scent of stale cookies and cigarettes.

"I remember his name," Dolores said wistfully.

"Who?" Jenny asked.

"The freckle-face boy." Dolores's very distant expression wavered behind an enigmatic smile. "His name was Linus."

Jenny smiled compassionately at the old woman. "The signs tell you what you can find down each path. Not *literally*—but what you'll feel. What you'll think. Every world works differently, so seeing or hearing or smelling is all mixed up. But if you've got a mind, in *any* world, then you have thoughts and feelings. And those thoughts and feelings are what you'll...um...think and feel. No matter what language, or what...experiences they're wrapped up in. Just the raw, basic core. The...*impulse*. Without the context. That's what you'll feel when you choose the path you want."

"So it's not my class trip," said Dolores. "Or the USO dance, or that Summer night with Linus."

"Right," said Jenny.

Dolores smiled and quietly said: "Didn't think so." She looked around. "It's just how I feel about them. And I can choose which one makes me feel best. And...follow that path?"

Jenny was relieved that Dolores could put it into words better than she could. "Yeah," she said. "But there are a lot to choose from. Follow me."

Leaving Rex standing patiently at the edge of the Lake, the two women skipped and danced around the shoreline, Jenny's sword flashing through the scintillating rush of wind with every turn and opening up just a taste, a sense, a quick glimpse of the paths surrounding Dolores. Silvery moonlight and the smell of smoke wafting through applause. Hard metal surfaces and the billowing of clean white linens. Sharp pinpricks and pipe tobacco with the squeaking music of balloons deflating. The rhythmic clacking of wheels on a tile floor accompanying the gentle rustle of a thick quilted blanket and the sharp but thrilling pressure of very tiny fingernails. Broken glass and sloshing liquid with undertones of dim lighting and a mournful saxophone.

Every cut the sword made tore a brief, ragged hole through the world, giving them just enough of a peek for Dolores to have a reaction. "Out on the boat," she whispered regretfully at one path. At another, she laughed and said: "He never did find his shoes!" One tear in the sky enveloped them with the scent of mint and a flickering buzz. "I could have done it myself," Dolores said defiantly. Each one inspired in Dolores a specific and defined emotion; even the ones that Jenny couldn't identify, she could see clearly displayed on the old woman's face. Not all of them were positive; more than once, Dolores was distinctly angry, or bored, or devastated, or frightened. A sweep of red cloth and a sour smell elicited a dark expression. "It wasn't my fault!" she insisted. Jenny twirled away to slash open another invisible hole in the air. Dolores self-consciously brushed back her hair and laughed nervously in response to a plastic and uncomfortably clean smell and bright white lights.

Jenny jumped and leaped along the edge of the smooth water, her sword slicing and dicing bizarre patterns that seemed to guide themselves. She felt both in control and controlled; the sword was alive with purpose and intention, but she couldn't entirely say that it wasn't her own will moving it. She could barely tell if she was dancing to keep up with the flying sword, or dancing to bring her sword to where it needed to be. It was as dazzling an experience for her as it was for the ghost of Dolores Meisel. The dance and whirl of events and moments, the music and lyrics of Dolores's life, were like a drug. Outside of herself, in that little area of the mind that somehow always manages to objectively observe and narrate, Jenny realized that it made sense—the Angels of Death had to get *something* out of their job, or they'd have no real reason to do it. The pure essence of Dolores's being, everything in her history adding up to the person following Jenny around the water, made Jenny's blood sing.

She was almost sad when the dance ended near Bow Bridge. Every path had been opened, and Dolores was drifting through memories and ideas. Jenny had lost count of the paths and the time; she may have opened hundreds, maybe thousands, without thinking about it. Judging from Dolores's face, though, she—like Jenny—still remembered every single one of them.

The old woman gazed back across the Lake, to where Rex stood watching them, a small figure in the near distance, blurry through the thick and fleeting air of Wonderland. "I can..." Dolores paused and collected herself. "I can choose whichever one I like?"

"Yes," Jenny said.

"How do I know which one to choose?"

"I don't know," Jenny answered simply. Dolores stared at her, lost but hopeful. Jenny smiled kindly. "It's a choice," she said, "but not a destination."

"Just a fork in the road," Dolores mused.

"Right," said Jenny. "Who knows? Maybe you'll get to choose one of the others later on. Maybe you can always come back and make new choices."

Dolores smiled a little. "You've...you've never done this before, have you?"

Jenny grimaced. "Um," she said. She shook her head. "No. You're my first."

"Didn't think so," Dolores nodded and grinned. "So I should just pick one, then?"

"It's up to you."

Dolores straightened herself up. She took a deep breath. "*That* one, then," she said, pointing.

Jenny was not surprised that she knew exactly which one Dolores was pointing to, and so did Dolores. They walked slowly and easily, side by side, back to a particular point on the shore of the Lake. Rex moved solemnly and quietly to meet them there.

The sword flashed up and twisted through the air, making the same cut there that it had only minutes ago. The crinkle of paper, the smell of glass and twine and salt and water, and the nearly comical noise of quiet squeaking on a flat surface spilled through the rip in the world. Dolores smiled happily, squeezing her fingers around the pickle jar cap in her hand. "I was wanted," she said, "and he was adorable."

"Maybe he's there," Jenny suggested.

Dolores made a face at her. "You don't know that," she said slyly.

Jenny made a face back. "Nope."

"Didn't think so," said Dolores, smiling openly. "But what does it matter if he is or not? Whatever it was in him that made me feel like that...*that's* there."

"Yeah," Jenny said. She planted the butt of her sword on the grass and held out a hand. "Are you ready?"

Dolores looked at Rex, then up at the phenomenal colors of Wonderland's night sky. She looked back at Jenny. "I guess I am." The old woman reached out to hold Jenny's hand.

"Wait a second." Jenny suddenly took her hand away. She fished underneath her hoodie and pulled out her camera.

"Do you do this with all your customers?" Dolores asked playfully. She struck a pose.

"I wouldn't know," said Jenny. "You're my first."

"I'm honored," said Dolores. She released her overdramatic pose and assumed a more natural one, waiting patiently as Jenny turned the camera on.

In the viewscreen, Jenny saw nothing but hypnotically swirling gray. She steeled herself against it, refusing to be pulled into a staring contest with the strange smoky place beyond Wonderland. Defiantly, she snapped a picture of Dolores, hearing the faint click and beep of the digital camera. For the few seconds that the camera previewed the shot, the viewscreen shone with a strange and gooey splatter of blue and white and yellow. Then the camera beeped again, resuming a realtime display, showing only the insidious twirling smoke of that place Jenny knew she didn't want to go.

Jenny let the camera drop back inside her hoodie again, the strap around her neck. "Thanks," she said to Dolores.

"No, thank *you*, dear," said Dolores. She flipped the cap in her fingers. "It's really okay to take this with me?"

"I don't see why not," said Jenny.

"Well then."

"Good luck."

Dolores laughed lightly. "I don't think luck will have anything to do with it. Looks to me like it's all about choices!"

Without another word, she jumped into the empty air and folded in on herself, flashing out of sight in an eye-bending display of extradimensional morphology. The smells of the market faded. The crinkling of paper died away, replaced by the usual pounding rush of windy Wonderland.

Jenny smiled at the place where Dolores had disappeared. The old woman had chosen her path. The first-time Angel of Death felt a definitive sense of accomplishment and pride.

Rex crept up and nuzzled her shoulder. Jenny reached up to rub his nose. "Yeah," she said. "Thanks." The horse *whuffed* quietly into her hair. Jenny sighed. The incredible high of dancing through Dolores's life was already crashing, bringing her down to normal, and she knew she'd need another hit to feel that way again. Whatever twist of fate had stolen her life, Jenny had to admit that this particular feeling—the buzz of slicing through the many paths that led away from this one—might actually make the loss worth it.

She tied her sword to Rex's saddle. The case still hung off one side, the strap around the saddle horn. Rex knelt for her, and she threw a leg over him, shifting comfortably into the saddle as the horse rose. Jenny leaned forward and kissed his neck. "Hey," she said. "Let's go out."

The horse didn't need to be told twice. He moved quickly from the edge of the water, paused for Jenny to grab hold, then shot across the park at top speed, heading south through the center of Manhattan. He hurtled down Seventh Avenue and made a sharp left through the West Village, leaping out onto the Hudson and soaring south. A dark figure loomed ahead: the slightly distorted and discolored version of Lady Liberty standing guard over the harbor, holding her torch high. Rex raced for the statue, making an impressive leap onto the pier on the north side of Liberty Island and slowing down as he wheeled around the statue's base to stop before her at the large, odd-man-out southeastern point of the eleven-pointed star she stood on.

Jenny untied her sword and raised it in front of her. Holding tight to Rex with her knees, she carefully grabbed hold of the gleaming blade and pushed through to the real world. The real Statue of Liberty bloomed into full color and switched hands, the torch held like an avenging weapon. Jenny looked up at the light burning in the dark blue night and breathed in the Summer wind sweeping over the sea.

Rex sighed, a stuttering whicker that released the tensions of the evening and forgave any mistakes. Jenny hugged his neck. "Thank you," she said. He leaned over to let her off for another disgraceful dismount. Straightening up, she dug in her pocket as she patted the horse's shoulder. "Let me check on Calvin—one sec."

She speed-dialed the magician; he picked up after the second ring. "Hey!" he said.

"Hi," said Jenny. "Just wanted to make sure you got home okay."

"Yeah, yeah, I'm fine," said Calvin. "What about you? How was it?" The staticky echo of the cell phone couldn't hide his excitement. "What happened? How did it go?"

"I'll come over in a bit," said Jenny. "Let's have dessert. Anything you want—just pick it up. I'll be there in an hour or two."

"Okay, cool," Calvin said.

"Wait," Jenny said. "What about the Raymonds?"

"What about them?"

Jenny frowned. "Anything...you know...weird?"

"Nah," said Calvin. "They just drove me home."

"That's it?"

"Well, Carrie came up to use the bathroom..."

"You *let* her?"

"Jenny!" Calvin snorted. "She's pregnant. I'm not gonna say 'No, you can't use the bathroom' to a pregnant lady."

"Okay, okay." Jenny sighed. "But that's it, right? She just...peed and left?"

"Basically." There was an obvious note in his voice. Jenny knew him too well.

"Calvin..." she prodded him.

"They, uh...they asked if I had a wand." She could hear his waffling over the phone.

"What do you mean?"

Calvin let out a big sigh. "Okay, it's not that big a deal," he said. "I just didn't want to tell you on the phone. They were just, like, 'Hey, why don't you have a magic wand?' And I was all, 'Well, I've got one, but I don't use it.' And they were all—"

"Yeah," Jenny interrupted. "We need to talk."

"Okay, okay—I know," said Calvin.

"I'll be there in an a few," Jenny said.

"Right. I'll get some ice cream."

"Make it pie," said Jenny. "And I'm buying."

"I'm sorry..." he started.

Jenny cut him off. "Pie *à la mode.* You get the ice cream. See you in a bit." She flipped the phone closed and looked at Rex.

The horse breathed an all too human sigh and knelt wearily to let her climb aboard.

CHAPTER TWENTY-THREE

Nursing dark suspicions toward an odd but delightfully amiable couple like the Raymonds was a tricky balancing act. The Amazing Quirk and his lovely but skeptical assistant had to be expertly subtle, or at least subtle enough to cover their bases in case it turned out that the odd but delightfully amiable couple was, in fact, only an odd but delightfully amiable couple and not something more sinister that would be less insulted by dark suspicions, and would instead more or less confirm them.

In practice, this meant that Jenny and Calvin avoided answering their phones when the Raymonds popped up on caller ID, though they checked their voicemails and occasionally called back in hurried tones as they rushed through New York City streets, giving them a plausible excuse to hang up as quickly as possible when the conversation drifted toward another odd but delightfully amiable evening together. They held off any specific plans, and whether the Raymonds understood the unrelenting pace of hectic city life or just gave up on them, the cheerful calls slowed down to a trickle. By mid-October, they seemed to stop entirely—it had been nearly two weeks since Carrie had called to invite them for dinner at the Raymonds' apartment.

Jenny felt guilty about shunning them, especially since the passing weeks were counting down to their ultimate demise. Of course, the upcoming doomed Halloween spelled death for everybody, it seemed, so as long as she focused on preventing the coming cataclysm, she didn't need to worry about Vincent and Carrie specifically.

She hadn't felt the twinge of any new appointments since she'd escorted Dolores Meisel down the Smooth Road. Over pie and ice cream that night, she and Calvin had exchanged stories. The Raymonds had been as charming and vanilla as ever on the drive to Calvin's apartment; it was Carrie who'd brought up the wand, perking up suddenly as they discussed some of their favorite magic acts. She was surprisingly knowledgeable about stage magicians. She and Vincent had even seen a number of other local acts—unknowns like Calvin, just starting out—and knew them by name and their trademark tricks. They were more well-versed on the subject than Calvin, who didn't get out to see other magicians very often since his successful run at the *Beau* started.

When Calvin had admitted to having a wand he didn't use, Carrie had brightly asked: "Did you buy it along with your other tricks?" At Calvin's affirmative answer, she asked: "What does it look like?"

"It's just a wand," Calvin had told her. "You know, just a shiny stick."

"Of course," Carrie Raymond had nodded pertly, and the conversation moved on.

When they'd arrived at his apartment, he'd quickly agreed to her request to use his bathroom, since the Raymonds had a long drive back to their place. Carrie *ooh*ed and *ahh*ed at his cases and shelves on her way in and out.

And that was that, as far as Calvin could tell. His lovely assistant was wary of the whole "where's your wand" line of questioning—it occurred to Jenny that Carrie was keenly interested in all of their unique prop magic, far more so than any of the coin or card tricks or even Jenny's gory physical feats—but it was hard to root out any specific ulterior motive that people like the Raymonds might have when it came to grilling a struggling stage magician on his devices. That was why she and Calvin had agreed to wean themselves off the Raymonds and concentrate on more important matters, like the End of the World.

Calvin had been excited to hear about her appointment, and Jenny had told him the tale of Dolores's journey to the afterworld as best she could. She showed him the picture she'd snapped: a bizarre splotch of blue and yellow on a stark white background. Calvin could see it clearly, only compounding the puzzling question of how vision worked in Wonderland. It was also hard to describe the thoughts and feelings that symbolized the paths Dolores explored, or even *how* they signified what they did, but Calvin got the general idea. It was an astonishing peek at the future for the magician; he just hoped it was a less immediate future than the Halloween deadline they were working against.

With no appointments tickling the back of Jenny's brain, and their social calendar shrinking back to normal without the Raymonds in their lives, the two of them fell back on standard routine: jobs, doing the magic act twice a week, attending the occasional after party, and searching for patterns that might theoretically culminate in some massive event on Halloween. They read the news online, researched old texts at the library, even followed zig-zagging and fruitless trails through Wikipedia that started with search terms like *armageddon, apocalypse,* and *end of the world.* They covered topics from terrorism and dirty bombs to astronomy and Earth-shattering asteroids to government conspiracies and alleged Mayan prophecies. The only solid conclusion derived from all this was that there were thousands of looney theories about the end of the world, and millions of people crazy or gullible or misinformed enough to believe them. Legitimate clues about what might actually happen continued to elude them.

Their lack of answers felt all the more crushing with Halloween only a couple of weeks away. Years of real life—school and work and family obligations—had conditioned them not to take deadlines very seriously; anything could be rescheduled if push came to shove. Now they were racing against a deadline that couldn't be postponed. This deadline pushed back harder than any mere mortal could procrastinate.

Despite the turmoil in their private lives as Defenders Against the Coming Apocalypse, their public lives as the Amazing Quirk and Jade were going very well. The show still drew a crowd—regulars (including their fan club, the Charmed Quirks) were now crowded in among a decent number of newcomers at each show. David Dennis's lazy publicity had teamed up with word-of-mouth to spread the news about the charming magician and the Jewel of the East. Though he still occasionally used the word *agent* as a pejorative, Calvin held out hope of getting noticed and moving up to a bigger and brighter level in show business. His blithely implied certainty that Jenny would prevent the end of the world gave Jenny almost as much confidence as it did extra pressure.

The crowd roared as Jenny's dismembered hand hit the floor and she dropped from the hanging rings hovering overhead. The audiences at the *Beau* had changed with the seasons, like trees trading in green Summer wardrobe for golden Autumn fashions. Like all of New York, the *Beau Regardez* was filled with heavier jackets and thicker coats, whether they were hung over seats or hastily pulled on before the front doors opened to the gray chill outside. The comfortably late Summer was finally settling down to doze through a bleak and damp New York Autumn, prepared to crash hard core when Winter stormed in with all the subtlety, if not the punctuality, of a squadron of Ku Klux Klan paratroopers.

Her numbness had practically developed into another superpower over the past month; Jenny didn't even flinch when Calvin's knife flashed and split her wrist, and she had mastered the sardonic gaze she leveled at the audience when an arrow or knife ran her through. Physical injury simply didn't faze her anymore; she saved all of her concern for their desperate investigations into the Halloween Holocaust.

The *Beau* audience thundered, Pilot's hit single "Magic" simulated pop Seventies orgasms in the sound system (David Dennis had taken to changing things up every few shows), and Jenny and Calvin spun off stage with the magic table.

Back in the dressing room, Calvin grinned. "Good show, huh?"

"At least I caught the card," Jenny said glumly, wriggling out of her tutu.

"You covered it," said Calvin. "Totally! Nobody even noticed."

"Yeah..."

"You got really good at this stuff," Calvin insisted. "Hey, even without your powers, we could probably do a really cool show."

"Without my powers, we'd still have your *stuff*," said Jenny. Despite the key role her indestructibility played in the act, Jenny felt it was really just a supporting character that gave them something dramatic to do with the chains and Calvin's other, crazier ideas. Her ability to read birthdays wouldn't even have come into play at all if it hadn't been for Calvin's exotic props.

The Big Plan to chop her in half might shift things to a new (if potentially paraplegic) paradigm, but they still hadn't been brave enough to try it. Calvin had bought some wood and constructed a traditional magician's box for the trick, and had tracked down a very sharp guillotine-like contraption, but he still wasn't quite ready to slice up his best friend. A hand or a finger was one thing; severing his lovely assistant on a larger scale was a different story. Jenny was inured to the actual pain at this point, though not the fear, which still drilled the back of her head like a nervous pre-med experimenting with trepanation. She felt strange enough wiggling disembodied fingers; she wasn't sure how it would work if everything from the waist down was yards away from everything from the waist up. The memory of her leg being torn off, that first time at the beginning of the summer, was overshadowed by the horror and confusion of the moment, and did little to encourage her. She was relatively sure that reattaching her body would be *possible*—but about the internal organs that would spill from her ruptured body like candy from a *piñata*, she was a bit less certain.

"Yeah, well," Calvin went on, "you're still getting really good at the sleight-of-hand."

Jenny smiled tightly. "Thanks," she said. She loosened up a bit. "Sorry."

"It's okay." He'd removed his bow-tie and thrown it on top of the magic table. Colby Cheese, her pink nose twitching in the musty funk of the dressing room, snuggled in a towel on the easy chair, nibbling contentedly on a lettuce leaf. "Party tonight?"

"You know what? Might as well." Jenny shrugged. "I'm too tired to Defend the Human Race tonight. Let's just go flirt with the Quirks and watch David kiss Paul's ass."

"Bleh," Calvin stuck out his tongue. "I've already seen that episode." He patted himself down and rubbed Colby's head absently. "You ready?"

"Yeah, let's go," said Jenny.

They headed out to the lobby, reeling from the massive blast of cheering and applause that met them as they entered. The Charmed Quirks, as usual, formed a bantering crowd around their idols, with plenty of other regulars weaving in and out of the throng. David Dennis tipped an imaginary hat their way; four months into their open-ended run, they still had some major pull, and he wasn't done milking that particular magic cow just yet.

Jenny thanked one fan, laughed appreciatively at another's joke, and put a hand up to scratch an itch on her cheek—she gave a start as she realized she was still wearing the magic spectacles. "Crap," she muttered. She tapped Calvin's arm and he leaned over. "Forgot the glasses," she told him. "I should put them in the table with the Window—I'll be right back."

"Sure," Calvin said softly. He smiled and went back to appeasing the adoring fans with the personal attention they all demanded. He'd learned all too well by now: fame was far less about the spotlight on the famous than it was about doling out pieces of that spotlight to keep it shining.

Jenny sifted through the crowd back to the hall. The sharp contrast between the orange glow of the lobby and the dimly lit hall dimmed even the sound, the *hummina-hummina* of the crowd fading as she passed the corner. Jenny gingerly pulled the spectacles off her face and folded the stems closed. She noticed the dressing room door was ajar—she could have sworn Calvin had closed it when they left to meet the audience.

The light was on, too. She would also have sworn they'd left only the desk lamp burning to keep Colby company.

A shadow flickered in the light streaming under the door onto the threadbare carpet. She would *damn well* have sworn that she and Calvin hadn't left *themselves* in there. Somebody was in their dressing room. It wouldn't be Kevin or any of the crew at the *Beau*; there were strict rules in place, thanks to the secretive nature of magic acts and David's favoritism. It was probably an overenthusiastic fan, or maybe the Raymonds had come to visit again, and decided against Carrie trying to wade her way through a pressing crowd with her delicately pregnant belly.

Jenny's immediate instinct was to look without announcing herself. She'd seen too many horror films where the daffy babysitter with little to no sense of genre flounced spunkily through the door with a loud: *Hello! Is anybody in here?* She softly pushed the door open, her heart skipping a beat as she remembered the few daffy babysitters who'd crept silently into a room only to be stabbed in the back with sharpened sporting equipment.

A hooded figure cloaked in black was bent over the magic table. At the slightest whisper of Jenny's soles on the dingy carpet, the bulky figure turned, and the hood fell back.

It had been a while, but there was no mistaking the Ice Cream Psycho.

"Hey!" Jenny shouted, part anger and part confusion. "You—"

Carrying an armful of items rummaged from the magic table, the Ice Cream Psycho charged and body-checked her into the door, slamming it all the way open. He probably counted on leaving her too stunned to react, but Jenny's death-induced numbness teamed up with a surge of adrenalin to shake it off in an instant. Her hand shot out to grab the guy's ankle—he was still wearing the same dirty sneakers and khakis underneath his billowing black robe. He tripped through the doorway, dropping the loot as he flung up his arms to avoid smacking his face into the opposite wall. Jenny saw Calvin's hat roll a short way down the hall; the Window to Your Soul thumped on the carpet, and the rings jangled into a heap just inches away.

The Ice Cream Psycho kicked back, pulling free of her grip. He turned and scowled; there was nothing cartoonishly evil about him, no homicidal grin blazing at her with a thirst for human blood. He just looked *mean.* The dressing room light gleamed off his bald spot; he glared at her from the shadows of the hall.

"What the—" Jenny started, still lying on her front, staring up at him.

He dashed forward and grabbed her shoulders, picking her up off the floor and steamrolling through to slam her against the far wall of the room in one surprisingly swift motion. This time, it took a moment longer to shake off the pounding inside her skull. The short man released her, and she felt like she slid down the wall in slow motion as he stalked out. Through the doorframe, Jenny saw him pick up the clinking chain of rings and the Window.

The wind still knocked out of her, she croaked: "Stop!"

He flicked his eyes her way, then suddenly looked down the hall toward the lobby. With a sweep of black robes, he ran the other way, where the magician's top hat had rolled.

Jenny caught her breath and stumbled to her feet, scrambling to follow the Ice Cream Psycho. She flew through the doorway and crashed into a heap of arms, legs, clammy T-shirts and sweaty boy smell.

"Whoa!"

"Sorry!"

Jenny looked urgently around and was stupefied to recognize the pair she'd just piled into. "Lyle?" she said incredulously. She looked from one to the other. "Lloyd?"

"Hi," said Lyle, breathing heavily and holding his pudgy belly where Jenny's elbow had hit hard.

"Told you she'd remember us, dude," said Lloyd, a goofy grin on his skinny face. Lyle beamed hopefully at Jenny.

"Oh, fuck," Jenny said.

Lyle's expression plummeted with his hopes. "Um, we saw a poster..."

"The guy!" Jenny demanded. "Where'd he go?"

Lloyd raised his eyebrows. "The wizard lookin' guy?" he said. He pointed up the hall, away from the lobby. "That-a-way."

Jenny sprang to her feet. She took a step, then froze, looking back at the two guys technically responsible for her death. Thinking about everything that had come about as a consequence of that one moment, her face softened. "Nice to see you, guys," she said kindly. Her eyes sharpened. "Wait." She dashed back into the room and snatched the instrument case with her sword in it, then swung back out into the hall, hopping over Lyle and Lloyd.

The two boys were baffled. "Um," Lyle called out.

Jenny looked over her shoulder as she ran, the instrument case slung over one arm. "Stay there!" she yelled back. "Don't follow me...tell the magician the Ice Cream Psycho stole our stuff!"

"What?" Lloyd giggled nervously, but Jenny had already rounded the corner.

The next leg of the hallway ended shortly, with only three doors the black-cloaked thief could have used to make his escape. One Jenny knew led back into the wings of the theatre. The other two stood side by side on the opposite wall. She did a brief, forced Eeny Meeny Miny Moe and shoved her way through one of them into a stairwell leading up and down. Another round of Eeny Meeny sent her bounding upward, rounding a landing, and reaching two doors at the top. One was an emergency exit. She doubted that the Ice Cream Psycho would have gone through the other door to the second floor of the building, so Jenny took a deep breath, squinted a silent prayer that the alarm wouldn't sound off, and pushed the lever on the exit door. The door opened without any blast of bells or sirens. Jenny breathed a sigh of relief and tiptoed quietly out onto a rusty old fire escape.

A cold, wet wind whistled through the alley behind the *Beau Regardez*. Jenny looked down and saw the Ice Cream Psycho, his hood back up, one hand snaked inside next to his cheek—holding a cell phone, she realized. He was facing the other way, and hadn't seen her. Jenny looked down and saw another door set just below her; she swore silently, realizing he'd exited on the ground floor, and she'd Eenied the wrong Meeny.

Jenny crouched by the railing of the fire escape, psyching herself up, and was just about to yell down at the guy when four more figures walked briskly around the corner of an adjacent building. All of them wore flowing black robes like the Ice Cream Psycho. Or, Jenny mused, like her fellow Angels of Death.

No, she thought vehemently. *They wouldn't.* But she was less sure than she would have liked. With the arrival of four more thieves, her initial wave of energy ebbed. She wasn't sure if they were living or, like her, kind of dead, but she also wasn't clear on how to approach the situation either way. She stayed quiet, trying to make herself as small and unseen as possible.

She couldn't hear the conversation taking place in the windy alley below, but one of the taller robed figures took charge, standing firm and nodding calmly while the others whispered harshly at each other and the Ice Cream Psycho. Finally, the apparent leader extended an arm, and the original thief handed over his stolen prizes: Calvin's hat, the interlocked rings, and the Window to Your Soul. The Window drew the most attention; the leader turned it over and over, peering from the recesses of a dark and shadowy hood.

A scut of sound echoed in the alley, and five hooded heads jerked around to look at the ground floor door: it scraped across uneven cobblestones and badly-laid asphalt with a wrenching racket. The black-cloaked gang watched impassively as Calvin McGuirk finally shoved the door fully open and came out.

Jenny winced.

"Uh, hey," said Calvin. He gulped visibly. "Any of you guys, uh...?"

"That's the one," announced Lloyd, running in after Calvin and pointing at one of the figures in black.

"No," Lyle followed quickly, "it's *that* one!"

Neither of them was pointing at the Ice Cream Psycho, but Jenny figured that was the least of their problems.

The tall leader whispered something to the others and stepped back, conspicuously carrying Calvin's magic props.

"Hey," Calvin laid some courage on the table. "Those are mine! What are you guys—"

The other four, including the Ice Cream Psycho, formed a rough line in front of the leader. Each reached into a voluminous sleeve and extracted a jagged knife.

"Dude," Lloyd said dramatically.

"Oh, man," Lyle added.

Calvin said nothing, frozen in place, arms out to instinctively shield the two younger men from knives that he wouldn't fare any better against.

The bad guy on the far end of the line suddenly reeled and collapsed, smacked in the head by a heavy case which clattered onto the broken cobblestones. Everyone in the alley looked sharply at Jenny Ng, straddling the fire escape railing.

"Stop it!" she commanded. Her voice echoing back sounded less threatening than she'd hoped.

The Ice Cream Psycho was closest, and broke the momentary stand-off by lunging at Lyle with his heavy knife. Trying not to let common sense or even thought get in her way, Jenny leaned over and let go, dropping on top of the round little man with an ugly thud. She wasn't hurt or badly shaken, thanks to her powers; unfortunately, neither was he, since she weighed barely more than the battered instrument case on the ground.

Thinking quickly, Calvin shoved Lyle aside with one arm and Lloyd through the door with the other. He hadn't thought much beyond that plan, though, and fear flashed in his eyes at the realization that he'd just halved his side's makeshift team.

Jenny did her best to make up for it. She wasn't exactly superhero material—she hadn't spent years in an underground bunker fighting robots and dodging lasers for practice—but her confidence knowing there was no way the bad guys could hurt her in a straight-on fight was her advantage and her secret weapon. She threw her arm forward with everything she had, safe in the knowledge that her broken fist would heal in seconds, while the Ice Cream Psycho's nose wouldn't. A sickening crack and the sound of squashed watermelons accompanied the man's screams. Sure enough, the oddly painless sensation in Jenny's hand faded as her split knuckles melted and flowed and mended themselves, leaving no marks or cuts aside from the Ice Cream Psycho's blood staining her skin.

Gargling in agony, the Ice Cream Psycho staggered away toward the tall figure who still carried Calvin's props. Jenny had never punched anyone before—she'd never been in any kind of physical fight—but she didn't allow herself time to stop and think. The crook she'd clobbered with the case was getting back up, and the remaining two were rushing forward, knives shining in the dim gray lighting of the alley.

"Calvin!" she shouted, kicking one of her charging opponents hard in the groin. He doubled over with a *whoosh* of soundless groaning as the other slashed viciously at Jenny's leg. "My sword!" she yelled.

Calvin ducked past the man who'd cut Jenny's leg and bowled into the bad guy who'd just stood up; the gangly magician wouldn't win any football scholarships, but his enthusiasm made up for it, knocking the already shaken man back to land roughly on his butt. Sprawled on top of the dizzy man, Calvin stretched for the instrument case.

"Dude!" Lloyd yelled out, hanging back by the door, but unwilling to abandon his friend.

Lyle shouted back fearfully, "Dude!"

The Ice Cream Psycho and the villains' leader whirled and ran, black robes fluttering behind them. They rounded a corner and disappeared into the winding maze of alleys.

Jenny shoved the man she'd kicked in the family jewels and he stumbled away to lean on the wall. The last bad guy standing tossed his hood for an unimpeded view of his target. He was a lean guy with dark skin and slicked back hair. His fuzzy facial hair wasn't so much Evil Henchman as Coffee House Poetry Slam Contestant. Like the Ice Cream Psycho, he didn't smile devilishly at her; his mouth set and his eyes cold, he focused on the task at hand.

They squared off, Jenny crouching in her best imitation of the Ultimate Fighter competitions she'd caught on Keith Heckler's television late at night. She understood that keeping a low center of gravity was a good thing, but she wasn't solid on why that was, or what she could do with an adequately low center of gravity.

The guy slashed at her, grinding his teeth fiercely. She dodged, and he only nicked her side. Her leg had already healed up, leaving just a frayed rip in her black leggings, now matched by the tiny hole torn in the white shirt she'd thrown on over her show costume.

Calvin's voice rang out: "Sword!"

Jenny barely glanced over as she caught the weapon the magician tossed her way. The sword was mostly hilt, so there wasn't much danger of accidentally catching it by the blade, but she flinched reflexively as the leather slapped into her palm anyway. She gripped it tightly and swung the sword in front of her, glaring a challenge at the Beatnik with the knife.

The exaggerated difference between his knife and her giant, curved sword threw off his rhythm.

The man beneath Calvin McGuirk bucked violently, toppling the magician into a splayed collection of long limbs on the asphalt. Rising, the man shouted unintelligibly—it wasn't another language, Jenny knew, because she would have understood it if it was. The groin-kick victim scrambled toward the turn in the alley, with Calvin's opponent following quickly. They paused at the corner and shouted back at the Beatnik: "Come on!"

Distracted by Calvin's fall and the escaping crooks, Jenny let her guard down for a moment; the Beatnik seized his opportunity. Lyle shouted a warning. The glittering knife plunged into Jenny's chest with a spurt of blood and the crunch of bone. The Beatnik tried to pull it out, but it was stuck; he tugged hard, jostling Jenny's body as she stared at back him.

It was the calm smirk on her face that must have done it. His eyes wide, the Beatnik let go of the knife and ran to join his partners, the three of them racing to follow the other two black-robed burglars into the humid darkness.

The echoes of crunching and scuffing died away, leaving only the heavy breathing of the four young people shuddering in the crashing final notes of the Fight or Flight Symphony. Jenny and Calvin stared, exhausted, at the corner where the thieves had disappeared. Lyle and Lloyd stared, wide-eyed, at the knife stuck in Jenny's chest.

"You're *totally* a Super Ninja Chick!" Lloyd exclaimed.

Jenny turned and gave him a weary smile. "No," she said.

Lyle scrambled to his feet. "Uh huh!" he insisted. "Dude, are you some kind of robotic super-cyborg from the future?"

"We're, like, totally important to the future of the human race, right?" Lloyd theorized excitedly.

"Yeah!" Lyle nodded. "And you're here to make sure we live to fulfill our destinies!"

Calvin, still breathing hard, picked up the instrument case by its strap and approached Jenny. "Here," he said, "let me help."

"Whoa!" said Lyle.

Calvin slung the case over one shoulder, then gripped the knife in one hand and pushed against Jenny's chest with the other. He politely—and awkwardly—avoided touching her breast as he yanked the knife out. Lyle and Lloyd walked slowly around to flank the magician, watching the procedure in awe. The grins on their faces only stretched wider as the knife wound weaved itself together into a smooth and unmarked stretch of skin just above Jenny's black bustier.

"Dude, can you *fly?*" Lloyd asked.

"No, no," Jenny waved them away. "I can barely ride a horse."

Lloyd scratched his chin fuzz ponderously. "So are we, like, your commanding officers in the future?"

"Am I thin?" Lyle added shyly. "Uh...ripped?"

"Guys!" Jenny cut them off. "I'm not from the future. I'm not a ninja. I'm not a cyborg!"

"But you're a superhero," Lloyd smiled pointedly.

Calvin laughed. "He's got a point," he said.

"Not helping," Jenny replied. "And we've got bigger problems."

Calvin's expression went dark. "They had my stuff. The h—um, the hat, and the rings and the glasses and the Window."

"They didn't get the glasses," said Jenny. "I dropped them in the dressing room. But the one guy who was there—the first guy, the one who took our stuff—is the one who chased me the first night I...you know, the first night with Wonderland."

Lyle and Lloyd looked back and forth at the magician and his lovely assistant, quietly trying—and failing—to follow the conversation. Their long hair and fanboy T-shirts were soaked with sweat.

"I don't get it," said Calvin.

"Didn't they look familiar?" asked Jenny.

Calvin looked at her blankly.

Lyle won this round: "They were like a whole team of Grim Reapers!"

"Totally," Lloyd agreed.

Calvin shook his head. "No way," he said. He looked hard at Jenny. "You don't think...?"

"I don't know," said Jenny. "It's either them or...or somebody *else* who's been really, really *interested* in your props...right?"

"No way!" the magician repeated, but with less conviction. "Crap! They've been after the stuff the whole time!" He slapped his forehead. "She asked about the *wand!*"

"But why?" Jenny wondered aloud.

Calvin shrugged. "Maybe they're working for another magician?"

"I don't know," Jenny said sarcastically, "is it normal for competing magicians to send *knife-wielding maniacs* after you?"

"Right, okay." He opened the case and held it for her. "But then, why?"

"I don't know, Calvin," said Jenny, more gently. She put her sword neatly into the velvet grooves of the instrument case. "But we need to find out. Because maybe there's something more about your stuff than you figured out. Maybe there's a *lot* more those things can do."

"The wand!" Calvin blurted, slamming the case shut.

Jenny nodded. "Let's go, quick."

They turned to the door.

"Hey," said Lyle in a tiny voice.

"Um, yeah," Lloyd said, standing beside his friend. "What about us?"

Jenny paused. "I don't suppose we could just forget all about this, right?"

Lloyd shrugged. Lyle squinted and thought. "Do you have something that can erase our memories?" he asked.

"No," Jenny answered uncertainly.

"Then, nope," said Lyle. Lloyd grinned and nodded.

Jenny sighed and looked at Calvin—he smiled sympathetically. "Okay, then," said Jenny. "Come on."

"Dude!" Lloyd cheered triumphantly.

"You're *so* not gonna regret it," burbled Lyle. "We've got, like, all kinds of skills and stuff."

"I'm good at crossbows," announced Lloyd.

Lyle gave his friend a look. "Dude, that was that *one* time, and you hit the *other* guy's target..."

"I was totally aiming there!"

"Totally weren't!"

Jenny shook her head as she and Calvin led the bickering duo through the door. "I am *so* gonna regret this."

CHAPTER TWENTY-FOUR

Without Rex, rushing Through the Looking Glass to Central Park didn't feel much faster than running there on the real world side of the mirror, but Jenny would later realize that it took only half the time it would have taken without her universal pass for Wonderland Transit. With no need to dodge aimless pedestrians, speeding cabs, or lurching luxury sedans with Jersey plates, Jenny sprinted through the empty, quivering Wonderland air without stopping. Every crosswalk gave her a dusky go ahead sign; they all simultaneously gave her a misty Don't Walk hand symbol, too, but she expected that by now. She was starting to catch on: a thing's appearance in Wonderland seemed to be about *permanence*, as if the Smooth Road was camera film that needed time to develop a counterpart to any given real world object. Jenny was proud of that realization. She was also proud of herself for quickly adapting to the reversed orientation of Wonderland this time around. Maybe the idea of being as competent an Angel of Death as Caravel or the others wasn't quite so out of reach as she'd once thought. She wasn't even out of breath when she reached the reservoir, clambered over the iron railing and ran along the retaining wall to the middle of the water. Her nerves buzzed, and her muscles felt fresh and ready.

Paranoia dogged her the whole way; while the Raymonds were more likely suspects than her fellow Grim Reapers, she still jumped at flickering shadows licking the corners of Wonderland buildings, not sure what she could do if a mob of black-robed figures swarmed out of the shimmering darkness to overtake her and steal the magic spectacles. As a precaution, she'd left the specs with Calvin. Accompanied by the two unkempt fanboys, the magician was on a Queens-bound express, hoping to find the wand safe and sound in his apartment when he got there. The plan was to meet at Heckler's place to take a breather and brainstorm their next move—they weren't sure if the bad guys, whoever they might turn out to be, knew where Jenny lived, but they didn't want to take that chance.

Jenny pulled a Sharpie and some loose sheets of paper out of her shoulder bag, and slowed at the center of the reservoir's retaining wall. The glassy surface of the water was awash with ghostly laps and waves that only partly existed. It occurred to her that she wasn't entirely sure what to write to Caravel. The senior Reaper had said leaving a note was sufficient, but Jenny was caught between needing help against a gang of Reaper wanna-bes and suspecting the gang were actual Reapers, the latter of which might mean Caravel herself was behind the burglary. Something coy might not convey the proper urgency; something straightforward might tip her hand if Caravel *did* turn out to be a bad guy.

With little time to make a firm decision, she scribbled six quick words:

We need to talk. Sunset.
—Jenny

She was still pretty sure she could trust Caravel, and didn't want to plant an outright accusation in the note, but she also didn't want to be played for a fool if she was wrong. She placed the note on the scratched stone. Despite the rushing wind of Wonderland, the paper lay still and flat, not a single corner flapping or twitching.

Jenny ran back and climbed over the fence. While the extra time she saved traversing Wonderland's empty streets was considerable, she still couldn't make it all the way back to her apartment that way; there was the issue of running across the East River without falling into it, which she couldn't do without Rex. She was confident that she could no longer drown in *real* water, let alone the ephemeral Looking Glass rivers, but climbing the opposite bank would be a tall order. She had to take the subway.

She found a secluded spot in the trees near the edge of the park, pushed through the gleaming blade of her sword, and fell back into the real world with a pop of darkness and the sibilance of brown dust. She stowed her sword in its case and raced out of the park, then downstairs into the Eighty-Sixth Street subway station.

It was Saturday night; the subways were running on the weekend schedule. Nearly an hour later, she bounded up the stairs at Prospect Park—on the opposite side of the park from her apartment. Without hesitation, she slipped between the trees, looked around to make sure she was unseen, and pulled her sword out. She hurled herself through a burst of non-Euclidean geometry and hit the Smooth Road running, crossing the park beneath the wildly painted night sky. Jenny flashed back to the night she'd met Rex. She thought to call out for him, to see if he would come running, but the idea that another Angel of Death might hear her voice reverberating in the warbling Wonderland breeze stopped her. It seemed like sound could travel the whole world on this side of the mirror.

She crossed the park in less than ten minutes, her hectic pace and heavy Doc Martens slapping weird echoing schisms on the dark, sepia-toned streets. She reached her building, shot through the front door, and scrambled up the stairs to dive through her own shifting, swerving doorway. "Rex!" she shouted. She was amazed that she still wasn't out of breath. It dawned on her that she probably didn't need to breathe *at all*, these days.

The horse loosed an ear-splitting whinny, growling and stomping on the hard floor. He was a part of her, Jenny knew, even if he seemed like a separate, sentient being; he was already well aware of the events of the night. She hugged his neck, smelling salty sweat and the slick hair of his mane. He always went a little stir crazy without her there; she'd made a habit of stowing him in Wonderland when she went out, on the off chance that somebody might get inside her apartment and discover the horse. It wasn't a decision she'd made lightly, but alternatives were hard to come by.

Rex made a low, guttural sound. She looked into one big, dark eye, and it hit her: while Rex was partly her, he always seemed a step ahead when it came to the death business. He'd been in it longer than she had; he'd belonged to Pauzok—the Coney Island Count—before Jenny had come along. He'd been a *part* of Pauzok. Two questions hit her. The first was: could he explain any of what was going on tonight?

The second was: could she trust *him* to be on her side?

A soft and earnest glint in his eye flooded her with relief. He was hers—he was *her*—and he wouldn't betray her, even if it meant facing an entire army of Grim Reapers riding his fellow pale horses. Jenny let out a long, shuddering breath and leaned into the stallion. He nuzzled her shoulder. "So who do I trust, then?" she asked quietly.

He stared at her.

"Was it them?" she asked. "Was it Caravel and all them?"

He stared harder. A rough, whiskery sound scraped from his throat. Rex was telling her plainly: *It can't be them.*

Jenny nodded slowly. "Okay," she said. "I believe you. But then we're *all* in deep shit."

The horse knelt down, but Jenny patted him and crouched, dropping the case and pulling out her sword. "If they *do* know where I live," she said, "I might not be able to come back." She gulped and looked around the mirrored version of her apartment. "Let me grab a few things."

She spun them both through the reflection on the sword blade, landing in the real world with a puff of bells and sparks. As Rex scuffed his hooves impatiently on the hardwood, Jenny grabbed her big backpack and started sifting through clothes, grabbing a decent assortment for a variety of contingencies, stuffing them unceremoniously into the backpack.

Thoughts snapped and popped in her head, vague plans congealing in the creamy center of a crunchy outer shell. Jenny looked around, and her eyes zeroed in on a pile of old receipts, papers, and Post-it notes. She fished through it and came up with the business card she was looking for. Jenny scanned the front: *Vincent Raymond, Doctor of Chiropractic, Licensed Physical Therapist.* The address was on the Upper West Side.

"Gotcha," she whispered, sticking the card in the front pocket of her shirt. Rex eyed her cynically, but kept any comments to himself.

She made a quick round trip through the bathroom to snatch her toothbrush, hairbrush, and a few other items, and shoved them into the backpack's side pocket. The clean white toilet made her pause: she hadn't actually sat on a toilet in at least a week. To Jenny, bathrooms had become useful private spots with easy passage to Wonderland, rather than places to go to relieve herself. Since she now knew how to use her sword, bathrooms were even less relevant.

Jenny shook herself and closed the backpack. She slipped it on her back, then slung her shoulder bag on one side and the case for her sword on the other. With a torn and slightly bloodied white shirt on over the bare bones of her show costume, she thought she looked like an East Villager going to camp out on the sidewalk for concert tickets.

She glanced around the apartment in a slow, ill-defined checklist, wondering if she'd forgotten anything. Most of her stuff could be abandoned without much loss. She had her most valuable possessions— her phone, her camera and her sword. Calvin had the spectacles and, hopefully, the wand, the only remaining magic props that hadn't been stolen. The rent was paid up through the end of the month, and Doc Kolachek wouldn't have much trouble finding a new tenant if he needed to. Either the world would end in some unnamed cataclysm by then, or Jenny would find a way to stop it—but even if she did, she had a strong feeling that she would never be back here again.

She nodded firmly. Rex knelt again, and she swung up into the saddle, grappling for balance with the backpack, bag and case all threatening to bowl her over. The horse rose, and Jenny *clucked* her tongue and patted his flank. She flipped the lid of the instrument case and pulled her sword out just enough to expose the blade. Hugging Rex's neck, she laid her palm on the blade and gave it a mental shove. The stallion landed solidly in the shuddering colors of Wonderland.

She secured the sword in its case, and they turned to the window. Rex nickered a soft question. Jenny nodded and rubbed his neck, then held tight to the saddle and reins. The horse kicked back and bolted forward, leaping right through the shimmering, shadowy window, soaring through empty space to land with a thud on the street below. With only a momentary pause to get his legs in order beneath him, the horse dug in and launched down the street, rounding a curve and heading up to the park.

He galloped flat out across Prospect Park, barely swerving for hills or trees, veering left, southward and eastward across Prospect Park Lake, and shooting out across Ocean Avenue. He swung down Flatbush and wheeled sharply right, putting on speed as they neared Heckler's place.

Jenny tugged the reins—she knew by now that bringing Rex to a halt was more a matter of *thinking* it than controlling him physically, but the symbolic gesture kept her psychologically sound. The horse slowed and pranced to the corner of Heckler's building, sneaking just a few steps down the narrow walk between that building and the next. He bent forward, and Jenny gritted her teeth, trying to focus on coordinating her legs and arms. The off-balance weight of her luggage doomed her dismount from the start, though; she fell into a heap on the ground.

Rex graciously looked away as she self-consciously picked herself up. Jenny scowled and adjusted the items strapped over her shoulders. She was an indestructible superhuman with an epic sword and a magical horse...and she still couldn't dismount the damn thing without a sit-com pratfall.

She flipped the latches on her case and pulled the sword out halfway again. "Let me figure out where I can put you," she told Rex. "Just wait here a sec." Still a little embarrassed by her dismount, Jenny stared through the shining blade at the real world alley on the other side and jabbed a pair of frustrated fingers at the surface, sending her back with a jolt.

She walked briskly around the corner to the front of the building. Lyle and Lloyd sat on the steps, looking down at the sidewalk with long expressions and furrowed brows. Calvin stood on the walk, facing the street, his arms crossed and his posture stiff. The magic table was in front of him, a duffel bag sagging over the top. A small pet carrier sat on the walk beside the table.

"Calvin," Jenny called.

The magician turned. His face was tight, his eyes flashing. "They took it," he fumed quietly. Jenny had never seen him truly angry before. Despite his lanky frame and goofy shock of red hair, there was nothing funny about it. "They got the wand. They didn't even mess up the place. They knew right where to go."

"They took the box?" Jenny guessed.

Calvin nodded. "She knew," he said, breathing hard. "She kept asking about all the stuff—but she never asked about the box. She *knew*."

"She knew it was there," Jenny agreed. "The antique stores and pawn shops—"

"She *was looking for it*," Calvin seethed.

"They weren't coming to see me," said Jenny. It was all coming together, crystal clear. "They've been going to *all* the magic shows, and the shops, and everything...looking for the box. With the props in it." She slammed the instrument case with her fist. "Fuck!" She looked over at Lyle and Lloyd, sitting forlornly on the steps, trying to stay small. "What's with you guys?" Jenny asked.

"Um," said Lloyd. Lyle said nothing, but glanced at Calvin nervously.

Calvin glared at them. "Don't you know who they are?" he said angrily.

"They're, uh," Jenny started. She looked at the magician uncertainly. "He's Lyle. He's Lloyd. They're just two guys I met."

"Uh huh," said Calvin. "Two guys you 'met' in June, right? The two guys you 'met' on that one particular day...?"

"Calvin..."

"Jenny!" he exclaimed furiously. "They're the ones who...who—damn it!" He didn't bother finishing. She understood well enough.

She put a gentle hand on his arm. "Calvin, stop," she said. "It doesn't matter."

"But they *killed*—"

"It doesn't matter," Jenny repeated firmly.

The fanboys perked up, eyes wide. "Killed who?" Lloyd said.

"We didn't kill anybody!" said Lyle. He looked back and forth between Jenny and Calvin.

Jenny took the magician's arm and pulled him away, keeping her voice low so the fanboys couldn't hear. "Yeah, it was them," she said quietly. "But they didn't know. They couldn't know. Do I *look*...you know...dead?"

"They don't even know what they did," Calvin said, quiet but steaming. "This whole thing's just a game to them. A comic book or a...or a video game. In real life."

"They couldn't know," Jenny said again. "Most of the time, people you kill don't get up and walk away. All they know is that they hit me. They felt really bad about it. I mean, they probably wanted my phone number anyway, but they felt really bad."

"Not bad enough—" Calvin started.

"Did you ever bump into somebody on the sidewalk?" Jenny asked. He didn't answer. "What if they went around the corner and dropped dead because you accidentally...I don't know...ruptured their spleen or something?"

"That's..."

"If you didn't know, how *could* you feel 'bad enough' about it?" Jenny said simply.

Calvin said nothing. Then he dropped his head and stared at the grass.

"They didn't know," said Jenny. "And they don't need to. Why ruin their lives? For what?"

"They ruined yours," Calvin mumbled.

Jenny lifted his chin to look into his eyes. "If it hadn't been for them, *none* of this would have happened," said Jenny. "We never would've met. We wouldn't be doing the show. I wouldn't have my...powers. And nobody would be around to save the world from...from whatever's going to happen."

Calvin bit his lip. He frowned, but his face softened.

"I don't know if I believe in fate or anything," Jenny went on, "but I believe in luck. My mom always said it the right way. Luck—good luck, bad luck—isn't something you *have*. It's just what *happens*. We're lucky they hit me. The whole *world* is lucky they hit me. I mean, if I can save it...right?"

Calvin swallowed and tilted his head in an almost imperceptible shrug. "I guess," he whispered.

"So they're just in this, now," said Jenny. "There aren't a lot of people we can tell about this. Since they already know—since they *saw* it, anyway—we can probably use their help." She smiled lightly at him. "Don't look a gift horse in the mouth, right? Even if it's a couple of comic book geeks."

"Yeah, well," Calvin said, hiding a tiny half-smile, "this stuff is probably their field of expertise anyway. If they help out, we'll give them exclusive rights to write the Adventures of Death Woman."

"Let's go with Lady Death...and her Lovely Assistant," said Jenny, poking his arm playfully. "It's classier."

He couldn't hide his smile at that one.

Jenny hugged him, pressing her cheek to his chest. "You're my best friend in the world, Calvin," she said. "I love you."

He squeezed her tighter. "I love you, too," he said, his voice skipping and scratching like a vinyl record.

They pulled apart and smiled at each other. After three seconds, the smiles got awkward. Jenny cleared her throat and turned away. "Hey, guys," she said to the two boys on the steps. "Sorry, don't worry about it. It's okay."

"*What's* okay?" asked Lloyd, scratching his fuzzy chin.

Calvin followed Jenny to the steps. "Just a...misunderstanding," he said. He avoided their eyes. "Sorry I snapped at you."

Lloyd scrunched up his skinny face. "Um."

"O...kay," said Lyle. "Sure. Thanks."

Jenny cleared her throat again. "Is Heckler home?" she asked.

Calvin shook his head. "He didn't answer."

Jenny laughed. "Well, I guess I can get us in." She gave Lyle and Lloyd a mischievous look. "You guys'll like this one," she said.

She gave her shoulder bag to Lyle, her overstuffed backpack to Lloyd, and dropped the case by the magic table, pulling the sword out completely. She looked up and down the street, but nobody was close enough to

315

clearly observe the small group at Heckler's front door. Winking at the fanboys, she touched the blade and slipped Through the Looking Glass. In moments, she went through the building's ambiguously secured front door, pushed back out of Wonderland, and opened the door from the inside. "Hi," she smiled at the boys' stupefied looks.

Calvin grinned. "You'll get used to it—sidekicks."

"Dude!" Lyle breathed.

"Dude..." Lloyd agreed.

"Bring our stuff," said Jenny, holding the door open. The four of them hefted the magic table, Calvin's duffel, Jenny's bags, the sword case, and the pet carrier up the stairs to the second floor. Colby Cheese peeked through the slats in the carrier, sniffing the unfamiliar air and sticking her whiskers out. Lyle reached out to pet her nose, and she gently nipped his finger.

Jenny pulled the Wonderland trick again to get into Heckler's apartment, and the gang piled inside, setting loads down among islands of laundry and magazines. There was no sign of Keith Heckler—presumably, he was spending his Saturday night in the company of flexible college students, copious amounts of liquor, and bright lights flashing to a driving techno beat. Lyle and Lloyd looked around with the awkward curiosity that follows from intruding on a stranger's life.

"Let me get Rex," said Jenny. She walked out the door, swinging her sword.

Lyle planted his round frame and stubby legs on a bare spot between a mountain of *Maxim* issues and a molehill of *GQ*s. He cocked his head. "Rex?"

"Rex is her horse," Calvin explained.

Lloyd shook his head, his mouth a big round question mark. "Like, a *horse* horse?"

"Of course, of course," said Calvin. His smile was closer to smirk than he meant it to be, but he was still getting over the sting of realizing who the fanboys were and what they had unwittingly done to Jenny.

A burst of wind and a slice of twirling lights heralded the arrival of Jenny, leading her giant stallion through improbable angles to the center of the apartment. Lyle cringed and Lloyd gave a shout, but fascination quickly overcame fear and they both dashed over to investigate the horse behind Heckler's couch. Seeing Rex through the eyes of Lyle and Lloyd, it hit Jenny all over again just how huge and impressive the horse was. She'd gotten used to him since he'd moved in with her, and his size had lost its impact; the fanboys' saucer-wide eyes and overlapping questions brought it back home with a vengeance.

Rex waited passively but impatiently while the pair gaped and stared and clamored just out of range of the horse's muzzle. Jenny clambered over the couch to settle in with the sword straight up in front of her, the butt end resting on the floor. The sharp blade gleamed like her personal pennant as she went into War Council mode. "So we're pretty much positive it's the Raymonds," she said, her eyes dark and pensive.

"Yeah," said Calvin, sitting down heavily on a folding chair. "Has to be. It was so obvious!" He glowered. "She knew all those other magic acts. I saw her at the shops. She kept asking about all our *stuff!*" The magician's lips twisted. "And all that Circle of Life stuff, you know, the creepy stuff. Jeez!"

Jenny tapped her fingers on her sword hilt in a quick percussive anthem. "Well," she said, "at least there's some good news." At Calvin's inquisitive look, she shrugged. "If it's not the other Reapers, then Caravel's not in on it. She'll get my note, and maybe she can help us figure out what to do."

"She never really seems to help," Calvin shook his head. "I mean, no offense, but she's always talking about *not* helping. That she's not allowed to—that *you're* not allowed to."

"Who's Caravel?" Lyle asked brightly. He and his partner were still behind the couch with Rex, but they'd quieted down and were actively trying to participate.

Jenny gave him a quick, tight smile over her shoulder. "She's like me. Another...um, another...." She paused, not sure how to phrase everything for easy consumption. She didn't want to explain her Superhero Origin Story, since it involved a lot of pretty heavy guilt for Lyle and Lloyd; but that left some big gaps in anything she *could* explain, and she was trying to avoid too many questions. "Okay, basically—I'm like a...Grim Reaper. An Angel of Death."

Lloyd nodded sharply. "Got it," he said. Lyle smiled.

She should have figured the two comic book geeks would accept that with no problem. She sighed inwardly, relieved. "There's a whole bunch of us," she continued. "I'm new, and Caravel's kind of like my...my teacher or trainer or whatever."

"Obi-Wan," Lyle said sagely.

"Roy Focker," said Lloyd.

Lyle shot back: "Ramirez!"

"Kambei," Lloyd offered smoothly.

"Nice," Lyle admitted, then parried, "Splinter."

"Merrick," Lloyd countered.

Lyle offered his pal a condescending smile. "Giles."

"It was *Merrick* in the *movie*," Lloyd started with a defensive *Duh* on his face.

"Movie's not canon!"

"He was in the—"

"Guys!" Calvin interrupted. "Focus?"

Lyle nodded quickly. "Sorry." He and Lloyd both looked appropriately abashed.

"Right," Jenny continued, "so there are all these rules, and they're— *we're*—not supposed to interfere with this stuff when people are going to die. We just have to help them get where they're going after."

Lloyd muttered out of the corner of his mouth, "*Shinigami.*" Lyle nodded, his cheeks jiggling, stifling a grin.

"But Calvin's stuff—the props we've been using in the show—they're something else. And they're real magic, kind of." She flourished wiggling fingers at them. "Like *magic* magic. And these people we know, they probably—"

"It's *them*," Calvin insisted.

"Yeah, probably," Jenny said. "They stole Calvin's stuff. We don't know what they want to do with it, but the thing is...it's Calvin's stuff that let me see that the end of the world is coming."

Lyle looked at her in disbelief. "The end of the world?"

"Yeah. On Halloween."

"Dude," Lloyd lamented.

"We've been trying to figure out how it happens," Calvin explained. "Like an asteroid or a nuclear war or something."

Lyle cocked his head. "But...how do you know about it?"

Calvin looked at Jenny. Jenny gamely replied: "Huh?"

"I mean, like, was it a vision, or a dream, or a prophecy, or what?"

"Yeah," Lloyd said. "How do you know it's the end of the world, but you don't know what happens?"

Jenny frowned. "It's—okay, I can kind of read all these kind of...invisible letters all over everything. And everybody." She gestured vaguely all around. "And I can translate them into...well, birthdays and death days. And places. Times and places when people are born or die," she summarized.

"Whoa," said Lyle.

"So the thing in the show?" Lloyd added, excited. "When you said everybody's birthdays on stage?"

Jenny nodded. "Yeah."

Lyle stared at her in awe. "You know when we're gonna die?"

"Well, no," she admitted. "I need the props to do that. To see the letters."

Calvin interjected. "But you *do* know when they're going to die." The other three looked at him. "Everybody dies on Halloween. Me, and the Raymonds and..."

"The Raymonds," Lyle echoed. He raised his eyebrows. "They're the bad guys?"

"The ones who stole our stuff, yeah," said Calvin.

Lyle looked at Lloyd. "Why would the bad guys kill themselves?" he asked.

"Yeah," Lloyd agreed. "That's weird. Unless they got caught in the crossfire."

Jenny shook her head. "No, no," she tried to explain, "they're not the ones who end the world. They're just the ones who I noticed first. Who die on Halloween."

"And the ones who stole your stuff," Lloyd pointed out.

"And your stuff told you about the end of the world," added Lyle.

"And you said they're creepy."

"And they've got scary guys with black robes and knives working for them."

"I mean, of *course* they're the ones who do it."

Lyle nodded smugly at his friend. "They're plot relevant."

"Yup," said Lloyd. "Definitely."

Jenny looked at them, dumbfounded. She turned to Calvin.

He looked back at her. "The Circle of Life," he said quietly. "You can't have beginnings without endings."

"Out with the old, in with the new," Jenny responded robotically. "It *is* them," she breathed, her heart pounding. "They're trying to blow up the world!"

"*Duh*," said Lloyd. The fanboys rolled their eyes simultaneously.

Calvin spread out his hands: "Wait, wait! Time out! *How* can they blow it up?"

Lyle looked at Calvin like the magician had just asked something as obvious as where Superman gets his powers from. "What does all your stuff do?"

"Huh?" Calvin said. "Hm." His brow lowered as he chewed on gristly, grisly thoughts.

Jenny checked them off on her fingers. "We know the chains just catch you and hold on tight."

"And levitate," Calvin added. "Plus they move through each other."

"Right." Jenny ticked another finger. "The glasses and the Window work together, and show you the letters."

"Which only *you* can understand," said Calvin.

"But only *some* of them," Jenny said.

"The hole goes...*somewhere*," Calvin mused, his elbows on his knees and his long fingers cradling his chin.

Lloyd perked up. "Hole?"

"In the hat," Calvin explained.

"Where does it go?" Lyle asked.

Jenny shuddered. Calvin shook his head. "Don't know—somewhere really cold and dark, though."

"And the wand..." Jenny began. She looked at Calvin. "We don't know what the wand does."

Lyle shrugged tentatively. "Maybe it blows stuff up?"

Calvin grimaced. "Good thing we never tried using it in the act," he said.

Jenny nodded glumly. A stray idea wandered through her mind—a quick thought of Calvin's old friend Griffin, the one who'd been into wizards and roleplaying games. She stood and turned abruptly, taking in the two fanboys who flanked her just behind the couch. "Okay, wait," she said. "You guys know stuff like this, right?"

"Jenny..." Calvin started skeptically, but she waved him off.

"Shush." She looked earnestly at Lyle and Lloyd. "Like, heroes and legends and the occult and all that, yeah?"

The boys looked stoked to find themselves useful. They nodded. "Yeah," said Lyle. "We're, you know, pretty much experts."

"Totally," Lloyd confirmed.

"Werewolves, vampires, zombies—hey, I can recite the *Necronomicon*," Lyle said proudly. "Well," he amended, "the parts they wrote in the books."

"Yeah, he can recite it in Latin," Lloyd said. "And I've got, like, every page of the *Monster Manual* practically memorized."

"Not gelatinous cubes..." Lyle needled him.

"Dude, you are so lame!" Lloyd shot back. "What kind of DM actually puts gelatinous cubes in the—"

"They're in the—"

"I was on a boat!"

"I *told* you it was a cargo ship for the Circus of Sorcery, you just didn't—"

"Guys!" Jenny barked.

"Focusing!" Lyle interrupted himself instantly. Both boys snapped to attention.

Jenny took hold of the situation. "Okay, so do you think you could tell us about Calvin's props?" She looked intently at one and then the other. "Like, if they're part of some ancient legend or old story, or some kind of mythology or something?"

"Huh," Lloyd mused, turning to Lyle.

Lyle looked at his friend and nodded slowly. "We'd need Internet access," he said.

"And some time," said Lloyd.

Lyle turned to Jenny and smiled hopefully. "And some snacks...?"

"You're on," Jenny said. She looked at Calvin.

He shrugged and gave her a willing smile. "Can't hurt," he admitted. "Like I said, this *is* kind of right up their alley."

"Right," Jenny nodded. "Okay, so let's get them set up. You have your laptop?"

"In the table."

"I don't know if Heckler has WiFi, but we can go to a coffee place."

Lloyd chimed in: "There's a cool place on Seventh, past the cemetery."

"Which?" Lyle asked.

"We went to Rich's LAN parties there," said Lloyd. "Remember? I totally fragged your—"

"Right," Jenny caught the geek gauntlet before it was thrown down. "Sounds good." She rummaged through her shoulder bag on the floor. "Calvin, you bring them there and we'll pay for whatever they need." She looked sternly at the boys. "No games, no fragging, no porn—we're paying you to *work*," she reminded them.

"Yes, ma'am!" Lyle replied. Lloyd gave her a snappy salute and nearly put out his eye.

"No," said Calvin.

Jenny stopped short, her arms full of clothing. "What?"

"Where are *you* going?" the magician asked pointedly.

Jenny stood, black sleeves dangling from her bundle. "Calvin," she smiled sweetly, "I have an open invitation to visit *Doctor* Vincent Raymond's office." She balanced her bundle in one arm and yanked the business card from her shirt pocket. "It's about time I took him up on it."

"I'm coming with you," Calvin said firmly.

"Calvin—"

"No arguments," he said. "Artoo and See Threepio here can see what they can find. They don't need a babysitter."

Lyle beamed. "I'm totally Artoo."

"Aw, man..." Lloyd whined. "Could I at least be Chewbacca?"

"I'm coming with you," Calvin repeated, looking Jenny right in the eye.

"Okay," she relented, "fine. But you'll have to come through Wonderland with me." She looked back just as hard.

Calvin nodded, understanding what he was getting into. If they were going together, they had to stick together; and they needed speed, which meant riding Rex on the Wonderland Transit. "I'll do it." He stood straight and tall, as if *looking* brave would make him *feel* brave. "I trust you."

"I know," Jenny said solemnly.

The fanboys didn't know what to make of the exchange. They had no idea what Wonderland was like.

"Let's get them over to the Internet place and we'll go together," said Jenny. She handed the business card to Calvin. "I'm going to change into my, um, Reaper clothes."

Lloyd burbled. "Dude! You've got one of those robes, too?"

"Close enough," Jenny said. "You guys get ready out here—Calvin, give them as complete a description of the props as you can." She felt weird assuming command of her little army against the darkness, but as the only genuine superhero present, she might as well. "Guys, we're counting on you—see what you can find. Anything, everything—even if it doesn't make sense, well...nothing's made sense for the past few months. It might be right." She smiled and a shrugged. "Weird is good. You find Weird, it might be what we're looking for."

"Weird is good," Lyle repeated obediently.

Lloyd tried another salute, and nearly poked his other eye. "Check!"

Jenny headed into the bathroom and looked back at Calvin through the doorway. "You ready for this?"

"Yeah," he nodded once, deeply.

"Let's do it," Jenny said. She closed the door and transformed into a very business casual Grim Reaper.

CHAPTER TWENTY-FIVE

Lyle and Lloyd were a little disappointed to see Jenny's black hoodie and jeans instead of something with spikes, chains, shoulder pads, and a gritty Nineties anti-hero sensibility. They got over it when Lloyd noted her resemblance to at least six popular *anime* characters who, as he was quick to point out, "Kick ass!" They begged Jenny to spike her hair up a bit more, and she reluctantly ran sink-splashed fingers through her hair to appease them. Their nerdlust sated, they put their coats on and followed Calvin outside.

Jenny taped a note on the door in case Heckler came home to find their stuff in his apartment. She took strange comfort in the knowledge that Keith Heckler wouldn't care one way or another if she and Calvin and the fanboys took over his apartment as their Heroic Headquarters. As with most things, Heckler would just take it in stride. She had to admit that his cheerful apathy was a genuine perk in some cases.

Jenny and Rex jumped into Wonderland and rode down to meet the boys at the LAN center. It was one thing heading for a general area or a place she knew, or letting the horse follow the tingling pull of an appointment, but locating a specific unfamiliar address in the mirror world was tricky, since she had to actually pay attention to the streets signs and numbers and mentally reverse them in her head. It was a straight shot down Fort Hamilton Parkway and a right on Sixtieth—which, of course, meant she had to turn *left* in Wonderland, a fact she kept repeating over and over in her head so that she would follow the intent of Lyle's directions instead of the literal directions.

She didn't have to worry, though; Rex kept her oriented and on the right course. In less than fifteen minutes, she saw the wide glass windows and darkly flickering neon sign that marked her destination: *GAMERNET.* Mirror-reversed in Wonderland, it looked like some vaguely Russian propaganda announcement. She watched the real world through the reflection on the glass. The boys soon pulled up in a taxi.

Another graceless dismount and a quiet trickle of profanity later, Jenny slipped into a recess between the game place and the next building over and pushed through her sword blade to the real world. "Over here, guys," she called.

Calvin and the boys turned her way, their faces glum. "They've got a private party going on," Lyle said, pointing at a sign on the door.

"All-nighter," Lloyd explained.

"We're not allowed in at all?" she asked. She let out a frustrated squeak. "Dammit, *Batman* doesn't have to deal with stuff like this."

"Well, Batman could just *buy* a—" Lloyd began.

Jenny cut him off: "Yeah, right, okay." She looked through the glass at the flashing lights of computer screens inside. She gave the place a thoughtful look, then set herself. "Calvin...?"

"I'll hold your sword," he said, taking it from her and trying awkwardly to conceal it beside one long leg.

"Back in a sec," Jenny said. "You guys come with me. Maybe I can talk to the guy."

Lyle and Lloyd trailed behind like two disheveled ducklings as Jenny braved the explosions and droning narration of twenty interconnected consoles and headed to the central desk. The guy behind the desk turned around, started to sigh sardonically at the fanboys, but then caught sight of Jenny. "Magic Jade!" he exclaimed.

Jenny was startled. "Um." She stared at his sandy hair and unsuccessful but familiar facial fuzz. The place hit her before the name. "Oh! Empire Tech...?"

"Yeah," he grinned. "Rob," he reminded her. It was the same guy who'd helped her track down Callie the day after John the juggler died— after the snarky receptionist at Empire Tech had told her off.

"Rob!" said Jenny. "Wow—you work here?"

"Assistant manager," said Rob. "Decent pay, free Internet, all the noobs I can frag." He made a point of glancing at the frustrated pair behind Jenny. "You get in touch with Callie that day?"

"Yeah," said Jenny, "yeah—thanks! Thanks for your help."

"Sure," said Rob. "No problem. So what can I do for you tonight?" He smiled suggestively.

Jenny had to admit that he was cute for a tech nerd. No immediately obvious awkward social tendencies, weight issues, or skin problems. Plenty of confidence without too much bravado. In an alternate world where she hadn't been killed by Lyle and Lloyd and ended up in an ill-defined romantic-Platonic relationship with Calvin, Rob would have been a welcome alternative to another night on Heckler's fold-out couch.

This wasn't that world, though, and she couldn't afford to dwell on the ethics of exploiting the guy's blatantly advertised interest in her. "Um, yeah," she said. "Rob, hey, listen: we've got a really, *really* important...um...research project we're doing."

He nodded, still smiling. "Yeah...?"

"And our Internet's down," Jenny added. "And, you know, if you have any computers free, we'd *really* appreciate it if we could grab a couple to just get some work done."

"Free?"

"What?"

"You asked if I have any computers for free," Rob said.

"No! Um, just if they're *free*...I mean, *open*," Jenny corrected.

He laughed. "Don't fall apart on me now, Magic Jade," he said. "Yeah, sure, no problem. Just need a valid ID for each one you want to use. There's a couple at the end these guys aren't using," he jerked a thumb over his shoulder at the party of trash-talking geeks blowing each other away with virtual bullets and grenade launchers.

"Thanks," Jenny breathed a sigh of relief. "Thanks so much, Rob."

"That's *two* you owe me, Magic Jade," he replied. He looked past her at Lyle and Lloyd. "You guys were at Rich's LAN party, right?"

They perked up. "Yeah," said Lloyd.

Rob grinned. "Nice move with the truck on the bridge. That was killer."

Lloyd smiled proudly. Lyle scowled. "Totally stole that from me," he said. "I showed him how to—"

"*Or* we could not," Jenny jumped in, "and just go get set up and start *working*." She looked meaningfully at the fanboys.

"Right," said Lyle. He and Lloyd pulled VelCro wallets out of their dark trenchcoats and slapped their licenses on the counter.

"Head back on the right," said Rob. "You guys can use Yomin and Golmac."

"Seriously?" Lyle asked incredulously.

"The manager's total Old School," Rob said with a grin. "Magic Jade, you're paying for this?"

"How much is it?"

"Two tickets, plus popcorn and drinks, on me."

Jenny squinted. "Huh?"

Rob put on his best Innocence. It was pretty good Innocence. "Movie? Next week? You and me?"

"That's blackmail," Jenny teased back.

"I've got your number anyway," Rob said pointedly.

Jenny laughed. "You are the non-nerdiest nerd I've ever met!"

"I'll take that as a compliment," he replied. His voice boomed: "Hear that, nerds? I'm the least nerdiest nerd of all of you! I am your Mutant God King!"

Choice insults and derogatory noises answered back as the explosions continued. Lyle and Lloyd rolled their eyes and exchanged glances.

"Okay," said Jenny. "You can call me—I probably can't do next week, but we'll figure it out." She looked at the fanboys. "You guys get to work—Calvin and I'll be back as soon as we can."

"Hey, uh," Lyle shoved his hands in his pockets, "*we* should have your number, too." His eyes flicked briefly at Rob like he could laser vision the guy to death.

Lloyd nodded emphatically. "Yeah, in case we...you know."

"Right," said Jenny, pulling a pen from Rob's shirt pocket and yanking a business card from the desk. She scribbled her number and handed it over—both fanboys reached for it, and Lyle snatched it away first. Glancing smugly at Rob, he sauntered past the desk. Lloyd followed, whispering fiercely. "I totally could've..."

"You'd never even..."

With the fanboys out of earshot and on the job, Jenny felt the plan rolling along. She smiled at Rob and put his pen back in his pocket. "Thanks again, Rob. I'll be back in a bit—just need to go, uh, check on a few things. For the project," she added quickly.

"See you later, Magic Jade," Rob said jauntily.

Jenny waved, laughed awkwardly, and backed out of the store. Calvin was leaning against the wall with the sword half-concealed behind him. "All set?" he asked.

She nodded. "I, uh, know the guy," she said. "He's helping us out."

"You *know* him?" Calvin said.

"Long story," Jenny brushed it off. "Okay," she said seriously, "are you ready to go? I'll try to make it as quick as possible."

Calvin nodded firmly, pushing every ounce of courage.

"While we're in there, just go where I put you," Jenny instructed. "If you don't feel me touching you, *stand still.* Don't move. I'll grab you...don't go stumbling around trying to find me."

"Got it," said Calvin.

Jenny took a deep breath and reached for her sword. The magician handed it over, and Jenny took his hand, guiding him to the small recess between buildings. It was a tight fit; they were close, holding on to each other, the sword held out to one side. There weren't many people on the street, and the flashing lights of the gaming storefront set a high contrast to the darkness of their little nook; nobody would see them disappear. Jenny looked up at Calvin. "Ready?"

He nodded tightly. "Do it."

With one arm around Calvin, Jenny pressed the flat of the blade against her forehead, focusing her will and energy and feeling the familiar twist of gritty air and cascading shimmers. Calvin stood solidly in front of her—she felt him let loose an involuntarily gasp. He was moving in a sightless, soundless world now, able only to feel her pressing against him, her arm around his waist.

Rex's *chuff* of horsey breath echoed, and Jenny turned. She could feel Calvin forcing himself to stay still, to not panic or move without her guidance. Rex politely knelt as deeply as he could, and Jenny guided the magician's hand to touch the horse, then carefully pushed him toward the saddle to give him the right idea.

"Right!" Calvin shouted deafly. He swung a leg over and got seated with Jenny's help. She climbed in front of him and guided his arms around her waist as Rex rose and tossed his head. "Whoa," Calvin said reflexively. Jenny couldn't imagine what it must be like for him, blind and deaf and on horseback in a confusing, pounding world. He squeezed her hips; she didn't mind.

Rex started slowly, giving Calvin time to adjust as their speed increased. Before long, they were racing out across the Upper Bay. Calvin couldn't see the smooth, bottomless water beneath them, and made no reaction; Jenny, acutely aware that she wasn't sure how she'd get him back if he fell beneath the translucent flickering waves, hugged his arms to her sides desperately.

They dashed up the Hudson. Rex held back a bit, reflecting Jenny's worry over Calvin possibly falling off. Ten minutes up, Rex veered left and went through a small marina eerily devoid of boats. The leafy trees and sketchy grass twitched and bobbed at least as much as the stop-motion waves on the flat water. The horse barged through a restaurant—Jenny tugged Calvin's arm down to make sure he ducked under the doorframe, and she felt his breath on the back of her neck—and out into a circular courtyard. They stormed up a wide curving staircase and away from the river. As they trotted to West End Avenue, Jenny smiled; she wasn't far from where she'd gone to meet Dolores Meisel, her first appointment.

Vincent Raymond's office was a few blocks up on West End; again, Jenny paid close attention to numbers and mentally flipped them to check their progress. It didn't take long to see the magic numbers, read in reverse: 529. The digits were big flat stainless steel characters on polished glass; even in the dim and dusky wind of Wonderland, the brushed steel gleamed. The building was tall and imposing, not imperiously classical but not pretentiously modern. Its understated perfection matched the Raymonds strikingly well, and Jenny knew at a glance it was the right place.

This time of night, the building was probably inhabited only by security measures. Jenny wished there was another way, but cameras and guards were too big a risk; they had to go up to Vincent's office through Wonderland, which meant Calvin had to stumble through darkness just a little longer.

She didn't want to subject Rex to seven flights of stairs, though, and elevators seemed out of the question on this side of the Looking Glass. Through the smear of revolving doors at the entrance, Jenny patted the horse's shoulder. He moved toward the stairwell and bent down. It was a nice gesture, but Jenny still tumbled off his back and staggered across the floor, smacking the wall with her sword to keep from falling. She cursed loudly, only slightly mollified knowing that Calvin couldn't see her impressive spill or hear her vent her frustration. Collecting herself, she reached up and carefully guided the magician to the floor; he barely swayed as he touched down, and Rex gave her a look.

"He's got longer legs," she said testily. "I'll get it eventually."

Rex straightened and waited morosely by the elevator.

Jenny took Calvin's hand and spread his palm, face up. She pressed two fingers into it, walking them in place and slowly lifting his hand upward. Calvin nodded. "Stairs?" he shouted at a Grandpa Lost His Hearing Aid volume.

Jenny placed a thumbs-up firmly into his palm and patted his elbow.

"Okay," he yelled. "Seventh floor, right?" He'd read the business card, too.

She gave him another tactile thumbs-up and guided him to the stairwell.

Calvin was breathing hard when they emerged on the seventh floor; Jenny felt fine, and a little bad for feeling fine. She made a mental note to keep in mind that she barely noticed physical effort or fatigue anymore, but had to be considerate of the living, who couldn't keep up that same pace. Apologetically, she hugged Calvin's arm tight and led him down the hall, looking for Vincent's office. Suite 703 was only two doors down, though it was hard to read—the numbers were on the doors, which were blurrily open and closed at the same time. Jenny slipped inside with Calvin and raised her sword. She kept one arm around him and thumbed the blade.

The pounding dimness of Wonderland was replaced with coolly quiet darkness. All the lights were off, and the only sound was the ambient hum of electronics and air conditioning. The air felt cool and clear, but very still.

Calvin immediately noticed the difference, though he still couldn't see anything. "Jenny?" he whispered.

"Here," she whispered back. "We're in Vincent's office. In the real world."

"Where're the lights?"

Jenny smiled brightly in the darkness. "One sec—stay here." She pulled away and went back through her sword to Wonderland, alone. In the mirrored echo of the office, the light was its usual dingy sepia, and

Jenny had no trouble locating the light switches. She stood next to them and popped through the sword blade to the pitch darkness of the real world. "Cover your eyes," she whispered into the dark, and reached for the switches.

Her hand hit empty air.

"Jenny?"

"Sorry, hold on—cover your eyes," she said again. She'd forgotten to reorient herself in the darkness; reaching backward, she found the wall and the switchplate, and flicked the lights on.

Illumination fizzled and bobbled and gradually bloomed in a domino chain of clinking modern fluorescence. Calvin peeked through his long fingers and gave himself a moment to adjust; Jenny's eyes adjusted almost instantly. They looked around the waiting room of Vincent Raymond's office.

It wasn't necessarily what they pictured, but it was in the ballpark. Tasteful beige and teal, subtle stripes, short speckled carpeting, comfortable contemporary seating and a wide, circular glass coffee table. The front door, still closed, was the kind of rich brown wood Jenny expected in a West End building like this. Two other doors led deeper into the office, one next to a sliding glass receptionist window. Jenny wondered if Carrie had ever been Vincent's receptionist. She could picture the deskbound Aphrodite perched regally behind the window, deciding who had earned an audience with the Adonis of back-crackers.

"Wow," said Calvin.

Jenny turned to see what wowed him. The walls bore a few chiropractic diagrams outlining parts of the spine and suggesting various symptoms that wrenching each vertebra back into place could alleviate. Among the artfully laid out schematics, though, was a small assortment of framed paintings.

They had to be Carrie's work.

Sweeping strokes of dark black and blue and green filled most of the canvases. Carrie claimed she didn't paint people—she wasn't entirely lying, but there were human figures in her work. Twisted, mangled, awful human shapes bowing or fleeing or flailing in the face of the approaching darkness, a darkness that writhed and slithered across the canvas with massive ripples and waves of blue and green and gory yellow. Weird irregular shapes and pencil-thin concentric circles took over the bulk of the paintings, along with odd markings that looked as if an elephant with a calligraphy kit had attempted to write a few stanzas of Arabic poetry.

"You recognize them, right?" Calvin asked her.

Staring, Jenny nodded in silent amazement.

"Me too," Calvin spoke in hushed, reverent tones. "I copied some of those down from the Window. Can you read them?"

Jenny shook her head. "I've seen them," she said. "I've seen some of them, anyway. Written on people or places or things. But those aren't ones I know."

"Who the heck *is* she, Jenny?" Calvin put a finger close to one of the dark and roiling paintings, stopping just short as if a mere touch might suck him into the cold holocaust frozen on the canvas. "I'm getting a little freaked out here."

"Me too," Jenny assured him. "Come on, let's see what else we can find."

Calvin pulled himself away from the paintings and walked with Jenny to one of the inner doors. Jenny covered her hand in her sleeve, as if fingerprints were a primary concern, and tested the doorknob—the door opened. She peeked in, holding her sword like a weapon, which of course it was, though she wasn't thrilled at the prospect of using it as one. A hallway with several doors led away from the waiting room before turning a corner. It probably went all the way around in a square that terminated at the other inner door, by the receptionist's window. The two of them crept quietly inside, not intending to steal anything, but tacitly agreeing that the stealth of blockbuster movie ninjas was a good call.

More diagrams and charts lined the walls in the hall—and more paintings hung at appropriate intervals. Jenny wondered what kind of clients Vincent had, who didn't run screaming and holding their sore backs at first sight of the eerie, oozing art. Casual words spidered through her memory: *What do you paint?*

Just whatever I see.

"In her nightmares, maybe," Calvin muttered. Jenny nodded and reached for his hand; he took it and they walked to the turning in the hall.

At the end of the next leg was a beautiful oak door with silver fixtures and a name plate: *Dr. V. L. Raymond.* They looked at each other and nodded; holding their breath, they pushed the door open.

The light switches in the waiting room had turned on overhead lighting throughout the suite, but Vincent Raymond's private office was still dark. Calvin groped for the switch, and the room was suddenly lit by a very post-modern chandelier in the center of the ceiling. It was a cluster of clear glass spokes and spikes that would have had Superman feeling a bit homesick for Krypton. The bright white light cast strange forms and translucent shadows on the dark carpet, the huge desk, and a variety of shelves and cabinets. The two dominant decorative features in the room, aside from the starburst chandelier, were another of Carrie's paintings and a framed photograph of Carrie Raymond herself, side by side on the wall behind the desk.

The painting was nearly four feet across and almost as tall, and continued the theme of swirling blackness with undulating blue and green overcoming a crowd of pale yellow figures raising their arms in terror or triumph or maybe just a celebratory home team wave. The figures were stark and simple and only nominally humanoid, a severe contrast to the whirling vortex around them, as if Keith Haring had finally surrendered to the bleak, cold, uncaring universe and thrown all artistic sensibility to the wind.

From the silver-framed photo beside the painting, Carrie Raymond gazed out lovingly and quite seductively. The apocalyptic painting sucked all joy and life out of the room while Carrie's warm and noble expression refueled that vital energy in a neverending cycle; as if she was the only succor and salvation that could shield them from the demented void and see them through to the other side of bliss. She was the Archangel of Beauty in the face of Armageddon.

"I don't know which is scarier," Jenny said, with more glib bravado than she felt.

Calvin cleared his throat. "She's got my vote."

"Yeah," Jenny said. "Let's see what we can find."

They separated and crept through the office, each jumping self-consciously at every unexpected click or jingle of sound as they searched cabinets and desk drawers. Jenny drew a sharp breath as her eyes fell upon a photo on one shelf. She was about to speak when Calvin called her name; she looked over.

"I don't think there's any doubt any more," said the magician. He held up a calendar from the desk and pointed at the final square on the page. October Thirty-First was circled over and over, emphatically, first in pencil, then in red marker over the pencil markings.

"Yeah, I know," said Jenny, and she pointed at the photo she'd found.

Calvin moved closer and looked past the reflective glare on the glass. In the photo were Vincent and Carrie with a small group of others, all dressed for Spring, leaning on the railing of a boat out on the water. Not far from Carrie, just above Jenny's fingertip, the Ice Cream Psycho gazed at the camera emotionlessly.

"Who is it?" asked Calvin.

Jenny realized he'd never seen the Ice Cream Psycho's face. "That's him—Ice Cream Man. The psycho who followed me that night, the one who stole our stuff."

Calvin's eyes wandered to the other photos on the shelf. "There he is again," he pointed, "and in that one."

"Yeah," said Jenny, examining each photo. "They must be pretty good friends." She pointed at one photo, Black-Tie Vincent and Wedding Gown Carrie happily skipping down the front steps of a church as a jubilant crowd clapped and smiled. Near the top of the stairs, back in the crowd, the Ice Cream Psycho squinted sharply in an ill-fitting tuxedo. "He was at their wedding."

"Jenny, we need to do something," Calvin said urgently. "It's them, it's definitely them, we *know* it now."

"I know!" she said, then caught herself being too loud. "I know," she repeated in a harsh whisper. "But we have to *find* them first."

Ruffling through papers in Vincent's desk uncovered bills and other documents with consistent addresses on them—addresses that weren't this office. One was on the Upper East Side, one was in Park Slope—not far from where Jenny had met them—and one was out in the Hamptons. It was the trifecta of New York City blue blood real estate. The Raymonds might be in any one of the three homes, or even somewhere else that wasn't listed in these papers.

"So," Calvin finished copying the addresses into his phone's Memo application, "if they've got our stuff, it could be at any of these."

"Or somewhere else," Jenny rubbed her jaw wearily. "Maybe one of the other Black Robes is holding onto them. Maybe," she cocked her head thoughtfully, "Vincent and Carrie aren't even the leaders. Maybe they're just part of the group."

"Carrie doesn't seem like the type to follow somebody else's orders," Calvin said.

"Yeah, I know." Jenny shrugged. "Just another possibility."

"So what do we do now?"

Jenny narrowed her eyes in a dangerous expression. "We need to get them to come to us."

"Huh?" Calvin looked skeptical.

"We need to take control of this," said Jenny. "If *we* can decide where they'll be next, we can follow them to where *they* go."

"How do we do that?"

"There's only one thing they don't have," Jenny pointed out, "that they probably want."

Calvin frowned. "The glasses."

"Right," Jenny nodded. "If we can get them to come after the glasses, then we can follow them to wherever they're hiding the other stuff."

"And they definitely want the glasses, 'cause the Window is useless without them." He reached into his pocket and pulled out the magic spectacles, letting them catch sparkling glints from the Kryptonian chandelier overhead.

Jenny smiled darkly. "They want the whole box set," she agreed. "So let's let 'em have it."

"And when they come to get it..." Calvin began.

"We'll be ready for them," Jenny whispered.

CHAPTER TWENTY-SIX

The damp fog of Autumn dawn made the whole city seem like it was waking up in a cold sweat from one of those unnerving dreams involving immediate family members and sex. Mist-slicked buildings avoided each other's eyes with the shameful guilt of twelve-year-old boys smuggling stained sheets to the basement. The sun valiantly attempted to take back Sunday and cheer things up, but could only offer an anemic gray light spidering through low clouds to poke feebly at the neighborhood like sleep-numbed fingers struggling to pry the lid off a can of coffee grounds on a far too early Monday morning.

Across the table from Lyle and Lloyd, Jenny and Calvin yawned. The diner was open twenty-four hours, though not always consecutively, near both the park and Jenny's apartment; she'd never applied for a job here so that she'd always have a place to go for a quick bite or a cup of coffee without any fear of recriminating glances. The service was quick, the place was tiny, and Jenny was relatively sure the food was edible, possibly even nutritious. They needed to refuel—well, the boys did, even if Jenny could have gone forever without it—and there weren't many options before six o'clock.

While Calvin picked tentatively at his scrambled eggs and Jenny sipped her coffee, the fanboys lost no time reporting their findings between bites of sausage, bacon, and pancakes drowning in syrup like steerage class passengers on the *Titanic*. Along with pop culture references and competitive barbs, they actually provided some solid information. What Jenny and Calvin might be able to do with any of it, they weren't sure. The divide between popular fiction and the reality that they lived in might be the span between Galaxies, or the narrow cracks between sidewalk squares. They had no feasible measuring stick to tell if reality operated like any of the stories Lyle and Lloyd described, and if it did, which of the many and contradictory tales fit best.

"I mean, sure," Lyle said through a mouthful of sausage, "you've got all kinds of glasses that see stuff nobody else sees."

"*They Live*," Lloyd offered, crunching six slices of bacon at once. The secret behind his skinny body apparently didn't lie in the realm of Eat Less and Exercise.

Lyle nodded, giving his friend a point. "Yeah, and Sailor Moon used to have that mask," he said.

"The Doctor wore those red-blue three-dees that one episode," said Lloyd.

Holding up two fingers, Lyle smirked. "It was a two-parter."

"The ghosts in *Thirteen Ghosts*," Lloyd took the moral high road while carving through a hunk of pancakes. "You could only see them with those goggles on."

In contrast to Lloyd's stick-thin build, Lyle's pudgy frame was all too well explained by the fanboys' eating habits. Genetic biochemistry was a fickle bitch. He swallowed a mouthful of pancakes and bacon and smiled patronizingly at Lloyd. "That's 'cause in the original, the *audience* got those special glasses to see the ghosts."

"The glasses in *Transformers*," Lloyd countered.

"Yeah," Lyle agreed. "And that gets closer. 'Cause you guys are talking about glasses that let you *read* stuff too. Like read those magic letters."

"Reading Spectacles," Lloyd suggested, "*D 'n' D*."

"Or the Glasses of the Arcanist," said Lyle. "You could read, like, any magical words and stuff with those."

"But there aren't a lot of, you know, *ancient* myths and stuff about that." Lloyd waved at the waitress.

"Right," Lyle said. "But that's only 'cause glasses really aren't that old."

"Yeah, they had those glass balls in, like, ancient Greece or Egypt and all—could I have another stack and some bacon?" Lloyd interjected as the waitress walked by. "Thanks! But glasses weren't really a thing until later," he resumed his report without pausing, "so any old-fashioned type legends about them didn't really come up."

"It's like looking for old Norse myths about fax machines," Lyle explained. "There might be some cool ghost stories about a fax machine, but they won't be written until after it's invented."

"But there's the seeing stone," Lloyd pointed out.

Calvin perked up. Jenny prompted the fanboys expectantly: "Seeing stone?"

"Uh huh," Lyle nodded, putting a whole sausage in his mouth.

Lloyd seized the opportunity and the lead. "It's an old folk tale about fairies. A stone that has a hole in it—"

"S'posed t'be c'by water!" Lyle garbled through sausage.

"Huh?" asked Calvin.

Lyle chewed desperately as Lloyd grinned. "The myth says the hole needs to be cut by water," the skinny fanboy clarified. "Like, you know, by erosion or something. And if you look through it, you can see all the fairies that are all around us, all the time."

"But that doesn't tell us anything about the glasses," Jenny complained, "or the Window."

"Well, yeah—"

Lyle cut in: "But we've got an idea about that." He shoved his plate in front of Lloyd, who was more than happy to shut up and devour Lyle's last pancake. "It's like, you can read all this stuff, and only understand some of it, but what you *do* understand, it's like...you know, stuff *about* what you're looking at. Right?"

Jenny nodded uncertainly. "Right...."

"So maybe it's, you know, like the Language of the Universe," Lyle said. "If the stuff you can read is when people are born and die—"

"And *where*," Lloyd added effortlessly through a mouthful of pancake.

"And where," Lyle amended, "then maybe all the other stuff is the other stuff about them. You know, like how much they weigh, or what color they are, or how strong or fast they are—"

"Their stats," Lloyd suggested. "But more than that."

"Yeah, like, maybe it's not just their *descriptions*," Lyle began.

Lloyd finished off: "Maybe it's actually what *makes* them...them."

Jenny sat quietly, thinking. Calvin took a stab at the idea: "So what you're saying is that everybody's...made of the letters. But we just see them in a certain way that the letters...describe?"

The fanboys beamed at the magician, nodding.

"But the glasses...and the Window...let you see the letters themselves," Calvin mused.

"And I can actually read some of them," Jenny finished.

"Huh."

Lyle shrugged. "Yeah, pretty much. Like you can read the ones about your job. You know, the Grim Reaper thing."

A beat passed as they all absorbed the concept. Jenny jumped back in. "Okay, so they're about information," she said. "They'll need those to figure something out. But what about the other stuff? The hole and the wand and the chain?"

"The chain's weird," said Lloyd. "I mean, the trick's been around forever—rings that you can move in and out of each other and all that, I mean."

"Chinese linking rings," Lyle added. "They were invented by this Chinese magician a couple hundred years ago."

"Maybe," Lloyd said with a touch of informed cynicism. "But in myths and stories, chains show up on ghosts and monsters and stuff, sometimes."

Lyle tapped the table for a point. "Jacob Marley."

Lloyd tapped one too: "The kyton."

"Spawn," Lyle tapped hard.

Lloyd was indignant. "Dude!"

"Okay," Jenny broke in, "but what about the levitating?"

"And the shrinking?" asked Calvin.

"I dunno," Lloyd shrugged. "Sounds to me like it's just supposed to catch you. You know—*capture* you."

"Yeah," said Lyle. "I mean, what else would it be for?"

Calvin sighed. "Okay, fair enough."

Jenny kept at it. "How about the hole? The wand?"

"Magic wands are a dime a dozen," Lyle waved that one away.

"Yeah, come on—awesome, thanks!" Lloyd happily grabbed a new plate of pancakes and bacon from the waitress.

"There's, like, a million stories with wands in them," Lyle continued as his friend chowed down. "Or staffs—"

"Staves," Lloyd managed to correct his shorter partner through the syrupy mess in his mouth.

"*Staves*," Lyle glowered, "or rods, or sticks, or whatever. And they all do different stuff. It's just like...a *thing* with magic stories."

"Sometimes the wand gives you magic powers," Lloyd waved his fork demonstratively.

"Sometimes it just focuses the magic powers you've got," said Lyle.

"Sometimes the wand *is* the magic powers," Lloyd examined his fork and licked off some syrup.

Lyle shrugged with an authoritative air. "It's, like, impossible to say, really," he said. "Every story's different. So we don't know what the wand's for."

Jenny rubbed her eyes, searching for connections behind her eyelids. "But we have to figure out how they're going to *use* it, or what it *does*..." she began.

"Nah," Lloyd shook his head and gobbled another strip of bacon.

"What?" Jenny looked at them hard. So did Calvin, after pulling out of another yawn.

"We don't think it's the wand you have to worry about," said Lyle. "It's the hat. The hole, I mean."

Calvin scratched his head and yawned again—beyond exhausted, he focused blearily on Lyle. "Wait...why?"

"Okay—so you can put stuff in it...?" Lyle prompted.

"Yeah."

"And you can take it out if you don't...you know, let go?"

"Like if you keep it on a string or something," Lloyd explained.

"Right," said Calvin.

"But the other side's somewhere else, somewhere—you know, like you said, dark and cold," Lyle went on. Talking to the fanboys was like talking to one person with two heads and an insatiable appetite for breakfast foods.

Calvin nodded. "Yeah."

"So if you don't know what's on the other side," Lyle asked, "then how do you know there wasn't anything there before you started throwing stuff in?"

Calvin and Jenny blinked. "What do you mean?" the magician asked with a sinking feeling.

"Okay, listen," Lyle launched into Geek Lecture mode, "your standard Bag of Holding doesn't really *go* anywhere. It's just a lot bigger on the inside than on the outside."

"Hammerspace," Lloyd said, wolfing down pancakes.

"Time Lord technology," Lyle volleyed. He turned back to the magician and his lovely assistant. "But that's all it is. There's a lot of space in there, but it isn't someplace *else.*" He compulsively tapped his fingers. "But from what you said, the hole you've got isn't that. It's not even a Portable Hole— that would let you go through stuff, but *right here*, not someplace else. No—what you guys have—"

"Had," Lloyd shrugged tactlessly.

"—is a portal. It *goes* somewhere." He looked at them with incredulous disappointment. "What you never really figured out is: *where?*"

Lloyd scraped syrupy pancake pieces off his plate. "Meddling with powers you can't possibly comprehend," he mumbled ominously.

A silent moment lingered. The squeak of the waitress's sneakers and the sloppy chewing of the old man at the counter were as loud as thunder.

The fanboys cleared their throats awkwardly. Lyle smiled weakly at Jenny and Calvin. "If you can just, you know, close it or something," he said, "then maybe it'll all be over."

"There's no lid," Calvin said tonelessly.

Lloyd finished his pancakes and looked around hungrily. Calvin pushed his scrambled eggs across the table. Digging in, Lloyd brightly suggested: "Hey, maybe you can just destroy the thing."

The magician shrugged. Jenny gave Lloyd a thankful smile. "Yeah, maybe," she said. "Okay, so putting it all together...do we have any idea what they're trying to do?"

"Yeah," said Lyle.

Jenny stopped short, surprised. "We do?"

"The paintings you saw at his office," Lyle said. Jenny had snapped digital photos of them to show the fanboys. She motioned for Lyle to continue. He said, "Well, you've got a portal to someplace freaky," he began.

"And a chain to hold someone—or some *thing*—in place," Lloyd contributed, licking eggs from his lips.

"A way to get information," Lyle said, miming the glasses. "And the wand..."

Lloyd nodded. "Whatever the wand does."

"And the bad guy lady is doing those weird paintings...."

The fanboys looked at each other, then nodded emphatically and turned back to their companions. "Summoning," they announced together.

"Summoning?" Jenny asked blankly.

"Summoning *what?*" asked Calvin.

"Dunno," Lloyd said plainly. "Whatever it is, it's gotta be big."

"Like, End of the World big," said Lyle.

"So you probably don't want to fight it," Lloyd advised.

"Yeah," Lyle said, "you probably just want to stop it from getting through."

"Stop them from summoning it, you don't have to fight it."

A tiny smile fluttered across Jenny's face. She looked at Calvin with the first small sense of hope in a while. "Makes sense," she said.

Calvin looked back with a combination of disbelief and affection. "I guess," he admitted. "So we just need to find them, and stop whatever they're doing, and take the hole away."

Jenny snapped her fingers. "Piece of cake." Ignoring Lloyd, who looked around and smacked his lips, she leaned like a football captain in a huddle. "Okay, then we just need to know where they are, and where they're keeping the hole."

The magician smiled. "Get them to come to us?"

"Uh huh," Jenny smiled back. She looked at Lyle and Lloyd. "You guys want to come to the show again?"

They looked curious. "Sure," said Lloyd.

"For free?" asked Lyle.

"For free," Jenny replied. "You guys aren't going to be just audience. You're going to be part of the show."

"The Farewell Appearance of the Amazing Quirk and the Mysterious Jade," Calvin grinned.

"Right," said Jenny. "But you guys aren't a part of *that* show." At their confusion, she dialed up a smooth and dangerous expression. "We'll be doing the *real* show for a much smaller audience. And when they show up, we're gonna give them an encore they'll never forget."

Lloyd burped, but it only partly ruined the dramatic moment.

CHAPTER TWENTY-SEVEN

The messy daytime sky in Wonderland exploded into the spectacular blast of the usual phenomenal night sky on the other side of the mirror, and Zé bolted out of the trees like he'd been waiting for his cue. Caravel rode low in the saddle, brown hair and black robes flying behind her. The stallion crossed the reservoir and clopped up onto the wall where Jenny waited. Beside her, Rex shook his mane and stomped a perfunctory greeting to his equine colleague; there was business to conduct, and the horse felt no need to stand on ceremony.

Zé stopped a horse-length away and Caravel slid gracefully off his back. Jenny frowned enviously; as usual, she'd staggered across the top of the wall when she'd climbed off Rex. Caravel rushed over, dark eyes wide in her smooth brown face, and held out her hands. "Jenny," she said urgently.

"Caravel, I need—"

"You were right, Jenny," Caravel said. "I don't know what it is, but you were right!"

Jenny took a step back. "Huh?" She crossed her arms, digging her hands into the opposite sleeves of her black hoodie out of habit. Cold didn't bother her anymore, and temperature didn't have much meaning in Wonderland, but Caravel's words were distinctly chilling.

"We're all appointed," said Caravel. "All of us. Every *Anjo da Morte* I've talked to, and I've talked to many, and every one *they* have talked to. Halloween night, and the morning after—it's just appointment after appointment, *menina!*" She grabbed Jenny's shoulders and hugged her close, shaking.

Jenny didn't know what to say. The sight of a woman like Caravel in such a state knocked her off her conversational strategy, and she had trouble getting back on track. "You mean...*appointment* appointments?" she asked, pulling back but not out of Caravel's grip.

The dark and beautiful Reaper nodded. "*Sim,*" she said, her eyes shining with uncried tears. "So many appointments, all at once, it has never been seen, *menina.* There are precedents—humans have such a talent for destruction—but never anything on this scale, before."

"What scale?" Jenny asked.

"*Todos.*" Caravel shook her head in disbelief. "*Tudo.* Everywhere and everyone, Jenny."

"The End of the World," Jenny whispered. The Looking Glass wind scattered the echo, returning her words in strange and spidery mimicry.

"Our kind are gathering from all over," said Caravel. "The disaster starts here, in New York—somewhere near the city, where there are millions of deaths in only the first few minutes. Then it spreads—quickly, in only hours...it spreads...."

"How far?" Jenny tried to be stoic, but her voice caught in her throat.

"The whole world, *menina,*" Caravel said quietly. "Around the Earth. *Em toda parte.*"

"It's okay," said Jenny, hugging Caravel back.

"Jenny, this is not okay," Caravel protested.

"We're on it," Jenny promised her.

Caravel looked at her like she'd suddenly sprouted a beard. "Who is 'we,' *menina?*"

Jenny pulled away and sat on the edge of the wall; the sudden role reversal with her Grim Teacher hit hard. She even patted the scratched surface next to her. Dumbfounded, Caravel sat beside her. The horses moved behind them, protectively.

After a second to gather her thoughts, Jenny spoke. "We know who it is," she said. "And we think we know how they're going to do it. So we can stop them"

"Who *what* is?"

"There's these...people," Jenny explained. "Really weird people. And Calvin and I and...well, some friends—we think they're trying to do some kind of thing with the magic stuff Calvin has. You know, like the glasses and the Window I showed you. We think they're going to do something, or create something, or call something...and it's going to destroy everything."

"How can they do that?" Caravel asked. "*E por que?*"

"We're not sure yet," said Jenny, "but we're going to stop them. I mean, that's the plan, anyway."

Caravel stared solemnly across the water. "How can you stop them?"

"They need Calvin's stuff to do it," Jenny said, swinging her feet beneath the translucent, intangible waves. "So we're going to get his stuff back. We just need them to take the bait."

"Bait?"

Jenny smiled tightly. "We're doing our last show this week. The last magic show." She looked down and stared through her fingers into the depths of the weird water. "We can't keep it going now anyway, not now that we know how dangerous the props are. But they missed one," Jenny looked up sharply, a glint in her eye, "they missed one of the props, and one of the others won't work without it. So we're going to give them a chance to get it."

Caravel nodded, thinking it through.

"And when they do, we can follow them wherever they're going...and get it all back!"

"What if it's too late, *menina?*" Caravel asked gently.

"It *can't* be too late," Jenny insisted. "We can't just let everybody *die.*"

"There are rules, *menina*," Caravel began.

"And I don't care!" Jenny snapped. She caught herself and held up a hand to apologize. "I mean...you know what I mean. I don't think we're supposed to just blindly follow these things...do you?"

"It's what we *do*, Jenny."

"Not me." Jenny stood up. "I've only done it the one time, and I didn't ask for this, and I'll do it if I have to, for the right reasons...but *this* isn't right. This wasn't supposed to happen. It *wouldn't* have happened if it hadn't been for me in the first place!"

"No, *menina*, you can't—"

"If I didn't become one of *us*, and I didn't join Calvin in the act, and I didn't meet the Raymonds, then maybe they never would've found his stuff, and they couldn't—"

"*No, menina!*" Caravel said sharply, standing up beside Jenny. "You are the one who tells me that fate can be changed. You are the one who tells me that appointments can be...rescheduled." She smiled lightly. "If fate is not set, then things just *happen*, and we do what we can in the aftermath. That's all we can do, *menina*."

"But you guys don't do anything," Jenny said bitterly.

"There are rules," Caravel shrugged. "You know that."

"What if I could help you?" Jenny said suddenly.

Caravel paused. "*Ué? Que você quer dizer?*"

"I can find out where Pauzok is," Jenny said. "I can find him, and help you take him back, so he doesn't have to sit forever in some looney bin somewhere."

"You know where he is?" Caravel asked.

"No," Jenny admitted, "but I can find out. And we can get him out of there, and bring him home, or whatever we can do with him."

"Send him on..." Caravel said, very softly. Her golden brown eyes sparkled. Jenny wore a poker face to hide that leaving Pauzok to not rot in an asylum bothered her, too—her shared concern might weaken her bargaining position. The light in Caravel's eyes suggested she knew, anyway. Her heavy lids closed as she took a deep breath. "There are rules, *menina*..."

"Caravel—"

"*But*," the Angel of Death went on, "I'm on your side." She opened her eyes and smiled. "I like how you think, Jenny. And I would like to help Pauzok. I don't like the idea of him wandering off, forever, after this...End of the World. Never knowing he could escape as easily as looking in a mirror."

"So you'll help?" Jenny asked excitedly.

"I'm not sure what I can *do*, Jenny," said Caravel. "But I won't stop you. And I'll do what I can."

"Thank you, Caravel!" Jenny said, throwing her arms around her mentor. "*Obrigada.*" She pulled away and reached for Rex—he bent over and let her climb into the saddle. "I'll get in touch," Jenny told Caravel. "I'll leave a note, or whatever I can do. I'll meet you back here."

"Where are you going now, *menina?*" Caravel and Zé stood politely aside for Rex.

Jenny shrugged. "I need to see a man about a horse," she said with a simple smile. "*Heeyah!*" She twitched the reins and leaned forward as Rex flew across the water and through the trees. A minute later, he vaulted the FDR and a fence before making a tremendous leap onto the East River, following it past Roosevelt Island and all the way down to Brooklyn. Rex raced beneath the Williamsburg Bridge and jumped up on the docks at the navy yard, losing no time dashing down Washington and then Ocean Avenue. In less than twenty minutes, he was slowing to a trot outside of a large building streaked with the dim sepia and clear flickering zephyrs of Wonderland. Even in mirror image, Jenny recognized the place.

One clumsy dismount later, she tied her sword to Rex's saddle. She didn't want to wave it around in public. In her shoulder bag was a new batch of Emergency Exit mirrors she and Calvin had bought; they would do the trick if she needed to get Through the Looking Glass and couldn't find a mirror.

Jenny was happy with the plan so far. She and Calvin and the fanboys had crashed at Heckler's place after breakfast. When he'd returned to find them all sacked out across his apartment, he wasn't the least bothered or even surprised; he headed back out for coffee, which he cheerfully served on his return—after turning the TV up full blast in a wake-up call that combined the worst parts of jet engines, Tasmanian devil arguments, and fingernails on a chalkboard.

It didn't take long to fill Heckler in, and the five of them mapped out their next moves. By the time Jenny had to leave for her sunset meeting with Caravel, at least five dozen people across the five boroughs, Long Island, and choice bits of New Jersey were putting up flyers announcing the Final Fantastical Performance of the Amazing Quirk and Jade, the Jewel of the East. Lyle and Lloyd put the flyer together with help from Rob, the Mutant God King of Nerds, who printed hundreds of copies on GamerNet's networked printers and mass e-mailed the image of the flyer itself to let others print their own, despite the trouble he'd get into for wasting so much company paper and bandwidth. Jenny and Calvin were depicted in dramatic and mysterious poses, thanks to Jenny's digital camera, and Jenny found it poetic that the fanboys had used the splotchy picture of Dolores Meisel in Wonderland as a special effect, though they had no idea what the photo showed. A squadron of Charmed Quirks had heeded the call when Calvin got in touch with a request for help, and once they were resigned to the fact that they couldn't change his mind and extend the show's run, they wandered the streets and shops of the Metro Area, plastering flyers on any available surface. Callie at Empire Tech eagerly put together another team of willing fans when she got the call, and Rob convinced the networked nerds at GamerNet to get in on the action with the promise of free gaming sessions and a few WiFi passwords he'd picked up hacking networks around the city. Even Heckler rallied some troops—most of them young and female, sparking genuine doubt regarding the organic content of their breasts and the efficacy of their brain cells—and sent them out to spread the word of Quirk and Jade's farewell performance. Friends of friends, and friends of those friends and *those* friends' friends, were working together in the biggest four-day publicity blitz the independent theatre scene had ever witnessed.

Other than feeling like Judy Garland to Calvin's absurdly tall Mickey Rooney, defeating evil real estate investors through the power of love and impromptu musical revues at Old Farmer Brown's place, Jenny actually had a good feeling about all of this. Calvin had even convinced David Dennis to get in touch with newspapers and entertainment magazines to hype the show, promising the behind-the-scenes theatre queen that the *Beau Regardez* would break box office records, which was probably true. The popularity of the act, coupled with its imminent conclusion, almost guaranteed that they would face a massive audience like they'd never seen before.

The fact that every flyer—and the publicity photos they'd e-mailed to David—featured extreme close-ups of the Mysterious Jade in her magic spectacles also guaranteed (they hoped) that the *right* people would be in that massive audience. That was key; the secret show within the show, featuring Lyle and Lloyd as two very lucky and forgetful fans, was meant for that select few.

Their private publicity army was set to work straight through to Wednesday night's performance. Caravel had joined the fight—and with any luck, some more Avenging Angels of Death would ride beside her. Calvin was devising the act and helping Lyle and Lloyd learn their parts. Their pieces were strategically arranged on a chessboard with higher stakes than Kasparov challenging Deep Blue for humanity's freedom from the dominion of Evil Robot Overlords. Jenny had one last stop to make on this eventful Sunday—one last piece to put into play.

Straightening herself—she tied her hoodie around her waist to avoid the indie Euro junkie look—Jenny pushed through the bathroom mirror into the real world version of the Coney Island police station.

349

Too late, she noticed a pair of legs under the door of one stall. As a loud flush sounded behind the door, Jenny fished past rattling Emergency Exits, pulled a lipstick from her bag, and started applying it, staring studiously at her reflection. Mirror Jenny winked and exaggerated her puckered pose, but fell into a more natural expression just as a woman in a dark gray suit walked out of the stall. She looked at Jenny in surprise, but only for a moment, and then moved to the sink to touch up her own makeup.

Jenny smiled at the other woman in the mirror and nodded a greeting, then smacked her lips, put her lipstick away, and walked out the door. She went down the hall to the front desk, where a familiar woman—stern, maternal, no-nonsense—sat answering phones.

"This *is* the Sixtieth, what can I do for you, sugar?" she purred into the phone cradled on her wide neck. She smiled at Jenny like she was sharing a joke, then continued: "No, Darlin', you need City Hall, but they're *closed* today." She listened. "Mm hmm. That's right, sweetie, you have a lovely evening too. So long!" She hung up and leaned on the desk to look at Jenny with a pithy but pleasant smile. "Yeah, honey, what I can do for you?"

"Um, hi," said Jenny. "I'm here to see Detective Monaghan...?"

"Mm hmm," the lady drawled genially, flipping through a two-ring binder full of index cards. "Sorry, sweetie, he's not in today. Can I get you another detective?"

Jenny dialed up pure youth, which wasn't hard, and a lost expression. "Um, actually," she said, "he knows me. He was asking me about a case. And I remembered some stuff I didn't remember before."

"Can I get you one of the other detectives, honey?"

"Um," Jenny thought quickly. "Actually, I'm a little nervous around all this stuff, and...and I really trust him." The truth made an easy lie, when the only lie was context.

"He's a good one, yeah," the desk clerk nodded understandingly. Her smile was astonishingly white. "You want me to leave him a note, honey?"

"Do you think you could get in touch with him?" Jenny asked. "I mean, it's kind of an emergency. *Not* an *emergency* emergency," she added quickly, fearing too much urgency might summon a whole squad of concerned cops who would just be in the way. "It's just that he asked me to get in touch with him if I remembered anything else, and I *really* think this is important."

The woman looked her over appraisingly, lips pursed and eyes thoughtfully narrowed. Focused on that matronly face, Jenny didn't even see the phone until it was at the woman's ear, gripped in a colorful dragon-clawed manicure. With a wink and a smile, the desk clerk dialed with her other hand, mindful of her decorative fake fingernails. She held up one finger to tell Jenny to wait. After a pause, she said: "Hello there, Detective Monaghan? This is Jolene, down at the Sixtieth, so sorry to bother you on your day off, darlin'." Her voice was like deep fried honey. "Mm hmm, that's right. Detective, I've got a young lady here named..."

Jenny gave a start at the woman's prompting look. "Oh—uh, Jenny Ng!" she said quickly.

Never slowing down, Jolene pronounced Jenny's name flawlessly, if skewed a bit by a *faux* Southern twang. "Jenny Ng, she's a young lady says you questioned her about a case?"

Jenny heard Monaghan's high-pitched voice burst through the earpiece. Jolene casually held the phone away until the detective calmed down, then moved right back in to reply. "Sure thing, detective, I'll let her know." She listened some more. "Well, then, you just hold on one second, sugar." She held the phone out, surprised but polite. "He'd like to speak to you, honey."

Jenny smiled blankly. "Oh! Thanks," she said, taking the phone. "Detective Monaghan?"

"Miss Ng!" Monaghan sounded even more scattered than usual. "Where are you? Ah, no," he immediately said, "don't, ah, answer that, sorry, of course. You're at the precinct."

"Yeah," said Jenny. "I wanted to talk to you. About...you know. The horse," she muttered the word as quietly as she could, "and all that."

"Right, right," the detective said hastily. "I can, ah, be there in an hour, maybe two..."

"I can come to you," Jenny interrupted. She caught the desk clerk's raised eyebrow. "I mean, I don't have to come to your house, but if there's someplace nearby we can meet, I can...uh...travel pretty fast."

"You've got a car? There's not much, ah, parking around here on a, you know, a Sunday..."

"No, it's okay," Jenny assured him. "I can get there in twenty minutes."

"I haven't even told you, you know, where it, ah, *is*," Detective Monaghan pointed out.

Jenny smiled, then looked up at the Jolene's polite but querulous expression and covered her smile. Lowering her voice, she told Monaghan, "I can get *anywhere* in twenty minutes. Trust me."

There was a pause. "All right, Miss Ng," said Monaghan, his voice suddenly less harried old man and more wise old cop. "There's a coffee shop around the corner from my house. 'Perk,' on Montague, just off Henry. I'm in, ah, Brooklyn Heights."

"I can be *there* in *ten*," Jenny grinned into the phone. "See you soon."

"I'll see you there, Miss Ng."

He hung up, and Jenny handed the phone back to the desk clerk. "Thanks," she said. At Jolene's bemused look, Jenny shrugged with a little laugh. "It's a...big case."

"Must be, honey," the woman said with a clever smile. "You need anything else?"

"No, I'm good," said Jenny, adjusting her shoulder bag. "Thanks very much. Have a good night."

"You too, honey," Jolene drawled, then turned to answer another ringing line. "NYPD, Sixtieth Precinct, what can I do for you, sugar?"

Jenny waved a tiny wave and mouthed: *Bathroom?* She got a smart, businesslike wave back and a finger pointing to the hall as Jolene continued her phone conversation without missing a beat. Walking away from the desk, Jenny headed back to the bathroom. Inside, she quickly crouched and checked the stalls: all empty. Turning to the mirror, she smiled at Mirror Jenny, who grinned and nodded in return. They playfully lunged at each other and high-fived, sending Jenny hurtling into Wonderland.

Rex was waiting by the steps of the Looking Glass police station; he barely had to bend down as Jenny mounted the saddle from two steps higher. "Brooklyn Heights, Jeeves," she intoned with an upper crust accent.

The horse twisted back to look at her and rolled his eyes unappreciatively.

"Too late to rename you?" Jenny joked. He was not amused. "Sorry...let's go!" She nudged his flanks with her heels, and he took off into the flickering darkness.

Rex could probably have reached their destination well under the ten minutes Jenny had boasted, but there was no need to push it, and he held back a bit as he raced up Ocean, onto the expressway and over to Carroll

Gardens. He made a sharp left on Henry Street and soared north, covering twenty blocks in under a minute. Through the window reflections, Jenny saw that Brooklyn Heights was a happening place, even on a Sunday night. There didn't seem to be any secluded spot she could pop through to go meet Detective Monaghan. She spotted the coffee shop—spending an odd moment mistaking its backwards Wonderland signage for some forgotten bit of trivia from high school biology—and decided that the bathroom was once again her best option.

Rex halted in front of the shop. He looked at her reproachfully, then leaned forward. Jenny sighed. "How am I ever going to learn if even *you* don't have faith in me?" she asked. The horse's withering look wasn't the only irony that hit her: he was a part of Jenny—if he didn't have faith in her abilities, then apparently neither did she. Jenny furrowed her brow as she thought about that one, and then entirely missed her dismount, stumbling into a sullen pile of Grim Reaper at the mirrored coffee shop's entrance. She cleared her throat and avoided Rex's eyes; he diplomatically avoided hers. If he was human, he would have whistled aimlessly.

Collecting herself and standing up, she self-consciously checked the sword tied to Rex's saddle, rattled the Emergency Exits in her bag, and headed into the coffee shop. A long mirror stretched along behind the service counter, and she saw an artistic, moneyed crowd spending a relaxing evening with laptops, books, and friends, sipping lattes and cappuccinos and flavored drinks that required impeccably delivered Italian tongue twisters to order them. In a far corner by the front window, Monaghan stared outside and anxiously stirred his drink. Jenny smiled, went through the Eigensmeared bathroom door, and looked at the mirror.

A young lady was on the toilet. The bathroom was a single-occupant room with no stalls. Jenny winced and tried to look the other way. The girl was about Jenny's age, a bouncy blonde in a thick cream-colored sweater, her leggings down around the ankles of big warm fleece-lined boots. Jenny dropped her face in her palm; she'd never thought about the implications of bathroom mirror travel depots. This was, after all, the inevitable result of depending on lavatory vacancies for access to transportation.

Still, the alternatives were finding another place or bringing her sword through with her, and she didn't want to waste time or get arrested just to avoid some vestigial human taboos. She sucked it up and waited by the sink, watching in her peripheral vision while the girl finished up, pulled up her leggings, and flushed the toilet. Jenny waited another six minutes as the girl took her time adjusting herself in the mirror, reaching through the neck of her sweater to grope her own armpits and then giving her fingertips a smell test, running water on her hands and teasing her hair...all the usual things anyone might do with privacy and time.

It was maddening.

The girl finally dried off on some paper towels, made one last adjustment, and turned the bolt on the door. As soon as she walked out, Jenny jumped through the mirror and turned to face Mirror Jenny, who laughed silently and hysterically at her predicament. "Right," she muttered at her reflection. "Very funny."

She opened the door and crashed into a scruffy guy in a sweatervest. He jumped back, surprised, and glanced over his shoulder at the blonde girl walking away from the bathroom, then looked at Jenny, doing the math.

"You know," Jenny said matter-of-factly. "We go in groups." She gave him a pretty smile and slipped past before he could reply.

Monaghan was still staring out the window as she approached his table, and Jenny cleared her throat. "Detective?"

He turned, startled. "Miss Ng!" he said. "I didn't, ah, see you come in." He glanced at his watch. "And it's been almost, ah, twenty minutes," he teased.

"Yeah, sorry," Jenny said, sitting opposite him. "There was...traffic."

He nodded, but his misty blue eyes drilled right into her brain. "Traffic, of course." He smiled avuncularly and gestured toward the counter. "You want some, you know, coffee?"

"No thanks," Jenny said. She wanted to trust him—she really wanted to trust him completely, but she wasn't sure how to start.

"Well then," he said, dropping his hands around his cup on the table. "You said you had something more to tell me about the, ah...the horse?"

Jenny looked him right in the eyes, almost positive this was a good man, a wise man, somebody who might not understand all of the craziness she was wrapped up in, but who would at least sympathize. Those translucent, watery eyes had seen a lot in years of police work, and even more in the many decades of life this man had obviously experienced. She bit her lip, then bit the bullet. "You never called Calvin," she said, no question in her tone.

She'd caught him off guard. "Ah...Calvin?"

"My friend," Jenny clarified, "my partner in the magic show. My *alibi*," she emphasized. "You never called him."

Monaghan's mouth flickered in a kind but inscrutable smile. "No, Miss Ng, I didn't."

Jenny asked, "Because you knew it was bullshit?"

"Because I smelled the horse shit—beg pardon." The inscrutable smile resolved to decidedly wry. "Miss Ng—"

"Jenny," she corrected. "If you're going to arrest me or believe me, either way...it might as well be Jenny."

He conceded the point politely. "Jenny," he started over, "I've, ah, got to tell you, you're not, you know, the world's most talented liar."

She chuckled ruefully. "Not even when you feed me all my lines."

"Heh, well," he raised his hands in surrender. "You needed some, ah, help. Miss Ng—*Jenny*," he amended firmly, "I'm a detective. I've been on the force thirty years. I know what I, you know, *look* like. It's just how I think. I find it easier to, ah, work out my thoughts verbally."

"Even if you're not saying everything you're thinking," Jenny said.

He smiled. "Now you're catching on." He took a sip of his tea. "So you've been hiding a, ah, giant horse in your apartment, then?"

"He's mine," she replied. She thought for a second. "Well, he's mine *now*. The guy you got—the guy you had me go see in the jail—the horse used to be his. But I kind of...inherited him."

Detective Monaghan shook his head just barely. "You *did* know him, then? Our, ah, John Doe?"

"No," Jenny said quickly. "I didn't. I mean, I know who he is now—I mean, I found out. Later. But I didn't know him when you asked me. I'd never seen him before."

"What's his name?"

"It's—that's not important right now," Jenny hedged, then gave up, flustered. "It's Pauzok, but it doesn't matter. I mean, he doesn't know who he is, but I do, and...well, it's complicated."

"Then maybe it would be easier to, ah...start at the beginning." Monaghan sat back, relaxing his posture and expression for the first time that Jenny had ever seen. He was opening himself up to her story, ready to listen.

Jenny poured it out.

She told him about the car accident. She told him about being indestructible, and about meeting Rex and getting the sword. She told him about the magic act, and Calvin's props, and the Raymonds. She told him about the Ice Cream Psycho, and Mirror Jenny, and journeying through Wonderland; about Ketch and Caravel and the other Angels of Death, and her first appointment with Dolores Meisel. She told the detective about the beautiful moments she'd sifted through with Dolores, and how the old woman had made her final choice and danced elseward to another world, on another path. She told him about the End of the World, and the plan to steal Calvin's props back, and the black-robed people they were up against. To her surprise, Jenny told him *everything*.

He sat and listened, cautious old eyes never wavering. He occasionally asked for clarification or more information; thirty years on the force had taught him to check up on details. But for the most part, he absorbed her story and nodded gently, a little smile spreading slowly across his lips.

Outside, rain pelted against the window. Inside, light jazz underscored Jenny's story of magic and horses, angels and monsters, criminals and comic book geeks.

Finally, her throat running dry, she stammered a little. Detective Monaghan pushed his tea across the table, and she gratefully took a sip. Jenny blinked blearily, drained emotionally even if she could no longer be physically exhausted. "So...we could use some help," she said quietly. "I mean, we can't go to the *police* with this, but I figured...I figured there was one police *man* I could go to."

The detective looked at her without a word.

"The one who didn't turn me in," she added unnecessarily.

He broke into a smile. "Jenny," he said. "I, ah, pride myself on being a good judge of character. You're not on drugs, I'm pretty sure of that. I don't know why you'd lay a story like, ah, *that* on me if it weren't, you know, the truth. Or at least, ah, how you see it."

"It's the truth," she said definitively, and took another sip of tea.

"I have to, ah, say...I'm inclined to believe it is." He took a deep breath. "Still, against this kind of thing, I'm not sure what help I could be." He scratched his head. "I don't have, ah, probable cause to go, you know, investigate a couple like the Raymonds for, ah, petty theft, let alone harboring weapons of mass destruction. You've got, you know, an eyewitness account of the man in their photographs attacking you and your friends, with four other men, but then it's your word against theirs. And I'd, ah, bet they've got some good lawyers." The detective exhaled a defeated sigh. "I'm just not so sure what I could help with."

"I guess I just need backup," said Jenny. "You know, somebody *in case* things go wrong."

"You're looking for insurance," Monaghan said.

"I guess. I mean, I think I can handle the sneaky stuff, and if the other...you know, the other death people come through, they can handle the rough stuff. But I'm just not sure if I've got all the bases covered."

Detective Monaghan nodded. "Well, then, I suppose I'm your, ah, military advisor. Your, you know, joint chief of staff."

"Um, yeah," Jenny grinned and rolled her eyes. "Maybe you can just go through this stuff with me, see if there are any holes."

"And fill 'em, yeah," Monaghan said dubiously. But he smiled and added, "If I can help, I'll help. It sounds like there's, you know, a lot more on the line here than my, ah, career."

"So I can count on you, detective?"

"Well, if we're going this far, you might as well call me Glenn," said Detective Monaghan.

Jenny nodded. "Right...Glenn." She listened to his name coming out of her mouth, then made a face. "Um, actually...?"

"No, it doesn't feel right at all, does it?" Glenn Monaghan grinned weakly. "I suppose 'Detective Monaghan' will have to do."

Jenny laughed, relieved.

"Now then," said Detective Monaghan. "Let's look at what you're up against. I may not be able to, you know, *arrest* these people yet, but maybe I can help you stop them."

Jenny and the detective ordered more drinks and discussed vital plans of cosmic importance to avert the End of the World. The very snotty barista somehow managed to blame them for getting their order all wrong, but Jenny knew even he didn't deserve being consumed in the monstrous cataclysm to come. On the other hand, neither did he deserve a tip.

CHAPTER TWENTY-EIGHT

The *Beau Regardez* was a madhouse, packed wall to wall with excited, jabbering spectators awaiting the last and purportedly greatest performance of the Amazing Quirk and his lovely assistant, Jade. The party was full-swing, with wine and beer in the lobby and plenty of fans dressed in whatever nearest equivalent to a tuxedo or evening gown each could afford or cobble together. So many New Yorkers getting this riled up on a Wednesday night did not bode well for the productivity of Thursday morning's workforce.

The publicity machine had done its job well; familiar and unfamiliar faces filled the room, and all reports indicated that the theatre couldn't seat everyone who'd bought a ticket. Standing Room Only was redundant; people were making deals to sit on each other's laps or armrests just for a chance to be part of the event.

Jenny and Calvin got infrequent updates from Kevin, who knocked at the dressing room door to keep them informed. Despite David Dennis's standing rule that all performers had to watch the majority of the acts that they weren't in, the magical duo had been excused in consideration of their fame and box office draw, and the momentous occasion of their final show. Their nerves vibrated as they bustled about the dressing room getting ready for more than just the show. The past three days had been non-stop activity, between keeping the publicity army supplied and marching, creating their final act, getting Lyle and Lloyd ready for their part, getting their more important plans in gear, and even sitting down for a Monday afternoon magazine interview that David Dennis had scored. David was interviewed, too, and had plenty to say as the man who "discovered" their talent. Neither of them complained as he waxed enthusiastically about the state of theatre and magical showmanship, claiming credit for everything from the success of the Amazing Quirk to the casting of the Jewel of the East. Giving him his due, he really did provide a lot of support over the last four months, both financial and professional. They may have been able to find what they needed without him, but his unshakable faith and unspoken affection certainly made it easier.

David had originally wanted to devote half the show to them, cutting down on the number of acts, but they'd requested just the opposite—their last act would be a short one, and they wanted to give more performers the opportunity to take advantage of the extra room on the program, performing in front of the largest audience the *Beau* had ever seen. Almost two dozen familiar and favorite acts were on hand, as well as a couple of new ones that had impressed David enough to be included in such a big night. David himself wore a flamboyant outfit of bright blue with stripes and a dashing scarf, and had hired extra crew for the extravagant lighting and sound concepts he'd added for the occasion. Tantalizing slogans and flyers adorned every wall, door and pillar, punching up the mystery and magic of the Amazing Quirk's last show. The magic spectacles were almost comically accentuated in all the new pictures—in one, Jenny even put her hands up around the frames like she was peering intently at the viewer through very short binoculars, divining the nature of their distant souls. No matter how much David Dennis pleaded, though, Calvin and Jenny refused to provide any clues about the new act. He badly wanted to customize the lights and sound to their script, but their decision was firm—as always, only *they* had advance knowledge of their tricks. Frustrated but still giddy with the spectacle and mystery of it all, David didn't press any further.

The opening acts featured music and dance, poetry and art. The juggling girls performed, as did the enormous burlesque poets Roberta and Verbena, and even the transvestite comedian who had auditioned the same night as Calvin and Jenny (his parrot perched proudly on his shoulder, supplying rimshots and snappy comebacks). Ellie and the guys in Sex and Violins rocked the crowd with wrenching string quartet versions of the Ramones and The Clash. Mike, the hyperkinetic comic who sang political opera at Calvin and Jenny's first show, sang a lengthy tribute to the Amazing Quirk and Jade, which he'd written to the tune of Handel's *Messiah*. He was backed by a couple of dueling pianists, Igor the hawk-nosed ukelele player, the Sex and Violins quartet, a poet on a pair of bongos, and a dozen fellow performers (from a skinny fire-eating Goth chick to the booming baritones of Roberta and Verbena) who sang back-up during the Hallelujah chorus. It was both funny and poignant, and the audience cheered and stomped enthusiastically, some even singing along—the attention-starved comic admirably kept the focus on the magician and his lovely assistant, rather than his own clever rhymes and puns.

As Mike's song ended and the crowd's response reached a crescendo, all the performers dashed off the stage to grab good spots snuggled in with the rest of the packed audience, and the lights suddenly went techno—dimming and flashing and sparkling with a dark and mystical flare. Barely audible beneath the noise of the crowd, music throbbed in the speakers, quickly becoming recognizable when the first climax of *Night on Bald Mountain* hit. The theatre exploded into yelling, screaming, clapping and thumping. Those who hadn't seen the show before were infected by the raucous tempest of those who had, and joined in without hesitation. As sinister strings brought the music back down, David's slithering tones filled the speakers, and the audience levels dropped to the occasional punctuation of cheers, whistles, and shouts.

"Ladies," said the recording of David Dennis. "Gentlemen. Visitors whose souls cannot be confined in terms of gender..." That one provoked hoots. "Old faces, new faces, and old faces that have spent enough cold hard cash to look new." Another round of laughing and hooting. "Some things are not meant to last," the recording purred, as the man himself, front row center, steepled his fingers and smiled a superior reptilian smile, "and some stars are too hot to hold. Like shooting stars, streaking across the dark sky, they flare up brighter than the sun, and explode in the kind of climax most of us need little blue pills to achieve."

Catcalls and laughter rang out. Sitting next to David, his boyfriend Paul smiled appreciatively and patted his partner's knee.

"But ever after, when that star has burned its way across the sky and left a flaming image scorched into our eyes, we'll remember the light...the glory...the *magic*."

The crowd began to rumble and hum in anticipation.

"Not all of us get to experience something so...*amazing* and *lovely*...in this short and bittersweet tragicomedy we call 'life.'" The callouts weren't lost on the audience, who howled and hollered. "But when we do...we know it was meant to be. No coincidence, no fluke. Just a...*quirk* of the universe, which bursts out of the frothing sea of spirits beyond our simple human senses." More cheers, louder, and earsplitting whistles. "You know them," the recording boiled toward a big finish, "you love them...some of you more than might be healthy." The Charmed Quirks shrieked, waving their posterboards and banners, while the rest of the audience laughed at the friendly jibe. "On your feet, and prove yourselves worthy of the *magical* feats you are about to witness—for the *very last time* on this stage—ladies and gentlemen, the *Beau Regardez* gives you...the *Amazing Quirk*, and his lovely assistant—the *Mysterious Jade*, the Jewel of the East!"

Drowning out the last words of the recording, the audience unleashed screams and cheers, pounding on the seats, jumping up and down, jostling each other in a shoulder-to-shoulder throng that took one look at the Maximum Occupancy sign and laughed the laugh of swashbuckling heroes. Even *Bald Mountain*'s painful volume couldn't compete with the uproar crashing into the stage like a tsunami taking out the entire California coast.

In the noise and lights, the mysterious Jade flowed dramatically onstage, spryly guiding a tall full-length mirror with a golden frame. The mirror rolled on wheels beneath a flowing black skirt at the bottom. The shining surface faced the audience squarely, reflecting flashes of light and grinning faces as it skated across the stage.

Her expression ineffable, Jade reached center stage and spun the mirror once all the way around, showing nothing behind it. The crowd was still cheering. She turned the mirror again, but halfway round, exposing its dark wood-paneled back, the reflective mirror facing upstage away from the audience. With a sly smile, she walked behind the mirror; after a moment of nothing but music, lights and shouting, the mirror spun again, revealing Jade—now sitting on the Amazing Quirk's magic table, which had appeared from nowhere.

The audience went nuts. The full-on magical "appearance" of the table, right before their eyes, wasn't a trick they'd seen before.

Jade tilted her head subtly in acknowledgement, her trademark spectacles flashing in the colored lights, then hopped off and rolled the table downstage. Dancing gracefully back to the mirror, she again turned the reflective surface upstage, out of view, and hid behind it. Seconds later, Jade's hand reached out from one side and sent the mirror spinning away, revealing the Amazing Quirk beside her, blinking in the bright lights, but smiling broadly.

If the crowd was nuts before, they were raving lunatics at the sudden manifestation of the magician himself. The cacophony thundered overbearingly through the theatre and probably spilled out into most of Chelsea, if not the entire lower portion of Manhattan. The Amazing Quirk was barely audible as he declared his usual introduction: "Hello! I am the Amazing Quirk...and this is my *lovely* assistant, Jade, the Jewel of the East!"

Half the crowd shouted it along with him. The adoration pervading the room had an almost tangible effect on the Amazing Quirk's beaming face. He smiled his love right back at them as he and Jade took their poses to either side of the magic table, each illuminated by a sharp, bright spotlight that followed their every move. The glitter-glued Q on the front of the table glistened in the bright stage lights.

The Amazing Quirk drank in the applause for a bit, then raised his arms for quiet. Aside from a few uncontrollable yelps and shouts, the crowd loyally quieted down, waiting breathlessly to see what the magician and his lovely assistant had in store.

"It's been a ride, hasn't it?" the Amazing Quirk grinned. The crowd clapped and laughed, and he laughed with them. "Like our esteemed benefactor said, nothing lasts forever." He bowed to David Dennis in the front row, and paused for the audience to applaud graciously. The producer feigned coy modesty, but everyone knew he was lapping up the recognition like a thirsty dog. "But," the Amazing Quirk went on, "if you're gonna go out, you should go out with a bang!"

A clap of his hands produced an explosion of light and colorful glitter, which set off another round of applause as the Quirk leapt into a new pose and Jade spun the table dramatically forward to meet him.

"You've all seen us do a lot of tricks," said the Amazing Quirk. "And we've loved doing them for you." Jade pulled a black top hat from the table and held it up. She upended it, demonstrating that nothing came out, then turned it back upward. "You all know the recipe for rabbits," he smiled mischievously, and with a flick of his hand he produced a wriggling white mouse. More claps and calls responded as he held his hand over the top hat and dropped the little mouse in. "Though sometimes," he admitted, "when you mix mice together—" he conjured another mouse in the other hand and dropped it into the hat "—all you get is...more mice."

He and Jade reached into the hat and each pulled out a handful of mice, crawling over sweaty palms and each other and sniffing at the stuffy air in the theatre. Applause and laughter underlined a brief chanting chorus of: "Colby...Colby...Colby...." Plenty of fans knew Colby Cheese by name.

Obligingly, they dropped the mice into the hat, which Jade exchanged for a wide red cape from the magic table as the Amazing Quirk moved aside. She held up the cape, showing off both sides, then offered a corner to the magician. Pulling the cape taut, the hem fluttering between them, they smiled at the audience. The Amazing Quirk said: "We've made a lot of friends over the past few months...some of them *literally*."

Jade snapped the cape away, revealing the Quirk's long left hand cradling an adorably fluffy rabbit. Colby peered around nonchalantly, her little sides moving in and out with her fast breathing. Over laughter and cheers, the Amazing Quirk added, "We made them over and over and over...." Another wave of laughter rippled through the audience.

Jade took Colby Cheese from the magician and carried her back to the magic table. The Amazing Quirk continued warmly. "You've seen the classics," he said, conjuring a fan of cards from thin air, then making it disappear just as rapidly, "and some twists on the classics." Jade returned, twirling three wide metal rings on each arm. She tossed some to the Quirk, who linked them together quickly and "lassoed" Jade's wrist, pulling her in for a dramatic tango dip. Jade held the other rings in her mouth, smiling prettily and winking through her glasses as she threw one arm out in a balletic tableau. The audience clapped at the corny moves and posing. Somewhere in the theatre, a high-pitched voice yelled out: "I love you, Jade!" Plenty of agreement and cheering cascaded through the theatre.

Jade smiled coyly as the Amazing Quirk eased her back on her feet, and she skipped lightly to the table to put the rings back.

The cards suddenly fanned out in the magician's hand again. "Through it all," the Quirk said, and he tossed a card out to land neatly in David Dennis's lap, "you've all stuck with us." He sent another card spinning through the air to Mike the comedian, who clapped it to his chest with a yelp of surprise. The Amazing Quirk sent a genuine smile his way. "Even when," he said, sending another card out to one of the juggling girls, who easily snatched it out of the air. "We missed the target," the magician finished, throwing another card out and watching it flutter limply somewhere into the third row. He smiled sheepishly at the good-natured jeers that came back at him.

He fanned out the rest of the cards in his hand, their intricately illustrated backs to the audience. "Go ahead and pick it up," he said, and there was the rustle of movement in the third row. A pretty brunette held up the card and laughed. The Amazing Quirk winked at her: "Yeah, it's my cell phone."

That one got them laughing, and the Amazing Quirk turned the fan of cards around to reveal a message in neat, unbroken letters: *C A L L   M E.* "I wasn't *that* off-target," the magician remarked. The laughter doubled and carried through as he gave the brunette another wink and deftly disappeared the cards. Jade came sauntering back downstage and posed beside him.

"So we're pretty close, all of us," said the Amazing Quirk. "We think of *all* of you as one great, big...kinda dysfunctional...family!"

Laughter and cheers, the latter loudest in the seats commandeered by the Charmed Quirks, filled the theatre.

"Out of respect," the Quirk continued as the audience quieted, "we should tell you *why* we're leaving. We should tell you," his voice took on a spooky tone as he gazed archly from beneath lowered brows, "the whole story."

Oobs and *aabs* set just the right atmosphere, and laughter appropriately lightened it. The audience hung on every word.

"As you know, our mysterious Jewel of the East is the most magical thing on this stage." The magician looked fondly at his assistant, who faltered for just a moment, giving him a shy smile back. Quickly recovering, Jade performed an adequate pirouette, finishing with a glittering flash of metal as she threw one arm wide to reveal a sharp knife. "She was transformed by an ancient Eastern prince into a thing of beauty that will last...forever." There was a slight catch in his throat. Then, their actions timed flawlessly, they each took a deep breath—Jade tossed the knife up in the air, where it glittered and spun as she put out a hand. The Amazing Quirk grabbed her wrist and spun her in a flashy flamenco whirl, ending with his arm around her waist as he expertly caught the falling knife and plunged it into her bare side, above her tutu and below her bustier.

The audience gasped and shouted excitedly as the Mysterious Jade collapsed in the magician's arms—only to open her eyes and smile. The Quirk spun her out, and she neatly yanked the knife from her body. While applause thundered and fans squealed, she grasped the blade and threw it in an easy arc to the magician, who caught it, twirled it, then launched it straight down, where the tip bit into the stage and the knife quivered impressively. The blade was dark and shiny wet, but Jade wiped blood from her skin to reveal that she was unbroken and unmarked.

The Amazing Quirk walked around his assistant like he was reciting the specs on a prized classic automobile. "No blade can mar her beauty," he said, "no blow can crush her perfect skin. No poison can drain the life shining behind those mysterious glasses."

The cheers and calls continued unabated, not interrupting the performance, but only enhancing the anticipation and celebration. The magician gently—almost romantically—removed her glasses one stem at a time, and pulled them away. He turned them slowly in his fingers. They glinted in his spotlight. "Jade's glasses help her bear the ugliness in our world...a world one as beautiful as she was never meant to dwell in. But she won't need these anymore."

With an energetic grunt, he swung his hand through the air, empty fingers fluttering as his gaze followed the arc of the glistening spectacles. The audience lost track of them in the darkness of the house, but a pair of shouts rang out from one side, a dozen rows back. The Amazing Quirk looked directly into the spotlight and, with a flick of his hand, directed the spotlight operator to shine his light on the audience.

"All yours, guys," the magician told the two long-haired young men who stood bewildered in the spotlight. The shorter, fatter one clutched a familiar pair of glasses over his head, the lenses gleaming in the white light. The tall skinny one, a risible thatch of fuzz on his pointy chin, gave everyone a goofy grin and waved.

The crowd cheered the fortunate fans who got Jade's glasses as a souvenir, and the two guys straightened their silkscreened superhero T-shirts and sat down awkwardly. The spotlight flew back across the audience to land on the Amazing Quirk, who smiled out at the lucky pair. The applause died down, and his smile faded, his expression growing serious, even earnest.

"No," the magician said firmly, as if to convince himself as much as his audience, "the Jewel of the East is not meant for this world." He stood beside her and looked down at her sadly. "She's too beautiful, too magical, too...*wonderful* to be trapped in a rough, tough, mundane world like ours."

Sharp-eyed spectators noticed Jade's eyes flick briefly toward the magician before resuming their stoic gaze outward. It had been a long time since anyone had seen her on stage without her glasses; they'd simply become a part of her character. Without the big round lenses shielding her eyes, there was something exotic, almost alien, about her face.

The Quirk moved upstage to the mirror, his eyes on the audience at all times. "The prince's evil brother—you remember him—knew this all too well. That's why he kept her floating over his tower, bound by her magical, levitating chains, never to escape him...or this world that couldn't hope to hold on to beauty like hers."

He rolled the mirror downstage, keeping the reflection toward the audience. Jade stared at the crowd, unmoving except for her gentle breathing.

"I knew the deal when I met Jade," said the Amazing Quirk. "From the day I met and studied with the ancient mystics who helped me learn her secrets, I knew that Jade couldn't...be mine forever. I could only share her beauty with you for a little while." His face was tight with emotion. "One day, when time had passed, just like all comets blazing past our little world...she would have to soar back out to the heavens. She would have to return to the farthest reaches of other dimensions, where all heavenly bodies reside."

The audience was tensely quiet, only the barest whispers and murmurs betraying their bottled up excitement.

"And, as you've no doubt realized by now," the Quirk announced, "that time has come. The time has come for me to...let go. Because true love isn't about capturing another's heart. True love...is when you release their heart, to soar through the stars and find its own destiny."

The Charmed Quirks' hearts melted at the veiled but unsubtle revelation of the Amazing Quirk's love for Jade.

"I'm only a magician," said the Amazing Quirk. "Just a man. But Jade..."

He gracefully guided her in front of the mirror. She still faced the audience.

"Jade is a legend," the magician finished simply. His hands lingered for just a moment on her arm, tracing a path to her fingers and locking on for a moment. Jade squeezed his hand tight, and they let go. "Jade!" he declared. "Mysterious Jade, Jewel of the East!" He was smiling through tears. "I release you! I set you free!"

The magician turned his lovely assistant around, and she looked deeply into the mirror—then she reached out, palm to palm with her reflection...and disappeared.

A stunned, outrageous silence cut the audience's gasps short. It lasted for a full eight seconds. Someone in the middle rows actually sobbed quietly. Jade's empty spotlight wavered and wobbled for a moment, as if trying to find the missing assistant, before finally zooming away across the stage and shutting off.

An avalanche of applause broke, bombarding the room, louder than anything before it. The pressure of the sound itself beat against the thin, lanky frame of the magician who stood alone onstage with a distant smile on his boyish face. He dropped his arms to his sides and turned to address the audience; the volume dropped, but not by much.

"Ladies and gentlemen," said the magician, just loudly enough to be heard, "I am the Amazing Quirk. And I bid you...good night."

Without another word, he plucked the knife from the floor, then rolled the magic table and the tall mirror off stage as classical horns and strings in the sound system competed with the maelstrom of cheering and stomping in the audience. The spotlight followed the Amazing Quirk to the wings, then flickered off as he exited. The audience—smiling, laughing, crying, cheering, howling, clapping, jumping—watched the magician go, knowing they'd just witnessed the definition of magic...not only in the mystical or mythical sense, but in the deeper and more emotional sense that all human beings long to experience at least once in a lifetime.

CHAPTER TWENTY-NINE

Jenny Ng chucked her tutu on the beat-up easy chair and kicked off her high-heeled shoes. She didn't even bother to remove her leggings or bustier, just throwing her hoodie on over them and sliding into socks before she jammed her feet into her big black Doc Martens. She zipped up the hoodie and slipped her cell phone in one pocket. She hung her camera around her neck and absently ran her fingers through her hair. As she bent down by the instrument case on the floor, a voice coated in chocolate and centuries flowed across the room like syrup across a comic book geek's plate.

"It was a lovely show, Jenny."

Jenny turned—Caravel emerged from the dressing room mirror as she spoke. Her mirror image wandered idly and independently through the reflection of the room, brushing gingerly past Mirror Jenny, who stood still and gaped at her mirrored mentor, looking like a girl in Ed Sullivan's audience anxiously awaiting the Fab Four with near-hysterical anticipation.

Jenny smiled and sighed. "Thanks."

"I wish I'd seen the other shows," said Caravel. "I'm sure they were amazing."

"Only 'cause Calvin's pretty amazing...and we had the magic props," Jenny said bitterly. A thought struck her, and she searched Caravel's face. "You're not mad I used the mirror trick in front of everybody, are you?"

"People are very good at jumping to the obvious but entirely incorrect conclusions." Caravel smiled kindly. "They all know it was a mere trick— cleverness and misdirection."

"Smoke and mirrors," Jenny quipped.

"Even when it isn't," Caravel nodded. "*É bem*. It won't reveal anything. I'm not mad, Jenny."

"Cool." Jenny took her sword from the case. "You got my note."

"You left it last night, yes."

"Did you get Pauzok out?" Jenny asked. With the heavy explanations out of the way, it hadn't been tough to explain to Detective Monaghan the urgent need to get Pauzok out of the mental hospital. He'd come through big time with the exact address and even ward number, which Jenny had written out for Caravel and left on the reservoir wall in Wonderland late Tuesday night.

Caravel smiled again. "It's happening tonight. Soon." She nudged Jenny's tutu out of the way and sat down in the big easy chair, plainly enjoying the quiet mundanity of just sitting in a chair. "A small group of us will go there in the dark, and take Pauzok away with us."

"What will you do with him?"

"Who knows?" Caravel shrugged. "I'm not sure if his memory can be restored. And even if it can, I'm not sure if he can rejoin us. *You* are him, now. You have his horse, and his sword...I don't think you can give them back." She grinned uncertainly. "This sort of thing doesn't happen often— we don't have any rules on what to do with it."

"With me, you mean." Jenny patted herself down in a final checklist. "Will he be okay?"

"He'll be fine," said Caravel. "He'll be with us, if nothing else, unless he chooses to go elsewhere. To be honest, he has choices now that none of the rest of us do. In a way, I envy him."

"Me too," Jenny said firmly. She didn't want to be rude, but she squirmed uneasily at the seconds ticking away. "Caravel—"

"I know, *menina*," the beautiful Reaper said. "Go."

Jenny flashed her a quick, tight smile, and then wrapped her fingers around the blade of her sword. In an instant, she splashed into the dusty, refracted air of Wonderland. She jumped, startled, when she saw Caravel still standing beside her—but she was on the opposite side, a strangely off-tone Caravel, blurry around the edges. Mirror Caravel smiled pleasantly and nodded at the door of the Looking Glass dressing room. Jenny nodded back. "Thanks," she said, and she headed out.

The perpetual existence of Caravel's mirror image in Wonderland set Jenny's mind racing, wondering once again what happened to Mirror Jenny when Jenny wasn't looking. She supposed Mirror Jenny must be just as visible to other Grim Reapers in Wonderland as Mirror Caravel was to her. But that still left her wondering where her reflected avatar went when Jenny herself went Through the Looking Glass.

She dismissed the distraction, focusing on more pressing concerns. She'd been worried enough about Calvin's journey on the Smooth Road before their performance. Jenny had hidden the magician in Wonderland, center stage in the mirrored *Beau Regardez*, at the start of the comedic musical tribute to their act—but she hadn't anticipated Mike the comedian's song going on quite so long. Though Calvin knew what he was getting into, she wondered how in the world he managed to stand so still, so patient, waiting for her to bring him back for his big reveal. He'd been blind and deaf to everything, probably including the passage of time itself; the agonizing limbo he must have endured made Jenny's spirit ache. The fact that he was still able to jump right into his role when he appeared on stage only magnified Jenny's intense admiration and affection for him.

Jenny took a deep breath and moved on to the clever bit of her plan: she held her sword up alongside her head, the blade against her cheek. Its curved tip swept out just next to her eye, and through the shining metal she could see the real world beside her in the hall. She'd devised a quick and easy way to "watch" what was going on in the real world while safely hidden in Wonderland. Thanks to the arcane geometry of Wonderland physics, what she saw wasn't actually on the side of her body that intuition demanded, but was most certainly on the side of her body dictated by the rules of reflections, which made it easy to wander through the crowd as she emerged into the lobby. Trying not to flinch as reflected figures seemed to walk right through her took some getting used to, and actually seeing the darkened reflections of internal organs as they passed through the plane of the mirror was off-putting, but she steeled herself and kept the blade next to her eye, carefully scanning the crowd in the bright lights of the real lobby while double-vision superimposed the view over the dim, sepia version of the same room.

The lobby was more full than she'd ever seen, and crowds still poured through the theatre doors. *Beau* regulars, performers and fans alike, laughed and jabbered away, intoxicated by the extraordinary final act of the Amazing Quirk and Jade. Jenny couldn't hear them from her side of the Looking Glass, but their faces and gestures were animated enough to tell what they were going on about. The Charmed Quirks were the most animated of the lot; some were even crying and consoling each other over the romantic finale of their idols. Known but less familiar faces threaded through the crowd as well, from Callie—with her boyfriend and a bunch of other Empire Tech students—to Rob the Mutant God King with a handful of loyal Nerd subjects. The woman who'd interviewed Calvin and Jenny and David was there, along with a photographer who stared fiercely at the viewscreen of his expensive digital camera, jabbing buttons to flip through photos he'd taken of the show. Some people in nice suits were scattered here and there, folks with enough money to be unaware of the Chelsea theatre scene, but also enough money to require them to attend such a highly-touted Arts and Entertainment event. David Dennis—holding tight to Paul's hand in a disarmingly endearing way—was beaming with big apple-red cheeks, rubbernecking for a sign of where his star performers had disappeared to, but just as excited to be baffled by the mystery. Jenny's spotlight operator, Tim, was spreading his hands and shaking his head at small group of crew and performers, obviously insisting that he had no more clue than anybody else about how Jade had performed her vanishing act. Two pleasant women, one white and one black, were chatting up David and a couple of the more charming performers. They exuded elegance and intelligence.

Over in one corner, just past the cute brunette who had been targeted by the Amazing Quirk's flirtatious overtures, was Keith Heckler, conducting some flirtatious overtures of his own with a couple of perky blondes and a very tall Chinese girl. Not far away were Lyle and Lloyd, talking excitedly as Lyle conspicuously waved the shining spectacles about.

The fanboys were playing their roles very, very well.

Jenny walked over to them, smiling at how easy it was to navigate through the fans on this side of the mirror, where none of them existed. Positioning herself right next to Lyle and Lloyd, Jenny slowly swept the room, looking very intently at faces, and more intently at eyes.

She found what she was looking for near the doors leading into the theatre. A man and a woman stood and smiled slim, uninviting smiles, like Upper East Side blue bloods forced to endure the flatulence and noise of a subway ride down the Lexington line because their chauffeur called in sick. Jenny wouldn't call them a couple—they stood just a little too far apart, and had too tenuous a connection for that. They didn't look at each other, didn't talk to each other; they simply smiled their lukewarm smiles and watched the crowd patiently.

But not arbitrarily. Their eyes far too often shifted across the room to look right at Jenny—or rather, right at Lyle and Lloyd, who occupied the same position on the real world side of the mirror. It was possible she was mistaken, but Jenny had little doubt that the duo's eyes focused a little too much on the glasses that flashed in Lyle's plump little fingers. The man and woman didn't look directly familiar, but they certainly fit the *type* Jenny was expecting—nice Upper Middle Class people who would look right at home tasting wine and watching a polo match at the Raymonds' place in the Hamptons. The kind of people who smiled and cheered all around the Ice Cream Psycho in Carrie and Vincent's wedding pictures.

"Gotcha," Jenny whispered. Then she remembered that nobody could hear her. "Gotcha!" she declared triumphantly. She winced nervously at the infinitely empty echo of her voice.

The crowd suddenly shifted wildly, and though Jenny couldn't hear the cheering, she tilted the sword to pan her view. Calvin McGuirk, the Amazing Quirk, walked slowly and calmly into the lobby from the hallway. He had a complicated smile on his face, and his bright green eyes were clouded and distant with the hard-earned wisdom of much older men. He nodded and smiled, then said something that set the crowd off. He settled them down again with a wave of his hands, and offered some words, gesticulating with his lanky arms and long fingers.

As Calvin continued, Jenny scanned back to the man and woman by the door. Sure enough, their eyes were on Lyle and Lloyd, not the magician who held everyone else's attention. As far as Jenny was concerned, that clinched it. Still, her job was to stick to Lyle and Lloyd—and the glasses— not to *prevent* the thieves from carrying out their plans. She just wanted a clear idea of who to look out for, in case they tried anything dangerous; she wasn't about to let the fanboys take a bullet for her, either literally *or* proverbially.

Calvin must have finished, because the crowd erupted in applause. A quick glance at the magician showed him shaking hands with the two pleasant women David Dennis introduced to him. Jenny turned back to take in a view of Lyle and Lloyd. She noticed the cute brunette biting her lower lip anxiously before plunging into the crowd away from the fanboys. Lyle and Lloyd were putting on their dark trenchcoats, yanking their ponytails out from the collars, and buttoning themselves up. Lyle jumped happily, holding the glasses high over his head like a trophy—hamming it up a bit, but that would hopefully work to their advantage. The boys inched toward the outer doors of the lobby, overtly waving to other fans in the crowd, the specs still glittering in the overhead lights of the lobby. Then

Lyle stuffed the glasses in his coat pocket and followed his friend out the door.

In Wonderland, Jenny traced their reflected steps and went out her own less well-defined door. Out on the dark sidewalk, Rex stomped the ground impatiently. Jenny nodded and put one hand through his reins, guiding him along behind her.

Still holding the blade near her eye, she simultaneously saw the dark windswept Wonderland version of Eighth Avenue and the busy city street lit by neon and fluorescence in the real world. Lyle and Lloyd walked up the street, still nattering away at each other. Jenny felt like she was watching a silent movie, or the final moments of a buddy cop flick as the heroes strode away from the camera, their words quickly obscured by closing credits and inspiring rock guitar. It was a pain keeping her head turned to watch the fanboys walk in the reflection; she essentially had to jog sideways, looking at the blade over her shoulder. Hurrying away from the reflected fanboys in the sword brought her closer to where they actually were, and the reflection zoomed in accordingly.

A few blocks up, the boys paused at the corner, waiting for the light to change so they could cross Eighth. With no cars to yield to, Jenny forged ahead, leading Rex to the opposite corner and waiting for Lyle and Lloyd, watching them through the sword blade. Once they crossed the street, they walked jauntily into a brightly lit deli. Leaving Rex outside, Jenny followed them in.

There were only a handful of tables and chairs, along with a counter featuring a giant case of desserts, sandwiches and soups, and refrigerated shelves offering water, soda, and other refreshments. A friendly lady behind the counter smiled at the boys; she was short and round, with dark skin and dimples. Lyle grabbed a grape drink and requested a large cookie from the case; Lloyd had a soda and a giant pastry that might as well have been half a birthday cake. They paid and snagged an empty table where they tucked into their post-show meal. Jenny knew for a fact that they'd had very large dinners; she'd eaten with them. She idly wondered if portly Lyle's eternal curse was to be best friends with a man who could not gain weight.

It wasn't long before the man and woman from the theatre walked in, smiling tightly at the harsh white light of the deli. The woman took a seat at a table not far from the fanboys. She wore a plain dark suit with matching boots and a stylish gray coat. The man, wearing a thick coat over a basic suit-and-tie combo, bought two coffees and sat opposite the woman.

They drank their coffee slowly, carefully and specifically *not* looking over at Lyle and Lloyd.

With perfect timing—Jenny would have hugged him if she could have—Lyle pulled the glasses out of his pocket and examined them casually. The boys traded the glasses back and forth, making comments to each other and tapping on the lenses and frame, obviously discussing the Cool Factor of being in possession of the Mysterious Jade's mysterious spectacles, or perhaps debating how much they could get for them on eBay. If they were following the plan, they were also speaking a little too loudly.

The moment finally came when Lloyd, fingering the glasses curiously, placed them on the table so he could finish off the rest of his pastry. Though she couldn't hear anything, the click of the glasses hitting the table rang in Jenny's head with all the subtlety of a rock falling from the sky.

The boys finished eating and were sipping their drinks when they got excited over something, snapping back and forth over some inane point of trivia, probably involving the precise Pantone color of an anime character's hair. Hands waved and fists shook, lips snarled and eyes flashed, and the fanboys lit into each other over whatever uncontroversial subject riled them up. Finally, Lyle stood up and firmly announced something, stabbing a finger out the window. Jenny hoped to whatever divinities might actually exist that he wasn't *actually* suggesting they step outside. Lloyd stood up, a head taller than his friend, and threw his arms up in exasperation. Still arguing, they started sweeping up the remnants of their meal: plates, napkins, crumbs and bottles. So intent were they on their fiery argument that they didn't even look down as they cleared the table. They returned their plates to the counter, tossed napkins into the trash, and marched outside with their bottles, surely about to do serious battle with the modern geek's weapon of choice: the Internet.

The cute little lady behind the counter hid a bemused smile behind her hand, and continued wiping cutting boards and shelves. She exchanged a smile with the equally short and round man washing dishes. Neither of them looked at the man and woman sitting at the table, sipping coffee. That man and woman stared right at each other, but their eyes widened in surprise—they couldn't believe their luck.

On the table, abandoned by the frenzied fanboys, were the forgotten spectacles.

Trying to be discreet, the man stood and returned to the counter, making some small request or comment to the lady behind it. Looking around casually, the woman at the table saw nobody watching; in an easy, fluid motion, she reached over and swept the glasses off the table. She put them in her coat pocket, and almost immediately rose and called out to the man. After a brief exchange, the man smiled at the lady behind the counter and dismissed his own request, then headed for the door with the woman he'd come in with. She nodded at him once, and he followed her out the door.

Jenny grinned. The trap was sprung.

She went out the blurry door and checked the view in her sword blade. The man and woman were at the curb, about to cross the street. Jenny clicked her tongue for Rex to follow her; his rolling snort suggested compliance.

The thieves didn't go far; they walked into a parking garage on Twenty-Third less than two blocks away. Jenny and Rex followed them in and waited as the valet went to get their car. She wondered if the thieves were as anxious to get moving as she was. Waiting in Wonderland for things to happen in the real world felt like waiting for a feather to sink in a jar of honey.

Finally, the valet returned with their car; spying through the sword blade, both her eyeball and her arm growing weary, Jenny saw a sparkling white Audi pull up. The scruffy valet got out, and the man and woman got in—he was in the driver's seat. Jenny took the opportunity as the man readjusted his seat and mirrors, and scrambled to climb into Rex's saddle and position the sword to reacquire her view of the garage. She honed in on the Audi just as the woman put a cell phone away in her pocket and fastened her seatbelt, saying something to her partner. He didn't respond, but put the car in drive and pulled out.

Jenny patted Rex's flank and dug her heels in. He immediately cantered out of the garage and followed the car. Anything Jenny saw through the mirrored blade, Rex would know; she had no need to guide him, as long as she kept track of the white Audi herself. Still, as convenient as Wonderland Transit was, and as convenient as it was keeping track of the real world through her sword, it was maddening to realize she had to match whatever pace her targets set, rather than racing ahead to their unknown destination. It was frustrating; the thieves might take hours for a trip that would take Rex only twenty minutes, since he traveled in a more "as the crow flies" or "as the Super Ghost Horse gallops" route. But unless she followed patiently behind the thieves, she wouldn't know where they went. Grumbling silently, she resigned herself to a potentially long journey.

375

Trotting slowly alongside the traffic-besieged car, Rex shared her annoyance with a noisy, throaty sigh.

The Audi wound its way up to Thirty-Fourth Street, then east to the Queens Midtown Tunnel. Jenny narrowed her eyes—Long Island was the likely destination, which meant excessive traffic and time. She rubbed her temple gently with the flat of her blade, and kept watching as the Audi rolled down into the tunnel. Rex followed in the Wonderland version of the tunnel, which was spiderwebbed with strange beams and arcs of light. They'd never used the tunnels before; running across the surface of rivers was so much easier. Both Jenny and the stallion started feeling claustrophobic in the strangely lit place, and it was a relief to ascend and exit, following the Audi onto the expressway. Traffic wasn't too heavy, but even so, the Angel of Death and her Pale Horse itched to cut loose, knowing they couldn't, limited as they were by the speed of the car they were chasing in a parallel reality. It wasn't hard to assume that this wasn't an officially sanctioned use of their abilities, which was probably why it felt like such a hassle. It was like trying to use a howitzer to assemble a brick wall—with enough time and technique, you might get it done, but it was clearly not the right tool for the job.

They followed the expressway for over an hour before zigging, then zagging to continue on another highway. After nearly an hour, the Audi forked off to a heavily wooded road, dotted with scattered lots, small buildings and driveways. After a few more turns, they followed the white car up a narrow road between the trees, where it took a sharp left into a long driveway. The driveway snaked back far from the main road to a large house nestled in among the trees.

It wasn't one of the *Lifestyles of the Rich and Famous* type houses she'd expected, but it was large, modern, and very well lit, with a separate garage at the end of the driveway and several cars already parked alongside it. Jenny was not at all surprised to see the Raymonds' sleek black BMW among them.

The Audi parked and the thieves got out. Jenny leaned over to dismount, and was so focused on keeping track of the pair in her blade's reflection that she didn't even notice when she only barely stumbled on the ground. Rex started pacing as Jenny followed the spectacle thieves up the walk to the front door.

They must have called on the way over, or the occupants of the house heard the car drive up, because the door opened without a knock or a bell. In the doorway, the Ice Cream Psycho glared coldly, wearing a golf shirt and khakis as usual. The man in the suit gave a little attitude back; the woman said nothing. The Ice Cream Psycho let them in, then peered outside before shutting the door firmly.

Jenny needed to see what was going on. More importantly, she needed to *hear* what was going on. Most importantly, she needed to see if she could find the rest of Calvin's props—especially the magic hole and the wand, which seemed like they might do the most damage—and steal them back.

She looked back at Rex. He tossed his mane, stomping all four feet, then stared at her solemnly. She nodded back, and walked confidently through the mirrored house's open-and-closed door.

The front hall was square, with a high ceiling, and halls led off in three directions. A staircase angled upward over the hall opposite the front door, leading to an unseen second floor. Where the outside of the house was brightly lit with big square lamps, the lights inside were almost all turned off. There wasn't much difference between the dull brown Wonderland version Jenny roamed and the real world version she saw through her sword. Down the opposite hall, at the end, a steady yellow light cast a square shadow down the hallway. Jenny followed the hall and came out into a fancy sitting room.

Her sword was redundant, since one whole wall of the room was a giant mirror. Past a few shelves and a squatting credenza, Jenny could clearly see the real world sitting room on the other side. Comfortable furniture, tiled floors, a striped area rug, and opulent lighting set the tone, but Carrie Raymond herself, wearing a flowing lemon-colored gown over her huge pregnant belly, dominated the room.

Carrie's calm and charismatic smile no longer seemed all that friendly; the other people in the room looked cowed into submission by her bare teeth. Jenny had to admit that there was something fearsome in Carrie Raymond's dark and stormy eyes, like an ocean tempest just getting started.

The man in the suit stood meekly before Carrie, his hands clasped in front of him, while his partner handed over the spectacles. The Ice Cream Psycho stood by the hall, just inside the room, watching everything through glowering, narrow eyes. Several other people were seated or standing around the room: a tall, thin man with a shining bald head, a plump woman with black hair and a scarlet dress, a blonde lady with enough makeup to drive a televangelist's wife into a jealous rage...and a skinny younger man with olive skin, slick black hair and a soul patch under his lower lip.

It was the Beatnik who'd stabbed Jenny in the alley. He sat on the edge of an overstuffed ottoman, hunched over with his arms on his thighs, staring sullenly at the striped rug.

Carrie Raymond plucked the glasses from the woman's outstretched hand and smiled, showing a bit too many teeth as she examined her prize. She said something breezy to the Beatnik, who nodded and continued staring at the floor, his eyes gray with sullen weather.

Jenny desperately wanted to hear the conversation. She scanned the room and saw another exit in the far corner; she went through its Wonderland counterpart and found herself in a room with wide, curved windows arching up and over her head to form a glass ceiling. The wrought iron furniture included little round tables and long lounge chairs. Jenny used her sword trick to peek into the real room, and even leaned into another adjoining room—a big kitchen extending to the front of the house—to make sure there was nobody there. Leaning back against the wall, just inches from the archway back into the sitting room, she put a hand on the sword blade and gave a little mental push, spilling outward into the real world. The pounding rush of Wonderland's swarming atmosphere transmuted into light classical music and Carrie's fluting voice.

"...only matters that we *have* them, Bruce," Carrie finished saying. "If we all are bound by our love in a single and glorious union, then individual accomplishments are shared by us all."

"Oh, yes," said one of the women. Jenny couldn't tell which one.

"We're all one," said a man in an old and cracked voice. That had to be the tall bald man.

Carrie said: "I'm so grateful to Warren and Mary for bringing us the eyes, just as I am grateful to you and our other friends for bringing us the rest of the artifacts." Jenny could almost *hear* the shark-like smile behind those words. Carrie's sing-song voice seemed less regal and charming, now, and more sugary and deceptive. "We are one day closer to bringing peace and joyous harmony to all our brothers and sisters. That we needed Warren and Mary to return for the eyes is just another reminder of how we are all connected, relying on one another in a great spiritual circle. Where you end, I begin, and where I end, he begins, and so on..."

"Everything is circular," said another woman.

"Endings and beginnings are the same," said the first unidentified woman.

"There is no renewal without completion," said the tall man.

378

If the Raymonds seemed a bit Stepfordish before, Jenny knew now this whole gang had chugged some off-color Kool-Aid. She thought most suicide cults limited their death count to Members Only; these people, though, were aiming to cheerfully and lovingly obliterate all life on Earth. She was almost embarrassed that the fanboys had to point out the obvious, even if it was only obvious in hindsight.

The sun room she stood in was lit only by moonlight and a few ornate torch lamps in the back yard outside; a nightlight in the kitchen didn't offer much illumination, and the archway from the sitting room cast an oblong shaft of light across the lounge chairs and stone floor. Jenny slid slowly down the wall, achingly careful not to bang her sword as she went.

"Now, with everything accounted for, I think our All Hallow's Eve ceremony is right on schedule," Carrie burbled happily. "We'll be at our house—Vincent has cleared a lovely area in the back."

"We don't mind holding it here," said one of the women.

"Certainly," said the tall man. He sounded perpetually on the verge of coughing. "It would be our honor—"

"No, thank you," Carrie said, a sharp edge cutting into her usual gracious melody. "That's very sweet of you, Eric, Melinda, but we really do have everything being prepared at our house. You'll each bring the artifact you've been holding on to for us. We'll have a lovely view of the ocean, and it's supposed to be a beautiful night. We've already bought plenty of wine, and we've arranged things with the caterers—thanks for Peg's number, Vivian, she's *wonderful.*"

"Of course, Carrie, anything I can do," replied the woman who, by process of elimination, wasn't Melinda or Mary.

Jenny shuddered; these people discussed their Destroy the World party the way they might discuss arrangements for a bar mitzvah. Safely and silently reaching the floor, she shifted to the edge of the archway to spy on the room without being seen. Bruce the Beatnik had his back to her, and blocked most of her view of Carrie. The others in the room were in clear view, though Warren and Mary, the ones who had stolen the glasses, blocked Jenny's angle on the front hallway, so she couldn't see the Ice Cream Psycho.

"Now," Carrie began, moving to rise. Bruce stood immediately and helped her up. "There's still so much to be done! We do need to have everything ready."

"It will be a glorious ending," said the woman in scarlet, whom Jenny recognized as Vivian from her voice. That made the blonde with the makeup Melinda, tall bald Eric's wife, the lady of the house.

"A joyous beginning," said Mary, the woman in the dark suit.

"Our circle completed," her partner Warren added.

"Consuming itself," said Mary.

"A perfect unity," Carrie beamed.

Eric nodded. "All in one."

"Consumed by love," said Melinda, taking his hand.

The entire group echoed, "Consumed by love."

A shiver went down Jenny's spine. *These people are fucking crazy*, she realized.

She had only a split second to react to a flash of movement from the shadowy kitchen as a thick hand roughly grabbed her shoulder. Jenny yelped involuntarily as the Ice Cream Psycho dragged her to her feet; her sword clattered against the wall and fell to the floor.

"Lawrence?" Carrie called.

"It's the girl!" the Ice Cream Psycho snarled, violently pinning Jenny's arms behind her.

Carrie gasped prettily as Lawrence the Psycho manhandled Jenny through the archway. "Jenny!" she exclaimed. She sounded more like a birthday girl pleasantly surprised by an unexpected guest than a cult leader unpleasantly surprised by an intruder. "Have you been here all along?" Her inviting smile was a hundred times more terrifying than any steely-eyed scowl.

Jenny was suitably terrified. It didn't help knowing she was indestructible and immortal; her fear of Carrie Raymond was visceral, even primal. She wanted to say something cool and calm, playing the hero under pressure, but she just stared back. Lawrence the Ice Cream Psycho held her arms so tight he nearly wrenched them out of their sockets.

"Have you come to join us, dear?" Carrie asked. She held up the glasses and smiled playfully. "Or did you come for these?"

Jenny looked at the glasses and nervous laughter bubbled in her throat. It came out in a strangled vibrato as she replied: "I want Calvin's stuff back." She put more confidence into her voice than she had, with none left over to bolster her paralyzed expression. She was once again acutely aware that her unbreakable body and unendable life would be no advantage if these lunatics tied her up or trapped her somewhere. She thought of Pauzok locked in a psych ward, living forever after all of humanity was wiped out; Jenny was horrified at the thought of meeting the same interminable fate.

Carrie's laugh rang like bells. "Jenny, dear, those items were never Calvin's in the first place," she said gently.

Her companions chuckled and murmured in agreement, shaking their heads at the silly little girl who didn't want to destroy the world.

"They're very old, you know," Carrie explained helpfully. "They've been around for thousands of years...maybe more."

"I don't care," Jenny snapped back. Her mind raced; fear fogged her thoughts. If she could get her sword, or reach the mirrored wall, she could escape.

"Oh, Jenny," Carrie said like a parent teasing a sulking child. "If only you knew what I know! The books I've read, the stories I've learned. There's so much more to life than you might think!"

"Then why do you want to end it?" Jenny demanded.

"Endings are just the start of beginnings," Carrie replied, infuriatingly calm.

Black-haired Vivian smiled broadly at Jenny. "Death is just the road to new life," she said cheerfully.

"Everything is circular," Eric and Melinda said, eerily at the same time.

Lawrence tightened his grip as Jenny struggled. He looked at Bruce the Beatnik and growled: "Get her sword. On the floor." He jerked his head back toward the sun room.

Carrie Raymond put a hand to her cheek and smiled happily. "Oh, she brought her sword!" She looked at Jenny excitedly. "I've been wondering about that sword, Jenny. 'Ancient Chinese secret, hmm?'" she teased.

Jenny said nothing. Bruce carried the sword in from the sun room. He looked at Jenny coldly as he took his place beside Carrie.

With a little sigh of delight, Carrie ran a finger along the sword blade. "You see, Jenny, I'm something of an expert on the very...very...old," she said. "And this sword...." She took it from Bruce, hefting it experimentally and regarding the blade with a trained eye. "This sword is even older than that." She looked at Jenny slyly. "Isn't it, dear?"

Jenny clenched her jaw and glared. Her shoulders were numb in Lawrence's iron grip.

"Eric, you have a safe, yes?" Carrie asked.

Eric nodded. "Of course, Carrie," he said, "I'd be honored."

"Thank you, dear. You can put this in there," said Carrie, handing him the sword.

He smiled at Jenny—his smile was repulsively friendly. "I'll take good care of it, young lady," he promised.

These people never matched their tone of voice or expression to what they were doing. Jenny felt like she'd landed in some backwards world even more reversed than the Wonderland past the mirrors.

Lawrence, at least, made sense to her. The Ice Cream Psycho wore his cold, ruthless anger on his sleeve and in his face. She wrestled with him, trying to break free, but he was surprisingly strong for a pudgy middle-aged man.

Eric walked out with the sword, and the rest of the cult members gathered around Jenny as if she were a party guest sharing the latest gossip. Except for Bruce and Lawrence, they all wore horrifyingly sweet smiles. Bruce's face was tight and controlled; while she couldn't see Lawrence behind her, she knew his face was still cold as ice and hard as steel.

"Now," said Carrie, "we certainly can't put *you* in a safe, can we dear?" The group laughed at her adorable joke. "No, we'll need to find someplace much safer than that."

"Why?" Jenny demanded. "You're going to kill us all anyway. Why not just kill me now?"

"Don't be crass, Jenny," Carrie said glibly. "We're not killers. We love you. We love all our brothers and sisters in this world."

Jenny mentally swore, wishing they'd taken the bait. If she got the chance to play dead, escape would be a simple matter of time and opportunity. "Then why are you blowing them up, or wiping them out, or whatever?" Jenny asked desperately. "Why are you trying to kill every...to destroy it all?"

"Oh, dear, you don't really understand at all, do you?" Carrie shook her head patronizingly. "It's not—"

Jenny kicked out, but Lawrence yanked her back and she missed Carrie wildly. "Don't care, don't care, don't care," she insisted. "You're fucking crazy. You're *all* fucking crazy!"

They laughed.

The worst part was: it wasn't Crazy Laugh. It was Oh You Poor Deluded Girl Laugh. They pitied her. Angry tears burned in her eyes. She'd never liked being laughed at, but this was far worse than a bunch of bitchy girls in a junior high locker room showing off training bras five years before she'd developed even a *hint* of breasts. For the first time in her life, Jenny knew what it felt like to actually want to beat the everloving shit out of somebody. It felt deep, and vital, and strong—even liberating.

A scream erupted from her throat that she didn't recognize as her own. Pounding her boot on the toe of Lawrence's canvas sneaker, she pulled harder than any survival instinct might have allowed, feeling a sickening yank and crunch as her left arm popped out of its socket, dangling by her side. With Grim Reaper control of her own disembodied limbs, she could still form a tight fist, and she whirled with all her strength, swinging her loose arm like a hammer and watching her fist smash into Lawrence's face.

The cultists backed hastily away from Jenny at the center of their circle. Bruce stood loyally before Carrie, protecting her from the crazy Kung Fu chick.

Lawrence fell to his knees, catching himself on the ottoman and holding his battered and bleeding face. Jenny fixed her blazing eyes on Carrie; she felt the familiar scratchy, squirmy feeling in her shoulder, and the cultists watched as her dangling arm twisted around and snapped back into place with an audible *pop*.

Carrie caught her breath and gazed coyly at Jenny over Bruce's shoulder. "Oh, Jenny," she purred, "you've got secrets of your own, haven't you?"

Jenny darted forward; the older cultists scattered, but Bruce shifted to block her from Carrie. He misjudged her goal, though—Jenny spun past the Beatnik and dove into the long mirrored wall. She barely had a moment to register Mirror Jenny's loyally outraged expression before she shifted back into Wonderland and landed heavily on the floor.

Tears of anger streamed down her face, which just made her angrier. She'd lost her sword, she'd tipped her hand, and—going by what Carrie had said—Calvin's magic props were distributed among various members of the Country Club Cataclysm Cult, meaning the hole and wand might be anywhere in the Tri-State area. The only thing she knew for sure was that the props would all be gathered at the Raymonds' house in the Hamptons, where they'd have "a lovely view of the ocean," on Halloween night.

She punched the floor futilely, trying to vent her frustration. Looking back through the mirror, she saw the cultists looking around in amazement, scurrying this way and that to search for her. Warren and Vivian were up close to the mirror, feeling its surface, looking for hidden catches or passageways while Melinda shook her head and shouted at them, obviously insisting that her house had no secret doors. Mary was by the hallway, calling for Eric. Lawrence was getting back to his feet, still holding his head and wincing—the entire side of his face, from temple to jaw, was bumpy and bruised, and there was a nasty gash that leaked blood down to his chin and neck. Bruce looked around suspiciously, posing near Carrie, waiting for Jenny to reappear out of nowhere and attack his gorgeous leader.

Carrie Raymond looked thoughtfully and calmly at the mirror, almost directly at Jenny. If her gaze shifted just slightly, Jenny would have been paranoid that the woman could actually *see* her in Wonderland, penetrating the Looking Glass barrier with charismatic, calculating blue eyes.

But no—Carrie's gaze swept the mirror, reflecting the chill that crept through Jenny's body. A tiny smile quirked one corner of the sinister beauty's lips as she rubbed her round belly idly.

Jenny shook herself and thought madly. If the sword was in a safe, she had no immediate way to get it. A copy of the safe *might* exist in Wonderland, if it had been in the house long enough, but there was no guarantee that it was big enough to get into, or that there was a mirror inside through which she could travel. For now, she had no clear way to recover her sword. She wasn't thrilled, but she made an executive decision to get back to her friends and work out their next move.

Standing up, she glared furiously back at Carrie Raymond through the mirror. The woman still stood, watching, preternaturally calm. Jenny scowled and hissed: "I'm coming back for my sword, you bitch."

The word *bitch* echoed viciously in the thumping wind of Wonderland.

CHAPTER THIRTY

It was October Twenty-Ninth—two days until the swanky party in the Hamptons that would bring about the End of the World—and Jenny Ng's makeshift Cultbuster squad was on pins and needles. The loss of Jenny's sword, and the knowledge that they had no way of locating all of Calvin's props until the apocalyptic soirée itself, had them working overtime to devise a Plan A, a Plan B, and various plans C through M, including sub-plans to account for sub-contingencies that might come up within the framework of the actual lettered plans. Lyle and Lloyd had taken the nick-of-time plans in stride, smiling sagely. "That's how these things always work," said Lloyd, as his round friend nodded emphatically.

On Monaghan's advice, Jenny and Calvin had contacted a friend of the detective's—actually a former collar and informant—to employ his unique set of skills, though they were careful not to give him too much detail. Jenny and Calvin weren't completely sure they could trust the skinny old man with a receding hairline and thin mustache who introduced himself as "Hinkley," but they were sure that neither of them knew how to crack a safe, and they didn't buy the fanboys' claims that they could learn how online. Getting Jenny's sword back might not be top priority, but it would certainly make Plans D through H easier, and plans A through C absolutely depended on having the sword. The closer they stayed to the beginning of the alphabet, the greater their chances of success would be. Since success in this case meant "saving everybody in the world from certain doom," they wanted to at least *try* to get the sword back into play.

Keith Heckler had managed to work out a few connections for his end of the plan, and was badly in need of a nice white shirt and black pants that didn't look like they were painted on his fitness trainer physique. Calvin finally pulled himself away from the hundred sheets of college-ruled paper laid out on Heckler's floor—each with plans, contingency plans, sub-contingency plans, and exhaustive lists of stuff that might come in handy for those plans—to go with Heckler and pick up a few things.

Jenny's trip to the Hamptons with their shifty safecracking associate was planned for the next day—the equipment he required took at least a few days to scrounge up at whichever seedy underworld K-mart supplied that kind of thing. With everything she could realistically do at the moment actually taken care of, Jenny had one more thing she wanted badly to do.

"I know it's important," Calvin said. He held her hand tightly. "But what do we do if something happens while you're gone?"

"You have my cell," Jenny told him. "I won't be more than a couple hours away. Whatever happens, going to that party and stopping them is Number One. Even if I'm dead in a ditch—"

"You can't die."

"—but even if I *can*, whoever of us is still alive has to finish this." She grinned. "Even if it's Lyle and Lloyd."

He couldn't argue, and didn't want to anyway. He hugged her close and kissed the top of her head. Jenny smiled and left through the mirror in Heckler's bathroom.

Less than two hours later, she rode Rex across the Betsy Ross Bridge into Philadelphia. Seeing the familiar sights and shapes of her hometown in the fractured sepia-tone of Wonderland gave her a spooky feeling, like returning to the hustle and bustle of a favorite vacation city only to find a ghost town. Jenny knew there were cars and people zooming by on the real streets, but without her sword, she caught only glimpses in the reflections on store windows and shiny façades, and those just looked like ghostly slideshows mocking her with memories of what once was. She felt lonely, out of place, and way too old. The phrase *You can never go home again* made sense for the first time: you *can* go home again, she realized, but once you're there, it can't ever be the same place you left.

Rex's hoofbeats echoed hollowly on the Looking Glass version of Spring Street. Jenny felt a lump rising, not quite at throat level, but just behind her breastbone and making good time on its way up the esophagus. She passed by dim echoes of familiar shops and restaurants, real estate agencies and grocers, and the Chinese Christian church that always made her wonder how Far East immigrants had been convinced by European transplants to believe in the divinity of a Middle Eastern prophet.

She gulped as she saw the two-storey building where she'd spent most of her pre-adult life after her father had died. Rex whickered gently; he walked to the front steps and knelt forward. Jenny tried her best, but the gravity of the moment teamed up with actual gravity and sent her tumbling to the ground. The horse respectfully kept quiet.

Jenny got to her feet and rubbed Rex's muzzle. "Be right back," she whispered. Then she went up the stairs and into the foyer.

The old apartment was on the second floor. Even when her hips had started feeling the years and mileage, Hua Yao Ng had refused to trade with the friendly Chinese man one floor down, and she still made the trek up and down at least three times each day. Jenny's mother was a proud woman, for those values of proud which also strongly implied *stubborn*.

Jenny smiled wistfully, trying to control the tide washing over her as she climbed the stairs. Walking up *this* particular flight of stairs in Wonderland gave the whole mirror world a hazy, dreamlike quality. She reached the top and went to the second door on the left...then realized her mistake and went across the hall to the second door on the right. Reorienting herself to the reflected geography was harder than ever in a place so firmly engrained in her muscle memory.

The apartment was just as she remembered, if smaller. It was a good-sized two-bedroom, with a den that her brother Peter had claimed as his room and their mother had reclaimed as a den when he'd gone off to college. The aching sameness of the place made Jenny want to cry; nothing had really changed much in ten years, to the point where even some of the odd pieces of junk or art—or some knick knacks that could be considered both—carved nearly substantial echoes of themselves into the tough four-dimensional surface of Wonderland. Near the kitchen door, the squat statue of a smiling, pot-bellied tiger was clear enough to make out the stripes on its face, though not its actual expression. Jenny realized it probably hadn't moved more than an inch in the past decade, giving the Smooth Road plenty of time to render a sketchy, smeared doppelgänger.

Jenny went into the bathroom, nearly turning the wrong way into her old bedroom first—she shied away from the room where she'd spent her formative years, wary of the torrent of emotion that might drown her. In the bathroom, she saw the old familiar fixtures, though reversed, and she peered out at the real world through the mirror. She figured she could shift back to the real world, sneak out, and knock, as if she had just arrived for a visit.

She put her palm on the mirror and slipped through, feeling the pressure on her ears release as the customary white noise of home settled into a dull buzz. It had never hit her so strongly before, how familiar places have their own ambient sound along with sights and smells—an invisible, unhummable tune that simply says: *You are here.* She hopelessly tried to memorize the silent music, as if she could store it away for a rainy day centuries from now. She wondered if it would make any difference to her then. Immortality put too many variables on the field—an infinite number of them, in fact—and prediction became an unwinnnable game.

Walking to the beat of that undetectable song, she went out and down the hallway, the difficulty of orienting to the reflected apartment matched by the ease of reorienting to the real thing. Former residences have unmistakable contours and unforgettable anatomy, like the bodies of long-time lovers. Jenny casually avoided the creaky spot on the hallway floor and headed for the door on a swift and quiet mission of stealth.

"Nearly give me a heart attack."

Jenny jumped fully a foot in the air, at risk of suffering a heart attack herself if she hadn't already been dead, and whirled to see her mother sitting on the couch, embroidering red thread into dark blue cloth. Hua Yao Ng looked like she always did: short, square, and more indestructible than any Angel of Death could hope to be. Her black hair—either still ungrayed, or surreptitiously colored—was pulled into a tight bun, smooth and sleek, not a single stray strand. She didn't even look up, focused on her embroidery, her mouth holding the tiniest trace of a smile.

"Why you no call, tell me you coming?" asked Hua Yao. She was perfectly capable of speaking proper English when she cared to, but frequently preferred sticking it to native English speakers who thought there was something magically necessary about articles, noun declension, and verb conjugation, even when they thoroughly understood her without those ingredients.

"Hi, Mom," Jenny said, ignoring the Automated Maternal Dithering and moving to hug her mother.

Hua Yao embraced her daughter quickly but warmly, then resumed her work, thin knobby fingers swimming like eels over the embroidery which appeared to practically stitch itself. She didn't need to watch to keep her fingers in line—they knew their job—and instead looked archly at Jenny, who sat down on the chair by the couch. "You're very thin. You eating?"

Jenny rolled her eyes, but relished it, like she was singing along with a favorite song she hadn't heard in years. "Yes, Mom." She backtracked to cover her entrance. "I, uh, had to use the bathroom first or I would've said 'hi.'"

"So you climb in the window," said Hua Yao. "We have perfectly serviceable front door, you know."

"I know," Jenny said, "I came in through—"

"And I been sitting here whole time."

"—the window," Jenny hastily revised. "So I...wouldn't...um. I forgot my keys."

"Mm," her mother said absently. The embroidery stopped short. "You want food? I make lunch."

"Uh, no, wait..."

Ignoring Jenny's protests, Hua Yao Ng put her embroidery aside and marched into the kitchen, instantly assembling pots and pans and water and a mix of ingredients that smelled too good to refuse. Jenny didn't strongly identify with her Chinese heritage—she and Peter were thoroughly Americanized—but there was something about her mother's authentic Chinese cooking, with fresh Chinatown ingredients from the local markets, that called to her tastebuds and settled her stomach the way that the standard Chinese take-out she'd gotten used to never could. *Real* Chinese cooking—the Cantonese style Jenny grew up with, not the faint imitation most American restaurants served—wasn't greasy or overpowering, and it never, ever left her hungry an hour later.

In minutes, Jenny and Hua Yao were tasting and stirring, teasing and chatting, falling into an easy, routine conversation among steaming pots. It had been years since Jenny had shared a moment like this with her mother; it had been almost eight months since she'd visited at all, and she kicked herself for not making it a priority. Being dead had given her at least *that* much perspective. Hua Yao pulled her usual trick, skating across the top of the conversation like a waterbug, never poking through the surface, but keeping a composite eye on the rushing waters beneath. She'd practically raised Jenny and her brother that way, always fully aware of their lives, always letting them get on with it offering only the slightest of nudges, and those only if they were wandering too near the edge. Jenny wondered how much she really got away with as a typical teenager—most likely, her mother was aware of every prank, transgression, and stupid mistake. Tersely practical Hua Yao Ng had a lot in common with deceptively stammering Detective Monaghan; both walked their beats without advertising how much their sharp eyes spotted.

They'd already eaten half a meal before the cooking was even done. Setting plates down on the dining room table, they brought out what remained in serving bowls. Jenny reflexively took the same seat where she'd spent every home-cooked meal, on her mother's right; across from Jenny was Peter's seat, and across from Hua Yao was the seat that had always been empty. They'd moved into the apartment after her dad died.

"So that it for the magic show, then?" Hua Yao continued the conversation from the kitchen.

Jenny hadn't offered details, but she'd mentioned the Amazing Quirk's last performance. "Yeah," she said, "but it's okay. I mean, it was cool for the summer, but I've got...you know...more important stuff I need to do."

"Yes, I know," her mother said, gently teasing. "Jenny need to *save* the world."

Jenny froze. "What?"

"Always going on about how you change the world," said Hua Yao, "taking your pictures. Make everyone look deep in the mirror and see what they are like."

"Right," Jenny let out a breath she didn't realize she was holding. "I was just a stupid kid."

"You a very good photographer, that's what you were," her mother corrected her.

Jenny smiled, embarrassed. "Thanks, Mom."

"You still taking pictures?"

"Oh! Um, yeah," said Jenny. Her bag hung on a chair in the kitchen; she went fishing in it and returned with her camera. "Calvin bought this for me. It's a really good camera."

"Look expensive," said Hua Yao, eyeing it.

Jenny laughed. "It's okay, Mom. We're doing pretty well right now."

"Oh," Hua Yao said brightly, "it's good to know you a *We* now."

"Mom...."

Hua Yao's smile showed more in her eyes than her lips. "He sound like a good man," she told her daughter.

"It's not like that," Jenny started.

"It is, if you want it to be," her mom shrugged. "You too smart, Jenny. Love isn't smart. It's not about thinking. It's just what happen. Love don't care about what it 'like.' Love don't even care about what *you* like."

From years of experience, Jenny knew that Hua Yao Ng's longer speeches—five or six sentences qualified easily—often said a lot more later on, when Jenny realized all that they implied. "Okay, yeah," she said. "Right."

Hua Yao patted Jenny's hand. "Can I see pictures?"

Jenny's face flushed, and she smiled. Her mother was a low-key woman; a simple question like that meant more than the words alone. "Yeah, sure," she said.

She turned her camera on and switched to Slideshow mode, shuffling through the pictures stored on the digital card. It surprised her how many pictures she'd taken; her recent life seemed to exclusively involve learning how to use her powers and stopping the end of the world, interspersed with work, magic shows, and rides through Wonderland. Somewhere along the line, after Calvin had bought her the camera, she'd rekindled her habit of lining up random shots as she roamed the city, letting her photographer's eye zoom in on an interesting face, or building, or tree, or trick of light.

Some shots of the beach where she'd played with Rex were pretty good, though she'd been learning to use the camera as she went. Later shots showed buildings and parks and people. She'd taken a few shots in Boston on her trip to see how far the End of the World spread, and plenty of shots of the woods where she brought Rex to take care of business. There was a beautiful shot of the Bank of America Tower, twisting upward across from Bryant Park, the sun reflecting off its serpentine sides in a late afternoon dominated by azure sky. There were some candid shots of a family in the park, their little boy letting go of a balloon destined to fly free into a cloudy day. A blonde girl with a very short skirt stood by a store window, while on the other side of the glass was a mannequin that could have been her sister. A homeless man slept next to his dirty brown dog, the dog sleeping on his cardboard sign, covering over the words that pleaded for help.

Pictures of performers at the *Beau Regardez* cropped up here and there, usually when they weren't aware of the camera. The fire-eating dancer was frozen forever in a perfect leap through an arc of fire sketched in the air with one of her torches. Roberta and Verbena looked like imperious giant mushrooms, caught in the middle of a comically irate

391

exchange, their eyes blazing but sparked with a tinge of mischief and affection, knowing the audience adored their brassy sniping. Mike the comedian was mugging at the audience, holding a grinning skull beside his own head during a funny *Hamlet* parody taking the American vice president to task for a very poor choice of words. One of the boys from Sex and Violins was smashing an old cello on the edge of the stage, splinters and shards caught in mid-shatter, frozen, racing away from the center of the exploding instrument as his bandmates played on behind him with very punk sneers. Dozens of people who'd been walking in and out of her life since Jenny got the camera, or running along with her, captured in dozens of photos on her camera.

And Calvin. Calvin in the dressing room, trying gamely to apply eye makeup as Jenny had taught him. Calvin at his apartment, feeding doomed mice their last meal, smiling so the mice wouldn't see it coming. Calvin making a silly face at her camera as he secretly fed Colby Cheese inside the magic table at a pub. Calvin looking glum and tired and beautifully human as he sat in the audience at the *Beau* for one of David Dennis's pre-show announcements. Calvin, his long arm extending out of frame in a shot he'd taken of himself with Jenny snuggling under his shoulder. Calvin, close up, his green eyes looking just offscreen, his mouth open to speak, freckles dotting his pale skin like he'd been covered in flakes of something for some Irish recipe.

Jenny had a lot of pictures of Calvin.

Her mother nodded, *hmm*ing and *huh*ing as Jenny clicked through the pictures one by one. Sometimes, Hua Yao made a short comment, like "Good colors" or "I like the sunlight." Mostly, she just looked, and Jenny felt proud to see her mother's reactions; Jenny felt almost normal again, like she really was pursuing the life of a professional photographer, and she was showing off her work to her mother.

She pressed the button, and electric swirls of blue and yellow appeared on a blank white background.

"Very pretty," said Hua Yao Ng.

Jenny pressed the button again before she could stop to wonder if her mother found the splotch of colors pretty, or Dolores Meisel herself. By the time she hit that wall, though, her mother was already commenting on the next few pictures.

The last picture was another shot of Calvin, glancing over his shoulder as he fixed his bowtie in front of the dressing room mirror. In the mirror past the magician, Mirror Jenny held her camera to one side, sticking a thumb in her ear and waggling her tongue. Jenny'd never noticed that before.

"Ha," her mother sighed, "always clowning, Jenny."

"Right...." Jenny stared at the rebellious reflection in the photo.

"They very lovely pictures," said Hua Yao.

"Thanks, Mom," said Jenny, shutting off the camera. She stood to go put it in her bag, and her mother began clearing dishes. Jenny helped, and they cleared the table in only two trips.

As she rinsed plates in the kitchen sink, Hua Yao asked, "So how long you here?"

"I can't stay," Jenny said, more quickly than she wanted. "I mean, I'd like to, but I...have to get back. Something really important."

"Yes, yes," her mother waved off anything so important it would cut short a visit from her daughter. "Do I get to meet the magician?"

"Um," said Jenny. "Sure. We'll see. Mom..."

"Yes, yes, you big important city girl with lots of things to do," said Hua Yao. Her smiling eyes belied her sharp words.

"I just..." Jenny wasn't sure where to start, or even where to finish. The reality that this might be her last meal with her mother—the last time she ever saw her mother in this world—was a giant stone sitting in her stomach. She swallowed, hard. "I love you, Mom."

Hua Yao raised her eyebrows and continued to scrub dishes. "What, I'm dying?" She jokingly checked her pulse. "Better tell doctors stop doing such a good job. I feel too good."

"I do," Jenny insisted. "I mean, come on, I know we don't always...say stuff all the time. Stuff that's important. The stuff we need to say."

"Jenny." Her mother shut off the water. "Since when you need to tell me stuff we need to say?"

"It's just, I want you to know," Jenny said.

Hua Yao scanned Jenny's face intently. "You think there anything I don't know about you?" she asked simply.

Jenny flounced into a kitchen chair, exasperated. "Yeah, Mom!" she said. "There *is*."

Her mother sat next to her and took Jenny's hand. Jenny looked up; Hua Yao was smiling gently. "Don't be so sure, Jenny." Jenny opened her mouth, but her mother raised a silencing finger. "I don't need to know everything," said Hua Yao, "to know you. You're my daughter, Jenny. You do the right things. No," she cut Jenny off again, "not always, and not always first time. But you do the right things. You a very good girl. And I love you too."

Jenny thought she would be crying, but she wasn't. Her mother's calm and understanding tone of voice made it all so easy; the tragedy of the moment evaporated, and all that remained was a mother and daughter, understanding each other, and saying goodbye.

She grabbed her mother, pulling her close. Hua Yao hugged her tightly. They were still for a minute or two, and then both dropped their arms and sat back at the same time.

Jenny Ng bit her lip and looked at her mother. "I have to go," she said.

"I know," Hua Yao Ng nodded. "You go. Do what's right."

"I love you, Mom."

"You my favorite daughter," Hua Yao teased.

"I'm your *only* daughter," Jenny replied by rote, rolling her eyes as per the practically scripted exchange.

Her mother smiled, dark eyes twinkling. "I'll say goodbye to Peter for you."

Jenny paused, wondering just how literally her mother knew what was going on. "Okay," she answered carefully. "Tell him I love him. And I'll...I'll see him soon."

"Not too soon," her mother said slyly, standing up and turning away. She wiped the counter with a dish towel.

Jenny smiled at the back of her mother's head. It didn't matter—either Hua Yao Ng really *did* know the truth, or she didn't really need to. Either way, her mother was right: Jenny had to go do the right thing.

She slung her bag over her shoulder and reached inside, fingering one of the Emergency Exits she'd brought with her. "I love you, Mom," she said.

"Love you too, Jenny," her mother said, not turning around.

"I'll see you later." Jenny pulled out the Emergency Exit and pressed her fingers against it; she disappeared, and the little mirror clattered to the kitchen floor.

Still not turning around, Hua Yao Ng nodded. She stood quietly for a brief moment. Then she bent down to pick up the mirror from the kitchen tiles. She looked at the bittersweet expression on her own reflected face, but like Jenny, she didn't cry. She tucked the cheap mirror into her breast pocket and tapped it proudly.

"Goodbye," Hua Yao said to the empty kitchen.

CHAPTER THIRTY-ONE

After reluctantly abandoning her sword to the cultists at Eric and Melinda's house, Jenny made sure to take a look at the street signs before riding back to Brooklyn. A round of Google Maps later, Lyle and Lloyd generated specific directions to get back there. Since they didn't want to give Hinkley the safecracker any more information than he needed to do his job, heading to Long Island by way of Wonderland Transit was out of the picture—Jenny sat in the back seat of Keith Heckler's Toyota, cramped by two heavy kits with serious looking latches. They'd picked up their guest of honor in Queens, and he hunched over in the front seat as Heckler floored the gas on Sunrise Highway, gray asphalt streaming through his headlights.

"Take it easy!" both Jenny and the weaselly crook said. Jenny felt weird saying something at the same time as Hinkley—the thought of sharing anything in common with the career criminal was unnerving. He was a skinny white guy, not far off Monaghan's age, with colorless thinning hair and the kind of throwback mustache that regularly showed up to casting calls for Forties detective movies. He seemed jumpy, even twitchy, his stony gray eyes scanning back and forth like he saw the world one line at a time. He wore a nice, well-pressed gray suit and an overcoat, which had surprised Jenny. At her dubious look when he got in, he'd tugged his stiff collar and sensibly pointed out: "Crooks who *look* like crooks get caught." He looked meaningfully at her black hoodie and jeans.

Jenny had to admit he had a point.

Speeding down the road, Heckler looked over at the safecracker and flicked a glance in the rearview. "We're on our way to save the world, and you want me to *slow down?*" he grinned.

Jenny looked nervously at Hinkley, who scowled at Heckler, and she inwardly fumed at her friend. "If we get *pulled over* with this stuff," she thwacked the top of one thick case, "it's gonna take a lot longer."

Hinkley agreed. "If you're going to clear out a safe," he said, "the people who put their stuff in there think it's *safe*. It's not going anywhere." He frowned professionally and scanned the road ahead and behind.

Keith Heckler toned down his grin. "Yeah, well, it's not their stuff," he argued—but he obediently slowed down to just five miles over the limit.

"That's what Monaghan said," Hinkley muttered at the window. "*They* stole *your* sword, you said." He twisted around uncomfortably to look at Jenny. "Whaddya got a sword for, anyhow? Girl like you?"

"You're getting paid, right?" Jenny replied hotly.

"No."

Jenny and Heckler both gave a start. "What?" said Jenny.

Hinkley shrugged. "I owe Monaghan a favor," he said bluntly.

"Oh," Jenny said quietly. That explained why Monaghan had said not to worry about money until later. He was getting them the work for free. Well—not for free, if he was using up a favor. From what she gathered, favors were a pretty big deal for men like Monaghan and Hinkley. Her face softened, and she smiled apologetically at the safecracker. "Sorry about that," she said. "It's, you know...complicated. I didn't mean to snap."

"Lady, I done a stretch in Sing Sing and two more I don't talk about," said Hinkley. "I'm doing my job here. I don't care if you snap."

Jenny exaggerated her smile. "I'm sorry *anyway*," she insisted angelically.

He stared a moment, then wavered and let a very small smile slip past his thin fish lips and fuzzy mustache. He had crooked yellow teeth and one exceptionally long fang. "Okay," he conceded. "Thanks. I'm not used to pretty ladies like you."

"*Nobody's* used to pretty ladies like *her*," Heckler said.

Jenny deadpanned his way. "Take a left at the light," she said.

397

"Yes, *ma'am*," Heckler grinned, flooring it again to beat the yellow light. He zoomed by just as it turned red, and slowed down on the smaller road curving north.

Watching the real world flash by gave Jenny a strange, dysphoric feeling—she'd seen the area in Wonderland, but hadn't ever seen it in full color, with real trees and cars going by. Even in the dark of night, the world was more vibrant and clear than anything on the other side of the Looking Glass. A few more turns and she recognized Eric and Melinda's street. "Okay," said Jenny. "Heckler, stop here. Don't move the car...or if you have to, send me a text."

"You got it, rearless leader," Heckler said. He waggled his eyebrows at her bored reaction as he slowed to a stop at the curb.

Hinkley looked over his shoulder at Heckler as he got out. "Read a map or something so it looks like you have a reason to stop," he advised.

"Gee. It's almost like you've done this before." His puppy-dog eyes and obnoxious grin didn't endear him to the old crook.

Hinkley snorted irritably and put his seat forward to grab a case. Jenny pulled the other one with her as she got out of the car. Hinkley frowned, concerned. "You sure you can handle that?" he asked her.

"I'm stronger than I look," Jenny said, though the case weighed on her arm like an anchor snagged on a black hole. She put up a good front and smiled. "See?" Hinkley looked skeptical, but didn't push. Jenny dropped the case and leaned into the car, grateful for an excuse to lower the heavy equipment. "Heckler," she said, her tone emphasizing the seriousness of the situation. "If anything goes wrong—*anything* at all—you *go*."

"Come on, Jenning..." he started cavalierly.

"*Anything*," she repeated with a deadly look.

Heckler shut up and nodded tightly.

"If you can get Hinkley out of here too, do it," Jenny told him. She looked at Hinkley: "If the shit hits the fan, you go with Heckler. Take care of yourself—don't worry about me." The crook shrugged nonchalantly—he had no intention of playing the hero. Jenny turned back to Heckler. "It's not fair to wrap him up in this shit when he's helping us out. Just get him out of here, get him home, get back to Calvin, and tell him to *keep going*. I can always get back to you guys...you know...*my* way. But even if you never see me again—*tomorrow night* is what's important."

"I got it," said Heckler. "Anything happens, return to sender, go ahead with the plan."

"Right." Jenny hefted the case again.

"Steal me something nice while you're in there," Heckler said. "This neighborhood's got *money.*"

"*Lan yeung,*" Jenny grumbled, but affectionately. She bumped the car door closed with her hip, but Heckler's irrepressible grin beamed through the window. "Let's go," she told Hinkley.

She'd had Heckler stop halfway down the street from Eric and Melinda's driveway; lugging their cases, she and Hinkley trudged the diagonal through the woods. She could see a neighboring house through some long branches decorated in dark and rust-colored fall leaves, but it quickly retreated into the darkness.

"How do you know they're out?" Hinkley whispered.

"What?" Jenny whispered back.

"The folks in the house," Hinkley whispered, louder. "How do you know they're out?"

"I don't," Jenny answered. At the safecracker's pained expression, she hurriedly added: "You said you could do it quietly..."

"Depends on the safe," he whispered unhappily. "And quiet won't be a big help if they're *in the room* with us."

"You do your part," Jenny said. "It's not even nine yet—I'm betting they're still helping get the party ready for tomorrow."

Hinkley gave a sidelong glance as he huffed and puffed with his heavy kit. "You don't gamble a lot, do ya?" He shook his head and crunched forward over dried leaves.

The house was in sight through the trees, and Jenny knelt with Hinkley at the edge of the lawn. Once again, the outside lights blazed while the windows were dark—either nobody was home, or Eric and Melinda had strange methods of saving on their electric bill.

"Let's check the back," Hinkley whispered, leaving his case and skirting the edge of the yard around the side of the house. Jenny followed. Not a single light was shining inside the house; just the big square lights illuminating the lawn and the pool out back.

Returning to the cases, Hinkley rubbed his receding hairline and thought hard. "Maybe we got lucky," he said. Raising a hand to stop Jenny before she started, he continued: "Or maybe they're asleep."

399

"Listen," Jenny said, "I know this isn't probably how you usually do things. But it's...*really* important that I get that sword back."

"Monaghan wouldn't've used up his favor if it wasn't," Hinkley cocked an eyebrow, "or got himself in line for accessory charges."

"Right," Jenny said. "If it goes wrong, and you get in trouble, call Monaghan. He won't let you hang."

"They don't hang you for burglary," said Hinkley.

"You know what I mean."

He took a deep breath, then blew it out ruefully. "Yeah, well, I said I'd help. Let's go."

They lifted their cases and, one at a time, hobbled hurriedly through overlapping edges of light on the lawn to hug the wall of the house, inching toward the front door. Hinkley's eyes spun, looking for anything resembling a camera, an armed guard, a guard dog, or something equally likely to earn him a reunion with his Sing Sing alumni. He reached for the doorbell.

Jenny froze. "What are you doing?" she whispered harshly.

He gave her a look. "If nobody answers, they're probably not here."

"No, wait," Jenny said. "I have a better way."

Hinkley dropped his arm and looked at her expectantly.

"Um," Jenny said. "I'll be right back."

"Take this," Hinkley said, producing two small flashlights and handing her one. It was heavy on her palm. Jenny jammed it in her back pocket and gave the man a quick smile of thanks.

With Hinkley waiting like a skittish deer on the front steps, Jenny slinked around the corner of the house and slipped an Emergency Exit out of her pocket. Pushing her fingertips against Mirror Jenny's, she popped into Wonderland and walked briskly back to the door, slipping through its ambiguous dual state. She looked around the front hall—no mirrors. She headed quickly down the opposite hallway to the sitting room and turned to look at the wide mirrored wall.

She couldn't see anything.

A moment of minor panic hit her. The mirrored wall was there, a dull sheen visible in the dim atmosphere of Wonderland, but the reflection showed only blackness. She wondered if it was really *that* dark in there, with absolutely no light leaking in from outside. That didn't seem right. She should be able to see *something*, like moonlight in the sun room or drifting down the hallway from the windows over the front door.

Jenny put a hand on the surface of the mirror and gave it a mental push.

She jumped back instantly, feeling like she'd been smashed in the forehead with a hammer. Holding her head and gritting her teeth against the pain, she staggered across the Looking Glass sitting room.

What the hell?

Her mind raced, blankly reaching for theories and coming up empty. She wasn't sure if the theories weren't there, or if she was too concussed by the weird mental attack to concentrate. It felt like a bug zapper in her brain, jolting her with a few million too many amps, far more than a light-addicted moth would ever have to face.

She forced herself to calm down, trying to focus and think things through. She wasn't sure what was wrong with the mirror, or why she couldn't get through, but there had to be other mirrors in the house. The safe was somewhere back through the hallway, that much she knew—most likely upstairs. If that's where Eric and Melinda's bedroom was, then they'd probably have a bathroom there, too, and Jenny could go through that mirror.

Following the hall through the guttering sheets of Wonderland air, Jenny swung around and dashed up the stairs. There was another hallway at the top, with half a dozen doors along the walls. Jenny peeked in each as she passed. A small bedroom, an office—no mirrors. The third was a big bedroom with a giant canopy bed. It wasn't the bed that caught her eye, but rather the shining mirror over an ornate bureau on the far wall. Through the mirror she saw the real world bedroom lit by silver moonlight.

Breathing a sigh of relief, she pushed through the mirror and found herself in the cultist couple's bedroom, mostly wood and a pinkish orange she was pretty sure interior decorators dubbed "salmon." The canopy over the bed bore a floral print considered tasteful three or four decades earlier, which these days qualified for Are We Going Over to Grandma's House Again status.

She took out Hinkley's flashlight and turned it on. In the bureau mirror, Mirror Jenny looked around curiously, as if examining the mirror frame, her nose wrinkling like she smelled something odd. Jenny turned to cross the room. The closet door was ajar, and the flashlight's beam shining on a bright pink robe caught her eye. She wanted to go downstairs and let

Hinkley in, but getting the lay of the land wasn't a bad idea, and she might as well play her hunch. Shouldering the door aside, she stuck her hands in and parted the hanging clothes sharply, flinching at the grating sound of hangers scraping the rod. She stopped short fearfully, breathing shallow, quiet breaths.

Nobody came to investigate. No calls or shouts sounded off.

Forging ahead, she looked inside the closet. There was a funny little handle on the back paneling—she tentatively pulled at it, then slowly opened the sliding panel to reveal the slate gray face of a floor-to-ceiling safe.

Jenny smiled; maybe she didn't gamble a lot, but she was paying her dues, and Lady Luck was grudgingly handing out the rewards.

The safe had a keypad, a little readout screen, and a giant handle. Jenny knew better than to mess with it—Hinkley would know better how to open it. She just needed to get him upstairs.

She tried her best to combine speed and stealth and wound up loping like a slightly shellshocked kangaroo out to the hall, down the stairs, over to the front door. She unbolted the door and opened it—Hinkley was nowhere to be seen.

"Hinkley," she hissed fiercely. "Mister Hinkley!"

"Shh!" came a harsh whisper. The old crook rounded the corner of the house and looked at her, breathing hard and leaning on his knees. "Christ almighty! Don't *do* that, girl!" He was whispering as best he could, but his labored breathing pumped the volume. "Ran when I...heard the bolt..."

Jenny lowered her eyes guiltily. "Sorry." She saw the equipment kits on the front steps. "You left the cases," she pointed out.

"Yeah, well," he breathed, "*you* try sprinting thirty feet with those monsters."

"Don't worry about it," Jenny said. "Sorry about that. Nobody's home, and I found the safe."

Hinkley worked to catch his breath as he walked up the steps. "How'd you get in?" He kept his voice down despite her assurance that the house was vacant.

"Um. Open window," Jenny replied. "I got lucky. Come on."

Ignoring his curious stare, Jenny grabbed one case and lugged it inside. Hinkley took the other and followed her in. He closed the door and turned on his flashlight, covering the lens to leave only a red, hand-shaped glow. "Up here," Jenny said. They went upstairs to the bedroom. Jenny dropped her case and gestured victoriously at the safe in the closet. "*Voilà!*" she announced with more flare than volume.

Hinkley dropped his case next to hers and approached the safe like a paleontologist moving in to check out a complete Diplodocus skeleton embedded in the wall of the Grand Canyon. His fingers twitched a silent sonata on an invisible piano as his eyes roamed up and down the safe.

"Can you open it?" Jenny asked him quietly.

The safecracker's face split into the first genuine smile Jenny had seen from him. "Not easy, but yeah," he said. "Gimme some time."

He started opening his kits and pulling out tools and gadgets, some of which he pocketed, some of which he laid out in front of the closet. Jenny kept watch, pacing between the window and the door, listening carefully for anything beyond the clicking and clacking of Hinkley at the safe.

It was taking a while; she knew Hinkley was working as swiftly as he could, but she grew more anxious and took short trips down the hall to listen for anybody returning home. On her way back, she passed a bathroom and peeked in, shining her light inside.

Jenny let out a strangled squeak. The space over the bathroom sink was bare: torn edges of wallpaper framing a blank rectangle in the wall. The bathroom mirror had been removed.

Her heart and lungs and stomach started banging together like her ribcage was a mosh pit. "*Diu*," she swore. "No, no, no...shit."

She pushed off from the doorframe and flew back to the bedroom, where Hinkley was still at work on the safe. She stared at the bureau in horror.

The mirror was covered over with a big black garbage bag, taped over the frame. It hadn't been there before.

"Mister Hinkley..." Jenny started with a warning note in her voice.

"Got it!" the old crook whispered triumphantly, turning a dial on one of his gadgets, stuck just below the keypad. The safe clicked sharply, and he yanked the handle, swinging the door wide.

"Mister Hinkley," Jenny repeated, moving forward to look over his shoulder.

He took a step backward and he pointed his flashlight to reveal a tiny glint of glass on the floor of the open safe. The stolen spectacles sat alone in the beam of light.

Jenny gaped. "Oh, fuck...." She grabbed Hinkley's shoulders and spun him toward the bureau. "Was that there a second ago?" she asked urgently, pointing at the garbage bag.

"Huh?" he asked, confused. "Don't remember. These folks Jewish?"

Jenny shouted: "Let's go! Now!"

Hinkley looked at her quizzically—then his eyes went wide as he looked past her. Jenny felt a *thump*, like a giant bug smacking aimlessly into the back of her skull, and the world burst into flashbulbs and disappeared.

She heard thunderclaps and shouting and thumping as if it was all echoing through Jell-O. Her limbs felt like safecracking kits, too heavy to lift off the floor.

Her indestructibility cleared her head slowly, and she tasted something acrid in the back of her throat, gagging like she'd tried to swallow a rock. Her vision was still fuzzy, and she choked and coughed, realizing she was on the floor. She pushed up on her hands and knees and hacked up the ugly lump in her throat, then spat it out. It bumped quietly on the carpet in front of her.

The world came back into focus. Jenny stared at a crushed and cracked bullet on the floor. Her knees felt shaky, her strength slowly returning. A footstep on the carpet caught her ear, and she jerked her head up to look.

Lawrence the Ice Cream Psycho stood at the door, a black gun in his hand. He looked at her with cold, unfeeling eyes and a twisted expression. "Guns either. Right?" he said. The right side of his face was covered in white gauze; puckered purple skin peeked out from beneath the taped edges.

Jenny shook her head hard to clear it. "What?" she said blankly.

He stalked over; she tried to react, but wasn't up to speed yet, and he wrenched her arms behind her. She felt metal edges bite her wrists, and when Lawrence let go, she dropped like a sack of misassembled Tinker Toys.

"Knives, guns," Lawrence mused cruelly. "Nothing gets you. Right?"

Jenny pulled at her arms helplessly, feeling the cold handcuffs on her skin. She glared at her attacker furiously. "I thought Carrie said you aren't killers," she snapped.

"They're not," Lawrence barked back. "That's why they have me." He grabbed the back of her neck and unkindly hauled her up, shoving her to sit on the edge of the bed. The mattress was so high that Jenny's feet dangled above the floor. "Didn't kill you, anyway. Looks like nothing can. Right?"

Jenny said nothing, but she said it very angrily.

"Some of us aren't so lucky," said Lawrence, running a finger down his bandaged face. The gun in his other hand didn't waver.

"You were uglier before," Jenny commented, more glib than she felt. She wiggled her waist a little, shifting farther back on the bed.

"That doesn't work," Lawrence said directly. "I don't get mad. This is my job."

"Nothing personal?" Jenny asked facetiously, still squirming on her butt and leaning over a bit.

"*Everything's* personal," he said calmly—and then exploded in a hurricane of arms. She screamed and tried to bite him, but he pinned her to the quilted duvet and reached into the pocket of her hoodie for the contents she'd been trying to secretly spill onto the bed next to her cuffed hands. He pulled out the Emergency Exits she'd brought with her. He looked at the little mirrors and a crocodilian smile contorted his battered face. "Smart," he remarked. "Does it have to be mirrors? Or does any reflection work?"

"Just mirrors," Jenny said quickly.

Lawrence nodded and grunted, his smile vanishing. He took aim at the bedroom window and blew away the glass with a deafening gunshot. "Bad liar," he said.

"Asshole," Jenny shot back.

"Anything else in the pockets?" he asked. "That's rhetorical. Don't answer." He flipped her like a slab of meat and fished in her other pocket, removing her phone. He patted down her jeans, front and back; Jenny was less ooged out by any sexual connotations than she was by the violence— nothing about this seemed sexual in the least. He pulled out her Metro card and a few dollars—she'd left everything else in her shoulder bag in Heckler's car. Lawrence chucked the card and money on the floor. He kept the gun on her as he backed up to the safe, where he took out the spectacles and dropped the Emergency Exits in their place. He shut the safe and twisted the handle down with a loud clank.

Rising fear tickled the base of Jenny's brain. "Where's my...friend?" she demanded, lacking a better word for Hinkley the safecracker.

"Dead," Lawrence said. He waved the gun. "Let's go."

"Where?"

"I don't need to bring you alive," he said menacingly. "Since you'll just come back to life when we get there." He jammed the gun into her side and dragged her off the bed, onto her feet. "I don't even need to bring you unharmed. You'll heal from anything I do. Right?"

Jenny's lip quivered.

"Can't be fun," Lawrence commented. "Maybe the body heals. But the mind," he tapped the side of her head with the muzzle of his gun, "remembers all of it. Right?"

His breath smelled like stale peppermint. Up close, she saw every crease and pore in his skin.

"Let's go," the Ice Cream Psycho repeated.

Jenny tried to drag her feet, tripping and falling to her knees as her captor shoved her forward. He walked in front of her, and she looked up.

"Fine," Lawrence said, with no trace of satisfaction. "The easy way, then."

He pointed the gun at her forehead and pulled the trigger. Everything went white.

CHAPTER THIRTY-TWO

The passage of time in the Ice Cream Psycho's trunk was hard to gauge. Seconds ticked by with the dull thump of seams in the road, punctuated by the occasional blinding glare of red brake lights. The trip could have been minutes or hours—every so often, after Jenny had lost count of the bumps in the road and how many lefts or rights they'd made, the car would slow to a halt and she would hear the door. The trunk would open, and Lawrence's chillingly emotionless face would appear behind his cold black gun. Another deafening shot, and the world would explode into white light and white noise—Jenny swore she even *tasted* white—before plummeting into gray nothingness. By the time she regained her senses and the latest crumpled bullet clattered on the fuzzy mat, expelled from her forehead the hard way, they were moving, and she had no way of knowing how many road bumps she'd missed in her count. She tried shouting, kicking on the inside of the trunk; she even tried engaging Lawrence in heated conversation whenever the trunk opened. But the very quick end to the conversation was always the same.

"You know—"

Bang.

"My friends—"

Bang.

"No matter—"

Bang.

"You can't keep—"

Bang. Yes, he could. She started just glaring defiantly at him, squinting in the dull light, each time he opened the trunk. It didn't make any difference to him, but it made her feel a little more heroic. Once, she even snarled vengefully and chomped down on his gun, eyeing him defiantly. He pulled the trigger anyway. The bilious taste in her mouth when she woke up changed her mind about trying that again.

She wanted to think Lawrence was getting a kick out of this—that he was just disturbed and depraved, and killing her over and over was how he got his jollies, a fringe benefit peripheral to his role as the Raymonds' personal Jenny collector. The truth, though, was simpler, and had nothing to do with some twisted psychotic sport: transporting her this way kept Jenny completely in the dark, with no clue about how far she'd gone, how long she'd traveled, or where they might end up. Since she wasn't sure how long it took her indestructible body to recover from each gunshot wound, rebuilding her brain and skull and recalling her from timeless gray emptiness to groggy consciousness, the car may have been circling the block for hours, or they might have gone thirty minutes on the highway back from Long Island.

If they were just going to end up at Carrie and Vincent's place in the Hamptons, the whole strategy was futile anyway—Jenny and Calvin already knew the address. But she kept her mouth shut about that, hoping that Lawrence's game would come back to bite him when her friends showed up just to spite him.

Since counting seams as the tires double-bumped over them became pointless, Jenny took the opportunity after each resurrection to assess her situation. There weren't any helpful reflective surfaces in the trunk—just the fuzzy mat and a pair of old jumper cables. The handcuffs were cold, but either they weren't made of a reflective material, or there was some requirement that Jenny had to be able to *see* reflections in order to jump Through the Looking Glass—she wasn't sure, but either way, pressing her fingers against the cuffs and concentrating accomplished nothing. They were still clamped tightly around her wrists, pressing into her butt as she curled into a fetal pose and pulled, straining against the cuffs or the chain, whichever might give way first. Despite her developing lack of aversion to pain, she was still a little timid about pulling her arms apart with her bare hands, so to speak. She wasn't sure if even a veteran Grim Reaper like red-bearded Ketch would have the stomach for that kind of thing; then again, since the other Reapers never interfered in mortal affairs, it was doubtful they ended up in this kind of situation to begin with.

Still, she worked at it each time she recovered from another death at the hands of the Ice Cream Psycho. She might have done it, too—but every time she wore away at the skin around her wrists and hands enough to almost pull them right through the cuffs, the car would stop, the trunk would open, and Lawrence would shoot her in the head again. By the time she awoke, her hands and arms were fully healed, and she had to start all over again, sometimes with the cuffs even tighter than before—Lawrence must have noticed her efforts. The only thing that didn't heal was the splitting headache she'd acquired from repeated bullets to the forehead.

Jenny breathed heavily, gagging on exhaust fumes, trying to calm down enough that her headache might fade away. The car slowed, blinding her with red light, and made a slow, sharp right. The reverse lights flashed, and the trunk went dark as the engine shut off. Jenny heard the rush of wind and the *chunk* of the car door slamming.

The trunk clicked and opened. Jenny blinked rapidly, her eyes adjusting to tall white lights outside. Lawrence stood over her, his gun aimed between her eyes. A crisp, star-studded night sky served as a breathtaking backdrop behind the squat, ruthless man.

"Out." He waved the gun for emphasis.

Jenny rolled herself towards the edge of the trunk; Lawrence grabbed her arm roughly and pulled her out. She staggered and fell and skinned her knee; the flesh healed instantly, but the hole in her black jeans didn't.

"Up," said Lawrence. He got her to her feet. Her legs very quickly recovered from the cramped conditions in the trunk; she had no real excuse to trip or stumble again, and Lawrence probably knew it. One of his arms was linked through hers, guiding her by the handcuffs; the other held the gun jabbed into her hip. She obediently walked in front of him, looking around to work out where they were.

Jenny hadn't been here before, but the smell of salty air and the sweeping thunder of nearby waves told her enough. The parking lot had more than a few cars in it—next to Lawrence's silver sedan was a black BMW she knew well enough. She looked longingly at sideview mirrors and shiny windshields, but knew her gun-toting chaperone wouldn't let her within five feet of a reflection before shooting her dead again and dragging her away to wake up with another pounding headache and nothing to show for it. A road snaked through some scrubby trees; Jenny saw a low building just past the trees with a wide deck jutting their way. There were lights and movement in the windows, but whatever the place was, it was too far away to make anything out.

Lawrence had the collar up on his thick brown coat. Jenny barely felt cold at all, though she could feel the bitter wind whipping in off the ocean. The tape had come unstuck on the Ice Cream Psycho's jaw, and a stub of white gauze fluttered in the strong wind.

He marched her away from the road and trees and building; on the other side of the parking lot, sandy paths led through dead vegetation to a narrow beach. It was less than a hundred yards to the ocean, which crashed into the tortured sand, closing the distance as high tide approached. To her left, where the sea was shepherded inland between man-made walls, Jenny saw a few people wandering along the edge, hands in pockets and eyes narrowed against the wind.

"If you want them dead," Lawrence growled in her ear, "call for help." He shoved the gun hard into her side. "You know I have no problem using this."

Jenny nodded curtly. She didn't resist as he marched her across the sand.

He took her away from the inlet, farther out along the beach, the frothing white caps dotting the darkness on their left. They were either on the south coast of Long Island, heading west, or the north coast, heading east. Jenny had no obvious way to tell. She'd never learned to navigate by the stars; she knew how to recognize Orion and the Big Dipper, but didn't know what directions they indicated even if she could find them. She wasn't sure which constellations twinkled in the deep darkness above, but the great hunter and the kitchenware subset of his ursine prey weren't among them.

They walked across the sand, slogging footsteps and crashing waves the only sound, and Jenny saw lights and shapes ahead. As they drew closer, she saw what looked like a luau: paper lamps were strung on poles, tents were set up and flapping wildly, and a few trucks and campers outlined the impromptu beach village. Fake Tiki torches were staked into the sand and cast a cheerful glow through sculpted plastic flames. Orange extension cords wove a complicated network tracing back to the campers, drawing power from either the engines themselves or from generators inside the mobile homes. People in fluttering black robes milled about, putting up lamps, laying out tables, fastening cloth to tent poles, and adding wood to the big circle of stones in the middle of the site, carefully stepping over the wires as they went.

Lawrence grunted wordlessly and brought Jenny into the circle of wires, ignoring the robed men and women who watched curiously but quietly as they passed. The Ice Cream Psycho marched her straight for the largest camper, a sleek modern take on the old-fashioned trailer home. A short set of metal steps was fixed to a hinge below the door. Lawrence stopped at the bottom and held Jenny's handcuffed arms tight. He rapped sharply on the doorframe with his gun.

The inner door opened, and Bruce the Beatnik looked sullenly through the screen. "Yeah," he said, and opened the screen door. Lawrence pushed Jenny up the stairs.

She'd always wanted to spend a week or two in a trailer, roaming with friends. The idea of living on the road, carrying your home with you, appealed to her in the spirit of youthful and utterly misguided adventure. In those fantasies, the trailer was cramped, with a half dozen or more college kids squeezed in to claim sleeping space where they could, on bunk beds or couches or curled up in the tiny booth around a table.

This trailer was surprisingly spacious, and occupied by people trying to end the world.

"Jenny!" Carrie's voice carried the same excitement she'd use to greet Jenny at the *Beau*, or at the restaurant for a dinner date. Context made no difference to Carrie Raymond; she was a bubbly, inviting sociopath for all seasons.

The Delightful Destroyer of Worlds sat comfortably on a striped silk sofa near the back of the trailer. Her thick black robe was open down the front, revealing a pristine white dress and her big, pregnant belly. Carrie smiled warmly, her teeth outdoing her dress, and clasped her hands together.

Another voice came from the front of the trailer. "This might be a little awkward," Vincent Raymond joked, moving past Jenny and the Ice Cream Psycho to sit with his wife. His voice poured into her ears like ambrosia, and Jenny squirmed at her involuntary reaction, hating the man for still being so *damn* attractive. He smiled, his eyes sparkling in the subdued lighting. He wore a big black robe, too, with a pale blue polo shirt visible where it hung open at the top.

"Lawrence," Carrie said, "I don't think that will be necessary anymore." She waved distastefully at his gun.

He didn't move. "It will," he said irrefutably.

Carrie sighed and gave Jenny an adorable little *I Tried* shrug. "Oh, well," she said endearingly. "Trust the experts, right?"

Jenny didn't know what to think. She'd had at least a basic assumption that the Big Reveal of Carrie and Vincent being evil homicidal maniacs would change the timbre of their conversations. These two were still the same scintillating, approachable couple of divine socialites she'd met the day Lyle and Lloyd hit her with a car.

"So, Jenny," Vincent dashed off another Greek God grin, "welcome to our celebration."

Jenny cleared her throat. She hadn't used her voice much since her rapid-fire resurrections in Lawrence's trunk. "Still fucking crazy, I see." She was proud that her voice only barely cracked.

"Bruce," said Carrie, "why don't you finish up and go help your mother with the hors d'oeuvres, dear? We'll be fine in here. Lawrence has everything in hand."

Bruce threw a petulant look at Lawrence—who thoroughly ignored him—and started for the door.

"Ah ah ah," Carrie cautioned with a wagging finger. "Don't forget what you came in for!"

Bruce paused and turned back. Pushing childishly past Lawrence and Jenny, he flipped open a tall, narrow cabinet and pulled out a couple of electrical strips.

Jenny stifled her gasp of surprise. Fastened to the inside of the cabinet door, now facing the door of the trailer with Jenny and Lawrence in between, was a thin full-length mirror. Standing next to the Ice Cream Psycho's stoic reflection was Mirror Jenny, peeking subtly past her own captor at the real Jenny. Mirror Jenny gave her the tiniest of smiles, doing a passable imitation of a regular mirror image, trying not to draw attention. Lawrence stared straight ahead, his gun still hovering next to Jenny's ribcage.

"Make sure you tell the boys not to overload any one generator," Vincent said wisely.

Bruce nodded and pushed through the screen door, letting it slam shut behind him. The inner door was still wide open.

"It's going to be a big event, Jenny," Vincent offered another charming smile.

"I thought you were having it at your house," Jenny said as breezily as she could. "This place is kind of like slumming for you guys, isn't it?" She looked around the trailer casually, briefly sweeping the mirror on the other side of the Ice Cream Psycho. Mirror Jenny had a barely contained smirk on her face, and wiggled her fingers mischievously—her arms were at her sides, no handcuffs on her wrists. Jenny tried to idly ignore her reflection, not lingering on the mirror for too long.

"Well," said Carrie with a cute little pout, "we were *going* to hold it at our house, but I know *you!*" She beamed a winning smile, like this was all a perfectly natural conversation to have on Armageddon's Eve. She playfully wiggled a reproachful finger. "You probably told Calvin all about it. And while I don't think there's anything your adorable little magician can do to interfere, we decided it would be best to change venues and keep this a...*private* affair."

Vincent patted Carrie's arm and they locked fingers romantically. "Yes, we don't want to attract too much attention here," he crooned. "Many people just aren't ready for this kind of commitment."

"Yeah, but you guys are really committed," Jenny said dryly. "Or you *should* be." She shifted just a little, lowering her center of gravity and angling her shoulder just ahead of Lawrence's chest. Past him and his stocky reflection, Mirror Jenny bent her knees and signaled with a barely perceptible nod.

"Now, Jenny," Carrie spoke like a parent admonishing her child for a racist remark. "True, some of us have our...quirks," she smiled at her cleverness and raised her eyebrows like a Vaudeville punster, "but in the end, we're really all the same."

"The greatest thing one person can do for another is to love them," Vincent declared.

"And the greatest love brings two people together as one," Carrie added.

Vincent smiled at his wife and held her hand up, kissing it. "So an even greater love would bring all of us together," he concluded, "together in one perfect unity."

"One perfect unity," his wife echoed, "of peace and harmony. All in one."

"Consumed by love," said Vincent.

"Consumed by love," repeated Carrie, gazing lovingly at her husband.

"Shit!" Lawrence shouted, swerving to tackle Jenny as she threw herself at the mirror.

They tumbled to the floor as Vincent and Carrie abruptly stood. Jenny struggled, on her back atop Lawrence's jiggling gut, but he dropped his gun and trapped her in a powerful bear hug. With no leverage, her handcuffed hands squeezed between her own butt and Lawrence's crotch, she couldn't break free. She tilted her chin forward, gazing over her own belly at the inside of the cabinet door.

"Mirror!" Lawrence grunted, still pinning Jenny to his chest.

Vincent moved forward to the cabinet. In the reflection, Mirror Jenny stood between the quivering legs of Lawrence's reflection. She looked aside at the mirrored version of Vincent Raymond approaching, then set her jaw. She gave Jenny a steely look and a grimly determined frown—and whirled to dash through the screen door behind her, not looking back, fleeing the trailer in Wonderland.

Vincent gaped at the mirror, where Lawrence's reflection struggled with empty air. The deviant Adonis looked back and forth between Jenny and her lack of reflection with a creeping smile of amazement. "That's new," he remarked.

Carrie joined him and looked in the mirror. "I told you," she said, her hand snaking into her husband's, "our little Jenny is just *full* of surprises." They beamed down at Jenny with perfect, white, even teeth.

Jenny felt the slimy nightmare sensation of being naked in school during a final exam. In a lecture hall full of man-eating sharks.

Trying to make like this was normal for her, her mirror image ducking out for lunch or shopping on a daily basis, Jenny stopped struggling and shot Vincent and Carrie a threatening smile, faking the confidence she didn't feel. "You just wait," she told them.

With Jenny no longer struggling, Lawrence rolled her over and climbed to his feet, one hand clamped on her shoulder as he picked up his gun. Leaning forward with her hands still cuffed behind her back, she had trouble balancing on her knees, but he gripped her shoulder tightly and kept her from smacking face-first into the floor. With the gun in his other hand, he slammed the cabinet and latched it shut.

"Oh, Jenny," Carrie sing-songed, "don't be like that. We brought you here to help us, after all. Remember..." She walked back to the sofa, leading Vincent by the hand, and fixed Jenny with a sly gaze as she sat down. "*We* helped *you*, once upon a time."

Vincent poured three glasses of wine. "Everything is circular," he said, smoothly turning the bottle to keep it from dripping.

"Life just goes round and round," said Carrie. "Each ending brings with it a new beginning."

Her husband put the wine glasses on a low round table before the sofa and sat next to his wife. "And the new can only begin when the old has ended."

"Just fucking *stop* it," Jenny snapped. Lawrence got her up and shoved her toward a chair across from the Raymonds.

"Now, Jenny," Carrie continued, "we did you a favor. In fact, we've done quite a lot for you, haven't we?"

Jenny said nothing.

Vincent smiled the sad smile of a high school principal disappointed to see the senior class valedictorian sent into his office. "Have a seat, Jenny."

She didn't move. Lawrence jabbed the gun against her shoulder and sat her down in an uncomfortably twisted position, her legs bent to one side.

"Life is all about circles, dear," said Carrie, swirling the deep red wine in her glass. "There are big circles, and little ones. And it's just that...*our* little circle is almost complete. We've almost gone all the way around." She took a cultured sip and smiled prettily.

Vincent picked up his own glass. "When we met, *we* were in a position to help *you*," he explained, his words writhing like the glittering scales of poisonous serpents. "Now, *you* can help *us*."

"That's how life works, Jenny," Carrie said. "Perfect circles, only perfect because they're complete." She and Vincent clinked glasses, then smiled cheek to cheek like the happy couple at the end of a home mortgage commercial.

Jenny arched one eyebrow. "Okay," she said tonelessly. "Where can I drive you?"

The Raymonds laughed. Lawrence stood like an ugly, balding gargoyle over Jenny's shoulder, his gun pressing against her neck.

Carrie held out a hand. "Lawrence?" The Ice Cream Psycho reached into his coat and handed her the spectacles he'd taken from Eric and Melinda's safe. Vincent twisted in his seat and produced Calvin's wooden box, placing it on the table. Carrie set the spectacles down with her wine glass on the table, then stretched her hands across the top of the wooden box.

Jenny watched in disbelief as Carrie's fingers danced across the box's brass fixtures, just as Calvin's had. A moment and a loud *clack* later, the black-robed blonde lifted the top. The wand lay from corner to corner,

415

neatly bisecting the box into two triangles. In one triangle was the Window to Your Soul, lying heavily and ominously on one broad face. In the other, the magic rings were piled in concentric circles on top of a flat gray disc—Jenny realized it must be the magic hole, removed from Calvin's hat and placed in the box with the portal facing down. The back side looked like scratched gray plastic with tiny bumps on it.

"I've been looking for these for a very long time," Carrie said in a dreamy voice, like reciting a favorite fairy tale. "I told you I've had an eventful life, Jenny. When I worked in the library, I was very partial to the...older books. Books that were dismissed as mythology and folklore. And it struck me as funny, one day—people are such imaginative creatures! We've come up with all sorts of stories and monsters and magic, haven't we?"

Jenny stared at the props. But for her handcuffs, she would gladly have endured a few more temporary gunshot wounds to just grab the box and run.

"But we're so much more than that," Carrie went on.

"So much more," said Vincent, smiling at his wife.

Carrie reached into the box and pulled out the Window, placing it on the table next to the spectacles. "Over the centuries, we've taken those things we've imagined, and we've made them *real*, Jenny! Look around you—we *live* in an Age of Magic. Oh," she said dismissively, "people can *call* it what they like. Technology. Science. But the things we can do now are *just* what older civilizations—ancient people, *our* ancestors—dreamed up in their stories. Science is mythology made real. Technology is just practical magic."

Jenny's eyes drifted up to Carrie Raymond's face. She swam through memories of all the conversations she'd shared with Calvin on the nature of magic, and the subject of *wizard-y* magic.

"We soar through the skies on gleaming chariots!" Carrie clapped her hands together. "We send messages to the other side of the world in an instant."

"We can send men to the moon," said Vincent, "and *talk* to them."

Carrie smiled approvingly at Vincent. "All of these myths and hopes and dreams, the impossible stories of generations past...we've made them come true." Carrie spread her hands over the table of props like a spokesmodel showing off her bejeweled showcase. "So why would we be limited to only *some* of those stories," she said suggestively, almost lasciviously, "and not others?"

Jenny looked back at the props. "Magic..." she whispered, adding it all up.

"*Technology*," proclaimed Carrie, finishing the math. "Not ours, of course. At least," she posed in a glamorous show of uncertainty, "I don't *think* they are. But wherever they came from, they've been here for a very long time. And the stories about them have been told, generation to generation, for just as long."

Jenny thought hard. "But...you *know* what you're doing. You *know* you're destroying the world. Don't you?" She mentally kicked herself for trying to reason with a crazy woman, but she was trying to piece everything together.

The beautiful couple laughed. "Of course I know what I'm doing, Jenny," Carrie said delightfully. "And you'll thank me for it, some day."

"But...why?"

Vincent chuckled. Carrie patted his arm in agreement. "Now, Jenny," she said. "I'm not some pulp fiction villain who's going to spend all night telling you the Caroline Raymond story. Suffice it to say, death and destruction are too often...unpredictable—"

"You don't know the half of it," Jenny muttered.

"—and I," Carrie continued uninterrupted, "prefer to take the bull by the horns, so to speak. All we want from you is some help with these devices. I just needed to clarify things for you, so you'll understand that they *are* devices...and that's all they are. Think of yourself as our 'Tech Support,'" she joked, sharing another relaxed laugh with her husband.

Jenny stared at them, aghast. "You want me to tell you how to *use* this stuff?" she exclaimed. "Are you fucking crazy?"

"No, that's fine," Carrie said reassuringly. "I'm well aware of how they work. We're just having a small, unexpected problem. A 'glitch,' you might say." She picked up the glasses and the Window, one in each hand. "The Eyes and the Aspect," she declared, naming the items. "I'd believed their use was...relatively straightforward. I should see the Scriptures when I look through one with the other, yes?"

Jenny said nothing...which unfortunately said everything.

"You obviously know how to use them," Carrie pointed out.

Vincent smiled helpfully. "You used them in the magic show. And for us, that night in your dressing room." He took a casual sip of wine. Discussing the implementation of the End of the World was mere after-dinner conversation.

"So I'm not sure why they won't work for us," said Carrie, a cute and plaintive moue on her face. "We need to know...did you have to do anything special? Anything unusual? To make them work right—to see the Scriptures? Any special words or...thoughts? Or motions?"

Jenny bit her lip. She shook her head.

"Well," said Carrie, visibly annoyed.

"Jenny's special?" Vincent suggested. "She's...in tune with the Eyes and the Aspect? Perhaps that's why she was given to us."

Carrie smiled slowly, her eyes narrowing on Jenny. "That could be," she said. She held out the spectacles. "Here, put them on, Mysterious Jade." Her teasing tone was entirely unwelcome in context.

Jenny tried squirming away, scrunching her head into her neck like a turtle, but Carrie leaned over and fitted the stems over Jenny's ears, adjusting the bridge on her nose to keep the glasses from sliding off. Carrie held the Window between herself and Jenny. "Do you see them?" she asked, clearly trying to contain her urgency. "Do you see the Scriptures? The letters—the text written on the fabric of existence?"

Jenny clenched her teeth.

Carrie exploded, her calm façade shattering: "Do you see them?!"

"Of *course* I see them!" Jenny snapped.

A giant, relieved smile lit up Carrie's face, and she regained her composure. Her husband hugged her and smiled gratefully at Jenny. "I knew it," Vincent said proudly, "I knew you were given to us for a reason!"

Jenny glared coldly at them through the dusty lenses of the spectacles.

The Raymonds picked up their wine glasses and clinked them together, each taking a genteel sip of the swirling red. "Lawrence, bring her outside," Carrie commanded. "We have wonderful news to share!" She handed Vincent her glass, and he put away the drinks as Carrie returned the Window to the wooden box and closed it. She left the spectacles on Jenny.

Lawrence pulled Jenny out of her chair and marched her outside, holding her on the way down the steps so she didn't stumble forward on the sand. Carrie followed them as Vincent put away the box of magic props.

"Everyone!" Carrie called out, pulling her robe closed against the chill cutting across the beach. "Everyone come, gather together! We have wonderful news!"

The people in black robes paused in their work, obediently setting things aside and forming a crowded circle around Carrie, Lawrence, and Jenny. As an assortment of men and women, they were all the more frightening for being so normal, so standard and varied. Nothing about them screamed Scary Killer Religious Cult; they would have looked perfectly natural attending a church picnic or a high school talent show. They were nothing more than husbands, wives, parents, even grandparents—the oldest, like tall bald Eric, were probably in their sixties or seventies, while the youngest weren't much younger than Jenny.

"Bruce, Matthew," Carrie said, her unearthly charisma washing over them faster and deeper than the dark, white-capped water behind her. Bruce the Beatnik and a clean-shaven young blond stepped forward, their black robes swatting back and forth like superhero capes. "Bruce, dear, take Matthew to our trailer, please, and get that mirror out of the cabinet—the one attached to the inside of the door. Bring it out here for us—thank you, dear."

The two men rushed off across the sand, passing Vincent Raymond, who parted the crowd of black robes as easily as he'd parted rubbernecking pedestrians the day Jenny had met him. He came to the center and stood by his wife, his glowing smile drawing in their followers like flies to very, very seductive flies of the opposite sex.

"Friends," Carrie proclaimed, "we have been rejuvenated—set back on the circular path to our destiny. Fate has given us this young lady—her name is Jenny!"

Happy phrases murmured and buzzed through the wind.

"Our needs are answered," Carrie declared, "because Jenny can read the Scriptures for us!" Actual applause broke out, subdued but genuine. "I would like to apologize to you all," Carrie added humbly, more softly, yet still loud enough to be heard over the wind and surf. "I had thought it would be my place—my destiny—to read the Scriptures, to call out the Name and bring about our New Beginning. I was...misguided. It was my destiny only to bring you here—to gather our artifacts and all of you wonderful friends for our celebration. It was my destiny only to find Jenny, and bring her here with us, so that our celebration can come full circle to its end...and a new beginning!"

More applause and appreciative murmurs, even some joyful laughter.

"Come," Carrie waved. The black-robed suburbanites moved aside for Bruce and Matthew, who carried the thin mirror between them. Carrie directed them to place the mirror upright on the sand, then turned again to her disciples. Jenny stood firm, scanning the crowd of happy, average faces. She saw several she recognized. Warren and Mary, who'd stolen the glasses, were there, though not together. Eric and Melinda held each other's hands, enraptured by the destiny the Raymonds were pitching. Black-haired Vivian, wearing her scarlet dress beneath her black robe, watched Bruce proudly, and Jenny realized the family resemblance—Vivian was Bruce's mother. This was apparently a family-friendly cult.

"Jenny is special," said Carrie. "She has been sent to us so that we can fulfill the destiny we've all embraced, and complete the circle!" With Bruce and Matthew helping, Vincent positioned the mirror behind Jenny, facing the crowd.

Jenny flinched as the cultists gasped—she knew they saw no reflection of her in the mirror. Only Lawrence clutching empty space, and their own faces staring in astonishment.

They applauded joyfully. Beneath the noise, Jenny heard Vincent's sharp command to Bruce and Matthew: "Bury it. At least a hundred yards away." The young men nodded and carried the mirror away.

Carrie Raymond basked in the adoration as if she could photosynthesize it. "Jenny is the human vessel of our circular universe," Carrie explained. "She shows us the cycle of endings and beginnings in her very being!"

As her words swept through the turbulent darkness, Carrie took the spectacles off Jenny's face and gestured at Lawrence. The Ice Cream Psycho put his gun to Jenny's head.

Glazed, Jenny scrambled desperately. "Wait! Don't!" she yelled to the crowd. "Don't listen to her! She's just *using* you! She—"

The gunshot split the night wind, and the black sky and black robes washed away in pure white oblivion. When Jenny finally pushed through smoky gray nothingness to blink at the sand beneath her cheek, the cheers and clapping of the black-robed crowd hit her ears like a flight attendant's announcement when your ears pop. Without an ounce of gentleness,

Lawrence heaved her to her feet again, holding her by one armpit like a marionette with the strings cut.

"Thank you, Jenny!" Carrie shouted happily, tears streaming down her face.

"Thank you!" Vincent said, smiling like a politician.

Their followers echoed them, some of them repeating Jenny's name like a prayer or a magic word, all of them clapping and smiling and flapping in the thundering wind.

"Tomorrow night," Carrie announced with the fervor of a Fire and Brimstone televangelist, "the circle will be complete!"

More cheers and clapping shattered the air, as if the pounding surf and powerful wind were mere reflections of the cult members' joyous sentiment. Jenny swayed like a drunk, dizzily searching faces for any sign of doubt, dissent, disloyalty. There wasn't any. Carrie and Vincent Raymond were going to unleash the apocalypse in twenty-four hours, and each and every one of these fine, upstanding citizens was enthusiastically looking forward to it with love in their eyes and joy in their hearts.

CHAPTER THIRTY-THREE

"No, man," Keith Heckler said fiercely into his cell phone, "that's not the one I signed up for. I want the one I signed up for!"

Calvin McGuirk had never seen the guy look so bothered. He hadn't known Heckler long, and didn't see him often, but the magician had never seen him look *at all* bothered. The knot in Calvin's stomach, already twisted over his own concern for Jenny, tightened harder out of sympathy for Heckler's heartbreakingly palpable concern. Highly trained asshole or not, it was clear he genuinely cared about Jenny.

The Great Sword Robbery had been a worse fiasco than the Summer Horse Heist, and not just because they didn't return with the sword. The air in Heckler's apartment crackled with nervous energy and outright fear— part of it stemming from their knowledge that the actual, factual End of the World was more nigh than any sandwich-boarded street prophet might guess, but more of it stemming from the simple fact that Jenny never came back. Their indestructible superpowered sword-slinging leader, on whom the first dozen or so alphabetically-organized plans to save the world banked, was missing in action, and they had no way of locating her.

Leaning uncomfortably on the low kitchenette counter across from Heckler, Calvin looked over at the couch. "You want some more water? Or tea or something?"

Hinkley the safecracker threw back a sardonic look, his eyes bugging out. "Yeah, that'll turn things around," he said sarcastically, then winced and cradled his hastily bandaged arm. His overcoat, suit jacket and white shirt were draped on the back of the couch; the right-hand sleeves of all three were torn and bloodied in the same spot, and his arm was covered in cloths and Ace bandages. His arm hair was matted from dried blood, antiseptic spray, and the soaked towels the boys had used to wash off his wound.

Calvin reined in any retort—the guy had taken a bullet for the cause, after all. "How are you feeling?"

"Almost good enough for a tea party," Hinkley grimaced through another jab of pain. He looked unexpectedly small and pitiable; aside from a bit of a pot belly, he was a terribly scrawny guy in just his white undershirt and nice gray pants. "I'm fine, forget it. I've had worse. Sure you ain't got anything stronger than tea?"

"Not here," Calvin said. "We'll get you something, though. Promise."

The safecracker attempted a weak smile. "Make it the good stuff."

Calvin smiled back. "You've earned it," he said firmly. He turned to Heckler, who was still sparring on the phone.

"Same pay?" Heckler exclaimed incredulously. "I wasn't in it for the money, Nellie Rockefeller!" He listened, then smirked. "Yeah, you got me— I just wanted to get close to you. McDonald's hired me to steal your recipe for stuffed crabs." He grinned maliciously at the squawking that exploded out of the phone. "No, no problem, I already got it. First—get crabs. Then—get stuffed! Bite me, Betty Crotch-Rot." He stabbed the button to disconnect.

"Yeah?" Calvin asked urgently.

"Should've checked my voicemail this morning," Heckler muttered angrily.

It wasn't Heckler's fault, Calvin knew. The whole morning—the last eighteen hours, in fact—had been a jumble of confusion, emergencies and frantic phone calls. Heckler had called Calvin from the road, sputtering about the disastrous burglary attempt while Hinkley moaned loudly in the background. By the time they got back, Calvin had texted Jenny five times—each time just a single question mark, since he couldn't be sure who might end up reading it—and received no response. The worst part was that she could be anywhere: captured and tied up, locked in a room with no mirrors, sunk to the bottom of the ocean with Mafia-style weights tied to her ankles...a hundred scenarios ran through Calvin's mind, each an appalling trap that would keep Jenny from answering her phone or even, in fact, from doing anything else, ever again. Jenny had told him about Pauzok, the Coney Island Count, potentially trapped forever in a psych ward with no way out—not even death—and panic rose in his chest at the thought of Jenny meeting the same fate. It even crossed his mind that she might be trapped in Wonderland, without her sword, unable to find a mirror back to the real world. Even though he knew that, unlike him, she could see and hear in the warped mirror reality, the idea still made him shudder.

They'd done what they could for Hinkley's bullet wound—he'd refused to go to the hospital, and Calvin figured he had a point. As far as they knew from cop dramas and action movies, gunshot wounds needed to be reported, and a tangle of bureaucratic red tape was the last thing they needed on the home stretch to the deadline of all deadlines. It turned out the bullet had just nicked the old crook as he'd dashed madly down the stairs in Eric and Melinda's house, but it took a while for the bleeding to stop, and his fish-white skin was an even more troublesome shade of pale when they bandaged him up. He slept it off while Calvin traded phone calls back and forth with Detective Monaghan, who agreed that a hospital visit wasn't a smart move (though the detective's worried tone was noticeable) and promised to do everything he could to help get Jenny back—of course, "everything he could" fell short, officially, of actually *doing* anything until she'd been missing for twenty-four hours, and they needed to come up with a more kosher Last Known Whereabouts than "breaking and entering a house in the Hamptons." As he'd done when he tracked down Hinkley, Monaghan tirelessly poked and prodded to find unofficial avenues that might prove more helpful. His latest call, a little after noon, assured the gang that he might at least be able to get some courteous, professional, respectful friends to take a look around, but he regretfully reminded them that there were no guarantees.

The morning had been spent in phone conversations, at the pharmacy to buy medical supplies for Hinkley's arm, grabbing cash at an ATM, and giving a large portion of said cash to the neighbors they'd bribed into revealing their WiFi password so Lyle and Lloyd could get online. The fanboys were looking for connections between the Raymonds, the other first names on Jenny's incomplete list of party guests, and any other bits of data that might congeal in a coherent picture of what was happening out on Long Island. They'd had some success: the house Jenny and Hinkley had tried to rob belonged to Eric and Melinda Polander, a retired real estate developer and his wife, and some clever Googling turned up the fact that Peggy Brazer, the owner of the catering company, had a cousin named Vivian Zlotnik, an upper-class widow with a son named Bruce who had been in the news several times in the past decade over some embarrassing but minor arrests. The fanboys even pinpointed the Zlotniks' address in the

Hamptons, following the winding maze of Internet links and search results to turn up other names and addresses that seemed relevant—names like Howard and Elise Merchant, Warren and Rita McCall, Richard Milliner and his daughter Alice, and an ex-cop from Chicago named Mary Saloma who had quietly resigned during an Internal Affairs investigation twelve years ago. Calvin was honestly impressed that the fanboys could pan through a few hours worth of Internet flotsam and jetsam and come up with so much gold dust. Whether that dust might be put together into a big enough nugget of useful information remained to be seen.

When the action had died down enough for Heckler to respond to the blinking light on his phone and check his voicemail, he'd howled in frustration and called the catering company he'd conned his way into—with the help of some unemployed actresses he knew—to find out why he'd been reassigned as a waiter at a different party for the evening. The conversation wasn't a friendly one, particularly the end Calvin could actually hear.

Keith Heckler stared daggers at his phone and smacked it down on the counter. "It's canceled. The Raymonds—or whoever—called the caterers and canceled yesterday, last minute. Didn't even argue about losing their deposit," he pointed out with a rueful shrug. "I don't think they're worried about getting the money back."

"*Agents*," Calvin swore, ignoring Heckler's uncomprehending look. "So our Inside Man isn't inside anymore."

"And I wasted sixty bucks on those clothes," Heckler said. At Calvin's glare, he spread his hands in wide-eyed innocence. "Hey, not priority, Quirk, but it still sucks!"

Calvin let it go and paced across the room. "And we don't know where Jenny is," he babbled uncontrollably, "and we don't know where the props are, and we don't know if they're still going to be at the Raymonds' house tonight, and..."

"We can try anyway," Lloyd suggested, looking up from the floor where he and Lyle were sprawled in front of two laptops. One was Calvin's, the other Heckler's; the fanboys had complained about not being able to go get their much more powerful computers, but time was more precious than RAM.

Lyle looked up at Calvin and Heckler hopefully. "We've got the Polanders' address," he said, "and we've got the Raymonds' address. We dug up a few others, and Lloyd even got ex-Sergeant Saloma's license plate number." He smiled proudly at his friend. "Nice one, dude..."

Lloyd grinned in a show of humility.

Calvin sighed. "You've done great, guys," he said sincerely, "but what are we gonna do? Visit every address you can find in the next eight hours? Hope we find the right one before they do...uh...whatever it is they're doing?" Their faces fell. "We can't count on that. And if we're roaming Long Island or Jersey or both or...*wherever*, all day long, what happens if Jenny comes back here and can't find us? Maybe she just *lost* her phone or something. Thanks for all the stuff you found—really, heck, you guys have been awesome—but I just don't know what we can do with it right now."

The fanboys looked devastated. Up to now, it had been almost like a game to them, a fully immersive roleplaying adventure that relied on their phenomenal Web mojo to provide backup for their fellow heroes. Heckler's arrival with a shot and bleeding ally had shaken that illusion already, and now they faced the possibility that all of their hard work might mean nothing after all.

"I gotta pee," Lyle said glumly.

"Me too," said Lloyd, but he put his hands up in a fair surrender. "You called first."

The shorter fanboy heaved himself to his feet and headed for the bathroom. Keith Heckler idly traced his finger across the counter, his perpetual grin only barely hanging on behind his doleful expression. "So what *can* we do, Stretch?" he asked.

Calvin shook his head, choking back a strangling feeling of helplessness. "I don't know," he admitted. "We've got *one* ace in the hole," he patted his shirt pocket, "but I don't know if that, you know, beats whatever *they're* holding."

"Can't count on it," said Heckler. He chucked a thumb at the fanboys. "If Mister and Missuz Geek are right—"

"Am I 'Mister'?" Lloyd asked hopefully.

"All yours, Tiger," Heckler winked, then continued: "—then missing just *one* of the eleven secret herbs and spices might not stop the Colonel and his Chick from battering and frying us. It might just fuck things up worse."

Before Calvin could answer, a shamefully girlish shriek pierced the bathroom door.

"What? What?" the magician responded, as he and Heckler and Lloyd ran to the door.

"Did you get it caught in your fly?" Heckler asked through the door.

"Again?" Lloyd tacked on.

Lyle yanked open the door, looking ashamed and amazed at the same time, one hand holding his unbuttoned jeans up around his waist. "Jenny!" he exclaimed.

Even Hinkley looked over from the couch, bug-eyed and baffled.

Not bothering to answer the three confused expressions through the bathroom door, Lyle rolled his eyes in exasperation and repeated: "Jenny!" He grabbed Calvin's arm and pulled him into the bathroom, then pointed. Heckler and Lloyd poked their heads in.

In the bathroom mirror, the reflection of Jenny Ng jumped excitedly as Calvin McGuirk walked into view. The effect was eerie, even after everything the magician had experienced; his own reflection stared, perplexed, from behind the mirror image of a Jenny who wasn't in the room.

"Jenny!" he shouted happily, his mouth open in a bewildered smile.

The reflection shrugged and sighed inaudibly, then held up her thumb and forefinger in a clearly significant: *Close.*

"Uh," said Calvin. "*Mirror* Jenny?"

Mirror Jenny gave him a winning smile and clapped her hands.

"Holy shit," Heckler said brightly.

"Wow," said Lloyd.

"Where are you?" Calvin asked quickly, waving his arms around in the space between them. His own mirror image nudged the reflected girl and she shooed him away, reacting ticklishly. "I mean...you know...*you*," he clarified. "The *real* you."

Mirror Jenny mocked a look of offense, her hands to her chest, then shook her head, laughing, before he could take her wounded pride seriously.

Hinkley's voice carried through the doorway: "...the heck is going *on* in there?"

"Just a second!" Calvin replied, then turned back to the girl in the mirror. "Do you know where she is? Can you bring us to her?"

She nodded emphatically, then pantomimed at him, one hand flat and the other moving her finger in loops across it.

"A pen?" Lloyd guessed.

Mirror Jenny beamed and confirmed his Charades victory with a finger to her nose.

"Heckler," Calvin said, "get a Sharpie or something."

Heckler bounded across the apartment and dug a marker out of a drawer. On his way back, he smiled at the perplexed safecracker. "It's Jenny," he explained cheerfully.

"*What's* Jenny?" Hinkley demanded, completely lost, but Heckler ducked into the bathroom and handed the marker to Calvin. "Thought she was *dead!*" Hinkley called after him.

Calvin uncapped the marker, waiting for a cue. Mirror Jenny put one finger on the mirror and waved him close. The magician leaned over and put the marker at the tip of the girl's finger. With her other hand, she again mimed writing, this time in the air in front of her. Calvin nodded. "Got it," he said. "I'll trace."

Calvin followed Mirror Jenny's finger with the marker, watching letters form as they went. Before they'd finished the second word, Heckler started sounding it out: "Gin...and tonic? Gin...bitch...be...Gin Beach!" he announced.

"I'm on it!" said Lyle, but he tripped and fell as his jeans fell down around his ankles. "Ow."

"*I'm* on it!" said Lloyd with an impish grin, jumping over his friend and racing back to the computers.

Calvin looked at the words written on the mirror by his own hand, but in Jenny's handwriting. His heart pounded, and he gave Mirror Jenny a high voltage smile. "Oh, man..." he breathed, overcome with hope.

"There goes my deposit," said Heckler, rubbing uselessly at the marks on his mirror.

Mirror Jenny stuck her tongue out at him.

"Can you...come with us?" Calvin asked. "I mean, can we bring you there somehow?"

She shook her head, then leaned over, her fists in front of her, and started rocking forward and back with a firm expression on her face. To drive the point home, she stomped the floor with her foot.

"Rex!" Calvin realized. "Right." Jenny had left Rex in Wonderland, just outside of Heckler's apartment. Calvin wasn't sure how any of this worked—he didn't think even Jenny was totally clear on it—but if Mirror

Jenny was confident, he was willing to accept that she could ride Rex and meet them wherever they were going.

"Yes!" Lloyd cried out in the other room. "It's on Long Island! Montauk! All the way out, almost, like a few hours away, but it's there!"

Buttoning his jeans, Lyle went to join his partner at the computers. Heckler and Calvin stood side by side as they faced Mirror Jenny.

"Think *this* one would do the kinky stuff?" Heckler asked with a lewd grin.

Calvin and Mirror Jenny both threw unimpressed, unappreciative looks his way.

He put up his hands apologetically. "Hey, it's okay," he said. "It'd just be nice to have *one* of them, you know?" He smiled at Calvin pointedly. "The real one's all yours."

The magician twitched. "Uh..." he began lamely. "What? I mean...I don't..."

"Don't be as stupid as you look, Red," Heckler chuckled. "We all know you guys wanna bang like rabbits in a hat."

Calvin looked nervously at Mirror Jenny, about to protest—but the girl in the mirror tilted her head with a gentle smile, cutting off any objections. She nodded plainly and sympathetically. She might not have been the real Jenny, but she knew damn well what that one was feeling, and Calvin's reciprocation was as clear as the sheet of glass between them.

"Shit," Calvin said, feeling as stupid as he looked to himself in the mirror. "Shit," he said again. He took a breath. "We've got to get her back. We've gotta go!"

Mirror Jenny nodded encouragement, waving him off to go get ready. She put a palm on the mirror.

Calvin put his palm against hers, feeling nothing but cold glass and an incredible warmth blooming inside him. His own reflection morphed mindbogglingly around her hand. "Thanks. I'll see you soon," he promised. "I'll see *both* of you soon."

Mirror Jenny smiled, then ran out through the mirror world's bathroom door.

"You know," Heckler mused philosophically, "it *is* technically necrophilia."

Calvin replied with a wordless, deadpan stare.

Heckler grinned and popped a guilt-free shrug. "Yeah, I know," he said. "Glass houses, stones. But it's been a long time since me and her, you know. If you don't judge, you Romantic Necromantic you, I can lay off too."

Calvin couldn't completely hide his amusement. "Come on," he said, pretending he wasn't laughing even the least little bit.

They emerged from the bathroom to find the fanboys poring over Internet maps and Hinkley sitting on the couch with an irritated expression. "Feel free to let me know what's going on any time," the safecracker declared, bluntly annoyed.

"Um," Calvin waffled, "Mister Hinkley—I'm not sure how to explain all of this..."

Hinkley's bulging eyes locked drolly on the magician. "You could, I don't know, admit that we're going after Ming the Merciless or whatever his name turns out to be," he suggested, "and that the girl and I were going to go get her lightsaber. And she's bulletproof. And talks to you through your bathroom."

Calvin and Heckler looked at each other for a moment.

"That about sums it up," Heckler remarked breezily.

Calvin nodded and admitted: "Yeah, that's pretty much it." He paused, then turned sharply back to Hinkley. "Did you say *we?*"

The old crook's eyebrows went halfway up his forehead as he sighed condescendingly. "You four and the little lady against the Evil Mongo Army? I may've been sleeping, but I'm not *deaf*," he shook his head, disappointed. "The end of the world is the end of *my* world, too. Think I'm gonna sit here and bleed to death and hope you idiots get your shit together in time to stop it?"

"Hope not," said Heckler. "I can't afford new couch cushions."

"You get us where we're going, I'll do what I can to help," Hinkley ignored Heckler's quip. "I owe her that much. If I knew that shot didn't kill her, I wouldn't've run off and left her with that guy." He set his good arm firmly on his thigh and exhaled a full stop, having said all he was going to say on the matter.

Calvin looked at the old man, vaguely surprised. "Okay..." he said slowly. "Okay. Okay! Let's do this. Guys!" he called to the fanboys.

"Uh huh?" said Lyle.

"You know where we're going?"

"Got it here," Lyle poked the screen.

"Two hours, twenty minutes on Google Earth," Lloyd said.

"Well," Calvin tapped his chin, thinking hard, "it's gonna cut pretty close, but we need to get our shit together first." He grinned at Hinkley, who rolled his eyes. An idea rattled around in the magician's head, and he looked at the fanboys thoughtfully. "You guys still have your car?"

"It was my mom's," Lyle said unhappily.

Lloyd helpfully added, "She took it back after he had the accident."

Calvin was too wrapped up in planning to react strongly to the mention of Jenny's accident. "Hmm," he said. "Well, we'll figure something out." A slow smile played on his face as he stuck his tongue into his cheek ponderously. "Hey...it *is* Halloween. You guys up for a little Trick or Treating?"

Hinkley snorted and shook his head. "Idiots," he muttered.

CHAPTER THIRTY-FOUR

The bonfire had been burning since long before sundown. The artificial Tiki torches and paper lamps became mere afterthoughts, celestial moons encircling a fiery star in the center of the campsite. Jenny looked desperately at the window frames on the Raymonds' luxury trailer and the other trucks and campers, but Lawrence had led a group of men around to systematically crack each window, pull out every glass or plexiglass pane, and lug them down the beach and out of sight. The ring of vehicles looked like an automotive ghost town. The Apocalypse Party Planning Committee was taking no chances, and Lawrence's little squad had been very thorough about removing every reflective surface they could find.

Jenny's handcuffs were gone, but only because she was now tied tightly to a tall wooden pole stuck upright between the ocean and the giant fire. The thick ropes securing her waist, shoulders, arms and ankles weren't the kind of thing she could chew through, even if that was her go-to plan for escaping ropes, which it wasn't. She hadn't had a cavity since she was nineteen and started being careful about her teeth, and while her Grim Reaper regeneration powers likely provided full dental coverage, she doubted her jaws were strong enough anyway.

Not far away, two more poles were staked deep into the sand and strung with twine spiderwebbing from one to the other. In the center of the web was the magic hole, carefully nestled in knots and loops. It was closer to the bonfire than Jenny was, so she saw only the silhouette of its plasticine reverse side; the actual portal faced the fire, and she noticed those who passed it carefully averting their eyes, no doubt unnerved by the ultimate blackness oozing invisible fingers of cold through the hole.

Laid out on the sand in front of the suspended magic hole was a long black cloth shot through with curves of gold thread. The other props—the wand, the rings, the Window, and the spectacles Carrie had plucked from Jenny's face—were laid out on the cloth, where specific golden swoops and designs seemed embroidered especially to encircle them. Whatever diabolical ritual was about to occur, the stage was set, and the actors knew their blocking.

The fact that Matthew and Warren were casually grilling chicken and burgers less than thirty feet away blew Jenny Ng's mind.

A few official-looking types had dropped by earlier, as the bonfire bloomed in the cold afternoon sunlight. Many of the larger men in the party seemed to be permanently stationed at either end of the encampment, making sure that random beachcombers and tourists didn't come too close, but they let these latest visitors pass through without protest. Jenny had still been handcuffed, sitting on the front steps of the big trailer—Lawrence had his gun by his side and one hand on the back of her neck. Vincent and Carrie had gone to talk to the newcomers, along with Mary, who flashed some identification and paperwork. There were smiles and handshakes all around, and the officials waved politely as they headed back to the parking lot. Jenny wondered if this was a private beach that the Raymonds had rented, or if it was public property that required permits. She tried to guess what they might have written on the application under Type of Event— *Occult Ritual to Unleash the Ultimate Destruction of All Civilization* would probably have raised a few eyebrows, but the typical Parks and Recreation bureaucrat might greenlight the permit anyway.

The celebration kicked in as the sun set far out over the water, past the little inlet back up the beach; Jenny realized she must be on the north coast of Long Island, though she wasn't sure how that information could help. The grills were fired up, and the very social sociopaths mingled around veggie platters, chips and dip, porcelain plates and fancy silver utensils, and coolers of juice, soda, and beer. One table was noticeably lower than the rest, sinking under the weight of dozens of wine bottles. Music played from one of the campers, and the buzz of conversation drifted around the bonfire, bursts of light laughter flitting about as the sky darkened and the ocean wind picked up. Those cultists who wandered by Jenny's post, even as they avoided the impenetrably terrifying view through the magic hole, smiled warmly and even waved, as if she were a wedding singer or a clown hired to entertain the party. They were eating burgers and grilled chicken. They were sipping wine or beer.

Jenny wanted to scream herself hoarse at them.

Carrie Raymond passed by, her teeth and golden hair gleaming in the firelight, her black robe sweeping dramatically behind her as it blew in the wind. She beamed. "Isn't this so much better than a stuffy old party in the back yard?"

Jenny glared through half-lidded eyes. "Fuck you."

The gorgeous hostess just laughed and fluttered gracefully to another knot of black-robed conversation. Another black-robed figure shuffled over—a young man, judging from his rolling gait. He was short and round, and had his hood up over his head. The guy paused and looked up at Jenny.

Her jaw dropped as Lyle gave her a wink and a boyish smile.

The fanboy put one finger to his mouth in a silent *shh*, then held it in front of his chest and shook it to emphasize: *One moment.*

Jenny refrained from replying, though she couldn't help staring as Lyle lowered his hood and wandered off through the party. His other hand stuffed the remaining half of a freshly grilled hamburger into the depths of his hood. She imagined she could actually hear the voracious bite he took.

Her eyes scanned the mingling crowd tensely, jumping from hood to hood, shadow to shadow, looking for puzzle pieces that didn't fit. Most of the black-robed people gathered in groups of three or four, or stood around the tables scarfing veggies or adding condiments to their burgers. Almost all of them had turned their hoods up to ward off the late October chill on the shore; Carrie's dazzling blonde hair was one of the few exceptions. One tall hooded figure walked away from the grills with four hamburgers on two plates; he looked around surreptitiously, then juggled all four burgers onto one plate and deposited the other on a table. He walked alone, munching his burgers and not moving to join any of the social circles gabbing away.

Leave it to Lloyd to find a way to get free food out of rescuing her and saving the world. Jenny tried her best to keep from shaking her head in disbelief, but a dazed expression uncontrollably crawled up her slack-jawed face.

It was hard to keep track of either fanboy as they drifted amidst the other black-robed partygoers, sometimes around the other side of the crackling bonfire. Jenny was pretty sure she spotted them a few more times—Lloyd had three grilled chicken breasts on his plate the next time she saw him—but she might have confused them with the other hooded men and women on the beach. She couldn't identify Calvin or Heckler in the crowd, if they were there—her heart pounding, she hoped they were, even as she hoped they weren't in danger—and she had just begun wondering if she had only imagined Lyle's quick exchange with her, a last desperate mirage before the end, when raised voices drew her attention to the west side of the camp, where Lawrence had marched her in.

Barely illuminated by the blazing yellow fire, two shadows cautiously navigated the sand, catching themselves as it shifted and their shoes sank in with each step. They wore blue uniforms, and called out to the party in sharp, official tones.

"...complaints about the noise," one voice drifted over on the wind. "...permit?"

There was no mistaking the voice. Jenny's heart leapt and her stomach plummeted, and she tugged vainly against her ropes, squinting at the coalescing confrontation and straining to hear.

Keith Heckler, wearing a policeman's uniform that Jenny had to concede looked incredible on him, rested his hands casually on his gunbelt and tilted his hat back roguishly as he addressed the men standing guard. Standing next to him...

Oh god, Calvin, Jenny thought with unbridled adoration and embarrassment, *only motorcycle cops wear helmets.*

His face was hidden behind the closed visor, but she would recognize the magician's gangling frame anywhere, even in a dark blue uniform that didn't fit as dashingly as Heckler's. Jenny stifled a nervous giggle. Her eyes drifted to the boys' waists, where shiny black guns rode high in their holsters. She didn't know where they'd managed to find guns, but she sincerely hoped they didn't have to use them. The thought of Calvin shooting someone—even a bad guy—broke her heart. The thought of Heckler aiming a gun within a mile of anyone she cared about curdled her blood.

The fake cops were getting plenty of attention. A general murmur spread and heads began to turn. Several robed figures headed off to meet them; Carrie's shining golden hair bounced effortlessly above her flowing black robe, like the star of a gothic salon commercial. From what Jenny could hear through the wind and music and the snapping, crackling bonfire, the discussion grew louder and even a bit heated.

"...reserve the right to revoke the permit," Heckler was saying, putting some swagger in his hips and obviously relishing his role of authority. "...complaints...the local residents..."

Mary's hood was down, and she brandished her paperwork at the cops. "...everything's in order..."

"Sorry," Heckler shrugged, raising his voice to be heard. "We're getting a lot of complaints about the noise!"

Mary's voice on the wind was distinctly unimpressed. "...*are* no local residents..."

Jenny gave a start when she felt something tugging on her legs. She looked down to see Lloyd, his hood flipped back, on his knees and sawing at her ropes with a very sharp knife. He grinned up at her—Jenny shook her head quickly in a warning, and he hastily nodded an apology and focused on the ropes.

She looked around—the campsite was lopsided, the cultists all flowing to one side to see what was going on between their leaders and the cops who'd come to ruin their party. Nobody was paying any attention. She took a risk. "What are you guys *doing?*" she whispered.

He looked up with an enthusiastic smile. "I'm Lloyd Clevenger," he whispered dramatically. "I'm here to rescue you."

"No fair," came a fierce whisper from her other side. Jenny turned sharply. Lyle, wielding another of Calvin's very sharp knives, was carefully cutting the twine web suspending the magic hole between the two poles. He looked unhappily at his partner. "I was so gonna say it."

"I got it first, dude," Lloyd gloated quietly, getting through the ropes around Jenny's legs and rising on one knee to work on the one around her waist.

"Clevenger?" Jenny asked blankly. Lloyd looked at her. She shrugged weakly. "I just didn't know your last name," she explained.

The fanboy grinned at her excellent trivial banter in the face of overwhelming danger, feeling like the black-robed, knife-wielding, superhero-rescuing badass he was, and went back to work on her rope.

Jenny looked at Lyle, who had severed a few strands of twine and was surgically selecting his next targets so as not to let the hole fall unexpectedly. Calvin's new top hat sat on the damp sand at his feet. "Hey, Lyle," she whispered. "What's yours...?"

His blade paused, and he smiled daringly. "I'm—"

A gunshot smacked the air and echoed across the beach as a little splat burst out of Lyle's flowing robe. He spun back and fell on the sand. Jenny screamed; Lloyd shouted and stood protectively in front of her. She appreciated the thought, but he wasn't as bulletproof as she was, and she was trying to see what was going on.

The black robes were muttering and nattering and exclaiming on the wind. Lawrence, also in a flapping black robe, stood by the bonfire, his smoking gun trained on Jenny and Lloyd.

"Hey!" shouted Heckler. "You! Trigger Happy! Gun down, now!" He yanked his gun out and aimed at the Ice Cream Psycho. Beside Heckler, Calvin drew his own gun and swerved frantically, as if trying to aim at everybody at once, though it was obvious he had trouble seeing as his helmet jiggled on his head.

Black robes swished as cultists ducked and dashed out of the way of the impending gunfight. Carrie and Vincent could both be heard above the ruckus, ordering calm and reassuring their followers.

Mary suddenly swung her leg around and landed a sharp kick in Heckler's side, toppling him as he yelped. Lawrence turned and aimed methodically, squeezing the trigger with another stark crack of thunder.

Jenny shrieked.

His cry muffled by his motorcycle helmet, Calvin McGuirk dropped like a stone.

A hazy red film filled Jenny's vision. Her eyes felt hot, her ears pounded louder than any trip through Wonderland, and her skin felt like millions of tiny little knives were slicing and stabbing away at her. She howled with pain that had nothing to do with her physical body and tensed her muscles, pushing the ropes as hard as she could, harder than she ever could have before.

The ropes stayed taut, easily withstanding her onslaught. She had no leverage, and couldn't hope to slide either arm out of the tight knots.

Lawrence swung the gun back at Lloyd. A voice boomed: "Wait!"

Vincent Raymond held his hands high, and silence quickly settled over the party. Lawrence still had his gun on Lloyd, who pressed back against Jenny, his arms behind him, hugging her in reverse. He trembled and fumbled with his hands on hers behind the pole, breathing hard with the effort. At the edge of the party, Mary roughly pulled Heckler to his feet with the assistance of two burly men in black robes. Vincent and Carrie stood by Calvin's body on the sand.

The cult leaders moved closer, and Vincent knelt down, gingerly removing the motorcycle helmet. "Calvin!" he said genially. "I thought that was you."

"Bring them to the fire, gentlemen," Carrie ordered. Several men swarmed in to pick up Calvin. "Gently, please!"

The cultists straggled back in, moving around the fire, as Lawrence came around to grab Lloyd and jam the gun in his side. The largest of the figures in the black robes—Jenny realized that these strong, tough men were likely chosen by Carrie and Vincent specifically as the cult's muscle— brought Heckler and Calvin into the circle, holding them captive not far from Jenny and Lloyd. Calvin groaned; as his face came into the light of the bonfire, Jenny saw his pain and frustration.

The crowd gathered before the magic hole like a Rockwellian family reunion around a black-and-white television set. As if they were taking the stage, the Raymonds came to stand next to Jenny, while Lawrence the Ice Cream Psycho held Lloyd on her other side. Lloyd's face was ashen, frozen in shock and abject misery; Jenny looked over at the crumpled black robes on the sand behind the magic hole, one sneaker and a pudgy denim-covered leg sticking out of the velvety folds. Her eyes welled up. Lyle's only crime—other than killing her, she supposed—was getting mixed up in all of this. He didn't deserve this. Revenge stirred in her stomach as she eyed Lawrence in cold silence.

Two big men brought Heckler in, and another handful of big men dragged Calvin McGuirk with them. The magician didn't resist, holding his left hip and limping. Mary held Heckler's gun, but didn't point it at him. As they stopped next to the Raymonds, the no-nonsense woman showed the gun to Carrie, then snapped it in half, tossing the halves distastefully on the sand behind her.

Jenny goggled. "*Plastic* guns?" she sputtered hotly, more out of fear than anger.

"They're called *balls*, Jenning," Heckler said. "You've licked 'em."

She ignored him. "Calvin! Are you...?"

"Almost," the magician replied weakly, clenching his side and twinging. He smiled feebly. "Merely a flesh wound." He winced, coughed, and doubled over, apparently entirely unaware of the definition of *flesh wound*.

"Oh, dear," Carrie said with a maddening note of concern. "I do hope you'll still be alive for the celebration, Calvin." She ran a hand down the side of his face and cupped his chin.

The magician glared at her, anger smoldering in his eyes.

"Ooh," she teased playfully, jerking her hand back like she'd touched a sizzling stove. "You redheads and your fiery tempers." She charmingly laughed off his Dirty Harry squint and moved to center stage.

"Friends," Vincent Raymond projected loudly, "you all know that there are those who don't understand us. Those who can't understand the beauty and simplicity of the circle. They are trapped in their rigid, linear thinking, unable to see the curve of our universe, the way it elegantly moves beyond and around to complete itself."

Carrie took her husband's hand. "But we don't hate them!" she reminded everyone magnanimously. "They're not evil. They're just uneducated. They're just unaware of our oneness, our unity, the peace and harmony that it will bring. But they will be! They will be gloriously welcomed into our circle, and consumed in our love, to travel the circles of endings and beginnings *with* us, forever, into eternity!"

A smattering of applause trickled, then strengthened and gained volume, as the Raymonds' charisma brought the cultists back from the brink of uncertainty.

"These," Carrie gestured at Calvin, Heckler, and Lloyd, looking at each as she spoke, "are friends of Jenny's. And they will be treated with respect and honor at our celebration, just as she is our respected and honored guest."

"Hey, Blondie?" Heckler said easily. "This is the worst party I've ever crashed. You can go fuck yourself." His perpetual grin had a definite edge. Jenny had never seen him look actually angry before.

"Tie him," said Carrie.

"Gotta warn you, I charge extra for—" Heckler's quip was cut short when Mary's clenched fist crashed into his jaw with a horribly audible crack. Blinking and working his jaw, Heckler offered no resistance as several strong men lashed him to the post on one side of the twine spiderweb with ropes as thick as Jenny's. A flick of Vincent's hand, and the other strong men moved to tie Calvin to the opposite post.

Carrie walked spryly to Lloyd, smiling pleasantly at him. "Hello, dear," she said. "You look awfully out of place here, don't you? You know...*rescuing* Jenny after you and your friend are the ones who nearly killed her?"

Lloyd's chin shook. He stared ferociously into Carrie's eyes. His were dry, but only because they'd already emptied themselves onto his streaked cheeks.

From the spiderweb, a voice cut in: "Wait." Mary moved around the cloth to Carrie and Lloyd. She eyed Lloyd appraisingly, then whispered in Carrie's ear. Carrie's eyes opened wide, and she smiled sunnily at the revelation sinking in.

"Really?" she said, amazed. Mary nodded. "Oh," Carrie continued thoughtfully, "I think that might actually change a few things. In fact, that might be absolutely...*wonderful* news."

As the black-robed crowd watched, Carrie moved to Vincent and spoke quietly in his ear. A striking smile painted his face, and he bent down to snatch the spectacles from the black cloth. He handed them to his wife, who theatrically displayed the glittering lenses in the firelight before crossing back to Jenny. "Jenny," she said affectionately, "you are *so* clever! I knew from the moment I met you that you were a special young woman."

"Carrie's very intuitive," said Vincent. "It's like she's psychic!"

"I don't think we'll be needing *these* anymore, right, dear?" Carrie said. She raised the spectacles in both hands and snapped them in half.

The cultists gasped and murmured.

"So." Carrie smiled serenely. "Would you be so kind as to give me the Eyes, Jenny? The *real* glasses that you used in your show?" Jenny tried to not even blink. Carrie shook her head. "Oh, that's okay. I don't think you would have brought them with you. I think it's much more likely you would have left them with...Calvin. Yes?"

Anticipating his wife's words, Vincent had brought Calvin forward. The magician's dark blue shirt bore an even darker spot, tendrils of wet darkness spreading down toward his pants. He involuntarily kept one arm hugged to his side; Vincent held the other in a powerful grip as he guided the limping magician forward.

"Now, Calvin," said Vincent, "we're working on a tight schedule here, sport, so if you could just hand over the glasses, that would really help us out."

Calvin squinted groggily at Vincent. "Not gonna happen, sir," he said.

"Remember—just Vincent," Vincent grinned. He waved a hand, and Lawrence approached, opening his robe and sticking his gun in his belt.

Calvin shook his head as the Ice Cream Psycho approached. "You won't find them," he said. He tried a smile but coughed instead, and a tiny trickle of blood spilled over his lips. "I'm a magician. We never reveal our secrets."

Lawrence grabbed the front of his shirt and ripped it open, buttons flying, Calvin's pale, skinny chest flickering in the light of the bonfire. The Ice Cream Psycho went through pockets, dug inside the shirt, looking for anything that might be concealed. He yanked off Calvin's belt and even dug inside the magician's pants.

"*Now* it's a party," Heckler called, grinning despite the ropes securing him to the post.

Nobody paid him any attention. Lawrence finished searching Calvin's clothes—socks and underwear, the motorcycle helmet, even his shoes—and came up empty. He looked sharply at Vincent and Carrie.

Carrie sighed, then moved away from Jenny with a little *Go Ahead* sweep of her arms. Lawrence took his gun and jammed it roughly beneath Jenny's jaw, looking menacingly at Calvin. "The glasses," he growled.

A hoarse, bubbling, coughing sound erupted from the magician. After a bit of wheezing, it became clear to everyone present: he was laughing. Jenny smiled wryly, and Heckler's grin widened.

"Aw, come on," Calvin said bravely. "If we all got this far and you *still* don't know—"

"They know," Jenny said.

Calvin smiled at her. "Uh huh, figured," he said. "Well, you don't really think that's gonna matter, right? Threatening a girl you can't kill?"

Lawrence pointed the gun at Calvin.

The magician smirked, still clutching his side. "Yeah, kill the only guy who knows where the glasses are," he said. "Right."

Lawrence wavered, then aimed at Lloyd.

"Barely know him," said Calvin, looking bored.

The gun moved to point at Heckler.

"Can't stand him," said Calvin with an amused snort.

"Enough," said Carrie, her bubbly tone diminishing as her eyes flashed with sharper intent. "I don't think you're quite as careless about any of them as you're pretending, dear," she told Calvin, "but let me explain something to you. Let me explain how this works. In a very short while, I am going to break the Beacon—that's your wand, dear. And something far greater than you or I could comfortably imagine is going to come through the Portal—that's your magic hole, dear." She put out a hand, and Vincent slipped the magic wand into her waiting fingers. The bonfire painted a gleaming line of yellow light along the length of the dark wand. "When that happens, dear little Calvin, the Eyes—those are your glasses, dear—and the Aspect—your little square of glass—will be the only means by which our guest can be controlled. Oh, wait one moment," she said, reaching again. Vincent placed the rings in her hand. "Actually, our guest might be easily constrained by the Bond—that's your magic rings, dear. But, of course, if the Bond were to be lost..."

All eyes were on Carrie, who made as if to hurl the rings into the ocean.

From the spiderwebbed post, Heckler cleared his throat. "Uh, guys...?"

"So if you have any hope of *stopping* this, Calvin, dear," Carrie said, ignoring Heckler, "then you're going to have to let it *start*." She smiled beatifically at him. "Isn't that just so marvelously poetic? There are no *endings* without *beginnings!*"

"Everything is circular!" the crowd chanted.

"One perfect circle," said Carrie, "of endings and beginnings and the endings to *those* beginnings...and the beginnings that arise from *those* endings!"

"Guys...?" Heckler repeated.

"Now, are you going to give me those glasses, Calvin, dear," Carrie went on, her voice still calm but hinting at the frenzy behind her eyes, "or do we find out just what Jenny's ancient Chinese secret really is?"

With a flash of motion, all eyes were on Vincent, who held Jenny's long curved sword just inches from her chest. He tilted his head with a firm but caring smile, like a parent prescribing a necessary punishment for a favored child. Jenny stared at the shining blade, her eyes frightfully wide.

Calvin cut his breath short. "Wait," he stumbled over words, trying to buy time. "I...wait..."

"Guys!" Heckler shouted, compounding the tension rather than cutting it.

Carrie whirled furiously: "*You* will be—" She gasped. "Oh, my!"

A murmur percolated and popped, erupting in gasps and giggles and squeals and shouts, as everyone looked at Heckler and the web of twine. Poking out of the magic hole, hanging over the rim and squirming with an otherwordly undulation that twisted the eyes in ways that three dimensions normally don't, was a greenish, bluish *thing*...a serpent, or a tentacle, or an interdimensional worm peeking through the interdimensional wormhole, exploring the boundary between worlds.

"I think your guest of honor showed up early," Heckler remarked. He looked back at the hole and gritted his teeth. "...*and* his Plus One," he added, attempting a brave chuckle.

A second tentacle slinked through the hole, feeling the edge and tentatively tangling with the first. A third suddenly curled around the top of the hole, looping in and out of the twine webs.

"Okay, I'm shitting myself," Heckler admitted bluntly. "Anybody else?"

The charisma that the Raymonds emitted like French perfume could only go so far. The murmur of the crowd began to rise, and it wasn't all positive. Black robes rustled as the cultists moved back unsteadily, looking for answers that tentacles emerging from the darkness didn't provide.

"Don't give in!" Carrie shouted. "Don't give in to fear! Embrace the love! Embrace our Redeemer! Complete the circle!"

Carrie tucked the wand into the silk rope around her waist, and her fingers danced over the rings. She wasn't as flashy as Calvin—she wasn't aiming for showmanship—but her speed was eerily comparable, and she quickly had the rings linked in proper order, from smallest to largest. Her disciples watched, fascinated, Carrie's impressive spell once again taking hold, and she let the chain swing free, the smallest ring between her thumb and forefinger.

The three tentacles were joined by a fourth, and a fifth. The first one explored the cold, smoky, salty air and curved towards Heckler; it looped around the pole and wriggled up the side of his pants, exploring the rough material and picking at the stripe down the outer seam. The other coiled downward like dough spooling out of a pasta making machine, its tip brushing the sand just beyond Lyle's bulky black sleeve.

Heckler laughed, flinching ticklishly. "This feels *so*...funky..."

Carrie raised the chain just above and in front of the magic hole, then tapped it quickly with her fingers. The smallest ring lodged itself in empty space, the chain swaying below it. She reached through the bottom ring, the largest, and ran a finger down the lowest tentacle.

The tentacle shivered and went rigid—the other tentacles hastily snaked back into the hole. Like a cobra hypnotized by a snake charmer, the lone remaining tentacle doubled back on itself, the tip exploring its own length until it met Carrie's finger. An unsettlingly delicious shiver ran through her body as she leaned back and moaned. "Yes...!"

The tentacle prodded her hand, sending quivering ripples through her, wrapping slowly and carefully around her fingers. Carrie slowly, luxuriantly drew her hand back through the bottom ring, leading the entwined tentacle through. She completely withdrew her arm, leaving only the tentacle stretched through the metal ring.

Lovingly, passionately, almost reverently, Carrie pulled the tentacle to her lips, kissing the writhing, wriggling skin. The fingers of her other hand glided along the tentacle in a reassuring, maternal way, moving closer to where it passed through the largest ring. Beneath the serpentine appendage, her fingers found the ring itself, and tapped a quick and deliberate pattern on the inner side.

Carrie snapped her hand back, and the ring began to contract. The tentacle, as if sensing the danger, detangled itself from her other hand, undulating waves flowing back toward the magic hole; but it was too late. As the tentacle released Carrie's hand, the ring hit its waving humps and coils and squeezed, rapidly shrinking to catch the tentacle in a cold metal embrace. The shining metal circle compressed the aquamarine skin itself, which puckered and wrinkled in odd patterns that hit the eyes more like herniated optic nerves than the mere reaction of rods and cones to photons of light.

The tentacle yanked back urgently, pulling at the chain, but it was held fast, the ring at the top glued to the fabric of this universe. All the tentacle could do was pull the chain in a kinked curve toward the magic hole. The thing was trapped.

A low hum sounded, just below any frequency that could comfortably be heard. It vibrated the skin of everyone present like the mesh screen in front of the woofer at a death metal concert. Jenny could feel her eyes swimming as the entire world buzzed in front of them.

"Give me the Eyes!" Carrie demanded, turning on Calvin, her eyes flashing. "This is our only chance, Calvin! The end is coming whether you like it or not—there's no stopping that now! But if I can't accept the Seed, the circle will be broken! The beginning will never come!"

Voices rippled and burst in the crowd of cultists.

"The circle must be completed!"

"Give us the Eyes!"

"She must bear the Seed!"

"Do it!"

"The Eyes!"

"The Seed!"

"The circle must not be broken!"

Calvin had dropped to one knee, still holding his side in exhausted pain. He shook his head as the buzz of the crowd blended with the strange, unearthly hum that made the whole world quiver. Their uncertainty had vanished; the black robes advanced, silhouetted in the blazing bonfire. Calvin looked at Jenny. She stared back, her brow furrowed and jaw set, her shoulder muscles tensed and writhing. She only barely shook her head.

"No—I can't!" Calvin hollered, but his refusal was drowned in the noise of the crowd.

"The Eyes!"

"The Seed!"

"The circle!"

"Finish what we've started...!"

"...and start anew!"

Vincent's voice soared powerfully above the storm. "Enough! Give Carrie the Eyes now," he commanded, "or I'll run her through." He set himself, the tip of the wickedly curved sword on Jenny's breastbone.

Jenny cried: "Give me time, Calvin!"

Carrie yelled: "There's no time, Calvin!"

Vincent boomed: "Time's up, Calvin!"

The sword twitched.

The tentacle writhed.

The hum got louder.

"Stop!" Calvin shouted. "Stop! I've got them..." He looked near to tears. "I've got them. Just...here. Here they are."

The noise of the crowd simmered down, leaving only the crackling bonfire and the visceral hum shaking their bodies as the tentacle thrashed against its levitating bond.

Jenny shook her head, tears streaming down her face. "...Calvin...wait..."

The magician held up one empty hand—with a twist of his wrist, he conjured the magic spectacles and held them up. The firelight danced and twirled in the twin reflections on the lenses.

Carrie's eyes drank them in thirstily. Vincent's heavenly face split in a hellish smile.

"Thank you, Calvin," said Carrie Raymond in a calm, breathy voice. She plucked the glasses from his limp fingers.

The hum was unbearable, pulsing in their bodies with malevolent intent. Some of the cultists at the front of the crowd were blinking and shaking their heads, their mouths contorting with words no one else could hear.

Carrie proudly perched the spectacles on the bridge of her nose, wrapping the stems around her ears beneath her cascading golden hair. Vincent was instantly at her side, holding the Window up in front of her with one hand, Jenny's sword still in the other. The black-robed followers around the bonfire began to cry joyfully, chanting and shouting and wringing their hands. Some continued to mumble incomprehensibly, their eyes uncontrollably twitching open and shut.

In fact, Jenny noticed, several more of them were doing that. And it didn't look pleasant.

Wearing the magic spectacles, Carrie peeked through the Window that Vincent held up and laughed gleefully. "The Scriptures...!" she breathed.

"The Scriptures!" half the crowd echoed happily.

"Nnn...grnnnh...nnn..." muttered the other half.

Carrie Raymond, her eyes blazing with feverish rapture, took the wand from her belt and held it high. She looked adoringly through the Window at the tentacle and nodded sagely, finding just the glowing words she sought. The wand was pliant, even springy, as Calvin and Jenny had discovered in their examinations of the props...but they'd never bent it hard enough to break it.

Shouting words in a language no human ear could fully comprehend, and very few human voices could fully pronounce, Carrie snapped the wand in two.

Jenny winced—a piercing pitch stabbed her temples like red hot knitting needles, slashing through the outer layers of her brain into a place that was too deep to hold against the pain. Her head rolled as she writhed in agony against the tall wooden pole.

The tentacle, too, tensed and writhed with renewed vigor, whipping back and forth between the magic hole and the linked rings.

The cultists' eyes were fixed on Carrie and Vincent. Jenny's were closed tight, trying to block out the shrill tone needling her brain through sheer willpower. Calvin's were on Jenny, alarmed and urgent. Heckler stared at the tentacle, his mouth twitching. Lloyd's gaze focused below it on the pile of black folds on the sand.

"Come!" Carrie Raymond shouted, transfixed. "Come plant the Seed! Complete the circle, and help me give birth to a new world on the ashes of the old!"

She threw her arms back in an overdramatic, messianic pose, and Vincent Raymond lovingly wrapped an arm around her, his hand on her pregnant belly, the other holding Jenny's sword aloft triumphantly.

"Complete the circle!" half the cultists echoed.

"Nggrghghaah!" howled the other half.

The hum built up to blood-boiling levels, and the ocean stirred behind the hole. A light flashed from the ocean, a bright white beam cutting through the darkness to cast a wild, webbed shadow on Carrie and Vincent Raymond.

But the light zoomed closer, and the hum tangled in a strange harmonic with a more guttural tone, a growling pitch that was far higher and less tangible, sputtering and grinding.

More simply: an engine.

With a torrent of seawater and a wallop of sand, a small motorboat crashed through the encroaching waves at top speed, hitting some rocks and soaring over the short stretch of wet sand toward the hole suspended between two posts. Heckler yelped as the boat crashed into the opposite post, ripping the twine and knocking the thick wooden pole into Mary, who grunted and dropped to the ground.

"Ahoy, there!" a reedy voice shouted over the bow.

Vincent had protectively tackled Carrie as the twine split. Incredibly, the magic hole fell neatly into Calvin's black top hat on the sand; as it fell, the tentacle was tugged farther through the portal, still caught in the constricting chain that levitated above, and now protruded into the world out of Calvin's black hat. Calvin blinked at the crashed boat's harsh lights flooding the campsite.

Lawrence's face was frosted with cold anger. He whirled and aimed his gun at the pale, bug-eyed face looking over the edge of the boat. Suddenly, he flipped head over heels as the embroidered black cloth was yanked out from under him—the gun fired into the air over the fire.

With a petrified, wide-eyed smile plastered across his fear-stricken pallor, Lyle looked up from beneath his floppy black hood and dropped the edge of the cloth.

"Yeah!" Lloyd crowed, rushing to his partner's side.

"Through my freaking robe!" Lyle shouted back, sticking a finger through the bullet hole in the black folds. He glared at the Ice Cream Psycho sprawled on the ground next to him. "I'm not *that* fat, asshat."

"Crowning moment of *kicked your ass!*" Lloyd taunted, kicking Lawrence in the ribs, hard.

Lashing out with a primal scream, Vincent Raymond launched to his feet, leaving his wife on the sand, and rushed forward with Jenny's sword swinging in a whistling arc that would terminate in Lyle's back by way of slicing through Lloyd's neck.

It never hit; Vincent's aim went wide as a hand smacked into his face and knocked him off target. The hand bounced from his cheek, flopped down off his shoulder and landed on the sand between Lawrence's legs. Its middle finger unfolded in a gesture that threw Vincent off even more than the attack had.

Jenny stood a couple of yards away, free of the knotted ropes and the wooden pole, one wrist ending in a ragged stump and the other ending in a fist clutching Lloyd's knife. Her eyes glittered with jet black outrage. "That's my sword," she said in a voice shaking with anger, "and those are my friends. *You* won't touch *either of them.*"

Vincent stared dumbfounded as Jenny marched forward...but she stumbled and dropped the knife, her hand grabbing her head as she winced in agony. Stretching from the top hat on the ground to the chain overhead, the tentacle stiffened and relaxed and stiffened again, several times, in quick succession, as if it had pushed the stern head nurse on the psych ward a bit too far and got electro-shock therapy for its troubles.

Seeing her falter, Vincent moved to swing the sword around, but Calvin tucked himself into a torn and bloody somersault and rolled into Vincent Raymond's legs, pitching him over onto Lawrence the Ice Cream Psycho. The fanboys dogpiled him, smacking and kicking his voluminous black robes with no regard for which bits they might strike.

"You cut off your *hand?*" Calvin asked hoarsely.

Jenny pushed through the pain and flashed a grin masquerading as a grimace. "It was quicker," she said. "Those ropes are *thick.*"

Carrie Raymond was on her feet, ignoring the scuffle, fervently watching the seizing and twitching tentacle with a bit of that Old Time Religion on her face. The Window in her hand, she read glowing words off the tentacle, enunciating strange and sibilant syllables that snaked off into directions that didn't exist in this universe. Behind her, a couple of dozen black-robed figures were wagging their heads back and forth, mouths frothing, spit flying, ferally intoning: "Nghghrhrghgh...!" The rest of the cultists were starting to catch on, lowering their voices and staring back and forth at the ones caught up in the humming frenzy. The ungodly growling was soon accompanied by rising shouts of panic.

"I'm here!" Carrie Raymond cried into the wind and thunder. "I'm ready! Take me! Plant the Seed! Complete the circle!" She reached up and touched the captive tentacle once more.

ZAP.

It wasn't so much a sound as it was a feeling deep inside the skull, like a bumblebee perched nervously on your brain stem finally growing a pair and jabbing its stinger into your pineal gland. A psychic dam broke, and the frothing, flapping, wild-eyed men and women in black robes suddenly whirled on their saner fellows in the mosh pit to end all mosh pits. Dozens of tentacles shot out of the magician's hat like gyrating streamers on a New Year's Eve acid trip, gracefully arching over the crowd and plummeting down to indiscriminately snare and shake and wallop the gathered disciples, including the ones already salivating and creeping about on the others like robotic breakdancers with faulty servos.

Another dozen tentacles shot out past the captured one, whipping around Carrie Raymond's arms, legs, body, neck, instantly tangling her up in a muscular Gordian knot. Carrie's face was frozen in ecstasy, a sensual rictus twisting her lips as more incomprehensible and unrememberable words spilled out. Her fingertips quivered orgasmically; her toes curled as her expensive shoes fell off into the sand, and the tentacles lifted her twenty feet into the air, waving and squeezing her slowly, methodically, like a giant shiatsu masseuse with an advantageous number of fingers.

Vincent Raymond rolled out of the dogpile, only to lie on his back and stare upward, wide-eyed and open-mouthed. Another score of tentacles sprouted from the hat and curved high into the sky, out and over the woods to the south, the sea to the north, spreading out in every direction along the beach. The screams and chanting and throbbing hum threaded together in a bloodcurdling symphony; Jenny squeezed her forehead with one hand as the unbearable high-pitched screech sang counterpart to the low thrumming music.

"Guys!" she yelled, screaming to be heard but wincing at the volume of her own voice. "Grab Calvin!" She looked at the demolished motorboat. "Mister Hinkley! What are you doing here?"

"I never got the signal, but that stuff didn't sound so good! And the water was getting rough!" he shouted back over the din. "So I thought I'd crash the party!"

Jenny gave him the best smile she could, her nerves wrecked from psychic nails scratching down a cosmic chalkboard. "Come on!" she shouted. "We've got to get out of here!" Hinkley tried to carefully and hastily lower himself over the side of the boat; hastily won, and he landed with a heavy grunt, breathing hard.

"No!" yelled Calvin McGuirk. The fanboys helped him up, one on each side. He shook his head. "We have to stop it! It's going to spread! More tentacles—"

"*I* have to stop it!" Jenny corrected him, bellowing through the cacophonous cataclysm. "We have to get *you* guys out of here!" She turned and called out. "Heckler!"

"Nnngnrghgahh!" Heckler replied, foamy specks spewing from his mouth. He was pulling frantically and unsuccessfully at the ropes tying him to the pole, tangled in the frayed remains of the twine webbing. The pole was tilted but still jammed firmly in the sand.

Jenny looked into his wild and unthinking eyes. "Shit!" She reached down and grabbed her disembodied hand.

Lawrence the Ice Cream Psycho clutched at her sleeve. "Let her finish!" he snarled. "Let her receive the Seed! The circle must be completed! Let her finish!"

Jenny regarded him with a look of disgust. "*I'll* finish it!" she snarled back. Wielding her own severed hand like a hammer, she pounded him in the face, right on the ugly purple wound she'd already given him. His bandage was gone. He howled in agony and rolled in the sand, letting go of her sleeve.

She jammed her hand on her wrist and took a deep breath, feeling the scratchy pull of bones and viscera reconnecting. As tentacles continued to shoot out, stretching out across the sky, the crowd of black-robed cultists started swimming past them, heading for Jenny and the boys. The thrumming madness must have been contagious; there were more cracking, creaking, crinkled victims than before, and less panic-stricken cultists still frantically running from tentacles and spitting lunatics in a macabre game of tag.

"Go!" Jenny waved back up the beach toward the parking lot. "I'll get Heckler!"

Stumbling in the shifting sand, Lyle and Lloyd supported Calvin and ran off, skirting the teasing waves and breakers. Hinkley eyed her; Jenny nodded, and he loped off after them. Jenny took a second to look over at Heckler. He was yanking his ropes so hard his wrists were raw and bleeding, and he didn't seem to care, his face caught in a lunatic snarl and his mouth still geysering saliva and profane gibberish like the demonic love child of Old Faithful and Sam Kinison.

The noise was tangible. The ocean sobbed and the air babbled; the sand itself was stage whispering the sad lament of madmen. The afflicted cultists growled and howled, gnashing and thrashing, while the few who remained in control of their faculties shrieked in terror, trying in vain to pull away from the crazies. High above, Carrie Raymond danced in the wind, cradled by writhing tentacles. Vincent crouched anxiously nearby, staring up at his wife and mouthing words that just didn't matter anymore.

Jenny took a hop, skip, and jump, and punted one weighty Doc Marten into Vincent's perfectly chiseled chin—the Übermensch's eyes rolled back in his head and he collapsed backward. She grabbed her sword with her newly reattached hand. "*Mine*," she said softly, not caring if he heard.

A hand clamped her shoulder, and Lawrence breathed hot, angry breath at her as she whirled. He pulled her face to face, holding his gun threateningly and almost farcically to her eye, shaking it furiously. "The circle must be completed!" he roared, spitting as much as the crazies crashing around the bonfire.

In such close quarters, Jenny couldn't pull the sword away to swing it; it was jammed obliquely between them, the blade curving behind Lawrence's shoulder. Jenny looked him in the eye, then glanced past him at the blade gleaming in the firelight. Her sudden smile only infuriated the Ice Cream Psycho further. She swept her hand up the hilt toward the blade. He howled and pulled the trigger just as she brushed her thumb across the blade and disappeared.

451

The bullet flew through empty air and thunked into the thigh of a crazy cultist who was swinging feral fists at anyone or anything that came near; the black-robed woman dropped to the ground, her leg buckling, but didn't stop her flailing.

Lawrence blinked and stumbled forward. He railed against forces of fate that couldn't care less. "The circle *must be completed!*"

A tremendous hoof clunked square in the center of his bald spot, and he fell face first into the sand, out for the count.

"What goes around, comes around," Jenny remarked coolly. "Happy?"

Beneath her, Rex snorted and let loose a titanic challenge at the fallen Ice Cream Psycho, holding one hoof up like a wary prizefighter eyeing the next contender.

Jenny squeezed his neck. "Good to have you back, boy," she said. He nodded and tossed his mane; he'd been cooped up in Wonderland for half the battle already, and he wanted some exercise. She spun him around and he jumped over a sweeping tentacle. Another crashed down near her, and she ducked beneath it, urging Rex forward.

"Nghgrhrhrhah!" Heckler complained pitifully.

"I'm *coming!*" Jenny snapped at him. She didn't appreciate his tone, considering the piercing siren still ringing in her ears.

One tentacle came dangerously close, whistling past her head. She reflexively swung the sword up, and the wiggling thing actually warped around it, dodging with an improbable kink in its sinuous undulations. Without pausing, Rex leaped and galloped the last few yards to Heckler, who shook his head like a rabid dog.

"Nice," Jenny replied, tumbling forward off the horse and not even trying for a graceful dismount. She reached out for Heckler's ropes. He snapped at her, and she bopped him on the nose with the flat of her blade. "*No,*" she commanded firmly. He stared at her, his eyes scarlet and curious, with none of Heckler's charm and style. Whatever was really Heckler was either gone for good, or locked away, hidden deep inside. She hoped she could get it back. "Let's go!" she told him.

She reached for his shoulder, and he unceremoniously chomped down on her hand. It was more annoying than painful; Jenny rolled her eyes. "Good enough," she said. She gave Rex a look: "Follow the guys!" she shouted. Then she tucked the sword under her arm and palmed the blade with the hand Heckler wasn't biting.

The rushing emptiness of Wonderland's silent heartbeat was an incredible relief after the riot of sound and fury in the real world. The flat, glass-smooth ocean was blurred by half-existent waves, and the sand dimmed down to coffee brown. The campers and tables and boat and bonfire were gone, of course. There was nothing but a mile of beach in either direction, the hissing white noise of the Looking Glass wind, and Keith Heckler gnawing on the ball of her thumb.

His nibbling weakened, then slowed, then stopped. He blinked, looking around blindly. "Shit!" he said. His deafness struck him hard as he heard his voice only in the vibration of his head. "Shit!" he repeated more desperately.

It was definitely Heckler; the madness was gone, the attitude back. She hugged him close, rubbing his back reassuringly, trying to let him know she was there.

"Jenning?" he called. "I can't see a fucking thing!" His eyes chased nothing back and forth in a desperate attempt to make anything out. "Wonderland, right?" Like Calvin, his voice was louder than he intended, overcompensation for his inability to hear himself. "What happened?"

"Uh..." Jenny began, knowing he couldn't hear her.

"Yeah, stupid question!" he shook his head. "Am I staying or going with you?"

Jenny tugged his arm, pulling him a few steps along.

"Got it," he overenunciated.

She ran as fast as she could over the almost insubstantial sand—it felt like running across a bouncy inflatable castle at a kids' party—keeping in mind that Heckler couldn't see where they were going. He kept up, though, clutching her wrist and high-stepping to avoid tripping over anything. They reached the Looking Glass version of the parking lot in minutes.

Jenny hugged Heckler and pushed through her gleaming blade to the real world. She offered a silent prayer to whatever agents of destiny might be listening that her friend wouldn't immediately revert to Tentacle Madness. She felt him tense up—and then exhale a giant sigh. "Now that's a *trip!*" he whooped.

Jenny pulled away and smiled. "The only way to fly," she said.

"Jenny!" Lyle called.

453

The fanboys hunched with Calvin and Hinkley in the relative safety between parked cars; Lyle and Lloyd had removed their black robes and thrown one over Calvin's ripped up police uniform to keep him warm. Rex paced anxiously nearby, looking up with a relieved and grumpy snort as Jenny and Heckler approached. Hinkley's big bulging eyes were fixed on the sky above—a sky criss-crossed with slippery, sliding, glowing blue and green tentacles stretching off into the distance. The throbbing otherworldly song still thrummed in the bass range, and the tiny needle of high-pitched buzz resumed stabbing Jenny on the treble end.

Lloyd's long face was equal parts exhausted and amazed. "I'm a lot less excited to meet Cthulhu than I ever thought I'd be," he said.

"Ditto," Lyle agreed emphatically.

"Tell me it got worse," Jenny said darkly.

Hinkley didn't even lower his eyes to look at her. "No, I respect you too much."

"They're going *everywhere!*" Lloyd exclaimed. "This is it...this is it..."

"*Game over,* man!" cried Lyle.

"Dude!" Lloyd scolded him.

"Shut up!" Jenny snapped irritably. "I'm sorry, guys. That *fucking noise...*"

"The whole world's humming," Calvin said sadly. "It's like...it knows..."

"No, not that," Jenny shook her head curtly. "The whistling thing. The high-pitched siren."

They all looked at her blankly. "The what?" Calvin asked.

Jenny abruptly crouched in front of him and looked at him angrily. "*Why* did you give them the glasses?" she demanded.

The others froze as Calvin stammered uncertainly. "I...what?" He shook his head and looked her in the eye. "Jenny, that thing was already coming. I don't know if Carrie even knows what she's doing—it was here before she broke the wand, right? With or without the glasses, it was already coming out. If they killed *you*, what chance would we have? And the sword's the only thing that can probably...kill...."

Jenny stared at him.

Calvin gulped.

She dove forward, and their lips met; Calvin's eyes, wide and surprised, closed blissfully, and they held the kiss long enough to make the rest of the guys uncomfortable...and then a little longer. Jenny wrapped her hands around the magician's chin and jaw and neck, letting herself fall into the passion and reality of their kiss.

Shifting feet and throat-clearing ended the moment.

Jenny broke away and smiled, sadly but warmly, at Calvin. "That's a pretty good excuse."

"I came up with it all by myself," Calvin grinned. Then he coughed and cringed again, holding his wounded side.

Jenny held the side of his face, her worried eyes looking him up and down. "You need a hospital," she said. "*Now.*" She looked up. "Anybody know how to hotwire a car?" she asked.

"Of course I do," said Hinkley. "But it'll be tricky..." He showed off his arm in a sling, then winced from the effort.

"My car's right around the..." Heckler started.

"No time," Jenny said. "Pick a car, any car. Make it a big one. Heckler, you're the only one of us who got affected by the Crazy, so far. You get away from here—Hinkley'll help you start it, you can drive." She looked at him earnestly. "You keep him safe."

"Hey, these muscles are just for show!" Heckler preened, his perpetual grin back in the driver's seat.

"Then give 'em a good view," said Jenny. She accepted his sly smile as agreement. "Mister Hinkley, you go with them—you look like you could use a hospital yourself." She looked at the fanboys. "Guys," she said heavily, "I hate to put you in this, but I could use the help..."

Lloyd instantly answered: "We're in!"

"I'm *so* gonna name my daughter after you," Lyle said proudly. "Jenny Hillengardner," he added, finally getting to say it.

"What if it's a boy?" she asked.

"Bruce Wayne Hillengardner," he replied like it should have been obvious. "I already picked that one."

"In eighth grade," Lloyd pointed out.

Calvin stood, leaning on Heckler's shoulder. "Jenny..."

She stretched up and gave him another, shorter kiss to cut off his protests. "Just go with them. I'll finish this." She smiled worriedly at him, her hand over his heart. "I don't want you to get hurt."

His expression was a soap opera starring petulance and a mournful frown. "*Life* is about getting hurt," he said stubbornly.

Jenny kissed him again. "But I'm not alive anymore," she said simply.

"Jenny—"

"I love you, Calvin," Jenny cut him off. "But I need to focus. Love isn't rational or thought out. It's spontaneous, and reckless, and has no regard for convenience, or timing, or common sense...or *anything*."

"I..."

"Go," she said, pushing his chest firmly. She turned to avoid his kicked puppy eyes. "Guys, let's go."

Lyle and Lloyd averted their eyes, sympathetically avoiding Calvin, and headed for the sandy path back to the beach. Jenny ran to Rex and swung up in the saddle in one deft maneuver. The horse turned and reared up, kicking his front hooves and neighing an equine battle cry.

"What siren?" Calvin shouted over the stallion's noise.

Rex dropped his front legs, and Jenny looked back uncertainly. "Huh?"

"What siren?" Calvin repeated, limping forward away from Heckler. "You said you heard a siren. Not the humming, the low noise, you hear something *else*."

Jenny stared at him blankly. "You don't hear it?" She already knew the answer. She looked at the fanboys, then Heckler and Hinkley. "Guys? Heckler? Mister Hinkley?"

"Uh," said Heckler. "You mean something other than the *Logan's Run* soundtrack? Sounds like Barry White taking a really hard dump?"

"The *high* note," Jenny insisted. She saw no recognition in their faces. "Like a..." her face went white. "*Dog* whistle," she suggested slowly, realization dawning.

Calvin nodded firmly. "When Carrie broke the wand?" he asked. "You flipped out...is that when—"

Jenny smacked her forehead, then winced as she only aggravated the pain in her brain. "Fuck!"

"The tentacle went nuts then, too," Calvin said pointedly. He stared hard at Jenny. "I love you too, damn it. And love might not be rational, but *we* are. I'm a magician—I'm pretty good at looking in the right place at the right time." He grinned. "Capes and breasts never distract me."

"What does it mean?" Jenny blurted desperately. "Why would I be the only...well, me and the monster..."

"How did Carrie say those words?" Calvin said, his brow furrowed in thought. "I mean, they weren't Latin or Chinese or Portuguese or whatever...she was speaking a whole different language. Like, sounds that don't even sound like someone *talking*."

"...with the glasses on..." said Jenny.

"Looking through the Window," Calvin finished.

They looked at each other; the others listened tensely.

"We need the glasses," Jenny declared firmly.

Calvin nodded. "You need to see what she saw. Read what she read."

Jenny nudged Rex closer and leaned over; even on the giant stallion, she wasn't much taller than the lanky magician. "I'm sorry," she said, guilty eyes looking at the ground. "I shouldn't have tried to—"

Calvin put a finger under her chin and lifted her face. His smile was gentle and unjudgmental. "Hey, you're just indestructible," he said quietly. "It takes a magician to figure out the tricks."

Jenny smiled back. "I just wanted you to be safe."

"If we don't do this, *nowhere* is safe," he replied.

"Guys!" Lyle shouted out in a panic.

On the path from the beach, two black-robed figures were racing into the parking lot, their limbs flailing like overenthusiastic mimes with severe osteoporosis. A crash of metal and glass exploded next to Rex as a tentacle shot down from the sky and pierced the roof of a silver SUV like a fondue fork—the vehicle caved in on itself, splashing broken windows all around.

Rex bucked, and the guys reflexively ducked.

"Shit, that's the one I was gonna pick," Heckler said, staring at the SUV and the giant muscular tentacle stretching off into the sky.

"I think you guys took too long with the dramatic moment of revelation," Lloyd suggested.

"Yeah," said Lyle, "if we're gonna do this, we should get going."

Calvin grabbed Jenny's hand. "I'm coming," he said.

"I know," said Jenny. She leaned down and kissed him. "Get on!" Heckler helped the magician climb up behind Jenny.

Calvin wrapped his arms around her waist and leaned his chin over her shoulder. He kissed her ear. "Let's go!"

"Guys," Jenny shouted out, "Stay behind us!" She drove her heels into the horse's sides, and he charged off toward the beach.

Rex bashed his way through the two Crazies, knocking them off the path; they twitched and thrashed without getting up. Heckler and the fanboys ran as fast as they could in the stallion's wake.

Another tentacle speared the ground just ahead, then another, splashing sand that spiraled into the powerful wind racing over the shore. The waves were growing and frothing, pounding the sand like they were preparing dough for a pizza pie. Underneath the cries and screams and shouts down the beach was the throbbing hum of an otherworldly dirge; above all of that, Jenny still heard the piercing whistle in the center of her brain.

The campsite was in shambles. Several campers, including the Raymonds' luxury trailer, were flipped over or torn apart. The paper lanterns and fake Tiki torches were out—obviously, the tangled bundles of extension cords had been interrupted somewhere along the line—while the bonfire still burned, spilling out across the sand on blown bits of driftwood and kindling. Flickering flames danced around the central blaze; Jenny realized that some of the black-robed cultists had caught fire, and were either running frantically from the inferno or running mindlessly, infected by the nightmarish Tentacle Madness.

"Lyle! Lloyd!" Jenny shouted. "What do you know about this thing?"

"It's fictitious!" Lloyd shouted back. Lyle was huffing and puffing too hard to answer.

"Crap," said Jenny. "Does it have any weaknesses? In the stories?"

"Stars, magic, bigger monsters..." Lloyd started.

"Steam boats!" Lyle managed between ragged breaths.

"*Bigger* monsters?" Jenny yelled. "What the hell is bigger than *that?*"

At the head of the campsite, where one lone pole still stood at a steep angle jutting out over the water, was a writhing mass of tentacles thicker than a massive tree trunk, branching only feet above the sand into the hundreds of tentacles filling the sky or chasing cultists or lifting Carrie Raymond high above, where she was hazily lit in the bonfire's smoke and light. Calvin's top hat was gone, no doubt torn apart as the magic hole itself *stretched* to fit all the tentacles pushing through from the cold black world on the other side.

"And that's just its *arms!*" said Heckler.

"That might not even *be* Cthulhu anyway," Lyle suggested.

"Yeah, I mean...where's the rest of him?" Lloyd said. "And does Cthulhu have that many tentacles?"

"Why don't you count them?" Heckler offered sarcastically.

More crazed cultists scrambled across the sand toward them.

Their precarious position hit Jenny hard. She and Rex were indestructible, but the boys weren't. "Guys, watch out!"

Skritching, scratching, clawing black-robed men and women spidered across the sand, and Heckler and the fanboys froze behind Rex, unsure what to do. Calvin squeezed Jenny tight.

With the sound of a million bedsheets snapping smartly out over a million mattresses, the number of black-robed figures on the beach suddenly more than doubled. Out of the darkness, dozens of pale horses charged forward, each bearing a cloaked rider and letting out a spine-tingling whinny. Each rider held a long, wickedly curved sword, the blade pressed flat against the side of their horse's muscular neck.

A silky voice threaded the wind behind Jenny. "Remind me never to doubt you again, *menina*."

"Caravel!" Jenny whirled the horse, almost knocking Calvin off—he squeezed tighter, which she definitely didn't mind. The beautiful brown *Anjo da Morte* smiled wryly, standing in the stirrups as Zé trotted forward in line with Rex. Sitting behind her on the saddle was another black-robed Grim Reaper: pale, skeletal, and regarding the chaos with calm curiosity, Pauzok hugged Caravel's waist loosely.

"This," Caravel said, scanning the scene, "is not what I expected. What's that awful noise?" She held a finger to her temple and rubbed vigorously.

"You came!" Jenny said gratefully. "You all came!" She looked at Pauzok, who regarded her cheerfully even as he squinted and clenched his jaw against the racket like someone who'd forgotten his glasses. Her face must have struck a chord. "And you got him," Jenny smiled at Caravel. "Thank you."

"Thank *you*," said Caravel. "Now, what is this? What's going on? These people are all appointed tonight...and so are many, many more."

"I don't care about these," Jenny said unkindly. She was surprised and caught herself, shrugging her head back and forth. "Or, well, maybe. But we just need to stop that thing. I need to find the magic glasses. And the Window!"

"That creature should not be here. Do what you need to do, *menina*," said Caravel. "And we'll take care of the rest. But do *not* use your sword against them!"

"Against who?"

"Any mortal," said Caravel. "These swords are not meant to take a human life. If they do, the consequences can be *muito perigoso*."

"Then what *good* are they?" Calvin complained.

Caravel winked coyly. "You know what they're for, Amazing Quirk. *Ya!*" She kicked her heels into Zé's flanks, and he bolted forward.

"*Lei ho*," Pauzok said brightly as his face flashed by.

"Hi," Jenny called after him.

"He seems happy," Calvin said optimistically.

"A future that goes on forever," Jenny remarked, "and no past to worry about."

"Let's make sure *our* future goes on at least a little bit," said Calvin. He grinned over her shoulder and hugged her.

Jenny snapped the reins. "Guys!" she called. "Just stay clear of anybody in black robes, and find the glasses and Window!"

The fanboys ran, Heckler running just a bit faster ahead of them. Rex marched across the sand, dodging cultists or just nudging them aside with a well-placed bump from his flank.

Ahead of them, Reapers on horses galloped through the party, even through the bonfire itself, leaving little puffs of black smoke in their wake. Some launched from the saddle and tackled cultists to the ground, disappearing as they thumped their swords to their chests. Some scooped up cultists and laid them across the saddle, bringing them along as they laid their sword blades against their horses' necks and disappeared, riding the powerful steeds through nothingness into the Smooth Road. The Grim Reapers weren't exactly a crack military outfit; for all their extraordinary powers, they weren't definitively faster or stronger than their foes, and since their swords were apparently only to be used as transportation—rather than as weapons—they were occasionally forced to grapple or struggle with the cultists as they swept through the party. Their horses were an advantage, but the crowded conditions reduced that advantage, forcing the horses to avoid each other and their riders in the unpredictable fray.

One thing Jenny noticed in particular, however, was that the tentacles didn't harass the dark riders and their horses. In fact, whenever they got close, the tentacles would bend and twist in sharp angles just to stay clear of the otherworldly Angels of Death. "Calvin...?"

"Yeah, I see it!" he said, staring in amazement. "I'm sticking with you!"

"Just hold tight," Jenny said, and pushed Rex onward.

Vincent Raymond stood near the disheveled and sand-covered black cloth, staring up at his wife. The dozen or so tentacles holding her well above tree height seemed to have no interest in joining the hellish rioting, and waved evenly in an imperceptible breeze, much slower and gentler than the howling wind ripping into the coast. Rex circled wide near the crashing waves, and Jenny yelled through the wind: "Vincent!"

Like he was waking up, he blinked and shook his head, then turned to her groggily. He wore a weak and wavering smile. "The circle...we're completing the circle...!" he said, just loudly enough to hear.

"Vincent, no!" Jenny said. "I need the Window. And the glasses!"

"She's so...beautiful!" He gazed lovingly up at the tangle of tentacles in the sky.

"Fuck, he's gone," Jenny muttered to Calvin.

A high-pitched voice slipped in beneath the wind: "Got it!"

Jenny and Calvin turned to see Lyle and Lloyd standing by the pole where Jenny had been tied. The taller of the pair was waving the Window to Your Soul back and forth in the blazing firelight.

"Stay there!" Jenny said, steering Rex away from Vincent.

Heckler converged on the fanboys just as the horse got there, and Lloyd handed the Window up to Jenny. She gritted her teeth. "We still need the glasses," she reminded them, "it's useless without them!"

"Blondie!" Heckler exclaimed. The others looked at him. "She never took them off—right?"

Five pairs of eyes traced the long path up the bundled tentacles to where Carrie Raymond swayed above them.

"Oh, shit," said Jenny.

"I'll get them!" Lloyd yelled excitedly.

"No!" Jenny said. "Stay there—I'll get them...somehow." She slipped inside the reins and shouted over her shoulder to Calvin. "Grab the reins—stay on Rex!"

"You're crazy!" the magician declared.

"And indestructible!"

"You'd better be!" he insisted, with a quick kiss on her cheek.

Jenny jammed the Window in her pocket as Rex made the quick jaunt to the magic hole, the source of all the tentacles squirming into this world from somewhere else. The hole had expanded to an absurd diameter, cinching all of the tentacles together like a plastic tie around a bundle of electrical cords. If she was going to reach Carrie at the top, though, Jenny had to start climbing from here.

She shoved her sword into Calvin's hand. Finding it hard to stay balanced, she brought her feet up on the saddle and turned in a crouch, her hands on Calvin's shoulders to help her stay up. Jenny reached up, faltered, caught her balance on Calvin's head, then took a deep breath and pushed off *hard*. She leaped, arms outstretched, aiming for the tentacles snaking up toward Carrie Raymond, trying to snag the first branch so she could climb the rest of the way up the serpentine tree.

The tentacles kinked into four ninety-degree angles, forming a perfect open-ended frame and neatly dodging around Jenny, who flew through the air and landed hard on the beach.

"Oh, crap!" Calvin exclaimed. "You can't!" Jenny looked up at him. "You guys...the Reapers...you can't *touch* the tentacles! It's impossible!"

Jenny let out a frustrated shriek.

It was answered by a low growl of fury as Calvin was suddenly yanked from the saddle, falling on the black cloth with a painful thud.

Lawrence the Ice Cream Psycho yelled incomprehensibly and tore Jenny's sword from Calvin's weak grasp. He charged at her, swinging the sword overhand, coming down to cleave her in half. Behind him, Lyle and Lloyd ran to catch up, but they wouldn't make it in time. The sword slashed downward. Jenny stared helplessly, trying to tell her legs and arms to scrabble her body out of the way.

The sword stopped short with a reverberating *clang* against another curved sword. Lawrence turned to snarl, but his eyes opened wide as Ketch, the big stocky Grim Reaper, smashed a meaty fist into his face. Lawrence's legs wobbled, and he dropped roughly and unwillingly to the ground, eyes unfocused and nose leaking blood like a faucet.

A huge smile parted Ketch's red beard. "An' it be miles down the road, so my calling comes to call," he rumbled gleefully.

"Yes!" cheered Lyle. "Go, Conan!"

Lloyd laughed and pumped a fist through the air.

Ketch helped Jenny up. "The road shakes, Little Accident, with more appointments than breaths." He came close and winked. "It will not break me worse to see the slate cleaned and written newly."

Jenny smiled. "I'll see what I can do," she said.

"Well! No accident, then!" Ketch declared in his gravelly roar, and he charged like a locomotive into the chaos around them.

"Calvin!" Jenny shouted.

He was sitting up. "I'm fine!" he lied, coughing and holding his side. Rex nuzzled his red hair comfortingly.

Lloyd yanked Jenny's sword away from Lawrence and held it out. She didn't take it; looking around, her heart skipped a beat. "Where's Heckler?" she asked urgently.

"Uh..." said Lyle.

"Jenning!" Heckler's voice echoed down from above. They all looked up to see him perched on the clump of tentacles wrapped around Carrie, barely visible, like a friend at the top of a ferris wheel on a dark boardwalk night. He waved wildly, a telltale glint between his fingers—he'd snatched the glasses right off Carrie's face.

"You got them!" Jenny hollered proudly. "How the hell...?" She stared at Lyle and Lloyd.

"He said to wait here!" Lloyd said quickly.

Even from a distance, Heckler sounded strained and growly. "Geeks can't even...climb the ropes...in gym!"

Lloyd shouted back. "Can too!"

"...not really," Lyle mumbled with a downcast glance.

"Jenning!" Heckler yelled. "Ngnghhr...!"

"What?" Jenny panicked. "Oh, shit!"

"Nghghrahh!" said Heckler. He shook his head furiously, like he was trying to get water out of his ears and the water was filled with tiny piranha. "...*catch!*" he spat out, chucking the glasses.

Jenny and the fanboys dove, all pop fly etiquette out the window. As the spectacles fluttered and spun, Heckler slid off the other side of the knot of tentacles. The glasses hit Lyle's fingertips and bobbled for just a second before they lay flat on his palm, neatly snagged. "Huh!" Lyle exclaimed, surprised and thrilled by what was probably the best catch of his life.

Heckler plummeted. "Nghrahhahh!"

"Keith!" Jenny screamed.

A streak of black and white blurred by, and Caravel caught Heckler's falling body expertly, not even holding the reins as Zé raced under the tentacles. Pauzok was no longer in the saddle with her. She turned and called to Jenny: "He's not on my list tonight, *menina*—and I think we can keep it that way!" Zé jumped and dodged around some frenzied cultists, and Caravel yelled over her shoulder, "I'll put him somewhere safe!"

"*Obrigada!*" Jenny said, jumping and spinning in celebration as Caravel rode off into the night. She ran to Calvin and grabbed his hand, helping him up. Lyle and Lloyd followed quickly.

"What's next?" asked Lloyd anxiously, holding Jenny's sword awkwardly in two hands. Lyle held up the spectacles gleefully.

"I guess we find out," said Jenny. She took the spectacles and pulled the Window from her pocket. "Let's see what we can see."

They held their breath as Jenny put on the glasses and held up the Window. She turned her gaze on the scores of tentacles bottlenecked in the magic hole. Then she nodded once, slowly. She wasn't smiling, but her face seemed serene.

"What?" Calvin asked. "What?"

Jenny didn't take her eyes off the tentacles. She moved forward, and Calvin grabbed her arm protectively to stop her. She turned to him with a calm, easy expression.

"What is it?" he asked again.

Jenny pulled him down to eye level and kissed his mouth. "It's his name," she said. "And I think we need to talk."

"Jenny—"

But she gently twisted away and approached the tentacles. Calvin stood back with the fanboys; Rex nickered softly behind them.

Jenny reached out, and the tentacles dodged sharply. She nodded, then paused, then opened her mouth and pronounced words that slithered across the ear and scrambled the brain, words that no human had any business knowing.

The tentacles all snapped into stillness. The Crazies all collapsed on the sand. The tempest of noise subsided. And the world held its breath.

CHAPTER THIRTY-FIVE

The high-pitched whine resolved, once she sounded out the symbols scrawled across the myriad tentacles in glowing letters, into a very specific and direct vibration aimed into her cerebral cortex, completely bypassing ears, eyes, or any other external sensory organs. It was the difference between the drone of an art history professor's slideshow narration in a darkened lecture hall and the distinct timbre of his voice when he catches you napping and calls you on it.

In that direct vibration was a sensation that made the hair on the back of her neck stand up, and her brain took the ingredients of that sensation and whipped up an omelette of unforgettable images: mostly eyes, looking at her sternly from somewhere above her head. They weren't strangers' eyes. They were eyes she knew. A third grade teacher. Her mother. A junior high principal. Her mother again. A government employee behind a counter. Her mother again, again. A hundred pairs of eyes, many of them her mother's, as well as firm-set mouths and folded arms and archly tapping toes, from a thousand different moments in her life, none of them related to the others...except by that sensation.

It was the sensation of being carefully scrutinized by a suspicious authority figure that was nevertheless waiting and willing to hear her side of the story.

She was lost in the sensation, feeling burning guilt and shame, mentally putting her hands behind her back and hanging her head, twirling a hypothetical toe on an abstract rug, unable to push through the overbearing scrutiny to provide any notion of defense or explanation. She felt crushed under the weight of those hundred pairs of eyes.

They blinked.

New memories flooded her: the taste of every piece of gum she'd ever chewed, the loud rattling hum and oily smell of an exposed engine, the bristling fur of some small wiggling animal beneath her fingertips, the smell and pale yellow of a wilted flower in the sweaty fist of a little boy who ate way too many hot dogs. The memories congealed into a conceptual capsule, a specificity that dissolved into something unutterable but clear; a meaning that made sense inside the snapping neurons electrifying her mind, but not in any human language she could speak, even though that included every human language ever spoken.

The meaning was softer than unblinking eyes. The meaning was patient, but expectant.

She tried to speak, but words exploded in her head like cold milk expanding in a bubble.

Shadows and colors snaked around her, stirring the darkest recesses of her mind. Holes opened in the present and the past, puffing with the smells of a million meals, the sounds of a billion insects and a trillion palpable squeaks of shoes on linoleum. In those, she flipped over the vague memory of a thousand rocks flipping over, and a sharp old woman's face smiled.

It came clear in that smile, the smile of a woman browsing thousands of recollections to pick just the right path. It *was* a language—just not a human one. It was the core, the basic understanding of the universe, a shared and common pidgin of experience that could be shared and understood across all cultures, every species, any intelligent minds. The memories and sensations weren't the language itself—they were just how her brain made *sense* of it, cobbling together contexts she could more readily understand from her own lifetime.

She sifted through surface memories, unskillfully trying to construct a semantic package through which she could communicate her meaning and intent. A hundred hands reaching, palms up; two hundred eyes opened wide, looking down; candy placed on a school folder on a small desk on a tiled floor on miles of dirt on the roiling miasma of fiery liquid stone pulling it all down toward the center...

Toes tapped again, and every member of a large audience waiting for a Broadway show yawned simultaneously, then assumed a polite expression and peered at the stage.

She tried harder, pushing everything together, ignoring names and places and facts and figures and actions and reactions, and going purely with the emotions she felt in response to them. She let an image flow through her: a greeting card scribbled with cartoon monkeys unfolded itself, and a slip of paper fluttered to the floor.

A dusty footprint in the sand answered. The terrain was cold and airless. The stars stared down, red and unsettled. She felt like somebody was reading her diary over her shoulder.

She responded with a million crying faces, some from her own life, some from the very moment she'd just left, some from television commercials with wise Clausian figures suggesting how her spare change could change the life of skinny children in other countries.

A foot stamped abruptly into the dusty footprint, then pulled upward and away, leaving smooth and unmarked dust. The red stars transformed into picture frames of all sizes and descriptions, each one defining the boundary of an empty white canvas.

She brushed shining reflections across the blank canvases, her own face staring back from each, not one with the same expression or pose as any other. A million million mirror images in a million million different flavors.

A pause lasted somewhere between a picosecond and an eon. The reflections shifted, like mirrors tilting on separate gimbals all at once, to the same degree, panning across blackness all around until something new came into view. It was a glow of green and blue, a swirl of goo and membranes and shells, varying from frame to frame: here elongated, there tangled, over there spiraling into itself in intricate and even beautiful mathematical progressions. Each image played a very specific note, a low note that couldn't be heard, but resonated in her bones and veins.

She smiled tentatively, and her smile echoed back in a pulsing yellow glow in each and every mirror.

A small square table with a clean white tablecloth was set beneath a sharp spotlight. The light illluminated only the table, leaving the surrounding room in blackness. On the table was an empty plate. Nearby was the smell of aftershave and the scribble of a pencil.

Her response was a quickly devoured stack of pancakes, the smell of a roasting June evening after a brief heavy rain, and a field of freckles showered with warm but insistent kisses.

The freckles crudely morphed into curious blobs of peanut butter and jelly, all glowing yellow. One by one, the points of light flashed and extinguished, the blobs disappearing with them, in quick and astonishing

467

succession. The humid air after a June storm dried to scorched desert. There were no more pancakes.

A catch in her throat spilled tears. She offered the humble smell of pine needles and the irksome but irresistible feeling of her fingernails scratching silk ribbons.

The ribbons were torn apart. A single round stone took their place, levitating alone in the void. It glowed with that same yellow phosphorescence.

She wasn't sure how to respond to that.

The stone sprouted white fur, and the glow dimmed to a foaming sea green. A dozen little girls burst into a bathroom where she was picking her nose on the toilet.

She hung her head sympathetically, the hot damp of a towel on her forehead and the hard tap of glass on the tip of her teeth or tongue driving like a sonata into an exhausting run around a park after a bad break-up.

The girls spun in place, pulling their arms tight, crinkling and stretching into long knobby sticks, which then fell over and splintered. The muted frustration of spilling your drink blossomed into the unspoken outrage against someone blasting their car stereo too loudly.

She offered only agreement; a pair of shoelaces satisfactorily and permanently tied on an old pair of sneakers that smelled like every field she'd ever run through.

Photographs of everyone she'd ever known shuffled like a flickering kinescope, circling through over and over and blurring into a single image of beautiful blonde hair and perfect white teeth.

She shook her head. The teeth stretched and fell out. The golden hair faded as the teeth ran outward in all directions.

Forcefully, stubbornly, the teeth veered back to the center and made stunning acrobatic *leaps* to crash into each other in explosions of pompously improvised jazz clarinet and loose change. As the coins jangled and cleared away, the blonde hair glistened again, mirroring her every pose and expression.

She shook her head again. Her own army of reflections, breaking out of the frames floating in the darkness, converged on the sneering yellow and screamed ugly colors and the taste of unwashed metal spoons at it.

A giant tub of dirt and hacking coughs fell on the silken hair, pounding it into a swarm of yellow bees with flowing black wings. The bees started to advance on the million surprised reflections of a skinny Chinese girl, but instead turned sharply upward and zoomed toward glowing green and blue images in the frames overhead, stingers waving with dripping dyskinesia that made her stomach and heart twitch.

With an ease she hadn't expected, she caught the bees with lassoes of thin red yarn and tangled them in one giant ball of buzzing knots.

The ball split in two, like an amoeba becoming a proud parent, and one faded away under a cool trickle of icewater.

She nodded. The other buzzing ball of yarn turned to powder that puffed away in a breath of fresh basil.

Everything faded to black. The noble strains of a single violin painted the black, curling around and returning her attention to the empty table. The pencil scribbled furiously. The violin settled into a single, long, sustained note, becoming more whalesong than Stradivarius.

She thought of the smell of makeup and city streets.

The pencil scribbled louder, drowning out the scents.

Powerful, sweeping oceans swept out of her, crashing into the unmoving table and teeming with life from the tiniest microorganisms to the biggest of blue whales.

The pencil tore through paper as the waters subsided. The tablecloth was bone dry.

The honesty of Calvin McGuirk was set on a silver serving tray. The compassion of Calvin McGuirk poured into a pristine crystal glass. The strength and loyalty of Calvin McGuirk patted the chair and pulled it out from the table as an invitation.

The pencil went silent. The cetacean violin tremolo wriggled to silence. Her mother's hands were holding hers and her brother's; a larger set of hands, with long agile fingers, handed her a brand new digital camera.

The warmth of hot tea spread across her tongue.

Again, the conversation dimmed to black, but this time there was the tiniest circle of light flashing in the darkness. Inside the circle, pain and anguish pushed futilely against the edges.

She understood. The circle shattered and the passionate tempest swirled outward, the expansion lowering its density and reducing it to a mere dull ache of cosmic background emotion.

There was the gentlest touch on her chin, and a flash of green eyes. A handful of mint-flavored bells rang softly and slowly in an unhurried and haphazard sequence.

Jenny Ng bowed her head respectfully. "You're welcome," she said. She figured that would translate well enough.

CHAPTER THIRTY-SIX

"Jenny!"

The ocean was still crashing, the world was still humming, and Calvin was shouting next to her as she stared up at the tentacles protruding through the magic hole. Her arm tingled numbly—she'd been holding the Window in front of her the whole time. She blinked and fell to the sand before the hole, dropping the Window from nerveless fingers. Calvin caught her and helped her down.

"We need to let him go," Jenny said, exhausted and very quiet. Calvin stayed close and heard every word.

"Him?" He stared, uncomprehending, then jerked back and looked up. "*Him* him? The monster?"

"The...yeah," Jenny said, nodding to avoid the weight of words. "Just release the chain, Calvin. *Please.*"

He hugged her and nodded firmly, the wind whipping his black robe around him. The flapping cloth barely went below his knees as he stood up and reached for the rings suspended in mid-air. With a quick flick of his fingers, he tapped the small top ring and it instantly popped free, cascading down with the other rings.

The bottom ring began to expand, but the captured tentacle was even faster—it whipped back into the hole past hundreds of other tentacles, taking the rings through to the unknown space on the other side.

One by one, tentacles unraveled from the sky overhead, slithering back into the magic hole like slurped spaghetti. The hole started squeezing back down to normal size as twenty, forty, eighty tentacles retracted, disappearing in the dwindling forest of tentacles still extending upward and outward. Another score vanished, then another hundred, and soon there was only one long, tangled bundle of tentacles left, extending to Carrie Raymond's body bobbing in the night sky.

Lyle and Lloyd moved quietly to Jenny's other side, standing over her protectively like Calvin, watching as the tentacles went home and the crazed cultists, collapsed around the bonfire, began blinking their crusty eyes and smacking their lips, looking around in dazed confusion. The Grim Reapers, some mounted and others guiding their horses, watched warily, many of them stomping out errant flames and helping weary cultists sit up. Some Reapers flashed out of view, only to reappear with more black-robed cultists in tow, leaving the bewildered mortals to wander through the remains of their failed apocalypse.

Above, the tips of the tentacles slowly descended, dropping Carrie with an unceremonious thump next to her husband. Vincent stood with his arms at his sides, staring at the waves with a dull and broken expression.

Free of their burden, the tentacles swept gracefully away from the Raymonds, past Jenny and the boys. Uncertain but solemn, Calvin and the fanboys watched the tentacles spiral through the magic hole like jungle vines swirling down a toilet. The weird pervasive hum died down to the simple ocean wind beating a pleasant rhythm against their hair and ears. The waves, still wilder than normal as the tide ebbed, began settling down to levels that wouldn't make a veteran surfer soil his wetsuit.

Jenny smiled easily, wistfully. "Thanks," she said.

"You're not talking to us," Lyle asked in a small voice, "are you?"

Jenny looked at him. "Well, thank *you* guys, too," she grinned. "Thank you, thank you, thank you!"

Lloyd stared at the magic hole lying in the sand by torn pieces of Calvin's black top hat. "What *was* it, though?"

"Just a guy," Jenny shrugged. "I mean, for whatever *his* kind thinks is a guy, he's just a guy. He was just coming to check out where all those *mice* and things were coming from..." She smiled wryly at Calvin. "And then Carrie...well. It was her fault. He wouldn't have done all that. She was hurting him. She was...well..."

"Raping him," Calvin said soberly. He glared at the Raymonds.

Jenny reached up, and Calvin helped her to her feet. They hugged tight.

Lyle and Lloyd looked at the Raymonds, then back at the hole. "Whoa," said Lloyd. "*Not* cool."

Jenny lay against Calvin's chest and looked through the hole. There was the barest flicker of blue and green flashing in the distant inky black. "The wand was a weapon," said Jenny, "or like...like a cattle prod. It's supposed to get his attention, I guess, but it doesn't work like that. It hurt him. A lot. I think that's what I felt, too—but it didn't affect you guys. And the rings tied him down. And Carrie...she could read his name—she must've been practicing that forever." She looked up at Calvin. "The letters on her paintings," she reminded him. "They're the alphabet that spells his name."

The magician held her head tenderly, brushing her hair back.

Jenny turned back to the hole. "But she only knew how to *read* it. She couldn't understand him. She didn't hear him when he said: *No.*"

"No means *no*," Lyle declared sternly.

"Yeah," Jenny smiled appreciatively, then looked over at Carrie Raymond, lying twisted and contorted at her husband's feet, a disturbing smile on her face. "I don't know if she knew what she was doing," Jenny went on, "or if she just thought of it like all those myths and folk tales she learned. Like he was just a part of her stories, instead of...instead of something else. Some *one* else. The...the *person* the stories were *based* on, not the *thing* in the stories themselves."

"But you *talked* to him?" Calvin asked, his eyes glowing with admiration and pride.

Jenny nodded, then pulled away and walked to the magic hole. "Once I said his name, he tried talking to me instead of her," she said, kneeling by the hole and staring in. "And I...I got it. It's actually a language I knew," she smiled a mysterious private smile.

Calvin knelt beside her. "You were only there for, like, seconds," he said.

"Huh?"

"When you said you were going to talk to him," Calvin explained, "and then you told me to release the rings." He shrugged. "It was just a few seconds."

"Oh," Jenny said thoughtfully. "Neat."

Calvin peered into the hole as the blue-green glow dimmed to total darkness. "So he's gone."

"Yeah," she said. "He just wanted to know what was going on. He came to get the kids off the lawn, and they jumped him. Once I explained...once I told him, it was just the one kid...or, you know...he understood. It was hard. I don't think he really *gets* that there are lots of us. That we're all different people. I think he's all alone out there. And has been for a really, really long time."

"Wow," Lloyd said softly. The fanboys leaned over next to them, looking through the hole.

"You know," said Lyle, "it's a lot less scary now."

"Yeah," Lloyd agreed.

"The unknown is always scary, *meninos.*" Caravel joined them, Zé following her, and several other Reapers moved closer. Ketch smiled encouragingly at Jenny. Curach got her attention with a friendly wave.

"But now we *know* it," Lyle said cheerfully. "It's like, we made friends with it, so...you know..."

Jenny laughed. "I wouldn't go *that* far," she said. "He's not our friend. Not really. He's just a neighbor. And we should stay off his lawn," she added pointedly.

"Right," Lyle nodded. "Makes sense."

"Um," Jenny rose, and Calvin got up quickly with her. She looked at Caravel. "I've got to go."

Caravel smiled kindly. "I wondered," she said. She pointed down the beach, away from the camp on the opposite side from the parking lot. "That way, I think?"

Jenny nodded, staring off.

"Jenny...?" Calvin put a hand on her shoulder.

"Not *go* go," she promised, holding his hand. She frowned darkly. "Not yet, anyway." She kissed him, then patted his chest. "I've got an *appointment.*"

"An...*oh*," said Calvin, surprised.

She'd been feeling the tug since she'd finished her conversation with the neighbor. An alarm buzzed in her head, and Rex impatiently scraped the sand with his hooves, *whuffing* and snorting. She smiled at Lloyd, reaching out—he nodded and returned the sword to her.

"But after that," Calvin began, his voice and face tight. "I mean...after the appointment..."

Jenny put one hand on the back of his neck and pulled him roughly to her, kissing him deeply, passionately, giving him everything she had...and then let go. There were tears in her eyes as she smiled. "I love you, Calvin McGuirk," she said loudly. "*Love* you. But," she shook her head. "It can't. *We* can't. It's just not fair. To *either* of us. And the longer I stay, the worse it'll get. The more unfair it'll get."

He swallowed and shook his head, but she covered his mouth bluntly.

"No," she said. "You are the best, smartest, kindest, most amazing person I've ever known. I love you so much it *hurts*. But you've got a whole lifetime ahead of you. I mean...fuck! Life...and time...they're two totally different things, you know? You've got so much life left, even if it's not a lot of time on a...cosmic scale."

Calvin couldn't help but smile back.

"But even if I've got all the time in the world," Jenny continued, "I've got no more life. I'm done, Calvin. I'm not part of this world. I'm just a part of *you*."

Now he was smiling and crying, too. "Absolutely," he promised. "Every day. The whole lifetime."

"But you need to let me go. And you need to make sure you find somebody else," Jenny ordered, playing stern eyes at him. "I don't want you pining away for me the whole time."

"I won't," Calvin said, crossing his heart with one finger. "I promise."

"*God*, I wish we'd done it back in July," Jenny blurted regretfully.

He froze, mouth open and brain grinding.

Jenny laughed. "Not gonna happen now," she teased. "There's no time." Cutting off any clever remarks, she smacked her lips against his. They held their kiss while the wind whipped around them and the cultists muttered and murmured around the campsite, warily eyeing the Grim Reapers and their swords. When the magician and his lovely assistant finally broke, Jenny hugged him tight, her head on his chest. She bit her lip and looked at Caravel, who nodded wisely at her unspoken question.

"You'll know what to do when you get there, *menina*," the dark and stormy Reaper said.

Jenny looked around, scanning faces under black hoods. "Where's Pauzok?"

Caravel shrugged. "He wandered off during *a batalha*," she said, sighing. "But at least he's not going to be trapped forever in a padded room, *sim?*"

A gruff voice blasted the beach, reverberating from an electronic megaphone. "People on the beach! This is the police!" The cultists all flinched, panic in their eyes. "Do not move! Stay where you are! Drop any weapons on the ground, and move away with your hands over your head!" Floodlights bathed the campsite.

Jenny smiled. "That'll be Monaghan's guys," she said. She kissed Calvin hard, then spun away, sprinting for Rex. "Don't worry!" she called back. "He knows you're the good guys—just tell them who you are!"

Other Grim Reapers vaulted onto their horses, slapping reins and nudging flanks, galloping away down the beach.

"What *else* do we tell them?" Calvin asked urgently.

"I dunno," she said, swinging into the saddle. "Think they'll believe the truth?"

They grinned at each other like idiots.

"I love you, Jenny Ng!" he shouted, long arms waving. "For the rest of my life!"

"I love you, Calvin McGuirk!" she shouted back. "For even longer!"

Rex whirled and took off after the other Grim Reapers.

Powerful police floodlights beamed bright whiteness far along the shoreline. The battalion of dark riders on pale horses was still illuminated as they began disappearing, one by one—each placing the side of their gleaming blade to their horse's neck and galloping into the slippery space Through the Looking Glass.

Jenny leaned forward and patted Rex's shoulder affectionately. "Oh!" she said playfully. "Why didn't you *tell* me?" He rolled his eyes, but charged onward, his powerful hooves throwing sand behind them in great shimmering gouts. Jenny put the flat of her blade on the skin of his neck, rising and falling with his thundering gait, and gave a little mental push. She and the horse folded through absurd dimensions and burst into Wonderland, still beating an exhilarating path past the sketchy waves and flat ocean water. Ahead of them, other Angels of Death charged through Wonderland, peeling off left or right as they went.

The pull of her appointment urged her forward. As the tingling reached its peak inside her head, Rex anxiously stopped and pawed the bizarre sand-substitute. She saw nothing but the jigsaw-puzzle mosaic of wind and air in Wonderland, overlaid on the sepia-toned beach. The modern art sky swirled above her. She looked down at Rex, who grumbled impatiently. "Let's go," she said. As the other Grim Reapers sped on ahead, branching out along their own paths, she touched her blade to Rex's neck and pushed back out to the real world.

She reoriented herself with the shoreline on her left, the campsite in the distance behind her. In the other direction, a figure slogged away from her, trying hard to run on the gritty, shifting sand, but stumbling and tripping. Jenny clicked her tongue, and Rex trotted after the man.

His black robes flapping, Lawrence the Ice Cream Psycho whirled and raised his gun, firing a shot that whistled past her ear with tangible heat. He carefully aimed again, and squeezed the trigger.

The second shot went wild as something shiny flashed behind him and smacked the back of his head, shattering with a tinkling clatter. Rex *chuffed* hard as he slowly approached.

Behind the Ice Cream Psycho, Hinkley the safecracker held the remains of a thin wooden frame with shards of mirrored glass in it. He hunched over, his bad arm swaying in his homemade sling, and smiled dryly at Jenny. "Figured when the going got tough, the tough would get the heck out of there," he said.

"Nice shot," Jenny said, keeping a cool eye on Lawrence. The man's face was distorted in bestial rage. He was lying on the sand, several feet away from where his gun had dropped when Hinkley hit him.

"Yeah, well," Hinkley said, "you might be bulletproof anyway, but I owed him one. Didn't have a gun on me, but I found this mirror buried in the sand."

"That works," Jenny remarked. She flashed a smile. "Thanks, Mister Hinkley."

Lawrence spat and snarled. "The circle is broken!" He eyed Hinkley, then glared back at Jenny. "She had to *finish!* The circle must be completed!"

Hinkley chuckled. "Yeah, they got nice shiny circles waitin' for ya back there," he mocked. "Clap right on your wrists. I've worn 'em plenty in my time—they're all the rage in Sing Sing."

With sudden speed and strength, Lawrence threw himself backward, *away* from his gun—exactly the opposite of what Jenny expected, so she nudged Rex the wrong way—and he bowled over Hinkley, who shouted as he fell on his wounded arm. Rex instinctively spun back the other way, but Jenny was off balance and tumbled off onto the sand. The Ice Cream Psycho just as quickly rolled forward off Hinkley and grabbed the gun, swinging it up to aim at Jenny.

"Oh, come *on!*" Jenny complained. "We've *been* here before—you know that's not going to do anything!"

With barely a pause, he turned the gun and put it under his own chin, poking up into the fold of fat around his neck. A mad light flared in his eyes.

Jenny shook her head, her expression gentle, almost sympathetic. "That's not gonna do it either, Lawrence," she said plainly. "Don't you get it yet? You won't get out of this *that* easy."

He sneered defiantly and pulled the trigger.

The middle of his bald spot burst like a bloody melon, and his body fell over, leaking blood and gumming the sand in sticky red.

"*Holy* shit," Hinkley snapped like a baseball announcer bucking for a fine. He stood woozily and looked at the corpse of the Ice Cream Psycho. "That was one crazy *bastard.*"

Jenny gazed levelly past the body. "Yeah, Mister Hinkley," she agreed. "He really is."

Standing on the sand behind his own dead body, the ghost of Lawrence the Ice Cream Psycho looked back at her with creeping dread. His limbs dangled and his chin shook.

"Mister Hinkley," Jenny asked, "you know your way back?"

"Yeah..." The old crook gave her a sidelong glance, trying to emphasize the bleeding corpse lying between them.

"Go ahead," she said. "Just let them know you're with Calvin...and Monaghan. You'll be okay."

"What about you?"

Jenny got up and squared off firmly against the glaring ghost. "I've got work to do."

"O...kay," Hinkley said. "I'll, uh...leave you to it, then."

He shuffled across the sand, headed back to the campsite.

Jenny and the spectral Ice Cream Psycho stared at each other over his dead body. "Are you ready, Lawrence?"

He grunted uncertainly, not sure what he could say. "I'm dead," he tried.

"Yeah."

He narrowed his eyes. "I'm...a ghost?"

She nodded. "Basically."

"But you can *see* me." He was trying to make sense of it.

"You're just dead, Lawrence," Jenny said slowly and seriously. "But me? I'm *Death*."

Lawrence shook his head, his double-chin quivering. He was dressed in an old white T-shirt and denim overalls. Jenny reached out. "Come on," she said. "We have to go."

"No," he babbled, "no, I'm part of the circle, I have to go back..."

"There *is* no circle, Lawrence!" Jenny boomed, swiping a shard of the broken mirror. "*You're* dead," she told him, not gently, "*that's* your corpse, and *you're* a ghost. He couldn't even see you," she nodded at Hinkley, shrinking in the distance. "*You* can't even see you," she pointed out, waving the shard in front of him.

He stared at the empty reflection. His eyes went hard and dark.

"Now let's go," Jenny ordered him. She moved behind the ghost, her arm across his back, and thumbed the blade of her sword, jumping them Through the Looking Glass.

Lawrence's ghost gave a start and looked around sharply, taking in the bizarre surface of the beach, the strangely flat water, the There But Not There leaves and waves.

"I don't understand..." he mumbled pitifully.

"Neither did I," said Jenny. She'd calmed down—she felt more in her element in Wonderland. No overweight psychopathic zealot could harm her here. This was *her* kingdom; he was just passing through. "I'll try to explain it, though." She moved away, holding her sword in one hand and the broken shard in the other. "You were wrong, Lawrence."

He stared with all the comprehension of a goldfish.

"There are no circles," Jenny went on. "There are no endings or beginnings. There's just us, going on and on, as long as we can. There's just roads that we travel, and paths that we take, and turns that we make. There's just *choices*."

He tilted his head. He no longer seemed scary. He wasn't the Ice Cream Psycho anymore. He was just a confused, angry, scared old man.

Jenny actually felt sorry for him. "So what I do here," Jenny said, "is let people make their choices. I show them the street signs, give them a peek down each street. And they decide where they're going from here."

She raised her sword and turned, poised to slice through the air, spilling a cascade of memories and sensations.

But she stopped. She lowered her sword and turned back to him.

"But here's the thing, Lawrence." She dropped her sword on the weird, rubbery sand and held the small, sharp section of mirror to her chest. "I think I'm only supposed to let people make their choices...if they haven't already made them."

Lawrence shook uncontrollably and dropped to his knees. He looked up at her with his mouth hanging open, no longer uncertain, but wracked with fear and guilt.

"You made your choice a long time ago," Jenny said quietly, removing the magic spectacles and putting them in her pocket. "I think you know that. I think it's time for you to follow that path to the end."

She bent low and faced him eye to eye.

"But I'll tell you a secret, Lawrence," she whispered.

His gaze dropped to the flat, unreflective back of the shard in her hands.

"That end isn't really an end," said Jenny.

She took the shard away from her chest.

"And it's not a new beginning, either."

She turned the mirrored shard around.

Lawrence stared, stupefied, into the swirling gray haze in the mirror. He raised a hand as if to ward off the unthinkable void.

Jenny looked stoically at the feeble ghost, not smiling or frowning, not judging, only witnessing. In a low voice, she said: "It's just another place to stop...and think..."

His fingers approached the surface of the reflected limbo, guided there as if by magnetism, and Jenny whispered in his ear.

"...and make another choice."

Lawrence the ghost touched the smoky mirror. He twisted and faded into the bizarre folds of space surrounding Wonderland, and disappeared.

Jenny held the mirror shard gingerly and leaned over to retrieve her sword. She slipped through the shiny blade in a scintillating cloud of wind and sound. The battering wind didn't sound all that different from the rushing, pounding beat of Wonderland.

Rex nodded solemnly, emitting a low, throaty sound of understanding and affection. Jenny dropped the shard on the sand, where it reflected only the clear starry sky above. She ran to her horse and jumped into the saddle, jamming her feet in the stirrups and pulling the reins as her nerves sang with the ocean waves and the whistling wind.

The pale horse raced across the sand and out onto the surface of the ocean. The dark rider on his back raised her sword to split the sky as they faded into the infinite black night.

CHAPTER THIRTY-SEVEN

A pale old man stepped gingerly across the warm sand. His hair was white, specifically that shocking, luxuriant shade of white that men lucky enough not to go bald tend to enjoy as they approach their personal centennial, and it practically glowed silver and pink in the dazzling rose-colored sunset boiling away across the clear blue ocean. The man—very tall and thin, though his height was diminished by his hunched shoulders and aged spine—leaned heavily on a long wooden cane, tracing a trio of prints along the cream-colored beach like a very well-hung frog. Topping the cane was an irregular chunk of glass mounted on a shiny silver ring. There's something to be said about the chunk of glass. It will be.

"You beautiful man!"

An old woman called from the deck of a large white house that stood prominently on a low cliff just above the beach. She was fit for her advanced age, though the wrinkles on her face could serve as European highway maps, each line and groove marking the many roads traveled in a long life of fun, sorrow, adventure, work, boredom, passion, and all the usual good stuff that human beings get to drive through on the journey from emergence to interment.

"It's later than it looks!" she yelled, her teasing tone carrying clearly. "Come up and clean up while I tidy up!"

A smile crossed the old man's face. He peered down at a watch that wasn't on his wrist, shook his arm, and pretended disgust at the shoddy non-existent timepiece. The woman laughed, bubbling bells echoing down the cliff, and went back inside the house of white walls and picture windows. Several tiers of rocky beach and brush led from deck to shore, or *vice versa*, with flights of sand-swept white steps leading from one to the next. Despite his slow pace and creaking bones, the old man limped courageously upward, reaching the deck as the sun dipped below the crashing blue waves miles out from shore.

Crossing the deck was easier than the sand or the long flights of stairs; the sliding glass door was open for him, and he ducked out of the dusk— still steaming from the heat of a long California Summer day—into the cool, air-conditioned living room. The room was bathed in twilight and tasteful floor lamps; the white stone floor glittered with specks and flecks of silver and gray. The place was opulent, but not ostentatious. Everything was simple, possibly even affordable, but as clean and beautiful as the old couple's money could buy.

As he walked through an arch to the kitchen, the old woman hung up the phone. "The kids got home okay," she announced. "It was so nice having them here today!"

The old man nodded warmly, his smile genuine and unbreakable. "A nice surprise," he said. He was short of breath, and it showed in a quiet and restrained voice, but his face clearly conveyed his deep appreciation. He leaned in and puckered up; the old woman gave him a big, gleeful kiss, lingering longer than the day's young visitors might have found palatable. The old man silently chuckled at the thought. He nodded toward the hall, posing a wordless question.

"I'll be right in," the old woman said. "Get yourself set up."

He smiled and croaked: "Love you."

"Adore you," she replied, giving him another quick kiss and heading back to the living room.

He shuffled down the hall to the bedroom. It took some effort to strip down and put on pajamas—balancing on his cane was a skill he'd obviously perfected—but he wouldn't have it any other way. Being waited on hand and foot just wasn't in any cards he cared to have in his hand. Once he had the pajama pants up to the knee, the rest was smooth sailing. He held the cane in front of him and slowly lowered himself until he sat pertly on the edge of the bed, waiting.

Weariness settled on his shoulders. He let himself drift a little, his spine slowly unrolling as his shoulders and neck and head met the cool sheets stretched across the mattress. His knees crooked over the edge of the bedframe and the toes on his huge feet brushed the hardwood in gentle, scratching scuffs of dry, aged skin. The sensation was familiar, comforting, just another piece of the world that he'd come to love in nearly one hundred years of kicking about.

He closed his eyes. He smiled. He exhaled.

"I am *so* glad you got your pajamas on first," a bright young voice pointed out thankfully.

He opened his eyes. He was standing, looking around the bedroom from his full height. He looked down on the bed and saw himself stretched out, eyes closed, peacefully still. He jumped a little as he turned to look at the short, skinny girl standing next to him dressed all in black.

"Hi, Calvin," said Jenny Ng, Angel of Death.

"Hi, Jenny," said Calvin McGuirk's ghost. He was grinning. Death at his age was far from a tragedy, and seeing an old friend was farther still. She hadn't changed a bit, of course.

"Seriously, that would've been pretty embarrassing," Jenny said. "Standing here talking to you while your naked body is...um...hanging out there the whole time."

Calvin looked down at his translucent form, a mere ghostly projection, even though he knew it wasn't the body she meant. He was wearing a very special tuxedo—at least, most of it. The jacket was absent, and his sleeves were cut short, just as they should be.

"Oh, wow!" he exclaimed. He swept Jenny up in a huge hug.

"Easy, cowboy!" she laughed. "Your wife's in the next room! You can hug me once we get to Wonderland."

"You're here to...?"

She nodded. "They used to be careful about that kind of thing," she explained. "You know, don't escort the people you knew—gets weird, or emotional, or whatever." She shrugged, the hood on her sleek black jacket flopping behind her. "They've been pretty cool about it for the last seventy years or so, though. A lot of rules have changed."

"You changed them," he guessed.

"I still don't know how it works," said Jenny. "But I got to be with my mom. And that was a start."

"That's incredible. It's awesome, it's..." Calvin trailed off and took a breath. "It's so great to see you."

"It's great to see *you*," she told him. She scrutinized his outfit. "Is that...?"

"No, it isn't," he grinned. "Actually, I wore this at my wedding." At her skeptical look, he quickly added: "I had a jacket on for the ceremony!"

"Yeah, but..." She reached out and wiggled his bowtie.

Calvin grinned sheepishly, the expression on his old face not a millimeter different than the one he'd frequently worn as a young man. "Yeah, it was a clip-on," he admitted, toying with his bowtie.

Jenny laughed again. She looked around the room, walking aimlessly. "So you did well."

"Thanks to you," he said earnestly.

She looked at him dubiously.

"Our final show," said Calvin, his eyes crinkling happily as he remembered. "I mean, really, our *final show!* It gave me *everything*, Jenny!"

"What?" Jenny sat on the bed and smiled absently at the peaceful old man lying there.

The old man's ghost laughed happily. "I got my agents!" he crowed. He waved off her attempt to scoff. "No, they were *good* agents. Changed my vocabulary and everything," he joked. "They were at the final show, and they were really into it. Even when I met them later and had to tell them there was no more Mysterious Jade, they were still interested. I'm still with the same agency! But, you know, it's the old lady's grandson, now, and I only do some talk shows and stuff..."

Jenny blinked in amazement. "Wow," she said. "That's incredible. So that's how you can afford all...*this?*" Her gesture took in the fancy house on a Malibu beach.

"Well, Mary Ann worked, too," Calvin said. "She's a writer and illustrator. She's a best-selling children's book author."

"She looks really cool, Calvin," Jenny said. If there was any regret there, she covered it with sincerity.

"She is," he agreed warmly. He gave Jenny a big, goofy grin. "I met her at the show."

Jenny did a double-take. "*The* show?" She gaped. "The *show* show?"

His grin went wider. "She's the one I gave my phone number to," he said, "on the card. She said 'hi' after the show, and called me a few weeks later."

"Jeez, you didn't even wait for the body to get cold," Jenny teased.

Calvin took her half-seriously. "No, we were just friends for a while," he protested. "We didn't even start dating until a few years later."

"It's okay," Jenny laughed, "you *know* that. I'm just really happy that you got all that."

"And my engineer," Calvin added.

"Huh?"

"My engineer," Calvin repeated, "the guy who helped design my shows. You knew him."

Jenny made a face. "I did?"

"Rob Lester." Calvin smiled, elaborating with his hands. "The guy who helped us out, the guy at the computer place, who—"

"Holy crap!" Jenny exclaimed. "Rob! Nerd King Rob! How did you guys—"

"He was at the show, too," said Calvin. "He liked what we did, and got in touch. He was working on his engineering degree, so we teamed up. He's still one of my best friends in the world."

Jenny clapped her hands together. "Holy *crap*," she said again. "And Lyle? And Lloyd?"

Calvin shook his head. "No, we didn't really keep in touch for long. They went their way...you know how it is. I'm not sure what happened to Heckler, either..."

"He died a few years back," Jenny said wistfully.

"Oh." Calvin spread his hands. "I didn't know, Jenny...I'm sorry."

"It's okay," she smiled. "He went happy. His third and fifth wives are *still* fighting over the will."

Calvin chuckled. "What about the fourth?"

"Well," said Jenny, "Three and Five are *sisters*."

"Oh, *man!*" Calvin laughed harder. "Yeah, that sounds like Heckler."

They laughed like no time had passed at all. As the moment faded, Jenny held out a hand. Calvin looked at it, and asked: "Did you...I mean...Heckler...?"

"No," she shook her head. "Somebody else took him. I only heard about it."

He took her hand. Jenny looked at the long cane that the old man's body clutched. She looked closer. "It's..."

"Yeah," said Calvin. "The wand was just broken bits, and the rings were gone. I wrapped up the hole and put it in a safe. We never found the glasses, but the guys and I decided it would be okay if we just broke the Window apart and each kept a piece. Lyle and Lloyd, and Heckler, and we gave pieces to Mister Hinkley and Detective Monaghan. That one's mine."

"The cane..." Jenny prompted.

Calvin shrugged and smiled, patting his hip. "They got the bullet out," he told her, "but I've had a limp ever since. The cane kinda became my 'thing.' Everybody knew the Amazing Quirk and his trademark cane," he grinned, mock humility masking the real deal.

She smiled back and carefully touched his side. Calvin almost winced, but then realized there was no pain, no dull ache—for the first time since that long ago October night on the beach. Pain was for the living; he no longer had to deal with it.

The absence of his old wound brought up the memories of that night. "They were arrested..." Calvin started softly.

"I know," Jenny said simply. "It wasn't long for Carrie. She never really recovered. Vincent went about twenty years later. No," she responded quickly to Calvin's look, "I wasn't there for either of them." Her expression hardened. "That was probably a good idea. I was still too connected back then."

The old magician wasn't sure what to say.

"Don't worry about it," Jenny said, shrugging it off and smiling. She guided him into the bathroom where they stared into the mirror together. Calvin's ghost had no reflection. Mirror Jenny waved from behind the glass and gave him an exaggerated wink.

"Nice to see *you*, too," he said, deeply grateful.

The girl in the mirror blushed theatrically.

Jenny squeezed his hand. "That's not all you're going to see," she said meaningfully.

Calvin stared at her. "Oh my god...Wonderland!" He looked from Jenny to Mirror Jenny and back again. "I'll be able to see it. To really *see* it. Right?"

"It's your turn," Jenny nodded. "Are you ready?"

Calvin bit his lip nervously and straightened up. He nodded.

Jenny pushed Through the Looking Glass. The world reversed and dimmed down to a pale, desaturated imitation of itself. Calvin gawked and smiled, pulling away from Jenny and skipping through the bedroom. Her friendly laughter echoing in the flickering air, Jenny followed him down the hall, through the living room, out onto the deck. Calvin stood tall, his arms on the railing, staring up into the stunning surrealism of the mirror world's night sky and shouting joyfully. He looked down at the shore, where blurry suggestions of waves rolled over a glassy surface to the weirdly insubstantial sand. "Rex!" he shouted.

The horse returned a raucous whinny, inviting the ghostly magician down. Without limping, Calvin dashed down the steps to meet him. Jenny caught up as Calvin threw his arms around the stallion. Rex nuzzled the ghost's shock of thick white hair affectionately.

"Say cheese," Jenny told him, snapping his picture as he turned to look.

He smiled, then looked closely at her camera. "You know," he said, "they've got *much* better cameras now. You can—"

"I like this one," Jenny interrupted. She smiled and turned it off, stowing it in a saddlebag. "Always have."

Calvin nodded, his chest bursting with emotions he'd learned from experience could keep a man going for decades. He buried his face in Rex's mane for a moment, then extricated himself and looked at Jenny. "So when did you get the appointment?"

"A few weeks ago," Jenny said. "I knew it was you. I don't know how, but I just knew." She looked at his quizzical expression and walked idly around her horse, leaving no trail in the strange sand. "I never...you know...kept tabs on you. It just would've been weird. And after a while— well, I started to understand the changes Caravel told me about. I still love you, Calvin, but it just means something different now. I don't really connect that much with the world anymore. Just with *you*. So when it came—when I felt the alarm, and Rex started acting up—the way it felt...I just knew it was you."

Her fingers danced over the knots on her saddle, and she pulled her sword free. It had been a long time since Calvin had seen that sword.

"So you had a good life?" Jenny asked. She studied his face intently.

Calvin smiled. "The *best*," he promised her. "And you were in it."

"Damn straight I was," Jenny smiled back.

A thought fluttered across his face. "Jenny," he asked, "was this the date? The date you saw when you read my letters, I mean. That night in my apartment, the night we met?" He moved closer and took her hand. "Is this the day I was always going to die?"

"Nope," Jenny answered. "You must've done something right." A broad grin broke across her face. "We're *way* past that day."

"Cool," said the old magician.

"You just chose a different path," Jenny suggested. She raised her sword and squeezed his hand. "Are you ready to choose another one?"

He nodded and squeezed back. With her sword sweeping across empty air and splitting open the chapters and episodes of Calvin McGuirk's life, Jenny Ng danced with him on an unearthly beach under a paint-splattered sky. And she graciously took only just the right amount of pleasure in noticing that some of the old memories that spilled out of his past were of her.

ABOUT THE AUTHOR

Geoph Essex is a man ahead of his time, as far as he knows, but he never wears a watch and can't read them anyway, so he could certainly be mistaken. He's a writer, an artist, an actor, a multimedia creator and a computer programmer, and will rarely pass up an opportunity to eat cookies. He currently lives near Manhattan with his incredibly talented wife Gulya, many cockroaches (some quick, some dead), and a deaf mouse who can't hear the sonic repellent that drove away the rest of his family.

Unless you're reading this long after the publication date, in which case he may have moved.

You can visit Geoph on the Web at www.semperbufo.com, or at the official Lovely Assistant Web site, www.lovelyassistant.com.

43681319R00277

Made in the USA
Middletown, DE
16 May 2017